# NO ONE SITS *THIS* DANCE OUT!

Major Mike O'Neal glanced at his ammunition counters without expression. In that one brief engagement, Bravo Company had used up fifteen percent of their ammunition and there was no end to the Posleen in sight. The plan had been for an orderly advance to the objective, but he was pretty sure that was out the airlock. The lack of an artillery curtain barrage and the frantic and fragmented nature of the mortar fire that replaced it meant they were going to have to run for it.

This was exactly the situation that he had feared. The battalion was strung out, in its most vulnerable possible position and still well short of its goal, the top of the ridge overlooking the river.

If they didn't have the ridge the Posleen could pour fire into the battalion from above. There would be no way to reduce the Posleen numbers, much less break their spirit. When the ACS finally got there, the battalion would come into the view of millions of still *unbloodied* Posleen. So far the battalion had been able to move with relative impunity because of the supporting fire from artillery battalions. If that went away the casualties would start to mount fast.

But there were tens of thousands of really angry Posleen starting to dig themselves out of the rubble. And they were getting ready to fall on Bravo Company like the hammers of hell. The only thing that would save their ass was more artillery, which they weren't going to get, or sacrificing the Ten Thousand, which he wasn't willing to do.

There just weren't enough resources to get the job done.

In other words, just another day fighting the Posleen.

"Okay," he growled, stamping downward on the dead Posleen at his feet to get a better footing. "Playtime's over. Let's kick some ass."

# WHEN THE
# DEVIL

# DANCES

## JOHN RINGO

WHEN THE DEVIL DANCES

Copyright © 2002 by John Ringo
All rights reserved, including the right to reproduce this book or portions thereof in any form.

A Baen Books Original

Baen Publishing Enterprises
P.O. Box 1403
Riverdale, NY 10471
www.baen.com

ISBN: 0-7434-3602-4

Cover art by Patrick Turner

First paperback printing, April, 2003
Third printing, November, 2005

Library of Congress Catalog Number 2001056460

Distributed by Simon & Schuster
1230 Avenue of the Americas
New York, NY 10020

Production by Windhaven Press, Auburn, NH
Printed in the United States of America.

DEDICATED TO:

Thomas Burnett, 38, father of three,
and all the other warriors of Flight 93. They
died that others might live.

Call me not false, beloved,
    If, from your scarce-known breast
So little time removed,
    In other arms I rest.

For this more ancient bride,
    Whom coldly I embrace,
Was constant at my side
    Before I saw thy face.

Live, then, whom Life shall cure,
    Almost, of Memory,
And leave us to endure
    Its immortality.

—Rudyard Kipling
"The Bridegroom"
*Epitaphs of the War*

# POSLEEN INVASION TIMELINE

| | |
|---|---|
| October 9, 2004 | First Landing Five Globes:<br>Landings: Fredericksburg, Central Africa,<br>S.E. Asia, Uzbekistan. |
| July 28, 2005 | First Wave 62 Globes:<br>Primary Landings: East Coast<br>North America, Australia, India. |
| August 15, 2005 | Last Transmission: Australian<br>Defense Command, Alice Springs. |
| April 12, 2006 | Second Wave 45 Globes:<br>Primary Landings: China, South America,<br>West Coast N.A., Middle East, S.E. Asia. |
| May 14, 2006 | Last Transmission: Chinese<br>Red Army, Xianging. |
| May 28, 2006 | Last Transmission: Turkic<br>Alliance, Jalalabad. |
| June 18, 2006 | Last Transmission: Combined<br>Indochina Command, Angkor Wat. |
| December 19, 2006 | Last Transmission: Allies of<br>the Book, Jerusalem. |
| January 23, 2007 | Battle of L3: Loss of Supermonitor<br>Lexington, Task Fleet 4.2. |

| February 17, 2007 | Battle of Titan Base. |
| March 27, 2007 | Third Wave 73 Globes: |
| | Landings: Europe, North Africa, |
| | India II, South America II. |
| April 30, 2007 | Last Transmission: Islamic Defense |
| | Forces, Khartoum. |
| July 5, 2007 | Last Transmission: Indian |
| | Defense Force, Gujarrat. |
| August 25, 2007 | Last Transmission: Forces of |
| | Bolivar, Paraguay. |
| September 24, 2007 | First Battle of Irmansul: Loss |
| | of Supermonitor *Enterprise, Yamato,* |
| | *Halsey, Lexington II, Kuznetsov, Victory,* |
| | *Bismarck.* Task Fleets 77.1, 4.4, 11. |
| December 17, 2007 | Second Battle of Earth: Loss of |
| | Supermonitor *Moscow, Honshu, Mao.* |
| | Task Fleet 7.1, 4.1, 14. |
| December 18, 2007 | Fourth Wave 65 Globes: |
| | Primary Landings: China II, East Coast |
| | North America II, Europe II, India III. |
| March 14, 2008 | Last Transmission: European |
| | Union Forces, Innsbruck. |
| August 28, 2008 | Fifth Wave 64 Globes: |
| | Primary Landings: West Coast North |
| | America II, East Coast America III, |
| | Russia, Central Asia, South Africa, |
| | South America III. |
| September 17, 2008 | Last Transmission: Grand |
| | African Alliance, Pietermaritzburg. |
| October 12, 2008 | Last Transmission: Red Army, |
| | Nizhny Novgorod. |
| October 21, 2008 | Official Determination: No coherent field |
| | forces outside of North America. |
| November 14, 2008 | Second Battle of Irmansul: Loss of |
| | Supermonitor *Lexington III, Yamato II,* |
| | Task Fleet 14. |

December 1, 2008          Senate Select Committee
                          classified report:
                          Earth Human Population
                          Estimate 1.4 billion
                          Posleen Population Estimate:
                          In excess of 12 billion.

May 26, 2009              Last operational Posleen force
                          destroyed on Irmansul.

# CHAPTER 1

*The Commando's Prayer*

Give me, my God, what you still have;
give me what no one asks for.
I do not ask for wealth, nor success,
nor even health.

People ask you so often, God, for all that,
that you cannot have any left.

Give me, my God, what you still have.
Give me what people refuse to accept from you.
I want insecurity and disquietude;
I want turmoil and brawl.

And if you should give them to me,
my God, once and for all,
let me be sure to have them always,
for I will not always
have the courage to ask for them.

—Corporal Zirnheld
Special Air Service
(1942 )

*Clayton, GA, United States, Sol III*
*2325 EDT Friday September 11, 2009 AD*

The night sky over the ruins of Clayton, Georgia, was rent by fire as a brigade's worth of artillery filled the air with shrapnel. The purple-orange light of the variable time rounds revealed the skeleton of a shelled-out Burger King and the scurrying centauroid shapes of the Posleen invaders.

The crocodile-headed aliens scattered under the hammer of the guns and Sergeant Major Mosovich grinned at the metronomic firing of the team sniper. There had been three God Kings leading the Posleen battalion, what the invaders called an "oolt'ondar," a unit over size varying from a human battalion to a division. Two of the three leader castes had been tossed from their saucer-shaped antigrav craft with two precisely targeted rounds before the last had increased the speed of his saucer-shaped craft and flown quickly out of sight. Once he was gone the sniper began working on the Posleen "normals."

The rest of Long Range Reconnaissance Team Five held its fire. Unlike the sniper, with his match-grade .50 caliber rifle, the tracers from the rest of the team would be sure to give them away. And then it would be wheat against the scythe; even without their leaders, the battalion of semi-intelligent normals would be able to wipe a LRRP team off the map.

So they directed and corrected the artillery barrage until all of the remaining aliens had scattered out of sight.

"Good shoot," Mueller said, quietly, glancing at the dozens of horse-sized bodies scattered on the roads. The big, blond master sergeant had been fighting or training to fight the Posleen since before most of the world knew they existed. Like Mosovich he had seen most of the bad, and what little good, there had been of the invasion.

When they first got orders to fire up any targets of opportunity while on patrols it did not seem to be a good idea. He'd been chased by the Posleen before and it was no fun. The aliens were faster and had more endurance than humans; getting them off your trail required incredible stealth or sufficient firepower.

However, the invaders never seemed to sustain any pursuit beyond certain zones, and the LRRPs *had* sufficient firepower to wipe out most of their pursuers. So now they took every chance they could to "fire up" the invaders. And, truth be told, they took a certain perverse satisfaction from a good artillery shoot.

"Took 'em long enough," Sergeant Nichols groused. The E-5 was a recent transfer from the Ten Thousand. Like all the Spartans the sergeant was as hard as the barrel of his sniper rifle. But he had a lot to learn about being beyond the Wall.

"Arty's usually late," said Mueller, getting to his feet. Like the sniper, the team second, who always took point, was draped in a ghillie cloak. The dangling strips of cloth, designed to break up the human outline and make a soldier nearly invisible in the brush, were occasionally a pain. But it was manifestly useful in hiding the oversized master sergeant.

The lines along the Eastern seaboard had been stable for nearly two years. Each side had strengths and weaknesses and the combination had settled into stalemate.

The Posleen had extremely advanced weaponry, hundreds of generations better than the humans. Their light-weight hypervelocity missiles could open up a main battle tank or a bunker like a tin can and every tenth "normal" carried one. The plasma cannons and heavy railguns mounted on the God King's saucers were nearly as effective and the sensor suite on each saucer swept the air clear of any aircraft or missile that crested the horizon.

In addition to their technological edge they outnumbered the human defenders. The five invasion waves that had hit Earth, and the numerous "minor" landings in between, had ended up dropping two billion Posleen on the beleaguered planet. And it only took two years for a Posleen to reach maturity. How many there were on Earth at this point was impossible to estimate.

Of course not all of those had landed on North America. Indeed, compared to the rest of the world the U.S. was relatively unscathed. Africa, with the exception of some guerrilla activity in central jungles and South African ranges, had been virtually wiped from the map as a "human" continent. Asia had suffered nearly as badly. The horselike Posleen were at a distinct disadvantage in mountainous and jungle terrain, so portions of Southeast Asia, especially the Himalayas, Burma and portions of Indochina, were still in active resistance. But China and India were practically Posleen provinces. It had taken the horses less than a month to cross China, repeating Mao's "Long March" and, along the way, slaughtering a quarter of the Earth's population. Most of Australia and the majority of South America, with the exception of the deep jungle and the Andes spine, had fallen as well.

Europe was a massive battleground. The Posleen did poorly in extreme cold, not from the cold so much as an inability to forage, so both the Scandinavian peninsula and the Russian interior had been ignored. But Posleen forces had taken all of France and Germany except portions of Bavaria and swept around in an unstoppable tide to take all the North German plain to the edge of the Urals. There they had stopped more from distaste for the conditions than any military resistance.

At this point there was resistance throughout the Alps and down through the Balkans and Eastern Europe but the beleaguered survivors remained low on food, manufacturing resources and hope. The rest of Europe, all of the lowlands and the bulk of the historically "central" zones, were in Posleen hands.

America, through a combination of luck, terrain and strategic ruthlessness had managed to survive.

On both coasts there were plains which, except for specific cities, had been ceded to the Posleen. But the north-south mountain ranges on both sides of the continent, along with the Mississippi, had permitted the country to reconsolidate and even locally counter-attack.

In the West the vast bulk of the Rockies protected the interior, preventing a link-up between the Posleen trapped in the narrow strip of land between the mountains and the sea. That narrow strip of land, however, had once contained a sizable percentage of the population of the U.S. and the effect of the dis-location and civilian loss there was tremendous. In the end most of the residents of California, Washington and Oregon made it to safe havens in the Rockies. Most of them found themselves in the still-building under-ground cities, the "Sub-Urbs" recommended by the Galactics. There they sat, working in underground factories to produce the materials the war needed and sending forth their hale to defend the lines.

There were many untapped sources of materials in the Rockies and all of them were being exploited, but what was missing was food production. Prior to the first landing all holds had been released on agricultural production and the American agricultural juggernaut had responded magnificently. But most of the spare

food had ended up being sent to the few fortified cities
on the plains. They were scheduled to hold out for five
years and food was their overriding concern. So there
was, elsewhere, a severe shortage when the first massive
landing occurred. Almost all the productive farmlands
in the west, with the exception of the Klamath Basin,
had been captured by the Posleen. So most of the food
for the Western Sub-Urbs had to be provided over a
long, thin link across the Northern Plains following
I-94 and the Santa Fe Railroad. Sever that link and
eighty-five million people would slowly starve to death.

In the east it was much the same. The Appalachian
line stretched from New York to Georgia and linked
up with the Tennessee River to create an uncrossable
barrier from the St. Lawrence to the Mississippi. The
Appalachians, however, were nothing compared to the
Rockies. Not only were they lower throughout, but they
had passes that were nearly as open as flatland. Thus
the Posleen found numerous places to assault all along
the line. And the fighting at all of them, Roanoke,
Rochester, Chattanooga and others, had been intense
and bloody. In all the gaps regular formations, mixed
with Galactic Armored Combat Suits and the elite Ten
Thousand, battled day and night against seemingly
unending waves of Posleen. But the lines held. They
held at times only because the survivors of an assault
were too tired to run, but they held. They bent from
time to time but nowhere had they ever been fully
sundered.

The importance of the Appalachian defenses could
not be overstated. With the loss of the coastal plains,
and much of the Great Plains, the sole remaining large
areas for food production were Central Canada, the
Cumberland plateau and the Ohio Valley. And although
the Canadian plains were high quality grain production areas, their total production per acre was low and

they were effectively unable to produce a range of products. In addition, while there was increasing industry throughout British Columbia and Quebec, the logistical problems of a broad-based economy in nearly sub-Arctic conditions that had always plagued Canada continued even in the face of the Posleen threat. It was impossible to shoehorn the entire surviving population of the U.S. into Canada and if they did the survivors would be no better off than the Indians huddling in the Gujarrat and Himalayas.

Lose the Cumberland and Ohio and that would be for all practical purposes the end of active defense. There would be humans left on the continent, but like all the other major continents, they would be shattered survivors digging for scraps in the ruins.

Knowing that the lower Great Plains were indefensible the forces there, mostly armor and Galactic armored suits, had retreated, never engaging unless they could inflict terrific casualties. This retreat had ended near the Minnesota River for much the same reason as the Siberian retreat. However, the Posleen had succeeded in one objective, whether they knew it was an objective or not. In the long withdrawal, the 11th MI, the largest block of GalTech Armored Combat Suits on Earth, was destroyed.

All of these defenses were predicated on the Posleen's major weaknesses: inability to handle artillery and inability to cross significant barriers. The God Kings were able to engage aircraft and missiles with almost one hundred percent certainty but still were unable to stop indirect, free-flight artillery. So as long as they were in artillery range of humans they were vulnerable. And because of their odd mental dichotomy, it was virtually impossible for them to overrun modern defensive structures. Posleen attacks that carried the first layer of a prepared defense normally involved

casualty rates of one hundred Posleen for every
human killed; even with their overwhelming numbers
they simply could not take more than the front rank
of a prepared defense. And virtually all the defenses
along the Rockies and Appalachians were layered with
large units up and multiple supporting units. So the
Posleen came on and they died in such vast numbers
that it was impossible to count. And they lost. Every
time.

Now, in most areas humans crouched behind their
redoubtable defenses while the Posleen created a civilization just out of artillery range. And in between was
a weed-choked and ghost-haunted no-man's-land of
shattered towns and ruined cities.

And it was this wilderness through which the LRRPs
patrolled.

"Let's head out," Mosovich said quietly, slipping his
binoculars into their case. The binos were old technology, not even light gathering, but in conditions like
this they worked well enough. And he liked to have
a completely nonelectronic backup; batteries, even
GalTech batteries, ran out. "I suspect those guys were
headed south towards our target."

"What, exactly, are we supposed to do against a
globe, Jake?" Mueller asked. But, nonetheless, he
headed down the slope to the south.

The week before one of the gigantic "battleglobes"
of the Posleen invader had been detected in a landing pattern. The vessel had landed with more control
than normal for the Posleen. Usually the landings were
more or less at random but this globe landed in one
of the few areas in the Eastern U.S. that was not
covered by heavy fire; the Planetary Defense Center
that would have interfered with the landing had been
destroyed before completion.

The globes were made up of thousands of smaller

vessels from multiple worlds. They formed at prede-
termined deep-space rendezvous then proceeded to
the target planet. When they reached the outer
strands of the atmosphere the globes broke up and
the subvessels, Lampreys and Command Dodecahedrons, would fan out in a giant circle around the
landing target.

It was one of these that had landed somewhere
around the already conquered Clarkesville, Georgia.
And it was the LRRP's job to find it and find out where
the forces from it were going.

So far it looked like they were *gathering* forces, not
leaving. Which was, to say the least, unusual.

"First we find it," said Mosovich. "Then we figure
out what to do."

Finding it would be difficult. There were parties of
Posleen moving everywhere throughout the rugged
countryside. Since the centauroid Posleen found mountains difficult, that meant they were confined to the
roads. That meant in turn that the LRRP team had
to be careful to avoid roads. The best way to do that
would have been to "ridge run"—follow ridges from
hilltop to hilltop. However, the general trend of the
ridges in the North Georgia hills was from east to west,
rather than north to south. Thus the team had to first
climb up one ridge, averaging from two to six hundred
feet, then down the other side. In the valley they would
carefully cross the inevitable stream and road, then
ascend the next ridge.

Mosovich took them wide off of Highway 441,
descending from their perch on Black Rock Mountain
and down into the wilderness around Stonewall Creek.
The pine and oak woods were shrouded in a medieval
darkness; the background light of civilization had been
extinguished for years. The primeval woods rustled with
wildlife and in the hills south of Tiger Creek they

startled up a herd of bedding deer that must have numbered in the hundreds.

Up the hill from Tiger Creek Mueller stopped and raised a hand. From ahead there was a low, constant rustling. He crept forward, cranking up the gain on the light amplification goggles.

When he saw the first of the beasts climbing laboriously out of a ten foot high mound of dirt, he just nodded and backed up. He looked at Mosovich and gestured to the south, indicating that they needed to go around. At Mosovich's gesture of inquiry he held out two fingers, formed in a V and curved down, then gestured as if driving them at the ground. The sergeant major nodded and gestured to the south as well; nobody wanted to go through an abat meadow.

The creatures were one of the pests brought by the Posleen. Like the Posleen they were omnivorous and capable of surviving on Terran vegetation. They were about the size of rabbits, white and looked somewhat like a cross between a rat and a pillbug. They moved like a rabbit, hopping along on a single rear leg that had a broad, flexible pod-foot. Individually they were inoffensive and, unlike Posleen, fully edible to humans; Mueller had eaten them and he had to admit that they tasted better than snake, something like capybara. However, they nested in large colonies dug into the ground like anthills and defended their colonies viciously, swarming out on anything that came near them and attacking with a pair of mandibles that looked like oversized rat-teeth. They also cleared large meadows out of the forests, felling the trees like beaver and chewing them up to create underground fungus gardens. They also ate a variety of vegetation and had been observed to scavenge carcasses.

They were eaten by everything at this point including wolves, feral dogs and coyotes, but their only natural predator was what the Posleen called "grat." The grats were much worse than abat, being a flying pest that looked remarkably similar to a wasp. However, grats were limited since the *only* thing they could eat was abat. With a mature abat nest in the area, Mueller made sure to keep a sharp eye out for grat; they were much more territorial than the abat and the sting from one was deadly.

The rest of the trip was without incident, however, and by dawn they were bedded down themselves on the hills overlooking Lake Rabun. Their movement had been slow but that was okay. By tomorrow they would be snooping around the Posleen encampment and sending back reports. Clarkesville was within range of the 155mm artillery batteries around the Gap so whatever the Posleen were doing they could expect to receive a warm welcome.

Sister Mary gave a thumbs up that communications were established. The commo sergeant had been preparing to become a nun when the word came of the pending invasion. She was released from the preliminary vows of a novice and enlisted in the Army. The first days of the war had her repairing field radios in St. Louis but when a Posleen globe surrounded the city, her service in a scratch company earned her a Distinguished Service Cross. The unit of odds and sods from the support units in St. Louis— no more than eight hundred personnel, none of them infantry—had ended up defending the Granite City Steel Works and shattering better than a hundred times their number. Her own exploits were too numerous to list, thus the simple "actions in and around the Granite City Steel Works" in her citation.

The communications situation Beyond the Wall was complex. The Posleen had become more and more adept at detecting and localizing radio transmissions.

After repeated losses, the LRRP teams began using automatic laser retransmitters for commo. Every team went out with large numbers of the bread-loaf sized devices and emplaced them on the ridges in their areas of operations. Since the retransmitters doubled as sensors they also gave the commands a feel for movement in their area.

Thus the short, stocky commo tech carried a huge load of retransmitters. And had to continually ensure that they were in communication with the rear.

Mueller rolled out his poncho liner and covered it with the ghillie blanket. Crawling under the combination he held up two fingers indicating he wanted second watch.

Mosovich nodded, pointed to Nichols and held up one finger then four fingers to Sister Mary. They would sleep most of the day and head down to the river near dusk. By the next morning he intended to be looking at Clarkesville.

Nichols dragged the ghillie blanket up to cover himself and his rifle then set up on a convenient rock. The march had been a bastard; the hills were pretty steep and the undergrowth was thick as hell. But he had a secret he was not about to share. The secret was that a bad day hiking up and down hills was better than a good day in the Ten Thousand. All in all he would rather be here than Rochester.

# CHAPTER 2

God of our fathers, known of old,
  Lord of our far-flung battle-line,
Beneath whose awful Hand we hold
  Dominion over palm and pine—
Lord God of Hosts, be with us yet,
Lest we forget—lest we forget!

—Rudyard Kipling
"Recessional" (1897)

*Rochester, NY, United States, Sol III*
*0755 EDT Saturday September 12, 2009* AD

Mike O'Neal looked down at the smoke shrouded valley where Rochester, New York, used to be. The embattled city was now flatter than any hurricane could have made it; the humans were adept at fighting in rubble whereas the horselike Posleen found it nearly impossible. But that didn't mean it was a human city anymore. Just that two different species of vermin battled over it.

The rain was misting, a thick, drizzly fog blown in from Lake Ontario. Mike cradled his helmet in one hand and a grav pistol in the other. Behind him was a distant rumbling like thunder and on the east side of the Genesee River a curtain of white fire erupted with the snapping of a million firecrackers. The heights above the former Rochester University were taking another misdirected barrage.

"These mist-covered mountains, are home now for me," he sang, twiddling the pistol in one hand and watching the fire of the ICM.

> "But my home is in the lowlands, and always
>     will be.
> Someday you'll return to your valleys
>     and farms.
> And you'll no longer burn to be brothers
>     in arms."

Dancing in front of him was a hologram. A tall, lithe brunette in the uniform of a Fleet lieutenant commander was talking about how to raise a daughter long distance. The commander was very beautiful, a beauty that had once been an odd contrast to the almost troglodytic appearance of her famous husband. She also was calmer and wiser in the ways of people, an anodyne to the often hot-headed man she had married.

What she was not was as lucky as her husband. A fact he never could quite forget.

Another wash of ICM landed and hard on its heels a flight of saucer shapes lifted into the air and charged west across the river. The Posleen were learning, learning that terrain obstacles could be crossed with determination and a well led force. He watched clinically as the hypervelocity missiles and plasma cannons of the God King vehicles silenced strong points and a force of normals crossed on the makeshift bridge. The wooden contraption, simple planks lashed to dozens of boats scavenged from all over, would have been easily destroyed by the artillery fire but, as usual, the artillery concentrated on the "enemy assembly areas" and "strategic terrain." Not the Posleen force, without which the terrain would no longer be strategic.

"They learn, honey," he whispered. "But we never do."

They hadn't learned in the unexpected skirmishes before the war officially started, when they lost Fredericksburg and almost lost Washington. When lightly armed "fast frigates" had been thrown willy-nilly at battleglobes.

The battleglobes were constructed of layer upon layer of combat ships. A direct hit by an antimatter warhead would strip a layer off a section of the exterior but the inner ships would simply blow the damage off and reengage. Thus the theory of using a massive punch to break them up and then engaging the scattered ships with "secondaries." But that required not only fleets of secondary ships, fighters, frigates and destroyers, but a massive central capital ship.

However, rather than wait until the Fleet was fully prepared the Galactic command had thrown more and more ships, practically right out of the shipyards, into the battle. Pissing them away in dribs and drabs not only in Terran space but over Barwhon and Irmansul. The loss of the ships, the secondaries that were vital to the overall plan, was bad enough, but the loss of trained personnel had been devastating.

The invasion of Earth had practically cut it off from space and none of the other races of the Galactic

Federation could fight. To provide the planned crews
for the Fleet, Earth had been stripped of likely can-
didates and they were put through months and years
of simulator training in preparation for when they
would venture forth to triumph in space. Instead, they
had been thrown away in skirmish after skirmish, none
of them doing any noticeable damage to the Posleen.
Thus, the limited number of off-planet forces had been
bled white before the first capital ship was completed.

The second invasion wave was fully in swing before
the first "superdreadnought" was launched. This massive ship, nearly four kilometers long, was designed to
use its spinal hypercannon to break up the globes. And
it worked with remarkable facility. Coming in at high
velocity from Titan Base the *Lexington* smashed two
of the globes headed for Terra. And then it was
swarmed.

Thousands of smaller ships, the skyscraper shaped
Lampreys and C-Dec command ships, surrounded the
beleaguered superdreadnought and pounded it to scrap.
Despite the heavy anti-ship defenses along the sides
and despite the massive armor it was stripped to a hulk
by repeated antimatter strikes. Finally, when no further
fire was forthcoming, the wreckage was left to drift.
So durable was the ship the generators at its core were
never touched and it was eventually salvaged and
rebuilt. But that took more years, years that the Earth
didn't have.

Mike wondered how many other wives and husbands,
mothers and fathers were pissed away by the goddamned Fleet. By "admirals" who couldn't pour piss out
of a boot with the instructions on the heel. By a high
command that kowtowed to the damned Darhel. By
senior commanders who had never seen a Posleen,
much less killed one.

And he wondered when it was going to be his turn.

He watched the ghost of his wife's smile as the cold autumn rains dripped off his shaved head and the artillery hammered the advancing centaurs. And flicked the safety of his pistol on and off.

Jack Horner stood arms akimbo smiling at the blank plasteel helmet in front of him. "Where in the hell is O'Neal?"

Inside his armor Lieutenant Stewart winced. He knew damned well where the major was. And so did the Continental Army Commander. What neither one of them knew was why O'Neal wasn't responding to their calls.

"General Horner, all I can say is where he is not, which is here." The battalion intelligence officer gave an invisible shrug inside the powered battle armor. "I'm sure he'll be here as soon as possible."

The colloquy of commanders and key staff from the Ten Thousand and the ACS were gathered on the hills above Black Creek. From there, even with the waves of cold, misting rain coming off the lake, the successful Posleen assault across the river was clearly visible. As was the ineffectual artillery fire of the local Corps. Whose headquarters, commander and staff were forty-five miles behind the Continental Army Commander's current position.

"We need to get this penetration contained," said Colonel Cutprice. The colonel looked to be about twenty until you saw his eyes. In fact he had been one of the most decorated veterans of the Korean War. Thanks to the miracles of Galactic rejuvenation, and a push for more "warriors" in the officer corps, the decrepit old warrior had been restored to youth. And almost immediately started gathering medals again.

The silver eagles on his shoulders were almost an affectation; the "Ten Thousand" force that he commanded was better than a brigade in strength and thanks to its converted Posleen equipment had the combat power of an armored corps. But he refused any rank higher than bird colonel and the one abortive attempt to replace him had resulted in something very close to mutiny. So a colonel commanded a pocket division.

"My boys and the 72nd Division have 'em contained along Genesee Park Avenue and there's a company or so of the 14th holding on in The Park; they're dug in hard on the hill. But more of the fuckin' horses are pushing over that damned bridge all the time. We need to drive in a counterattack and destroy the crossing. It would be helpful if we could get some combat suit support on that."

Stewart winced again at the neutral tone. For conventional forces, or even the unarmored Ten Thousand, assaulting the Posleen was a brutal business. The railguns and plasma cannons of the enemy turned troops in the open into hamburger and the God Kings opened up main battle tanks like tin cans. It was why the ACS, the Galactic supplied Armored Combat Suits, were *always* used for assaults. But that meant that the ACS had been whittled away in attack after attack, especially on the Great Plains and here in the Ontario Salient. And with Earth interdicted and the only factories for making suits off-planet that had meant "ten little suits, nine little suits." Until there were none.

There was a trickle of resupply from the Galactics. Stealth ships slipped onto Pacific Islands and transferred their cargoes to submarines. These, in turn, visited high latitude ports such as Anchorage. The cargoes then would be trucked to where the lines were still holding. But that resupply route was pitifully inadequate for making up losses. Which was why the U.S. had gone from two *divisions* of ACS to less than two *battalions,* a ninety percent reduction in total force, in the last four years. And it had used up more than *four* divisions of suits along the way.

1st Battalion 555th Mobile Infantry, "The *Real* Black Panthers," had lost fewer units than the other battalions and it still maintained a solid core of veterans who had survived every battle. But even they had had a nearly two hundred percent turnover rate. And with the slow rate of resupply that meant eventually even "First Batt" was doomed.

Whereas the supply of Posleen just seemed to be growing.

Horner shook his head and turned to the other suit in the conference.

"If Major O'Neal does not appear soon, I am turning command over to you, Captain Slight." His blue eyes were as cold as agates. Mike O'Neal had once been his aide and was a hand-picked protégé but if Rochester got turned the next fall-back line was just east of Buffalo. And the front there was twice as long. Holding the Rochester defenses was, therefore, the number one priority in the eastern United States.

"Yes, sir," said the Bravo company commander. "Sir, it would help if we could free up the artillery. We need it to hit that bridge, not the, pardon my French, fucking 'logistical tail,' sir."

Horner smiled even wider, a sure sign of anger, as Cutprice snorted.

"We're working that out. As of twenty minutes ago General Gramns was relieved by my order. The Ten Thousand artillery coordinator is up there right now trying to convince them that a pontoon bridge is a better target than 'assembly areas.'"

"With a platoon of my MPs," Cutprice added. "And two saucers. I told him the first one of those chateau generaling bastards gives him shit, he's to blast him right in fucking public. With a plasma cannon." The lean colonel was so utterly deadpan it was impossible to tell if he was joking.

"Whatever it takes to get their attention." Horner sighed. "And it might take a summary execution. I'd put you in charge of the Corps, Robert, but I can't spare you. And you can't do both jobs."

"I'd end up killing all their rear echelon asses anyway," the colonel grumped. "And all the goddamned regular Army assholes that can't get their divisions to fight."

"The 24th New York and 18th Illinois are reassembling near North Chili," Horner said. "But I don't want to just slot them into the hole. Once we get the pocket cleared out I want you to throw up bridges and press a counterattack. I've sent for Bailey bridge companies and I want you to use them. Harry those horses. Drive them as far east as you can. I guarantee you that there will be infantry for you to fall back on. On my word."

"What is the target?" Stewart asked. "Where do we stop?"

"The goal is the Atlantic Ocean," Horner answered. "But don't outrun your supports. I'd like to see the line pushed back to Clyde. The front would be narrower and the ground is better for us."

"Gotcha," Cutprice said with a death's head grin. "Our flank's gonna be as open as a Subic Bay whore, though."

"I'll have the ACS out there," the general said quietly. "Whether O'Neal shows up or not."

Ernie Pappas sighed. The hill was a moraine, a leftover of the glacier that had carved out Lake Ontario. On the back side, facing southwest away from the fighting, a former children's hospital had been converted to tend to the thousands of wounded produced by the month's long battle. Including at least a dozen ACS troopers too busted up for their suits to fix.

Even up here in the clean, fresh air the miasma of pain could be sensed. But the hill provided a fine view of the battle that VIII Corps was in the process of losing. A fine view.

Which was undoubtedly why the Old Man had chosen it for his meditations. The major had gotten more and more morose as the war went on and the casualties just kept mounting. There wasn't anything that anyone on Earth could do about it, but the Old Man seemed to take it personally. As if saving the world was all on his shoulders.

That might have come from the early days when his platoon was credited with almost single-handedly stopping the Posleen invasion of the planet Diess. But that was revisionist history. Some of the best and most veteran NATO units had been involved and it was the Indowy-constructed Main Line of Resistance, and the conventional American, French, British and German infantry units that manned it, that stopped the Posleen butt-cold. O'Neal's claim to fame, besides being the only human to ever detonate a nuclear device by hand and survive, was in freeing up the armored forces that had been trapped in a megascraper.

But it might be that that had the Old Man thinking he could single-handedly save the planet. Or maybe it was just how he was; the lone warrior, Horatius at the bridge. He really believed in the ethos of the warrior, the philosophy of the knight, *sans peur, sans reproche*. And he had made his troops believe in it too, by his shining vision and his intensity and his belief. And that shining vision had sustained them. And maybe this was the cost.

Gunnery Sergeant Ernest Pappas, late of the United States Marine Corps, knew that knights in armor had been nothing more than murdering bastards on horseback. And Ernie knew that what you did was survive. Just survive. And maybe you managed to stop the enemy and maybe you didn't. But as long as you survived to cause them grief that was good enough.

But Gunny Pappas knew that wasn't what got the boys to get up and shoot. The boys got up to shoot from the shining vision and because they believed with Ironman O'Neal beside them there was no way they could lose. Because that was how it *should* be.

Pappas looked down at the smoke and flames drifting off the rubble of the city and sighed. This sure as hell wasn't how it should be. And if Captain Karen Slight tried to carry the battalion into that fire they would evaporate like water on a griddle. Because they wouldn't *believe*.

"Major?" he said, putting his hand on Mike's shoulder.

"Ernie," the major answered. They had been together since O'Neal had taken command of Bravo back in the bad days when it seemed like the entire Army had lost its mind. They'd been through the ups and the downs, mostly downs. Whether they knew it or not it was the team of Pappas and O'Neal that defined the 1st/555th and made it what it was.

"That was a long goddamned climb you just forced on an old man."

"Great view, though. Don't you think?" Mike smiled sadly and carefully spit into his helmet where the biotic underlayer picked up the spittle and tobacco juice and started it on its long trail back to being rations.

Pappas glanced at the pistol and winced. "You need to quit listening to Dire Straits."

"What? You'd prefer James Taylor?"

"We've got a situation."

"Yep." Mike sighed and rubbed his eyes with his free hand. "Don't we always."

"The 14th Division high-tailed it." The battalion sergeant major took his own helmet off and shielded his eyes. "They're halfway to Buffalo by now."

"What else is new?" O'Neal intoned. "Nice artillery fire, though. Not hitting anything, but very pretty."

"Corps arty. I doubt they'll stick around much longer. The whole corps is thinking the 'bugout boogie' by now."

"Ten Thousand plugging the gap?"

"Yep."

"Yep."

There was a long silence while the sergeant major scratched at his scalp. The biotic underlayer of the suits had finally fixed his perennial dandruff but the habit lingered on long after the end of the problem.

"So, we gonna do anything about it, boss?"

"Do what?" the battalion commander asked. "Charge heroically into the enemy, driving him back by force of arms? 'Disguise fair nature with hard-favored rage'? Break the back of the enemy attack and drive them into rout? Retake positions lost for months? Drive them all the way back to Westbury and Clyde where they are supposed to be?"

"Is that what you're planning?" Pappas asked.

"I'm not planning anything!" Mike answered shortly. "But I suppose that is what Jack is expecting. I notice he turned up."

"It's how you know it's serious," Pappas joked. "If CONARC turns up the shit has truly hit the fan."

"I also notice that there are no artillery units responsive to calls for fire."

"They're working on that."

"And that both flanking divisions are defined by Shelly as 'shaky.' "

"Well, they're Army, ain't they?" the former Marine chuckled. "Army's always defined as 'shaky.' It's the default setting."

Artillery fire dropped on the rickety pontoon bridge and the wood and aluminum structure disintegrated.

"See?" said O'Neal. "They didn't really need us."

"Horner wants a counterattack."

O'Neal turned around to see if the sergeant major was joking but the broad, sallow face was deadpanned. "Are you serious?"

"As a heart attack. I thought that was what you was bitching about."

"Holy shit," the major whispered. He reached down and put on his helmet then shook his head to get a good seal on the underlayer. The gel flowed over his face filling every available crevice then drew back from mouth, nostrils and eyes. The Moment, as it was known, took a long time to get over and a lifetime to adjust to. "Holy shit. Counterattack. Grand. With Slight in command I presume? Great. Time to go pile up the breach with our ACS dead."

"Smile when you say that, sir," the NCO said, putting on his own helmet. "Once more into the breach."

"That's 'unto,' you illiterate Samoan, and I *am* smiling," O'Neal retorted. He rotated his body sideways, turning the snarling face of his battle armor towards the sergeant major. "See?"

"Gotta love his armor," Cutprice chuckled.

"I wish I had a thousand sets," Horner admitted. "But I'd settle for a thousand *regular* sets so that's not saying much."

The armor was a private gift to then-Captain O'Neal from the Indowy manufacturer and included all the "special" functions that he had requested when he was a member of the design group. Besides the additional firing ports on wrist and elbows for close range combat, it was powered by antimatter. This eliminated the worst handicap of powered armor, its relatively short combat range. Technically, standard armor was designed for three hundred miles of range or seventy-two hours of static combat. In practice it had turned out to be about half that. Several suit units had been caught when they simply "ran out of gas" and were destroyed by the Posleen.

The drain on suit power had just gotten worse with the ammunition shortage. Because it was impossible for any terrestrial factory to produce the standard ammunition, which had a dollop of antimatter at the base to power the gun, it had been necessary to substitute simple depleted-uranium teardrops. Thus the grav-gun, which should have been powering itself, was forced to "suck" power from the suits. Since the rounds were still accelerated to a fraction of lightspeed, and since that required enormous power, the "life" of the suit batteries had been cut to nearly nothing. It was getting close to a choice of shoot or move for most of the standard suits, the exception being O'Neal's, which had almost unlimited power.

The flip side, of course, was that if anything ever penetrated to the antimatter reservoir, Major O'Neal and a sizable percentage of the landscape for a mile around would be vapor.

But all of those things were invisible. It was the "surface" that attracted attention; the suit gave the appearance of some sort of green and black alien demon, the mouth a fang-filled maw and the hands talons for ripping flesh. It was startling and barbaric and in some ways, for those who knew O'Neal, very on cue.

"It suits him," said the colonel from long experience.

The ACS went wherever it was hottest. And the Ten Thousand followed.

The Ten Thousand—or the Spartans as they were sometimes called—was an outgrowth of a smaller group called the Six Hundred. When the first Posleen landing occurred, early, by surprise and in overwhelming force, the green units sent into Northern Virginia to stop them were shattered in the first encounter. Many of them, especially rear echelons, escaped across the Potomac. A large number of these gathered in Washington so when the Posleen forced a crossing of the river, right on the Washington Mall, thousands of these soldiers who had been in the rout were directly in their path. All but a tiny handful fled. This tiny handful, six hundred and fifty-three to be exact, had decided that there were some things that were worth dying for in a pointless gesture. So they gathered on the mound of the Washington Monument for the purposes of a stupidly suicidal last stand.

As it turned out it was not, quite, a suicide. Their resistance, and the confusion among the Posleen crossing the bridge, slowed the enemy just enough for the armored combat suits to arrive. Between the ACS and artillery fire the Posleen pocket in Washington was first reduced, then eliminated.

A special medal was struck for those six hundred and fifty-three truck drivers and cooks, infantrymen and artillery, linemen and laundrymen, who had stood their ground and prepared to go to their God like soldiers. After a brief ceremony, they were to be spread throughout the Army with nothing to remember the encounter but the medal. The leader of the resistance, however, successfully argued that there should be a better use than dissemination. Thus the Ten Thousand was born. Most of the Six Hundred were given promotions and used as a nucleus of the force which was then armed from captured and converted Posleen weapons. Once completed, the Ground Forces commander had at his fingertips a fast, heavy and very elite unit.

But it did not assault swarming Posleen; only the ACS could survive that.

"Major," General Horner said. The use of O'Neal's rank was the only sign of reproof for his tardiness.

"Jack?" O'Neal answered.

Horner smiled coldly. The ACS was not an American unit; it belonged to the Fleet Strike, a part of the Galactic Federation military. Therefore it would only be common military courtesy, not regulation, that would require O'Neal to use the general's rank. But the blank name was as much a rebuke as his use of a blank rank. In better times O'Neal had referred to him as 'sir' or 'general' and even 'colonel.' Calling him 'Jack' in public was as good as a slap.

"We have a situation," the general continued.

"People keep saying that," O'Neal snorted. "What we have is a Mongolian Cluster Fuck, sir. Is General 'the ACS is an unnecessary expenditure of resources' gone?"

"Gramms has already been replaced," Cutprice interjected. "And Captain Keren is currently explaining to his staff the words 'fire support' and 'responsive fire.' "

"Do we have a plan?" O'Neal asked. "Or are we just going to get on-line and charge at them screaming?"

"We hold the heights on this side of the river," Cutprice answered again. "But they're pressing into the city and up along the canal and the heights on their side are higher so the ones on this side are getting fire support from the groups gathering on the far side. They're also about to cut our supply line at the Brooks Avenue bridge. I'd like you to open up a pocket between the river and the ridge. My boys will follow in support but you're going to have to take the first shock."

"Why not just pin them and hammer them flat with artillery?" Stewart asked. "If you need Keren, by the way, we can always send Duncan over to 'reason' with them."

"Hell no! I want the damned headquarters *standing*." The boyish colonel gave the broadest grin anyone had ever seen and burst out in a belly laugh. "I've seen Duncan on a roll!"

"We need a crossing and we need it fast, Lieutenant," Horner said gravely. "Not because I want my name in the news but because the Posleen are just as susceptible to rout, once you get them running, as humans. And we *need* them to be back at the Clyde lines. Long range recon teams tell us that the defenses haven't been touched. If we can harry them all the way back to the Clyde half our problems in the East are done."

"I've been watching their numbers building," Mike pointed out. "They're headed into this battle like ants headed to honey."

"So what then?" Horner asked. "You have an idea."

"Yes, sir," the major responded, forgetting his anger. "What I'd really like to do is use a flight of Banshees to land behind them; but given the terrain I don't think it would be possible and I doubt that we could hold out until the reinforcements arrived. Barring that, I want to hammer them flat then paint the lines for once. Nukes are still out?"

Horner winced. He was personally in favor of the use of tactical nuclear weapons in situations like this one. Tac-nukes had a wider "footprint" than any other form of artillery including Improved Conventional Munitions.

The majority of China had fallen in less than two

months; it had taken the first major Posleen landing only forty-two days to go from Shanghai to Chengdu. And along the way the Race of Han had been reduced to a shallow splinter as over nine hundred million humans and a five thousand year old culture were wiped from the face of the earth. There were still pockets of resistance in the previous regions of Chinese control, the most notable of which was a small contingent in the Luoxia Shan led by the former head of Red Army procurement and "Radio Free Tibet."

But in the process of disintegration, the panicking Chinese military had fired off a nuclear arsenal that was six or seven times larger than prewar intelligence estimates. The last spasm had been in the region of Xian, where the rearguard of the column retreating into the Himalayas had expended itself in a nuclear firestorm whose net effect was to slow the Posleen by only a day. The result was that China's death throes had consumed enough nuclear weapons to poison the Yangtze River for the next ten thousand years. And to poison the political climate for nearly as long.

"No nukes," Horner said. "There's things the President will waffle on. And she turns a blind eye to the fact that SheVa rounds and your handgrenades are essentially micro-nuclear weapons. But we're not going to nuke Rochester." He held up a hand to forestall the argument he knew was coming and smiled tightly. "Not even neutron bombs or antimatter. No. Nukes."

Mike turned away and looked at the far heights. The Genesee Valley was an obstacle to the Posleen and conventional forces but nothing to the suits; they were as comfortable in water as in space. However, there were *millions* of the Posleen swarming in the valley and only a bare handful of suits to oppose them.

"They're still going to have to be cleared out of the

valley before we can move," Mike said. "That *has* to happen before we cross the river. I will *not* perform this assault without artillery fire that *I* consider adequate. Nor will any member of *my* battalion."

He could hear the in-drawn breaths around him but he also could care less. The ACS was, in a very real and legally binding sense, a separate military from the United States Ground Forces. Technically, by the treaties which the U.S. Senate had signed in all innocence, he was Jack Horner's superior officer. Technically, O'Neal could *order* a nuclear preparatory barrage and *technically* General Horner would have to follow his orders. Technically.

Realistically, no ACS major had ever refused an order from a Terran general. Not even "Iron Mike" O'Neal. Mike had occasionally argued about specific orders. But point-blank refusal was new. Call it the result of having watched the battalion have two hundred percent casualties over five years and slowly dwindle away to nothing.

Call it experience.

Horner considered his options for a moment then nodded coldly. "I'll go get the artillery preparations arranged. I assure you that when you come up out of the water there will be nothing living between the Genesee and Mount Hope Avenue."

"Ensure that the artillery is prepared to *maintain* that support," O'Neal said. "We'll need a curtain of artillery; I want to walk under a back-scratching all the way to our primary positions. And we'll need an ongoing curtain until the support is in place. If we don't get that, I'm not sure this is doable."

"Agreed," Horner said with a tight smile. He looked to the east as well and shook his head. "I'll give you all the artillery I can scrounge between now and tomorrow morning. On my word."

"Do that, General, and we'll eat their souls," Stewart said softly.

"We're gonna do that little thing," O'Neal said definitively. "Whether any of us survive is another question. And, Stewart: massage your AID. I want you to see if you can identify the incredibly smart Kessentai that came up with this bridge idea. Such intelligence should be rewarded."

# CHAPTER 3

Oh, East is East and West is West,
    and never the twain shall meet,
Till Earth and Sky stand presently
    at God's great Judgement Seat;
But there is neither East nor West,
    Border, nor Breed, nor Birth,
When two strong men stand face to face,
    tho' they come from the ends of the earth!
              —Rudyard Kipling
    "The Ballad of East and West" (1889)

*Clarkesville, GA, United States, Sol III*
*1350 EDT Saturday September 12, 2009 AD*

Tulo'stenaloor regarded the young Kessentai coldly. "Tell me again about this skirmish."

"This what, estanaar?" Cholosta'an asked. The young scout-leader was clearly confused to be discussing the encounter. Especially with the "estanaar" of this large band. The term was both new and old, it was to be

37

found in the Net, but it had not been used in the memory of anyone in the Horde. It had connotations of "Warleader" and "Mentor" and even "King" in human terms. However, the days of the last estanaar were recorded thousands of years before.

"The sky fire," Tulo'stenaloor said with a snarl. "This small battle."

"There was no battle, estanaar," the God King admitted. "There was only the sky-fire . . ."

"Artillery," Staraquon interjected. Tulo'stenaloor's intelligence officer flapped his crest in derision. "Start learning the words."

"I am not a nestling," snarled Cholosta'an. "I do not have to take this from you, Kenstain!" The term was a terrible insult, the equivalent of calling someone a eunuch. Kenstain were God Kings who had been removed for all time from the Battle Rolls, either by their own choice or by the decisions of the Posleen Data-net. Some were God Kings that had chosen not to engage in battle, but most were those unlucky in battle or who were unable to garner riches through either fighting or deceit.

Kenstain were useful on a certain level, they provided the minimal "administration" that could not be provided by the Net. But since they were unrecognized by the Net, they could not engage in legitimate trade and had to survive at the whim of their luckier or more courageous brethren.

No one liked Kenstain.

Tulo'stenaloor leaned forward and raised his crest. "If you say that one more time I will have you killed. You agreed to obey my orders if I led you to victory. Learn now that I was serious. I want your information, but not so much as to have my intelligence officer called such. Do . . . you . . . understand?"

"I . . ." The young God King slumped. "No . . .

estanaar, I do not understand. I do not understand why it matters and I do not understand why I must be put through this. It is not the way of the Path."

"Do not speak to me of the Path," spat the older God King. He fingered the symbol dangling from one ear and snarled. "The Path is what has led us to this impasse. It is the Path which has hurled us into defeat on Aradan and Kerlan. We will use the Path when it is the way to victory, but the only Path in my encampment, the only *mission*," he said, using the human word, "is to defeat the humans, utterly. It goes beyond this small ball of mud, it goes to the survival of the Po'oslena'ar as a race. If we do not destroy these humans, they will destroy us. And I *will* destroy them, root and branch, here and on Aradan and Kerlan and anywhere else they exist. Not for the Path, but for the Race. And you will either aid me in that, without question, or you may go. But if you say you will aid me and you question me or the officers I appoint to you then you will *die*. Do you understand me now?"

The young God King had been born on Earth in the heat of battle and since leaving the slaughter of the pens had heard nothing but the stories of defeat at human hands. Not for him the riches of the initial landing when vast stretches of land fell before the onslaught of the Race. Not for him the easy way to pay his edas debts, the crushing weight of the cost of outfitting his oolt. Until that was paid there was no way he could do anything but be a servant to more capable or lucky Kessentai. Thus, his first battle had been like all the others, a blindsided slaughter in these hills, shredded by artillery that they could never reach and he and his fellow Kessentai pecked at by snipers that were impossible to distinguish through the mass of fire. There was no glory, and certainly no loot, to be gained from those pitiful assaults. Not even by picking over their own dead.

He had seen the weakness of the Path, the Path of War that called for berserk assaults no matter what the target, and he knew there must be a better way. It was because of this that he had responded to the messages filtering through the Net. There was a new Way, a new Path, and a new messiah that would lead them beyond these trackless wastes into the promised land of the interior. It was a new Way and it was a hard Way, but he had never expected how hard.

"I . . . will obey, estanaar," the scoutmaster said. "I do not understand but I will obey." He paused and thought back. "The sky-fire . . . the artillery . . . fell without warning. Rather our tenaral told us it was coming, but only when it was on top of us. Then Ramsardal fell and when I saw the damage I began weaving; I knew it was the human 'snipers' but with the sky . . . artillery fire the tenaral were unable to find them. I bonded as many of the oolt'os as I could on the way past and moved as quickly out of the fire as I could."

"Can you read a map?" asked Staraquon.

"I . . ." The young Kessentai fluffed his crest nervously but finally laid it flat. "I do not know what a map is . . ."

"Call me 'Esstu,'" Staraquon said calmly. "I gather information about the humans. You will be given a lesson in maps later by the Kessentai of Essthree, but a map is basically a picture of the ground from in the air. I would like to know where the encounter was. Since there was sniper fire, it was from a reconnaissance team, one of the human *'lurp'* teams, rather than fire directed from their sensors. If there is a reconnaissance team out there, it is probably coming to see what we are doing. We don't want that; we don't want the humans seeing what we are doing. Therefore we want to know where the encounter was and when."

The God King fluffed his crest again and clacked his teeth. "It was last night and it was closer to the human lines. I . . . knew a way to this area but it passed close to the human lines. It was the only way I knew so I took it. I could *show* you where it is, but I cannot tell you."

"All right," Staraquon said with a flap of his crest. "It would have been good but not necessary." He turned to Tulo'stenaloor. "I wish to send out more patrols and I want some of my *esstu* Kessentai included. There are detectors we have been working on that might help us find these pesky *lurps*."

"Was there a transmission from the area?" Tulo'stenaloor asked. He admitted that he did not have the expertise in figuring out how to gather information that Staraquon did. But that was why he had recruited him as his "esstu."

"No," the intelligence officer said. "It would appear that they are using some nontransmissive form of communication. Probably these laser retransmitters that they have scattered around the hills."

"Is there some way to gather the information from them?" the older Kessentai mused. "Or some way to feed it in?"

"Both," Staraquon said with a bark of humor. "But shouldn't we wait on that for when the attack takes place? I want these humans to suspect nothing until then."

"Agreed," Tulo'stenaloor said. "Very well, do what you need to, you may even draw on the Kessentai force if you think it can be kept secret. But find this recon team and kill it."

Jake took another look through the binoculars and scratched his chin in thought. The Tallulah River drained the northeast Georgia mountains, joined by numerous smaller tributaries until it became a substantial stream. At that point, however, humans had taken a hand and the river was repeatedly used for hydroelectric power generation. Currently he was observing the bit of it that flowed out of the Lake Burton Dam and, in very short order, became Lake Seed. Between the two lakes was a short stretch that, according to the map and their intel report, was supposed to be fordable. Only about thirty meters from side to side and knee deep at worst. What was even better about this point for a crossing was that there were steep, heavily wooded slopes on either side of the river. All the team would have to do was move down through the woods, pass through a blessedly small open area, cross the river and move back into the sheltering woods.

Unfortunately, the intel reports neglected to take into account the sumptuous rains of the previous few months and the power plant on the dam.

The plant was old, possibly as much as a century passed since its construction, the large multi-pane windows and antique lights scattered around made that clear. The generators inside would probably be signed by Thomas Edison himself, but the plant still functioned and it was evident that the Posleen were using it to supplement their fusion plants.

Which, by itself, was no skin off of Jake Mosovich's nose. But the problem was the generation had raised the level of the river to nearly chest height and the power of it would make any white-water kayaker happy. But the objective was on the far side. Which created a number of unpalatable options. They could turn around and cross Lake Burton on the north end. But if they did that it would make more sense to extract to behind the lines, *drive* around to the Highway 76 defenses and start all over again.

Alternatively, they could move closer to Toccoa and

make a crossing. The problem with that was that the most dangerous point of the insertion would take place practically on the target. A landing zone for a globe was commonly almost ten miles in radius. It would be expected that landers were at least as far out as Toccoa although telemetry had indicated this landing was remarkably tight. Whichever was the case, crossing further down would be much more dangerous. If anything went wrong on the crossing, they might find upwards of four million Posleen chasing their asses. And while Jake had developed a fond affection for Posleen stupidity, he had also gained a strong appreciation for their tenacity and speed. There was no way they would survive a globe-force on their ass.

That left one option.

"The bridge is up," he whispered.

"Yeah," Mueller said. "And by that you are suggesting what?"

He and Mueller had been together a long time. Along with Sergeant Major Ersin they were the only survivors of the first, disastrous human encounter with the Posleen on Barwhon when a hand-picked team of the best the U.S. Special Operations Command had to offer was sent out to learn about this amazing and unlikely reported extraterrestrial threat.

All went relatively well until the small team was ordered to retrieve some live Posleen for study. It was then that the team learned, to its cost, about the efficiency of God King sensors and how very fast the "dumb" Posleen could react to a direct and recognizable threat. He had completed the mission, but at the cost of six legends in the SpecOps community. And he had never again underestimated the Posleen.

But there was a difference between underestimation and necessary risk.

"I don't see a choice," Mosovich pointed out. "And

there's not much traffic. We've seen, what? One group cross it in the last few hours? We move down to right on top of it, make sure there aren't any bad guys around and then sneak across. What's so tough?"

"Getting killed is what's so tough," Nichols interjected. "What happens if a God King wanders by? I guarantee you that if we're 'on top' of the bridge, their sensors are going to scream, even if we don't get spotted by sentries on the dam!"

"What sentries?" Mosovich said. "Posleen don't *post* sentries. They never do."

"They never send out patrols, either," Mueller pointed out. "And it sure as hell looks like that's what's going on here. How many of these damn groups have we seen, just milling around. Usually they're constructing something or farming or working. These guys are acting like . . . soldiers."

"You spooked?" Mosovich asked seriously. Mueller had been at the Posleen killing business as long as the sergeant major; it made sense to listen to his hunches.

"Yeah," Mueller answered. "Something ain't right. Why land a globe out here in the middle of nowhere? Why're all these guys doin' what look like patrols? For that matter, how many times have you seen one of these dams generating?"

"And then there's *why* we're here," Sister Mary added quietly.

Much of the intelligence that humans gathered on the Posleen was from one of three sources: the sensor net scattered through the woods, high-intensity telescopes scattered across the face of the moon and special scatterable, short-lived mobile "bots" that could be fired from artillery shells.

Since this latest globe landing, all of the sensors in line of sight of Clarkesville had been systematically eliminated, every set of bots sent in had been localized and destroyed and the Posleen had put up a blanket of smoke over most of the area they were organizing in. It bespoke something very unusual. And now they seemed to be actively patrolling.

"We gotta get into the area," Jake pointed out. "To get there we gotta cross the stream."

"Next time, we're humping in SCUBA gear," Mueller grumbled. "Then we swim across the lake."

"I don't know how to SCUBA," Sister Mary whispered.

"I don't know how to swim," Nichols admitted.

"Babies," Mueller grumped. "We're taking out babies. Don't they teach you anything in Recondo?"

"Sure," Nichols said. "How to do a repulsion jump. I think I've used it as much as you have SCUBA training."

"Tonight," Mosovich said. "We'll move out at two ohmygodhundred. Standard formation. If we make contact, follow SOP, rally here. Sister Mary, call up the arty and make sure they're awake for our crossing."

"Gotcha."

"Chill until then. Tonight's going to be busy."

"You have had a busy day, eson'sora."

Cholosta'an laid his crest down and bobbed his head to the older Kessentai, uncomfortable with the unusual term. Like many others it had been ferreted out of the Data Net by acolytes of the unusual master of this Globe-force, but it was unfamiliar to the majority of Posleen. It had echoes of a genetic relationship, father to son or sibling to sibling. But they were overtones only; the term meant neither father nor master but something similar to both. Defining the relationship, however, was an ongoing process.

"It has been . . . interesting." The ever-present smoke of the main camp stung his eyes but at least now he understood the reason for it. The humans, too, had maps, and ways of seeing from the sky. Most of those had been destroyed automatically, the reason, apparently, that the Alldn't equipment engaged what appeared to be harmless targets. But there were other ways; communications had been . . . intercepted from the orbital body. The humans even had eyes there.

Orostan fingered his harness in thought as he idly drifted his command saucer back and forth. The continuous movement of the tenar was a habit the smarter God Kings learned. On this benighted ball the less smart didn't last long. "You understand maps now?"

The young Kessentai looked around at the purposeful activity of the encampment and flapped his crest. "I believe so. They are similar to the graphics of a construction survey. Once I connected the two it got much easier, but thinking of them flat rather than raised was tricky. And learning is one thing, but it takes experience to set a skill." He had been born with many inherently transferred skills, not least the skills of battle but also a large nonviolent skill set ranging from how to construct a polymer extrusion machine to how to build a pyramid made of nothing but one foot blanks of steel. However, gaining new skills was harder, it required both time and materials to repeat the processes over and over again. Map reading at a "skill" level would take some time.

The oolt'ondai clacked his teeth and pulled out a roll of paper. "Well, for today you need to send half your oolt out on patrol. The rest will move to an outlying camp that is being prepared. Can your cosslain handle the patrol?"

"What is the nature of this 'patrol' . . . thing?" the young Kessentai asked.

"Another of Tulo'stenaloor's human practices. Oolt'os are sent out to walk on the roads and in the hills looking for humans that might be spying on us. We lose a few to their damned artillery, but it keeps prying eyes away."

"But . . ." The Kessentai fluttered his crest in agitation. "I can send them forth and tell them to keep an eye out for humans. But it sounds like you have something else in mind."

"Indeed," the oolt'ondai said with a clack of humor. "Other groups already go forth. Send them to the attention of Drasanar. He will have them follow a patrol group on their path. After they know it they will be set to follow it until told to stop. Can they be trusted out of your sight?"

"Oh, yes," Cholosta'an admitted. "My cosslain are actually quite bright and I have three in my oolt. Any of them will be capable of following those directions."

"Good, send one half of the oolt to the attention of Drasanar, he is the patrolmaster. Then send the other half to the," the oolt'ondai paused as he tried to get his mouth around "Midway." Finally he got out a map and pointed to it. "Take them to the camp here. Turn them over to one of the Kessentai in charge of constructing the camp and return. We've many things to do and not much time to do it in."

"What is all the rush?" Cholosta'an asked. "I thought the battle was not to take place so soon."

"Ask Tulo'stenaloor," Orostan said with another clack of humor; while the leader of the force was always glad to answer questions, he rarely had time. "He wishes us to be spread out in 'well-defended camps.' He is having them expand the production caverns, as well, to hold the entire host and shield it from this human artillery." The older God King flapped his crest and snorted. "He is in love with the humans I think."

Cholosta'an looked at him sideways, swinging his long neck around nervously. The oolt'ondai was far older than he, with tremendously more experience. It showed in the outfitting of his tenar and the weapons of the cosslain that surrounded him. While Cholosta'an understood the draw of Tulo'stenaloor for himself, he had to wonder what drew the old ones, the long time warriors like Orostan.

The oolt'ondai noted his regard and flapped his crest until the wind raised a small dust cloud. "Don't get me wrong, I follow Tulo'stenaloor and I believe."

"Why?" Cholosta'an asked. "I know why I'm here; I was born on this mudball and I intend to get off of it. But every battle I've been drawn to has been a slaughter. I've replaced most of my oolt twice over to no gain. Three times I've had to return to my chorho, bowl in hand, asking for a resupply. If I return again I will be denied. But you don't *need* a chance. You don't even have to *be* on this Alldn't cursed planet."

Orostan considered his answer for a moment then flapped his crest again. "If you have actual needs, for thresh or ammunition, even replacements for damaged equipment, tell me and it will be made good; you shall *not* go into battle with the Host of Tulo'stenaloor underequipped. There will be a bill if we succeed, otherwise it will be charged to the Host. To the rest of the question, call it another way, The Way of the Race. The humans are the first race to challenge the Po'oslena'ar in many long years. For the Po'oslena'ar there is only the Way. If we do not defeat the humans, if we do not continue on our Way, the tide of orna'adar will sweep over us and we will perish as a race. This is the homeworld of the Humans, the queen of the grat's nest. We must seize her and destroy her or we shall be destroyed in turn."

He scratched at a scar on the tenar and ruffled his crest. "The People almost took this planet by storm. We *have* taken most of it, but a few geographic areas remain. The most troublesome is surely this one. And I think that Tulo'stenaloor's plan will work. We have to think like the humans to defeat them and we must copy some of their ways while using our own also. But the most important thing we must do is we must *surprise* them. The humans have a saying 'to take somebody from behind.' Like many human sayings it has several overtones which don't translate well.

"You are right, I don't have to be here," the oolt'ondai admitted, looking to the mountains to the north. "I have four estates that are not in orna'adar; I have gathered the treasure of eight worlds and could live wherever I wished if I wanted to settle into death. I am an oolt'ondai, commander of my own oolt'poslenar. I can go anywhere in the galaxy that my drives will carry me and my personal oolt is armed with the finest weapons the People make so once I get there I can take any lands I desire. But for the race, for my genetic line, I am here. And, for the race, for our clans and for our lines, you and I, young eson'sora, we're going to crack this *stev*. We are going to take their passes, take their valleys and drive to the heart of the grat's nest, 'rolling them up' from behind. We are going to smash these humans flat."

# CHAPTER 4

*Rochester, NY, United States, Sol III*
*0547 EDT Sunday September 13, 2009* AD

"Just as soon as the arty arrives, we are going to smash these Posleen flat."

Mike didn't bother to look around; the silty water would have prevented a "real" view of the company commanders gathered in a crouch. Besides, his attention was fixed on the symbology being trickled into his eyes.

The inside of a suit of GalTech armor was filled with a semibiotic shock gel. The silvery gel was the medium that supported the billions of nannites that fed and cared for an ACS trooper, but it also served to prevent high speed impact injuries. Since these affected the head as much as, or more than, any other part of the body, the helmet was cushioned on all sides by the gel, leaving only a small portion open for the eyes, mouth and ears. The exterior of the helmet was opaque; what the "Protoplasmic Intelligence System" inside the armor saw was a fully conformable construction of the external view. This "construction" was, in turn, conveyed to the eye by small optics that were extruded from the helmet. A similar audio system threaded out of the wall of the suit and into the ear canal for hearing while air was pumped to the opening around the mouth.

This engineering, some said over-engineering, had stood O'Neal in good stead on Diess. There, when it all went to the wall, when a Posleen battlecruiser had come in for direct support of the invaders, he had taken the only road to "victory" he could see and used the last bit of his suit energy to fly up to the ship and hand detonate a cobbled together antimatter limpet mine.

He knew at the time that he was committing suicide; had sent a note to his wife to the effect. But through a series of low order physics probabilities and the "over-engineering" of the suits he had survived. Since then, many troopers had survived nearly as strenuous situations, although none *as* strenuous, and these days no one used the term "over-engineered." "Hideously expensive," yes. A command suit cost nearly as much as a small frigate. But not over-engineered.

The armor also permitted degrees of control that were both a blessing and a nightmare. A superior could control every aspect of the battle down to the smallest action of a subordinate. Which was the nightmare. However, it also permitted a commander to lay out a very detailed and graphic plan, then monitor events and intervene if necessary when, not if, the plan went awry.

Now, though, it permitted the major to cover last-minute changes with his company commanders and battle staff while standing on the bottom of the Genesee River.

"Word is we have an additional artillery battalion," he continued, updating the schematic with the icon for on-call artillery. "It's still not what I would prefer for this assault. But I think that it's all that we're going to get in less than five or ten days. And if we wait that long all that we'll really get is more Posleen.

"That brings us up to close to two brigades but only one of them is fully coherent and effective. That brigade will initiate with a time-on-target over our initial movement area. With luck that will plaster the Posleen in our way and this will be a walk in the park."

"Riiight," Captain Slight said, to assorted chuckles. The captain had come a long way from the newbie lieutenant who had joined Mike's company before the first landing of the Posleen and she was well respected by her company, what had been Mike's company. She was also trusted by her battalion commander.

"When we move forward, our right will be aligned on the canal," Mike pointed out. "So it will be covered. But our left flank is going to be as open as a gutted whale."

"I thought we were going to have a curtain barrage covering it," Captain Holder said. The Charlie company commander was responsible for the left.

"We are," Mike said with an unseen grimace. He worked his dip and spit into the pouch the somewhat prescient gel produced. "But Duncan is defining the battalion responsible for the barrage as 'shaky.' "

"Who'd he get that from?" Slight asked. The icon for the artillery coordinator was firmly fixed on the hill previously occupied by the battalion commander and for some of the same reasons. Among other things, it gave a lovely view of the battlefield. More importantly, it permitted the suit's sensor suite a lovely view of the battlefield, and what the suits could do with that information continued to astound everyone. Including, from time to time, the artificial intelligence devices that drove the suits.

However, the artillery that would be supporting the push was miles back, nowhere near the location of the battalion's artillery expert.

"I understand he is liaisoning with the Artillery Coordinator of the Ten Thousand," Mike answered in a lofty tone.

There was a grim chuckle from the officers.

"Colonel, I'll ask the question one last time," the captain said with a grim smile. The junior officer was slight, café au lait in complexion and furious. Furthermore, his reputation preceded him.

"Captain, there's nothing else to do," the older officer said seriously. "The guns are getting in place as fast as possible. I know it's not up to standard, but it's as fast as this unit is capable of. You have to understand, we're not some sort of super unit . . ."

"No, Colonel, you're not," the captain spat back. For most officers it would have been suicide, but Keren, and every other member of the Six Hundred, already knew what suicide was. Suicide was huddling around the Washington Memorial, damn near out of ammunition and completely out of hope, because you'd rather pile up the mound with your dead than back up one last yard. And the one thing that the Six Hundred never, ever accepted was an excuse. From anyone. "What you are is an artillery battalion of the United States Ground Forces. And you are expected to perform as such.

"Unless your command is laid in in the next three minutes, prepared to fire, I will ask for your relief. And General Horner will order it. And then *I* will take command of this battalion. If I have to *kill* every member in this unit, until I get to the last ten reasonably competent people, I will do so to get fire on target. Am I making myself perfectly clear?"

"Captain, I don't care who you are," the colonel said harshly. "I do *not* have to take that sort of tone from any goddamned O-3."

"Colonel," the officer said coldly, "I have *shot* superiors that failed to perform to my satisfaction. I don't give a flying fuck how you *feel* about getting reamed out by a captain; we no longer have time for your incompetence. You have one of three choices, lead, follow or die. Choose."

The colonel paused as he realized the captain was absolutely serious. And there was a pretty good chance that if a captain of the Six Hundred asked for his relief, it would be granted. That was what the Army was coming to, damnit.

"Captain, we will not be laid in in three minutes," he said reasonably.

"Colonel, have you ever heard of the Spanish Inquisition?" Keren asked tightly.

"Yes," the officer said and blanched. "I'm . . . sure we can get laid in to your satisfaction, Captain."

"Try," the captain rasped. "Try like the Posleen were about to eat your ass. Because if you're caught between the Posties and the Six Hundred, choose the Posties. Do I make myself clear?"

"Clear," the colonel answered and checked his salute before turning away.

Keren watched him leave with cold, dead eyes then stepped around the command Humvee by which they had been carrying on their quiet conversation. He assured himself that no one was watching, then, retaining the identical expression, casually threw up.

He washed out his mouth with a swig from his canteen and shook his head. It wasn't that he was unprepared to shoot the arrogant, incompetent bastard in command of the artillery. It was that it wouldn't help. The unit had been on support duty in

Fort Monmouth for so long they weren't in any way, shape or form prepared to do anything but fire, from exactly the same positions, on the same azimuths and elevations, day after day.

Unfortunately, they had been pulled out of their comfy positions as the ones "most excess to need" and sent to support the assault in Rochester. What "excess to need" was turning out to mean was "excessively incompetent." It was an old problem, when a unit called and said "we need your best for something hard" the unit that was losing the capability *naturally* did not want to send their best. Whether it was a levee of individuals or a shift of units, the commander always tended to send whoever they felt the most comfortable with losing.

And any commander in his right mind would be willing to get rid of this battalion of artillery. Keren had to wonder how many "friendly fire" incidents they had been involved in.

Keren shook his head again and pulled a cellphone out of his pocket. There were still plenty of the towers and, as long as the Posleen weren't jamming, they were a pretty decent way to communicate. And they weren't monitorable by most military units, which was a real plus at times.

"Hey Duncan, man, I think it's time for the Spanish Inquisition. . . ."

Mike watched the quality marker of the new artillery battery switch from Quality Two to QualFour and smiled. If things like that didn't happen, he'd wonder what was wrong.

"And it appears that Keren just downchecked them," he continued as the rumble of the brigade time on target started, right on time.

"Oh. Joy," Captain Slight said with a slightly hysterical

laugh. "We're going out there with our ass in the breeze, sir."

"And such a nice ass it is," Mike said in an abstracted tone. He was flipping at icons and as they changed back and forth knew that Duncan was doing the same. "The choice is the curtain barrage or on call fire. We can put down the curtain with mortars or shift the mortars to on call. Your call, so to speak. I want to shuffle the companies and put Bravo on the left flank. Your orders will be to spread yourself along the left flank and hold that zone until relieved by the Ten Thousand or other similar units. Since you'll be the most spread out, I'll give you the majority of the supplementary fire. For what it's worth, this number of mortars will make a lousy curtain barrage."

He knew that if he set the suit systems to simulated vision, the female officer would be tapping her fingers on the front of her helmet. It was a nervous habit that was the best substitute she had for nibbling her fingernails. Which, when she was out of armor, was what the commander did constantly. He could practically hear the plastic on plastic thunking sound from here.

"On call, sir," the captain said. "I'll want to make the company even more of an 'L' shape. And they'll eventually get in behind us."

"We'll make that bridge when we come to it," Mike answered. "Captain Holder, d'you have a problem taking the center?"

"Negative, Major," the commander replied. "We'll hammer them flat."

"Okay," O'Neal answered, resetting the markers for the three line companies. The three units were already short of bodies and inverting Bravo to cover the flank, necessary as that was, would reduce the density of fire, the "plowing the road" that the ACS depended on to reduce the Posleen swarms. The only reserve was going to be their Grim Reaper heavy weapon suits. Since the suits were configured for indirect fire support, if there was a breach in the line, the only people to take care of it would be the battalion command and staff. Not a pleasant thought, but it had happened before. He reconfigured the companies while the Artificial Intelligence Devices spread the line of attack for each individual trooper in the companies. The lines of attack were only recommendations, though. The ACS troops knew that if things changed they were supposed to think on their feet and get the job done. "Maximum aggression" was the byword. From the saying their commander used all too often, they just called it "Dancing with the Devil." "The artillery's getting ready to wind down support. Let's get reconfigured, fast."

The commanders handled it without even moving and from the surface the movement would have shown nothing but a series of odd ripples. The suit troopers accepted the change without comment; their systems gave them more than enough individual data to understand the reason and they were all chosen for more than just their aggressiveness. It was apparent that they were going to lose the support of the curtain barrage. Without it, the main threat changed to the left flank. And that meant, naturally, that Bravo company would be reassigned. Much as Mike tried to rotate the companies, everyone agreed that when it was really tough, Bravo got the call.

The troopers therefore handled the unexpected move with equanimity and dispatch. They had been arrayed on a line, ready to move out. This required shuffling nearly two hundred suits, under ten feet of water, but that, too, was no problem. The AIDs in each suit gave the path and the troopers followed the guidance, "flying" with their suit drivers in and around each other until all of them reached their assigned positions.

O'Neal didn't even look to see if there was a problem. The Panthers had been hammered until all that was left was bare metal; they could handle the move in their sleep. They could handle the next battle the same way, but the casualties would be steep. And then the battalion would be even shorter, with no significant resupply in sight.

He glanced at his timer and grimaced. He had hoped to move forward in the last stages of the artillery strike; the barrage wasn't going to hurt the suits. But the time-on-target was lifting already and they were just getting into place. It would have to be good enough.

"Move out."

Karen Slight grunted when she saw the actual conditions on the land. Until the suits had crested the water the situation had been a thing of icons and readouts. She could have slaved a view off of Duncan's suit, but it wouldn't have told her anything the sensors didn't. In fact, it would have been far less clear. But what the sensors couldn't give her was the graphic image of the shot-torn hell that was central Rochester.

The time-on-target had been a mixture of variable time, impact and cluster ammunition that stretched in a one kilometer box with the canal on the south side, Castleman Avenue on the east, the river on the west and Elmwood Avenue on the north, and it had flayed the Posleen in the pocket. There had been thousands, tens of thousands at least, of the centauroids preparing to push across the river and most of them had been killed outright by the fire. The bodies of the Arabian horse-sized aliens were strewn across the shattered rubble of the city, three and four deep in spots.

This left a ruined wasteland of piled rubble, scattered bodies and the wispy miasma of propellant fumes, smoke and dust that lingered over a battlefield. But in that fire-laden mist, shapes were moving.

Some of the Posleen, many of them even, had survived the initial time-on-target and were now reacting to the walking barrage. Some were running away and others were standing up and waiting for it to come to them. But a few were learning the human trick of finding cover. It was hard with a variable time barrage; to avoid the slashing overhead shrapnel of VT required overhead cover and the damage of the last few weeks of constant battle had destroyed most of that. But some few of them dove for remaining cellars and bunkers. And they would surely be back after the barrage moved on.

The battalion moved to its first phaseline, the high banks of the river, and flopped to its belly as if it were one beast. The suits had activated their cloaking holograms and the only sign of their presence was a brief series of mud splashes. Some of the survivors of the barrage had been God Kings, however, and they used their sensors to track on and fire at the cloaked combat suits.

The humans responded immediately, the mass fire of the battalion seeking out the better armed God Kings for lethal attention, but the far more numerous "normals" were now aware that there was an enemy on their flank and they turned towards the threat and opened fire more or less at random.

Most of the fire was high, but some of it was punching into the ground and even into the troopers of the battalion. It was under these conditions that the ACS proved its worth. Hunkered flat to the ground as they were, they made poor targets at best and most of the rounds that hit them, that would have demolished a Bradley fighting vehicle, glanced off harmlessly.

Not all of them, though, and Slight grunted again

when she saw the first data lead go dead from her company. The location and name of the trooper, Garzelli from third platoon, flashed briefly on her heads up then faded. She didn't allow herself to focus on it, she just noted it and marked it for pickup. Her first sergeant would have done the same thing, but no harm in being sure.

She looked up at the heights overlooking the battlefield. The slope was actually sharp and the battalion was enjoying some cover from the Posleen that were massed above. They had not been under the hammer of fire and were fresh; when they moved to engage things would be hot and Bravo would be in the thick of it.

Most of the remaining fire on the flat had been suppressed, however, and she noted and passed the battalion commander's orders to begin the movement to the next phaseline.

This was when it got a tad tricky. Only one of her platoons, third, was actually going to be "on-line" with the rest of the battalion, the other two were going to be echeloned to provide cover for the left flank. This required that the two platoons wait as the battalion moved forward and string themselves out like beads along that side. She waited until about half of them had started forward and then moved out herself. After a few steps she stumbled and looked down at the Posleen she had tripped over. It was impossible to tell if it was a God King or a normal; the entire front half had been devoured by one of the 155mm impact rounds. But there was enough left to get in her way and as they progressed it was only going to get worse. She was having a hell of a time watching the whole company while also watching out for herself and she sometimes wondered how in the hell O'Neal did it.

Mike didn't even notice, consciously, the icon for

friable ground, but he stamped down, shoving his boot through the chest cavity of the Kessentai then kicking to free it as he moved on. The symbology for the ground around him would have been impossible for anyone else to read, a hyper-compressed schematic showing ground level and conditions. The original schematic had replaced a lower screen view that he had originally used after falling through ice a couple of times. Then the half screen of images had been compressed laterally until all that was left was an inch-high readout stretching all the way across his view.

His "view" of the battle, after five years of command, was nothing *but* a mass of icons and graphs; an external view was nothing but a distraction. He ran his eyes across the readouts with satisfaction. All the companies were moving out in good order and Captain Slight was doing an excellent job getting Bravo in position along Elmwood Avenue. Sooner or later the mass of Po'oslena'ar around the Strong Memorial Hospital, what was left of it, was going to come tear-assing down in a tena'al charge and smash into Bravo like an avalanche. As long as they waited until Bravo was fully in the groove it shouldn't matter. And so far all was in the green.

A couple of the bridges were showing as questionable, the icons outlined in yellow. He didn't bother to try to find out why; his AID was processing data from a thousand sources and any of it could have led to that conclusion. Over the last few years Shelly had become remarkably adept at gauging the quality of units and if she said the bridges probably would take a bit longer than anticipated to move into the hot zone she was probably right. Another screen showed the symbology for the Ten Thousand getting into position.

There were high buildings across the river and he ⸱d the fact that Kessentai on the heights were beginning to drop. The snipers of the Ten Thousand were obviously getting into the act, using both their own weapons and tripod mounted "teleoperated" systems. At those ranges, though, it was unlikely that they could get rounds into the power storage compartments of the tenar, which was unfortunate; when one of the .50 caliber sniper rounds hit the storage crystals the unstable matrix tended to turn into a good copy of a five-hundred-pound bomb.

The battalion had reached the Conrail line, and he ordered a short stop to get everything set. The Reapers, who had been responding to calls for fire all along, yanked charging tubes out of the huge ammo baskets welded on their backs while the regular ACS troopers checked ammunition levels and shifted as necessary. The standard suits carried hundreds of thousands of the depleted uranium teardrops but the grav-guns fired nearly five hundred a second. This meant that the suit troopers occasionally had to worry about running out of ammunition, a situation that would have been considered impossible before the war.

Bulbous bodied medic and engineer suits moved forward supplying additional ammunition to the fighters and checking on the dropped data links. Such damage usually meant that the trooper was terminal, a DRT or Dead Right There in the cold battlefield parlance of the medics, but occasionally it was just massive suit damage that the trooper had survived. In that case, nine times out of ten, the medic would leave the trooper anyway.

A few troopers had fallen back from the fight with serious injuries or damaged weapons. Usually anything that penetrated a suit was fatal, but, again, if the trooper survived the initial shock the suits *would* keep them alive until pickup, sealing the injury, debriding the wound, attacking infection and either putting the trooper out or shutting down the nerve endings depending on the tactical situation. And even such injuries as lost limbs were, at worst, an inconvenience as O'Neal was well aware; he came away from Diess with only one functioning limb. Regeneration and Hiberzine were perhaps the two greatest boons the Galactics had presented to humans and the suit troopers well knew it; most of the veterans had lost at least one limb at some point.

Mike spit a bit of dip into a pocket in the undergel. The icons for the Posleen on the heights indicated that they were starting to get their shit together. Among other things, there were signs of Kessentai going ground-mounted. If they were also smart enough to keep their crests down, the snipers across the river were going to have a damned hard time spotting them. Even if the snipers *could* pick them out it was a bad sign. It meant there was a God King who knew what he was doing and could command the obedience of others. Now was when the battalion was really going to earn its pay. Time to Dance.

Duncan hunched forward and wished he could get a Marlboro in the suit. He'd done it a couple of times before, but the suit had a hell of a time handling the fumes. The undergel acted . . . real strange for a couple of days afterwards. He didn't know if it was toxic shock from the smoke or if it had just gotten pissed off; the underlayers developed "personalities" after a while that were still something of a mystery. But whatever the reason, he finally decided it was a bad idea and gave it up.

Which left him trying to direct nearly a division of artillery while having a nicotine fit.

He was watching the same icons as the battalion

commander and if he didn't have Mike's instincts for how the Posleen moved he could tell they were shaping up for an attack. He'd been calling for fire from the two battalions of 155 tasked for "on call" fire, but they were half useless. He'd finally switched to using the organic mortar elements of the waiting divisions and the Ten Thousand. There were quite a few of those that were not very responsive, or bloody inaccurate, but there were also nearly twice as many of them as the artillery. Coordinating all of them was a bastard; some of them wouldn't respond to electronic commands while others would . . . but incorrectly. It left his AID "faking" his voice all over the nets. But they were starting to get some good fire going on the Posleen assembly areas just as the main force began its push.

He took a look at the flow of the icons and wished he could scratch his head. His *guess* was that they were going to come down the sidestreets around PS 49. Most of them had been using West Brighton and Elmwood Avenues to move up to the flimsy crossing. If they followed the same route they'd be filing right into the "corner" of the battalion and cutting hard into Bravo company.

The problem was time of flight. The Posleen moved more or less like horses and just about as fast. So he had to decide where the majority of them were going to be in four or five minutes, the time it took to send the order and have it turned into fire commands then have the artillery or mortars fly, rather than where they were right then.

It was tricky. But that's why he got paid the big bucks and didn't have to be in the line anymore.

Now they seemed to be angling towards Elmwood Avenue and with a short plea for luck to anyone who was listening he concentrated all his available fire in and around PS 49.

✧        ✧        ✧

Mike noted the shifting call-for-fire icons and nodded. It was a good call and that would probably catch a large percentage of the assault. But there were still going to be leakers, through the fire and around to the sides. That was up to Captain Slight to handle and it was time to move out; the walking barrage in front of them had already completed its timed halt and was preparing to move on.

Captain Slight relayed the order to move out and returned her attention to the north. The massive mortar barrage was just getting into swing and the Posleen were trying hard to get ahead of it. Somewhere around the hospital there was a God King or God Kings with sense and they were not only pushing "their" forces towards the humans, but pushing the undirected mass of normals who had lost God Kings ahead of them. This was just about like herding cats, since normals that were not immediately bonded after the death of their leader caste tended to get chaotic and grouchy. But in this case there was no place for the unbonded to go but straight into Bravo.

It started as the battalion moved out again. Most of the unbonded that were carrying heavy weapons had dropped them and most of the fire was from 1mm railguns and shotguns, neither of which was even noticeable by the suits. Unfortunately, buried in the mass of normals was the occasional one with a heavier 3mm railgun, that could penetrate a suit if the Posleen got lucky, or a hypervelocity missile launcher that could smash a suit like a walnut. And with all the bodies in the way it was hard for the AIDs to point them out for special attention.

There was also the problem that the company could not just *ignore* the huge mass to concentrate on the more dangerous companies behind it. Every one of those centauroids was carrying a monomolecular boma blade. Enough chops from one of those and the suit integrity would be gone; one of the greatest fears of any suit trooper was getting stampeded by the horses.

So as the avalanche of Posleen started down the narrow streets, dodging in and out of the rubble, the company took it under fire.

The Indowy-made grav-guns fired 3mm droplets of carbon-coated depleted uranium that were accelerated to a small fraction of the speed of light. The carbon coating was added after it was discovered the DU rounds tended to "melt" at about ten kilometers in standard air pressure, but the carbon didn't prevent them from creating their characteristic "silver lightning" of plasma discharge. In addition, because of the relativistic speed of the rounds, when they hit a solid object they converted most of their kinetic energy into a racking explosion.

Thus the wave of Posleen was met by nearly a hundred lines of actinic fire, reaching out to waves of racking explosions as the tiny "bullets" converted themselves into uranium backed fire. The first wave was shattered by the volley; any of the rounds that missed traveled on to hit succeeding aliens.

Fighting the Posleen in a situation like this was often likened to trying to stop an avalanche with fire hoses and that was precisely what was happening here. As long as Bravo kept the fire up, none of the Posleen could get a good shot off before being swept away in a tide of grav-gun fire. At the same time, the mortars and artillery were thrashing them in the pocket.

However, this was simply ground they had to cross to get to their objective. The battalion couldn't stop to wait for Bravo to kill all the Posleen around the hospital. Even if it was possible, and it probably wasn't,

# CHAPTER 5

*Rochester, NY, United States, Sol III*
*0633 EDT Sunday September 13, 2009* AD

Mike glanced at his monitors and watched the movement without expression. The worst part about it was
the ammunition counters. In that one brief engagement,
Bravo had used up fifteen percent of their ammunition and there was no end to the Posleen in sight. The
plan had been for an orderly advance to the objective,
basically a horseshoe by the Genessee Bridge, but he
was pretty sure that was out the airlock. The lack of
a curtain barrage and the frantic and fragmented nature
of the mortar fire that replaced it meant they were
going to have to run for it.

This was exactly the situation that he had feared when
he had had his confrontation with Horner. The battalion
was strung out, in its most vulnerable possible position
and still well short of its goal, the top of the ridge overlooking the river.

If they didn't have the ridge the Posleen could pour

fire into the bridgehead, and the battalion, from above. There would be no way to effectively direct fire and there would be no way to reduce the Posleen numbers, much less break their spirit, from in the valley. But when the ACS finally got there, the battalion would come into the view of literally millions of Posleen, millions of still *unbloodied* Posleen. They needed all the artillery *there* to suppress the Posleen fire and for smoke missions so that the normals couldn't target the battalion. So far the majority of the battalion had been able to move with relative impunity because of the supporting fire from the "better" artillery battalions. If that went away the casualties would start to mount fast.

But there were tens of thousands of really angry Posleen starting to dig themselves out of the rubble around the hospital. And they were getting ready to fall on Bravo Company like the hammers of hell. Bravo Company needed all the artillery *there* to keep from being overrun. If they didn't get some support, and fast, they were going to be thresh-in-a-can before you could say "Spam, spam, spam, spam and rat."

The only thing that would save their ass was more artillery, which they weren't going to get, or sacrificing the Ten Thousand, which he wasn't willing to do.

There just weren't enough resources to get the job *done*.

In other words, just another day fighting the Posleen.

"Duncan, shift all artillery to the north in support of Bravo Company. Battalion . . . prepare for tena'al charge." He touched a series of imaginary keys and the scene started to change. Where before the holographic camouflage had been blending the suits into the background it now shifted to reveal larger versions of the demon worked into his own armor. As it changed the armor began to boom out a driving electric drum solo.

"Okay," he growled, stamping downward on the dead Posleen at his feet to get a better footing. "Playtime's over. Let's kick some ass."

"Jesus, Mike, it's not *that* bad?" Horner whispered as the suit units seemed to go into hyperdrive. All of them had shape-shifted into large demonic creatures and then started sprinting for the heights, laying down a curtain of fire as they went. The silver lightning was *chewing* the ridgeline, sweeping away the front rank of Posleen as they came into view.

He looked to the north and it was apparent that the company there was in serious trouble. The artillery on the hills had stopped and he could only presume that meant it was shifting to the north in support of that unit. The company did not seem to have taken major casualties yet. But there was a huge mass of undirected normals heading for it and if they could not be stopped they were going to hack the beleaguered company to bits. It was clear that O'Neal had chosen to remove the artillery support from the majority of his unit in the belief that the company could hold out. Overall it did not look like a good bet to Horner; spread out as they were, the ACS were inviting defeat in detail. They might take and hold the bridgehead, but it looked like it would be at the expense of most of the battalion.

On the other hand, the overall requirement had been laid by one General Jack Horner. So he couldn't exactly complain when they did whatever it took to perform the mission.

"Another day at the races," Colonel Cutprice said from the other window. "I'm not going to wait for the bridge. First Batt is fully airmobile; I'll send them across immediately using their tenars in support of Bravo company then start ferrying the rest across to support the ridge. Otherwise we're going to end this day without a battalion of ACS."

"I'll go down and see if shouting at people gets the bridges up any faster," Horner said with a smile, his version of a frown. "And find out why the boats aren't already assembled."

"That would be nice," Cutprice said in a disinterested tone. "It's going to be kinda lonely over there for a while."

"'Course, what else is new, sir?" Sergeant Major Wacleva asked. "I'll go get your body-armor."

Horner looked over at the colonel and smiled again, tightly. "Do you really think that is a good idea, Colonel? Leading from the front is for squad leaders, not colonels."

"As opposed to, say, watching the ACS slaughtered from across the river, General?" Cutprice asked, pulling out a cigar and slowly lighting it. "Yeah, I think it's a grand idea." He looked east where a cloud shadow seemed to be moving rather fast and frowned.

"Ah yes," Cutprice said after a moment. "Right on time. Wouldn't be a really screwed up battle without a five percenter."

Horner looked to the east and up. "Well, that, at least, we can take care of." He tapped his AID and gestured out the window. "Nag, tell SheVas Twenty-Three and Forty-two to engage the approaching Lamprey at will."

"Colonel, you know that discussion we had the other day?" Sergeant Major Wacleva asked, walking back into the room with two sets of body armor.

"Which one?"

"The one about 'when do you know it's really bad'?"

"Sure."

"Well, it's bad if the Ten Thousand shows up. And it's worse if the ACS shows up. And it's really, really bad if General Horner shows up. But the ultimate in bad has to be when *two* SheVas show."

Attenrenalslar was what the humans had taken to calling a "five percenter." Ninety-five percent of Posleen God Kings understood only the simplest imperatives. Eat, screw, fight, take territory and repeat until death. However, that remaining five percent was, in some ways, more trouble than the other ninety-five. The "five percenters" were the ones that jammed the humans' frequencies at seeming random, but always it seemed at the worst possible time. It was the five percenters that occasionally took over a fire net to the consternation of all. It was the five percenters that organized groups of Posleen to act in what was an almost concerted action. And it was the five percenters that used their Lampreys and Command Dodecahedrons as airmobile units.

One of O'Neal's nightmares was somebody who would organize all the five percenters into one massive unit.

Currently, though, Attenrenalslar was one of the very few God Kings that had determined that the best way to turn the tide of this battle was to take his lander across the river and attack the humans from behind. He might be the only one; the percentages on "air-mobile" had gotten worse and worse for the Posleen of late.

Early in the war it was a nearly guaranteed tactic. The humans had very few weapons that could engage the landers and as long as they stayed below the horizon from one of the few remaining Planetary Defense centers, the humans almost had to wait for them to land before having any real chance to attack the Posleen within. Since the landers also mounted anti-personnel weaponry, not to mention space-to-space weaponry that was good for taking out most of a battalion, they could attack ground units with impunity. The wonder was that the Posleen didn't use them all the time.

However, that weakness had been noted even before the enemy made their first landing; Mike O'Neal's first Medal of Honor accrued from almost single-handedly taking out a command ship. But the method was not considered survivable.

In the first major Earth landing it appeared that a battleship had managed, through a fluke more than anything, to take out a Lamprey. From that was born the concept of the SheVa Gun, the sort of weird bastard weapon that is only created in the midst of really terrible wars.

The gun was named after the Shenandoah Valley Industrial Planning Commission, the group that had first solved all the various design problems inherent in the new system, and the majority of the first parts and pieces of the massive construction were made in the Roanoke Iron Works.

The basic parameters for the weapon were simplicity in themselves. The gun was an extended barrel, smoothbore, 16" battleship cannon. Because of the occasional necessity of rapid fire, the standard 16" "bag and round" method of loading, which involved sliding a 1200-pound round followed by fifty-pound bags of powder, had been replaced with a single shell the size of a small ICBM. The SheVa gun carried eight rounds as a "standard load" and a tractor-trailer could haul two "four-packs" that permitted reloading in under ten minutes. Each gun was loaded with standard rounds, but there were at least two tractor trailers "on-call" carrying special munitions, including both sensor and antimatter area effect weapons, at all times.

The other parameters were that it be able to fire from two degrees below horizontal to ninety seven degrees above with a swiveling turret and that the system be fully mobile. It was this combination that had caused all the design teams to almost give up in despair. That was, until the good old boys (and girls) from the Shenandoah went ahead and admitted that the parameters just meant it needed to be bigger than anyone was willing to admit, even privately.

The monstrosity that was finally constructed defied belief. The transporter base was nearly a hundred meters long with two fifty-meter-wide treads on either side supported by four-story-high road wheels. The "gun" was mounted on shock absorbers the size of small submarines and constructed using some of the same techniques. The swivel turret was two stories *thick*, constructed of multiple pieces "welded" together by an explosive welding technique, and nearly fifty meters across. The upper deck was six-inch steel plate, not for any armoring purpose, but because when the gun fired anything else would buckle.

When the design was mostly done the power source was obvious; there wasn't enough diesel in the entire United States to support the projected requirements for the guns. On the other hand, Canada's supplies of pitchblende were plentiful and above the weather-line that the Posleen preferred. Therefore, nuclear was the only way to go. However, putting a large "reactor control crew" onboard seemed silly. Finally, they "borrowed" a South African design for a simple, practically foolproof nuclear vessel called a "pebble-bed helium" reactor. The system used layered "pebbles" that automatically mitigated the reaction and helium—which could not pick up, and thus release, radiation—as the temperature transfer medium. Even if the coolant system became totally open, that is if it started venting helium to the air, no radiation would be released and the reactor would not "melt-down." Of course, if the reactor took a direct hit there would be "hot" uranium scattered all over the ground but other than that, no problem; the system was absolute proof against "China Syndrome."

The control center and living quarters were actually located underneath the behemoth and were the size of a small trailer. It wasn't that it took a large crew; the system could actually be run by one person. It just made more sense that way. The designers looked at the physical requirements for the three-man crew and finally settled on a small, highly armored command center. But the monstrosity had so much power and space to spare that they added to the design until they had a small living quarters that would permit the crew to live independent of the surroundings.

The designers also included a rather interesting evac vehicle.

So when the crews of SheVas Forty-Two and Twenty-Three got the word that a lander was on the way, they dropped their cards, dropped their Gameboys and slid smoothly into action.

"This is Forty-Two, General," said Lieutenant Colonel Thomas Wagoner. Forty-Two was a brand new SheVa, *the* newest until there was a "Forty-Three." And Lieutenant Colonel Thomas Wagoner was a brand new SheVa commander. He had just been transferred, over his howling objections, from command of an armored battalion and was having trouble adjusting to being a tank commander, by any other word, again. But he was pretty sure he could remember how to crank a track, by God. "We're on it.

"Okay, boys, blow the camouflage; it's time to lay some tube."

Duncan felt a rumbling in the seat of his pants and configured his view to "swing" westward. The remains of West Rochester were shuddering as if the town had been hit by a minor but persistent earthquake and he could see boulders being kicked loose from the hill he was sitting on. When the viewpoint finally swung to the west it became obvious what had caused the effect.

Behind him, about four miles to the rear on the south side of the canal, an oddly shaped hill was shuddering apart. As the greenish foam fell away the enormous shape of a SheVa gun was revealed.

The thing was just *ugly*. There was no other word to describe it. The bastardized cannon required something like a crane cantilever to keep it from bending and the massive construction of the whole system didn't permit anything on the order of beauty. Like a steam shovel for a giant open-pit mine or a deep ocean drilling platform, the only things prior to the SheVa to be built on its scale, it was pure function.

The scale of the guns was hard to grasp until you realized that the tiny ants running alongside weren't even *people*, they were trucks.

He shook his head as the thing first waggled from side to side to warn all the little "crunchies" that it was preparing to maneuver and then accelerated up the side of a small moraine, smashing a factory to bits on the way.

"Fucking show-off," Duncan muttered, turning back to the east.

"Forty-two," called the commander of SheVa Twenty-Three, "be aware that we have two more lift emanations including a C-Dec."

"Got that," said Colonel Wagoner. His intent was to use the moraine as cover until they could get a good hull-down shot at the Lamprey. The problem with SheVa guns was that "hull-down" generally required something like a small river valley; the moraine was as good as he was going to get.

But when the other two lifted, they would be in a position to rake Forty-Two's position from the north. The question was whether to engage them as they came in view or after the leading Lamprey.

"Sergeant Darden," he called to the driver. "Swing us around to the south side of the moraine with the gun about forty degrees to the angle of the slope. We'll take the current Lamprey as it bears then continue around the slope to engage the others." He switched to the SheVa frequency and glanced at the battlefield schematic. "Twenty-Three, prepare to move out. As we engage the first Lamprey, engage the first of the trailers. Then we'll gang up on number three."

"Got it, sir," called the other gun. "Time to show these ACS pussies what 'heavy metal' really means."

Duncan just sighed as the ground *really* started to shake. The secondary screen showed another hill—this one much less artistic; it had buildings sticking out of it—coming apart as the second SheVa went into action, its cantilevered gun pointing to the east.

It suddenly occurred to Duncan that the gun was not pointing particularly high in the sky. He looked at the gun, looked towards the probable target and had just enough time to say: "Oh, shit," before the weapon fired.

The rounds for the SheVa guns used the equivalent of a battleship 16" gun "max charge." The bullet, however, was a sabot round, a depleted uranium "arrow" surrounded by a thermoplastic "shoe." The bullet, therefore, was very light compared to the standard 16" gun "round." And instead of a rifled barrel, which permitted a round to stabilize in flight by spin, but also retarded the speed of the round, it was a smoothbore. The barrel was also extended to nearly three times the length of a standard sixteen-inch barrel, thus permitting more of the energy from the charge to be imparted to the bullet.

Since round speed is a function of energy imparted versus round weight and barrel drag, the round left the barrel at speeds normally obtainable only by spacecraft.

The plastic "shoe" fell off within half a mile and what was left was an eight-inch-thick, six-foot-long, pointed uranium bar with tungsten "fins" on the back. The fins stabilized its flight. And fly it did, crossing the twenty kilometers to the target, trailing a line of silver fire, in just under two seconds. However, such speed and power do not come without some minor secondary effects.

Duncan dug plasteel fingers in the bedrock as the hurricane of wind hit. The sonic boom, which shattered windows and even walls in the hospital down the hill, was almost an afterthought to the wind. It was the wind, driven to tornado speed, which tore at buildings and people throughout Rochester, ripping off roofs, toppling walls, turning trucks on their sides and pitching troops around like bowling pins.

Whatever secondary effects the round might have had, its primary effect was even more spectacular. Simple kinetic impact would usually destroy a Lamprey or even a C-Dec—when the rounds did not explode they tended to punch all the way *through* the ships. But the designers of the SheVa guns weren't satisfied with "usually." So at the core of the SheVa round was a small charge of antimatter. Only the equivalent of a ten-kiloton nuclear weapon.

The effect of the round punching into the ship was obliterated by the rush of silver fire that gouted from every seam and port. For a moment the ship seemed like it would hang together, but then it just came apart in a blossom of fire that consumed the Posleen for a quarter of a mile around. Large pieces, the size of cars and trucks, flew out as far as the human battle lines and bits the size of a human head reached even to Duncan's location.

"Show-offs," Duncan muttered, dusting off some dirt. He picked up a piece of Lamprey that had impacted on the hilltop and tossed it in the air. "Sure, it's easy to do with the right equipment. Try doing it with just a suit sometime."

"Target," said Twenty-Three. "Your turn, Colonel."

"Right," Wagoner said. "Try to get some elevation next time; the secondaries on that one shook up the whole corps."

"Crunchies," Twenty-Three called. "What can you say?"

"You can say 'Yes, sir,'" said Wagoner. "And get some cover."

"Yes, sir."

"Forty-Two out." He tapped a control and nodded as the line of travel dropped into place. The target line was plotted and potential secondary damage noted. They would be firing over the edge of the corps, but not near any of the hospital like that idiot in Twenty-Three. And they would be higher off the ground by at least a thousand feet. The damage should be minimal.

"Forty-Two, prepare to engage," he said over the intercom. "Target in three, two, one . . ."

Attenrenalslar cursed as the trailing command ship exploded and began moving his Lamprey from side to side, hoping to throw off the aim of those demon-cursed weapons.

The vehicle that had engaged the command ship had already disappeared behind one of the small mountains that dotted this plain and he was sure the instruments had detected another for a moment. But deciphering the cursed technology of the Alldenata was a task for those who had studied it; most of the icons were unfamiliar to him.

"Come out, though," he whispered, caressing a weapons control that was targeted on the distant hillock. "Come out little abat and see what Attenrenalslar has in store for you. . . ."

"Fucker's maneuvering, Colonel," Sergeant Pritchett called. The gunner turned the SheVa gun to full auto as the Lamprey came in sight and clamped down on the firing circuit. "Solution coming up."

Millimeter wave radar on the side of the gun "painted" the target, comparing it to the electronic pictures it stored of various Posleen equipment. The onboard computer determined that, yes, this was a lander and the lack of return from an "Identify, Friend or Foe" query indicated that, yes, this was a valid target. It then ran a laser down the barrel, determining that it was in good condition to fire and another on the outside determining that all the support structures that were supposed to be supporting were in fact functioning. Last it computed barrel distortion, number of rounds fired through the barrel, temperature of the air and a myriad of other variables to arrive at an adequate firing solution.

It also noted in passing that the target was slowly maneuvering. But when the distance to target is less than ten kilometers and the round is traveling at twenty-five hundred meters per second, that is less than four seconds of movement on the part of the target. And it was a *biiiig* target.

❖     ❖     ❖

"Fuscirto uut," Attenrenalslar snarled. "There *are* two." It was unlikely that the secondary weapons would scratch that thing; it was the size of a oolt'pos. But he tried to slew the ship to get a plasma cannon to bear.

"On the way!" Pritchett called as the entire world went red.

The gun used more energy in one shot than a brigade of armor and although the gun was heavily reinforced and the platform was the size of an oil rig, it still shook the entire beast like a terrier shaking a rat.

But before the last rumble had faded away, Darden had thrown the monster in reverse and Pritchett was ensuring the automatic loading sequence was progressing properly.

"Target!" Colonel Wagoner said with a note of satisfaction. "Now *that* is what I call laying tube." Maybe he could get used to being a tank commander again after all.

Mike grinned inside his armor as a wash of overpressure blasted Posleen off the ridgeline. "Cool. Now if we could just get a little of that over by Slight."

The battalion had covered the thousand meters to the heights in just under sixty seconds, long enough for the Posleen landers to react and be neutralized in turn by the SheVa guns Horner had called up. There had been several thousand Posleen in the pocket. Most of them were still dazed from the artillery fire, but quite a few had put up a struggle. None had survived.

Now the Posleen were just below the ridgeline, at the point called the "military crest." The wash of nuclear fire had probably opened up a fair-sized hole in the Posleen on the height, so it was undoubtedly

time for the ACS to earn their pay. Mike tapped a
control and the entire battalion took one leap to the
edge of the natural parapet. They probably weren't
going any farther and with the way the ridge was
shaped it wouldn't even be necessary to dig in. After
ensuring that that was the case, he elevated his main
gun and took a peek through the sensor system.

"Oh, shit," Mike whispered. At the first view of the
conditions in the valley beyond, his readouts had gone
blood red and he just had to clear the visor to see
what was really there as the entire battalion opened
fire.

From his perch Horner had been able to see some
of the forces beyond the ridge, but the view from the
ACS made his belly clench; as far as the eye could see
the ground was a seething mass of Posleen. Earlier
estimates had been something on the order of four
million; assuming the density that they saw there and
continuing only four miles out of sight Little Nag was
calculating it at over for-*ty* million.

"We can't do this, we can't do this . . ." Mike heard.
The circuit was open to the entire battalion and he was
picking up bits and snatches of conversation. The suits
were protected by the cover of the top of the hill, with
only their guns elevated above the crest. But a plasma
cannon or hypervelocity missile fired from the far side
of the other valley could tear through the ground and
take them out with just a couple of hits. For that
matter, the number of Posleen meant that some of
them were bound to make it through the fire, if for
no other reason than that others were masking them.
And once the Posleen got to hand-to-hand range, their
boma blades could get through the armor. Not to
mention point-blank cannon and railgun fire.

"Steady down," Mike said. He'd turned off the unpleasant view and had pulled up the schematics again. They were saying the same thing, but the view wasn't so visceral. "Steady down, keep your barrels low and maintain fire dispersion." He glanced at his readouts and chuckled. "The good news is that even *we* can't miss." Because of the automation of the systems and the fact that the ACS was designed to "spew" fire, it was an article of faith among the conventional forces that they couldn't hit the broad side of a barn.

"Major," said Captain Holder. "We're getting heavily flanked to the north. It's not like they're meaning to do it, but that's where they're being pushed."

"I'm aware of that, Captain," O'Neal said calmly. The numbers on Bravo did not look good. They had twice the separation, which meant half the fire pressure, that the rest of the battalion did. And in the face of forty million Posleen the main battalion's fire lanes seemed woefully inadequate. For that matter, Bravo had already expended forty percent of their onboard ammo. "Duncan, get all available fire in front of Bravo Company."

"What about us, sir?" asked Captain Holder.

"Well," Mike answered, "we're just going to have to kill all these Posleen by our own selves."

"We're in the right place, though," Mike whispered to himself. Shelly, correctly, didn't transmit the mutterings. "We've got the heights, we've got the position, one flank, at least, is secure. We can do this. All we have to do is hang on."

The majority of the Posleen directly in front of Alpha and Charlie company for a half kilometer or so had been killed by the explosion of the second lander. But that dead zone was quickly being filled up by the tremendous pressure from the rear. The Posleen, as normal, were coming on fast, hard and blind, charging right into the fire. But this time there were so many of them it might just work.

Mike had gamed out scenarios just *about* this bad and "won." That is, some personnel survived and they held on long enough that the follow-on forces were able to get into position. But in this case he had no artillery support and the battalion was just too spread out. It didn't take him long to calculate their odds of survival.

"Slim to none," he muttered.

"Battalion," he called. "All units lay down interlocking fire with your sharpshooters concentrating on the God Kings. Bravo, you need to tuck your corner in a little. All Reapers from all companies to the corner and dig in. All medics and technicians just became ammo runners; start ferrying ammo and power packs. And bring up the Reapers flechette cannons; I think this is going to end up being some close-in work." He worked his dip and spat as the first hypervelocity missile flew overhead. Over the past five years he swore he'd used up his entire fund of motivating things to say at moments like this. "I can't get my boots off to count on my toes, but if we win this one I do believe it will be one for the record books."

# CHAPTER 6

*Rochester, NY, United States, Sol III*
*0817 EDT Sunday September 13, 2009* AD

Staff Sergeant Thomas ("Little Tommy") Sunday realized that he just loved this shit too much.

He stepped off the platform attached to the side of the tenar and shot one of the Posleen in the head and smiled. The normal had been hacking at one of the pieces of shattered combat armor adorning the ridgeline. The extender for the suit's grav-gun was blown away and Sunday couldn't tell if the ACS trooper had tried fighting in direct view or if he'd been killed by one of Posleen at short range. Whatever, the position looked just about right for him to hunker down and do some killing of his own.

Reaching onto the tenar he hefted a two-hundred-pound battle-box in one hand and then marched up the hill, firing the twenty-pound railgun one-handed at any Posleen that showed its head over the ridge.

Thomas Sunday, Junior, had joined the United States

Ground Forces on his seventeenth birthday. In the intervening years he had grown into the spitting image of his father, an All-Pro linebacker in his time, and "Little Tommy" now stood six foot eight inches tall in his stocking feet and weighed in at nearly three hundred pounds. He hadn't been this big when he joined, though. His seventeenth birthday had been four months after the fall of his hometown of Fredericksburg, Virginia.

In the first landing, Fredericksburg had been surrounded and cut off from any aid by an estimated four million Posleen. A scratch force of the local Guard unit, a combat engineering battalion, and the local militia had held off the advance of the Posleen force for nearly twelve hours while a special shelter was prepared for the women and children. At the end of that long night the defenders had detonated a massive fuel-air bomb as cover for the hidden noncombatants and to remove any capability for the Posleen to use the bodies of the defenders as food, "thresh" as the Posleen called it.

The Posleen had come away from Fredericksburg with a healthy respect for the twin-turreted castle that was the symbol of the Engineers. Thomas Sunday had come away with a girlfriend and memories.

Of the people that he had grown up with, only four were left alive. Of the defenders of Fredericksburg, people with actual guns in their hands, he was one of only five still alive, including his girlfriend.

Not one member of his militia group. Not one friend, only a few acquaintances. His mother and sister had survived in the shelter and were now in a Sub-Urb in rural Kentucky. Everyone else was gone.

All of them were gone, wiped from the face of the earth as if they had never existed.

The Posleen had gone away with a respect for the Engineer, and by extension all humans. Little Tommy had come away with memories. And a burning desire to kill Posleen.

He did so now, dropping into the prone, snuggling up to the shattered combat suit for better cover and sticking his head up over the ridge to get a look at the conditions.

"Man, I have just *got* to get a transfer," he muttered.

The slope downward from his position was just *carpeted* with dead Posleen. There were still millions left to kill, sure, but the ACS must have accounted for nearly a million all by itself and at this point the remaining ranks were finding it hard to make it up the hill for all the bodies. There was no single bit of ground *visible* for at least a klick from the very top of the ridge down to the valley. Every single square inch was covered in bodies, most of them two, three, even four deep. And it was apparent to Sunday that very little of it had been artillery fire; Posleen that had been hit by artillery looked more chewed up for one thing.

He set the railgun up on a tripod and set it to autofire as he opened up the battle-box. There were four cases of ammunition and a dozen battery packs in it as well as a second railgun which he set up alongside the first. Then he ganged the ammunition cases together, giving two to each of the guns, and ganged up the battery packs. When all of that was done—he pulled his personal weapon—a 7.62 Advanced Infantry Weapon that had had the original barrel switched out for a "match grade"—off his back and adjusted his shooting glasses.

"Now to have *real* fun," he chuckled.

Crouching down he ran down the ridgeline a few meters, ensuring that the rest of his section was emplacing their weapons. Each of them was armed with a railgun and each three-man team manhandled a battle-box into place. Then as two of the members covered the third, the "layer" installed the last railgun in "auto" mode.

Basically, Sergeant Sunday had emplaced nearly as much firepower as half his team.

Now he found a comfortable spot to set up and peeked past a shattered cornerstone. The Posties were getting their shit together again and they just *couldn't* be allowed to do that.

Whistling the opening bars to "Dixie," Thomas Sunday, Junior, took a bead on a God King and gently squeezed the trigger. Just like a tit.

"Speaking of which," he said to himself as the first God King pitched backwards off his tenar. "One of these days I've just *got* to get down to North Carolina."

The first thing that Wendy noticed was the glow-paint. It was set to the flattest, whitest intensity. The room was almost painfully neat. Part of this was an intentional minimalism; there was very little of a personal nature at all. The walls were undecorated Galplas. The standard building material of the Galactic manufacturers of the Sub-Urb could be adjusted to reflect light in practically any tone or shade so naturally some bureacrat had decreed that there were only four that could be used: institutional green, institutional white, institutional blue and institutional salmon. These were institutional white and looked as if they'd just been extruded. Since this was an outer portion of Sector F that might, in fact, be the case. The combination of the light, the impersonal nature of the room and the lack of ornamentation gave the quarters a greasy, clinical feeling.

The second thing she noticed was the locker. The dull gray, unmarked polygon squatted in the far corner like some sort of mechanical troll. The material looked like regular Galplas, but it clearly was plasteel; the container was more proof against burglary than a steel safe. The Indowy manufacture was readily recognizable to any resident of a Sub-Urb—all the high security sections were sealed with the same stuff—and nothing but a high-watt plasma torch or a molecular grinder could cut it. There was a standard issue wall-locker in the room as well, so the plasteel safe was probably for security purposes.

With those exceptions, the room was otherwise standard for the Sub-Urb. By the memory-plastic door was an issue emergency locker, the only thing unusual about it being that it hadn't been vandalized. According to the seal and the inventory on the exterior, if she opened it up it should contain four emergency breath masks, a limited first aid kit and a pair of Nomex gloves. If it did, it would be the first complete set that Wendy had seen in four years. One wall sported a 27" flat-screen viewer and the carpet was basic polylon. All in all, it looked like an original issue personal living quarters. Or what they had looked like when Wendy had first been dropped in this underground hell.

The girl sitting on the room's single bed was wearing only a pair of running shorts and a midriff top. That was not terribly incongruous because she was *very* good looking. Her skin had the teenager fineness of a recent rejuvenation and her clearly unsupported breasts were high and firm. Strawberry-blond hair cascaded over her crossed arms and the white coverlet in a titian waterfall while sharp green eyes regarded her visitors with wary intelligence.

"Annie," said the doctor, "this is Wendy Cummings. She's going to help you with your recovery." The psychologist smiled cheerily. "We think it will help you at this stage in your development to get out a little more."

What Dr. Christine Richards did not say was that the post-op team was petrified. The latest round of cognitive tests had shown that, despite the speech impediment, Anne O. Elgars was fully recovered from her multi-year coma and experimental surgery. What they were not sure of was that it was, in fact, Anne Elgars.

"Hi, Anne," Wendy said, holding out her hand and giving a lopsided smile. "We're supposed to be 'compatible' as friends. We'll see. Sometimes psychologists can't tell their ass from their elbow."

The person who might or might not be Anne Elgars tilted her head to the side then returned the slight smile with a broad grin. "A . . . Ahm A . . . Annie tuh fr . . . en."

"Glad to hear it," said Wendy with a blinding smile in return. "I think we'll have lots to talk about. I understand you were in 33$^{rd}$ Division at Occoquan?"

"Well," said Dr. Richards. "I think I'll leave you two girls alone. Annie, if you would, I'd like you to help Wendy with tasks. Now that you're recovering it's important that every pair of hands help."

The expression slid from the redhead's face like rain: "Unnnnkay Derrrr . . ."

"Don't worry," said Wendy with a glance at the psychologist. "We'll be fine."

As the door closed on the doctor Wendy stuck her thumb behind her upper teeth and flicked it in the direction of the retreating specialist.

"I hate psychologists," she said making a moue of distaste. "Fucking shrinks."

Elgars' mouth worked for a moment then with an expression of frustration she held both of her hands palm upward.

"To qualify for front-line combat as a female you have to pass a psych eval," said the blonde, tying up her ponytail in frustration as she sat next to Elgars on the bed. "And it's a real Catch-22. They won't admit anyone who is 'unstable,' but a fighting personality is considered borderline unstable for a female."

Elgars' mouth worked again and she grunted a laugh. "Fum . . . fu. Umbitch!"

Wendy dimpled. "Yeah. They're all sons-of-bitches. I agree. But they can fuck themselves. So, you've got amnesia? And a speech impediment, obviously."

"Uhhh . . . yuhhhh," Elgars said with another flash of impatience.

"Don't worry about it," Wendy said with a smile. "We've got plenty of time to get the story. But can I ask one question?"

"Yuhhh."

"Is that a weapons locker? Because if it is I'm really pissed. They took all my shit away when I got to this damned hole. I go to the range at least once a week, but they won't even let me try out for the security force."

"Yuhhh," Elgars said with a quizzical expression. "A . . . Ah doooo." She stopped and her mouth worked. "Ah . . . don'n . . . know wha . . ."

"You don't know what any of it is?" Wendy asked. "You know the words, you just can't say them, right?"

"Yaaah."

"Okay." Wendy hopped off the bed and walked over to the featureless polygon. It was about two meters high, with six "facets" on the side and no apparent locks or doors. "How does it open?"

Elgars slid off the bed and swayed over to the locker. Her speech may have left much to be desired, but her movements were efficient and graceful.

Wendy regarded her carefully and smiled. "Have you been working out?"

"Phy . . . skal ther'py," Elgars answered, placing her hand on the face of the polygon. "A' so' o'r stu'."

The front of the cylinder opened to either side with a blast of gun-oil scent, and Wendy's jaw practically hit the floor. It wasn't a couple of personal items, it was a damn arsenal.

The left door was hung with dress uniforms. The officer's dress blues on top, with rank marks for a captain, were practically coated in awards and medals. At one point, besides being expert in rifle, pistol and submachine gun, Elgars had passed, in succession, the Army Advanced Marksmanship Program and Marine Corps Sniper School, the last of which was practically unheard of. She was a veteran of infantry combat, as denoted by her Combat Infantry Badge, and had apparently earned two Purple Hearts and a Silver Star along the way. But the capstone was the simple device on the right breast, a gold "600."

"Oh, shit," Wendy whispered. Besides the uniforms—the right door was hung with camouflage and Fleet Strike grays for some reason—there were a half dozen weapons in the locker. Taking place of prominence was something Wendy had only seen pictures of: a Barrett M-82A1 .50 caliber sniper rifle. It clearly had seen use, but before being put away had been factory serviced and sealed in PreserFilm. There also were two different submachine guns, with loaded clips dangling on harnesses, a couple of pistols, one a silenced Glock and the other something odd and bulky with a laser sight and silencer, and a "bullpup" style assault rifle. Hanging in the back was a combat harness with full loadout for a team sniper.

"How the *hell* did you get this in here?" Wendy asked. "The Sub-Urbs are zero-tolerance zones!"

"Uah . . . Ahmmm 'ct've . . . Aaaaactive . . ."

"You're active duty?" Wendy said with a laugh. "Sorry, but . . ."

"Ahmmmm Ssssixssss . . ."

"Six Hundred," the former resident of Fredericksburg said with a sober nod. "And even the *dead* of the Six Hundred are still listed as active duty."

Elgars smiled and nodded. "Buuuu . . . wha'sssss," she gestured into the locker.

"And you don't know what this stuff is, do you?" Wendy asked.

"Nuuuu."

Wendy regarded her levelly and green eyes met her blue.

"Okay, let's find something out. Do you have something that shows you can have this?"

Elgars gestured at the uniforms, but Wendy just shook her head.

"No, for the shit-head panic children in Security we'll need more than that. Any documentation specifically stating you're authorized? You got a gun card?"

Elgars reached in and extracted an envelope. Inside, on driver's license-sized card, was a simple note:

"Captain A. O. Elgars is a currently serving member of the United States Armed forces on detached duty and her right to carry weapons irrespective of type or caliber in any portion of the United States or its Territories for any reason she at her sole discretion shall deem reasonable and prudent shall not be infringed. Any questions regarding these orders shall be directed to the Department of War." It was endorsed by the Continental Army commander and the commander of the Ten Thousand. The back had her picture and personal data.

The license was standard issue. At the beginning of the war the right of the Federal military to conduct maneuvers in and around non-threatened zones had been repeatedly questioned. Among the questions raised was whether military personnel should be restricted in access to their weapons, especially in and around cities which had anti-gun laws.

Most of the complaints had ended after the Fredericksburg landings, but when a detached brigade of infantry was surprised and overwhelmed in Seattle, with their weapons still in the unit armory, the question was settled once and for all. Serving members of the armed forces were not required to wear uniforms at all times. But for "the duration of the current emergency" serving military personnel were required, by Federal law, to be armed at all times with a "basic load" for their primary weapons. Posleen landings occurred at random and on the balance it had been decided that the occasional irrational act was balanced by the security of an armed response to the invasion.

"Now the important question," said Wendy with another smile. "What to wear."

Elgars smiled back and reached for the Battle Dress Uniform. She fingered the lapel with a puzzled expression.

"Do you recognize the uniform?" Wendy asked. "It's BDUs. That rank shows you're a captain. Do you remember being a captain?"

Elgars shook her head and shrugged. "Ser . . . sar . . . sar'nt."

"You were a sergeant?" Wendy asked. "Why do you have captain's tracks?"

"Sarn' . . . pri'ate." Elgars face worked and she banged her head. "Staaaa . . . No . . . Ahhhh!"

"Calm down," Wendy said, shaking her shoulder. "Whatever you *were*, you're a captain now." Wendy looked at her for a moment and shook her head. "Have they given you *any* background on why you're here? Or even where 'here' is?"

Elgars shook her head and gestured around at the room. "Is an' off'ce a' I see."

Wendy took a breath and thought about where to start. "Okay, you know you're underground, right?"

"Righ'." Elgars nodded at that. "Su'-ur'."

"A Sub-Urb," Wendy agreed. "Have they shown you a map?"

"N'."

Wendy picked up the remote for the flatscreen and punched in a code. "This is the information channel. Did they show you that?"

"N'."

"Christ," Wendy said. "Okay, here goes." She flipped through a menu and brought up a schematic of a cube. "Welcome to the Franklin Sub-Urb. Here's Getting Around One Oh One.

"The Burb is a cube. The top of the cube is one hundred feet underground with the area over it reinforced with 'honeycomb' anti-shock armor. The cube is broken into eight sectors and each sector is broken into subsectors. The primary sectors are letters, A through H. The subsectors are numbers and once you figure out the way that breaks down if I say something like 'C8-8-4' you know right where you're at. The subsectors are each four stories high and four blocks wide and deep. They start numerically at the center and work outward both from the center and from the joining line to the next sector. The sectors are eight subsectors, or eight blocks, wide and eight deep, but they are still under construction and a few of them continue out beyond eight subsectors.

"Right now you're in Sector F, Subsector 1-1-4. That means that you're right at the top of F, on the border with E and four blocks out from the center. Sector A is security, emergency services, administration and a few living quarters, mainly for administration and security. Sectors B through D are living quarters. Although some of C and D are given over to support.

Sector F is hospital and environmental support and E through H are generally given over to support including a fusion reactor in H and an extensive hydroponics and waste reprocessing section in G.

"The main personnel entrance is above Sector A and joins A near the juncture of the other three living sectors. Just outside of it is a large parking garage where most of the vehicles used by the evacuees are parked. On the southwest quadrant, adjacent to Sector D, is the main resupply route. Supplies come in there and are transported down elevators to Sector H.

"There are primary movement routes running along primary sector junctures—that is, where four sectors converge—and at four points within each sector. Prime Corridors have slide-ways, walkways and cart paths. Secondary movement routes are found at every other subsector juncture point. Secondary Corridors do not have slideways and you have to be careful of carts and vice versa. The small corridors where residences are found also can be used to move around; they are referred to as tertiary corridors. Except in special cases, carts are not permitted in residential corridors.

"If you get lost," she continued, hitting a command so that a list of icons came up, and pointing to an icon that looked like a computer, "look for this symbol. That's an info-access terminal. You can query one as to your location and how to get to just about anywhere in the Urb. You also can ask for a 'sprite,' which is a Galactic supplied micrite. It's about the size of a fly and glows. It will leave and take the shortest primary route to your destination. Follow it. It will stop if you stop and leave when you reach your destination."

She gestured to the rest of the icons. "There's other symbols you need to get to know. There's symbols for security, bathrooms, cafeterias and stuff like that. Most of them are sort of self-explanatory, but you need to get familiar with them.

"You are permitted to leave the Sub-Urb, but it is strongly discouraged and no unauthorized personnel are permitted into the Urb and no military personnel are permitted unless they have written orders or are on hospital status and assigned . . . like you."

"You' gi' 'is for," Elgars said.

"Yes, I've given this lecture a few times," Wendy said with a grim smile. "I've been in this fucker since it was just a giant echoing hole." She thought about it for a moment. "That's all you really need to know for now. There's some minimal emergency information you should get familiar with, but it's available on channel 141. I'd recommend watching that fairly religiously for a couple of weeks; there's all sorts of tips to getting around. Any major questions for now?"

Elgars shook her head and went over to the other locker to get a bra. The locker had a chest of drawers in it and several sets of civilian clothes, mostly blue jeans and dresses. On the right hand side was a shoe rack with one pair of running shoes, two sets of shined combat boots and nine pairs of high heeled shoes, most of them black. The only thing that showed any sign of use was the running shoes.

"Man," Wendy breathed. "You've got enough clothes for five people down here."

Elgars made a questioning sound in her throat and Wendy shrugged.

"There aren't any clothes getting made these days; all the mills make stuff for the Army. So whatever people brought, and most of 'em only brought a suitcase or two, that's what they had to wear." Wendy gestured at her own outfit of a dungaree type shirt and slightly oversized jeans. "They make a few things to keep people dressed and shoes, but none of it is 'fun clothes.' You've got more dresses than I've seen in three years."

Elgars looked at them then at Wendy. They seemed to be about the same size so the captain gestured. "Yuuuh . . . waaa . . . ?"

The blonde dimpled prettily and pushed the air off her right ear. "Not now. Maybe some other time if I can borrow something that'd be great."

Elgars reached into the locker and pulled out one of the dresses. It was a violet wrap, consisting of multiple layers of lace in a variety of shades. She looked at it with distaste for a moment then thrust it at Wendy. "Take."

"Are you sure?" Wendy asked. The dress was beautiful.

"Suuurre." Elgars' face worked for a moment as if she was going to spit. "Ah don't lahk purple," she continued in a soft southern accent. There was no trace of a lisp.


Elgars looked around with interest. The corridors were wide—wide enough to slip a car through with difficulty—and high. And they seemed to go on forever. Every fifty meters there was a set of stairs and every hundred meters there was an escalator flanked by an elevator. At each such intersection there was another emergency pack, but unlike the one in her room, most of these were hanging open and empty. The plastic walls changed color, but all were calming pastels. The tones were pleasant, though, not institutional in any way. Occasionally there were walls of what looked like stone but with a smooth look as if it had been extruded or melted.

Overhead there were regular sprinklers and innumerable pipes with cryptic markings like "PSLA81." At intervals the one of the pipes that was marked with a red-and-blue pattern would have an extension downward to a double-headed ending. Since it was valved and capped, Elgars imagined that it was probably designed to supply emergency water for some purpose.

The main corridors were open but there were memory-plastic doors on either side, some of them marked and others not. Most of the ones that they passed seemed to be residences although a few were marked with names like "The Cincinnati Room." At intervals in the main corridors there were open doors with control panels on both sides. These were heavier and seemed to be designed to close in the event of an emergency.

At every set of stairs or escalator was a sign: "Primary evacuation route" with an arrow up, down or pointing into the corridor. Flanking it was another: "Secondary evacuation route" pointing in a different direction. In addition to the emergency signs there were signs with some of the icons that Wendy had pointed out. Elgars was fairly sure she could figure out the bathroom and the cafeteria signs. But what was the one with three things that looked like feathers?

As Wendy had pointed out, there were regular markings on the walls, a letter followed by three numbers. In their perambulations they had proceeded out of Sector F and into B. It seemed to Elgars that they were taking a very roundabout route; they seemed to be staying in personnel quarters corridors and away from the main thoroughfares.

Most of the residential corridors were narrow, no more than two persons wide, and showed signs of wear. In one area most of the glow-paint had been damaged, leaving long sections of near total darkness. Wendy didn't stop but Elgars noticed that she seemed to be much more cautious in her movements, slowing as she approached intersections as if to listen for other footsteps, and the few people that they passed seemed to avoid eye-contact.

"This is the older section," Wendy said quietly as they were headed down a secondary corridor. This one had scorch marks on the walls as if a fire had once raged through the area and the damage was never completely repaired. "I was here when this corridor was as new and shiny as your room. But it's near a maintenance section now and . . . well . . . it's sort of a bad neighborhood. On the other hand, the security pantywaists don't like it much, so I don't think we have to worry about them."

What they did have to worry about became evident as they came to a residential intersection. In the better sections there was a slight widening of the corridors at the intersection, a water fountain and signs to the significant support facilities in the area. Two of the three corridors leading to this spot had had their glowpaint almost entirely stripped away and the water fountain had been ripped out of the wall and was sitting in a pool of rusty water.

As Wendy stepped cautiously into the shadows along one wall, there was the rasp of a match and a group of figures emerged from one of the darkened corridors.

"Well, whatta we got here?" the leader asked, lighting her cigarette. The girl was below normal height and unhealthily skinny. Her face had been badly tattooed with a figure that was probably a spider and her hair was pulled up in patches that had been dyed a variety of colors. She was wearing heavy boots, short shorts and a midriff top. Elgars would have laughed at the combination if it wasn't for the aluminum baseball bat she was swinging in one hand.

"I think we've got trespassers," giggled another. This one was above average height and heavyset with wide hips and pendulous breasts. The two would have made a comical couple were it not for the weapons in their hands.

"Whatcha got in the bag, cutey," the leader said as the other three started to spread out.

"Nothing you want," Wendy replied quietly. "You just go your way and we'll go ours."

"Oh, I don't think so," the heavier one said, pulling a chain out from behind her back. "I really don't."

"Do we kill them?" Elgars asked with perfect clarity. She was standing quite still, her weight forward on the balls of her feet and her hands at her side. The question was asked in an absolutely toneless voice.

"Uh, no," Wendy said. "Security gets all pissy when you do that."

"Okay," Elgars said and *moved*. From Wendy's perspective, one moment she was totally still and the next she was practically chest to chest with the leader.

The captain blocked the swing of the bat with her forearm—she was well inside the arc—and ripped the ring out of the leader's nostril. "That's to get your attention," she said in a deep voice just before she head-butted the leader into the far wall.

Wendy's hand dipped into the bag and came up holding the Glock, which more or less stopped the other three in their tracks. "Oh, look, there *was* something you guys could have used. And, lookey, it's got a silencer on it. Which means that when I blow you all over the wall, security won't even hear. Now, why don't you three just take off while my companion finishes playing?" They took one look at the pistol and decided there were corridors that needed their attention. Like, now.

Wendy winced as Elgars kicked the henchman in a place that is, arguably, more sensitive in women than in men. The chain had disappeared somewhere down a corridor and a knife was already on the floor broken at the tang. The woman was waving one hand in front of her face, fighting to get a word out, when Elgars followed it up with a kick to the side of the head.

"If you didn't want to play, you shouldn't have brought the ball," the captain said, bouncing on her toes with her hands up at shoulder height, fingers folded and palms out. Again, the voice was decidedly deep and clear.

"I think you're done here, Annie," Wendy said, stepping over to the leader to check for a pulse. There was a good solid beat, which was nice considering the bang her head had taken. Wendy flipped out a penlight and checked the pupils. The right pupil was a little sluggish but Wendy figured she had a better than fifty/fifty chance of waking up. The henchman was even better off, already starting to groan into consciousness.

"Damn, you two are luckier than you have any right to be," Wendy said, straightening up. "I'd suggest you run by the infirmary, though." She kicked the leader in the shin. "You've got a pretty good concussion going there.

"Right," Wendy said, "I think we should get as far from here as possible."

"'Ka," Elgars mouthed, lowering her hands. "N'd t' ge' ou' o' D'ge."

A few turns, a short secondary corridor and they were back in well-maintained corridors as if the encounter had never taken place. These corridors were, for the most part, not crowded. The one exception was an open area where at least four hundred people, mostly older but with a scattering of younger women and children, sat on metal chairs playing board games, talking and sipping drinks. One end of the area was an elaborate playground, like hell's own hamster trail.

It was mainly around this centerpiece that the children ran screaming happily.

Wendy didn't even pause, continuing her unerring navigation towards their eventual goal.

"We're almost there," she said, taking another up escalator. "This place is laid out really logically. Once you get used to it you can find anything. All the security stuff is up and towards the main entrance which is on the inner corner of A."

Elgars pointed to a large red box on the wall of the corridor. It was the second one that they had passed. It was marked in a similar manner to the emergency packs in the rooms, but had a large sign "For ER Personnel only." And it apparently hadn't been looted.

"It's an attack pack," Wendy said. "There is one in each subsector, located at the subsector's 4/4/4 point; that's short for the middle of the subsector. It's got basic rescue and fire gear in case of an emergency. There's some class B breath packs, a trauma kit including foldable stretcher, a defib kit, firefighting gear and an entry kit. They can only be opened by qualified emergency/rescue personnel; there's a palm print scanner on them. I can get one open; I'm in the fire/rescue reserve force. I'm hoping to get on a regular crew soon, if I can pass the Physical Performance Eval."

Elgars pointed to the sprinklers on the ceiling. "F'r'?"

"Yeah, they're for fire suppression," Wendy agreed. "And some of the areas that have a lot of computer equipment are Halon fed. But even with them, there's the possibility of a large breakout. And if a *big* fire breaks out, we're screwed. This thing is like a ship; you have to kill the fire before it kills you. The alternative is going to the surface, and if we wanted to be up there, we wouldn't be stuck down here."

"Wur ahh . . . are we?" Elgars asked gesturing around.

She apparently had decided to ignore the earlier adventure.

"You mean in the world?" Wendy responded. "They didn't tell you?"

"Nuu . . ." the captain said. "Ne'er ask . . ."

"Didn't want to ask the shrinks, huh?" Wendy said, taking another turn. This corridor was less well lit and appeared to be unused. The doors along both sides all showed the red panel of being locked. "We're in the mountains of North Carolina. Does that mean anything to you?"

"Nuuu . . ." Elgars said with a shrug then frowned. "S . . . saw a m . . . map. A . . . Ash . . ."

"Not near Asheville," Wendy said with a snort. "It's a long story."

"Tell."

Wendy shrugged. "When the Posleen dropped on . . . Fredericksburg," Wendy said with only a slight catch in her voice over the destruction of her hometown, "most of the Sub-Urbs weren't ready for people to move in. But there were nearly two million refugees from Northern Virginia. Some of them could go back but . . . well most of F'Burg was just *gone*. I mean, between the battleships and the fighting and the Bomb it had been smashed flat. And we were going to have to move out soon because the Posleen were just coming back. And most of the survivors were . . . well . . . not in the greatest shape. . . .

"Anyway, this was the only Urb that was almost finished on the East Coast. It was the first one started; the local congressional representative had managed to wrangle getting it placed in his district even though it's in a really stupid spot."

Elgars made another sound and Wendy grimaced.

"Well, first of all, all the other Urbs are placed near interstates, usually near existing cities. Asheville has two really huge ones and they're both full. But we're near a place called Franklin. It's just a little town in southern North Carolina, a dot on the map. The only reason we're here is because of the congressman; he'd been in Congress for just about forever and was the committee chairman for the procurement process. So this was where the first Sub-Urb went.

"Supplying us, what little supplies we get, is a real pain because the trucks have to compete with the supplies for the corps that's defending Rabun Gap. And the corps is practically on top of us; their main rear area supply point is Franklin, so at first we had all sorts of trouble. There's a Kipling poem that points out that soldiers aren't 'plaster saints.' Mix a corps of soldiers with an underground city full of women and things got . . . bad for a while. So now they stay out there and we stay in here and almost everybody's happy."

She shook her head after a moment. "We're just about the only Sub-Urb that has that problem, too. You see, we're just about the closest Urb to a defense line. I mean, there are a couple of others that are this close and then there was the Rochester Urb . . ." She paused and shuddered.

"Ba . . . ?" Elgars asked.

"Yeah," Wendy said quietly. "Worse than F'Burg really. The Posleen got into the Urb and after that there just wasn't anything to do. There's really only one way in and out. The defenders put up a good fight, or so we hear. There . . . weren't any survivors."

"Urgh . . ."

"Yeah," Wendy said. "That's why whenever the news mentions fighting around Rabun Gap we sort of tense up. If the Posleen come through there's not much we're going to be able to do."

Elgars just nodded and kept looking around. Like Wendy, most of the people were poorly dressed. The exception were one or two teenage females who were wearing flashy shorts and midriff tops. The clothing was clearly new, but the style was . . . different from the rest of the inhabitants.

Wendy noted her glances and frowned. "Corps whores," she whispered.

"Whuh?"

Wendy shrugged again. "Everybody finds their niche here. Some of them turn into drones, some of them decide to have some fun running the corridors and acting like they're bad. Others . . . find a party. The soldiers up top are restricted from coming down here; there were just . . . too many problems when they had unrestricted access." She frowned and it was apparent that there was a wealth of stories in that simple sentence. "So after a while the head of security and the corps commander reached an agreement and now the soldiers don't come down here. That doesn't mean we're restricted from leaving. So some of the girls, women too . . . ply a very old trade on the surface."

"I do' . . . n'er'stan'," Elgars tried to enunciate.

Wendy looked at her with an arched eyebrow. "You don't know what I'm talking about, do you?"

"Nu."

Wendy sighed and hitched the bag higher. "They trade sex for money, Captain. And goods. Like better clothes and food than you can get down here. And electronics gear: that's almost nonexistent these days."

Elgars looked around at the high plastic walls and the unending corridors. She thought about being stuck in here for years and shook her head. "So?"

Wendy looked at her again and shook her head. "Never mind. It would take too long to explain why people find that bad."

The captain nodded as they turned into a door

marked "S&A Securities." There was a small alcove on the far side and another door which was locked.

Wendy pressed a buzzer and looked up at a security camera. "Lemme in, David, I bring a visitor."

"You're carrying, honey. I'm surprised you made it." The deep voice came from a speaker almost directly overhead as the door buzzed.

"I just walked around all the detectors," Wendy said as she entered the sparse room beyond. "And it was a good thing I was."

There were steel weapons lockers with mesh fronts along the left hand side of the room. The shape of rifles and submachine guns could be seen faintly through the mesh. Opposite the door was a low desk; as Wendy and Elgars entered the room a dark, burly man pushed a wheelchair out and came around to the front.

"You have problems?" the man asked.

"Nothing we couldn't handle," Wendy said with a shrug, still bleeding off adrenaline.

"Who's your visitor?" the man said, watching her with eyes that knew darned well that it hadn't been something minor.

"David Harmon, meet Captain Anne O. Elgars," Wendy said with a smile. "Captain Elgars took a little damage a while back and she's not quite up to form." Wendy frowned. "Actually, she's got amnesia, so she doesn't have a clue about weapons. But she used to. We need to see what she remembers."

"Remembers?" Harmon said with a frown. "My legs don't remember running. How are her hands going to remember shooting?"

"The doctor said she's remembering most of her motor skills; she can write and eat and all that stuff. And . . . well . . . I think the Blades would safely say that she recalls some basic fighting skills. I thought we could try at least."

"You ever been on a range?" Harmon asked Anne. "Blades?" he queried Wendy.

"Crazy Lucy and Big Boy," Wendy said, jerking her chin at Elgars. "She spent most of her time toying with them."

"I do-o . . ." Elgars said with a frown. "I do-o-o 'member . . . W'a'n't toy'ng."

"The captain's still recovering," Wendy said quietly. "She's . . ."

"Got a serious speech impediment," Harmon said. "Yeah, well ain't none of us whole in this fucking place," he continued with a snort and a gesture at his legs.

He unzipped the ballistic bag and started extracting hardware. "MP-5SPD. Nice. Silencer package. Did you used to do point, Captain?"

"Du-du-dunno," Elgars answered. "Do' 'member."

"She also had a Barrett in the locker," Wendy added.

"That doesn't make sense," Harmon said with a frown. He pulled out the next piece and frowned. "Desert Eagle .44. This is not the weapon of a sniper. At least, not one from a regular unit. Were you in special forces or something?"

"No," Elgars said and frowned. "At least, I d-d-don't thin'. P-p-papers s-s-say Th-th-Thirt'-Third. Then uh S-s-six hunnert." She frowned again and snarled, bearing even, white teeth. "S'all wrong."

Harmon looked over at Wendy with a lifted eyebrow. "You didn't mention that."

"She's on 'detached duty,'" Wendy said with a shrug. "Hospital detachment. I don't know if they're going to put her back through training or what. But it makes sense for her to re-learn the basics."

"Uh huh," the weapons instructor grunted. "Makes as much sense as anything else that has happened to me in the last six years."

He cleared the chamber on both weapons and

rolled over to a locker. "Get her a set of earmuffs and I'll set up the range."

Harmon extended the Glock to the captain and watched her hands carefully. "The weapon is not loaded, but you never take a person's word for that. Keep it pointed downrange and keep your finger off the trigger."

Elgars took the pistol with a puzzled expression and rotated it from side to side. The indoor range had been set up with man-sized targets placed at various distances between five and thirty meters. She glanced in the chamber and cocked her head to one side like a bird then picked up one of the magazines. "S'fam-uh . . . famil'ar. Kin ah lock an' load?"

"Go ahead," said Harmon watching carefully.

Elgars swept the unloaded weapon back and forth keeping it pointed downrange. "Th'somethin' wrong," she said, turning to look at the instructor. Following her body the pistol swung to the left and down. Directly at the wheelchair-bound range-master.

"Up!" Harmon said sharply, blocking the swing of the pistol up and out. "Keep it pointed up and down-range! Go ahead and pick up the magazine and seat it, then lock and load. This time, though, keep it pointed downrange, okay?"

"S'rry," Elgars said with a frown. "S'all wron'. S'righ' an' wron' a' same time." She picked up the magazine with a puzzled expression, but there was no fumbling as it was seated and she jacked back the slide.

"Uh, 'The firing line is clear'?" Wendy said with a grin.

" 'Re'y on uh lef'?" Elgars muttered with a frown.

Harmon smiled. "Ready on the left? The left is ready. Ready on the right? The right is ready. Firing line is clear. Open fire."

Before the former police officer's chin could hit his chest all five targets had taken two shots in the upper chest and one in the middle of the face. The sound was thunder, a series of blasts like a low speed machine gun, then the magazine dropped to the ground and the weapon was reloaded. He had never seen her hand move to pick up the spare; the weapon seemed to reload itself by magic.

"Bloody hell," Harmon muttered while Wendy just stood there with her mouth open.

"Was that okay, sar'nt?" Elgars asked in a shy little voice.

"Yeah, that was pretty good," Harmon said, waving away the cordite residue. "Pretty good."

# CHAPTER 7

"I think this is goin' pretty good," Colonel Cutprice opined. He ducked as a stray railgun round glanced off the shot-up piece of combat armor shielding him. "Could've been worse."

"*Would've* been worse if it hadn't been for that late shipment of Bouncing Barbies," Sergeant Major Wacleva grumped. "And the Spanish Inquisition."

" 'I've got a list, I've got a little list,' " Sunday said, belly-crawling over to their position. "We could use a few Bouncing Barbies out here, sir." He popped his head up over the armor and ducked back down. "There has been a fine killing, but it could always be better."

Cutprice shook his head. "You know why they're called 'Bouncing Barbies,' Sunday?"

"Yes, sir," the sergeant replied. "They really ought to be called Duncan's Folly. But they call 'em 'Barbies' because it is alliterative and, like Barbie, they just up

113

and cut you off at the knees if you get anywhere near them. You know she would. The cold-eyed bitch."

The M-281A anti-Posleen area denial weapon was one of the few commonly available bits of "GalTech," the technology that the Galactic Federation had first offered then been unable to supply in any significant quantity.

The device was the bastard child of a mistake, a mistake made by one of the members of the 1st Battalion 555th Mobile Infantry. In the early days of the conflict, Sergeant Duncan, who was a notorious tinkerer, had tinkered a Personal Protection Field into removing all its safety interlocks and then expending all of its power in a single brief surge.

The surge, and the removed safety interlocks, had created a circular "blade" that cut through several stories of the barracks he was in at the time. And, quite coincidentally, through his roommate's legs.

It took quite some time for all the right questions to be asked and in the proper way. But finally it was determined that the boxes were relatively easy for the Indowy technicians to produce, even one at a time. And they easily could be fitted into a human device called a "scatterable mine platform."

The resultant artillery round threw out forty-eight mines, each of which was slightly mobile and had a conformable appearance; the mine was a flattened, circular disk, somewhat like a "cow-patty." The surface could change color and texture depending upon the background, but the default setting was the yellow of Posleen blood, for reasons that became obvious.

After being released from the artillery round in flight, the disks would scatter across a "footprint" about two hundred meters long and seventy meters wide. Then if anything came within two meters of it, the mine would "hop" up one meter and create a field of planar force that extended out fifty meters in every direction. The field would cut through anything except the most advanced Galactic armor, which meant sliced and diced Posleen.

What was nice about the system, from the humans' perspective, was that it had up to six attacks on "onboard" batteries. After its attack it would scuttle sideways slightly and "hide" again, waiting for the next wave of Posleen and looking for all the world like one of the unpleasant "Posleen bits" that was left behind. Although the piles of chopped up Posleen generally gave away the fact that there were Bouncing Barbies in the area. Even to the moronic normals. Since the Posleen generally reacted to minefields by running normals over them until they were clear, this gave the capability to deal with multiple waves, which normal mines did not.

"We really need some out here, sir," Sunday insisted. "For one thing, when they fall on a big pile of dead like this they chop 'em up into bits. It would make it easier to move out. And it's a hell of a lot of fun to watch."

"You're so ate up you make O'Neal seem like a piker, Sunday," Sergeant Major Wacleva said with a death's head grin. He obviously approved.

"Call but upon the name of Beelzebub," Mike said striding up the hill. He knelt down by the armor and patted it fondly. "Juarez. He's been with the battalion since before I took over Bravo Company. He used to be in Stewart's squad. Good NCO. Hell of a loss."

Cutprice really looked at the armor for the first time; something, an HVM or a plasma cannon, had *eaten* the top of the armor. "How many did you lose, Major?"

"Twenty-six," O'Neal said, standing up to look over the slight parapet. His appearance was apparently ignored for a moment then a hurricane of fire descended on him. "Most of 'em were newbies of course. They do the stupidest things."

Cutprice and Wacleva ducked and huddled into their heavy body armor while Sunday cursed and crawled sideways to retrieve one of the railguns. The fifty-pound combination of motorized tripod and railgun had been hit by a stray round and tossed backwards. One glance determined that it was a goner.

"Damnit, Colonel," the sergeant called. "You just got my gun shot up!"

"Oh, sorry about that," O'Neal said. He sat down in the mud and reconfigured his visor to external view. "Cutprice, why are you hunkering down in the mud? Oh, never mind. Do you know if there are any more Barbies around? We need to get them out on the slope. They chop up the Posleen real fine; that will make it easier to move out when the time comes and besides it's fun as hell to watch."

"Were you guys separated at birth or something?" Cutprice asked. "And we're huddling in here because the ricochets from your armor were just a tad unpleasant."

Mike took off his helmet and looked over at him. "What are you talking about?"

"You were just taking fire, hotshot," Wacleva said. "You *did* notice, right?"

"No," Mike said simply. "I didn't. Sorry about that. I guess . . . it wasn't all *that* intense."

"Maybe not for you," Wacleva said, pulling a spent 1mm railgun flechette out of his body armor. "Some people, however, aren't covered in plasteel."

"And that's the problem of course," Cutprice said grumpily. "If we try going over that ridge, we'll be so much hamburger."

"We need to break up this force some," Sunday said. "Nukes, nukes, nukie nukes."

"That *would* be nice," Cutprice said. He was well aware that they barely had the Posleen force stopped, much less "backing up," which was the requirement. "Unfortunately, the President still says no. The artillery is getting into battery . . ."

"Spanish Inquisition time?" O'Neal asked, opening up first one armored pouch then another. Finally he gave up. "Sergeant Major, I apologize most abjectly for causing you some temporary discomfort. Now, could I bum a smoke?"

"Yeah," Wacleva said with a laugh, pulling out an unfiltered Pall Mall. "Keren started the Spanish Inquisition. Send in a platoon of MPs each with a sheet of questions and answers. Walk up to the senior officers and NCOs and ask them three questions off of the sheet. If they don't get two out of three right, they're relieved. Before you know it, you've lost half your dead weight and people who know what they're doing are all of a sudden in charge."

"The only thing I've got against it is that I didn't think of it first," Mike said. He put the cigarette in his mouth, lifted his left arm and a two meter gout of flame suddenly spurted from one of the many small orifices on the surface of his suit. He took a drag on the cigarette and the flamethrower went out. "It's not much good with infantry and armor units, but artillery is a *skilled* branch. If you don't know how to shore a fucking trench, you shouldn't be in the engineers. If you don't know how to calculate the proper size of an antenna, you shouldn't be in commo. And if you don't know how to compute winds aloft, you shouldn't be a artillery battalion-fucking-commander."

"I *gotta* get me one of those," Sunday said, pulling out a pack of Marlboros. "Can I try?"

"Sure," O'Neal said.

Sunday leaned back from the gout of flame and sucked on the cancer stick. "Love it."

"It's not standard," Mike pointed out. "It's one of the modifications I suggested that got nixed in committee. I *believe* in a Ronco suit."

"It slices, dices and makes Julienne fries?" Cutprice said with a laugh.

"You got it," O'Neal said soberly. "Obviously it's not just for lighting cigarettes. So, how do we get these fuckers reduced to the point that we can get them backing up? And maybe have somebody standing after we're done."

"I take it you're not up to the task?"

"Nope," O'Neal said, leaning back on the late Sergeant Juarez. "We took about one in four casualties this morning. Not as bad as Roanoke—that was a real shitstorm—but if we go over that ridge they'll eat us alive. We can hold the box but not move out of it. And we only hold the box because the arty is holding one side."

"They're getting slaughtered down there," Wacleva said with a gesture of his chin towards the hospital. "That'll cut down on 'em some."

"Have you really *looked* over the hill, Sergeant Major?" Sunday asked incredulously. "They're losing maybe a thousand a minute, which seems like a lot. But at that rate we'll be here for forty days and forty nights."

"Yeah, and in the meantime they'll be reproducing all up and down the coast," Mike pointed out. "The horny bastards." He scratched his chin and took another drag on the cigarette. Reaching over he picked up a shattered boma blade and held it overhead. After a few moments, railgun rounds started to crack overhead followed by the occasional missile. Finally a stream of rounds smashed the sword out of his hand, taking half of the remaining blade away in the process.

"Fire pressure's still up there," O'Neal opined as the others dug themselves out of the ground again. "Sometimes if you pin them in place and *don't* kill the first million or so they run out of bullets. But when you're killing wave after wave the guys behind are always fresh and have full loads. We used that in . . . Christ . . . Harrisburg One, I think. Pinned the front-ranks down until they ran out of fire, moved forward and dug in again so the rear ranks could come forward a bit then did it all over again. Sort of. I think. It's been a long time. But if we try that here, we'll get flanked. That was when we were retaking the outer defenses and we were covered on a narrow front."

"So obviously *that* is out," Cutprice said sourly. "Any other ideas?"

Mike rolled on his back and looked at the sky. It was still overcast, but the light rain had faded. The sun was up in the east and it might just burn off sometime after noon. He thought about that and realized it was already after noon.

He rolled over to the side and fingered the dirt. The brick buildings of the area had been pounded to a fine red clay that reminded him of home. And underneath? He sniffed at the ground for a moment, looked down the hill towards the river with his head sideways as if measuring the angle then flicked the cigarette over the crest of the hill and put his helmet on.

Cutprice hit the ground again as the thermal signature attracted a storm of fire. "Are you just communing with nature or do you have a plan?"

Mike held up one finger in a "wait a minute" gesture then rolled back over. "I have a plan," he intoned. "My mother would be proud; reading is finally going to save my ass."

"Reading what?" Sunday asked.

"Keith Laumer short stories."

✧      ✧      ✧

Colonel Wagoner looked at the video in his heads-up-display in disbelief. "Pardon me, General. Would you mind repeating that?"

Horner was smiling. Which as practically everyone in the *world* knew at this point meant the fecal matter had really and truly hit the rotary air impeller. "You are to cross the Genesee River and go into direct support mode for the ACS and the Ten Thousand. They are pinned down on the ridge that parallels Mount Hope Avenue. Cross the river, climb the ridge and give them on call direct fire support."

"General," the colonel protested, thinking about all of the really *bad* aspects of that order, "you do realize that . . . well . . ."

He paused for a second to collect his thoughts. "Well, for one thing, the rounds aren't exactly howitzer rounds, General. If they *do* hit something they're going to make an atomic fireball about a quarter the size of the Hiroshima bomb; it's going to be noticeable on seismometers from here to Tibet. Second, they go for a *looong* ways; there's a couple of fortress cities out there. New York comes to mind. Last but not least, we're not a tank for all we look like one. We don't have any armor over our tracks or on the gun mantlet. In other words, we're vulnerable to Posleen fire. And if we sustain a critical ammunition hit you're going to have an explosion that makes the Shanghai Strike look like a firecracker and you'll lose *everyone* in the pocket. *And* most of the forces on *this* side of the river."

He waited for a moment as Horner appeared to be waiting for him to go on.

"Is that it?" Horner asked.

"Well, yes, sir."

"Okay. You forgot that without infantry support the Posleen would be able to close in on either side and attack you from underneath. Which, all things considered, really is your most vulnerable direction. You don't have anti-Posleen secondary weapons."

"Yes, sir," the colonel said. "You have a point there."

"Also that unless the Ten Thousand pulls back, you'll almost surely crush them in large numbers. And that moving you *through* the assaulting corps is not going to be what you would call easy."

"No, sir, it won't," the colonel admitted.

"You also missed the more significant aspect of your possible demise," the general continued inexorably. "If you sustain a critical ammunition hit, the resulting ground level explosion will be on the order of seventy kilotons. While this will, undoubtedly, kill Posleen for miles around, it will also create a very large crater. This crater, based upon the subsurface structure, will probably dam both the Genesee River and the Erie Canal. While the large area of marsh that will result will somewhat impede the Posleen, they will then have crossing points over both water structures. Just at the time when the local defense forces will probably be in full-scale rout to Buffalo."

The colonel suddenly recalled the tiny and almost forgotten datum that Horner's original education was engineering. "Ah. That's . . . not a point I had considered, sir."

"Colonel, listen very carefully," Horner said with a broad smile, speaking as if to a child. "Move your vehicle over to the Genesee Valley. Cross the river. Engage the Posleen in direct fire mode in support of the ACS on the ridge. Fire your weapons low. As often as possible, engage concentrations on hilltops that you can impact; if there are occasional detonations of your antimatter munitions this is an unfortunate side effect for which neither of us can be held responsible. As you move up, the Ten Thousand will shift left to cover that flank. The ACS will provide you with close infantry support. Use the slope of the ground for hull down fire; it is, I am told, almost perfect for it. Try not to hit New York City. Is this understood?"

"Yes, sir," the colonel said quietly. He was beginning to get the impression that this was not entirely the general's idea. And that the general was not particularly happy with it.

"And Colonel Wagoner."

"Yes, sir?"

"Don't get hit. *Especially* in your magazines."

"I'll try, sir. Sir? One question?"

"Yes?" Horner snapped.

"The Ten Thousand are getting out of my way. What about the ACS? What if we roll over one of *them*?"

Horner paused and for just a moment frowned slightly, a sign of amusement. "Colonel, have you ever watched the Coyote and Road Runner?"

"Yes, sir."

"Well, if you run over an ACS, he'll just have to dig himself out. There's one over there painted like a green demon; you have my personal permission to show him why you call infantry 'crunchies.'"

# CHAPTER 8

*Near Seed Lake, GA, United States, Sol III*
*1147 EDT Sunday September 13, 2009* AD

"Good cosslain," Cholosta'an said, rubbing the superior normal on the back. The half oolt had returned from its first "patrol" on its own and from all appearances had made all the turns perfectly.

Many of the cosslain, the higher intelligence normals that were almost high moron level, could not have remembered all the turns in the complex patrol pattern they had been assigned. But the one good thing about his oolt was the cosslain, and this one sometimes seemed almost intelligent enough to handle God King duties. He couldn't talk, but his hand gestures were occasionally almost eloquent.

"Did you see anything of note?" Cholosta'an asked, signaling the half oolt to begin their daily feeding.

The cosslain gestured in the negative as he pulled a ration pack out of his harness. The food resembled a small mineral block and was just about as hard, but it gave the oolt'os something to do with their time.

"You'll go back out in a few hours," Cholosta'an continued, pulling out a slightly more palatable ration pack. It wasn't much better than oolt'os food, though, and he longed for a victory to give him the funds to afford better. "If you see any sign of the humans you are to fire off a magazine to bring the nearest Kessentai, you know that?"

The cosslain gestured in the affirmative, his triangular teeth grinding through the rations sounding like a rockcrusher.

"Good," Cholosta'an said. All the oolt'os seemed healthy and reasonably well fed so there wasn't much else to do.

"You do a good job," said Orostan.

Cholosta'an stifled his start and turned around slowly. The oolt'ondai had come up so softly that the younger Kessentai never even heard him. "Pardon me, Oolt'ondai?"

"You care well for your oolt'os. Many Kessentai, especially young ones, don't pay any attention to their care. It is good to see."

"They can't very well care for themselves," Cholosta'an said, wondering why the oolt'ondai was paying any attention to *him*.

"Let me ask you something," the oolt'ondai said, gesturing for the younger Kessentai to precede him. The newly dug cavern rang to the sound of devourers and the cries of the oolt'os manning them. It was only one of dozens that the hard-driving Tulo'stenaloor had ordered. It was his intention, apparently, to put the entire host underground, out of sight of the observers in the sky and out of danger from the human artillery. With more and more young and hungry Kessentai arriving every day, it was a matter of continuous construction.

The oolt'ondai fluffed his crest as he made his way

through the thousands of waiting oolt. The bodies of the oolt'os, and the occasional Kessentai, stretched for acres in every direction. The smell was an interesting admixture of home and fear. The smell was of pack, but the continuous battle for survival and status in the pens never quite left Posleen subconscious. The oolt'os would wait stoically until called upon, but if something wasn't done with all the Kessentai, such as having them manage patrols, they would begin to bicker, gamble and fight. A firefight in the cavern, once started, would butcher the majority of the force.

"Look around you. How many of these Kessentai do you think are doing more about their oolt'os than assuming they are fed?"

"Very few," Cholosta'an admitted. "I see many oolts who appear to be underfed and with poor equipment. I'm sure the Kessentai have many problems as I do, but I also doubt that the reason their oolt look so terrible is that they can't afford to trade for resupply."

"Agreed and agreed," Orostan said with a hiss of humor. "The host cannot make good every piece of junk shotgun and broken strap this flock of poorlings has brought with it. But we have more than sufficient thresh'c'oolt for the host. But it is not my duty, not my 'job' as the humans would put it, to care for every oolt'os in the host. So, why am I ensuring that *your* oolt is cared for? And, by extension, why are you under my . . . guidance?"

"I . . ." The young Kessentai paused. He realized that no one had ever told him that he should care for his oolt. It just seemed . . . natural. It would be through his oolt that he could, perhaps, take new lands and acquire possessions to make his life better. Without his oolt, functioning well, he would be nothing but a Kenstain. "I do not know."

"The reason you are working for me is the appearance of your oolt," Orostan said. "When I was told to go choose from among the new forces I chose on the basis of how the oolt looked, not how it was armed as some of my equals did. Your armament is, frankly, crap. But it is well cared for."

"It was all I could afford," Cholosta'an admitted. The shotguns that the oolt'os carried were the simplest, and therefore, cheapest systems available. And even at their small cost, the debt he had incurred was ruinous.

"Perhaps," Orostan admitted. "But a light railgun costs less than twice as much as a shotgun. And it is far more than twice as effective. Why not have *half* the number of oolt'os and railguns? Or, better, a third and a mixture of railguns and missile launchers. If you had that you would have a far smaller force to look at, but it would be much more effective."

Cholosta'an thought about it for a moment. It was a new concept; the assumption was that more was better. And he knew why. "The . . . the Net assigns spoils on the basis of how much you have contributed to the Taking. To . . . to get the best spoils, the best lands and the functioning manufacturing facilities, requires that you have more oolt'os, a larger and more powerful oolt." He paused. "I think."

"The net assigns spoils on the basis of *effect*," Orostan said definitively. "If you had half your number of oolt'os and railguns you would have a greater effect, everything else being equal, than your current balance. At some point in the future I may ask you to release half your oolt'os; will you?"

"If..." The young Kessentai paused again. "If you think it best."

"I do," the oolt'ondai said meditatively. "We'll sell off the guns—I know a Kenstain that specializes in that sort of thing and we'll get a good transfer on them—

and re-equip the remainder more heavily. The released oolt'os will go to the Kenstains who are working on the encampments and will be . . . 'supporting' us when we move forward." He hissed grimly. "Better that than the alternatives."

"What is the 'alternative'?" Cholosta'an wondered. "Thresh, one would presume."

Orostan hissed in laughter. "There are worse things than becoming thresh. We have to have something to clear these human 'minefields.'"

The younger Kessentai looked around at the thousands of Posleen normals in this single cavern. "Oh."

"Waves of disposable oolt'os for the minefields, oolt Po'osol for the walls, the tenaral to pin them in place and destroy their hated artillery and then, my young Kessentai, we feast."

The rest of the shoot had been without incident as Elgars demonstrated a tremendous proficiency with each of the weapons in the bag. She could strip down an MP-5, Glock .45, Steyr assault rifle and an Advanced Infantry Weapon, prepare any of them for firing and fire each expertly. But she didn't know any of the names.

All of her shots were in the "sniper's triangle" area of the upper body and head. Her reloads were fast, smooth and perfect and she always reloaded immediately after all targets had been engaged. That last was a clear indication of background in special combat techniques. But she did not recognize the term.

Now they carefully made their way back to her room. It was apparent that Elgars now recognized the roundabout path for what it was; an attempt to avoid security. She seemed mildly amused about it.

"S'okay fer me to c-c-carry?" she asked, hefting the bag of weapons.

"Technically, yes," Wendy answered, checking a cross corridor before she stepped into it. "Technically, you can't move around *without* weapons. But security is so anal-retentive about guns they *freak* whenever anybody is carrying."

"No gu' here?" Elgars asked, shifting the bag uneasily.

"Oh, there are guns aplenty," Wendy answered with a snort. "Well, not aplenty. But there are guns, pistols mostly. Hell, there's plenty of crime here if you don't know where to go and what to avoid. And people break into the cubes all the time, what they call armed invasions. You can get any kind of gun you want if you know who to see."

"So, why no . . . ?" Elgars stopped frustrated by her inability to speak clearly.

"Well, 'less guns, less crime,' right?" Wendy said bitterly. "It's part of the contract on the Sub-Urbs; they are zero weapons zones. When you get inprocessed, they take away all your weapons and hold them at the armory, which is up by the main personnel entrance. If you leave, you can reclaim them."

"So, leave," Elgars said slowly and carefully.

"Haven't you been following the news?" Wendy asked bitterly. "With all the rock-drops the Posleen have been doing it's the beginning of a new ice-age up there. It's a record low practically every day; you can't move for the snow and ice from September to May. And there aren't any jobs on the surface; the economy is shot. Then there's feral Posleen."

"F'r'l?" Elgars asked.

"The Posties breed like rabbits," Wendy said. "And if they're not around a camp, they drop their eggs at random. Most of them are fertile and they grow like crazy. Since there's been landings all over, there have been eggs scattered almost across the entire U.S. Most of the feral ones can survive in the wild quite well, but they flock to humans for food. They're as omnivorous as bears and have absolutely *no* fear of humans; they tend to attack any person that they run into. So it's like having rabid Bengal tigers popping up all over."

Wendy shook her head sadly. "It's bad down here, but it's *hell* up there."

Elgars looked at her sideways. The way that Wendy had said that didn't ring quite true. After a moment she frowned and nodded uncertainly. "Joi' s'cur'ty?"

Wendy shook her head angrily at that, striding along the corridor. "I don't have the 'proper psychological profile,'" she snarled. "It seems that I'm 'uncomfortable with my aggressive tendencies' and 'present an unstable aggression profile.' It's the same excuse that was used for why I couldn't join ground forces. Catch-22. If you're a woman and you think you'd make a good soldier, you must be unstable. Same for security."

"S'crazy," Elgars said. "No women 'n s'cur'ty?"

"Oh, there are women," Wendy answered with a snort. "They wouldn't have a security department if there weren't; all the males that aren't Four-F are in the Ground Forces or buried. But the women in security are 'comfortable with their aggressive tendencies.'"

"Huh?" Elgars said as they came to another cross corridor. "Whuh that m'n?"

"Well, what do we have here?" a voice asked from the side as an alarm began to beep. "If it isn't Wendy Wee. And who's your friend? And why don't you keep your hands where I can see them. And put the bag on the ground and step away from it."

Wendy moved her hands away from her side as the three guards spread out. All three were wearing blue vaguely military looking uniforms, bulky body-armor and ballistic helmets. Two were carrying pulser guns, short barreled weapons vaguely resembling shotguns that threw out small, electrically charge darts. The darts transmitted a high-voltage shock that would shut down the human, or Posleen, nervous system. The leader, a stocky female, had a charge-pistol dangling from her hand. The GalTech weapon projected a line of heavy-gas that acted as a charge carrier for a massive electrical field. The weapon was short ranged, but it was capable of penetrating all but the most advanced armor.

"Hello, Spencer," Wendy said with a thin smile. "My 'friend' is Captain Elgars. And she is authorized, as you know, to carry whatever she wants."

"I could give a shit what you say, Cummings," said the leader. "I've got you dead to rights smuggling guns." Spencer turned to Elgars and gestured at the bag with her charge-pistol. "Put down the bag and step away from it or you're going to get a taste of my little friend."

Wendy glanced over at Elgars and blanched. The captain was still as a statue, but it was not, by any stretch of the imagination, a stillness of fear. The redhead was staring at the guard like a basilisk and it was clear that she was on the ragged edge of violence.

"Annie, put down the bag and show the nice guard your ID, slowly," Wendy said.

"Shut up, Cummings," snarled the guard sergeant stepping up to Elgars and tapping her on the chest with the pistol. "Are you going to put down that bag or are you going to drop it 'cause you're twitching on the floor?"

Elgars slowly looked down at the pistol then held the bag out to the side and dropped it. As it fell she reached up and twisted the pistol out of the sergeant's hand. A short flurry of hand motions had the weapon in nine pieces which she scattered across the corridor. The captain reached down as the guard started to draw her truncheon and seized Spencer's wrist in a bone-crushing grip.

The guard sergeant froze, caught by pit-bull-like grip and the lambent green fire of the captain's eyes; the two other guards didn't have a clear shot since their team-leader's body was in the way. Elgars slowly reached into her hip pocket and extracted her ID pack. She flicked it open a handspan away from the struggling guard's eyes and cocked an eyebrow. "Now, are y'all gonna put them sticks away, or am I gonna stick 'em up yo' ass?" she said in a soft, honey-smooth southern voice.

"Let go of my wrist," Spencer ground out, wrenching at the viselike grip.

"Tha's 'Let go of mah wrist, ma'am'," Elgars whispered, leaning into the guard sergeant so that she could whisper in her ear. "And if you don't quit struggling Ah'm going to feed you yo' arm, one inch at a tahm."

"Let go of my wrist, ma'am," the guard ground out. As the pressure from Elgars' grip increased instead, she ground out a: "Please."

Elgars relented and Spencer finally wrenched her arm away. She shook her wrist, trying to get some circulation back in her hand, and it was clear that she would prefer to just leave the confrontation. But her pistol was scattered all over the ground. She looked up at the captain, who over-topped her by at least an inch.

Wendy smiled brightly and stepped behind Elgars to pick up the bag. "We'll just be going now," she said, grabbing Elgars' arm. "Right, Captain?"

Elgars leaned forward and looked carefully at the guard's nametag. "Yes," she said softly. "O' course. Ah'm sure we'll be seein' quaht a bit of each othah, won't we, Sarn't . . . Spencer is it?"

"Of . . . of course, ma'am," Spencer answered. "Sorry about the misunderstanding."

✧         ✧         ✧

"This is one of the cafeterias," Wendy said turning off of a main corridor into a large antechamber. There was a series of roped off "mouse mazes" leading to four open blast doors. Beyond the blast doors was a long, low room with a fairly standard cafeteria line down the middle. There was a stack of trays, cups, a beverage dispensing unit with a limited selection, utensils and sundries and a short section of food. The food consisted of rather bland dishes, weighted heavily towards starches.

Wendy took a tray and moved down the line accepting a helping of corn and a small piece of badly overcooked pork from the unsmiling servers. Elgars followed, carefully mimicking her choices.

At the end of the line Wendy turned to a small box mounted near eye height. The screen lit up and identified her correctly then scanned her plate. It noted that she had received their midday ration and indicated a large calorie balance.

Wendy gestured at that. "Unless you're a real pig, you can make it on less than the calories that you're allotted every day. You can transfer a percentage of it to somebody else's account and you get increases for community service. It's the main medium of trade in the Urb."

Elgars stepped up to the box which repeated the performance noting an even larger ration balance.

Wendy raised an eyebrow quizzically and looked at the details at the bottom of the readout. "Oh, that makes sense," she said with a nod. "You're on active duty ration levels; which basically means a double ration."

"Why's that?" Elgars asked as they headed for the door.

"Active duty is assumed to be doing physical labor,"

Wendy pointed out. "Anyone that does day in and day out physical labor has a higher ration level; it's based on 2600 calories per day so that individuals can have some to trade. But if you're in the infantry, say, you're usually expending that much every day. So they double the ration level." She shook her head. "That's not real well known, but once you've been in this hole for a while you learn stuff."

They passed through a second set of open blast doors and into the eating area beyond, where Elgars stopped to look around.

The ceiling was about twenty meters high with glow-paint along the upper portions of the walls and onto the ceiling that gave a fairly pleasant indirect lighting. The walls, with one exception, were floor to ceiling murals, this one being a southwestern motif. The exception was a wall that was clearly stone, but unlike most of the other stone walls that Elgars had seen, this was a pattern of red on red with yellows shot through. It was pretty and clearly fit with the overall motif, but something about it waked an unpleasant memory. Elgars shivered and looked away.

The room was filled with tables and had six marked exit doors on the far side from the entry. In addition, on the parallel walls were large blast doors marked "Authorized Emergency Personnel Only."

"The cafeterias double as emergency shelters," Wendy said, gesturing at the doors. "There's nothing in them which is a fire hazard, just the tables and some drink dispensers that are pressurized in another room. In the event of a fire in the sector, people are directed to the cafeterias. The blast doors close and internal ventilation goes on; the ventilators are on the other side of those doors.

"There are eight in each of the housing sectors, two in Sector A, two in Sector F and one in each of the others. The ration level varies day by day and what's here is what you get; there's not much variety. There are a few 'restaurants' scattered around, but they're not much better and they all get the same food. There's a couple of 'bars' for that matter. Not that there's anything much to drink, either."

Elgars nodded and gestured with her head towards the rock wall. She still didn't like the look of it, but she wanted to know how the designer had gotten the pattern into it and what it was made out of.

"That's actually sandstone," Wendy said, guessing her question. "Each of the cafeterias are a different motif. For this one, the designers had some sandstone rubble shipped in and they vitrified it. That's what that melted rock is. It's been broken down by Galactic diggers—which shatter the rock by ionizing some of the molecules in it—then put in forms and melted."

As they sat down Elgars sniffed the offering then carefully cut the pork into tiny bites and slowly ate each one. Wendy was done eating before the captain was done cutting.

"Your voice changed again," Wendy commented, dabbing at her lips with a cloth napkin. "Back there dealing with security."

"I' ha'?" Elgars asked. She carefully cut out a bit of fat and flipped it off her plate. "How?"

"You keep sliding in and out of a southern accent," Wendy noted. "And when you're speaking with that accent, you don't have a speech impediment. Where are you from?"

"Nuh J'sey," Elgars answered.

"So, where's the southern accent come from?"

"Ah dunno, honeychile," Elgars answered with a thin smile. "An' Ah wish you'd drop it."

Wendy's eyes went wide and a shiver went down her spine. "Did you do that on purpose?"

"Whuh?"

"Never mind."

They ate in silence for a period while Elgars looked around with interest and Wendy carefully considered her new acquaintance.

"Do you remember what a southern accent 'sounds' like?" Wendy asked carefully.

Elgars turned from her examination of their surroundings and nodded. "Yuh."

"Have you thought . . . would you want to try *talking* with one?" Wendy asked. "It sort of seems like . . . you want to be talking with one. It's the only time you're clear."

Elgars narrowed her eyes at the younger girl and clamped her jaw. But after a sulfurous moment she took a breath. "You mean lahk this?" she said. Her eyes widened at the smooth syllables. "Shee-it, thet's we-eird as hay-ll!"

"That's a bit thicker than you were," Wendy said with a smile. "But it's clear."

"What the hayll is happenin' to me?" Elgars said, the accent smoothing out and the voice softening. She set down her knife and grabbed her hair with both hands. "Am Ah goin' nuts?"

"I don't think so," Wendy said, quietly. "I know people who are nuts, you're just eccentric. I think the shrinks were driving you nuts, though. I don't know who is coming out of that head, but I don't think it is the person who went into the coma. For whatever reason. They kept telling you that you had to be what they reconstructed that person to be. And I don't think they were right."

"So, who am Ah?" Elgars asked, her eyes narrowing. "You're sayin' Ah'm not Anne Elgars? But they did a DNA check and that's the face Ah'm wearin'. Who am Ah then?"

"I dunno," Wendy said, setting her own implements down and regarding the redhead levelly. "We all wear masks, right? Maybe you're who Anne Elgars really *wanted* to be; her favorite mask. Or maybe you're who Anne Elgars really was and the Anne Elgars that everybody thought they knew was the mask."

Elgars regarded her in turn then pushed away her tray. "Okay. How the hell do Ah find out?"

"Unfortunately, I think the answer is talk to the psychs," Wendy said. She shook her head at Elgars' expression. "I know, I don't like 'em either. But there are some good ones; we'll just have to get you a new one." She glanced up at the clock on the wall of the cafeteria and her face worked. "Changing the subject, one of the things we haven't discussed is work. As in what I have to go to. I think you're suppose to help with it; at least that is what I think the psychs meant. God knows we could use a few more hands."

"What is it?"

"Ah, well," Wendy said carefully. "Maybe we should go look it over, see if you like it. If you don't, I'm sure we can find something you'll enjoy."

"So," Elgars said with a throaty chuckle, "s'nc you can' be in s'curity or t' Arrrm'uh, whuh *do* you do?"

The door must have been heavily soundproofed because when it opened the sound of shrieking children filled the hallway.

The interior of the creche was, as far as Elgars could tell, a kaleidoscope that had experienced a hurricane. There was one small group of children—most of them seemed to be five or so to her admittedly inexpert eye—that was not involved in movement. They were grouped around a girl who was not much older, perhaps seven or eight, who was reading a story. And there was one little boy sitting in the far corner working on a jigsaw puzzle. Other than that the remaining ten or so children were running around, more or less in circles, shrieking at the top of their lungs.

It was the most unpleasant sound Elgars had ever heard. She had a momentary desire to pounce on one of them and eviscerate it just to get it to Shut Up.

"There are fourteen here during the day," Wendy said loudly, looking at Elgars somewhat nervously. "Eight of them are here all the time, Shari's three and five others who are orphans."

A medium height blond woman carrying a baby made a careful path through the circle of playing children. She could have been anywhere between thirty and fifty with a pleasant face that had probably once been exceedingly pretty. The years had clearly been hard, though, and what looks were left hovered between rough and beautiful, like a tree that had been battered by a century of winds. Despite that she seemed to be almost completely imperturbable as if she had seen the world at its worst and until something to equal it came along it was a *good* day.

"Hi, Wendy," she said in a husky contralto that bespoke years of cigarettes. "Who's your friend?"

"Shari, this is Anne Elgars. Captain Elgars, technically, but she's on convalescent status," Wendy said in one rush. "Captain, this is Shari Reilly. She runs this creche."

"Pleased to meet you, Captain," Shari said, holding out her free hand, which happened to be the left.

"Pl'sed," Elgars croaked.

"One of the reasons Captain Elgars is on convalescent status is that she's still in speech therapy," Wendy explained. "And the psych suggested that she sort of 'follow me around' for a while to get her bearings; she lost most of her memory at the Monument."

"You were at the Monument?" Shari said neutrally.

"S' the' tell muh," Elgars responded. One of the kids maneuvered out of the swarm, trying to escape a pursuer in what Elgars had finally determined was a sort of free-form game of tag. The little girl, about six or seven, came swooping around the group by the door, shrieking like a banshee.

"You handle this very well," Shari said with a faint smile. "Most people would have flinched at Shakeela."

Wendy cocked her head to the side and nodded. "That's true. But I've never seen you flinch at all."

As the tension from the sound built up, Elgars felt herself getting more and more still as if a blanket was coming up to protect her senses. She still could hear, even faint noises, but as long as she stayed in this place, not drifting but not really feeling connected to the world around her, she was fine. Unfortunately she found she also couldn't talk. Which precluded staying "safe."

"I don' fl'nch," she finally answered. "Don' know why."

Shari nodded after a few seconds when it was apparent no more was forthcoming. "Wendy, I've got to go change the twins. Little Billy had an accident and that set Crystal off. Could you hold Amber?" She held out the infant.

"Why don't I start cooking lunch instead?" she asked. "I think that Annie can probably handle it."

"Okay," Shari said with only a moment's hesitation. "Do you know how to hold a baby?" she asked.

"No," Elgars answered, eyeing the little mite doubtfully.

"Just put it up on your shoulder like this," Shari said, tucking the baby's head under her neck. "And support it from underneath like this," she continued, lifting Elgars' left arm to hold it up. "The most important thing is to not let the head flop. Okay?"

"No h'd fl'p," Elgars repeated, patting the baby

lightly on the back with her free hand. She had seen Shari doing it and it somehow seemed right. Not particularly important, sort of like tapping your fingernails on a table or flipping a knife in the air. Just something to do with the hands.

"There you go," Wendy said, headed for the door at the back. "You're a natural."

"I'll be back in just a second," Shari said, grabbing one of the running children and carrying it over to the changing station. "Won't be a moment."

Elgars just nodded as she continued to tap the baby. With no one talking to her she was free to experiment with the feeling she had had. It was not just a stillness, but a sort of unfocused awareness of her surroundings. Although it seemed to reduce the effect of the children's voices she could still hear them clearly. And she found herself noticing little details. It was a moment of transcendent stillness and perfection that she had rarely enjoyed. And all because she found herself wanting to rip the little bastards' throats out.

At which point the little twerp she was holding threw up half its lunch.

"I work there six days a week, six hours per day," Wendy said as they made their way back to Elgars' quarters. "Since you're supposed to follow me around . . . I think you're supposed to work there too. It will fulfill your community service obligation anyway." She looked over at Elgars, who had had that strange stoniness to her countenance ever since Amber had burped. They probably should have explained about the towel.

"So, uh, what do you think?"

Elgars thought about it. She had become familiarized with making large quantities of something called "grits" which seemed to be the staple food for children. She had also learned how to change diapers. She'd tried reading a book, but that hadn't worked out too well.

"I di'n't l'ke it," Elgars said and worked her mouth trying for more clarity. "I's not as ba' as sur-ge-ry with no drugs. Close but not as bad."

"Oh, it's not that bad," Wendy said with a laugh. "It is a tad noisy, I'll admit that."

Elgars just nodded. She supposed it was one of those things that you had to put up with. Like vaginal exams and pain threshold tests.

"That's sort of my day," Wendy continued, looking at Elgars worriedly. "Except extraction drills. Like I said, I'm a reserve fire/rescue. That's Monday, Wednesday and Friday. Tuesday, Thursday and Saturday I go to the range. And one hour in the gym every day except Sunday."

Elgars just nodded. It was different than the hospital, but that was good. The hospital mixed unpleasant sameness with occasional bouts of pain. This at least was consistent.

"Are you okay?" Wendy asked.

"Don' know," Elgars admitted. "Want to kill something."

"From the kids?" Wendy said nervously.

"Maybe. M'stly wanna kill whoever decided I needed to be 'fixed.' Or ge' ou' where I can do some'ing."

"Your speech is already improving," Wendy pointed out. "Maybe the psychs will let you go soon." They had arrived at Elgars' quarters and she shook her head. "Maybe you should write to your commanding officer and ask him to intervene. Even though you're on hospital status you're still on his books. He's got to want to get you back. Or get you off the books. And he can't do that without the shrinks getting off the fence."

"How d' I d' that?" Elgars asked with a frown.

"There are public e-mail terminals," Wendy said. "Let me guess, they didn't tell you you have e-mail access, right?"

"No," Annie said. "Where?"

"Do you have an address for your commander?" Wendy wondered. "If not, I bet I know who could forward it. . . ."

# CHAPTER 9

The tumult and the shouting dies;
      The captains and the kings depart:
Still stands Thine ancient sacrifice,
      An humble and a contrite heart.
Lord God of Hosts, be with us yet,
Lest we forget—lest we forget!

             —Rudyard Kipling
             "Recessional" (1897)

*Near Cayuga, NY, United States, Sol III*
*1723 EDT Sunday September 13, 2009* AD

Mike sat in the sunshine on Fort Hill looking down over the interleaving ridges and marshes running north and south from Lake Cayuga to Lake Ontario that comprised the Montezuma Defense Zone.

The terrain had been perfect for the human defenders; with all the roads and bridges cut, the Posleen assaulting out of fallen Syracuse had been cold meat in the first days of the war. Whether slogging through the numerous marshes or rushing the slab-sided hills they had fallen by the hundreds of thousands. And human losses, while high, had been a bare fraction; it was believed that the Battle of Messner Hill had achieved over one *thousand* Posleen deaths for every human defender.

Therefore, the decision to retreat barely a month into the war had been a critical blow. It had been on the plains between Clyde and Rochester that the Ten Thousand was born and the ACS died. It was in the politically driven decision to defend every hamlet, to counterattack every hilltop, that six divisions of veteran soldiers had been turned into food for the alien invaders. In the process, over three thousand M-1 tanks and two thousand irreplaceable suits had been lost. It was on the Ontario Plain that the war was nearly lost.

But now it was all returned. The Posleen, once broken in the brick-dust ruins of Rochester U, had run. And the ACS and the Ten Thousand hammered them for it. The Ten Thousand needed no encouragement; from the lowest buck private to their commander, every single soldier believed in "keepin' up the skeer." And any time a Posleen force turned at bay they would call on the supporting artillery and ACS.

That last, however, had cost the ACS battalion dear. Every suit was precious and they had lost better than two dozen troopers or suits in the pursuit. Supposedly a few new ones were on the way. But when they arrived would be problematical.

Looking down over the sparkling marshes, though, Mike had to believe it was worth it. The Ontario Plain was the weakest point in the Eastern U.S. With it back in human hands not only was there defense in depth—unlike at the beginning of the war the plain was now being covered with line after line of trench works—but the strongest points were held by veteran soldiers that knew the Posleen, however fierce, were not invincible. Posleen could die and their crested heads made great decorations over a mantelpiece.

Mike didn't even raise his head at the sound of a helicopter behind him. That was the definitive sign of a secure area; any aircraft was vulnerable to God Kings' fire and helicopters were worse than planes. If a helicopter was buzzing around it meant that all was right with the world. He smiled and recrossed his feet on the headless God King propping them up. Life was good.

Jack stepped out of the OH-58 and shook his head. It looked like the orders he brought were none too soon. There were quite a few signs that both the 1st/555th and the Ten Thousand needed a break. But the crests that some of the Ten Thousand troopers had attached to their rucksacks was nothing compared to the head of a God King stuck on an upthrust sword. The dripping yellow trophy had stained the weapon, probably the God King's own boma blade, and pooled under the ACS commander.

But Mike didn't seem to notice that little fact or the smell, despite having his helmet off. He just kept looking to the east, towards Syracuse and the distant Atlantic. Towards the enemy that held the plains.

The general walked up behind his former aide with a glance at Mike's staff. The group of officers and NCOs kept a respectful distance, also looking to the east and conversing in low tones. Most of them were young, like the commander, and all had learned in a hard school. But Horner understood the difference, the reason they were not starting to act oddly; they didn't have the added weight of command.

From the very first contact with the Posleen, O'Neal had been in one position of command or another. Frequently, in the early days, these were thrust upon him unexpectedly. And unlike Horner he had not had the time before the war to come to terms with the weight of responsibility or the little tricks that commanders learned to manage the load. The result was his psychological management techniques took unexpected and, arguably, unwise directions.

No question, it was time for a break.

"Morning, Mike," said the general.

"You will note that it is Tuesday," the major said, standing up. "And while we are not in Syracuse that is not our fault; I was informed that to go further would be 'logistically insupportable.' Thanks for the armor support, by the way."

"It's okay," said Horner. "We got back Savannah. And, believe it or not, there are *no* problems anywhere in the Eastern U.S. As a matter of fact, the worst I have to worry about is a globe in Georgia that's not acting the way it should."

The ACS commander turned around and looked up at the much taller general. "So you're telling me we're going west."

"Nope," said the Continental Army Commander. "You're not going anywhere. Except back to Buffalo for at least a week of R&R."

Mike frowned. "Harrisburg?"

"The assault got beaten off. And we managed to slip in a resupply of critical parts so they're back in full form."

"Roanoke?"

"The 22nd Cavalry retook the forward positions. And the Posleen look like they're licking their wounds. Actually, they'd better be 'cause General Abrahamson boxed 'em in and pounded them into scraps. He couldn't get a good count, but it looked like over two million lost there. Better than Richmond."

"Chattanooga?"

"Hasn't been a probe in a couple of months."

O'Neal tugged at the collar of his armor and worked his neck around nervously. "California?"

"There hasn't been any activity in weeks," Horner sighed. "Mike, you need to take a break. You're propping your feet on dead Posleen and screaming 'eat me' at my corps commanders."

"You heard about that, huh?" the major asked without chagrin. "He deserved it, though. We'd been ready to move out for two hours when his first unit showed up."

"Probably," Horner admitted. "But you still need a break. There's not enough time for you to go see Cally, though. Is that okay?"

"Yeah," said the ACS commander looking around as if awakening from sleep. "I just . . . I don't know what to do, Jack!"

Horner snorted. "Keep your battalion on standby, but one day recall is fine. I'll go tell Duncan; he can handle the details. Go back to Buffalo. Get some dress greens, flash the medal around, get your tubes cleaned. You're a widower, not an ascetic."

"That's cold, Jack," O'Neal said with a touch of anger.

"And that is something you haven't figured out, yet," the general responded. "War is cold. You have to be colder."

"Yeah," Mike said, wiping his gauntlet over his face and glancing at the head of the God King with distaste. "Maybe a couple of beers *are* in order."

"Two weeks," Horner said. "After that there's that globe landing in Georgia I want you to go check out. I had the local corps commander put a Fleet LRRP team on it, but they don't appear to be moving. So take a couple of weeks. Besides, we're getting ahead of the game on SheVas and I sent SheVa Nine down there to backstop Fourteen. If *two* SheVas can't handle it, what's the point of sending the ACS, right?"

"Okay," O'Neal said. "I got the picture." He took one last look at the marshes and hills to the east. "All in all, though, I think I'd rather be in Georgia."

"I need you functional, Mike. This war has cost us too many good soldiers already."

Mike nodded and scratched at one of the newer gouges on his suit. The nannites would eventually clean it up, but the repairs left visible traces like scars, slightly off-color. The sign that a suit had seen wear.

"Did you *really* tell that SheVa colonel to run me over?" he asked.

"Who?" Horner said with a frown. "Me? Whatever gave you that idea?"

"'Twas a terrible cruel thing to do," Mike grumped. "I got half a dozen ports clogged."

"Face it, Mighty Mite," Horner said, slapping the suit lightly on the shoulder. "You needed a good shellacking. It was a tough job, but somebody had to do it."

Mueller crouched on the slope above Bridge Creek Road and regarded the bridge sourly.

The rest of the team was gathered around, belly down on an outcrop of schist that gave a fairly covered view of the dam and the bridge at the same time. In spring or summer the slope of mixed white pine and hardwoods would have obscured the view of the dam and vice versa. But this late in the fall the only thing protecting the team from view was camouflage and stillness. Which meant that crossing the bridge was going to be tricky.

Coming out of the dam the river curved around the slope they were on, slightly to the east, then straightened back out in an "s." The bridge was a strikethrough in the middle of the "s," slightly out of sight from the dam. On the north side of the road, the side they overlooked, was a low field of white pine that came within twenty meters of the road and ran right up to the water's edge. The road's right-of-way hadn't been bushed since before the invasion from the looks of things and was thick with weeds and brambles. The cover down on the flat was going to be much better than anywhere on the slope.

On "their" side of the river was a power substation that appeared to be still functioning. At least, the road up to it had been recently regraded and the fence metal looked to be in good repair. If it wasn't in use, the Posleen probably would have salvaged it long since.

From long years of experience, Mueller was fairly sure which way Mosovich would hop, but he had to be sure.

"Well?" he whispered.

Mosovich's camouflage-painted face was set and still for a moment, then he grimaced. There were two problems in the crossing. The first was the slope, which was not only open—it was steep as hell. Most civilians would have referred to it as a cliff, but it was really just a very steep, standard Appalachian, forested slope. The trees alone would reduce the difficulty in going down and it was cut by both the back-and-forth trails of deer and a couple of what looked like old logging roads. The team, with the exception of Nichols, had been spending enough time climbing up and down similar slopes that they were as good as any mountain troops, with the possible exception of the Gurkhas, in the world. So they would be able to negotiate it. But it was still steep as hell and that meant the possibility of somebody getting injured on the way down.

If they went straight down they would also be in view of the dam. For all his words about the Posleen not posting sentries he wasn't about to take an unnecessary risk. Just to their left, moreover, was a very shallow gully. If they moved around to that they would be out of sight of the dam, any Posleen coming from the east would have to look back over their shoulder to spot them and the ground was a tad less steep.

Once they were on the flat they could get into the trees by the stream and have fairly good concealment right up to the bridge. Crossing that would be tricky thing number two.

"Left. Take the slope fast. Go for the drainage ditch by the road then into the trees."

"Gotcha," Mueller said, swinging off the gray rock outcropping to get ready to go down the hill.

"Fast is a relative term," Nichols pointed out. "I ain't gonna win any hundred yard dashes with this heavy mother."

The sniper's rifle weighed thirty pounds and the ammunition for it was not exactly light. Although the snipers carried relatively few rounds, their "loadout"—the amount of material and equipment they carried—rounded out at over a hundred pounds. Nichols wasn't a slouch, but Godzilla couldn't dash with a hundred pounds on his back. Not very far.

"Mueller, take one end," Mosovich hissed. "I'll take the lead. When we hit the flat, trot, don't dash. But for God's sake, keep an eye out, don't trip and don't slow down." He crouched as well, looked both ways and nodded. "Let's go."

The safest and quietest way to go down the leaf-covered slope would have been to follow the deer paths step by cautious step. In places they might have been able to drop a level or two, moving onto the occasional outcrop or fallen tree so as to get down on the flats a bit quicker, but by and large it would have been a slow, serpentine, back-and-forth trail to the valley floor.

However, that serpentine trail would have meant

being exposed for ten or fifteen minutes on the lightly wooded hill. Mosovich had considered and discarded that method, preferring to get to the flat, and some reasonable cover, as fast as possible. Which meant tobogganing.

The most deadly part of the descent was that each step was in danger of sliding on the leaves. But that slide could be used to the advantage of the team and Mosovich was more than willing to go for it. He sat down, planted both feet lightly and kicked off.

The sensation was similar to tobogganing on snow and just about as fast. It was also reasonably quiet, not that that would matter; if there was a Posleen close enough to hear their passage they would be spotted as well. The technique was different from sledding on snow in that it was easier to slow yourself and Mosovich was careful not to let it get out of control. Fortunately, there were not only trees to occasionally catch himself on but several natural breakpoints.

He reached the first of these, a broken section of what was probably once a logging road blasted into the slope and went flat to listen for a moment. The Posleen companies weren't quiet and there was a chance that if one was coming from the east they would hear it before it came in view. The same couldn't be said for the west, which was the more dangerous direction, but life was a gamble much of the time, especially for the LRRPs.

After a brief pause he started down again. This portion of the slope was, if anything, steeper and he had to catch at trees several times, banging himself painfully on the inner thigh on a small, concealed stump and catching a small beech sapling just before going over the steep bluff at the bottom. He paused again to listen, but there was nothing to hear except the soughing of wind in the trees and the faint hum from the power substation no more than twenty meters away. And ten meters down on the flat.

The ten-meter bluff was not quite ninety degrees. Once upon a time he would have turned around and carefully found his way down using hand- and foot-holds. But, once upon a time and far away in a land called Vietnam, a visiting Gurkha had first laughed himself sick then shown him the *proper* way to traverse such a slope. So, standing up, he leaned forward and started to run. The movement could best be described as a controlled fall; there was no stopping it until you reached the flat and could coast to a stop. Or keep running as the case might be.

He was never able to determine where he had put his feet in these situations and it didn't really matter because a second after he started he'd dropped the ten meters, feet flying from one friable bit of quartz-embedded clay to another, and was on the flat pounding towards the drainage ditch by the road. He flopped on his belly in the stagnant water in the ditch, extended a camera to cover both directions and popped up a directional antenna.

"You guys coming or what?"

It was exactly two minutes and thirty-five seconds from when he had kicked off of the ledge.

The rest of the team descended more circumspectly, but with Mosovich in place he had a view that would give advanced warning if a Posleen patrol was approaching. As long as the team could freeze in place their camouflage and the darkness would probably prevent their being spotted. As it turned out, there were no patrols in the time it took them to descend the hill and join him on the flat. A small patrol, no more than twenty, came by while they were making their way through the grove of white pine along the river. But they just crouched in the close-packed trees—the area looked almost like a Christmas tree farm—until the Posleen passed, then the human patrol closed on the bridge.

The bridge was a simple, flat, concrete structure that just spanned the rushing waters. Checking both ways as if for traffic, Mosovich hopped over the near guardrail and started across the span with the rest of the team not far behind. On the far side, to the left, was another small field, the intersection of the main road and a washed-out side road that paralleled the river on the west side. The field was covered in brambles and small white pines, none of them more than knee-high, but it looked like some concealment to Brer Mosovich and he jumped the far guardrail and went to ground again.

As soon as the rest of the team was in place, and making sure again that there was no sign of Posleen, he trotted through the brambles to the side road. The nearest woodline was up a chest-high embankment and across another small, sloping, weed-covered field. Once they crossed that, no more than another seventy meters, they would be in the woods and out of sight; the woods on this side were much more "bushy" than on the far slope.

Jake jumped up the embankment and waited for Mueller and Nichols. After helping the sweating sniper haul the rifle up the embankment the team leader headed for the woodline.

Daffodils, some roses run wild and a shallow crater showed that this had once been a homestead. There was also a low, stone terrace to be negotiated. As Jake scrambled up that—reaching the deeper shadows under an enormous pinetree—he looked to the east and went flat on his stomach; a Posleen patrol had just come around the bend on the far side of the river.

The rest of the patrol saw him go down and followed suit, hoping for the darkness and their camouflage to conceal them. Sister Mary took a calculated risk and reached back to flip down her own ghillie net, which was kept in a bag at the top of the rucksack. It only took a few twitches to cover herself and a human could have walked within a few feet and never realized she was there.

The Land Warrior suits they all wore had a nice suite of "sensors," one of which was a fiber-optic periscope. Mosovich, and everyone else, used theirs now as they slowly extended them above grass height and looked back towards the bridge. The small diameter of the optics, even with the best processing in the world, did not give much detail in the extreme darkness, but some gross outlines were possible to make out. The Posleen patrol had come from the northeast, from the general direction of Tiger, and now they broke rhythm and ranks to cross the small structure.

As the patrol watched, the Posleen force, about two hundred in number, formed up on the near side of the bridge, no more than fifty meters away, turned up the far hill and trotted away.

Mosovich waited a moment for them to get out of sight then stood up carefully. "Now why the hell didn't they see our trail?" he wondered.

"I dunno," Mueller responded, picking up the barrel of the sniper rifle. The four trails were clear in the vision systems, with bent down grass and weeds pointing directly to their position. "I dunno," he repeated. "But let's get the hell out of Dodge."

"Concur," Mosovich said, heading towards the trees again at a moderate but steady pace. "No reason to look a gift horse in the mouth."

The Posleen normal had very few desires in life. Eat. Sleep. Reproduce. Satisfy the desires of its God. Kill anything that threatened it or its God.

Currently it was satisfying its God that had it bugged. The orders it had been given were right at the edge of its competence. Most of its limited intelligence was bent on keeping to the complicated patrol path that had been laid out for it. The rest was burdened with determining what "signs of the threshkreen" meant. It knew threshkreen; it had survived all three of the fights its God had been involved in. They mostly wore green and brown. They carried weapons not dissimilar to the People. They were generally tough and stringy.

But, by all reason, threshkreen either should be or should not be. This . . . being in potential, having been, but are not now, but might be again, this was rocket science to the poor normal.

However, as it passed over the bridge, ready to make its programmed turn, it paused. Around it the part oolt formed, looking for the threat that had prevented their temporary master from continuing on. No threat. No thresh, no threshkreen. Just the dark silence of the moonless night.

For the superior normal, however, there was a problem. The last time the God had spoken to him— he recalled it with a thrill of pleasure—the God had asked if he had seen anything not-normal. This, then, these . . . trails through the high grass and thorn bushes, this was not normal. By extension, it was possible that he should call for help if something was not normal. However, those were not his orders. His orders were to fire off one magazine if he saw "sign of threshkreen."

But . . . this could be the mysterious "sign." Running thresh made such trails; it was a good way to find the thresh for gathering. Threshkreen, though, tended to leave things on the trails themselves, so walking on them when gathering threshkreen was contraindicated.

But even the four-legged thresh of these hills made trails like that from time to time. Another patrol could have scattered them, driving them away from the road by their presence. It could even have been wild oolt'os; there were some of those in these death haunted hills.

Rocket science indeed. Finally, cautiously, the normal moved towards the trails, searching and scenting for any clue. The trails came off of the road, crossed the field with some evidence of scattering or bedding, then went up into the hill beyond. He cautiously paralleled one of the trails. There was a scent of oil, a bite of gun-smell, that combination of propellants, metal and cleaners. But that could have come from anything. It could be in his nose from their own weapons. Finally he paused.

The field was covered in thorn and grass, a simple triangle between the trees along the river, a road that paralleled it and the main road they were patrolling. The parallel road, a washed-out track now after the first onslaught cleared these hills, was also torn in the passage of whatever had made the trails. And in the mud on the far side, under the short cliff that terminated the field beyond, was a clear and unmistakable boot print.

The normal didn't *know* it was a bootprint. But he now knew what his God had meant by "sign of thresh-kreen" for he had seen *this* before as well. And when he saw it, he lifted his railgun in the air and fired.

"Oh, bloody hell," Nichols said quietly.

"Somebody spotted the path," Mueller added unnecessarily. "Jake?"

"Sister, call for fire on that field, call for scatterable mines on our trail, too. Let's didee-mao, people."

Cholosta'an scratched up behind the head of the superior normal as he drew his blade. It bothered him to gather this one. The normal was, without a doubt, the best of his oolt'os, but he was wounded sore and the path of duty was obvious. Cholosta'an scratched the cosslain and told him how good he had been to find the trail of the threshkreen as he laid the monomolecular blade against the normal's throat.

"Wait," Orostan said quietly. "Is that the one that found the trail?"

"Yes, Oolt'ondai," the younger Kessentai answered. "It . . . bothers me to gather him. I have none better. But the way is clear."

"Leave him. We will provide him with food. With enough food and rest he may grow well."

"Even if he survives he will be crippled," Cholosta'an protested feebly. The idea was attractive, but the oolt'os would be nothing but a weight on his balance sheet.

"If you will not support him, I will," Orostan said. "Keep the genes. Keep the material. Put him to the work of a Kenstain, that which he can do. We need such as he. And you have other things to do."

"As you bid, Oolt'ondai," Cholosta'an said, sheathing the blade. He gave the oolt'os some of his own rations, a singular honor, and stood up. "Well, you suggested I give up half my oolt and that is, more or less, what has occurred."

"Not exactly as I had intended," Orostan said. "But not without some good. We now have these damned threshkreen, this *Lurp* team, localized. We can put all our patrols on a few roads and narrow the area down even more. Once we have them in a tiny box we will find and destroy them if it takes the entire host to do it."

"Good," Cholosta'an said savagely. "When we do I want to eat their hearts."

Orostan hissed in humor. "I am no human lover, but they do have some good expressions. They refer to that as 'payback.'"

# CHAPTER 10

*Near Seed, GA, United States, Sol III*
*0623 EDT Sunday September 14, 2009 AD*

Mosovich cursed bitterly. "I'm getting too old for this shit."

"Yeah," Mueller whispered. "Tell me about it."

Oakey Mountain Road was a tiny thread paralleling the Rabun/Habersham county line. The line itself followed the ridges that the team was using to avoid detection, but the road, not all that far away at most points, was generally obscured by the thick forests of the hills. This was their first clear glimpse, paused on the mountains above Lake Seed, and it was horrifying; the narrow trail was crawling with Posleen.

"That's a couple of *brigades'* worth, Jake," Mueller whispered.

"Yeah, and if they're there, they're going to be on Low Gap Road . . . They're boxing us."

"Jake, Posleen don't do that," Mueller protested, ignoring the evidence of his own eyes.

"Yeah, well, these Posleen do," Mosovich answered. "Sister Mary, are we secure?"

"Yep," she answered. "There's a box over on the other side of Lake Rabun and I've put in a couple of new ones. We're solid laser back to corps."

"Wake somebody up. I want a human being, not a machine. I think this mission is a bust and we're going to have to cut our way out."

The officer rubbed his eyes sleepily and took the proffered headset from the communications tech. "Major Ryan, FSDO. Who is this?"

Ryan sometimes wondered if he wouldn't have made a greater contribution to the war effort in the Ten Thousand, a posting that came automatically with the tiny "Six Hundred" embroidered on the right chest of his BDU uniform. However, a brief but memorable "counseling session" with the Chief of Staff of the Army Corps of Engineers had convinced him that there were better places for him, and for the Army.

The Ten Thousand generally depended on other units for their engineering support and their senior engineer was basically a liaison. Sergeant Leo, now suitably promoted to warrant rank, fulfilled the position perfectly. And it would be a dead end for a junior engineer who had realized he *liked* being an officer.

Thus had started a series of usually high profile, and always critical, assignments. The first had been as junior aide to the Commander of the Corps of Engineers and almost all the others had involved positions equally challenging and career advancing. Even this last, a redesign of the Rabun Gap defenses, was a high profile job. He was, technically, just the Assistant Corps Engineer, but in reality he was directing not only the brigade of engineers but all the divisional engineers in a complete rebuild of the valley's defenses.

The defenses for Rabun Gap were extremely heavy, make no mistake. The gap was a relative low point in the eastern ranges with a major road passing through it, so the United States had spared no expense in preparing for the Posleen onslaught. The primary physical defense was a curtain wall that stretched across a narrow point south of the former Mountain City like a slightly smaller Hoover Dam. The wall stretched, on an only slightly less massive scale, up both of the steep slopes on either side running along a line of ridges up to to the east and west. The "long wall" was being worked on constantly and would soon exceed the Great Wall of China as the single most massive human construction on Earth.

However, beyond The Wall, and behind it for that matter, was a different story. Originally The Wall was intended to be the centerpiece of a defense structure that stretched down past Clayton and filled the entire Rabun Gap, which, technically, began behind the primary structure about two miles.

Early landings and different priorities had meant that much of the preparations had not been carried through. None of the defenses in front of the wall remained; succeeding waves of attempted assaults had swept them all away and there had been no replacement. Furthermore, the defenses behind The Wall that were supposed to extend in depth for miles, had either never been completed or, in many cases, had been obliterated by the corps units as they jostled for space.

On a tour that had finally included the relatively low-priority Rabun Gap region, the current commander of the Corps of Engineers had gotten one look at the defenses and nearly died of shock. Defenses three or four times this quality had been repeatedly gained and lost around Harrisburg and Roanoke so she knew damned well that these could be taken by a sufficiently determined Posleen assault.

She first considered calling in John Keene. The civilian engineer was another special trouble-shooter that the COE kept in reserve. But not only was he deeply and inventively involved in rebuilding the Roanoke defenses, the local corps commander was General Bernard of 29th Infantry infamy.

It was by the order of General Bernard that the Posleen who had settled in to feast on the corpse of Fredericksburg in the first landing were induced, instead, to come swarming out and attack the forces gathering to their north and south. General Bernard, ignoring orders to the contrary, had ordered his division artillery to fire on a concentration of Posleen that had no apparent interest in continuing in a hostile manner. This had the effect, metaphorically, of poking a stick into a wasp nest, with similar results.

John Keene had successfully designed and implemented an engineering defense plan for Richmond to the south, literally at the last minute. The plan was implemented in opposition to the one suggested by General Bernard and had to be rushed through due to the poor tactical judgement of the general.

The corps to the north of Fredericksburg, however, through a combination of bad political decisions, poor training and an apparent computer hacking by renegade forces, was overrun almost to a man. This left only Engineer Officer Basic Course student Second Lieutenant William Ryan, fellow classmates and other engineer trainees pulled from Advanced Individual Training to harass and delay the Posleen. With a little help from the *USS Missouri* they had fought their way back to the Lincoln Memorial, where they basically got tired of running and held the basement until the ACS arrived to dig them out.

Which brought to the COE Commander's mind Lieutenant Ryan, now Major Ryan, who would be the perfect party to put in an operational position. Especially if the major was put in place with a very quiet word to the prickly Bernard that if he didn't give the major all the support he needed then get the hell out of the way, a certain court-martial board could be reconvened to "discuss" his failures in Virginia.

Thus Major Ryan found himself explaining to administrative units that they could either move their facilites *back* from the wall or to the other side of it and he really didn't care which.

And pulling Field Grade Staff Duty Officer.

Jake winced. He didn't know who this turkey was, but given that he was pulling staff duty in a nice dry headquarters it was pretty unlikely that he knew which end of a rifle a bullet came out of much less how vitally important getting fire to a cut off patrol was.

"Major, this is Sergeant Major Jake Mosovich, Fleet Strike Recon. And we've got us a situation here."

Ryan tugged at the lock of hair that always seemed to dangle on his forehead and tried to remember why the name sounded familiar. "Go ahead, Sergeant Major, you have my full and undivided attention."

Jake dialed up the magnification on the night vision system and sighed. "Sir, we are surrounded by Posleen. Our position is southeast of Lake Seed and the Posleen have apparently figured this out and are patrolling all the surrounding roads. Our objective was an overlook of Clarkesville, but at this point that is impossible. If we can cut our way out alive we'll be lucky. Are you with me, sir?"

✧        ✧        ✧

Ryan shivered and remembered the mingled shame and relief when his own platoon was permitted to leave the Occoquan defense. He knew, only too well, how Mosovich was feeling at the moment. Or maybe not: in Ryan's case he had always had the option of retreating.

He glanced at the artillery availability board and blanched. The sergeant major was not going to like what he was about to tell him; it was likely that he wouldn't believe it either.

"Sergeant Major, I've got some really shitty news. The fighting up north has had CONARC calling for available artillery from all over. We've lost both additional heavy artillery regiments in the area, the additional special arty we were supposed to get was diverted to Chattanooga and Asheville and half our corps arty is gone. We don't have any of the heavy, special guns at all, except one SheVa and they don't have any useful ammunition. And you're out of range for anything else except one five-five. And half the one five-five is tasked to emergency protective fire. I can't get that released without the corps commander's permission."

Ryan could hear the sergeant major swearing softly over the open circuit and something about it made the memory click. "Sergeant Major Mosovich? From Richmond?"

There was silence over the circuit for a moment. "Yeah, that's me. Why do you know about that, sir?"

Ryan stroked his mustache. He had grown it as an affectation back when he thought he was a little too young to suddenly be a captain. Then, after a while, he noticed that people tended to avoid looking him in the eye. Oh, not the combat types, but around corps headquarters you didn't run into many of them. But for the rest . . . they tended to look away. Some of them said he didn't look like he was still in his twenties.

But he kept the mustache.

"I know Mr. Keene. Pretty well." He'd studied under Keene's tutelage in Chattanooga during the rebuild and they had become more than acquaintances; Keene was one of the ones who could look the young major in the eye. And Keene had some good stories about Richmond. Better than Ryan's, which mostly ended "and then we ran away again" or "and then he died."

"Better than Barwhon, Sergeant Major," Ryan added, realizing now, how he could get the NCO to work with him. If they worked together rather than at cross-purposes, which would just *happen* if Mosovich assumed he was dealing with an arm-chair commando, they could, maybe, get the LRRP team out.

"Better than Barwhon but not as good as Occoquan," the major added. "I had the *Missouri* on my side there." Ryan paused again and clicked icons, reconfiguring data. "You now have everything I have the authority to release, Sergeant Major. I'm going to send a runner over to the corps commander with the request that he release the fast reaction forces, all but one batt. Some of these guys are probably asleep, so it will take waking them up. But in just a bit you'll have the better part of two brigades of artillery at your beck and call."

Mosovich smiled as his AID showed all the available artillery in the corps transferring to his control, but he suppressed his chuckle. "So that was you, sir. Yeah, I wish the *Mo* was in range. Or any of the railguns. But what we've got will have to do."

Ryan pointed at the nearest senior NCO and towards the corps commander's quarters. The headquarters was on a hillock in the middle of the Gap and had once housed the Rabun School. Now the dormitories were officers' quarters and the headmaster's home was the corps commander's quarters. Generally, the commander did not prefer to be disturbed in the middle of the night, but one look at the major was enough to send the staff sergeant scampering. And he wasn't going to return unless he had the release of the artillery.

"I'll see if I can scrounge up anything else. Can you think of anything?"

"Just one, sir," Mosovich added. "It might make sense to wake up Major Steverich in S-2. These guys are *not* acting like normal Posleen. Way too controlled, way too . . . something. They seem to be anticipating us in a way I don't like one bit. Like they're anticipating everything we do."

"Or reading the mail?" Ryan asked. "You're secure, right?" He checked the notation on the communicator. "Right."

"Yes, sir," Mosovich answered. "We're using the laser system, I'm not even trusting ultra-wide band. But we've been losing sensors. That's why *we're* out here; because we've lost all our sensors on this side of the mountain. What have they been doing with them?"

Tulo'stenaloor looked over the shoulder of the God King and reined in his impatience. Goloswin had been almost impossible to find, and even harder to dig out of his comfortable rut on Doradan. From the point of view of the young hotheads that made up the majority of the Host, Kesentai like Goloswin were not much more than Kenstain. They may have fought well enough to get a few small possessions, a square of property and a factory or two. But then they *quit*, leaving the fighting to their betters. And they had odd . . . hobbies was not a Posleen word, but it fit.

In the case of Goloswin the hobby was . . . devices.

He seemed to understand the Alldn't equipment better than its long dead Alldn't and Posleen designers.
He could improve, another human word, "tweak" came
to mind, a tenar so that it was faster, smoother and
the sensors interacted even better with the guns. His
sensor suites were a thing of legend and many well-
to-do Kessentai waited years for one of his systems to
be built and eventually catch up with them.

And one of them cost more in trade credits than a
basic oolt, fully equipped.

But the technician's real love was new discoveries,
new devices to tinker with, such as the sensor box
floating in the stasis field.

"These humans, so endlessly inventive." The God
King sighed. "Look. Not just a communicator, not just
a relay and not just a sensor, but all three rolled into
one. Crude in places; I think that some of these com-
ponents undoubtedly came from something else. But
quite, quite inventive."

"And now a defense device," Tulo'stenaloor pointed
out. "The last one that we tried to take down blew up
when it was moved." The loss of an oolt'os and a
Kessentai who was supervising was not worth commenting on.

"I need a sample of one of those," Goloswin said.
"I have an oolt'os who will probably be able to take
one down successfully."

"After this little problem is rectified," Tulo'stenaloor
said. "They are dependent for untraceable communication on these things. I would like to remove that link
if I could."

"Oh, it's not untraceable," Goloswin pointed out. He
slid his talons through some glowing dots in the air
and a new holofield opened and configured. It was a
rough map of the region and Tulo'stenaloor realized
that the "bright" areas were where the human sensors

could see. And he realized immediately what he was looking at.

"You're in the sensor net?" he breathed.

"Oh, yes," Goloswin agreed. "Trivial exercise, quite trivial. The nice part is this." He highlighted a field and four purple icons sprang to life on a ridgeline. "There are your pests. Now go take care of them and get me a sample of the new sensors. I look forward to examining this 'boobytrap.' And the next human you talk to, please ask it what a 'booby' is *before* you eat it."

Mosovich looked at the map and got a sick feeling in his stomach. The fact was that, no matter how much artillery fire they got, they were in a box. There were only three places where crossing the Talullah River would be a reasonable proposition. As Mueller had pointed out, if they had SCUBA gear they could have crossed any of the lakes at any point. But without the gear they would be four obvious targets, out on the flat nowhere and open to fire from any passing patrol. And the crossing would not be quick. Even if they could "drownproof" Sister Mary and drag her across on a float. But otherwise it was a matter of choosing the bridges; crossing the streams would be nearly impossible and—between having to rig ropes to keep from being swept away and making their way across— sure to take too long as well.

However . . . these Posleen were acting like humans. They seemed to be thinking about the possible actions of their quarry and reacting in a reasonable manner. Which meant that they would be *expecting* the team to either cross the bridges or the lakes heading more or less directly towards the lines. They might or might not know that the latter would be virtually impossible.

If they could break through the lines to the *west*,

then break contact, two very big ifs, they could make their way towards the lines around Tray Mountain. That was a wilderness area and the roads were few and far between, making it much better from their perspective.

But getting there would be a long damned walk with, apparently, damned little support. The artillery, though, what there was of it, would be able to cover them the whole way. The important point would be to make sure they didn't get spotted by where the artillery was firing.

He chuckled silently. This was almost as bad as fighting humans.

"There is a reason that fighting humans is so hard," Orostan mused. "They apparently have been warring amongst themselves, and surviving at it, for their entire history. Their legion of dirty tricks comes from those millennia of experience. We Posleen, on the other hand, have either fought those with no experience of war, or fought the ornaldath. And the ornaldath has always lasted for such a short period of time, and been so chaotic, that little can be learned."

"With humans, every day is ornaldath," Cholosta'an muttered bitterly. "They . . . cheat."

"Yes," Orostan admitted in an amused tone. "But it is not ornaldath. They do not use the greatest weapons, much. Tulo'stenaloor's . . . 'intelligence' people have learned that they have a great reluctance to use those that are not chemical, those that use fusion and antimatter for their propellants. So it is not, by any stretch of the imagination, ornaldath. Except when you corner them. And then, sometimes, they use those weapons. Rarely."

"They are not cornered now?" Cholosta'an asked. "They are only a bit of one continent. The ones that are to the north have no materials to fight with and other than this remnant it is all tribes scattered in the mountains. Except for this remnant, they are broken. Isn't that the point of gathering this host?"

"Don't count the humans out until the last one is dead and you have hacked its body to bits and eaten it," the oolt'ondai cautioned. "Many of them got off the planet before we landed and those 'scattered tribes' are still strong enough to be a challenge in many areas. We have taken the bulk of the planet for our lands, and the bulk of the human population for our feed, but their fleet rebuilds and rebuilds seemingly endlessly. And these humans, these 'trapped abat' are no joke. Every day they find new ways to confound us."

As if on cue the sky began to scream.

"Splash out," Mosovich said, listening to the fire-cracker rattle of ICM landing in the distance. The team had moved down the mountainside, using every bit of concealment, until it was within two hundred yards of Oakey Mountain Road. The biggest worry were the God Kings scattered among the normals. It was hard, in the heavy foliage, to spot the occasional passing saucer, but whenever one came in view the team went to ground and held their breath in anticipation. But, so far, so good.

Now, with the firing behind them, if the Posleen stayed true to their current form they should hurry towards the bridge in anticipation of the team's movements.

And that did appear to be happening. The normals in view, almost immediately after the artillery began to land, began to stream to the north. With any luck in a few more minutes there would be enough of a reduction the team could consider trying the road.

They were on a ridgeline perpendicular to the road,

bedded down in a thick stand of white pine saplings. At the point they would be crossing the road it went through a small saddle and there was a hilltop on the far side. There had been a house or small farm to the right of the saddle in bygone days, but now all there was, was another weed-covered field and the overgrown right-of-way. The open area was small, as well, no more than fifty meters including the torn up grassy track that had been Oakey Mountain Road.

On the far side of the hill that was their objective the ground fell off down a steep slope to the Soque River. Although that would normally be a tough crossing, the area was densely grown and there was small chance the horselike Posleen could keep up with the team in there. They would have to cross Highway 197, but unless the Posleen were patrolling everywhere, any movement over there should be slight. And, again, the ground should be overgrown enough to permit them to slip past any patrols.

From the crossing of the Soque they would swing west of Batesville. If they weren't spotted on their crossing, corps would maintain harassing fire on the Posleen in regular spots near the Talullah. With luck, it would be some time before the Posleen commander discovered that they had slipped out of the trap. By that time they should be well outside the main search area.

If. With luck.

In a remarkably short time the masses of Posleen that had been in the area were gone. The road was empty and still in the pre-dawn night.

"Time to move out," Mosovich whispered. Steep slope again. Time to slide.

"Well, at least it is falling on others," Cholosta'an observed. The tenar's sensors were set to replicate the activity on the far side of the mountain.

The town of Seed had often been described as not much more than a stop sign; it really wasn't even that. The "main" road was Oakey Mountain, a two lane winding bit of nothingness going from nowhere to nowhere in the hills. And there wasn't even a stop sign on it, let alone a convenience store. The other road was Gap Road, a macadam track going over the mountains to Lake Seed.

And it was less now. Where before there had been a few houses now there were only weedy fields, scrub and the occasional shallow crater that indicated a home with a "Scorched Earth" home defense system.

Currently the fields were covered with the oolt'ondar of Orostan and the many additional newcomer oolt attached to it. This force had been primarily responsible for patrolling Low Gap Road. Orostan had ordered in road construction materials and the track over the mountains was in the process of being graded for the first time since the initial invasion. But most of his force was now consolidated at Seed in case the humans broke in another direction. As opposed to the forces over by the lake that were closing in, presumably closing in, on the human team. And it was clear that these latter were getting hammered.

"Yes," Orostan said. "And Lardola is being conservative. Most of the loss has been among the new forces. And especially among those marked as the least favorable."

"I'm glad I wasn't marked as 'unfavorable,'" the younger Kessentai commented sourly.

"No, you weren't," the oolt'ondai agreed. "Or you'd probably be in there getting turned into thresh." His communicator chimed and he touched one of the glowing dots, receiving the call.

"Orostan, this is Tulo. The humans appear to have tricked us; they are attempting to break to the west.

Again, they are preparing to cross the road on the western side. The patrols over there have scattered and headed for the firing. Cut the humans off if you can get there in time, pursue them if not." A holo map blossomed over the older Kessentai's tenar showing the relative position of the human team and the Posleen force.

"Understood," the oolt'ondai said. "I will do that immediately."

"And," the distant commander added with a hiss of humor, "I take it I don't have to suggest that you use caution."

"Agreed," the oolt'ondai answered.

"I will take my oolt immediately, Oolt'ondai," Cholosta'an said, starting to swing his tenar to the north.

"Softly, Kessentai," Orostan said, flapping his crest in negation. "I did mention that you were not considered entirely expendable, right?" The oolt'ondai ran his finger down the readouts until he grunted in satisfaction. "Oldoman," he said into his communicator. There was a moment's pause, which evoked a snarl, but the communicator finally lit.

"What?" came a harsh answer.

"The humans have been seen trying to make it across the road. Go north and cut them off; I will follow with the rest of the force."

"I go!" came the reply. "Enough of this waiting in the dark!"

"An expendable one?" Cholosta'an asked.

"Eminently," Orostan agreed. "His oolt'os are on their last legs from hunger, not because he does not have the credits to afford it, but because he expects them to find food on their own. Terrible equipment, not a decent gene line in the group. Damned few usable skills and all replaceable. He's not worth the air he and his oolt breathe." For a group called "The People of the Ships" it was the ultimate insult.

"And will we follow with the rest of the force?"

"Oh, definitely," Orostan said, sending orders to his key subcommanders. "But carefully and slowly, the least worthy scouts out to the front. It is not worth losing a thousand oolt'os to catch one small group of humans, no matter how dangerous."

"I don't see that it's worth this expenditure to cover one group of lurps," the corps artillery commander complained.

It was inevitable that everyone would want to get their two cents in just as soon as they woke up. And with the corps commander fulminating in the pre-dawn hours the word had quickly woken his staff. Who had descended in full fury on one lonely major.

Who didn't have an ounce of back-up.

"I don't see that it's worth the expenditure to keep you fed, Colonel." Major Ryan was tired and getting just a bit cranky. And trying to follow the battle around Seed while surrounded by chateau generals was getting on his nerves.

"Enough of that," General Bernard said. He was a big, florid commander who filled his BDU uniform like a bass drum. This also described the occasional military genius in history, but unfortunately that particular description, "military genius," did not extend to General Bernard. He had been the Virginia National Guard commander prior to the invasion, what is called the Adjutant General. Upon the Federalization of all forces he had retained command of the 29th Infantry Division up until the debacle that was generally called the Battle of Spottsylvania County. During the first landing individual units of the division had fought bravely and occasionally brilliantly. But the general had been shown to be completely out of his depth and when he ordered his division artillery, against standing orders, to initiate contact with the Posleen, it had contributed, markedly, to the ensuing massacres of the 9th and 10th Corps.

However, his political skills had stood him in good stead in the following war of blame-calling and finger-pointing. Certain prominent generals had gone down in flames, the President at the center of the controversy had, of course, died, but a few others, both deserving and undeserving of blame, had managed to survive. In Bernard's case he had even prospered, pointing out that the general that ordered his relief was shortly thereafter soundly defeated by the Posleen. The fact that General Simosin was also the victim of a very deliberate and subtle hacking of his control net was missed in the debate. Indeed, the fact that the battle took place at the time and in the way that it did being at least partially the fault of General Bernard and his single rash and stupid order was missed in the debate. Thus he was reinstated and even, eventually, promoted. However, everyone who was "in the know" was aware that as a field commander he was incompetent at best and dangerous at worst. Thus his posting to the relatively low priority Rabun Gap Defense Zone. This was not a guy you were going to trust at Chattanooga or Roanoke or Harrisburg.

General Bernard was also aware of this thin ice. And thus he did not immediately hop to the defense of his artillery commander. "One of the things we are here to decide is how much support they need. And I released the FPF batteries."

"We *probably* won't need final protective fire right away, sir," Colonel Jorgensen said. "They seem to be expending most of their attention on these lurps.

But if they follow them all the way back to the lines, assuming they make it, then we might have problems."

"The indications so far are that this group is sitting on its hands," Colonel McDonald pointed out. The corps intelligence officer was well aware that those were, technically, "his" lurps out there. What was even more important was that if he lost them it was unlikely he'd get a new set with the same capabilities any time soon. He had some "home grown" teams, but they didn't have the experience or the equipment of the long-service Special Operations types that had been transferred to Fleet Strike. Which would mean local patrols with standard equipment. Including regular radios. And since the Posleen seemed to be learning to track in on radios pretty quick, that would mean teams with not much in the way of communications ability.

So for a variety of reasons, not excepting the milk of human kindness and the interests of one soldier looking out for another, he didn't intend to let these two jerks hang Mosovich out on a limb.

"We have plenty of movement in the sensor areas," McDonald noted. "They're getting ready to move out of the sensor coverage. But even if they do we can get good fire on the approaching forces. It's only ammo; bullets not bodies, remember?"

"It's only ammo to you, George," Colonel Jorgensen said. "But it's my boys and girls feeding the guns. It's my cost for replacing tubes. I've got to explain the trunion damage and, for that matter, the ammunition expenditure. And we've got a *globe* sitting out there, planning who knows what. What happens when they come swarming at the wall? Where do we get the ammunition then?"

"Colonel, I've seen your ammo dumps," Major Ryan said. "You've got enough ammo on hand for five days of continuous fire, especially with all the units we lost to Tenth Army. Five . . . days. Trust me, those defenses will not last five days if the Posleen come at us in force. Five hours will be about right. So you've got plenty of ammo on hand in that case."

"I think we'll give a better accounting of ourselves than that," Bernard said. The wear and tear on the artillery would just mean he got new tubes sooner and this damned major would undoubtedly make some sort of a report of his "fighting spirit." "But we do have a sufficiency on hand. Fire them up, Red. Take every call for fire, fire on every sensor target. Major Ryan has been on this from both ends; let him handle the interface and you give him all the support he asks for."

"Thank you, sir," Ryan said. "I have been on their end and I *do* know what it's like." He paused for a moment. "And I'll admit this is way beyond my level, but I think you need to call Army and ask for your arty back, sir. I'll double that through COE if you like. Those Posties *aren't* acting right."

"I concur on that analysis, sir," Colonel McDonald said. "Just watching them on the sensors you can see they are staying way more coordinated. Look at this group over by Seed. Or the one that has been pinning down Low Gap Bridge and the 441 Bridge. Usually when you get shooting the Posties swarm towards the fighting. These guys are sitting the fighting out, holding key terrain. That, sir, in my *professional* estimation is a nightmare."

General Bernard paused and rubbed his almost totally bald head. That was a horse of a different color. He'd protested having the artillery pulled away when it occurred. If he called Army now and complained about nebulous reports of a Posleen globe force that was acting "funny" then nothing happened it could be the final nail in his professional coffin. The Army still had institutional memory all the way back to the Civil War of officers who were too quick to take counsel of their fears.

"Colonel, I want a full intelligence analysis," he answered. "Get a good count, or a good estimate. Detail all the ways they have been acting strangely and what the possible increase in combat effectiveness is from that. If it looks like a significantly increased threat, I'll take that to Army. I'll take it to CONARC if I have to. But I need more than 'these Posties are acting funny.'"

"I wish we had a Mike Force," McDonald said softly. "I hate just leaving the lurps to their own devices."

"I've heard about Mosovich before," Ryan said, tugging at his forelock. "He's not a guy to go down easy."

"I'm *really* getting too old for this shit," Mosovich growled as they darted across the road.

"Not that again," Mueller gasped. He'd given up trying to support one end of the Barrett and was carrying it on his own, along with his own weapons, equipment and ammunition, leaving the heavy ammunition pack to Nichols. Making it down the steep slope to the road had been . . . interesting. "You just got a rejuv; you're under warranty for another century."

"'It's not the years, honey, it's the mileage,'" Jake answered. This field was thankfully untorn and he led the team across it at a lope towards the woodline. "I'm just getting really tired of trying to make it to woodlines before somebody starts shooting at me."

"Try flying on the outside of a saucer into the middle of a Posleen swarm," Nichols gasped, sweat pouring down his face.

"Well, it looks like we cheated death again," Mueller answered, as they made it into the woods. This area, however, was a fairly open decidous slope, leaf covered but with little undergrowth. They were open to being spotted until they made it halfway up the hill where there was a large thicket of rhododendron. The slope was reasonably gentle and Nichols took the Barrett back.

"Thanks, man," Nichols said in an embarrassed tone. "This is the first time in my life somebody's had to hump some of my gear."

Mueller just nodded. He and Nichols were of similar build, heavy, stocky bodies with a lot of muscle on a heavy-boned frame. But he overtopped Nichols by almost eight inches. "Don't sweat it," Mueller said and looked over his shoulder. "Oh, shit."

To the southeast there was a small valley that was surmounted by another saddle slightly higher than the one they had just crossed. It was out of sight of the one the humans had used and the road ran through it, bent to the left to pass down the valley then up through "their" saddle.

Another Posleen force was coming over the far hill, but this was no patrol. At its head was a God King saucer and although it was clear the humans hadn't been spotted yet, the saucer was headed straight for "their" hill.

They had left a laser retransmitter on the far hill, but there was no time for Sister Mary to hunt for it with an antenna. "Fire Control," Mosovich snapped into his UWB transmitter. "Fire concentration Juliet Four. Say again, Juliet Four. Now. Now. Now." The ultra-wide band system was difficult to detect, difficult to find and difficult to jam. That didn't mean the Posleen couldn't do all three, just that short transmissions were, generally, safe. However, if they had to *depend* on it the Posleen would eventually localize and destroy them.

But the operative word was "eventually." Right here

and right now it was the only way to call for fire. And if they didn't get some metal on target, and jack quick, that was all they would have wrote for Mama Mosovich's son.

The God King was a good four hundred meters away and there was only one. The sensors of the saucers had been shown to be able to "see" humans at that range, but could not "discriminate" them if they were not firing. If the Posleen company had been headed down the hill the team would simply have dropped and hoped they weren't spotted. But it was clear from the movement of the force that it *knew* where the humans were and was headed over there to wipe them out.

Given that fact, there was only one thing to do; get the God King and hope they survived. The problem was that once they opened fire, despite their flash-suppressed weapons, if the God King was still up the sensors would point right to their position. So the God King *had* to be taken out, first, and the God King *had* to be taken out with the first shot.

Nichols flipped out the bipod of the Barrett and dropped to his stomach. He was heaving from the exertions of the last few hours, but he figured he could catch his breath for one decent shot. That was why they taught the technique at sniper school and he was starting to hyperventilate even as he was dropping. His heart was racing so it was a good thing the shot was only a few measly hundred yards; if it was over a thousand, and he had made shots like that, the shot had to be taken between heartbeats.

He took four more deep breaths, let the last one out in a long blow and leaned into the rifle.

Orostan shook his head as the data-link from Oldoman's tenar went dead. "Not even maneuvering; what a stupid abat."

The majority of his force was headed down Oakey Mountain road towards the last reported position of the human team. A few oolt had been left behind in case the humans slipped by, but the better part of six thousand Posleen were on the road with Orostan and his picked Kessentai near the front. At the front, however, were a few more of the more "expendable" oolt.

Who were trying to run through a rain of steel. The majority of the artillery available to Mosovich had not been pointed at the Rabun Lake area. The fire down there was from one battery of 155, trying to draw the attention of the Posleen off of the real moves of the team. The rest of the artillery, nearly two brigades, had been prelaid for support along their actual line of march. Some of it was set on the actual target that he had called for fire on, while the other tubes were set to fire on additional possible target points.

At his brief call for fire, the guns that were already set up simply pressed the firing button and went into reload. The other guns, those set on other Target Reference Points, were required to swing from their initial azimuth and elevation to reengage. But the system was fully automated for such a tiny adjustment and within fifteen seconds they had fired.

The time of flight was nearly forty seconds, so the Posleen force was given time to flay their surroundings for upwards of a minute before the first rounds began to impact. And then, forty seconds later, fifteen more batteries rained down.

After that it got bad.

"Their artillery is killing us," Cholosta'an muttered. "As usual." The God King swept his tenar back and forth as they went down the road towards the distant thunder of artillery. The habit had stood him in good stead in the face of human snipers and, because he never assumed that there were none around, he had survived when many of his age-mates did not.

"Hmmm," Orostan said noncomittally. "It is killing *some* of us. But we have them definitely localized," he added, tapping at the hologram in front of him. "They are transmitting now. Two bursts of communication have come from this hill. As soon as we crest the ridge they will be in view."

"Yes," Cholosta'an noted. "But so will *we*, Oolt'ondai. And I note that *you* are not maneuvering."

"So I'm not," Orostan said, flapping his crest in agitation at his own stupidity as the symbol for another Kessentai dropped off the hologram. "But they are quickly retreating up the hill. They should soon be out of sight and the artillery will abate. And we will soon be in position to pursue them closely; they will not be able to adjust their artillery then."

"Are we going to try to cut them off?" Cholosta'an wondered. "Where do you think they are going?"

"I think we can directly pursue them," Orostan commented. "The hill on this side is not heavily wooded. Once we get through this artillery we can charge the slope. Humans are slower than we are; we should be able to run them to ground."

"That sounds . . . easy, Oolt'ondai," the younger Kessentai noted, suddenly remembering that Orostan had never actually *faced* humans. "But are you only going to send those who are *expendable* into the artillery? Or are *you* going to run through it?"

Orostan paused momentarily in thought. "That's not a bad question," he admitted, looking at the three dimensional schematic. "I think, all things considered, that we'll send the majority of the force through the notch, because that is the only route that will accept it. But you and I will swing to the east of the road, out of the main artillery fire." He tapped the map, which gave a good view of the immediate area. "There is a hilltop here to the east. It's still across the valley from the humans, but it will give us a view of their approximate position without going through the main fire." He paused again as the next oolt entered the hammering artillery. The data-link of the Kessentai stayed up, but the condition marker of the unit indicated that it was, more or less, shattered with better than forty percent casualties. "And I'll probably send a few more units around as well."

"Sergeant Major, this is Major Ryan."

Mosovich didn't reply; he knew the UWB was detectable, but he could listen just fine. As long as the Posties didn't start jamming.

"You're leaving the edge of the sensor zone, so we won't know where you are. But we've got a good read on the Posleen and there's damn near five thousand of them on your tail. I've called for some obscurement and I'll adjust fire to follow you up the hill, but you'd better scram. Good luck."

Mosovich glanced at the far saddle and nodded to himself. A salvo of variable time rounds was coming in at the moment and the air was filled with black puffballs. The beauty of the scene belied the shrapnel that he knew was flying downward from the red-cored explosions. A rank of Posleen was shattered under the line of fire even as he watched.

But even as the line of Posleen went down another God King stumbled out of the fire and then another. It was definitely time to leave.

Nichols peered through the scope and hammered out another round. The big rifle pushed his stocky body back at least four inches, but he quickly brought the weapon back into battery and started searching for another target. It had long been determined that the artillery messed with the sensors the God Kings used to find snipers so the shots were not as supercritical as the first had been. But every round helped and the team was laying down fire right alongside.

Mosovich swore softly as he picked out another target in the gathering light. Their position was not as concealed as he would have liked. And, despite the artillery, some of the normals were surviving the gauntlet in the gap to spray the hillside with fire. None of it was aimed—they couldn't see where the team was firing from—but as soon as the sun came up that happy circumstance would surely change.

Mosovich, however, could see the normals fairly clearly. The Land Warrior system was proving its worth again, giving him the capability to easily direct and redirect fire on the targets in the gap, enhancing the team's vision and permitting them to communicate clearly. Shoot, move and communicate was what war at all levels was about. But it was especially critical at the level of the small team and the suits were a real boon.

They weren't perfect though. Advanced research on them had more or less been halted at the start of the war and even with the Galactic power systems they were fairly heavy. They also did not have GalTech clarity levels in low light; there was a particular problem with depth perception that seemed insoluble without the Galactic ability to make continuous micro-sensors.

But what they did, they did very well. Mosovich picked out another target, bringing the aiming bead onto the target and squeezing the trigger of the Advanced Infantry Weapon. The system used a series of sensors in the suit and the weapon to determine the accuracy of the shot and whether any inaccuracy was the fault of the weapon or the operator. If any inaccuracy was an environmental input, whether a temperature change in the barrel or a shift in the wind, the system automatically compensated on the next shot. If it was the fault of the operator it simply sulked in electronic silence. In this case it determined that the 7.62 round would miss its target point by less than three centimeters in the four hundred meters of flight. Since this was well within its margin of error, it made no adjustments.

Mosovich knew, intellectually, what was going on, but he wasn't really worried. The system had proven to be better "straight out of the box" than he had had any inkling would be possible and he had come to depend upon the accuracy of the system. It occasionally "threw" shots, but it enhanced his own already expert marksmanship to stellar levels. Especially in this half-light, half-dark.

Nonetheless, there were already several hundred Posleen forming up out of the artillery box and the system revealed a seemingly unending stream coming up the road from Seed. There was also a smaller group trying to probe around to their right. As soon as it came into view, he'd have to split his artillery and some of the God Kings were bound to get through.

All in all, it was an unpalatable situation.

"We're going to have to move out," he yelled. "Nichols, I need you to stay in place until we move up the slope. Then we'll take over potting the God Kings and you can move. I'll call for fire on that group coming around the hilltop from there. Clear?"

"Gotcha, smaj," the sniper said. In a different unit the person being left behind might consider that they were being sacrificed. But Nichols knew that if that was *really* Mosovich's intent, he would say "Nichols, I'm going to use you like a cheap pawn."

"Mueller, Sister, move it," Mosovich snapped, throwing himself to his feet and turning to scramble up the slope. "Time to didee."

# CHAPTER 11

*Near Seed, GA, United States, Sol III*
*0715 EDT Monday September 14, 2009* AD

Orostan snarled as artillery started to land on the hill.
The thick deciduous and white pine secondary growth
should have concealed their movements, but the fire had
followed closely on another call from the human reconnaissance team. Now it seemed to be closing in on his
more elite forces and that was not to be tolerated.

"I am getting tired of these insufferable humans,"
the oolt'ondai snapped. The team was also slipping out
of their sensor range, clearly escaping over the hilltop
beyond even as the pincer movement appeared to be
closing on them.

Cholosta'an flapped his crest with a great deal more
resignation. "Artillery happens. I don't like it, but I have
yet to find a battle where the humans don't use it."

"Well, these will not for much longer," the oolt'ondai
replied, yanking a weapon up from around his feet.

The gun looked not dissimilar to the shotguns of

Cholosta'an's oolt'os. However, when the oolt'ondai fired it was clearly different. For one thing, since the humans had dropped over the back side of the hill and were under cover from direct fire, he would not have been able to hit them. But the senior Kessentai did not seem to be trying to, rather firing into their general vicinity. Another change was that the round was clearly visible, travelling at relatively low speed to drop into the distant white pine and hardwood forest. The last difference was that there was no apparent effect except a slight flicker in the tenar's sensors.

"What was that?" Cholosta'an asked warily.

"A little present Tulo'stenaloor cooked up," Orostan said. "Now to see if it worked."

Nichols peered through the mountain laurels, trying to get a clear shot at the new Posleen force coming around the shoulder of the far ridge. The good news was that his position, hunkered down under two granite outcroppings and surrounded by mountain laurel, was both well concealed and protected from most fire. But the problem was that he would be firing through heavy vegetation. Although the .50 caliber rounds were unusually massive, they nonetheless tended to tumble and stray off course if they hit a branch. So it was critical to get a clear shot. And that didn't seem likely. But when he saw the distant God King lift a weapon and fire something at the hill, he thought he could almost take the shot.

Then his sniper scope went black.

"Sarge," he whispered into his radio. "What the hell just happened? My scope just went blank." There was no immediate reply and he noticed that there was no sound from his earbuds, not even the usual background hiss of the frequency carrier. "What the fuck?"

He turned around and slid down the hill towards

where the team had assembled. He was taking rear-end Charlie again, but the position had been good so it was no big deal. But now, with his scope down, he was going to need some help. He hit the diagnostic button on the side as he slid but nothing lit up. It was as dead as a doornail.

The area under the white pines was still fairly dark here on the west side of the ridge and this early in the morning so he flipped down his helmet visor and nearly slammed into a tree in the utter darkness.

"Sergeant Major?!" he yelled.

Mosovich slapped the diagnostic box on his Land Warrior suit and looked up. "Sister Mary?"

"I got nothin', sergeant major," she whispered. None of the communications gear was functioning and even some of the medical devices were not responding.

"Dump anything that doesn't work," he said, slamming his helmet into a tree. "Shit!"

"We're golden, Jake," Mueller said easily. "We can do this."

"We can't call for fire!" the team leader snapped back as Nichols slid to a stop. The team was gathered on a reasonably flat spot that was probably another one of the ubiquitous logging roads from the 1920s and '30s. "Nichols, you down?"

"Everything, Sergeant Major," the sniper said, furiously starting to change out the batteries on the sniper scope.

"That probably won't help," Sister Mary said. "I already tried on the commo gear."

"Did you see anything unusual?" Mosovich asked.

"Yeah," Nichols said, looking at the scope and shaking his head. "That group that was coming around the side of the ridge. One of the God Kings fired something, it looked like a grenade. I thought I was done, but there wasn't an explosion, just my scope going dead."

"EMP," Sister Mary said. "Unbelievable."

"Yep," Mosovich replied. "Just fucking duckey."

"EM-what?" Nichols asked.

"EMP," Mueller answered, beginning to strip his Land Warrior suit. "Electo-fucking-Magnetic-mother-fucking-Pulse."

"Yep," Mosovich said again. "Nichols, might as well shitcan that scope. And your helmet systems; keep the helmet, and all the other electronic gear. None of it's going to work now."

"How in the hell did they do that?" he asked, starting to dismount the scope. "And what is electro-magnetic Mfing pulse?"

"It's kind of like a big electro-magnet," Sister Mary answered, starting to dig all the commo out of her rucksack. "It scrambles electronics, completely shuts down anything with a microchip in it. Most military stuff used to be partially hardened, but I guess since the Posleen weren't using anything that generated EMPs they backed off on that."

"The suits were supposed to be," Mosovich said. "Same with the scopes. My guess is that it was just a mother of an EMP burst." He looked over at Nichols, who had nearly finished unbolting the scope. It was not designed to be removed in the field and acted like it. "Can you shoot that mother without a scope?"

"I have," Nichols said, yanking off the last recalcitrant bolt and, just for the fun of it, whacking the $50,000 anchor into a tree. "There's a ladder sight and a ghost ring. I shot with both of them in sniper school." He paused. "But sniper school was a long damned time ago."

"Okay, gather up whatever you're going to carry," Mosovich said, flipping the last piece of nonfunctioning electronics away into the brush and hefting his rucksack. "Just because we got hit doesn't mean the Posties slowed down. So we need to get a move on." Mosovich moved to flip up the map on his visor and frowned when he realized he didn't have a paper backup.

"AID," the sergeant major said, wondering if the Galactic technology had survived. "Do you have maps for this area?"

"Yes, Sergeant Major," the light soprano of the system answered, bringing up a local map as a hologram. The map was three dimensional, which the Land Warrior suit could only do with difficulty, and Mosovich wondered for a moment if the AID was jealous of how much more he used the human systems.

"Okay," he said, pointing to the faintly glowing dot on the hillside that was the team. "We're about a klick and a half from the Soque, if the ground was flat. But it's practically vertical instead. So we get down this hill fast. Unless the Posleen react really fast we should be able to make it across 197 before they get there."

"And if they are there already?" Nichols asked.

"We cross that stream when we come to it," Mueller growled.

Orostan grunted as it became clear that the artillery both at his location and in the gap had ended. "It appears to have worked."

"Yes," Cholosta'an said. "But they still have slipped away," he added, gesturing at the sensors.

"There are oolt moving to the far road," Orostan said with a shrug. "Sooner or later we will box them and without communications they will not be able to call for fire on us. Then we will finish them once and for all."

Mosovich frowned as he caught another tree to keep from falling down the mountain. "AID, can *you* get a communication back to the corps?"

There was a pause that did not seem to be entirely for effect and the AID answered. "I *can*, Sergeant Major. The Posleen will be aware that you are communicating."

"Will they be able to find our location?" he asked. "Or decipher it? I assume it will be encrypted."

Again there was a pause. "I calculate a less than one tenth of a percent chance that they will be able to decipher it while in the GalTech net. There is no chance that they will be able to physically localize you. However, I do not have secure entry into the military communications system; all AIDs were locked out of it after the 10th Corps blue-blue event. I can only contact the corps by standard land-line. That system is not only non-secure, it has occasionally been hacked by the Posleen. The alternative is contacting someone in the corps chain-of-command and having them set up secure communications. There is a secure land-line system, but AIDs do not have standard access to it so I can't just connect."

"Why don't I like that option?" Mosovich said quietly.

"The first person in the corps chain of command with AID access is the Continental Army Commander."

Jack Horner balanced his cheek on one closed fist as he watched the hologram. The speaker was a spare man with dark eyes. Dark pupils, dark irises and dark circles. In better days the Continental Army Commander and the commander of the Irmansul Fleet Strike Force had spent some good times together. At this point both realized that there were no more good times. That was not, however, something that they mentioned in anything other than private e-mails. Such as this one.

"With the 'unfortunate' loss of Admiral Chen and

his replacement by Fleet Admiral Wright we might get some movement," the speaker said. He turned to the side and picked up a piece of paper. "To give you an idea of how precisely useless it is to have us sitting here, our total actions on Irmansul for the last month were forty patrol-sized actions against unbonded, and in most cases unweaponed, normals. This is what our mutual amie would call 'fucking bullshit.' Not that I would use such language about our benefactors the Darhel. Wright has at least allowed the detachment of a few 'scouting' forces. And I am told that the armor team on Titan Base has made some breakthroughs, so there may be help available from that quarter."

The speaker spat out an untranslatable French epithet that had something to do with donkeys. "My own forces realize that there is nothing for which to return. However, we strain at the leash nonetheless. Yes, there are still Posleen on this planet. There are now and probably always will be; there are too many wilderness areas to eliminate them all and they are in the food chain at this point. But they can be 'managed' by a small police force and the killersats. The Fleet won the last action decisively and with small loss, but if Earth is totally lost it will be for nothing. We *must* return and we must return soon. And if the Darhel do not release us, soon, we *will* take that signal honor upon ourselves.

"No matter what.

"Crenaus, out."

Horner smiled like a tiger as the image winked off. It had been clear to him from almost the First Contact by the Galactics that the Darhel were playing their own game. And that the survival of the human race was, at best, incidental to it. However, it was not until fairly recently that he realized the extent to which the Darhel were *inimical* to the concept of Earth surviving as a functional planet. The Galactic society was very old, very stable and, above all, very stagnant. The humans were more than just physically dangerous; the philosophies, thoughts, processes and methods that they would bring with them would be a deathblow to the Galactic society, a society that the Darhel controlled absolutely. Just the concept of democracy, true, unfettered democracy, and human rights, would in all likelihood destroy the Galactic Federation if they were allowed free rein. Thus it was imperative that the human race be turned into a non-threat.

He had begin to wonder lately why, exactly, the Darhel had waited until practically the last minute, only five years before the invasion, to contact the humans. There were a thousand and one hints that they knew about Earth long before that, from the prepared medicines to the knowledge of all world languages. Some of it was certainly "fear"; the Galactic aliens were nonviolent and nonexpansionistic and the humans were anything but.

General Taylor, the previous High Commander, had wondered some of those things aloud. Just before he was assassinated by "Earth First" terrorists. Of course, five senior Darhel were killed in that spasm of violence, so suggesting it was the Darhel assumed that they were willing to cover their actions by killing five of their own. And it also assumed that the Darhel could kill, period. There were indications that in fact they could not even *order* killing, much less kill someone themselves.

But that didn't mean that Jim Taylor had gone down to terrorists, either.

It might all be paranoid delusion, but the arguments for not redeploying the Expeditionary Forces were becoming more and more specious. *All* the arguments were becoming more specious. And even if the EFs left Irmansul orbit at this moment, the only major country with any continuity left was the U.S.; everyone else was for all practical purposes gone. India had some significant hold-out areas and Europe as well. But the fractions that existed there were insignificant compared to the Cumberland basin.

What were the Darhel waiting for? The Americans to lose too?

His AID chimed a priority message and he regarded it balefully for a moment. The device was Galactic provided. And it was more likely than not that the Darhel could read anything sent over one, such as the last message from General Crenaus. Which Crenaus knew as well as he did. So had they already taken the hint, that the message was directed as much at them as at him? He smiled again, a sure sign of displeasure, and tapped the device to answer the call.

"Incoming message from Sergeant Major Jacob Mosovich, Fleet Strike Reconnaissance."

Horner vaguely recognized the name; Mosovich was one of the old hands who had been transferred to Fleet when they swallowed the U.S. Special Operations Command. He also vaguely recalled that Mosovich was the team leader of the LRRPs at 12th Army so he was probably the team leader sent out against the globe that had landed opposite Rabun Gap. But that didn't explain why the sergeant major was calling him directly. "Put it through."

"General Horner, this is Sergeant Major Mosovich," Jake said.

"Go ahead, Sergeant Major," the general said. "What is the reason for the call?"

"Sir, we just got hit with an EMP round by the Posleen and you're just about the only person we *can* talk to."

Horner rocked back and smiled broadly. "Better and better. From that globe down in Georgia?"

"Yes, sir," the sergeant major replied. "These guys aren't acting like Posleen at all, sir. They've got patrols on all the roads, real honest to God patrols, they're taking out sensors, they're using some half-way decent tactics from time to time, they seem to have expected us personally and now they are all over our asses. And using some sort of EMP round to take out our Land Warrior suits and communications."

"What's your status at present, Sergeant Major?" the general asked, waving at the AID to bring up a map.

"We've temporarily broken contact, sir, and we're trying to put some distance between us and the main force. We hope to be able to *stay* out of contact, but I won't put money on it. The primary mission is blown, though, sir."

Horner looked at the map and smiled again, tightly. He'd driven through that area a couple of times in better days and the terrain the team was entering really didn't favor humans all that much. "Looks like it's getting ready to flatten out, Sergeant Major. I'd send a flying team of ACS down there if I had anything to give you."

"Oh, we'll make it out, sir," Mosovich answered. "But we *do* need to talk to our artillery folk. And we can't at present."

Horner gave an unseen nod to the distant team. "AID, connect directly to secure communications and get the sergeant major back in touch with his artillery, will you?"

"Yes, sir," the device answered.

"Will that be all, Sergeant Major?" Horner asked.

"Yes, sir. Thank you."

"Well, good luck," the general said. "I've made a note that I want to see your raw debrief. But that can wait until later. Make tracks."

"Roger that, General. Mosovich out."

❖     ❖     ❖

Ryan looked up as the planning officer came in the Tactical Operations Center.

"It looks like they're gone, Major," the PO said.

"I sincerely disagree, Colonel," the engineer replied. "We lost a sensor at the same time. It looks like they used something along the lines of an EMP to take out their communications. Which means they might or might not be out there someplace. Their intention was to cross the Soque and swing west of Batesville. So I have the arty laid in to cover that movement."

"That's the point," the planning officer snapped. "That artillery is laid in there 'covering' what is probably a terminated team. We need to talk about retasking."

"We can 'retask' when we're sure they are gone," Ryan snarled. "Until then the damn artillery can just stay pointed. It's not like it's going to wear out the tubes or the personnel to stay up."

He snatched up the buzzing secure phone and snarled: "What?"

"Stand by for connection to Continental Army Command," an electronic voice chirped.

"You might want to tell the commander we have an incoming from CONARC," Ryan said to the planning officer.

The lieutenant colonel gave the major another look and left the room as the tone on the line changed.

"This is the Office of the Continental Army Commander," a light soprano said. "Stand by for direct transfer to Sergeant Major Jacob Mosovich. All connections on this system are fully secured. A directive has been issued for the full debrief of the sergeant major and his team to be forwarded to the attention of the Continental Army Commander. Stand by for transfer."

"Bloody hell," Ryan said with a chuckle.

"That you, Ryan?" Mosovich asked.

"Good to hear from you, Sergeant Major," the major said with a laugh.

"Yeah, I can imagine what was being said. Well, the report of my demise was exaggerated. As usual."

Ryan laughed as the corps commander strode into the TOC. "Well, Sergeant Major, we're set up at three or four points on 197. I'll list 'em out for you and you can get ready to call."

"Gotcha," Mosovich said. "Glad to be back. I've got to slither down this damned mountain now."

"I'll be standing by," Ryan said. "That was Mosovich, sir," he continued, turning to the corps commander. "He's using his AID to bounce through CONARC's AID and then into the secure phone net."

"So it wasn't CONARC calling?" General Bernard asked.

"Not directly, sir," Ryan agreed. "But there is a directive to send Mosovich's full debrief to him, direct and personal. I get the feeling he wants to know what the hell is going on out there."

"The directive to take a look at the globe came from Army," the S-2 said. "But it looked like a rephrase of CONARC."

"Well, I guess if General Horner is going to get his debrief we'll just have to get the team back, won't we?" General Bernard asked tightly. "Is there anything we've missed?"

"We could try to send a flying column out of Unicoi Gap," the planning officer said. "We've got a battalion of mech up there. There's no report of heavy Posleen presence near Helen. If they didn't run into one of these heavy patrols they could, possibly, make it to Sautee or so. South of Sautee there's indications of the outer forces of this globe landing."

"Send a battalion in in support," Bernard said. "And have them send out a company. Tell them to move down to the vicinity of Helen, get in a good hide and stand by for further orders."

"I'll get on it, sir," the planning officer said, heading over to the operations side.

"I hope I haven't just sent out a forlorn hope," Bernard commented.

"Well, we already did *that*, sir," Ryan said, looking at the map. "The question is whether we can get them back."

Mosovich looked down the hill and shook his head. There was a very steep, very high road cut then the road, which was clear at the moment, then another cut down to the river, then the river and on the far side a short bank and dense underbrush. The best bet, again, would be to go down the hill fast, but that would mean doing a rappel. The distance wasn't far enough for their static rappel systems to engage effectively. And they didn't have a rope that was long enough to loop around a tree. So when they got down, the rope would dangle there as a marker. So they'd have to take it in stages.

"Mueller, rope," he hissed, pulling on heavy leather gloves.

"Gotcha," Mueller said, pulling the line out of his rucksack and shaking it out. The Army green line was the sort of stuff to make a serious climber blanch, simple braided nylon with a very high stretch rate and rather high bulk, but it had a number of features in its favor. One of them was that when doubled over you could "hand rappel" if the slope wasn't absolutely sheer. "Good" climbing ropes were much thinner than the green line and had smoother outer layers. The benefit of the first was reduced bulk and the benefit of the second was reduced wear from "rubbing." But there was no way anyone could slow themselves going down a slope with "good" line without using, at the least, a "figure-eight" rig, and a ladder rig was better. So, using the "bad" green line, the team would not have to stop and get full climbing gear out. Just hold on and hope for the best.

Mueller flipped the rope around a fairly well rooted hickory and slithered both ends so that they were even. If they had any sense at all they would have quick knotted it as well; if anyone lost one of the doubled ropes they would be holding thin air, but sometimes quick knots got stuck and while if the rope slipped *one* of them might die, if the rope got spotted *all* of them probably would.

"Me first," Mosovich said, picking the rope up and slipping it under his thigh.

"Let me go," Mueller said. "I'm the heaviest; it'll be the best test."

"Nope," Mosovich said with a chuckle. "We're going in order of weight. I want as many of us as possible to make it down. You go last. And carry the Barrettt."

"Screw you, Jake," Mueller growled. He put one hand on the rope. "Just remember who's at the top with the knife."

"I will," the sergeant major said. He leaned back and started to walk backwards down the slope.

Although he probably could have gotten away with a simple "hand" rappel, holding onto the rope with both hands, Mosovich had set up a "body" rappel with the rope run between his thighs and up over his shoulder. It was much safer and more controllable and he was, frankly, getting a little tired of living on the edge. As it was, it worked well. He went down the slope about seventy feet, well short of the end of the rope and better than two thirds of the way to the road, and found a sort of ledge where a vein of quartz created a shelf. There was just enough room to stand with relative ease. Mountain laurels grew all around it so there was some concealment, and another largish tree jutted out of the soil-covered cliff. This tree wasn't quite as robust as the one Mueller had secured the rope to above and was on a worse slope, but beggars can't be choosers.

Sister Mary came next, fast and smoothly. They had been training together for nearly six months, but she had come with mountain climbing experience from somewhere and she showed it now. She actually bounded down the slope, something Mosovic preferred not to do when on a body rappel, and still managed not to dislodge much in the way of debris. She hit the ledge a bit hard—the quartz was friable and rotten—and dislodged a fairly large rock. But it hit in the mud of the drainage ditch along the road and disappeared into the muck; no harm done.

Next came Nichols, who *hadn't* had any mountaineering experience before joining the LRRPs. He took the slope very carefully, both moving slowly and making more of a trace than Mosovich or Sister Mary. But he made it, one-hundred-fifty-pound rucksack and all, and shuffled sideways to make room for the next team member, very carefully *not* looking at the straight drop to the roadbed below.

Instead of coming down, Mueller pulled the rope up. It took Mosovich a second to figure out what he was doing, but when the Barrett and the master sergeant's rucksack came down the slope it was fairly obvious. Mueller followed them in rapid succession, dislodging another rock when he hit.

"I dunno, Jake," Mueller said, looking at the best available tree. It was a twisted white pine that was growing out of the juncture of another decaying quartz vein and the schist it was intruded into, which was weaker.

"I'll take it," Mosovich said, throwing the rope over his shoulder. "Sister, on rappel."

"Okay," Sister Mary said without demur. If the sergeant major said he could hold the rope, he would hold the rope. She took it and slipped it around her body. "I'm going to cross right away."

"Oh, yeah," Mosovich agreed. "And hit the stream. But wait there."

"Roger," she said, dropping over the cliff. Her descent, again, was fast and smooth. When she hit the road she crossed quickly, grabbed one of the saplings on the edge of the bank and dropped out of sight into the streambed.

"Nichols," Mosovich said. "And take the Barrett. Mueller, gimme a hand."

Both of them bracing were able to support Nichols and his massive load. The weight caused the sniper to drop far faster than he had probably preferrred, but he made it to the road and crossed quickly, dropping out of sight on the far side. There was a faint cry that reached their perch over the chuckle of the river and the two NCOs traded glances and a shrug.

"You sure you can support me, Jake?" Mueller asked. "I could go last."

"Sorry man, I'd rather trust myself," Mosovich said. "I can handle it. 'He ain't heavy . . .'"

"Right," said Mueller with a laugh. He dropped over the side of the ledge, but was careful to catch his weight on as many footholds as he could find in the eroded cliff. At the bottom he threw the rope aside and darted across the road.

Which left only Mosovich. Jake looked at the tree he was supposed to depend upon, the eroded hillside and the woods across the way. "What a screwed up situation," he muttered. Then he coiled up the rope, tucked it in his rucksack, turned around and dropped off the ledge.

The technique was another picked up in too many years of risking his life. On a cliff like this, with outcroppings, brush and trees sticking out all over, it was barely possible to slow yourself by catching various items on the way down. It was not a matter of stopping, that was going to happen suddenly at the bottom, but just slowing yourself enough that you didn't break anything.

It was not the sort of technique that anyone but mountain troops used, and then only in extremis, because it was so stupidly dangerous. *But*, Mosovich thought, *that's my life all over*. There were two things uppermost in his mind on the short descent. One was that if he dug in too hard, it would leave a path a blind normal would notice. So he couldn't slow himself the way he would have preferred, placing both hands and feet into the slope and "dragging down." The other thing that was uppermost in his mind was that, at the speed he was going, if one of these damned white pine saplings jammed him in the groin there weren't going to be any more little Mosoviches.

The cliff flattened out a bit at the bottom from runoff and caught one foot sending him into a backwards roll. He tucked into it and fetched up, hard, against a rock fallen at some previous time. But all the pieces were in place and nothing appeared to be broken. So it was clearly time to cross the road.

He trotted across and grabbed one of the saplings on the edge to swing down on. He was going to drop directly into the streambed and that was damned near as dangerous as going down the slope; the rounded and slimy rocks of the stream would turn an ankle sideways in a heartbeat and with all the gear they were carrying that would mean a broken tibia just as fast.

He slipped down the slope and looked at the team huddled against the streambank. "Everybody golden?"

"No," Nichols gasped out.

"He broke both ankles jumping off the bank, smaj," Sister Mary said, putting a splint in place.

"Well, Stanley," said Mueller leaning back until his head was in the stream. "Isn't *this* a fine mess you've gotten us into."

# CHAPTER 12

*Near Seed, GA, United States, Sol III*
*0825 EDT Monday September 14, 2009* AD

Lying in a freezing cold mountain stream was not one of Jake Mosovich's favorite pastimes. And doing it next to a troop with two broken ankles wasn't adding to the experience any a'tall.

"Jesus, I'm sorry about this smaj," Nichols gasped. Sister Mary had used a neural stunner to deaden the ankles, but it still wasn't going to feel all that good and the cold water obviously wasn't improving the sniper's shock; his face was a pasty gray.

"I didn't figure you did it on purpose, Nichols," Mosovich whispered. "Shit happens."

So far there had been no sign of the Posleen on this side of the mountain, but crossing the stream with a busted up sniper and all their gear was not going to go fast and a patrol could be along any time.

There were basically two choices: take off like jack-rabbits, hoping to make it across the stream and the mercifully narrow open area on the other side, or find a hide along the streambed and hope the Posleen eventually gave up and figured that the team had moved on.

Of course, there *was* a third option.

"Okay," Mosovich said. "Change of plan. Again. Mueller, move up the stream. Look for a better hide, someplace we can stash Nichols, you and Sister Mary. Nichols; we're going to put you under with Hiberzine. Moving you is going to tear up your legs something fierce. This way if they're bad enough, Sister Mary can just tie 'em off and forget about them."

"I can make it, sarge," Nichols said, shivering with cold.

"Can it, you idiot," Mueller said. He looked at Nichols under lowered brows. "If we don't put you under, your own body is going to put you down before the day is out. This is not a good way to grow old, Jake."

"What is?" the sergeant major said, starting to strip his combat harness. When he started pulling off Nichols' harness, the sniper grunted.

"You've got to be joking, right?" the specialist said, rolling over so the sergeant major could yank the harness, with its pouches of .50 caliber magazines, out from under him. Nichols was not as large as Mueller by any stretch of the imagination, but he made Mosovich look like a shrimp.

"No, I'm not," Mosovich said, folding up the bipod on the sniper rifle and submerging it in the water. "I was humping a Barrett when you weren't even a gleam in your daddy's eye." He looked over at Mueller. "Go to ground while I raise a ruckus. When the Posleen pull their patrols off wait a bit then hump buddy-boy out of here. Head for Unicoi; I'll lead 'em off to the southwest."

"Okay," Mueller said. "Have fun."

"Oh, yeah," the sergeant major said, submerging in the icy water until only his mouth and nose were exposed. "Never better."

Mosovich was shivering from the cold, but he hardly noticed. The current was strong as it pushed him downstream over rocks and occasional rapids and he floated backwards on his stomach, hauling the Barrett behind him and moving slowly and carefully from one bit of cover to the next. The river was full of old snags and boulders, fallen limbs and natural dams so there was more than enough concealment to be had and the river actually had passed *under* the road without his being detected.

He was lying on his belly behind a long fallen white pine, getting ready to move over a set of falls, when he saw the first Posleen patrol. It was better than two miles downstream from the team's crossing, but moving up the highway in the general direction. Mosovich froze when he realized it was being led by a God King. The indications were that at anything under a hundred yards the God King sensors could detect humans no matter what; they certainly had done so one time to him on Barwhon. But in this case the group of about three hundred passed on oblivious, no more than twenty meters from where his ghillie clad body crouched.

After that he was a little less circumspect since he had a particular point he wanted to make and not much time. The team was, apparently, not spotted by those Posleen, but it was only a matter of time before they *would* be detected. Unless, that was, the Posties had something better to worry about.

Finally Mosovich reached the position he had been looking for, where the stream made a sharp bend to the east and was intersected on the west by an old forestry road. In this case the road had been recently repaired, that is not much prior to the war, and was in fairly good condition. However, it only went "straight" for a short distance before angling south towards Ochamp mountain. It was across the highway, but beggars can't be choosers.

Mosovich carefully looked both ways, up and down 197, then heaved his dripping form up and began trotting. A trot was the best he could do, weighted down with the Barrett and nearly a hundred pounds of ammunition. But he made it across the road, continuing to trot up the forestry road and leaving as little trail as he could manage.

The road was grown up with a variety of weeds and scrub, so if he had to he could go to ground. But this time he was careful to move around the worst of the grasses, preferring to drift through the more resilient white pine and beech. The careful movement stood him in good stead because just as he was reaching the bend where he would have been safely out of sight, he heard the unmistakable clatter of Posleen headed up the road.

It only took a moment's thought for him to swing around, crouch down and swing up the ghillie cloak. He was better than seventy meters up the road, in light scrub and covered in a ghillie cloak. With humans there would have been no question that he was invisible, but these Posleen were starting to spook him.

The column of Posleen seemed like it would never end, a contiguous mass of alien centauroids. He automatically started a rough count, but when he went over four thousand he just gave up. This must be the brigade-sized force that had been menacing them at Seed. He wondered if it *knew* where they were, as it seemed to have on Oakey Mountain Road, but whatever prescience it had seemed to have deserted it and the last of the force passed quickly by.

He briefly wondered if he should have called for fire on the unit, but he wanted to put a bit more distance between them before he started playing artillery games again.

As soon as the last straggler had apparently passed he stood up in a half crouch and began backing slowly out of sight. As soon as the road was completely around the bend he turned and started trotting up the winding mountain trail. He clearly had a rendezvous to make.

Thirty chest-heaving minutes later he had climbed about five hundred feet and was on the top of Ochamp Mountain. The "mountain" wasn't much more than a hill, but it afforded a good view of the Soque valley and, again, had a well wooded backside that he could use to break pursuit.

As soon as he found an open area—another former homestead from the weedy flowers growing in the torn ground—he pulled out his binoculars and started scanning. Without too much trouble he found the brigade force, or at least a bit of it, continuing up the road towards Batesville. The problem was, they were practically on top of where the team should be, more or less.

Mueller scanned to the south and found another God King patrol, this time well away from the team's position. In fact, they were a just-possible sniper shot. With a scope they would have been dead easy, but using the ladder sight it was going to be tricky.

But if he missed the God King that would just make it better.

Lakom'set was beginning to wonder if following Tulo'stenaloor was the best decision he had ever made. So far the "Great War" had consisted of travelling up and down roads doing nothing. Given his preference he would be killing humans. But even being *shot* at by humans would be better than this endless wandering.

"This is boring, boring, boring," he said aloud. Naturally, his normals didn't respond. They could follow simple commands, but as conversationalists they left something to be desired.

Fortunately for him, just about then a .50 caliber round cracked by just over his shoulder and blew out the chest of the cosslain at his side.

"Maybe boring is good," he said as he whipped his tenar around in the direction of the sniper.

Mosovich ducked as the rocks around him were flailed by fire, then slid backwards on his belly. Clearly these Posleen were no longer taking his little pot-shots with any degree of humor.

Time to didee-mao.

Mueller didn't move as the shouting Posleen force headed to the south. Despite the fact that they passed less than fifty meters from the team's position in the stream, the God King sensors did not detect them. He suspected there was something to be learned from that, but what he wasn't sure.

It took nearly a half an hour for the whole to pass by. It was fortunate that the aliens hadn't taken longer. Both of the recon team members were on the verge of succumbing to hypothermia; if they didn't get out of the cold, running water soon they were going to drift off into the long sleep.

Their plan was simple. While Mosovich played rabbit and led the majority of the Posleen to the west, they were to head almost due north, passing through the human lines somewhere around the thinly held Lake Burton Line. The defenses in that section followed the trace of the Appalachian Trail and if the Posleen attacked or even took a section, they would be easy enough for light human forces to contain and push back. The roads into the sector had been demolished, walls thrown up in the lower sections and other than that the only activity was patrolling by infantry forces.

He glanced over at Nichols' still body and shook his head. The sniper didn't have to worry about hypothermia. The Galactic Hiberzine medication used a combination of drugs and nannites to slow human internal functions to close to zero and the nannites prevented, to the greatest degree, anything but gross mechanical damage to the body. So as long as they made sure some blood stayed in his system, he was "good," under virtually any conditions, for about three months. When administered the anti-drug, or after the nannites ran out of energy, the patient woke up with no memory of the time in between; to them it was as if no time had passed.

On the other hand, he wasn't light.

Mueller jerked his chin at the hills to the west. "We'll move out to a new hide," he whispered over chattering teeth. "Wait for nightfall then move out. Try not to make any tracks getting out of the water."

"Who gets the first carry?" she asked.

Mueller grimaced and looked at the river to be crossed. The water was rushing over hundreds of smooth, rounded, slimy rocks.

"The hell with carrying," the NCO said, grabbing the unconscious sniper by one wrist. "I'm gonna drag his ass."

A big hayfield on Lon Lyons Road had nearly nailed him as he was faced with the choice of crossing it, and probably getting spotted, or going around it and taking an extra ten minutes. He finally took the time and was glad when he spotted the Posleen patrol coming to the edge and looking at the open area askance. The God Kings had developed a healthy respect for human snipers and the open area probably looked like a good way to go to whatever gods the Posleen worshipped.

The patrol had taken long enough, waiting for another God King to join them, that he made it all the way across the road and into the heavy woods on the far side. In scrubby undergrowth he had no fear of the Posleen keeping up or even coming close. As he trotted through the woods, following deer trails when he could and breaking new trail when he couldn't, he had wondered which way he should go. He could turn to the south, towards Amy's Creek, and continue to "menace" Clarkesville, or he could continue more or less due west towards Unicoi Gap. After a moment's thought he decided on west; why throw away a perfectly good baseline for the Posleen to follow?

This position though, just to the east of 255 Alternate, was getting untenable so he slid down the hillside and started moving again. Crossing 255 would be a bear, but the map showed woods on both sides and most of the stuff around here was young and, therefore, thick white pine. It should be possible to move completely undetected on either side.

So it was with this happy thought in mind that he trotted completely out into the open.

The area on both sides of the road, that was shown as forest, had been cleared long before. Where he stood looked to have been the back area of some sort of small manufacturing facility. The buildings were gone, but there was too much unscavenged metal on the ground for it to have been anything else. On the far side of the road was a still-paved road and an intact farm. The paved road curved around behind the facility, which looked to have been a horse training facility, and the sudden incongruity, given what was baying at his back, caused a momentary snort of half hysterical humor to slip out.

He glanced quickly at the map the AID had brought up and shrugged. He and the Posleen had been playing a constant game up until this point. He would cut through the woods between these mountain roads, firing them up with artillery and sniper fire whenever he spotted them. A few of the, apparently, junior God Kings would push along on his backtrail while the majority of this brigade force swung around from one direction, or both, on the roads he had to cross. Assuming that the same situation was going on here, trying to bolt in either direction was just as likely to run him into the Posleen.

After only a moment's pause, he made the only decision he could and started jogging towards the road.

Cholosta'an looked up from his instruments at a warbling cry from one of his scouts. There, silhouetted on the distant ridgeline, was a figure that could only be the human they had been hunting for so long.

He swung his railgun towards the silhouette; the automatic tracking system, as usual, ignored the human, but before he could target the scout the figure had trotted across the road and out of sight. He reached down to loft his tenar, but Orostan raised a claw.

"Softly, Kessentai," the oolt'ondai said. The older Kessentai looked at the three dimensional map on his screen and grunted. "I think we may have him trapped." He began tapping at keys and sending commands to the nearer and farther Posleen forces, sending them out in fans to the west off of the road.

For one thing he had noted that this opened them out and made them less vulnerable to artillery fire.

"How?" the oolt'os leader asked with a frustrated snarl. "They move through these hills like Sky Spirits."

"But they cannot fly," the oolt'ondai said with a flap of humor and pointed at the map.

After a moment the younger Posleen hissed in humor as well.

Jake leaned against a relatively ancient hickory and gasped for air. He was sure that some time in his long career he had been this utterly exhausted, but when was a good question.

He was on a saddle just below the summit of Lynch Mountain and all the hounds of hell were on his path. The wood was open, mostly big old hickory, oak and beech, and showed sign of heavy foraging from deer.

To either side of the saddle, to the north and the south, the ground fell off in sheer cliffs. The spot would have been a good place for a last stand if Jake Mosovich had any intention of committing suicide. As it was it was just a damned good place to stop and catch his breath before the last push.

The last four hundred feet of Lynch Mountain loomed above him, looking just about straight up. The only way up was a narrow ridge that led from this knife-edge saddle up around in a curve to the left and then eventually to the summit. The path was, fortunately, covered for most of the way. Fortunately because the Posleen, as far as they were concerned, had him well and truly trapped and the entire brigade force was dead on his trail.

He glanced down the hill and shook his head. Give the bastards credit for tenacity. He had called for fire on his backtrail again and he was fairly sure that the lead, at least, of the brigade force was getting shredded by the artillery. There had been a number of unreduced houses on the hill, but by the time the artillery was done they might as well have been destroyed by the Posleen.

Now, though, it was time to go. He pulled a small device out of the side of Nichols' rucksack, pulled a pin, set a dial and tossed it on the ground. He was both lightening his load and putting a "sensor" in place; the effect of the device would be practically nothing compared to the artillery. Then he threw the Barrett over his shoulder and started out along the saddle. The path was actually about ten feet wide, but it fell off a couple of hundred feet to the east and west so in a way it felt narrow as a string. On the far side an old path continued up the ridge and there were occasional very old trail blazes, the faded orange paint pale against the grey of the tree-bark.

He scrambled up through the mountain laurel and rhododendron, grabbing at the granite and schist that were jutting up now through the thin soil, and climbed as fast as his quivering legs could carry him. The alternative didn't bear thinking on.

About forty-five seconds after he dropped it, the plastic oblong quivered, turned over and—with a slight "huff" of expelled air—threw out three fishing lines, complete with treble hooks. Then, with an almost unnoticeable clicking noise, it slowly pulled the lines in until the treble hooks caught on the surrounding vegetation. At that point the device was apparently satisfied and settled back into quiescence.

Orostan flapped his crest in agitation and glanced at the portable tenaral again. The humans had not cut back to either side, so they could only be continuing up the hill. The oolt'ondai had split his force around the artillery fire—it was clear that it was not being observed—and thus had avoided significant casualties there. But it would be necessary to cross a narrow lip of land to reach the crest of this hill and that would entail tremendous loss.

"This is not going to be pretty," Cholosta'an said.

"Tell me to eat, nestling, why don't you," the oolt'ondai snapped back. "Sorry, but that is obvious. Nonetheless, if we are going to run this abat *lurp* to ground, we *must* close with it."

"Well," the younger Kessentai said, with a slight flap of his crest, "we *could* just sit here and starve them out." He looked over at the oolt'ondai and hissed at the expression on his crocodilian face. "But I guess not."

The oolt'ondai appeared not to hear as he took a series of breaths. "Fuscirto uut!" he cried. "Forward!"

Jake dropped into a small "cave" between two large granite boulders and breathed deep. The position was just about perfect and, coincidentally, about as far as his legs were going to take him. The two "boulders"— both the size of a large truck—were actually outcrops that had been worn away until one dropped onto the other. In between was a small, rather dry gap about head height on the west side that narrowed to barely knee height on the east. Located slightly below the true military crest of the mountain and to the west of the mountain's summit, it looked over the last nearly vertical climb, which was on the *east* side of the mountain, and down to the saddle the Posleen would have to cross. Not only would the Posleen have to cross the saddle, struggle up the trail and then cross the actual summit, in full view most of the time, the position was darn near impregnable to anything but their heavy weapons—a concrete bunker might be a slight improvement, but not much—and had a back way out. Of course, the "back way" led to a four-hundred-foot-high vertical cliff, but beggars couldn't be choosers.

The wind-swept mountain had once, clearly, been a popular hangout. There was still a vague outline of some old lean-tos and two fire pits. It was well covered in gnarled trees, white pine and oak with a scattering of maple, their twisted trunks and branches leaning primarily to the south. The reason for their twisting was clear; what had been a light breeze down on the flats was a blowing gale on the heights and the wind whipped the leaves around him in a fury.

There were several large boulders and outcrops, but most of the mountain was covered in loam and brush. The exception was by the cliff, where the loam came to an abrupt end about four meters from the edge. The first few meters of the cliff were broken, with a fair-sized cave on one side, a fair number of wind-twisted white pine and several ledges. However, beyond the ledges the cliff fell away sheer for over four hundred feet to the tree-covered base of the mountain. The trees swept out for almost a kilometer from there before hitting the beginnings of "civilization" and another open field.

Jake flipped down the bipod on the Barrett, flipped up the ladder sight and pushed an old Jack Daniel's bottle out of the way. The range to the saddle, actually to the upper edge of it where the trail was clear of obstructions, was just at eight hundred meters. Judging distance like that, downhill in the mountains, was usually tough. But Jake's AID just laid a hologram on the hill and marked various points with range markers.

What the AID could *not* judge quite so well was the wind. At that distance the bullet would tend to drift rather strongly, perhaps as much as six inches given the wind and its direction.

Fortunately, Posleen were big targets.

The sergeant major rolled Nichols' rucksack off his back and rummaged around in it. He'd lightened it up on the way up the hill by some judicious disposal of devices, but it was the first "down-time" he'd had all day and all he'd had to eat since the previous night was a handful of hickory nuts he'd picked up on Ochamp Mountain.

Mosovich pulled out four one-hundred-round boxes of .50 caliber BMG, a bag of peanut hard candy, two packs of Red Man, three packs of some sort of apparently homemade jerky, and three MREs. Apparently Nichols wasn't big on "pogie-bait." No Fritos, no Pringles, no soynuts, trailmix or cornnuts, not even a damned Ramen package. What the hell were they teaching these kids? The MREs were spaghetti and meatballs, tortellini and lasagna. Either Nicols had eaten everything else before these or he had packed out mostly Italian. Mosovich dove back in and rummaged for a while, but came up empty. Nothing else, but socks.

"Damn, no hot sauce. What kind of a soldier goes out on a mission without hot sauce?" He could stomach the Army's version of "Italian food" if it had enough hot sauce in it. Otherwise it was just south of fried salamander—which wasn't half bad really—in his personal view of military food. Somewhere *way* down from fried grasshopper and just above kimchee. After a few moments' thought he pulled out one of the pieces of jerky and sniffed at it. His brow rose and he took a bite.

"Where in the hell did Nichols get venison jerky?" he asked no one. "And how come he was holding out?" After a moment's thought and another bite he answered the second question for himself. "I'm gonna have to speak to that troop about his choice of rations."

The sergeant major leaned on the pack and listened to the artillery in the distance. As he did he realized that the position also gave the first clear view he'd had of Clarkesville. The town was darn near fourteen klicks off, but it was as close as the team had gotten and the day was clear.

Mosovich pulled out his binoculars as he masticated the jerky. The stuff had the consistency of shoe leather, but it tasted heavenly. Bit light on the spicing, but perfection exists only in the mind of Allah.

"Lessee," he murmured around the jerky. "There's 441 . . . And there's Demorest. Probably." The town was noticeable mostly for the cleared areas; there weren't many buildings standing.

The day was as clear as a bell, one of those beautiful fall days when it seemed that from a high hill you could see creation. In this case the NCO could easily see all the way to where Interstate 85 used to be and Clarkesville was more than a tad easier.

The Posleen had covered the area with a smoke curtain, but the smoke pots, hundreds of them, were located on hilltops and left a "side" view of the area only lightly obscured. There were thousands of figures moving in the area, but that was only to be expected. What he hadn't expected to see was a gaping hole in the side of one of the hills just to the north of Demorest.

"Damn, they're digging in."

The humans had observed that behavior before, but only on Earth. Although the God Kings invariably lived above ground, usually in large stone or metal pyramids—although there didn't seem to be any evidence of those here—most of their *manufacturing* facilities seemed to be underground.

Apparently this was a "late conquest" activity. After an area had been fully reduced and all the human evidence cleaned up the Posleen generally put in farms. They primarily grew local crops having, apparently, none of their own. While this was going on the local God King's pyramid was constructed and the multitude of items necessary for that and day-to-day existence was created from the "factories," mostly nannite "vat" production, on the ships. But as soon as an area reached a certain level of production, underground facilities started being built. And when they were complete, the ships were passed on to the next generation and took off for either another planet or another part of the same planet. And the local settlement started working on the next ship out of their surplus.

The evidence for this process was gleaned mostly from overhead imagery observing the digging process and what went into and out of the caverns. The process was probably going on on Barwhon as well, although there was no way to get overhead on that planet. On Diess, which the humans had mostly retaken, the Posleen had *not* dug in their facilities. But the entire arable area of the planet was covered in megalopoli so they had just occupied the Indowy megascrapers. Digging them out of them had been interesting.

Most of the Earth though was in Posleen hands and thousands, millions, of the manufacturing facilities were scattered across the planet at this point. When it came time to reclaim the world, digging the centaurs out of the holes would be tough. On the other hand, it was expected that most of the factories could be put back in commission so Earth was looking at a whole new world of productivity. Usually, though, such facilities were in well-settled areas outside the war zone and Clarkesville was inside the artillery envelope. So seeing them digging in like that was unusual.

And so was the column of Posleen pouring into the dugout.

"That's not a factory, then," he muttered, working a big wad of jerky into his cheek. He wondered just what those sneaky yellow bastards thought they were doing. The Posleen under certain conditions dug like gophers; they apparently had very good mining technology, along the lines of the Galactics' ionic miners. But they generally left their normals on the surface farming, strip mining and gathering.

Then he saw what was following the column into the cavern and nearly choked to death.

Ryan looked over at the fire control officer and tapped his monitor. "Send a sensor round in the next volley."

As the day had progressed more and more people had gotten in on the act but, by and large, that had been good. Controlling this many artillery batteries, and their care and feeding or at least resupply of rounds, was no job for a single engineer major. Among other things, dozens of intelligence specialists had gotten into the act, massaging every bit of data collected for hard evidence of the Posleen's intentions.

So far the information was ambiguous. There was no question that the Posleen seemed to be acting in a more "logical" fashion than they usually did. But that didn't mean they were a greater threat. With the exception of the EMP grenade, there had been no new weapons. And while there were some improved tactics, they had not notably improved as shown by their chase of Mosovich.

It had been quite a while since the sergeant major's last call for fire and they had been desultorily pounding the hilltop, with only one battery now, for the last two hours. But there had been lulls like it throughout the day and it was, judging from past experience, just about time for another call.

"Sensor round inbound, sir," the lieutenant said, shunting the data to his monitor.

The round was based on a standard 155 millimeter round. But instead of explosive it carried more dangerous weapons: a camera and a radio.

As the round left the distant artillery gun, a shroud fell away and the camera was uncased. Using an internal gyroscope it compensated the sensor mount against the spin of the round and kept the camera pointed at the indicated target, which in this case was the ground.

The camera was only a sophisticated visual light system; transmitting systems such as millimeter wave radar were engaged by every God King and lander in sight. But the visual light system was able to pick out the shapes of Posleen and Posleen devices from the background clutter, sending the data back to the intelligence center in narrowly directed, short, encrypted bursts.

Despite the short, directed transmissions, the Posleen were able to detect and destroy the rounds most of the time in flight and they did so in this case, catching the round as it passed over Lake Burton, but leaving all its non-transmitting brethren, who only carried high explosives and lethal shrapnel, alive.

Ryan shook his head in bafflement. None of the humans could understand why the Posleen were so damned effective at destroying anything that maneuvered or transmitted, but left "ordinary" artillery alone. He checked the FireFinder radar, which actively worked with the gun targeting systems to ensure accuracy, and, sure enough, the rest of the rounds went on their way to the target.

The picture that had come back from the round was interesting enough. The artillery had reached over fourteen thousand feet in its parabolic arc, and the "visual footprint" had stretched from Dahlonega to Lake Hartwell. There were red traces of Posleen throughout the area, but the majority of them were concentrated around Clarkesville and Lynch Mountain. In other areas the centaurs were scattered. Clarkesville was still obscured because of the angle of flight of the round and the resolution on the Posleen around Lynch Moutain wasn't all that great.

"Get the intel guys to massage this as much as they can," Ryan said, scrolling his view around the snapshot of the battle and zooming in on the area around Mosovich. "In the next volleys I want you to have them set the sensor rounds so that they don't go active until they are a few seconds out. That way we may not have as wide a field of view, but we'll at least be able to see what we're hitting. Or not hitting. It's pretty clear that the Posleen are beyond our current fire point."

"Should I adjust fire, sir?" the lieutenant at the artillery control station asked.

"No," Ryan answered. "When Mosovich wants it, he'll call for it." Ryan pulled up a topographic map of the area, zoomed the resolution and then laid on recent overhead. After scratching his chin for a second he grunted. "But take everything that's not tasked and put it right . . . there," he continued, pointing to the saddle with a feral grin. "It's the only place there's a path the Posleen could use."

"Do you think that the sergeant major is up on the mountain?" the lieutenant asked, scanning his own system for a trace of the NCO. "I don't see him anywhere."

"Oh, he's there, somewhere," Ryan answered. "What I don't know, is where in the hell he thinks he's going."

# CHAPTER 13

*Rochester, NY, United States, Sol III*
*1925 EDT Monday September 14, 2009 AD*

Major John Mansfield crouched low, hiding in the shadows of the roof of the trailer. He could hear the crunch of gravel as his target approached and this time there would be no way to escape. He'd been tracking him for the last four days and tonight would be the time of reckoning. Preparing to spring he pulled his legs under him and clutched the sheaf of paperwork attached to a clipboard in one hand and a pen in the other; being adjutant for the Ten Thousand was no picnic.

As the official personnel officer for eleven thousand eight hundred and forty-three soldiers, officer and enlisted, all of whom were about as safe as Bengal Tigers, his was not always the funnest job. But the worst part was trying to pin the colonel down long enough to do his paperwork.

It had become something of a game. Cutprice would

set up an obstacle course, human and often physical, between himself and his adjutant. Mansfield would try to pass it to get the colonel to take his paperwork in hand. Once a human being put something, anything, in the colonel's hand, he was very concientious about completing it. But forget putting it in an "In" box.

But this time Mansfield had him dead to rights. The colonel had become a little too complacent, a little too regular in his schedule. And Mansfield had used all the tricks. A dummy was occupying his bed so no one would know he was stalking the night. No one had seen him crossing the compound so none of the troops would give him away this time. And a female trooper who really needed the colonel to sign a waiver so she could be promoted out of zone, a waiver that had been approved by her company commander, the sergeant major and the adjutant, had spent the evening plying the colonel with Bushmills. With any luck his defenses would be low enough that Mansfield would surprise him for once.

He crouched lower and leaned to the side, peering around the sign announcing that this simple single-wide trailer was the residence of the commander of the Ten Thousand. He glimpsed a shadow and consulted his watch. Yes, it was precisely the time the colonel should be showing up. He readied the pen and prepared to spring as a voice spoke over his shoulder.

"You lookin' for me, Mansfield?"

Major Mansfield stood up and looked at the figure that was now standing on the stoop of the porch. Now that it was in the light it was clear that the figure was both shorter and darker than the colonel. And wore the wrong rank.

"Sergeant Major Wacleva, I am, frankly, shocked that you would stoop so low as to assist this juvenile delinquent over my shoulder in his avoidance of duty!"

"Ah, don't take it personal, Major," the young-looking sergeant major responded in a gravelly voice. "It is the age-old dichotomy of the warrior and the beancounter!"

"Since when did you get cleared for words like 'dichotomy'?" the adjutant asked with a laugh.

"Since the colonel spent half the night getting plastered with Brockdorf," Wacleva responded sourly. He pulled out a pack of Pall Malls and tapped out a cancer stick.

"Yeah," Cutprice said with a laugh. "Did you know she was a philosophy major before she enlisted?"

"Yes, I do, Colonel," Mansfield answered testily, finally turning around to look at the officer. "Which is why she's one of the very few people I know who can read the Posleen mind. And did you know she needed your signature to get her promotion to E-6?"

"Why the hell do you think I'm standing on a roof in the freezing cold?" Cutprice asked. He took the pen out of the S-1's hand. "Which one is it?"

"Oh, no, you're not getting away that easily," Mansfield answered. "Among other things there's a real strange one in here. I think we might need to send a squad down to North Carolina to spring one of our officers."

"Who's in North Carolina?" Cutprice asked, stepping lightly off the roof and landing on sprung knees. "Goddamn it's nice to be young again."

"No shit," the major responded, landing next to him. "I think the last time I could be assured of doing that and not killing myself was in '73."

"With all due respect, sirs, yer both wimps," the sergeant major growled. "Try being old *before* '73. *I* couldn't do that when I was datin' yer mothers."

Cutprice chuckled and reached for the sheaf of papers. "Gimme the 3420, I promise I'll do the rest."

Mansfield and the sergeant major followed the

colonel into the trailer and Mansfield extracted a sheet of paper from the pile as the sergeant major went to the sideboard. "One 3420, complete and ready to sign," Mansfield said.

"Hmm." The colonel read it carefully. The game went both ways; Mansfield had twice inserted orders transferring himself to a command slot so the colonel was now careful to read the documents he signed. "This looks kosher," he said, scrawling a signature.

"So is this," Mansfield said. "There are two documents here. One is from Captain Elgars and the other is from her original shrink."

"Elgars doesn't ring a bell," Cutprice said, picking up the printout of an e-mail.

"And it shouldn't, she's never been 'with' us, so to speak," Mansfield said. "She was at the Monument, the sniper who is the reason it has a brand-new aluminum top."

"Hang on a bit," the sergeant major rasped. "Red-head, broken arm. What's she doing as a captain?"

"Just about everybody that was there got battlefield commissions," Mansfield pointed out. "Unless they specifically turned them down," he added with a "hrum, hrum."

"Well, I didn't turn it down, it's just a reserve commission and I'm acting in my regular rank," the sergeant major said with a grin. "That way when I retire I get major's pay and in the meantime nobody can make me a fuckin' adjutant."

"Elgars was in a coma so she wasn't in a position to turn down a promotion to first lieutenant," Mansfield continued. "And she got promoted in her zone automatically, since she was officially on the roll as patient status."

"That's the silliest fucking thing I ever heard," the sergeant major said, pouring himself a drink and setting the bottle on the table. Then he paused. "Naw, I take that back. I've heard sillier stuff. But it's close."

Cutprice glanced at the two letters. He had come up from the ranks himself and he was a little short on college education, but he was a fast and accurate reader. The letter from the psych was the normal bureaucratic gobbledygook. The patient was refusing "treatment" and acting manifestly crazy. The shrink tried to cloak that with words she thought the colonel probably hadn't heard, but in that the psychologist was wrong; the colonel had heard them before from shrinks talking about him. The letter from the captain was a bit different. Straightforward, spelling wasn't too great, but that was normal for enlisteds which was what she really was. She wanted to see another shrink, her original one was treating her like she was nuts. Yada, yada. Huh?

"She says she's got two people's memories?" Cutprice asked.

"Apparently so, sir," Mansfield replied.

"No wonder her shrink thinks she's nuts," the colonel mused. "She says she thinks the Crabs did it to her."

"Her treatment was experimental, sir," Mansfield noted. "It . . . sort of hangs together. And she doesn't want to discontinue treatment, she just wants to continue with a psychologist that doesn't think she's nuts."

"Sure, if you're willing to believe she's not," Cutprice said.

"We've got a lot of people who are a few bricks short of a load," Wacleva pointed out. "Look at Olson, I mean, nobody is sane if they go around wearing a God King crest all the time."

"Well, sure, but . . ." Cutprice paused. The captain had apparently been a pretty good shooter and she might be a good addition. He read the postscript and frowned. "She says she knows Keren and it got

forwarded by Sergeant Sunday. Both of those are recommendations in my book. Better than any fucking
shrink's."

"That is one of the reasons I'm here, sir," Mansfield
noted. "I talked to Keren and he really went off. He
didn't know she was out of her coma and he wants to
go see her. Now. He really had good things to say about
her. 'Greatest shooter on Earth. Natural leader. Crazy
as a bedbug . . .'"

"But I can't afford to send him to North Carolina
just to straighten this out." Cutprice picked up the
bottle of bourbon and poured himself a drink. "I'll tell
him that myself and why. Next suggestion."

"Nichols," said the S-1. "He's not an officer, but
I cross-checked the records for any of the Ten Grand
who have been in contact with her and they both
went through the 33rd sniper course before the Fredericksburg drop. In the same class no less. He transferred to the LRRPs and he's stationed down in
Georgia or North Carolina, in that corps zone. If you
send him orders to go see her, he could stop by and
talk. Get an idea if she's nuts or what. But he'll need
written orders; they won't let the riff-raff in the Sub-
Urbs."

"Nichols?" the sergeant major replied dubiously.
"He's a decent troop, but for one thing he's not Six
Hundred and she is and the other thing is he's . . . just
a troop. Nothing against Nichols, but he's just a spear-
carrier."

"Well, the other suggestion is that *I* know his
teamleader," Mansfield said. "And Jake Mosovich ain't
just a spear-carrier. If I ask Jake very nicely, he'll
probably even do it."

"I know Mosovich too," Cutprice said with a chuckle.
"Tell 'im if he doesn't, I've got pictures from an SOA
convention he doesn't want to see the light of day. *And*

video from a certain AUSA convention elevator. Okay, send Nichols and *ask* Jake to backstop. Tell Nichols you just want him to stop by and say 'Hi,' but tell Mosovich the real reason they're there. It's pointless to add, but tell him to handle it as he sees fit and ask him for an after-action report. Also, put him in touch with Keren. If she's *not* crazy, according to Mosovich, I'll tell her psych to take a running jump at a rolling donut. If she *is* nuts, and unusable nuts, I want her off the rolls. She'll always be Six Hundred, but I don't want her messing up the rolls of the Ten Thousand. Clear?"

"As a bell," Mansfield said with an evil grin. "I'm sure that Mosovich could use a little authorized 'comp' time away from his daily rut. He's probably getting bored at this point."

Mosovich swallowed the last of the jerky and washed it down with a swig of water from his Camelbak just as there was a "crack" and a puff of smoke from the saddle.

The device he dropped on the trail had started life as a scatterable mine. The devices were packed into artillery rounds and fired into battlefields to "scatter" and create a problem for the enemy to deal with.

The Posleen response to minefields was to drive normals across them. It was an effective method of clearing and, from the Posleen's point of view, very efficient since they would scavenge the bodies for weapons and equipment then butcher the dead for rations.

Therefore, generally the humans didn't use scatterable mines. While "every little bit helped" in killing Posleen, by and large minefields were pretty inefficient. There were, generally, and with the exception of Bouncing Barbies, better uses for artillery.

Scatterable mines themselves, however, were a different story. In bygone days the sergeant major probably would have stopped to set a claymore. While that might have been more effective, it also took more time. Or, if he was in a real hurry, he would drop a "toe-popper," a small mine that would detonate if stepped on. But toe poppers were, at best, wounding. And, unless you dug a small hole and hid it, which took time, they were also easy to spot.

One of the modified scatterable mines, though, was just about perfect. The "fishing lines" were monofilament trip-wires. They threw out the hooks then pulled them in until there was a graduated resistance. At that point, the mine was "armed" and if the lines were disturbed in any way, either by pulling or cutting, the mine would detonate.

No matter how it was dropped, the first thing the mine did was right itself. So when detonated, as in this case when the lead oolt'os of the approaching company charged up the saddle, it would fly up one meter and send out a hail of small ball bearings.

A claymore had a similar number of bearings in it, and sent them in a single line, which made it more deadly. But the "Bouncing Betty" tore the head off of the Posleen and scattered it over the trail. Good enough.

And it alerted Mosovich. Who lifted his AID.

"Ryan, listen up."

Ryan leaned forward as the distant AID poured information into the net. The Posleen charging up the saddle were clear and so was Mosovich's position.

"Are you going to be able to get out of there?" Ryan asked.

"I'll be fine," the sergeant major said. "I want fire on that saddle, right now, please, sir."

"On the way," Ryan said, sending the fire commands to the prelaid guns. "Twenty-seven seconds. I figured you'd fire up the saddle."

"Right," Mosovich said, leaning into the rifle and taking his first shot as the Posleen came into view. "Until we're done here my AID will give a continuous feed; keep the fire on the pass, though, I don't want you to follow the Posleen up the hill. And, if you wouldn't mind, sir, pass this on. I can see Clarkesville from here and I figured out why they're trying to keep us from observing them. They're digging in, like they do with their factories, but these are apparently barracks."

"That's not a surprise," Ryan said, watching the artillery flight clock. "Why would they be so worried about that? I mean, we have a pretty fair count on their numbers, so it's not like they're hiding anything."

"Well, they're barracks and motorpools, I should say," Mosovich added. He knew that firing the Barrett was giving his position away to the God King's sensors, but apparently they were all still in the trees. He saw one plasma round hit a poplar and turn it into a ball of fire.

"Motorpools?" Ryan asked suspiciously. "Splash, over." The rounds were only a few seconds away from impacting.

"Yes, sir," Mosovich said, as the first rounds started to land in the trees. "For the flying tanks. Splash out."

"A kenal flak, senra, fuscirto uut!" Orostan shouted. He shook his arm and glared at the flash burn. "I am going to eat that human's GET."

"Perhaps," Cholosta'an said, running up the trail behind the oolt'ondai's forces. "But only if he doesn't adjust that artillery onto us!"

The two Kessentai along with the first oolt of

Orostan's force, by pure luck, had been off of the saddle and out of the beaten zone by the time the first round hit. But behind them the sound of superquick detonating in the treetops was mixed with the scream of oolt'os and Kessentai caught in the barrage. That included what was left of Cholosta'an's oolt, but he wasn't going back for it either.

A normal ahead of Cholosta'an grunted, slapped at his side and fell sideways screaming down the slope.

"The artillery is masking the fuscirto fire," Orostan snarled, pointing his plasma gun towards the hilltop. He had had a bead on the sniper earlier, but the thrice-damned trees had gotten in the way. His crest on his left side was scorched so badly it might have to be cut away.

He fired at approximately where he thought the sniper was and the normals around him followed the target point slavishly.

"Uh, Oolt'ondai," Cholosta'an said, darting past the older Kessentai, "you might want to move around a little."

As the words left his muzzle, Orostan let out a bellow of rage and clapped at the furrow that had appeared along his flank. "Sky demons eat your souls! Come out and show yourself, you gutless bastard!" he screamed. But he started back up the path anyway, ducking and weaving among the limited cover while peppering the smoking hilltop with shots from his plasma gun. "Gutless abat!"

Jake slapped at the leaves in front of his position to put out the fire. Fortunately the God King seemed to think he was firing from about fifty meters to the west. Unfortunately, he'd missed the one shot he got at the bastard. It was difficult to tell which ones were God Kings at this range, unless they lifted their crests and these seemed to be keeping them down. There was usually a little difference in size, but not enough to be noticeable at eight football fields. God Kings were generally more heavily armed, as well, but judging by this group headed up the hill that wasn't clear. Most of the Posleen had either heavy railguns or plasma cannon with a few hypervelocity missile launchers thrown in for giggles. Which one was the God King on the basis of weaponry was anyone's guess. The last difference was "attitude" or at least who did what first. In this case, one particular Posleen sporting a plasma gun had fired, then all the other Posleen followed suit.

Fortunately they all fired at the *wrong* place, but the misses, thermal wash and ricochets had been mighty interesting for a few seconds there. A chunk of the hilltop the size of a house had been flattened and was surrounded by a growing forest fire. The trees, shrub and dirt in the area were just *gone* and most of the exposed rocks were smoking. If they'd fired at the right bit of mountain, or if they spotted him, his ex-wife would be getting a telegram and a check.

It wasn't dying so much that worried him, but it really ticked him off that his ex would get the check.

"I gotta find a better beneficiary," he muttered, taking a bead on the next Posleen in the line.

Cholosta'an darted around the oolt'ondai and put his hand on the older Kessentai's chest. "Let the oolt'os go first, Oolt'ondai," he said.

"I will eat the heart of this thresh," Orostan ground out. "I swear it."

From just up the trail came a crack of another mine and the descending scream and clatter of a Posleen falling off the narrow track. "Yes, Oolt'ondai," the younger Kessentai said. "But you can't do that if you are dead."

The oolt'ondai lifted his crest for a moment then lowered it as more oolt'os trickled by. There was a steady stream making it through the artillery beaten zone and there was no way the human was going to escape this time; the other side was too sheer for even one of these damn rock-monkeys to scale.

They had made it far enough up the trail, apparently, that the human could not observe their location. But as he looked back he saw another oolt drop off the trail with a fist-sized hole through his midsection and this one, in its flailing, knocked another off the path. The human was up there and still stinging them, but Cholosta'an was right; he would have to live to get any revenge worth savoring.

"Very well, youngling," Orostan finally said with a hiss of humor. He stepped to the side to clear the path. "We'll let a few more oolt'os get ahead of us, yes?"

"Yes, Oolt'ondai," the oolt commander said. He recognized a few of the oolt headed up the trail by sight and smell and that indefinable sense of "mine" that said they were of his oolt'os. But damned few. "So much for being unexpendable."

"Not at all, youngling," the oolt'ondai said with a limited crest flap, lest the sniper still have an angle on them. "Again you prove your worth. How many Kessentai in your position would have had the head to hold back? And of those, how many would have thought to stop *my* impetuousness? And, last, of those very few, how many would have dared?"

"Few, fewer and fewest," the Kessentai agreed as another "crack!" came from up the trail. "But I could wish that my oolt'os were not so few as well."

"That we will make up for after this," the oolt'ondai said, getting back on the path. "But I want to be there at the kill."

✧   ✧   ✧

Mosovich stroked the trigger one more time and rolled to his feet. He had been carefully counting the mines on the hill and the last one was, indeed, the last one. If it did not kill the Posleen that had detonated it, a short dash would take the centauroid to the crest of the mountain. That spot was in a thick stand of rhododendron and mountain laurel, but just beyond there the Posleen would be in position to flank Mosovich's position, and, what was worse, cover the back door to the hide with direct fire.

Mosovich backed out leaving most of the boxes of ammunition and all of Nichols' dirty socks behind. He wouldn't, frankly, need either where he was going.

He moved over to the edge of the cliff and hefted the big rifle so he was pointing it unsupported. He couldn't hold it up for long, and God knows, he wouldn't be able to fire many rounds. But he wouldn't have to.

"Don't eat them!" Orostan bellowed as the boom of a rifle came from over beyond the obscuring vegetation. "They are mine!"

The only response was a burble from beyond the brush as another boom echoed on the mountain. The trees were whipped in a gale as the God King reached the summit and started to descend. The trail was tricky, more broken even than on the way up and the rhododendron, laurel and white pine was whipping in his face as he finally came into the open.

The human seemed to have been waiting for that, for Orostan would always remember the smile. The apparently sole survivor just smiled that tooth-baring human smile, jumped back and fired.

And flipped backwards into nothing.

✧   ✧   ✧

It was tricky. As expected the shot, which undoubtedly went off into nowhere, gave him a few extra feet of boost. The Barrett had always pushed him backwards a few inches no matter how hard he braced and when he fired it off-hand it had pushed him back a couple of steps with each shot. So firing it completely unsupported, effectively in midair like some sort of damned Coyote/Road Runner cartoon, actually turned him for a somersault.

The good part about this was that the combination took him well out from the ledge. He had chosen his spot carefully and he had actually been standing on an overhang. However, the ground started to slope outward after only a few hundred feet long so it was important to get prepared quickly.

The static rappel system was one of the first that used the more advanced Galactic sciences in a device of purely human design and manufacture. Humans had implemented "old" Galactic technology, some of which was close to the cutting edge of human tech and theory, in many designs. New gun barrels were the most common devices, but there were also some small railguns designed for humans and "human only" fusion plants, that were only five or six times the size of equivalent Galactic and about a third as efficient.

This device was the first that used theories that were beyond human ken. The Tchpth considered gravity to be, at best, a toy and, at worst, a minor nuisance. A few of their "simpler" theories were explainable to humans, such as the theory that led to the Galactic bounce tube.

When Indowy wanted to travel up or down in their megascrapers, they generally travelled by bounce tube. This was a narrow tube that went to a specific floor. You entered it and if you were at the bottom it shot you to the top and if you were at the top it let you drop to a screaming (in initial usage this was literal) stop at the bottom. What it took humans a while to discover was that while bounce tubes were "active" devices on the lift side, they were "passive" on the drop. That is, a device at the bottom detected something coming in at high velocity, generated a very minor field and when the item hit the field it was decelerated using its own positive momentum for energy.

The Tchpth and Indowy considered this purely efficient. The humans initially considered it magic.

However, after staying up for several days, smoking a large amount of an illicit substance and taking a *very* long shower, a research grad at CalTech suddenly realized that if you took some of the things that the Tchpth were saying and turned them on their sides . . . sort of, it was a lot of very good stuff . . . it made a certain amount of sense. Then she wrote them down and slept for three days.

After deciphering what she wrote, which, as far as anyone but her mother was concerned was apparently Sanskrit, she created a little box that when thrown at a wall "threw back." The energy usage involved was no more than that of a small sensor and it *always* threw back, even when fired from a low-velocity pneumatic cannon. (The cannon was called a "chicken gun" and was usually used to test aircraft windshields. But that is another story.)

There was a current upper limit on the device, that is, when fired at *very* high velocity it tended to break the windshield, and it was better at stopping *itself* than it was at stopping stuff coming at it. So there was no "personal forcefield."

In other words, it was a very fast way to get to the ground in relative safety.

The device was modified and adjusted until it didn't just stop itself, but created a "static repulsion zone" which, when there was a situation of sudden kinetic change, damped that change. Then it was turned over to TRW for manufacturing purposes. The device was being installed on every vehicle still on the roads and in other places where sudden stops happened in a bad way. And it was issued to all the LRRP teams.

Mosovich looked down at the rapidly approaching ground and swore he was never, ever going to do this again. "It's not the fall that kills you," he whispered.

Generally, if you're going down a cliff or the face of a building, the best way is to rappel. Tie off a rope, hook up any number of devices and lower yourself on the rope. However, there are any number of cases where this is impractical; ropes are not infinitely lengthy. There was another device available that used a very thin wire for the same purpose. And Mosovich really wished he had one with him. But they were much harder to construct than the static repulsion boxes and weren't standard issue. Given the number of times this sort of thing came up, he was definitely getting one for everyone in the team and keeping them.

The problem was that static repulsion systems didn't slow your fall at all until they came near *solid* materials. For example, this system was going to completely ignore the trees he was just about to hit.

"Fuscirto uut!" Orostan shouted, jumping over the corpse of the last oolt'os and darting to the edge. His talons scrabbled on the rock as he almost slid over the side then he looked down the cliff face just in time to see the human disappear into the trees below.

"You cannot escape me that easily!" the oolt'ondai shouted to the winds, knowing that the words were a lie. "I will *still* eat your heart!"

Orostan looked out over the valley below and screamed in rage. The sun was sinking to the

northwest and before anyone could get to the landing area the human, if it was alive, and he doubted
that it had just committed suicide, would be kilometers away. In any of three directions.

Cholosta'an came up beside him and looked down.
After a moment he pointed downwards with a flap of
his crest.

"Yes," Orostan ground out.

"Alive?" the younger Kessentai asked.

"Probably," Orostan snarled. "And there was only
one."

Cholosta'an thought about that for a moment. "The
last time we had a good count it was over by the town
of Seed. There were four."

"Yes," Orostan said. "Four."

"And now there was only one," Cholosta'an said.
"One. And no bodies."

"No."

"Oh. Fuscirto uut."

"I'll send someone around to look for a corpse,"
Orostan said after a few moments' contemplation. "But
I doubt they'll find anything." He looked at his tenaral
and started to wonder who. Finally he turned away and
started back down the hill. The human might have
escaped today, but it undoubtedly was "based" beyond
the Gap. Its time would come. Soon.

As the last Posleen normal faded out of sight, the
"rock" that Mosovich had been standing on shifted and
rippled, revealing something that looked very much like
a four-eyed, blotchy, purple frog. The creature, if it was
stretched out, would have been about eight feet from
four-fingered foot-hand to foot-hand and was perfectly
symetrical; it had two hands and two eyes on either
end with a complex something in the area where a nose
might be.

The Himmit scout leaned out from the rock, its rear two foot-hands spreading out over the surface for purchase, and noted the faint heat signature moving away that was probably the human. He then levered himself back and looked towards the retreating Posleen. Such decisions. Human/Posleen, Human/Posleen? Finally, deciding that humans were *always* more interesting than Posleen—who basically ate, killed and reproduced and who could make a story from that?— it leaned sideways and started flowing from handhold to handhold down the cliff.

Such exciting times.

# CHAPTER 14

Mike looked around the room and then undogged his helmet. The command and staff of the 1$^{st}$/555$^{th}$ was grouped in a kindergarten schoolroom, sitting on the floor to use the undersized tables. The battlescarred combat suits made an unpleasant contrast to the colored drawings on the walls and the prominent poster of the five food groups.

"Well, we've had worse meetings." He chuckled as the last of the gel underlayer from his suit streamed off into his helmet. "Much worse."

"Yep," Duncan agreed as he set his helmet carefully on the desk in front of him. The plasteel was still heavy and hard enough to mar the stick drawing of a little girl with "Ashley" written below it. "At least nobody is shooting at us."

"We'll get back to that pretty soon," Mike said. He worked the ball of tobacco from one side of his mouth to the other and spit into his helmet. The nannites of the semibiotic underlayer gathered up the disgusting glop which, from its perspective, was simply moisture, nutrients and complex carbon molecules, and carried them off to be reprocessed. "There's groups of Posleen holed up all along the bottom of the Plain. We're going to help with the mop-up for the next week or so as reaction forces. After that, Horner has ordered us to move to our barracks and take some time off. Given that we had to reconsolidate without Alpha company, I think some time in barracks is called for."

"We've got barracks?" Stewart asked with a chuckle. "I mean, like, real barracks that are ours and everything? Or are we going to a 'rest and recreation' barracks?" he asked with a grimace. The facilities were run by Ground Forces and varied wildly.

"They're ours," O'Neal said with a grin. "They've been on my books the whole damned time. They're in the mountains in Pennsylvania. A place called Newry, just south of Altoona. We've even got a rear detachment."

"We do?" Duncan asked, bemusedly. "I would have thought the S-3 would know about that sort of thing."

"It's not all that big," Mike said. "And they're all seconded from Ground Forces. But there's a supply officer and a personnel section."

"And barracks?" Captain Slight said with a light chuckle. "With beds and stuff?"

"The same," O'Neal said with another grin. "I'm not sure I'll be able to sleep in one; the last time I tried I was up all night tossing and turning."

"I think the troops will adjust," Gunny Pappas said, shaking his head now that he'd doffed his helmet. "They seriously need some down time. And there's gear that needs work, even the GalTech gear."

"We'll do all of that," Mike said. "My basic plan is

this. We should arrive, transportation being available, on Monday or Tuesday. We'll spend a day cleaning up the barracks and our gear and morguing the suits. Then a day or two on short days around the barracks, getting used to wearing silks again and working on our dress stuff. Friday we'll have a real honest to God 'payday activities' with an inspection of the barracks and dress uniform inspection followed by a battalion formation and dismissal by noon. Everybody to be back in formation no earlier than noon the next Tuesday."

"You know, I don't know how that will go over," Captain Holder said. "Frankly, I think some of the troops will view it as . . . well . . ."

"Chickenshit, sir?" Gunny Pappas said. "With all due respect, Captain, I disagree. . . ."

"So do I," Stewart interjected. "And I disagree as a former troop. All of these troops are volunteers. You don't get to the point that we're at without realizing that there's a reason for all the happy horseshit in garrison. Sure, you ignore most of it in combat, but the best, the most elite troops, have always been the snazziest dressers."

"Waffen SS," Duncan noted. "Now there were some guys who knew how to wear a uniform."

"The 82nd," Captain Slight noted. "They were chosen for the role of Honor Guard in post-WWII Europe mainly on the basis of how well they dressed out. And nobody can fault their combat record."

"Rhodesian SAS and the Selous Scouts," O'Neal said in agreement. "Two of the baddest groups ever to come out of the Cold War and they were like peacocks in garrison; Dad still has his uniform and it looks like something from a Hungarian opera."

"Okay, okay," Captain Holder said, holding up his hands. "But do the *troops* know that?"

"We'll give 'em evenings off," Mike said. "Short

passes; they'll need to be back to barracks by a curfew. There's a reason for it. Gunny?"

"You don't just rip soldiers right out of combat and drop them on a town, sir," Gunny Pappas said with a nod. "You have to . . . acclimatize them first."

"We'll give them a week of 'chickenshit' to acclimatize, and a week for the town to get used to the idea and more or less prepared, and then we'll let them go for a weekend. I don't see us having more than a couple of weeks, maybe a month, in garrison. We'll let them unwind for a bit then train back up and then . . ."

"Back to killing Posleen," Duncan said with a growl.

"Back to making Posleen sausage," Mike agreed. "What we do best."

"We getting any replacements, sir?" Pappas asked. "We're . . . getting a little low on bodies in case nobody had noticed."

"There are twelve suits in the pipeline," O'Neal said. "They're all supposed to be waiting for us when we get to Newry."

"And bodies?" Captain Slight asked. "Even with the troops we picked up from Alpha, we're under manning."

"And bodies," Mike agreed. "Given that we have some mopping up to do, the bodies should be there in time to get the suits fitted and even dialed in. I understand we're even getting a couple from the Ten Thousand."

"Ten shut!" Sunday called as Colonel Cutprice entered the room.

The conference room was in the offices of a factory, long since abandoned, just west of the Genesee River. The blasts from SheVa rounds, which had levelled practically every prominence east of the Genesee, had blown out the windows of the room and Cutprice strode across crackling glass as he entered. But it was better than being outside; the rains had set in again and it looked to be turning to snow soon.

"At ease, rest even," Cutprice said, striding over to the group of four troopers. He was trailed by Mansfield, carrying a set of boxes, and the sergeant major, similarly weighed down.

"Smoke 'em if you got 'em," he continued, suiting action to words as he pulled out a pack of Dunhills. They were getting hard to find so he saved them for special occasions.

"You might be wondering why I called you here and all that . . ." He smiled and nodded at the boxes. "All of you transferred in from other units, and when you got here we took a rank away from you to make sure that you could cut the mustard, that you weren't just garrison rangers with great counseling statements and no damned heart for war." He looked at Sunday and shook his head.

"As it turned out, you all were what the Ten Thousand wanted; warriors to the core, psychotic motherfucking Posleen killers, willing to walk into the fire over and over and never flinch." He shook his head again, this time in sorrow. "And now we're losing you to those ACS bastards.

"Well, those ACS bastards do the same thing," he noted, taking the first box. "They take a stripe away when you get there, just to make sure you're what they need in a warm body. Then they stuff you in a can until you look like a worm that crawled out from under a rock." He glanced at the note attached to the box and nodded.

"Sunday, get your ass over here," he growled. "I don't know if your old unit did this before you came here, but they should have. Most of you is getting bumped a rank before you leave, that way when you get to the damned clankers you'll end up at the rank you have, by God, earned.

"The exception," he continued, looking up at Sunday, "is you, Tank. I'd been thinking about doing this for a while and I don't know what took me so long." He glanced at Mansfield then looked away. "Some paperwork problem. Anyway, I'm going to screw you for all time. You ready?"

"Yes, sir," Sunday said in confusion. "Whatever you think is best."

"Okay, if you're *that* trusting," Cutprice said with an evil grin, "you *deserve* this. Attention to orders!

"Staff Sergeant Thomas Sunday, Junior, is released from Service of the United States Ground Forces September 17, 2009, for the Purposes of accepting a commission as a Regular Officer of the United States Ground Forces and concurrent reentry to the United States Ground Forces as First Lieutenant. First Lieutenant Thomas Sunday, Junior, is ordered to active duty this September 17, 2009, with date of rank September 17, 2009." Cutprice stopped reading, reached in his bellows pocket, pulled out a battered pair of first lieutenant's bars and replaced Sunday's staff sergeant collar stripes. "You don't owe me anything for these, by the way. I had them rattling around in the back of my desk."

"Very well, Orostan," Tulo'stenaloor said. "I'll send Shartarsker in to make sure they are not coming closer to the base." He looked at the map and considered the report the oolt'ondai had sent in. "Good luck."

Goloswin looked up from the sensor readout. "It does not go well?"

"The team apparently has escaped," Tulo'stenaloor said. "After ravaging Orostan's oolt'ondar."

"Well, they are not in the sensor region," Goloswin

said, gesturing at the map. "Or at least not marking themselves as such. I'm not sure if they can at this point. There is a way to communicate with these boxes without other devices, but this assumes the humans are as clever as I am."

"So even if they are in the sensor net, we might not know it?" Tulo'stenaloor asked.

"Yes," Goloswin answered, ruffling his crest. "There is a way to modify their software to make them detect humans. The sensors 'see' the humans, but they also see the thresh of the woods and all the greater thresh of this planet. The 'deer' and 'dogs' and suchlike that have survived. The humans have designed the systems, quite efficiently I might add, to sort through the information they collect in several different ways. And it sorts out anything but Posleen and humans that are 'in the net' and telling it they are there and want to be tracked. Thus I would have to tell all the boxes to change their filters to find humans. And even then it would assume the humans are not cloaking themselves in any of several ways. I could do it—I am, after all, clever. But the humans might, probably would, notice. They, too, have clever technicians."

"And then they would know that we . . . How did you put it?" Tulo'stenaloor asked.

"They would know that they have been 'hacked,'" Goloswin said. "That we 'own' their system."

"We don't want to do that," Tulo'stenaloor mused. "Yet."

"What do you want to do in the meantime?" Goloswin asked. "Or can I go back to tinkering?"

"Just one last question," the War Leader said. "Can you set the system to 'filter' out the Po'oslena'ar?"

Wendy shook her head as she watched Elgars finish up her workout. The sniper always closed with an exercise that was peculiar to her. She had suspended a weight, in this case fifty pounds of standard metal barbell weights, from a rope. The rope, in turn, was wrapped around a dowel; actually a chopped-down mop handle.

Elgars would then "winch" up the weights by twisting the rope in her hands. Up and slowly back down, fifty times. Wendy was lucky if she could do it five times.

"I gave up on that one," Wendy admitted. They generally worked out once a day for about an hour switching between strength and cardiovascular sessions. Lately, though, they had been concentrating more on weight training; Wendy was trying out for a "professional" emergency services position and Elgars was backstopping her training. Today Wendy had stuck to warm-ups; when they were done she was going to go to the tryouts and she didn't even want to *think* about going through that SOB after a full workout.

"You ought to start at a lower weight and rep," the captain said. "It's good for the wrists."

"I can see that," Wendy admitted, looking at the captain's; the woman's forearms were starting to look like a female Popeye's.

"Makes it easier to climb ladders among other things, most of the stuff in your PPE."

"Yeah, well, time to go to *that* now," Wendy said nervously.

"One of these days I will figure out the purpose of a fire department in this place," Elgars said, wiping off her face with a towel and wrapping the towel around her neck. "Every fire that has broken out was extinguished before the crew arrived; that is what sprinklers and Halon are for. I think they're just a very overtrained clean-up crew."

"Well, at least it feels like you're doing something," Wendy said sharply.

"And caring for screaming children is not doing something?" Annie asked with a thin smile.

"Do *you* want to do it the rest of your life?" Wendy asked.

"No," the captain said, leading the way out of the gym. "But, then again, *you* don't get the desire to disembowel the little bastards."

"You get along with Billy," Wendy said with her own tight smile.

"That is because he doesn't say *anything*."

"Well, there is that," Wendy snapped. "You weren't in Fredericksburg; you can't know what it was like."

"No, I can't," Elgars said. "Thank you very much for pointing that out. I was not in Fredericksburg and I wouldn't remember anyway."

Wendy stopped and looked at the officer for a moment. "When did we start fighting?"

Elgars stopped in turn and cocked her head. "I think when I complained about the fire department."

"Okay," Wendy said. "It's something to do that *helps*. Yes, I'm tired of the daycare center. I was tired of it when most of this damned place was open cavern and it was just a couple of hundred shaken up Virginians. I'm *sick* and tired of it now. I've watched those kids grow up without sunlight or anyplace to play but a few rooms and I just can't do it any more.

"I'm tired of wiping noses. I'm tired of not making a contribution. I'm tired of being treated like some sort of brood mare, especially since the only guy I'm willing to be one with is NEVER HERE!"

"Okay," Annie said, raising a hand. "Gotcha."

"As to Billy," Wendy continued, leading the way down the corridor, "Shari was the last person out of Central Square. Billy . . . looked back."

"I don't know what that means," Elgars said with a sigh. "What and where is Central Square?"

"It was the big shopping center outside of Fredericksburg," Wendy explained patiently. "The Posleen dropped right on it. Shari just . . . walked away. Carrying Susie and leading Kelly and Billy. Billy . . . looked back. He's never been right since."

"Okay," Elgars said patiently. "I *still* don't understand. Looked back? At the shopping center? Whatever that is."

"The Posleen were . . . eating the people there."

"Ah." Elgars thought about that for a second. "That would be bad."

"And they apparently were . . . spreading out towards Shari. She says she doesn't really know because she wouldn't look back. But Billy did."

"Okay," the captain said with a frown. "I guess that would be bad."

"You don't get it, do you?" Wendy asked. She'd noticed that sometimes the sniper was sometimes almost inhumanly dense about stuff.

"No," Elgars replied.

"It was like one of those nightmares," Wendy said with a shudder. "Where something's chasing you and you can't get away no matter how fast or where you run. The docs think he's sort of . . . locked up in that. Like he can't think about anything else; he's just replaying the nightmare."

"I still don't get it," Elgars opined. "I don't have that nightmare."

"You don't?" Wendy asked. "Never?"

"I did once," Elgars admitted. "But I turned around and killed the thing that was following me." She shuddered. "It was one of the octopuses again."

"Octopuses?" Wendy stopped and turned to the captain. "What octopuses?"

"You don't dream about giant purple octopuses?" Elgars asked in surprise. "I do. Usually I'm watching from the outside and they're pulling out my brain. It's like it's all squiggling worms and they lay it out on a table and hit the worms with mallets to get them to quit squiggling. Every time they hit one of the worms, I can feel it in my head. You never have that dream?"

Wendy had gone from astonishment to wide-eyed shock and now turned back towards their destination shaking her head. "Huh, uh. And, friend that you are, I have to admit that that falls into the category of TMI."

"TMI?" Elgars asked.

"'Too Much Information.'"

"I wouldn't have run, for that matter."

"Even with three kids that were your responsibility?" Wendy asked.

"Ah . . ." Elgars had to stop to think about that. "I probably would have fought anyway. I can't imagine running from the Posleen. It seems like a losing proposition."

"Shari's alive," Wendy pointed out. "So are her children. All the other people, adults and children, who were at Central Square are dead. Unless you've got the force to hold ground, *staying* is a losing proposition."

Elgars shrugged as a double set of high blasplas doors, similar to an airlock, retreated into the walls. The room beyond was large: high-ceilinged, at least sixty meters across and even taller than it was wide. The walls were covered in white tiles and there were large fans on the distant ceiling.

In the center of the room was a large structure made out of vitrified stone. It looked something like a small, separate building, about six stories high, but it was covered in black soot and had dozens of different pipe-ends sticking out of it. The numerous windows were all unglazed, with edges cracked as if from hammering or, perhaps, really intense heat. A series of catwalks led off of it to lines arrayed up to the ceiling.

Arrayed along the base of the walls were hundreds of small openings. As Elgars and Wendy entered, the overhead fans kicked on with a distant howl and a faint draft came out of the nearest opening. The fans were drawing the air in the room fast enough to slightly reduce the pressure; if it was not for the hundreds of air-vents along the floor wherever the air did enter would be a hurricane.

The walls were lined with lockers and rescue gear and near the structure in the middle were some of the "fire-carts" that the rescue teams used for transportation in the Sub-Urb. The carts were sort of like a large golf cart with a high pressure pump and racks for rescue gear on the back. With the pump removed they could double as ambulances.

There were about twenty people gathered in the room, most of them females in good to excellent condition. Elgars had met a few of them when Wendy went to her EMS meetings and the captain had to admit that Wendy was in the middle range from a physical perspective. Wendy worked out every day, but she wasn't very well designed for high-strength, especially upper body strength; among other things she had parts that got in the way. It also appeared that a once a day workout was not quite enough; more than half of the women waiting to try out looked like female triathletes; their arms were corded with muscles and their breasts had shrunk to the point where they were practically nonexistent.

There was a group of emergency personnel confronting them, ten of them in a line. They were wearing the standard day uniform of the emergency, a dark blue Nomex jumpsuit. All of them were female and most looked like ads for a muscle magazine;

Elgars had the unkind thought that they probably opened doors by chiseling through with their chins. In front of them was an older female in a bright red coverall. As Wendy joined the group, she glanced at her watch and nodded.

"Okay, I think everybody's here that's going to try out," the firechief said. Eda Connolly had been a lieutenant in the Baltimore Fire Department until she received a politely worded order to leave Baltimore as "excess to defense needs." She had found herself one of the few fully trained emergency personnel in this hole, but in the last four years she had built a department to be proud of. And she was fundamentally uninterested in lowering her standards.

"You all know what you're here for," she continued, gesturing behind her. "You want to join this line. You want to be in emergency services instead of whatever hole the powers that be have stuck you in.

"Fine," she said with a nod. "I'd love for you to be in emergency services too. I think that if we had three times the number of emergency personnel it would be grand; too many times we find ourselves being run ragged because we don't have enough hands. But every single hand that we have can do every single job that needs to be done. And that's not always the easiest thing in this hole.

"There are two million people in this hole. Two million people that, every, single, day, seem to find a new way to get hurt. Arms caught in drains, knifings, shootings, industrial explosions. There are grain elevators that catch on fire, a situation where if you turn off the ventilation the whole thing just blows up. There's chemical plants and showers to slip and fall in and four thousand foot vertical air shafts that kids manage to climb out into and then panic.

"And all there is keeping them alive, half the time,

are these gals," she said with another gesture behind her. "Every one of them have passed this test. And then, within a week or two, found something harder than this test that they had to complete. Or someone, probably themselves, would die.

"So today you get tested," she said with a sigh. "And if you complete the course in time, making all the requirements, you'll be considered for inclusion. I've got seven slots to fill. My guess is that only five or six of you will pass. But . . . I'd rather have five that pass than seven that don't."

One of the group behind her stepped forward and handed her a clipboard. She glanced at it and nodded. "As I call your name, step forward, join up with one of the officers behind me to draw bunker gear and get ready to start your evaluation." She looked up one more time and smiled thinly. "And good luck. Anderson . . ."

Wendy threw on the bunker-coat and buckled it up. Once upon a time she had heard that there were multiple ways to put on a bunker-coat, most of which could get you killed. It had always seemed silly to her; like having a gun that shot you if you loaded it backwards. The gear was heavy and hot, but it had its purpose. On the wall above the lockers was a sign: "Like a rich armor, worn in the heat of the day." She'd tried for years to find the source of the quote, but the firefighters weren't telling and she'd never been able to find it anywhere else.

She reached into her locker and pulled out the breath-pack, spitting into the facescreen and wiping the saliva around to prevent condensation. There were various products to do the same thing, but strangely enough saliva was the least unpleasant at high heat conditions; you could use baby shampoo but it had a vaporization point well below that of the lexan visor and the fumes were unpleasant. Saliva had a low vaporization point as well, but it just smelled a bit of burning hair. Which, if you were vaporizing it off your faceshield, you were *already* smelling.

She checked the air and all the rest of the gear. There weren't supposed to be any booby traps built in at this point, but she wasn't willing to go for "might"; among other things, for part of the test the firehouse would be filled with smoke and she'd *need* the air.

Everything appeared to be right, though, so she donned the breath-pack, put on the respirator, put on her helmet and turned around.

By that point, the smoke was already streaming out of the smokehouse. The smoke was generated—there was no actual fire involved in the event—but it looked real. It looked as if the smokehouse was going to billow with flames at any moment.

She was supposed to be the fifth person to take the test, but there was only one person in front of her. As she noted that, the first testee exited the smokehouse on the roof and started the rope portion. The various lines above the smokehouse, which stretched around the room in a spiderweb, were an integral portion of the event. The Urb had some awesome chasms in it and emergency personnel never knew when they might be dangling over a two-thousand-foot drop. Being able to do specific rope work—and more importantly, being fundamentally unafraid of heights—was an important portion of the test.

Wendy shivered. She was *not* fundamentally unafraid of heights. Quite the opposite. But she could still do the job.

"Cummings."

She shook herself and tore her eyes away from the

testee who had just jumped across a small gap onto a swaying platform. "Yes?"

"You're up," said the firefighter who had led her through the preparations.

"Okay." She knew the firefighter; she knew most of them. But at the test it was all supposed to be totally impersonal. She knew why; she understood why. But it would be nice if somebody acknowledged her; acknowledged that she'd been a reserve ER for four goddamned years and this was the first time she'd managed to even make the *pre-quals* for the PPE. She paused a moment, but there was nothing else. Then she stepped forward.

"Cummings," Chief Connolly said. "Eight events. Ladder move, ladder raise/lower, high-rise pack, hydrant manipulation, the Maze, door breach, vertical environment, hose drag and dummy drag. You are familiar with each test?" she asked formally.

"I am," Wendy answered just as formally, her answer muffled behind the faceshield.

"At each station there will be a firefighter to direct you to the next station. Each station is timed. Movement from station to station is timed. If you 'bump up' on the person in front of you, you may wait and rest and the time does not count against you. The entire course, method and time, is graded and you must make a minimum grade of eight hundred points to qualify. Do you understand?"

"I do."

"In addition there are specific items that are automatic fails. If you lose the high-rise pack, it is a fail. If you skip a step of the door breach or misevaluate it is a fail. If you enter the smooth tube in The Maze instead of the corrugated it is a fail. And if you drop the dummy, it is a fail. Are you aware of these fail points?"

"I am."

"Do you fully understand the requirements to pass the evaluation?"

"I do."

"Very well," Connolly said. She looked around for a moment then leaned forward and whispered, very definitively, "Don't. Drop. The dummy." Then she straightened up, looked at her watch, pointed at a rack of ladders and said: "Go."

Wendy trotted over to the ladders at a fair pace. She could have run, but this evaluation was as much about pacing as capability; she'd seen women in fantastic condition wear themselves out halfway through.

Three ladders were racked on the wall, hung vertically. Beside each one, to the left, was a spare, empty rack. The test was simple; lift off each ladder and move it over one rack.

The ladders weighed forty-seven pounds and were awkward in addition; it was quite a test of upper body strength and balance for a one-hundred-and-twenty-pound female to lift and move one, much less three. Add in forty pounds of bunker gear, a breath-pack and all the rest and it was a challenge. And only the first.

She managed the ladders in good time. And managed the second evaluation which was to fully raise and lower, "extend and retract" one of the ladders. Harder than it sounded, it had to be done hand over hand, maintaining control, or the ladder simply "dropped." A drop was not an automatic fail, but it would count heavily against her.

The third evaluation, the high-rise pack, was the first that she knew was going to kick her ass. This involved carrying an "assault pack," two fifty foot sections of 1¾-inch attack line, a nozzle, a gated Wye valve and a hydrant wrench, to the fifth floor of the smokehouse. Forget that the smokehouse was living up to its name, with thick black smoke belching from a generator on the ground floor and billowing up through the stair-wells. Just lifting the pack—which was about a hun-dred pounds, or more than seventy percent of her body weight—off the ground was a struggle. The require-ment was to move "expeditiously" up the stairs, but in reality nobody managed so much as a trot. Each step was a struggle and by the time she reached the third level she knew that if she paused for even a moment she could never get going again. But finally, panting in the heat from the suit and gasping for air, she saw the firefighter at the top. It was through a haze of gray that was only half to do with the smoke, but she'd made it. She carefully lowered the pack to the ground and just rested on her knees for a moment until the red haze over her vision cleared. Then she stood up and, following the pointed finger, went back downstairs to the Maze.

The Maze was the confined spaces test chamber on the third floor. A plywood and pipe "rat-maze," it filled only one room but encompassed a total of a hundred and sixty-five feet of linear "floor." The Maze was multi-level with a series of small passages and doorways, many of which could be slid open or closed at the whim of the testers. None of the passages permitted so much as crouched movement; the entire maze was done on the belly, sometimes crawling at an angle or twisting through three (some suggested four) dimen-sions to reach a new passage.

Strangely, Wendy had never had a problem with the Maze, even when it was blacked out. Perhaps being buried alive in Fredericksburg had some com-pensations; she had come out of it with a fundamental *lack* of claustrophobia. Much the same could be said for Shari, who had waited out the weeks *awake*. If she had tended to claustrophobia, she would have put

herself under like the firefighter who was trapped with
her.

That didn't mean it was easy. The movement method
was difficult. But Wendy didn't have a problem, including remembering not to take the smooth tunnel. The
plastic tunnel was greased after a few feet and anyone who went in wasn't backing out. And it dumped
them out right at the feet of the grader.

Wendy, on the other hand, came out the corrugated
tunnel and popped to her feet reasonably refreshed. She
knew she had made up time on the Maze and the next
test, the door breach, was another "good" one for her.

She trotted up the stairs to the roof and picked up
the essential tools for the door breach test: a backpack
of liquid nitrogen and a $CO_2$-powered center-punch.
The testing device was in the center of the roof; an
apparently freestanding doorway with a closed memory
plastic door in it.

The design of the door necessitated the unusual gear.
For safety reasons, memory plastic doors were designed
so that their "base" configuration was "closed." That
meant that a precisely graduated charge had to be
applied to them to get them to "open" or collapse into
a tube along one side of the door.

When in their extended configuration the doors were
very tough; you could hammer at them with a sledge
all day long and not get them to break. And for security
purposes the charge had to be applied along a recessed
edge. When first confronted with this design, emergency personnel were momentarily stumped. However,
a former Marine firefighter pointed out that lexan
shatters fairly easily when chilled. Thus, a new entry
method was born.

The tester nodded when Wendy had the gear on,
held up a stopwatch and pressed the start button with
a shouted: "Go!"

There were several steps to the door breach and each had to be done precisely. She trotted to the door, positioning herself on the left side, and removed her Nomex gloves then began running her hand over the door and doorframe. She started at the top and ran her hand rapidly across and down. As she reached the bottom left-hand corner of the door she suddenly noted increasing warmth. The bastards.

She stepped back and shouted "Hot door!"

The tester hit the stopwatch and made a notation on her clipboard as Wendy took the opportunity to put her gloves back on. "The door is to be considered hot, but breachable," the tester said. She did not bother to note that if Wendy had not detected the heat she would have been disqualified; that went without saying. "Continue," the tester added, hitting the stopwatch again.

Wendy stepped back and looked at the pressure gauge for the LN bottle. The bottle had a line running out of it to a nozzle similar in appearance to a flamethrower. The outlet pressure, which was controllable at the nozzle, determined how far the stream of nitrogen would go. There was a maximum effective distance, but that really didn't matter. What was important was to reduce, as far as possible, splashback.

The nitrogen gushed out of the nozzle in a white, foaming stream, exploding into vapor as it heated in the room-temperature atmosphere. The reason that the test was on the roof was two-fold; it permitted the gas to be carried off and it prevented having a supercooled room.

There was a limited splashback zone, about a foot out from the door, and the small amount of liquid quickly boiled off. Before it had entirely vanished, however, Wendy stepped forward, avoiding the drops, and placed her punch against the left side of the door.

Normally she would have placed it against the lower

left, but with the single point of high temperature being there, she felt a need to adjust. As cold as the nitrogen was, the memory plastic of the doors had a fairly high specific heat and the lower left might not have cooled off enough to be cleared.

Placing the punch, she angled it so that it would go straight in but, in the event of a refractory door, would not kick into her body, and pulled the trigger.

The punch, which looked somewhat like a cordless electric drill, contained a twenty-centimeter steel spike, charged by a $CO_2$ cartridge in the handle. When triggered, the spike flew out at over three hundred meters per second, penetrating the door and, if it was cold enough, shattering the plastic.

In this case it was cold enough and the door shattered from top to bottom, breaking into chunks ranging from dust up to a few centimeters across. The sole exception was an almost perfectly circular point on the lower lefthand corner. It looked like her decision not to punch the door there was a good one.

She looked at the person in a silver suit on the other side of the doorway. The firefighter was holding a propane torch in one hand and faintly through the layers of lexan Wendy could see a grin.

"Bitch," she whispered under her breath with a returning grin. You *always* popped the door on the lower left, if you were right-handed anyway. It was the safest side and generally the bottom of a door was cool in all but the most intense fires.

The firefighter just pointed at the start of the rope course.

God, this was going to be a long day.

She managed to survive the gear drag and rope course. Both of them were basically gut-checks, in one case for strength and in the other for fear of heights. She wasn't the strongest person on the course and she hated heights, but she could take gut-checks all day long.

But at the end of the rope course, the only thing left was the buddy drag. She started to trot over to the station and realized that she just didn't have any trot left. She kept wondering when that famous second wind was going to kick in, but so far the only thing that had kicked in was utter fatigue. The buddy drag was going to be a hell of a lot of fun.

The test involved lifting a 225-pound dummy and dragging it. The dummy was on the ground, lying on its back, dressed in a bunker-coat and trousers. The candidate was required to lift the dummy up, holding it from behind with their arms wrapped around to the front, and drag it one hundred feet without dropping the dummy.

"Don't drop the dummy," she whispered, grabbing it by the shoulder of the bunker-coat and pulling it up to a sitting position. The head flopped to the side and the arms dangled, all of the appendages getting in the way no matter what she did. Finally she maneuvered herself behind it, her arms under the dummy's, right hand gripping the front of the bunker-coat and left hand locked on her right wrist.

With a grunt she straightened her legs, getting the dummy up, and then just paused, trying not to sway. The dummy was taller and much heavier than she was and just staying on her feet was a challenge. Finally, she leaned carefully backwards and started dragging.

Every step was an agony and a struggle. There was no momentum to build up, that evil enemy gravity prevented anything along those lines. She just had to drag it step by painful step. Two thirds of the way there, her grip on her wrist slipped, but a quick snatch with the left hand got a handful of bunker-coat and the dummy didn't, quite, fall. Now all she had was its coat and her Nomex gloves had gotten slippery with sweat so maintaining her hold was problematic. But she could still do it. She was nearly there.

Then disaster hit. She was within ten feet of the line, almost completely done, when she felt the first snap give way.

The dummy, unfortunately, had been used for thousands of drags. It had been lifted and carried and hauled hither and yon and always in the same bunker-coat. A bunker-coat which chose that moment to decide to open up.

She felt the snaps give way and frantically started scrabbling at the front of the coat, trying to get a handhold anywhere. The dummy poised for a moment on her knee, but then her last handhold slipped and it hit the floor.

She just stood there and . . . looked at it. The dummy was on the floor. She'd dropped the dummy. After all that . . .

She wanted to scream. She wanted to beg for another chance. And she knew that if she did either one, she'd never be accepted for another evaluation. So she just stood there, tears streaming down her face, unable to move as one of the examiners came over, buttoned up the bunker-coat and lifted the dummy into a shoulder carry to reposition it.

Finally, Chief Connolly came over and took her by the arm. She led her over to a bench and pulled off her helmet.

"There'll be other events," Connolly said. "All you have to do is as well as you did and don't drop the dummy."

"How did you know?" Wendy whispered.

"I didn't," Connolly answered turning to watch the next candidate. "I jinxed you. I knew you had screwed up your courage for the rope sequence so I decided to throw you a curve on the dummy. I didn't fiddle with the buckles, though. That was just bad luck."

"Bad luck," Wendy whispered. "That's the story of my life."

"And that's why I jinxed you," Connolly said calmly. "You don't really have your head around this yet. It's all a game to you, even when it's tough. I don't want anybody going into the fire with me that's in it for the 'fun.' Or the uniform. Or anything, but the burning desire to kill the flame and save the people."

Connolly turned back to look at her and shook her head. "You're still playing fireman, Wendy. That's what your psych profile says; that's why you're not in Security either. You're not sure that you can do it, you're not sure you can handle it and you want to play at it for a while to see if you like it. I don't want anybody in the department who's just playing. I don't want anyone who isn't perfectly, completely, confident and competent. We've got too big a responsibility for 'might.'"

Wendy looked up at her for a moment and nodded her head. "Fuck you." She pointed her finger at the firechief as she opened her mouth. "If you say another fucking word I will kick your ass," she whispered, getting to her feet and then getting to her feet again to stand on the bench so she could look the taller firefighter in the eye.

"Let me tell you about bad luck, Chief 'I am God' Connolly," she whispered again, carefully stripping off the bunker gear. "Bad luck is knowing, not worrying, not wondering, but *knowing* that the Posleen are going to kill you and then almost assuredly eat you. Bad luck is having every single member of your family, everyone that you are going to school with, everyone you have ever known, killed in one day. Bad luck is seeing your life wiped out in an instant.

"You came here from Baltimore before it was even invested," Wendy continued softly. "You've never seen a Posleen except on television. You've never seen them in their waves, cresting the hills and filling every corner of your town. You've never heard the crack of railgun rounds overhead or had your ears ringing from missiles slamming into the houses around you.

"You're right. I don't want to be a fucking fireman. I don't want to pull hoses and run up and down stairs all day. I want to kill fucking Posleen. I hate them. I hate them passionately. You think you hate fire, but you love it at the same time; most firemen do. Well, I don't love Posleen at all. I take it back, I don't even hate Posleen. I despise them. I don't respect them, I don't think they are fascinating, I just want them to cease to exist."

She'd stripped out of the bunker gear by then and she stood in the coverall tall and stone faced. "You're right, I'm playing at firefighting. Because compared to killing Posleen, firefighting ain't shit. So. Fuck you. Fuck your tests. And fuck this department. I'm done."

"You're right," said Connolly. "You are. I'll keep you on the reserve rolls, but don't bother turning up for drills. Not until you can keep it together."

"Oh, I've got it together," Wendy said, turning away. "Never better."

"Cummings," the chief called.

"What?" Wendy asked, pausing, but not bothering to turn around.

"Don't do anything . . . stupid. I don't want to be cleaning you up from someplace."

"Oh, you won't be cleaning *me* up," Wendy said, walking away. "But if anybody gives me any shit, you might as well bring the toe-tags."

"I hate these fucking holes," Mueller grumped. And Mosovich had to agree. Mansfield was going to owe him. Big time.

The "request" to go check out this crazy bitch came at a good time, anyway. After the last reconnaissance debacle, the corps commander had ordered a halt to long-range patrols for the time being. The gap was being taken up by increased use of unmanned aerial vehicles and scout crawlers. The former were small aircraft, most of them not much larger than a red-tailed hawk, that hovered along in the trees, probing forward against the Posleen lines. The problem with them was that the Posleen automated systems identified and destroyed them with remarkable ease. So they would only get a brief view of any Posleen activity. Crawlers—which looked like foot-long mechanical ants—did a little bit better. But even they had not been able to penetrate very far; whoever was commanding the Posleen had the main encampment screened tighter than a tick.

Mosovich had heard rumor that Bernard had requested permission to nuke the encampment with SheVa antimatter rounds. It had been denied of course—the President was death on nuclear weapons—but the fact that the question might have been asked was comforting. It meant that somebody was taking the landing seriously.

However, until they figured out a way to probe the Posleen, Mosovich, Mueller and Sister Mary didn't have a job. Since sooner or later somebody was going to notice and figure out something stupid for them to do, Mosovich was just as glad to have this "request" forwarded through corps. It had ensured a written pass from headquarters, without which getting in would have been nearly impossible. And it got them away from corps and the various idiotic projects that the staff would be coming up with.

The flip side to it was t̶
Sub-Urb. He'd been in a co
and they were depressing as h̶
people shoved underground
Especially since ten years before,
had been living in comfortable n̶
lines there were times when you c̶
that, yeah, there was a really big w̶
tally the United States was still ther̶ ̶ ̶ ̶ ̶̶ioning.
And once the off-planet forces retu̶ ̶̶d, everything
could go back to being more or less normal.

Then you went to a Sub-Urb and realized that you
were kidding yourself.

The Franklin Sub-Urb had a particularly bad reputation and he wasn't surprised. Half the escalators on
the personnel entrance they used had been out of order
and the reception area was scuffed and filthy with trash
and dirt piled up in the corners. And the security point,
an armor-glass-fronted cubicle something like a movie
theater ticket booth, was even worse. Every shelf in
the booth was piled with empty food containers, half
of which were filled with cigarette butts.

Realistically, though, the conditions weren't too
surprising. Not only was it one of the oldest ones,
meaning that it had people from the first refugee waves
when the Posleen were really hammering civilians, but
its proximity to the corps support facilities had only
managed to degrade the condition. They'd had to catch
a ride from their barracks in the Gap to Franklin and
it was apparent on the ride that even though the Line
forces in the Gap weren't the greatest, the support
groups were worse. No wonder they'd placed the Urb
off limits; he'd have kept these "soldiers" out and he
*was* a soldier. And from what he'd heard the first few
months when they *hadn't* kept the soldiers out boiled
down to a sack.

security was jumpy about letting
cially armed.

ch shifted his rifle as the female guard
ed with an older male. The newcomer was over-
eight, but not sloppily; it was clear that a good bit
of the body was muscle. He was wearing rank tabs for
a security major which meant he was probably the
senior officer on duty. No wonder she'd been gone for
a while.

"Sergeant Major—" the security officer said, looking at the e-mail orders, "—Mosovich?"

"The same, and my senior NCO, Master Sergeant
Mueller."

"Could I see some ID?" he asked.

"Okay," Jake said, fishing out his ID card and gun
orders.

"This is fairly irregular," the security officer continued. "We have a few personnel that have open permission to pass back and forth. But for all practical
purposes no military personnel are permitted other than
that."

"Unless they're on orders," Mosovich said. He supposed that he could bow and scrape and it might help.
But the hell if he would to this Keystone Kop outfit.

The officer carefully considered the two IDs and
then sighed. "Okay, it looks like I have to let you in. . . ."

"Then would you mind opening the door?" Mueller
growled.

The officer put his hands on his hips. "First, a few
words . . ."

"Look, Major . . ." Mosovich leaned forward and
peered at the badge, " . . . Peanut? We're not support
pogues. We're not the barbarians you had coming down
here before. I may look 22, but I'm 57; I was in the
Army when you were a gleam in your daddy's eye.
We're here on a mission, not to fuck around. And

there's only two of us; if your department can't take down two soldiers then you need to shitcan it and get some real guards. And, as you noted, we've got qualified passes. So open the door."

"Well, that covers part of it," the major said dryly. "Here's the rest. People down here don't have guns. They don't like guns; they're afraid of them. Except for the ones that want them and will gladly take yours if you give them half a chance. Carry them slung across your back, not combat slung. Make sure you maintain control of them at all times. If you lose one, I guarantee you that the corps commander will make your life absolute hell."

"He'd be hard pressed," Jake said. "We're Fleet. But I take your meaning."

"Okay," the major said with a sigh, activating a solenoid. "Welcome to the Franklin Sub-Urb."

Mueller shook his head as they passed through another one of the open gathering areas. "Strange looks." The sprite turned left out of the commons and onto another slideway.

"Yeah," Mosovich replied. "Sheep."

Mueller knew what he meant. The people of the Sub-Urbs were giving them the sort of look sheep gave sheepdogs. They knew that the dog wouldn't bite them. Probably. This time. But they definitely did not like to see the uniforms or the guns. To sheep, all sheepdogs are wolves.

"Probably worried about an attack," Mosovich added.

"I would be," Mueller agreed. The Sub-Urb was an easy drive from the front lines; whatever idiot put it this close should be shot.

"No way out," Mosovich said. "Stupid."

"Lots," Mueller contradicted. "All marked. And the armory at the front."

Mosovich just snorted. If the Posleen ever came up the Gap, the people in the Sub-Urb were so many food animals caught in their pens. And with the Armory on the upper side of the Urb, unless they got the word in *very* good time, the Posleen would be sitting on their weapons.

The decision had been made to make the Urbs zero weapons zones and in the eyes of Mosovich and plenty of other people that was just wrong. If everyone in the Urb was armed it would *probably* mean a higher murder rate. But compared to the one hundred percent loss in the event of an attack, even one by a random landing, a few murders would be worth it. Besides, the improved defenses if everyone was armed might keep the Posleen *out*.

Nonetheless, through a combination of politics and Galactic intransigence the Urbs had been disarmed.

"Stupid." Mueller shook his head.

Mosovich nodded as he turned down a brightly lit corridor. The walls had murals on them, which was unusual, and each of the doors had the nameplate of a different doctor on it. The sprite stopped in front of a door marked "Dr. Christine Richards, Psy.D."

Mosovich touched the entry pad and the door chimed.

"Yes?" a voice asked through the pad.

"Doctor Richards? It's Sergeant Major Mosovich. I'm here to talk to you about Captain Elgars?" The good doctor was supposed to have received an e-mail, but who knew what was really happening.

"Could this wait?" the box asked. "I'm preparing a report right now, but it's not complete."

"Well, you can report all you'd like, doc," Mosovich replied to the speaker. He was getting a bit ticked about talking to a closed door. "But I suspect that the Army is going to pay more attention to me than you.

And I'm going from here to run down Elgars. So this is your one chance to convince me that Elgars is crazy."

The door opened and Dr. Richards sighed. "She's not crazy, she's possessed."

Dr. Richards had spread out all the case files for Annie Elgars on her table, trying to explain why *she* wasn't crazy. "I want you to look at this," she said, laying down a long strip of paper with squiggly lines on it.

"Okay, I know my line here," Mosovich said. "I'm supposed to say 'Is this a brain map, doctor?' But Special Forces guys used to get shrunk all the time and I've seen an EEG before."

"Fine," Richards said, pulling out a textbook. "You're right, that's an EEG and it's Elgars' to be exact." She opened up the book to a marked page and pointed to the lines on the paper. "This is a normal EEG when a person is awake, or not in alpha mode. Look at it."

Mosovich did and then at Elgar's EEG. There was no comparison. "What are all these extra notches?" he asked, pointing to Elgars'.

"You tell me," Richards snapped. "And here, look at this." She riffled through the readouts until she came to another one that was marked. "When you do stuff that you've done thousands of times, the sort of stuff that they say 'He can do it in his sleep.' What's really happening is that your brain switches to alpha mode, which really *is* like you're asleep. It's one of the bases for zen, that 'state of nothingness.' Look, when you're shooting, do you actually *think* about what you're doing?"

"I know what you're talking about here," Mueller interjected. "You're talking about like when you're in a shoothouse. No, you have to turn your brain off and let go, let your training do the thinking for you. When you're really clicking we call it 'being in the Zone.'"

"Exactly," Richards said, pointing to a different set of spikes. "This is alpha state. In Elgars' case, she doesn't have many specific memories, but she can perform a remarkable series of actual manual tasks. If a person is that badly injured, you expect them to have to learn to walk and eat and go to the bathroom all over again. When Elgars was wheeled into the recovery room, she was lucid and capable of performing almost all normal daily functions. Furthermore, we have since determined that she has a wide variety of basic skills, including driving and operating a variety of hand weaponry from knives to very large rifles."

She pointed to the chart, running her finger along the normal rhythms until she got to the alpha rhythm and then pulling the book up alongside. "This is the transition point, where she goes from beta to alpha. And here is a normal transition."

Mosovich and Mueller both leaned forward and looked. Again, the transition area was completely different than the textbook version. It was somewhat longer and had numerous extraneous spikes. Mosovich pointed to the alpha rhythm on the chart.

"Her alpha looks almost textbook, though," he noted.

"Yes, it is," Richards said. "The differences are just those of being a different human. And that's the other scary part; her alpha is absolutely normal."

"So that's why she's possessed?" Mueller asked with a raised eyebrow.

"Look," Richards said with a sigh, leaning back in her chair and taking off her glasses to rub her eyes. "None of us are experts at this. I was a damned family counselor before they sent me down here. We have one, repeat, *one* clinical psych researcher, and he was an expert on *sleep disorders*. We're *all* out of our depth on this . . . phenomenon. But . . . yes, we have come to the conclusion that there is more than one . . . person,

not just personality, person, living in Elgars' head. And
that the primary personality might not be, probably is
not, Anne Elgars."

"Why not Elgars?" Mosovich asked, thinking that
Mansfield was *really* gonna owe him *big* time.

"Memories mostly," Richards said, putting her glasses
back on and scrabbling through her notes. "Anne Elgars
has memories that she really shouldn't have." The
doctor finally seemed to find the notes she was looking for and frowned. "Ever seen the movie *Top Gun*?"
she asked.

"Yeah," Mosovich admitted. "A few times."

"You're a rejuv though, right?"

"Yeah."

"Did you see it when it first came out?" Richards
asked.

"I think so," Mosovich said with a shrug. "Probably.
That was, what? '82? '84? I think I was at Bad Tölz
then. If I saw it, I saw it on post."

"The movie came out in 1986," Richards said, glancing at her notes. "Elgars has distinct memories of
seeing it for the first time in a movie theater then going
over to a friend's house, *driving* herself to a friend's
house to, as she put it, 'jump his bones.'"

"So?" Muller asked.

"Anne Elgars was two years old in 1986," Richards
said, looking up and taking off her glasses again. "Even
the most open-minded of parent is going to question
her two-year-old driving. At the least. And she has
*another* memory of watching it for the first time on
TV in a living room."

"Oh," Mueller said. "What about . . . what's it
called . . . 'implanted memory syndrome'?"

"Up, got me there," Mosovich said. "Whassat?"

"We considered classical implanted memory,"
Richards said, leaning back again. "Implanted memory

used to be called 'regression analysis.' It turned out that the process for regression analysis implants a memory that is *absolutely true* to the person with the memory. I could run you through a little scenario right now and you'd end up with a memory of having been a giraffe. Or a woman. Or that you were sexually abused as a child. Guaranteed. And none of them would be real.

"It caused *huge* problems for a while with child molestation cases; I was still dealing with the repercussions when I got moved down here. Still am for that matter. Women who have a distinct memory of having been molested by a parent or a family friend and it's very unlikely that it ever happened. The only way to get them to even *consider* that the memory is false is to go through the same process with one that is clearly impossible. And then they end up with this really impossible memory. Which has its own problems."

She shrugged and put her glasses back on. "What can I say? I've dealt with dozens of implanted memories in my time. This one doesn't show any of the classic signs. She recalls small details that are not germane to the memory. That's one sign of a 'true' memory versus implanted. Then there's the EEG." She picked up the alpha rhythm sheet and pointed to the transition. "We think that weird transition is where she is hunting for the right . . . call it 'soul' . . . to manage the action. It only happens the first time she engages a skill, so new examples are getting harder and harder to find. But it's consistent. And she goes alpha when she shouldn't. When she's writing, for example. That's not a normal alpha moment, except when typing."

"So what's going on here?" Mosovich asked in exasperation.

"Like I said, we're not experts," Richards answered. "We can only speculate. You want our speculation?"

"Yes," Mueller said. "Please."

"Okay," Richards said, taking off the glasses and setting them on the table. "Anne Elgars sustained a massive head wound in the battle of Washington. The damage was extensive and large portions of her brain showed no normal function. She was in a coma, effectively a permanent one, for nearly five years.

"The Tch . . . Tchfe . . ." she paused.

"We usually just say Crabs, doc," Mosovich said. "Although the best pronouncement a human can get along with is Tch-fet." He smiled. "I'm one of the few people I know who has ever had to try to speak Crab. And even *I* don't try when I don't have to."

"Very well, the . . . the Crabs approached the therapy team, us that is, with an offer to try to heal her. They noted that she might die in the process, but that if it worked it would permit various others who had sustained damage to be recovered as well.

"We had . . . authorization to do whatever we liked, except cut off her lifeline, so we acquiesced. She disappeared with the . . . Crabs and reappeared . . . as she is. In less than a week, with significant muscular improvement. 'Miraculous' was the most minor word we used."

Richards paused and shrugged. "From there on out, it's speculation." She frowned and shook her head. "Crazy speculation if you don't mind my using the word.

"Say you have a computer that is broken. You pull out the broken parts, clear out the memory and load on new software. We think that's what the Crabs did. . . . All of it."

"Shit," Mueller whispered. "You mean they . . ."

"They probably had to cut portions of the brain away," Richards said. "Or something just as radical. The damage was extensive and not just a result of bruising; she had some comintuated *fractures* in her tissue. Repairing that would require cutting and regeneration in, say, your liver. At least for us humans. But whatever the Crabs did, it was just as extensive. And when you finish that, you still have a 'dead' computer. So we think they took a . . . personality, a *person* if you will, that they had . . . hanging around, and loaded it in Elgars. And the memory stuff that we're seeing is the result of the sort of little fragments of code you just have . . . hanging around. You rarely can get rid of all of it in a computer, much less a human."

"So, Anne Elgars the person is dead," Mosovich said. "This is a different person entirely."

"Sort of," Richards said with another sigh. "Don't ask me about souls. Who or what a person *is* is a religious debate as much as a psychological one. For one thing, nature *does* have some influence on it; that's been repeatedly proven. People seem to tend to . . . fill a mold that is somewhat prepared. They're not locked in deterministically, but it is unlikely that the person Anne Elgars eventually becomes is either Anne Elgars *or* the person that the Crabs apparently 'loaded into her.'"

"What about the thing with the alpha waves?" Mueller asked.

"Ah, that's different," she answered. "Anne not only seems to have been loaded with a person, but also, separately, loaded with skills. And we think that some of them are 'integral' to the base personality, or even the original Elgars, and others are separate. So when she runs across a new situation, she has to 'hunt' for the right file so to speak. It's quite unconscious on her part; she has no idea what she is doing. But that's the reason for the odd transition."

"Well, I don't know who she is," Mosovich said. "But

the question is, can she do her job? Right now we need every rifle we can get. Can she soldier or not?"

"She can do *a* job," Richards answered. "Quite easily. She's *programmed* to be a soldier, arguably a 'supersoldier.' She has skills ranging from advanced marksmanship to field expedient demolitions. She can *certainly* soldier. The question is, what *else* is she programmed for?"

Wendy opened the door at the buzz, tucked a squirming Amber under one arm and frowned at the figure in camouflage filling the door. "We gave at the office."

Mueller frowned. "I'd think this was your office."

"It is, but we already contributed," Wendy answered. "In other words, what are you here for?"

"Ah, we were told we could find Captain Anne Elgars here," Mueller said. "From the picture, you are not Captain Elgars. However, it is nice to make your acquaintance Miz . . . ?"

"Cummings," Wendy said, wincing at the anticipated joke. She had lived with her name her whole life. "Wendy Cummings."

"Master Sergeant Mueller," Mueller said. "Charmed. And is Captain Elgars available?" he continued as the baby let out a howl like a fire engine.

"Sure, I'll get her," Wendy said. "Come on in."

She stepped around Kelly, who had chosen the middle of the floor as the obvious place to do a life-sized Tigger puzzle, and walked towards the back.

Mueller looked over his shoulder at Mosovich and shrugged, then stepped through the door. The room was filled with the sort of happy bedlam you get with any group of children, but the noise was dying as the kids noticed the visitors. Before too long Mosovich and Mueller found themselves in a semicircle of kids.

"Are you a *real* soldier?" one of the little girls asked. Her eyes were brown and just about as big around as saucers.

Mueller squatted down to where he wasn't much over their height and nodded his head. "Yep. Are you a *real* little girl?"

The girl giggled as one of the boys leaned forward. "Is that a real gun?"

"Yes," Mosovich said with a growl. "And if you touch it you'll get a swat."

"Guns aren't toys, son," Mueller added. "What's your name?"

"Nathan," the kid said. "I'm gonna be a soldier when I grow up and kill Posleen."

"And that's a fine thing to want to do," Mueller opined. "But you don't start off with a big gun. You learn on little guns first. And someday, if you eat your vegetables, you'll be big like me. And you can kill Posleen all day long."

"Without getting tired?" one of the girls asked.

"Well . . ." Mueller said, flipping a surreptitious finger at Mosovich for laughing, "you do get tired."

"Okay, let's start getting ready for lunch, children," Shari said, coming out of the back with Elgars and Wendy. "Leave these gentlemen alone. Wash hands then sit down for grace."

"I'm Elgars," said the captain, ignoring the children. She had white powder on her hands and a cheek.

"Captain, I'm Sergeant Major Mosovich with Fleet Recon and this is my senior NCO Master Sergeant Mueller." He paused and then nodded as if he'd done some sort of a mental checklist. "Your commander, Colonel Cutprice, sent a message to one of my troops asking him to come down here and find out if you needed rescuing from the shrinks. I don't know if you remember Nichols, but you two went through sniper school together. He got banged up on our last op and is still down in the body-and-fender so I came down here with Mueller instead. Anyway, here I am."

"Okay," Elgars said, with a nod. "So am I being rescued from the shrinks?"

"Is there someplace we can talk, ma'am?" Mosovich temporized. "Someplace quieter?" he added as the children trooped back from the bathroom.

"Not really," Elgars said, raising her voice slightly over the children. "The kitchen isn't much better. We'd have to go to my quarters and I can't really afford the time for that."

"Is this where . . . Do you *work* here, ma'am?" Mosovich asked.

"Sort of," she answered. "I help out. I'm following Wendy around, getting my bearings again."

"Well," Mosovich frowned. "Okay, the question, ma'am, is, how do *you* feel about going back on active duty?"

"I feel okay about it," Elgars said. "Can I ask a question?"

"Of course, ma'am."

"Are *you* here to evaluate me?"

It was this question that had made Mosovich pause early in the discussion. The question was whether to answer honestly or do the two-step. He finally decided that honesty was the right policy even if it wasn't the best.

"I guess you could say that, ma'am," the sergeant major admitted. "I got told to come down here and check you out then report back to your commander in writing as to your perceived fitness. You don't normally use a sergeant major to report on an officer and I'm not a psychologist. But I've been beating around this war for quite a while and I guess the powers that be trust my judgement."

"Okay," Elgars said. "In that case I'll be honest too. I don't know what the hell a captain does. I can shoot, I know that. I can do other stuff. But I keep finding holes. And I have no idea what the job of a captain even is. So being a captain would be tough."

Mueller tapped Mosovich on the shoulder and whispered in his ear. Mosovich turned and looked at him with a quizzical expression and held a finger up to Elgars. "Captain, could you excuse me for just a moment."

He and Mueller went over into a corner of the daycare center and spoke for a moment. Elgars could see Mosovich shaking his head and Mueller gesturing. After a moment, Wendy came over to ask Elgars what was going on.

"I dunno," the captain replied. "But I don't think I'm gonna like it."

Mosovich came back over and looked at both of them. He opened his mouth for a moment, stopped, glanced over his shoulder at Mueller. Looked at Wendy for a second then looked at Elgars.

"Captain," he said over the shrilling of the children in the background. "I don't think we can get a good read on how you really feel about your abilities in this environment."

Elgars looked at him for second, looked at Wendy then looked back. "So, what would you suggest?"

"Mueller suggests that the four of us go take a turn up on the surface. Maybe go to dinner, go to a range, see how you feel about being in an environment other than . . ." at which point Shakeela started with one of her patented howls " . . . a daycare center."

"Sergeant Major Mosovich," Wendy asked with a raised eyebrow, "are you suggesting a double date?"

"No," Mosovich said. "Just a chance to talk somewhere other than in here."

"Uh, huh," Wendy said, glancing at Mueller, who returned a look that said butter wouldn't melt in his mouth. "Well, Shari can't take care of the children alone. I think that *Captain* Elgars is capable of taking care of herself, however, so why don't the three of you go?"

"Okay," Mosovich said with a shrug. "Works for me."

"Hold it," Elgars said. "Wendy, how long has it been since you've been to the surface?"

"November?" Wendy asked with a frown.

"Uh, huh," Elgars said. "What year?"

"Uh . . ." Wendy shook her head. "2007?"

"And how long has it been since *Shari* had anything resembling a break?" Elgars asked.

"Taking the kids to the surface wouldn't be a break," Wendy noted. "But . . . I don't think she's been out of the Urb since we came here from Fredericksburg. And the last time *I* was up there was . . . was to give testimony," she continued with a stony face.

"Well, I think we should *all* take a trip up to the surface," Elgars said.

"With the kids?" Mosovich asked incredulously.

"Sure," Mueller said. "With the kids. Stress testing for the captain."

"Christ, okay, whatever," Mosovich said, raising his hands. "Stress testing for *me*. We'll all go up top and have dinner someplace in Franklin. See how Elgars handles being out and about. I'll include that in my report and we'll see what Colonel Cutprice says."

"I could use some help," Shari said, walking over.

"Well, that clarifies that," Wendy said with a laugh.

"Clarifies what?"

"The sergeant major needs to spend some time around Captain Elgars," Mueller noted. "I recommended going to the surface, along with Wendy so that the captain wouldn't be completely alone. Wendy pointed out that you needed too much help with the kids for her to leave. So it came down to inviting *all* of you to the surface."

"Where, on the surface?" Shari asked nervously.

"There's at least one decent place in Franklin, I think," Mosovich noted. "It's an R&R area for the corps. There's got to be someplace."

"I dunno," said Shari, reluctantly. "Franklin? It . . ."

"It doesn't have a very good reputation down here," Wendy noted with a grim chuckle.

"We don't go there much either," Mueller said. "But, trust me, the food's better than down here."

"I'm not sure . . ." Shari said.

"Well, I am," Wendy argued. "How long have we been down here? Five years? How long since you've seen the sun?"

"Long time," Shari whispered with a nod. "Except for Billy, I don't think any of the kids remember what it looks like."

"There will be three trained soldiers with us," Wendy noted. "It will be safe. It will be a chance for the kids to look at the surface. How bad can it be?"

"There's basically no Posleen activity at the moment," Mosovich pointed out. "There's a globe around Clarkesville acting funny, but they haven't done anything either. Except chase us around the hills."

"Okay," Shari said after a moment's thought. "Let's do it. Like you said, Wendy, how bad can it be?"


"You've completely outgrown this, Billy," Shari said, adjusting Billy's windbreaker as Wendy negotiated for her personal weapon.

"This is . . . unbelievable," she said looking at the weapon. It was an Advanced Infantry Weapon, the standard issue weapon for the Ground Forces, a 7.62 semi-automatic rifle with a 20mm grenade launcher on the underside. This one had been personalized with a laser sight on the top.

Had.

"Where's my laser sight?" she asked angrily, turning the rusted weapon over and over. "I turned this in with a Leupold four power scope that was laser mounted. There does not appear to be a Leupold scope on this weapon. There also were three more magazines. And you made me turn in my two hundred rounds of ammo that *weren't* in the mags. So where *is* all that?"

"The inventory just lists the weapon," the guard said, looking at his screen. "No ammo, no scope, no magazines."

"Well, bugger that," Wendy said, leaning forward to shove a faded receipt against the greenish glass. "You want to read this motherfucking receipt, asshole? What the fuck am I supposed to do with a weapon and no goddamned rounds?"

"Wendy," Mosovich said, pulling at her arm. "Give it up. There's no scope. There's no rounds. These assholes shot them off long ago. And the scope is probably on this dickhead's personal weapon. That he hasn't shot in a year."

"You want to get out of here at all you better jack up that attitude, Lurp-Boy," the guard snarled from behind the glass.

Mueller leaned forward until his nose was within inches of the armored glass and smiled. "HEY!" he shouted, then laughed as the guard jumped. He reached into the billow pockets of his blouse and pulled out a charge of C-4. Pulling off an adhesive cover he applied it to the glass then began patting his pockets, muttering "Detonators, detonators . . ."

Mosovich smiled. "You wanna open the doors or you want *I* should come in and press the button?"

He smiled and nodded as the armored doors

behind him slid back. "Thanks so very much. And if you're thinking about dicking around with the elevators, let me just point out that that means we'll have to come back."

"And . . . have a nice day," Mueller said, taking Kelly's hand and heading for the door.

"I can't believe this," Wendy snarled as she turned the rifle over and over in her hands. "I dropped this thing off *immaculate*. Like the day it came from the factory."

"I doubt it would even work now," Mueller said with a sigh. "Those things are a bastard when they rust. It's the firing mechanism; it's fragile as hell."

"Don't worry about it," Mosovich said. "It's not like we're going to get jumped by the Posleen in Franklin."

"We heard they were all over the place," Shari asked nervously, as they reached the elevators to the surface. "That people are killed every day."

"Oh, they are," Mueller said walking over to hit the elevator button. The elevator was *huge*, easily large enough to carry a semi-trailer, separated into lines by a chain and post arrangement. Several of the chains dangled free and one of the posts rolled on the ground as it lurched sideways. "There must be three or four civilians killed every day by ferals. You know how many people were killed every day in car wrecks before the war?"

"Yeah," Mosovich agreed. "Death rates, excepting combat casualties, have dropped in the States."

"Why are we going sideways?" Elgars interjected.

"Oh, sorry, I forgot you've never been in one," Mosovich said. "There are multiple elevators for each shaft, so that incoming refugees could be shuttled down really fast. There's an 'up' shaft and a 'down' shaft and they slide between the two." He nodded as the structure shuddered and began to rise. "I've been on one that got stuck; wasn't pleasant. Anyway, where were we?"

"Reduced death rate," Shari said.

"Not reduced overall, mind you," Mueller said. "Combat casualty rates have made up for it."

"How many?" Elgars asked. "I mean, combat casualties?"

"Sixty-two million," Mosovich said. "In the U.S. and of American military forces. And that's just the *military* losses. Pales compared to China and India, mind you, but still pretty bad."

"Six . . ." Shari gasped. "Could you say that again?"

"Sixty-two million," Mueller said quietly. "At the height of the war there were nearly that many under arms in the Contiguous U.S., what they call CONUS, and in the Expeditionary Forces. But in the last five years, most combat units, most infantry battalions, have had three casualties for every position in them. That is, they have had three hundred percent casualties. At its height, the American portion of the EFs had nearly forty million personnel. But the total casualties have topped that and the AEF is below twelve million, and only half of that is actual 'shooting at the Posleen' fighters."

"And there's a steady attrition in the interior," Mosovich added. "There's still landings from time to time; there was a globe that made it down, mostly intact, near Salt Lake just last year."

"We heard about that," Wendy said. "But . . . nothing like those casualty figures."

"They're not very open with them," Mosovich agreed. "Add in the forty million or so civilian casualties and the fact that we're fighting this war in the middle of a 'drop' in males of prime military age and we're . . . well, we're getting bled white. Even with rejuving older guys, taking a person that has never held a weapon in their hands and teaching when they are eighteen is one thing, doing it when they're fifty is . . . different. They, generally, aren't stupid enough to be good soldiers. Not cannon fodder soldiers. Young guys want to be heroes so the women will love them and have their babies. Old guys just want to live to see the next sunrise."

"Which just makes keeping women out of combat units stupid," Wendy said, shaking her head at the condition of her rifle. "This is . . ." She shook her head again. "I know that I can depend on you big strong men to protect me. But I don't *want* to have to!"

"Don't sweat it," Mosovich said with a chuckle. "We'll find you a weapon. And women generally aren't stupid enough either; they can have babies any time they want. That being said; I don't agree with the policy either, but nobody can seem to get it changed."

He stepped through the door into a concrete room. It was about fifty meters wide and a hundred deep with black lines painted on the floor. The walls were covered in condensation and a steady breeze blew out of the elevator towards the glass doors at the end. Halfway down the room there was a series of small bunkers. As they approached them it was clear that most of them were half filled with dirt and garbage, some of it blown in, but much of it dropped into them by passersby. Many of the lines on the floor had peeled up and there was trash all over the room, although clearly little of it was new.

"I think I know the *real* reason that it's nearly impossible for females to get in Ground Force these days," Mosovich noted. "But it's a nasty reason and you won't like it."

"I've dealt with a lot of stuff I don't like," Wendy said. "My life seems to consist of dealing with stuff I don't like."

"In that case I think the casualties are the answer, two answers really," Mosovich said.

"The first reason is that we're being bled white. We've lost about eighty percent of our productive-age male population. But even with combat casualties, we've only lost about thirty of our productive-age females . . ."

"We're breeders," Wendy said.

"Yep," Mosovich agreed. "The powers that be are obviously thinking that when the Posleen are kicked off planet, it won't do much good to have nobody left but a bunch of old women and a few children to 'carry on.' So they're conserving the breeding population."

"It takes two to tango," Shari pointed out, adjusting Shakeela's coat. The bunker was quite cool compared to the underground city they had left and it was clear that the fall had settled in up here. "Where are the 'breeders' going to find . . ."

"Guys?" Mueller asked. "It's not a nice answer, but it doesn't take many guys to make lots of babies, but it's a one for one ratio with women."

"He's right," Mosovich said. "It's not nice, but it *is* true. That's only half the story, though.

"In the first wave there were *massive* conventional casualties. There was a real question whether we were going to hold everywhere and we *didn't* hold a couple of places. Losses among combat formations were huge. And there was a . . . a disparity in female losses versus male. Losses among women in combat units were nearly equal to males, but they only comprised a third of the force at the maximum.

"I read your whole packet, Captain," he continued doggedly. "And I'd already read a classified after-action report in which you were a minor bit player. You did a good job at the Monument, no question, but if it hadn't been for Keren, you'd be dead right now.

And your . . . experiences in the retreat from Dale City are one of the classic egregious examples."

"Who's Keren?" Elgars asked. "And what do you mean by that?"

"Keren is a captain with the Ten Thousand," Mueller said as they reached the doors. There were two sets with a chamber in between and they acted as partial airlocks, reducing the blast of wind that was trying to escape the bunker. "He was in a mortar platoon near the rear of the retreat. He apparently picked you up during the retreat and you rode with him all the way to the Monument."

"You'd been dumped by another unit," Mosovich said tightly. He turned left and headed up the wide stairs on the exterior. There were two sets of those as well, one on each side of the entrance. There was a walkway on the wall opposite the doors that joined them near the top. Running along the surface on that side were small concrete combat positions, which were accessible from the walkway. On the far side was an open area nearly two hundred meters across and then a large parking lot filled with dirt-covered cars and trucks and one Humvee, parked on the grass on the verge.

"That was what happened to a good many females in that retreat and others. Some units returned with nearly one hundred percent female casualties versus fifty to sixty percent casualties among the males."

"Well, the actual incidence of *why* she was dumped wasn't that high," Mueller pointed out.

"Why *was* I 'dumped'?" the captain said carefully.

"You'd been raped," Mosovich said tightly. "Then they took away your sniper rifle and dumped you with an AIW and a single magazine."

"Oh," Elgars said. "That's . . . annoying in a distant way."

"So, you're saying that they don't want me in the Ground Forces because I might get raped in a retreat?" Wendy said angrily. "Then they shouldn't ought to let their damned soldiers in the Sub-Urbs!"

"Am I to take it that's why you were so uncomfortable coming to the surface with us?" Mueller said. "In that case, I'm sorry I asked. And if you'll give me a name and unit I'll take care of it."

"I was just giving testimony," Wendy said. She stopped at the top of the stairs blinking her eyes against the light and looked down at the town.

Franklin had been a small, somewhat picturesque city nestled in lightly inhabited hills before the war. Its main industry was supporting the local farmers and retirees who had moved up from Florida to get away from the crime.

With the change to a war footing, it became a vital linchpin in the southern Appalachian defenses. Units from just south of Asheville to Ellijay depended upon it for supply and administration.

The city was now overrun by soldiers and their encampments stretched up the hills on either side of it. The small strip mall that the entrance overlooked had been taken over by pawnbrokers and T-shirt shops with the only sign of "normal" presence being a dry cleaner.

She looked down over the bustle and shrugged. "When . . . when the Urb was first set up anyone could come and go at any time. That was . . . good at first. The corps did a lot of good in the Urb. And . . . there was a lot of dating. Most of the corps was male and most of the Urb is female so . . . things naturally happened. Then . . . the . . . the attitude sort of changed."

"A lot of the girls in the Urb were . . . lonely," Shari said. "They would take up with the soldiers and some of the soldiers practically moved into the Urb. A lot of what you could call 'black market' transfers went on; you used to be able to find coffee even. But then things started getting out of hand. The security force wasn't large enough, or effective enough, to keep the soldiers under control and they had an authority dispute with the corps MPs, who *were* numerous enough and quite ready to crack heads."

"We ended up having a . . ." Wendy shrugged her shoulders and shuddered. "Well, one of the officers that was involved in the investigation referred to it as a 'sack' during a long weekend. Something like a riot with *a lot* of rapes. I made it to the range and Dave and I sort of stood off the couple of groups that came around us."

"I had a . . . well, a group of . . . boys really that were like kids I was taking care of," Shari noted. "A couple of them were there when the riots started. I was okay."

"Others weren't," Wendy said darkly. "So we don't *like* the corps in the Urb. Anyway, the Urb was put off-limits to military personnel . . ."

"Unless they had orders," Mueller pointed out.

"Unless they had orders to go there," Wendy agreed. "And now they stay up here and we stay down there and any girls who want to go . . ."

"Ply a trade?" Mosovich asked. "I get the point. But you don't have to worry about *human* threats either."

"Oh, I'm not worried," Wendy said, stroking her rusted rifle. "It might be a bit screwed up, but it will do for a club if it comes to that . . ."

# CHAPTER 16

*Ground Force Headquarters, Ft. Knox, KY,*
  *United States, Sol III*
*1453 EDT Thursday September 24, 2009* AD

General Horner read the debrief of the recon team with a blank expression. His intelligence section was of two minds about it; Mosovich had an excellent reputation, but nobody had ever seen flying tanks before.

Horner didn't have a problem in the world with the information. It was bad. That was normal.

He sighed and pulled up a graph that he *knew* he looked at too much. It was his own AID's estimate, based upon all available information, of . . . relative combat strength in the United States. It took into account that the casualty ratio of humans to Posleen tended to be about one thousand to one, but it also took into account the dwindling supplies of soldiers and Posleen birthrates. What it said was that sometime in the next twelve months, when the current crop of

Posleen nestlings reached maturity and were given their weapons, there would be enough Posleen to swamp every major pass in the Appalachians. And it wouldn't even take smart Posleen.

Add in smart Posleen and things just went right down the old tubes.

The report from Georgia, though, was very troubling. He knew that Rabun was considered one of the less well maintained defenses, mostly because it had hardly been hit. There was a defense specialist down there, the name hovered on the edge of his recollection, but they needed more than that.

And Bernard was there. That would give the Posleen all the advantage they needed.

What to do, what to do . . .

First he typed in orders for the Ten Thousand to prepare for movement. They could stay in place, they needed the break, but they went to a four hour recall and were ordered to begin packing all their gear for a move. Cutprice was probably already packed, but it never hurt to be sure. He considered doing the same for the ACS, but if he did O'Neal would probably put everybody in suits and head for . . . Oh . . . shit.

He looked at the map again and shook his head. That put a twist in the whole plan. He really needed to *not* mention the situation to O'Neal, who really needed a few more days rest. Getting the battalion south fast, though, would be tough. Or not.

He checked the inventories and they had a sufficiency of Banshee stealth shuttles in inventory. The shuttles had been ordered when it appeared the Galactic largesse was unending. In twenty-twenty hindsight he wished they had the same relative value of suits, but they had to play with the hand they were dealt. If it really dropped in the pot in Georgia he could fly O'Neal and the Black Tyrone down by shuttle.

Most of them were out west, but he should have some warning before it dropped in the pot.

That was the extent of the forces he had immediately available. He would have his staff start looking at what else was available to reinforce in the Gap. But then he noted that it only had one SheVa. Moving one of those was *not* a short-term operation.

He tapped the controls and noted that there was a SheVa in movement to Chattanooga.

Not any more.

Mosovich looked at the façade of the building. The business had once been a family-owned barbecue restaurant and Mosovich had vaguely recalled it from years before when he visited the area. The local VFW had been next door.

Now it was a bar designed to separate soldiers from their money in the shortest possible time.

The front deck was packed with soldiers, most of them lightly armed and heavily drunk. Squeezed into spaces in between were the waitresses and other working girls.

He winced as a soldier stumbled out the main door. The unshaven sergeant was supported by a lightly clad female who couldn't have been over the age of consent. The sergeant squinted at the sunlight, grabbed the girl by a tit and stumbled off down the street, weaving on and off of the sidewalk towards a nearby motel.

"Not," he said.

"Not," Wendy agreed as she shivered in the wind. "Five gets you ten he gets rolled. Any other bright ideas?"

"Just one," Mosovich said, looking up at the sun. They had managed to pack the whole group into the appropriated Humvee by much sitting on laps and packing some of the children in the bed. But travelling much further would be problematic. And the afternoon was upon them; it was October and most of the kids were underdressed for nighttime fall temperatures. "How you doing, Captain?"

"I'm . . . fine," Elgars said, shifting her body to track on the sergeant as he stumbled past. "The . . . number of armed personnel is throwing me. I'm . . . feeling twitchy."

"That's normal," Jake admitted. "And not out of reason; there've been some hellacious firefights in these military towns." He looked around and shook his head. "Franklin is out. There are probably places frequented by the locals, but it would be pointless to look for them."

He looked at the sun again, counted on his fingers then looked at Wendy. "Do you trust me?"

She regarded him calmly for a moment and then nodded. "Strangely enough, yeah. Why?"

"I've got a buddy who's got a farm near here. He's got a granddaughter not much older than Billy and he'd probably be more than happy to have some company. We could go there, but it would be an overnight stay."

"Oh." Wendy looked at Shari, who shrugged then looked at the sun herself. "We need to get the kids out of the cold before dark."

"That won't be a problem," Mosovich said. "Getting *back* might have been a problem, but not getting *there*. And, frankly, he's probably got some clothes that would fit them; they're the worst outfitted kids I've seen in years."

"All we've got for the surface is what we arrived in," Shari said quietly. "Billy's wearing a jacket I borrowed a couple of years ago. And none of the other children have *anything*."

As if on cue, Kelly pulled at Shari's hand. "Mommy, I'm hungry."

"That's it," Mosovich said. "The farm or go back to the Urb as a bad plan."

"I don't want to go back underground," Elgars admitted. "Not just yet. I . . . like it up here."

"So do I," Shari admitted, looking up at the sky. "I miss the wind. Okay, if you're sure this friend of yours won't completely freak at having five adults and eight kids descend on him out of the blue."

"Not a problem," Mosovich said. "He can handle anything."

Michael O'Neal, Sr., pulled the Palm from his belt and frowned. Since the interesting events a few years back he had updated his security systems. The cameras at the front gate now transmitted back to a webserver that, in turn, sent a compressed video stream to the device. So he found himself looking at a Humvee piloted by Mosovich. Not a big deal, Jake had been up a couple of times in the last year. But the fading light showed that the Humvee was packed with other bodies.

O'Neal rolled the huge wad of Red Man in his cheek from one side to the other and frowned in thought. He was not a huge man, but he had an aura of squat stolidity that was almost preternatural; it appeared as if it would take a bulldozer to move him. His arms were overlong for his body, reaching, simianlike, almost to his knees, and his legs were just a tad bandied, adding to the overall aura of a slightly annoyed male silverback.

He jacked up the gain on the distant cameras and zoomed in on the front seat. Jake was driving and the guy next to him had to be Mueller from past descriptions. But Mueller had two kids on his lap and unless Papa's eyes were deceiving him there was a female leaning between them. Hot diggety. Just what he'd been praying for this last few months; maybe there was a God who took care of fools and drunks.

As he activated the gates there was a scream from upstairs like a panther with its leg in a trap.

"WHERE'S MY GUN-SMITHING KIT?" came a shriek from above.

Ah, Cally had apparently found something to her dissatisfaction.

"Have you looked in your desk?" he called calmly.

"DON'T YOU TAKE THAT TONE WITH *ME*, GRAMPS!" she yelled. "Of *course* I looked in my DESK! I keep it . . ."

He nodded at the cutoff sentence. Time to get out of the house before she got down the . . .

"I *just* looked there!" she said, breathing angrily and waving the cloth-wrapped tools above her head as if she was going to use them as a weapon. The young woman was as tall as her grandfather, long of hair and leg with wide, cornflower blue eyes. Her grandfather had often considered that it was a good thing she'd gotten her looks from her mother rather than her father. But those looks, along with the fact that she was barely thirteen and a few . . . incidents had gotten surreptitious pictures tacked up on barracks walls. With the caption: "Warning: Jailbait. To be considered ARMED AND VERY DANGEROUS."

"Cally," Mike Senior said calmly. "Calm down. You found it and . . ."

"DON'T YOU *DARE* SAY HORMONES!" she shouted.

"And what I was going to say was we're about to have visitors," he continued as if she hadn't said anything. "Mosovich and a packed Humvee full of women and kids it looks like."

"Refugees?" she asked calmly, setting down the smithing kit and holding her hand out for the Palm Pilot.

"I don't think so," Papa O'Neal said, handing it over and heading for the door. "Visitors at a guess. But that's just a guess."

"Okay," Cally said, unconsciously checking the H&K P-17 in her waistband. "I'll stay back."

"Just follow procedure," Papa O'Neal said. "Don't get . . . don't go overboard."

"Not a problem," she said with a quizzical expression. "Why would I go overboard?"

"Jesus Christ," Mueller whispered. "Who is *that*?"

"That is Michael O'Neal, Senior," Mosovich said. "I knew him a long time ago in a much hotter place we generally just called Hell."

"Not the guy," Mueller said, gesturing into the shadows of the front porch. "The *girl*."

Mosovich looked again and frowned. "She's . . . twelve or thirteen, Mueller. Waaay too young. Even in North Carolina."

"You're kidding me," Mueller said as the Humvee pulled to a stop. "She's like, seventeen if she's a day!"

"No, I'm not," Mosovich said coldly, holding onto the door handle and staring at the NCO with dead eyes. "And if you want to live through the next few minutes, put your tongue back in your head. If *O'Neal* doesn't kill you for being an idiot and a drain on the genepool I will. And if you somehow manage to survive both us old fucks, that little bit will kill you without a word or a whisper; there is no proof, but there is some indication that she has done so before, possibly more than once. Last, but not least, her *daddy* is Major 'Ironman' O'Neal of the ACS, Mighty Mite his own self. And if *he* comes after your ass he is, first of all, a *Fleet* officer with the legal authority to kill a *Fleet* NCO out of hand and second of all god-damned unstoppable. You don't have the chance of a snowball in hell if *any* of the three of us think you're going to try to make time with her. Do *not* make eyes at Cally O'Neal. Understood?"

"Gotcha," Mueller said, holding up his hands. "I don't go for jailbait, Jake, and you know it. But . . . Jesus, I want an ID or something! I swear she looks like, seventeen, even eighteen!"

"Sorry about that," Mosovich said over his shoulder.

"Not a problem," Elgars said. "It was a pretty professional dressing down. I've filed it for future reference. Can we get out yet?"

"Sure," Mosovich said, taking a deep breath to clear the anger. Just let *something* go right today.

"What was that about?" Cally asked quietly.

"Dressing down," Papa O'Neal responded just as quietly. The throat mike was nearly invisible against the collar of his shirt and the receiver in his ear *was* invisible to the naked eye.

Just because his military background stretched back to the dawn of time, or Vietnam, which was close, that didn't mean that Papa O'Neal wasn't up to date. His security systems were as state of the art as he could accumulate and a few of the items were, technically, restricted to Fleet personnel only. But when you're guarding the daughter of a living legend, people make exceptions.

The grounds were scattered with sensors, cameras and command detonated mines and the house behind him had enough surveillance equipment in it to be a demonstrator. This had occasioned some embarrassment, in ancient times when he used to have friends in the area. From time to time he would host rather . . . raucous parties at which his friends, mostly retired military who had moved to the North Georgia mountains for the air and the proximity to Ranger students they could mess with, would occasionally forget or ignore that the entire house was wired for sound. And video.

He was *still* humorously blackmailing people with those tapes.

The friends were gone, now. Many of them were dead on one battlefield or another and all the rest of them had been rejuvenated and were scattered throughout the United States. He was the only one left, one used up, worn-out old warhorse that was, in the eyes of the U.S. government, too tainted to be called up under the *worst* duress.

Which, fortunately, left him to guard the farm. And a Farmer's Daughter who was practically its Platonic archetype.

"What over do you think?" Cally asked as the door opened.

"At a guess, 'If you mess with Cally O'Neal you will die a quick and painless death.' "

"Why?" she asked as the rest of the doors opened and people began spilling out. "He's kind of cute. In a great big teddy bear sort of way."

*Why me, oh lord?* Papa O'Neal thought. *Couldn't you just have killed me on some battlefield? Slowly? Under the knives of the women? Why this?*

Wendy looked around as she unloaded Susie from her lap.

The farm was set in a small pocket valley, a "holler" in the local vernacular, set off of the main valley that comprised Rabun Gap. The valley was an almost perfect bowl with steep, wooded sides and a narrow opening where a small river dropped down a series of cataracts. The opening to the valley was to the south and the two-story stone and wood house, which was backed up onto the north side, faced it across a checkerboard of fields. One of the fields had just been stripped of its corn and another was covered in wheat or barley that was just about ready to be harvested. Others were devoted to hay or lying fallow under clover. On the east side where the valley started to slope up was a small orchard of mixed trees, some that she recognized as pecans and others that were probably fruit trees. The western edge was devoted to a large barn and a massive rifle and pistol range.

The house had the look of a fortress; the windows were generally small and, especially on the stone ground floor, set back in the thick walls. There was a large front porch overhung by the upper story, but that looked like a defensive item as well; anyone trying to get through the front door could be terribly discommoded by people on the upper story. On the western side, where most houses would have a garage, was a low sand-bag and wood bunker with the snout of a tarp-covered gun jutting from the center loophole and on the eastern side there was a large outdoor cooking area that clearly had seen more active days.

She finally unwedged herself from the back of the Humvee and nodded as she stepped down from the vehicle. She had to admit that despite the cool evening, and the temperature really *was* dropping like a rock, this was much better than the Sub-Urb or Franklin. Now if the locals were just friendly.

Mosovich shook Papa O'Neal's hand. "I'm throwing myself on your mercy here, Snake."

"Visitors are always welcome," O'Neal said with a smile. "As long as they are either pre-cleared or female."

Mosovich laughed and shook his head. "It's a long story."

"Come in to tell it," Papa O'Neal answered. "It's getting cold and those kids are kind of underdressed."

Cally started fading backwards as the group entered the living room. It had been so long since they had had unknown visitors that her defenses were screaming about threats that didn't exist. Finally she stopped by the couch and smiled in welcome, her left hand by her side and her right on her hip. Where it could access the H&K better. It would be okay. And if it wasn't, it would simply be very bloody.

Papa O'Neal saw Cally and realized she was wound tighter than a string. He knew that he had to defuse that situation quickly.

"Sergeant Major, you've met my granddaughter, Cally. But I don't think she's met any of the rest of you."

Mosovich smiled and ran through introductions on the adults. "I'll admit I don't know the names of all the children."

"Billy, Kelly, Susie, Shakeela, Amber, Nathan, Irene and Shannon," Shari said, pointing to each child. "Thank you for taking us in like this. We won't be here long."

"Nonsense," Papa O'Neal said, shaking her hand. "Feral Posleen move more after dark and, frankly, as packed into that rattletrap as you are it would be hard to defend. Except by running one over, which is admittedly a technique." He realized he hadn't let go of her hand and released it quickly. "No, staying overnight would be better. I insist. We have plenty of room."

"Uh . . ." Shari said, turning to look at Wendy.

Wendy shrugged her shoulders. "We don't have so much as a toothbrush with us. On the other hand, we're not exactly dressed for the fall and that Humvee is pretty uncomfortable."

"Seriously," Papa O'Neal said. "Stay the night. We've not only got beds, there's spare clothes around; I'm the designated storage point for . . . well, a lot of people. And . . ." he looked at Wendy and Shari somewhat pleadingly, " . . . I'd consider it a personal favor."

Shari looked at him with a puzzled expression then shrugged her shoulders. "Well . . . okay, if it's not an imposition."

"Not at all," Papa O'Neal countered forcefully. "Not. One. Bit. Please stay. At least overnight and part of tomorrow."

"Okay," Wendy said. She shrugged one arm where her coat covered the shape of a rifle. "On one condition; do you guys have any cleaning kits?"

Cally cocked her head as Wendy rubbed naval jelly into the barrel. "You're really pretty."

"Thanks," Wendy said, looking up. "You're one to talk."

They were attempting to repair the damage to Wendy's rifle in the O'Neals' gun room. The room was in the basement on the back side of the house, but well ventilated. It had to be; the air reeked with gun oil, propellants and solvents.

The west wall was taken up with a workbench that included a lathe, drill press and various rotary polishers. There was also a large tumbler, some buckets of soapy water and an elaborate reloading kit. Under the workbench were blanks of metal and several barrels marked "Explosive: No Smoking."

The east wall had three large blue barrels, each apparently filled with solvent. Wendy was just about ready to plunk the weapon in the one marked "Warning: High Molar Acid." But since she didn't know what the O'Neals used it for, she was still of two minds.

The north wall, towards the mountain, had a few gun racks and a large, heavy steel door with a numeric keypad in the center and a lever handle. It looked like the door to a safe.

In the center was a large table, with various cleaning supplies under it and six barstools. It was around this that Elgars, Wendy, Cally, Kelly and Shakeela had grouped. Billy had started to come with them and then decided to beat feet.

"What do you mean?" Cally asked.

"Well . . . you're friggin' gorgeous. I'm surprised you don't have fifteen boyfriends hanging around. I did when I was your age and I wasn't nearly as good looking."

Elgars set down the disassembled trigger mechanism and picked up a corroded spring. "What's a boyfriend?"

Cally laughed. "Good question. There aren't any families left in the Gap; they all moved out because of the Posleen being right over the ridge. So there aren't any boys around to have as boyfriends. And . . . well, given who my daddy and granddaddy are, I'm not impressed with the quality of the soldiers. And they're all too old for me. And only interested in one thing."

"Yeah, let me write the book about that one," Wendy said with a laugh. "Fortunately I have a magic charm to use on them. All I do is show them a picture of *my* boyfriend and they tend to leave me alone. And I can deal with the ones that don't."

"Oh, they're not so much trouble these days," Cally said with a shrug. "Not since I shot the 103rd Division sergeant major."

"You're joking," Wendy coughed, trying to suppress a laugh.

"Nope," the thirteen-year-old said with a grin. "That's when I switched from a Walther to the H&K. We were in town and this fat old soldier followed me around until he cornered me in the hardware store. He wouldn't take no for an answer so I pulled out the Walther and put a round through his kneecap. That got his attention.

"They initially tried to charge me as a juvenile with intended murder. Then I got the grand jury to go out to the range with me. They dropped the charges—the foreman noted that if I was attempting murder the sergeant major would be . . . how did he put it? 'pushing up privet hedge'—and charged him with attempted rape instead. I understand he's limping around a prison to this day. Since then, and since Pappy quit letting most people come over to the farm, there haven't been any problems."

"Why'd you switch?" Elgars asked. "Guns I mean."

"Ah, they were holding the Walther as evidence," Cally answered with a shrug. "And my hands had finally gotten big enough for the H&K. Besides, that bitty little 7.62 just made a neat little hole in his knee. If I'd had the H&K it would have blown the back right out of the sucker. I really regretted that when I was in juvie hall; anybody tried to cop a feel on me I want to see bits of bone on the floor. I swore I'd never use a damned little 7.62 to shoot somebody again."

Elgars chuckled and then shook her head as the spring in her hands snapped. "I don't think we can fix this, Wendy."

"I think you're right," Wendy said with a sigh, putting aside the barrel. "This really pisses me off; it was a present from my boyfriend."

"Well, I can't fix your present," Cally said with a shrug, holding the separated grenade breech up to the light and turning it back and forth. "Not quickly anyway. I think I could remachine all the action parts, even the ones for the grenade launcher which are a stone bitch. But the electronics are shot and I'm doubtful about this breech. I could probably make one of those with a few days work, but really, Wendy, I think it needs to be cannibalized for parts rather than used. Whatever you ended up with probably wouldn't be safe *or* reliable.

"However, I *think* we can find a suitable replacement." She walked over to the back wall, keyed in a code on the safe and opened it up. "We have a few choices in here."

"Good God." Wendy laughed, looking at the row on row of racked rifles that were dimly visible in the gloom. The "safe" was really a door to a large room, apparently set back into the hillside. She walked over to the door as Cally stepped through and flipped on the light switch.

"I think we probably can," Wendy continued with another chuckle.

There were four rifle racks in the room with just about enough weapons to equip a rifle platoon. If it was a very eclectic rifle platoon.

The left-hand side was the "heavy" weapons, including at least three crewed machine guns, Barrett sniper rifles and a couple of other heavy rifles that were similar. The center double rack was devoted to rifles, both military style and hunting, while the right-hand rack was mostly submachine guns.

The back wall was pistols—Wendy was pretty sure there were over a hundred—and a large variety of knives.

Stacked on the floor, on both sides, under the racks, and in every corner all the way to the ceiling was case on case of ammunition.

"Good God," Wendy said again. "This is . . ."

"Kind of over the top?" Cally said with a grin. "*I* haven't even shot most of these. I still don't know what some of them are. And you don't even *want* to ask about the ammo. There's stuff in that pile I don't think the Feds realize they let into the country. I'll have to check with Granpa, but most of these," she continued, gesturing at the center and right racks, "are pretty standard weapons. You can pretty much take your pick."

"It would just get fucked up again," Wendy noted darkly. "I'd have to leave it at security on the way in."

"We can drop this one with Dave," Elgars pointed out. "I can carry it to him and he'll hold onto it. That way you can work with it and keep it in shape."

"If you're sure," Wendy said, pulling a bullpup configured rifle from halfway down one rack. "I think you have two of these."

"A Steyr," Cally said. "Good choice. That used to be mine as a matter of fact and I can let you have it on one condition."

"What's that?" Wendy asked.

Cally looked around as if anyone but the girls might hear, then shrugged. "I've got a few . . . girl questions I need answered."

"Ah," Wendy said with a grimace. "Well, men and women are designed to be sexually complementary . . ." she said in a rote voice.

"Not *that* kind of question," Cally said with a laugh. "You only have to listen a couple of times to Papa O'Neal when he's drunk and reminiscing about R&Rs in Bangkok to find out all about that you need to know. No, it's . . . something else."

"What?" Wendy asked doubtfully.

"Well . . ." Cally looked around again as if seeking inspiration from the weapons on the walls. "Well . . . how do you put on eyeshadow?" she asked plaintively.

✦     ✦     ✦

"You're kidding," Shari said with a laugh. She was up to her elbows in corn on the cob and she couldn't have been happier; she couldn't remember the last time she had fresh corn and this was from the O'Neals' garden, a delicate hybrid that positively reeked of sugar.

"No, I'm serious as a heart attack," Papa O'Neal countered as he sliced steaks off a beef portion. "She has *no* female influences at all. No female friends, hell, no friends near her age at all. For all practical purposes it has been me and the occasional screwball I let up here like this shrimp."

"Just because I don't look like a gorilla, he calls me a shrimp," Mosovich said washing the potatoes. Given the suddenly descending hordes, Papa O'Neal fell back on easy and tried foods. But considering the rations that were standard among the combat troops, much less the Sub-Urbs, the meal would be ambrosia.

"He doesn't look like a gorilla," Shari said in an off-hand manner. "So you want me, us, to talk to Cally about 'girl things' while we're here?"

"Well, I don't want to be offensive," Papa O'Neal said. "But . . . the only thing I know about makeup is how to tell when somebody has been KGB trained to apply it. And I got her a book on . . . well . . . the whole feminine hygiene 'thing.' I . . . kind of need somebody to make sure she's doing it right."

"Has she had her first period?" Shari asked calmly. She took a sniff of one of the ears and picked off a worm. There had been several in the corn, but she suspected that was the nature of having it fresh.

"Yes," Papa O'Neal said uncomfortably. "I'd . . . laid in stocks. Fortunately."

"Has she had to go to the doctor for 'female problems'?" Shari asked with a smile.

"No."

"Then she's doing it right," Shari said. "Why don't you have her discuss this with her OB-GYN?"

"Uh, she doesn't have one," O'Neal admitted. "There's not one short of Franklin, and that one has a several month waiting list. And the local general practitioner has talked with her about . . . that sort of thing. But . . ."

"Is it a 'he'?" Shari asked with a grimace.

"Yeah."

"I'll talk to her," she said.

"And she's got some . . . control problems," Papa O'Neal continued carefully.

"She's going through puberty," Shari said with a laugh. "Who doesn't?"

"Would you marry me?" Papa O'Neal said plaintively. "Never mind. I didn't ask that."

"I understand," Shari said with a smile. "This has got to be tough. I think I've got some of the same problems with Billy, but they're not so obvious. Or they're overwhelmed by the other problems."

"That's the . . . little boy?" Mosovich asked. "The one that never says anything?"

"Yes," Shari said, stacking up the cleaned corn. "He's been that way since Fredericksburg. He's listening; he learns. He's not unintelligent and he'll even communicate through sign language, occasionally. But he never, ever, talks." She sighed. "I don't know what to do about it."

"Make him a monk," Papa O'Neal said with a grim chuckle. "There's groups of them that are sworn to a vow of silence. Then he'll be right at home."

"I suppose that is *one* choice," Shari said tartly.

"Sorry," O'Neal said, stacking the beef. "Me and my big mouth. But if you decide to take that route, I know a few of them. They're good people." He frowned and looked at the pile of meat. "How much do you think the little kids will eat? I've got a steak for all the adults, Cally and Billy. You think one steak for all the others?"

"That should work," Shari said. "Where do you get all this food?"

"It's a farm," O'Neal said with a grin. "What, you don't think we give it *all* up, do you? Besides, it's harvest time. We just slaughtered some cows and the pigs were going to be tomorrow. I'll probably harvest one for a pig roast in the morning then roast it all day. That's if you guys are willing to spend another night."

"We'll see," Shari said with a grin. "Ask me in the morning."

# CHAPTER 17

We aren't no thin red 'eroes, nor we aren't no
    blackguards too,
But single men in barricks, most remarkable like you;
An' if sometimes our conduck isn't all your fancy
    paints,
Why, single men in barricks don't grow into plaster
    saints . . .

             —Rudyard Kipling
               "Tommy"

*Newry Cantonment, Newry, PA, United States, Sol III*
*1928 EDT Thursday September 24, 2009* AD

"It's a real cantonment," Gunny Pappas said, staring
out the windows of the converted bus.

Moving ACS had been a problem from the beginning. Packaging their suits and moving them separately
effectively disarmed them; most ACS troopers were
fairly incompetent without a suit wrapped around them.
And moving the suits with people in them was a

horrendous operation; even with their pseudo muscles turned "down," suits tended to destroy normal structures when the two came into contact.

Finally, standard forty-five-passenger school buses had been converted to carry the units. The seats, basically bars of raw steel welded into benches, were intensely uncomfortable for anyone *not* in a suit. But they had the benefit of being able to survive even a *long* bus trip with ACS enlisted infantry onboard.

The sole concession to comfort in the buses was an adjustable headrest. The first thing ACS troopers tended to do once they were out of combat was remove their helmets and that habit had been recognized in the design. It was a well understood action; ACS sometimes spent weeks in continuous contact with the Posleen; after that long in a virtual environment the need to breathe uncanned air and feel wind on their face became overwhelming.

Stewart picked his head up from the rest and looked at the approaching gates. "Well, with any luck we won't have to E&E our way across this one."

"Long time," Pappas answered with a sigh. The sergeant major had brought a platoon of new recruits with him to their former base at Fort Indiantown Gap, back when he was Gunnery Sergeant Pappas. At the time the Ground Forces were in a state of only slightly controlled anarchy and the platoon had found it necessary to sneak in and fight their way across the base to their barracks. Once there they found the acting first sergeant engaged in black-marketeering and, possibly, murder. With the help of the acting company commander they had settled that idiot's hash and managed to maintain a semblance of order in their company until O'Neal and the new battalion commander arrived almost simultaneously.

"Roanoke?" Pappas asked.

"Harrisburg," Stewart corrected. "I was the second platoon leader."

"Harrisburg," Pappas agreed after a moment. He remembered the shattered armor of Lieutenant Arnold well, but while his recollection of battles was often too clear, inessential details like *where* they occurred had started to fall by the wayside. "HVM."

"Yep," Stewart agreed.

"Quit weirding each other out," Duncan said from the next row. He leaned forward and pointed at the barracks and the neatly trimmed parade grounds. "Garrison time. Time to get drunk and laid, not necessarily in that order."

"If everything's ship-shape, sir," Pappas pointed out. "I'll believe it when I see it. I mean, these are *garrison* troopers forwarded from *Ground Forces*. How good are they going to be? There's probably a foot of dirt on the barracks floor."

Mike heard the challenge of the MP at the gate distantly and the response of the driver sounded like it was at the bottom of a well. But he swiveled his vision sideways to watch the exchange.

The MP could not have known he was being watched by the battalion commander; the suit did not move and the helmet remained facing forward. But he was punctiliously correct anyway, checking the driver's orders and receiving a confirmation download from Mike's AID. When he was sure everything was correct he stepped back and saluted, undoubtedly waiting for the vehicle to move on before dropping it.

Mike touched the driver on the arm to keep him from pulling out and inspected the MP's turnout minutely. Most of his gear was clearly designed to look good and stay that way. The holster for his service pistol was patent leather as was his brassard and his battle dress uniform, a pattern still called Mar-Cam, was tailored and pressed.

But he was also well shaven with a fresh haircut and in good physical condition. The fact that they were coming was well known, but up until today Mike had not been sure of their ETA. So the soldier had either cleaned up quickly or maintained good grooming even when "the cat was away." On reflection Mike decided that it was probably the latter. After a moment, during which it must have been like looking at a statue, he returned the salute and waved for his Humvee to move on.

The MP must have called ahead because by the time the convoy reached the battalion area there was a small group of officers and NCOs gathered on the front lawn.

Mike clambered carefully out of the seat and walked over to the group, casually returning the salute of the slightly overweight captain who appeared to be in charge.

"Major O'Neal," the captain said with a nod. "I'm Captain Gray, your adjutant; we've never met, but we have exchanged e-mails."

"Captain," O'Neal said, taking off his helmet and looking around. Besides the captain there was a single second lieutenant. Other than that there were no officers. And the few senior NCOs did not seem to have been rejuved. However, the personnel were in good looking uniforms, Mar-Cam again rather than silks since they were only seconded to Fleet, and the junior personnel were in good physical condition. All in all, it was a decent looking body of REMFs. "Do I have a part in this little ceremony?"

"Not a ceremony, sir," the captain said. "But I thought you might want to get familiar with a few of the faces." He gestured at a sergeant first class in the

first rank. "Sergeant McConnell is the battalion S-4
NCOIC. He's actually the *regimental* S-4 NCOIC . . ."

"But since there's not a regiment to be NCOIC
of . . ." Mike continued. "Good afternoon, Sergeant. And
do you have a boss?"

"I think you're it, sir," the sergeant said. He was
short and also overweight, but he gave the impression
of being an india rubber leprechaun: hard, mischievous
and very elastic. He had bright eyes that regarded
O'Neal warily.

"We don't have an S-4 at the moment, sir," Captain
Gray said. "We've been promised one a time or two
but . . ."

"But there are places that they'd rather be," O'Neal
filled in. He looked at the group and cleared his throat.
"I'm sure we'll get to know each other very well over
the next couple of weeks. For the time being, continue
as you have been. I'd like you to get with the battalion command sergeant major and the company first
sergeants as to billeting. The troops will need to do an
issue draw," he continued, looking at the S-4 sergeant.
"We're basically here in the suits we stand in and not
much else."

"I took the liberty of looking up everyone's sizes, sir,"
Sergeant McConnell answered. "And everyone is
assigned a room and a wall-locker. The wall-lockers all
have a complete issue in them. They'll have to *sign* for
them of course . . ."

"We have a team on standby to examine deficien-
cies," Captain Gray said, anticipating O'Neal's question.
"I hope that your commanders find the barracks to be
acceptable; I had a full unit GI of the Bravo and
Charlie barracks last week and the inspection showed
that they were in pretty good shape. They're brand new
so there's some indications of that that we haven't been
able to work out; paint around the edge of the windows

and stuff like that. But otherwise I think you'll be pleased."

"Hmm," Mike said, not knowing quite how to respond. "Very well, get with the sergeant major, as I said." He paused and thought for a moment. "Do *officers* have an issue?"

"Officers have to buy their uniforms, of course," Sergeant McConnell said. "But there is a temporary issue in their quarters and they can choose what they want and buy it with a comment to their AID. We also have uniforms standing by in your lockers in the Morgue."

Mike looked around again and shook his head with a frown. "*Tell* me that this isn't as rikky-tik as it seems. I mean . . ."

"You mean 'what the hell are REMFs doing getting something right,' sir?" Sergeant McConnell asked with a puckish grin.

"I probably would have put it more politely," O'Neal noted as Pappas walked up behind him.

"I've been a REMF ever since I got out of Delta Force, sir," the sergeant answered. "Where I was a . . . not a REMF. I got recalled as my final MOS, which was supply. I decided that, all things considered, I'd stay there. I *had* my salad days. But, if I do say so myself, I'm a pretty damned good supply sergeant."

"Everything okay, sir?" Pappas rumbled.

"The only thing wrong seems to be that there's nothing wrong, Top," O'Neal said with a shake of his head.

"We've had plenty of time to prepare, sir," Captain Gray pointed out.

"And you have done so," O'Neal agreed. "Which is all too rare."

"There are also some combat replacements, sir," Captain Gray said. "They're in barracks and have been issued their basic equipment. They've been fitted and the lieutenant that is in charge has been having them work their suits in."

"What did we get, sir?" Gunny Pappas asked, taking off his helmet.

Gray's eyes fixed on the line of what looked like semi-intelligent water, or maybe a silver slug, that gathered on the side of the NCO's head and then humped itself down the armor and into the helmet. "Ahhh . . . we received four NCOs and an officer from the Ten Thousand and a group of privates from other Ground Force units. All of them have had some combat experience."

"Sounds good," Mike said. "Sergeant Major, these gentlemen have the billeting mapped out. Why don't you get with them and get the troops moved through in . . ." He paused and looked around. "Where are the Morgues?" he asked.

"In the basement of the barracks, sir," Captain Gray said, pointing at overlarge side entrances.

"Cool," O'Neal responded. "Company commanders and staff to battalion headquarters as soon as they're in silks. Troops fall into the barracks and get their issue squared away." He glanced at the sun and shook his head as he sneezed. "Damn. Shelly, what time is it?"

"Just past fourteen hundred, sir," the AID replied out of the helmet.

"Seventeen hundred formation for all companies," Mike continued. "I want everybody in silks and standing tall by then. The companies can release the troops to the cantonment area at that time, if they so choose, but they cannot release them off post."

"Clear," Pappas said. "You know that if we wait too long it'll just build up the pressure."

"I know," Mike said with a slight smile. "I used to *be* a grunt back when, smaj. Friday night. Payday procedures. By then I'll have had a chance to meet with the locals and get them marginally prepared. *Then* they can tear down the gates."

"Man," Mueller said, leaning back from the table. "If the troops in the corps knew you ate like this they'd be tearing down the gates."

"They could try," Cally said with a laugh. "I think we could probably turn 'em around with the first line of claymores though."

Papa O'Neal looked at Shari's half finished steak and frowned. "Are you okay?"

"I'm fine," Shari said with a wan smile. "It's just that this is as much meat as I can remember eating in a month."

"Well, you ought to come around more often," O'Neal said with a smile, poking her in the arm. "You're as thin as a board. We need to get you fed up."

"I know," Wendy said, scraping up the last of her baked potato. "In the Urb we both eat about the same amount and I have a problem keeping my weight *down*. Shari *never* gains weight."

"Oh, I used to have to diet," Shari said, wiping her mouth and setting the napkin down alongside the half full plate. "But the food in the Urb isn't . . ."

"Much good at putting on weight," Elgars finished, wiping up steak juices. "It's also lousy for putting on muscle; the protein portions aren't large enough. I have a hell of a time with it; I always feel like I'm being starved to death."

"It's one of the reasons I stopped exercising," Shari said, pulling a sated Kelly onto her lap. The two youngest were already in bed and most of the rest were outside in the dark, having borrowed warm clothes from the O'Neals. The kids were revelling in the freedom to just run and play; that was all too rare in the

Urb. "I'd just get exhausted. Between the lousy food and taking care of the kids. And there was nowhere to send them where they were safe like here; so they were always *right there.*" She hugged Kelly and rubbed her cheek on the sleepy girl's head. "Not that I minded, sweetie. But it's nice to have a break."

"Well, you're not getting any lousy food here," Papa O'Neal said definitely. "And you can definitely take a break. I want you to stay over tomorrow night. And we'll *really* have a feed then."

"Oh, I don't know," Shari said rocking back in the chair. "There's so much to do . . ."

"There's nothing critical," Wendy said. "We *are* the creche. We don't really ever *have* to go back."

"Not true," Shari said. "The children are in our care, but we don't have custody. That would be kidnapping."

"Okay," Wendy said, admitting the point. "But we don't have to go back in the morning. We can stay over."

"And what about the sergeant major?" Shari asked. "He has to get back, right?"

"Nope," Mosovich said. "If anybody wants us, they can page us; I can get to corps headquarters as fast from here as from my barracks. We're on duty anyway; the orders that I got cut say so. And both the food and the scenery are better here," he finished, winking at Wendy.

"So there," Wendy said, sticking out her tongue. "And I think that Annie's doing better here than in the Urb."

"I do too," Elgars said. "I don't know if it's the air or the food or what. But this is the first time I've really felt . . . alive. Whole."

"Well, if we're not an imposition," Shari said one last time.

"If you were an imposition, I wouldn't have insisted,"

Papa O'Neal said with a grin. "I'm looking forward to feeding you up," he continued, poking at her ribs. "You're too skinny. Skinny, skinny, skinny."

"That, frankly, sounds heavenly," Shari said with an almost giggle, slapping at his hand until he desisted. She ended up holding his fingers and released them. But not too quickly.

"It is nice," Wendy said with a smile as she leaned back and stretched. "But it has been tiring. I think we should all go to bed . . ."

Mueller suddenly coughed hard. "Oh, sorry," he gasped, quickly looking away.

Wendy stopped in mid stretch and regarded him out of lowered eyelids. " . . . And I was going to say, 'and get some rest for tomorrow.' Master Sergeant Mueller, have I ever shown you a picture of my boyfriend?"


"Oh, my," Captain Slight muttered. "I think he *must* have been the biggest one in his class."

First Sergeant Bogdanovich suppressed a snort. Bogdanovich, Boggle to a very select few veterans of the battalion, was a short, muscular blonde whose fine skin was as translucent as paper from years in suits. She had been in the battalion since before its first blooding and she *thought* she had seen it all. But Boggle had to admit that the first lieutenant reporting to the company commander *was* rather oversized. He actually seemed to have trouble making it through the door straight. She hoped there was a suit that was fittable to him. On the other hand, he looked like he could survive an HVM round to the chest *without* one.

"Sar . . . Lieutenant Thomas Sunday, Junior, reporting to the commanding officer," Sunday said, rendering a hand salute.

Sunday wondered at the timing of this meeting; the majority of the company had been released and he could hear the racket of their settling in throughout the barracks. But the officers and NCOs were apparently still going strong. He'd noted that was usually the case in the Ten Thousand, unlike his first Ground Forces unit, and he wasn't sure what it meant.

"At ease, Lieutenant," Slight said. "This is First Sergeant Bogdanovich. Later she'll be introducing you to your platoon sergeant." Slight paused and went on delicately. "It seems that you might have recently been promoted . . ."

"Yes, ma'am," Sunday admitted. "I was promoted to first lieutenant about five minutes before I left the Ten Thousand."

Slight smiled as the first sergeant chuckled. "Well, you have to admire Cutprice's chutzpah. What were you before you were so abruptly promoted? A two L-T?"

"No ma'am," Sunday said with a frown. "I was a staff sergeant."

"Hmm," Slight muttered with a frown. "I'll have to think about that one. I think the message we were supposed to get was that he thinks you'd make a good ACS platoon leader. What do you think of that?"

"With all due respect, I don't particularly like it, ma'am," Sunday admitted. "Lieutenants don't get to kill Posleen. I wanted suits to kill horses, not to pull George and 'determine zones of fire.' And . . . there are some benefits to being a Fleet sergeant or a Ground Forces staff that you . . . don't have as a lieutenant. *Besides* getting to kill horses."

"I tell you what, Lieutenant," the captain said with another slight smile. "Let's slot you in at platoon leader for the time being. And if we decide it's not right for you, we'll break you back to sergeant with no hard feelings; Fleet Strike moves people around like that all the time with no real effect on their record. How does that suit?"

"Whatever you say, ma'am," Sunday rumbled.

"Have you met the battalion commander?" she asked. "He wants to meet any officers we receive."

"No, ma'am. I was told to report to the company commander first."

"Okay," she said. "AID?"

"Major O'Neal is in his office reviewing the training schedule," the AID said promptly. It had a deep male baritone unlike most of those Sunday had heard, which seemed to be all female. "His AID says he'd be happy for the interruption."

Mike nodded at Sunday and returned his salute. "Chill, Lieutenant," he said as a grin violated his habitual frown. "Sit, even."

The office was small, smaller than the company commander's and like hers almost completely unadorned. Behind the major a private from the rear detachment was up on a step stool painting in a motto on the wall. So far he had gotten to "He who" in thick black, Gothic lettering.

The major leaned back and picked up the cigar that had been smoldering in his ashtray. "You smoke, Lieutenant?"

Sunday paused for a moment then shook his head. "No, sir." He remained sitting rigidly at attention.

"Well, if you've been with the Ten Thousand for the last few years there's no point in trying to corrupt you," O'Neal said with another grin. "I got an e-mail about you from Cutprice. He explained that if I try to take any of your rank, he will personally . . . what was the phrase? 'Boil me in my own suit like an undersized lobster.'" The major puffed a few times on the cigar to get it started again and peered at the lieutenant through the smoke. "What do you think of that?"

"Uh, sir . . ." Sunday said, frozen. "I . . . uh . . . I

wouldn't presume to comment on your interaction with Colonel Cutprice or on your decisions in regards to my position in the battalion."

"Sunday . . . Sunday . . . ?" Mike mused. "I swear I recognize that name . . ."

"We . . . have met briefly a time or two, sir," the lieutenant said. "The last time was at . . ."

"Rochester," Mike completed. "That one I remember; your physique is . . . distinctive."

"So is yours, sir," Sunday said then froze. "Sorry."

"No problem," Mike said with another grin, flexing one arm. His forearms were still the size of most people's thighs. "I take it you work out?"

"Yes, sir," Tommy answered. "At least two hours per day, duties permitting."

"Yeah," O'Neal said with a nod. "You'll be glad to hear that the suits permit weight exercise while in them. Otherwise there is *no* way I could maintain this. But I wasn't thinking of Rochester or even, I think, other battles . . . Shelly: Thomas Sunday, Junior, encounters and relationships, not while he was a member of the Ten Thousand."

"Thomas Sunday, Junior, is one of five combat survivors of the Fredericksburg defense . . ." the AID started to answer.

"That's it!" O'Neal said excitedly. "The kid wrapped up with the blonde! Even then I knew that anybody that could survive that *and* wind up with the girl was going to go far."

"Thank you, sir," Sunday said with the first smile since he'd entered the room.

"Thomas Sunday, Junior, is also the developer of 'Bridge over the River Die,'" Shelly continued doggedly. "That is all known connections."

"Hell, that was you?" Mike said. "That's a great module! We used it in Washington in the first landing.

I remember being told that it was written by some-body from F'Burg but . . . well . . ."

"You figured they were dead?" Sunday said. "That was a good guess, sir," he continued with a grimace. After a moment he shook his head. "You actually used it off the shelf?"

"Even the smoke," Mike said. "Everybody thought I was some tactical genius. Thanks."

Sunday laughed. "You're welcome. If it makes you feel any better—" He paused and shrugged. "Well, I ripped some of *your* code from the Asheville Sce-nario."

"I know," O'Neal said with another grin, taking a pull on the stogie. "I reversed it and read the code; you even left in my trademark."

"Well . . ."

"S'alright, it's still a good module. So, what happened to the girl?"

"Wendy?" Tommy shook his head at the change of direction. "She's in a Sub-Urb in North Carolina. We . . . keep in touch. Actually . . . we keep in touch."

"Uh, huh," the major said. "In one of the ones around Asheville?"

"Uh, no, sir, Franklin. It's a little town . . ."

"By Rabun Gap," Mike finished with a frown. "I'm from there. My dad and daughter are still in the area. I doubt they'll meet up, though; people who go into Urbs rarely come out."

"Well . . . sir, I was wondering something," Tommy said carefully.

"Spit it out," Mike said with another pull on the cigar.

"Well, it's like this. Ground Force does not recog-nize dependents for anyone under E-6. I'd just made staff when Rochester came up. But if I'd stayed in Ground Force, we could have . . ."

"Gotten married," Mike said with a frown. "You ever hear the thing 'lieutenants shouldn't marry'?"

"Yes, sir," Sunday answered quietly.

"Shit," the major said with a shake of the head. "Fleet's started to get some very 'old fashioned' types in its upper echelons; and some of them are getting downright nasty on the dependents issue. I'm not sure if it will fly for a lieutenant. The fickle finger of fate, eh?"

"Yes, sir," the lieutenant answered. "I still wanted to transfer, sir, I'm still glad I'm here, however that affects Wendy and I. I . . . killing Posleen is what I do."

"That's a bit of an understatement and an underestimation, son," O'Neal answered. "I've seen your code. It's good; you even know what to rip off and what not to. Killing Posleen isn't all of what *anyone* should do."

"Well, sir, with all due respect I don't *have* much more," the lieutenant said. "My mom is in an Urb in Kentucky; she and my sister were in the Bunker. But, really, we hardly keep in touch. With the exception of Wendy, everything I ever knew is gone. And it seems like to make a real life, I have to kill all the Posleen I can. Until they're gone, we can't begin to get back to normalcy. So . . . I kill Posleen."

"Well, this conversation has taken a turn for the morbid," Mike said with a shake of his head. He pulled on the cigar for a moment looking at the lieutenant in the blue haze then shrugged. "You're not the only one with a story, L-T. Yours is well known, but it's not the only one. Gunny Pappas lost a daughter to the Posleen in the Chicago drop. Duncan's family farm is nearly five hundred miles behind the lines. Captain Slight's lost her mother and brother to the war; both of them were civilians.

"If all that any of us do is kill Posleen, they've won.

When this war is over, we're going to have to go back to being humans again. If the only thing we know how to do is kill Posleen, if we've forgotten how to be human, to be Americans not to put too fine a point on it, we might as well not even fight it. You can feel free to hate the Posleen as long as that doesn't eat you up as a person. Because at the end of the day what we're fighting for is the right to wrap ourselves around a blonde in *peace*."

"Understood, sir," the lieutenant said. But Mike recognized the closed expression; the lieutenant understood the argument, but wasn't willing to admit its validity. "I've got a question, if I may, sir."

"Shoot."

"Do *you* hate the Posleen?" Sunday asked warily.

"Nope," Mike answered instantly. "Not a damned bit. They're pretty obviously programmed to be what they are. I don't know who programmed them—I'm pretty sure in other words that the tin-foil hat types are wrong and it wasn't the Darhel—but if we ever meet them, I'll damned well hate *their* asses. I don't know what the Posleen were like before they got tinkered with, but I doubt they were interstellar conquistadores. The Posleen can't help being who they are and we can't help resisting them. Not much room for hate in that situation. But if it helps you to hate them, go right ahead.

"Look, let's change the subject for a bit. It's after seventeen hundred and none of this crap is really vital. Let's go find the officers' mess together and talk games design. I'll think about the marriage thing and try to find an out. In the meantime I hear Mongolian Barbecue and some really lousy beer calling to me."

"Hell, sir, it's practically free," Sunday pointed out. "And free beer is, by definition, good beer."

"Boy," the major said with a shake of his head. "You

even drink love-in-a-canoe beer. You're going to fit right in."

On the back wall the battalion sign painter shook his head and carefully cleaned up the last part where his stifled laugh had caused his hand to slip. Then he continued with painting the new battalion motto on the commander's wall.

But he had to wonder. Most mottos made sense. "Fury From the Sky," "The Rock of the Marne," "Devils in Baggy Pants" and, of course, *"Semper Fidelis."*

But somehow he was having a hard time getting his head around: "He Who Laughs Last, Thinks Fastest."

# CHAPTER 18

*Rabun Gap, GA, United States, Sol III*
*0925 EDT Friday September 25, 2009* AD

Shari awoke with a start and rolled over to look out the window of the small bedroom. The sun was already high and the bedside clock, which she had set and wound up last night, showed that it was nearly 9 A.M., an unheard-of time for her to still be sleeping.

She looked over where Amber had been in her crib and felt a stab of fear when she noticed she was gone. But then, faintly through the house, she heard her squealing in glee at something and the sounds of children playing outside. Apparently someone had crept into her room and slipped out with the baby while she slept.

She stretched and ran her fingers through the tangle of her hair. She'd only been awakened once in the night, to give Amber a change and a bottle, and that was another miracle. All in all she felt as well rested and comfortable as she had felt in . . . about five years come to think of it. Maybe longer.

Everyone referred to the destruction of Fredericksburg in hushed tones, but her life had come apart well before then. Marrying one of the football team was considered a coup in high school, but twelve years, repeated battered women's referrals, three kids and a divorce later and it didn't look like such a good idea. Having the Posleen land and destroy the town had just seemed like a natural progression.

Now she found herself thirty . . . something, with three kids, a GED, wrinkles to shame a forty-year-old and—she took off the night dress she had found in the closet and looked down—a skinny body with . . . okay still fairly decent breasts, and stretch marks. She also lived in a cubicle with eight children. A catch she was not.

She shook her head and looked out the window; it looked like a beautiful day, she'd gotten a chance to sleep in and there was no reason for her to be falling into this melancholy mood. With a deep breath she picked up her neatly stacked clothes off the bedside table and then wrinkled her nose. It had been a long and active time the day before and they were still slightly damp with sweat. Shari was a fastidious woman and wandering around smelling like a bag lady was not her idea of a good time. After a moment's thought she looked at the chest of drawers and the closet. After her shower last night she'd peeked in the closet hoping to find something to wear to bed and had glimpsed a large number of plastic wrapped dresses. Now she opened up the top drawer of the chest of drawers and shook her head; the room was packed with clothes.

She pulled out a pair of bikini briefs and sniffed them. They were musty with long storage, with a faint hint of a spice that had probably been in the drawer as a preservative, and slightly . . . fragile in feel, as if they were quite old. They still smelled better than what she had been wearing . . . and they fit. They were on the large side, but they were close enough; the elastic had apparently survived storage.

Rummaging further she found bras and, in lower drawers, blouses, T-shirts and jeans. Whoever's clothing this was had been addicted to jeans; there were at least seven pairs, most of them hip-hugger bellbottoms.

Shari pulled one out and shook her head; there was no question that these were "originals" and not from the brief pre-Posleen renaissance. Not only did they have that same old, fragile feel as the panties, that she now realized must have been at least thirty years old, but someone had taken a pen to them in some bygone fit of insanity and covered them in graffiti. Kids of the turn years had rarely known who "Bobby McGee" was, although the peace sign and the "I got laid at Woodstock" would be recognizable. The strangest, scrawled on the seat in a different hand, was "Peace through superior firepower."

She shook her head and carefully put away this artifact then chose a simple pair of straight-leg jeans that were barely worn.

Bras turned out to be a problem. Shari had often felt that her only two saving graces were planted on her chest; indeed, her endowments were often the only thing that Rorie could not find to fault in her. However, whoever's clothing stocked this chest of drawers did not, apparently, have that particular grace/curse. After much searching she managed to find one that wasn't actively painful to wear. After managing to get it snapped, she looked at herself in the mirror and snorted.

"That's the answer, girls. Find a bra that is both undercut and a size too small and *you too* can have cleavage."

She initially pulled out a very pretty flowered blouse then looked at the neckline. Looking down she shook her head and pulled out a T-shirt emblazoned with "Led Zeppelin World Tour, 1972." It was a tad tight, but at least it didn't plunge and if, when, she fell out of the bra she wouldn't be into public view.

Digging around in the bathroom exhumed a brush, old, but serviceable, and a toothbrush, new, still in the box. She used both to good effect then looked in the mirror and stuck her tongue out at the reflection.

"I don't think so, girlfriend," she said to the sag-face wreck in the mirror.

The first set of makeup that she found had obviously been stored for decades. If anybody was still collecting memorabilia, this house was a gold mine; there was even an unopened box of L'Oréal hair coloring with the faded picture of an actress who hadn't looked that good in thirty years.

"Thanks," she muttered. "I know I'm worth it, but I just did them last week."

The makeup case was a loss, though. Oh, there was plenty in it, whoever had owned it must have occasionally made herself up like a kewpie doll, but it was all dried up. The foundation broke away into chunks when she opened the jar.

Next to the case though, hidden by it until she pulled it out, was a small, plastic container. It looked like Galplas, but Shari thought that was unlikely; where would a Galplas zipper bag have come from? However, on the top of the bag was a small green dot and when Shari touched it and slid her finger along the top the bag opened along an invisible seam. Galplas all right.

Inside was what Shari mentally decided were someone's "bare essentials." There was a tube of mascara, a light lip gloss, a single eyeshadow case with an eyebrow pencil and a pair of eyebrow tweezers. The colors were not perfect for her—if she wasn't careful she'd end up looking like Britney Spears—and she *really* wished there was a base and some rouge, but they would do. And this was practically brand new.

She quickly applied the makeup, sparse as it was, and then stepped back to consider the overall effect.

"Baby, you look like a million dollars," she said. Then: "Liar."

She made the bed then followed the smell of bacon downstairs to the kitchen. Kelly and Irene were at the table nibbling on biscuits, Amber stuck in a high chair just to the side, and Mr. O'Neal was at the stove, frying another pan of bacon and cracking eggs.

When she came through the door he did a double-take and missed the bowl, the hand with the uncracked egg in it flailing in the air for a moment before he looked down and lined back up.

Shari tried not to smile and walked over to the stove, sniffing at the food. "That smells heavenly."

"How would you like your eggs, milady?" Papa O'Neal said. "I'm scrambling some more for the bottomless pits over there, but I'll be happy to fix some any way you please."

"Scrambled is fine," Shari said, trying not to smile again as she caught a surreptitious peek in her direction. She shook herself internally. *Don't you dare arch. Don't do it or you'll never forgive yourself.* Despite the internal debate she felt a stretch coming on and stretched and, yes, she couldn't help herself, arched.

A piece of bacon hit the stove top as Papa O'Neal missed the frying pan.

"Damn," he muttered. "Clumsy . . ." He picked the bacon up with his fingers and juggled it to the cloth covered plate. "Would you like bacon or a . . . would you prefer some sausage?"

"Bacon is fine," Shari replied, walking over to the

table to give the poor guy some space. As she did she realized that she was putting some extra sway in the walk and wanted to hit herself on the side of the head.

*He's . . . well, he's got to be at least sixty and what in the hell is he going to see in you, but a has-been divorcee refugee with kids and stretchmarks?*

"I . . . uh, I see you found something to wear," O'Neal said, filling up the children's plates and carrying them over to the table. "I thought some of Angie's stuff might fit you. I meant to tell you to take your pick last night. Actually, I was talking to Elgars about the supply situation in the Urb; I had no idea. The house is packed with stuff; you should take anything you see that you want. I'm . . . surprised you found a bra that fit, though."

"I appreciate the offer on the clothes," Shari said. "It feels like charity but, what the hell, I'm willing to take a little charity. There really *isn't* anything available in the Urb." She smiled and stretched again. "I will admit that I'm unlikely to find some stuff, though."

Papa O'Neal coughed and went back over to the stove while Shari looked around for something neutral to comment on.

"Where are the rest of the kids?" she asked. Irene got down and climbed up on her lap, bringing the plate with her. She then went back to the serious business of stuffing biscuit and bacon in her mouth.

"Some of them are still asleep," Papa O'Neal said. "The rest are out with Cally doing chores. They *like* them. She took them egging this morning and then they got to *eat* them. Billy even helped milk the cows and that's really above and beyond the call of duty."

"Kids always like doing chores," Shari said with a chuckle. "Once. And as long as it's not too hard."

"Well, it's kept them outside and running around,"

O'Neal said. "And out of your hair; I could tell you needed a break."

"I like my kids," Shari protested. "Even the ones that aren't mine."

"Sure, and I like 'em too," O'Neal replied. He picked up a cooled-off piece of bacon and put it on the baby's tray. "But having to be on them all the time is too much for anyone, even Super Mom."

Shari frowned and cleared her throat. "Uh . . . should you be giving Amber bacon?"

Papa O'Neal frowned in turn and shrugged. "I don't see why not. I got given it as a baby and so did my son from what I hear. And that's the third piece she's gummed to death so far this morning. What do you *think* I should give her?"

Shari paused and watched as Amber picked up the slightly undercooked bacon and began gumming on it. "I . . . well, if you're sure it's okay," she said doubtfully. "We usually serve her cream of wheat. . . ."

"Semolina," Papa O'Neal said. "Got that. Fresh off the farm. Got two different varieties as a matter of fact."

"Or creamed corn?" Shari continued.

"Got that too," Papa O'Neal said. "But how about some nice cornmeal mush? That's good baby food. With some bacon ground up in it for flavor and texture."

"Do you always eat like that?" Shari asked. "I'm surprised your arteries don't clang closed with a boom."

"Got the lowest cholesterol my doctor's ever seen," Papa O'Neal said with a shrug. "It's all the cold baths and healthy thoughts."

"Uh huh," Shari said, picking up a slice of bacon that Kelly had overlooked. "One question and I hope I'm not prying. Who is 'Angie'?"

Papa O'Neal grimaced and shrugged. "Angie's where Cally got at least half her looks; she's my ex. She lives on a commune in Oregon and has ever since she was in her forties and discovered a true calling for . . . well, for Wicca."

He shrugged and put the eggs, bacon and a biscuit on her plate and brought it over to her.

"We never *were* real compatible. She was the communal nature-lover artist type and me, well," he shrugged. "The best you could say about me is that I never killed anybody that didn't deserve it. She never *liked* what I did, but she put up with it, and me. Part of that was that I was gone a lot and she sort of got to be her own person. She lived here, raised Mike Junior here for that matter. Pappy was still alive back then, but he practically lived up in the hills so she ran the farm her way.

"Anyway when I came back for good, we got along for a while then we commenced to fighting. Finally she discovered her 'true calling' to be a priestess and left for that commune and I understand she's been happily living there ever since."

"The 'Woodstock/Peace through superior firepower' graffiti," Shari said with a smile.

"Ah, you saw that," O'Neal said, laughing. "Yep. That was us all over. She got *massively* pissed at me for scrawling that on her butt. My point was that she shouldn't have gotten so stoned she *let* me. I *told* her what I was doing and she thought it was a cool enough idea that . . . well . . . she thought it was a good idea at the time."

"So no grandmother to help out," Shari sighed. "And somebody has to have a girl talk with Cally."

"Assuming you can find her," Papa O'Neal said. "I haven't seen her all morning. I've *heard* her; she's using her drill-sergeant voice on your kids. But I haven't *seen* her at all. We're usually up around dawn, but she was up even earlier and out the door before I got up."

"I thought you were getting up and slaughtering the fatted pig this morning," Shari said with a smile. The eggs and bacon had been wonderful and she had more of an appetite than yesterday.

"I did," O'Neal said, grinning. "And it's on the barbeque, slow roasting even as we speak. And Cally *normally* would have been right there with me. But not this morning; she hasn't gotten within fifty yards of me this morning."

He paused and rubbed his chin then looked at the ceiling in puzzlement.

"She hasn't been within fifty yards of me all morning," he repeated thoughtfully.

"I wonder what she's done wrong," Shari said with a grin.

"You have to tell him," Shannon said. "You can't go on hiding all the rest of your life."

"I can too," Cally answered. She forked another load of hay over into the stall with more vehemence than it actually needed. "I can hide as long as I have to, put it that way."

The barn was huge and quite old. The original structure dated to just after the War of Northern Aggression, as Papa O'Neal called it. There were several horse stalls, an area for milking and a large hay loft. Along one wall several hay rolls had been stacked. Leaning against them was an odd rifle with a large, flat drum on top of it. Cally *never* left the house unarmed.

"It's a natural thing," Shannon argued. The ten-year-old slipped off the hay round and picked up a chunk of clay on the floor of the barn. She waited just a moment until the mouse stuck its head out of the hole again and pitched the clay at it. The chunk shattered on the wall above the hole and the mouse disappeared. "You have a right to live your own life!"

"Sure, tell that to Granpa," Cally said with a pout.

"Tell *what* to Granpa?"

Cally froze and stuck the pitchfork into the hay without turning around. "Nothing."

"Shari and I were just wondering where you'd been all morning," Papa O'Neal said from behind her. "I notice you've got all your chores done. But you somehow managed to get them all done without coming within a mile of me."

"Uh, huh." Cally looked around, but short of actively fleeing by climbing up into the hay loft and then, all things being equal, probably having to climb out the side of the barn through a window, there was no way to escape. And sooner or later she'd have to turn around. She knew she was caught fair and square. She thought briefly of either turning around and shooting her way out or, alternatively, jumping out the window and going to Oregon to live with Granma. But she doubted she could get the drop on the old man. And as for living with Granma, the commune depended on the local military for protection; they'd take her guns away. Blow that.

Shannon, the fink, had actually made an escape. Bolted. What a jerk.

Finally she sighed and turned around.

Papa O'Neal took one look and pulled out his pouch of Red Man. He extracted about half the pouch, laboriously worked it into a ball just a bit under the size of a baseball and then stuffed it into his left cheek. Then he put the pouch away. The whole time he had been looking at Cally's face.

"Granddaughter," he said, his voice slightly muffled, "what happened to your eyes?"

"Don't you start, Granpa," Cally said dangerously.

"I mean, you look like a raccoon . . ."

"I think she was going for the Britney Spears look," Shari said delicately. "But . . . that density doesn't really . . . suit you, dear."

"I mean, if you go into town, they're gonna arrest me for beating you," Papa O'Neal continued. "I mean, your eyes are all black and blue!"

"Just because you know NOTHING about fashion . . . !" Cally said.

"Oh, *fashion* is it . . . ?"

"Uh, whoa, whoa!" Shari said, holding up her hands. "Let's all calm down here. I suspect that everyone in this barn, except me, but probably *including* the horse, is armed."

Papa O'Neal started to say something and she laid her hand over his mouth.

"You wanted me, us, to talk to Cally about 'girl stuff.' Right?"

"Yes," O'Neal said, pulling the hand away. "But I was talking about . . . hygiene and . . ."

"How to make guys complete doofuses?" Cally asked. "I already *know* those things."

Shari slapped her hand over his mouth again and he pulled it back.

"Look, I'm her grandfather!" he argued. "Don't I get to say *anything*?"

"No," Shari answered. "You don't."

"Arrrr!" O'Neal said, throwing up his arms. "This is what I *hate* about having women around. Okay! Okay! Fine. I'm wrong! Just one thing." He pointed at Cally and shook his finger. "Makeup. Okay. I can handle makeup. Makeup is even good. But *no raccoon eyes*!"

"Okay," Shari said gently, turning him towards the barn door. "Why don't you go check on the pig and Cally and I will have a little talk."

"Fine, fine," he muttered. "Go ahead. Clue her in

on how to make a guy insanely angry without even opening her mouth. Put her through girl academy . . . Fine . . ." He continued to mutter as he stalked out of the barn.

Cally looked at Shari and smiled happily. "You seem to be getting along."

"Yes, we are," Shari admitted. "Whereas you don't seem to be getting along with him at all."

"Oh, we're okay," Cally said, sitting on the hay. "I just spent so many years being his perfect little warrior child and now . . . I don't know. I'm tired of the farm, I'll tell you that. And I'm tired of being treated like a child."

"Well, get used to that continuing for a while," Shari said. "Both of those things. Unless something very unpleasant happens. Because you're only thirteen and that means you're going to be in parental control for five more years. And, yeah, they'll wear. And, yeah, you'll want to find any way out from time to time. And if you want a really stupid one you can find some cute jackass with a hot car and a nice butt and have a passel of kids and find yourself out in the cold at thirty with mouths to feed."

Cally pulled at a strand of hair and examined it minutely. "Wasn't *exactly* where I was going with that."

"That's what you say now," Shari nodded. "And in about two years you'll be in town talking to one of those nice young soldiers with the wide shoulders. Trust me. You *will*. You won't be able to help yourself. And I have to admit that if you're doing that with, as your grandfather so delicately put it, 'raccoon eyes,' your chances of ending up holding somebody like Amber a year later is really high."

Cally sighed and shook her head. "I was talking with Wendy and Elgars last night and we didn't have any makeup, but Wendy was telling me a few things. So I got up real early this morning and . . ."

"Tried it," Shari said. "Totally normal. Not a bit of problem. Want to go inside and try it again? This time with some help?"

"Oh, could we?" Cally asked. "I *know* I look goofy. I just don't know how to fix it. And I love what you did with whatever you used!"

"Well," Shari said with a grimace. "I prefer a bit more than this; I no longer have your perfect skin. But that was all I had to work with. It was in a pouch under the sink. It looked like Galplas . . ." She stopped at the look on Cally's face. "What?"

"That's . . ." Cally shook her head, obviously having a little trouble speaking. "That was my mom's. They . . . sent it back from Heinlein Station, from her quarters. It's . . . about all there was in the way of personal effects; everything else went up with the ship."

"Oh, Cally, I'm so sorry," Shari said, her hands going to her face.

"It's okay, really," Cally replied. "You can use it. It's just . . . junk."

"It's not junk," Shari said, walking over to her. "Are you okay? I'm sorry I used it."

"It's okay, really," Cally said with a set face. "I'm glad you did. I really am. I . . . I just wish mom . . . Ah!" She grabbed her hair. "There are four billion dead in the last few years! I will *not* blubber because my mother was one of them! I. Won't."

Shari sat down next to the girl and carefully put her arms around her. "You can mourn your mother any way you choose, Cally. Strength and even denial are forms of mourning; trust me, I know. But don't . . . blot her out. Don't . . . leave her behind." She rubbed at the teen's eyes and rocked her for a moment.

"Let's go get that stuff off of you and then pull out

your mom's bag of essentials and see what works. I think that would be a good start. In more ways than one."

Papa O'Neal looked up as Mosovich and Mueller rounded the corner.

"Isn't it a little early to be hitting the booze?" Mosovich chuckled.

Papa O'Neal held up the bottle of homebrewed beer and peered through it. "I'm raising jailbait in a valley full of horny soldiers; it is *never* too early to start drinking."

"Well, they're going to have a hard time getting in here," Mueller admitted. "We were wandering around checking out the defenses; I've seen firebases with worse killzones than these."

Elgars wandered up behind the two soldiers then walked over to the barbeque. She looked at the pig, which had been butterflied onto a large grill and was slowly grilling over hickory.

"This is a pig, right?" she asked with a sniff. "Like you have in the cells."

"Pens," Papa O'Neal said with a smile. "Yes."

"And we're going to eat it?" she asked. "They are . . . very dirty."

"I cleaned it up before I threw it on the grill," O'Neal answered. "And you can feel free to refrain. But I'm, personally, planning on, pardon the expression, pigging out."

Elgars nodded and pulled off a piece of half burned meat. She juggled the piece of pork for a second, blowing on it until it cooled enough to pop in her mouth. She chewed on it for a moment and then nodded. "It's good," she said.

"Why thanks," O'Neal said with a snort. "I try. Just wait until the skin gets to cracklin' stage."

"This won't be ready until this evening, right?" Mueller asked.

"Right," Papa O'Neal said, pouring a little of the beer on the fire to cool it. The hickory hissed and spat, making a succulent smoke. "It'll probably be ready a little before dark. But I don't have to stay here the whole time; Cally can watch it to make sure it doesn't flame up too far. I was thinking of taking y'all up on the hill. I've got a couple of caches that might come in handy if it drops in the pot and there's a couple of trails for coming over the ridges, places you'd be surprised about, that you might be able to use some time."

"Works for me," Mosovich said. "Would you care to accompany us, Captain?"

Elgars looked up at the steep-sided hills. "I think I would like that very much. I have been interested in wandering around here, but I was unsure of the protocol. And there was some mention of mechanical defenses."

"I can't leave anything live," O'Neal pointed out. "Too many large animals. We've got sensors and we get the occasional feral Posleen, but we only turn on the automatics for an attack."

"You know," Mueller said. "I feel like a real idiot. Here we are wandering around and there's ferals in these woods. We've run into 'em before. And without a gun, we might as well be walking larders."

"He doesn't have a gun," Elgars said, pointing at Papa O'Neal. "And he lives here."

"O ye of little faith," O'Neal answered, reaching up and behind him. What he pulled out looked like a hand cannon.

"Desert Eagle?" Mueller asked, holding out his hand.

"One up the spout," Papa O'Neal answered, handing it over by flipping it around and offering it butt first. "Desert Eagle chambered for .50 Action Express."

"Cool," the master sergeant said. He dropped the magazine and jacked out the round up the spout. The brass and steel cartridge was as big around as his thumb. "Jesus! That's a big goddamned round!"

"You can lose a .45 cartridge in the shell casing," Papa O'Neal said with a laugh. "I did that one time reloading. And the bullet's the new Winchester Black Rhino .50. It'll put a Posleen down with one shot almost anywhere you hit it. And there are seven. I got tired of carting around a rifle all the damned time."

Elgars took the weapon and handled it carefully then lined up a shot with a perfect two-handed grip. "I love it, but the grip's too large for my hands."

"There is that," Papa O'Neal said. He slathered some more barbecue sauce on the meat then reloaded and reholstered the gun. "And the recoil is a stone bitch. But it's got authority, by God!" He finished the beer, rinsed out the bottle in the outdoor tap and set it upside down in a rack that was clearly intended for the purpose. Then he burped and looked up at the sun.

"If we take off now, we can get up to the caves and be back by lunchtime. That gives us all afternoon to drink beer, lie about our exploits over the years and act as if we're not tired old farts."

"Works for me," said Mosovich with a grin.

"Then let's go load up," O'Neal said. "You don't walk *these* hills armed with a pistol. Even one this big."

Wendy smiled as Shari and Cally entered the kitchen.

"I see you took my advice," she said. "Nice job. Very understated."

"Ah . . ." Cally said.

"We had to do a little revising," Shari admitted.

"Granpa said I had raccoon eyes," Cally said bitterly.

"You *did* have raccoon eyes," Shari said. "And later Wendy can show you how to do raccoon eyes the *right* way; I've seen Wendy do the 'Britney Spears look' and it's a very good similarity."

Wendy stuck her tongue out, but otherwise forbore to comment.

"Until then," Shari continued, "go with the minimum. You don't really need it, you know. Most makeup work is designed to make women look like you do naturally. And, be aware, one of the reasons not to ladle it on like warpaint is that that's what the young ladies who are *selling* their affection do. And if you are walking around with that sort of makeup in dowtown Franklin, don't be upset if one of those soldiers gets the wrong impression."

"I'm just tired of being 'one of the boys,'" Cally said. "I mean, up until I started to get breasts and the boys started following me around with their tongues hanging out, Granpa treated me like I was a guy. Now he wants to stick me in a tower until my hair is long enough to climb down!"

Shari smiled and shook her head. "He's a father. Well, a grandfather, but arguably it's the same thing. What he really wants is what's best for you, in his eyes. He might be right, he might be wrong, but that's what he's trying for. That's what every parent tries to do," she finished with a sigh.

"The other thing is that he's a guy," Wendy said. "He used to *be* one of those boys with their tongues hanging out and he knows what they're thinking and he knows what they want. And all that ninety-nine percent of them want is to get laid. They'll say anything, do anything, to get that. Some of them are even willing to use force. He knows what they're thinking, he knows what they're saying to each other in the barracks and he knows what they are willing to do to get it. So he's *very* paranoid about it."

"I'm paranoid about it, too," Cally said. "You only have to get stalked a couple of times to get *really* paranoid. But . . ."

"But me no buts," Wendy said. "I spent four, heck, six years with the reputation of school slut because I was the only girl *not* putting out. I spent I don't know how many summer dates perspiring in a long sweater and tied tight sweat pants. And don't even get me started on fumbling with electronic locks. I got to where I knew not to get in the backseat because they might have engaged the damned child locks and I wouldn't be able to open the door. I walked home at least six times in four years. When it comes to guys and hormones there is *no* such thing as *too* paranoid."

"There's worse," Shari said darkly. "If you choose wrong in one of those back seats, you can get to the point where you really believe that you're in the wrong. That the hitting is because it's all your fault. That the abuse is okay because you're not good enough, not pretty enough, not smart enough." She stopped and looked at Cally shaking her head. "Don't get me wrong, men are great and they have a place . . ."

"Plumbing, electrical," Wendy said with a snort. "Carrying heavy loads . . . killing spiders . . ."

" . . . But choosing right is the most important choice you'll ever make," Shari continued, looking at Wendy severely. "But at that point, my advice is all dried up; I've never been able to choose worth a damn."

"Well, I did okay," Wendy said with a smile. "So far. And if you want some advice on that, it's just this; if he tells you he wants you to put out, run like hell. Shoot your way out if you have to. If he's not willing to wait for *you* to say you want to, he's not worth your time."

"How do you know he really likes you if he's not asking?" Cally asked. "I mean . . . what if he *doesn't* like you?"

Wendy smiled in recollection. "Well, in my case I *knew* he liked me because he carried me out of a firefight instead of putting a bullet in my head as we'd agreed. So I was pretty certain he liked me. But I'd sort of come to that conclusion before that anyway. You'll know. If you don't, he doesn't like you enough."

"This is too complicated," Cally said. "What about I shoot him? If he comes back, he really likes me. And I can guarantee he won't try anything until I say it's okay."

"Well . . ." Shari said.

"I was *joking*," Cally said with a laugh. "At most a broken arm." Cally looked pensive for a moment then shrugged. "So, to decide whether a guy is worth going to bed with, I wait. And if he doesn't ask . . ."

"Or beg or whine or bully," Wendy said. "They're all *much* more likely . . ."

" . . . Then it's okay?"

"If *you* want to," Shari noted. "And . . . wait a while, okay? Thirteen is *way* too young to make a good decision, however grown up you feel."

"I wasn't planning on testing it out tomorrow," Cally said. "Okay, so we've got the basic rule down."

"Yeah, and it's *really* the basics," Wendy said with a sigh. "It's the deciding if *you* want to that's tough."

"If he doesn't ask, but you're still getting a creepy feeling, or he's always making fun of you or talking you down, especially in front of people, don't, even if you want to." Shari shook her head with a dark expression. "Don't, don't, don't."

"This is getting complicated," Cally said. "I think I should just shoot him and see what happens from there."

"It'll drive away some good ones, you know," Wendy said with a smile. "Actually, I can't think of a guy it *wouldn't* drive away."

"I could just shoot 'em lightly," Cally said plaintively. "With a .22. In a fleshy spot. No pain, no gain."

Shari laughed out loud and shook her head: "Okay, it sounds like a plan. If you like 'em, and they seem to be okay, and they're not asking for you to go to bed with them, shoot 'em lightly in a fleshy spot. If they never come back, you know they weren't for you. But don't get in a habit of shooting him every time you disagree, okay?"

"Just one question," Wendy said with a mock serious expression. "Where are you going to get a .22? I mean, I've seen .308s and .30-06s, but .22s seem to be in short supply in this household."

"It's what I carry as my main weapon," Cally said with a snort. "It's not like I'm going to carry around a special 'guy test' gun just to shoot guys if I think I like 'em."

"You carry a .22?" Wendy said with a laugh. "Wow, that must really scare the Posleen no end! You're joking, right?"

Cally smiled thinly. "Let's go down to the range. And see who laughs last."

# CHAPTER 19

"So that's a .22?" Wendy asked in disbelief. The weapon was odd looking, resembling nothing so much as an undersized "Tommy Gun" with the drum magazine placed on top. She could see the tiny aperture in the barrel, but she found the concept of this warrior-child carrying a .22, a round usually used by eight-year-old boys to shoot rats, ludicrous. The gun *looked* like a toy, which she knew was a dangerous mental attitude.

"Yep," Cally said, walking around onto the range. "Range is *cold,* people, no locking, no aiming, no, no, no firing; safe your weapons." She picked up a broken cinderblock off of a stack and, with remarkably little difficulty, carried it halfway to the first target and set it on a section of tree trunk that had apparently been set up for the purpose. "This is the standard demonstration for the American 180," she continued, walking back to the firing line.

There were two ranges set up on the O'Neal property. The first, where they were preparing to fire, was a standard target range. There were a variety of pop-up targets, scoring circles and man- and Posleen-shaped silhouettes, ranging out to two or three hundred yards. The other range, which ran along the road to the entry, was a tactical firing line.

Cally looked at the group and frowned. "Papa O'Neal usually covers this, but I think I'm elected. How many of you have been on a range before?"

Most of the children had wandered over and she frowned when none of them raised their hands. "None of you have been on a range? Where do you do weapons training?"

"It's illegal to let a person under sixteen handle a weapon in the Urb," Wendy said with a frown.

"That's . . . ridiculous," Cally said.

Wendy shrugged. "You're preaching to the choir; there were kids in the Hitler Youth that were younger than that. They tended to surrender pretty quick and they weren't much good. But they fought in a real war."

"I won't even go there," Cally said with a frown.

"Have you ever shot a Posleen?" Shari asked. "I only ask because . . . I don't see somebody Billy's age being . . ."

"Useful?" Cally said with a snort. "You see the bunker by the house? I killed my first Posleen when I was his age, covering Granpa with my rifle; he was manning the mini-gun. It was during the Fredericksburg landing cycle and a Posleen company landed at the head of the valley and ended up coming up the trail. None of them left the holler; we hit 'em with the band of claymores and then stacked the survivors. So, yeah, I think Billy could be pretty useful if you let him be."

"It's not my rule anyway," Shari said with a shrug.

"Whatever," Cally replied. "You gonna mind if he fires one here?"

"Will it be safe?" Shari asked, looking at the odd little rifle in trepidation.

"Of course it will," Cally said. "The first thing to cover is range safety."

She ran through an abbreviated range safety briefing covering hearing protection, ensuring that the weapons were safed and cleared if anyone was to be downrange, keeping fingers off the triggers and always assuming a weapon was loaded. "The most important thing is that; never, ever point a gun, even an 'unloaded' gun, at anything you don't want destroyed. For the purposes of safety, every gun is loaded. Guns aren't evil magic; they're just tools for killing something at a distance. Treat them as useful, but dangerous tools, like a circular saw or a chainsaw, and you'll be fine."

She picked up the rifle and flicked on the laser sight; a tiny red dot settled on the cinderblock. "If not, this is what happens." Holding the weapon by her side, the dot barely shivering on the block, she opened fire.

The weapon was quiet: a series of pops like a distant, poorly tuned outboard motor. An outboard motor going *very* fast.

Wendy shook her head as the cinderblock *disintegrated*. The individual rounds were tiny, an individual .22 round was about as big around as a drinking straw. But the gun was spitting dozens of them in under a second and with negligible recoil; Wendy could see the rounds impacting in the haze of dust and the laser aiming point *still* wasn't moving.

After a few moments the bolt clicked on an empty chamber and Cally pulled the drum off, a single round falling into the dust at her feet, and replaced it. The cinderblock had been hammered into a pile of dust and chunks no larger than a thumb.

"It runs through its rounds in a jiffy," Cally noted, setting the weapon down. "And it's no good at any sort of range. But it's good in close, even against Posleen, and it's fun as heck to fire. However, if we're going to fire anything else, we need to put on our earmuffs."

Cally gestured to Wendy to hand over the Steyr then waved to Billy. "Your turn."

She jacked a round into the chamber and settled the weapon into his shoulder. "Left hand on the stock, right hand on the pistol grip, finger *off* the trigger," she continued, gently moving it away. "Safety is by your right thumb. Look through the rear ring, lay your cheek onto the stock and find the front sight and focus on it. Lay the top of the front sight on the target. Take a breath and let it out and when you're comfortable, *slowly* squeeze the trigger. Squeeze it gently; the shot should feel like a surprise."

Billy looked at her and nodded then leaned into the rifle, pulling it into his shoulder hard.

"Don't tense up so much," Cally said. "This is a bittly little .308 round. The recoil is not going to knock you on your ass."

Billy nodded again and slowly squeezed the trigger, putting a round into the center of the man-shaped target and knocking it down.

"Good," Cally said as he grinned. "Now, I'm going to pop up a target of a Posleen. There's a head-sized patch on its side, right behind the shoulder, marked in red. I want you to shoot it there. Okay?"

Billy looked unhappy, but eventually shrugged and nodded. So Cally popped up the target.

The Posleen was twenty-five meters downrange, a cold shot for a rifle, and in line with where the human silhouette had been. Billy was so startled that his first round went high, but he quickly settled down and put the second one into the target area.

"You don't like Posleen, do you?" Cally asked. Billy shook his head.

"They die," she said with a grin. "You shoot 'em and they die. Fall down and go boom. The point is that you have to shoot 'em, and you have to shoot 'em before they shoot you. Now shoot it again."

They spent the next few hours on the range, eventually going back to the house for a picnic lunch, feeding the baby and more ammunition. All the children were permitted to fire something, even if it was the target air gun from the armory. After putting a couple of thousand rounds, combined, downrange, Cally called a halt.

"I think that's enough for one day," she said, taking a Sig-Sauer .40 from a reluctant Kelly; the six-year-old had just scored two bull's-eyes at twenty-five meters and was suitably awed with herself. "Maybe you guys can come back some time and we'll do some more. But I have to go make sure the pig hasn't caught on fire."

"That *would* be a shame," Wendy said. "I'm going to be hungry. And I'm sure the walkers are as well."

"Speaking of which, I wonder where they are?" Shari said.

From high on the mountains a resounding "Booom" echoed across the holler.

"Somewhere around Cache Four, it sounds like," Cally said.

"What was that?" Wendy asked.

"At a guess, Granpa's hand cannon."

"Is he all right?" Shari asked, shading her eyes against the glare to fruitlessly look up the mountain.

"Oh, yeah," Cally said, setting the kids to policing the brass. "If he wasn't you would have heard everyone else open up as well."

✧　　✧　　✧

Papa O'Neal pointed down what appeared to be a sheer bluff about fifteen meters high then to a hickory sapling growing on the edge.

Looking closely, Mosovich could see where there was a worn patch on the trunk of the sapling. He nodded and gave the farmer a quizzical look.

Papa O'Neal smiled, shouldered his rifle and swung his feet out over the edge, dropping straight down.

Looking over the edge, it was clear now that there was a thin ledge below, upon which O'Neal was now perched. With a grin he ducked and disappeared into the mountain.

Mosovich shrugged and grabbed the tree, repeating the maneuver. He noted that O'Neal was now crouched in a cave opening, apparently prepared to catch the sergeant major should the likely event of his falling outward have occurred.

Mosovich shook his head at the local's grin and shuffled to the side; Mueller would have a tougher time than he did. Mueller, though, came down slightly more circumspectly, grasping a hand- and foothold on the wall and lowering himself carefully to the ledge. He then shuffled past O'Neal and deeper into the cave.

Elgars looked down the cliff and shrugged. She grabbed the tree and dropped, landing slightly off-balance. But before Mosovich or O'Neal could react, one hand reached up in a smooth slow-looking maneuver and grabbed a small protuberance between index finger and thumb, seizing the tiny handhold like a mechanical clamp. She slowly pulled herself vertical then ducked to enter the cave.

There was a short passageway, high enough at the center that a person could duckwalk through, and then the cave opened up and out to either side. On the right the roof sloped quickly down to the floor, bringing with it a trickle of water that collected in a small apparently man-made basin. On the left the wall was more vertical and the floor extended further back. At least, it seemed to; the actual left-hand wall was obscured with boxes.

There were metal and wood ammo boxes, plastic "rough tote" waterproof containers and even a few Galplas ACS grav-gun and grenade cases. There were also about a dozen cases of combat rations.

"It's not all ammo," Papa O'Neal said, going over and hauling down a long, low case that had "Ammo, 81mm, M256 HE" stamped on the side. The box turned out to contain several old style BDU combat uniforms, wrapped in plastic and packed with mothballs. "There's a full outfit, including combat load out, for a squad. And four days rations. Water?" he gestured to the pool. "And there are filters in one of the boxes."

"How many caches like this do you have?" Mosovich asked, shaking his head. "This is . . . Jesus, just the thought of the cost makes my teeth ache."

"Oh, it took a few years to set them all up," Papa O'Neal said with a laugh, sending a stream of tobacco juice to the floor. "And I did it bit by bit, so the cost wasn't all that bad. Also . . . there's some government programs now to do this sort of thing. At least that's what they're really about if you read the fine print; The BATF would shit if Congress had come right out and said as much. And recently, well . . ." He grinned and shook his head. "Let's just say that my son has done pretty well financially in this war."

Mosovich had to admit that was probably the case. The Fleet used something similar to prize rules, a combination of Galactic laws and human application. Since the ACS was generally the lead assault element, they got the maximum financial benefit of all the captured Posleen weaponry, ships and stores that generally were lying around in a retreat. He also noted that Papa O'Neal had neatly sidestepped the question of how many similar caches there were.

"And he's a great source of surplus," Mueller said, kicking a grav-gun ammo case.

"Uh, yeah," Papa O'Neal said with another grin. "They go through a lot of grav-gun ammo." He duckwalked back to the entrance and gestured down the hill where the farm and the pocket valley beyond were faintly visible. The main valley of the Gap was still shrouded by a shoulder of the hill, but Black Mountain was in clear view—it dominated the southern horizon—and a corner of the wall was faintly visible. "This spot makes a fair lookout, but of course there's no back door. I don't like going to ground when there's no back door."

"Yeah, I been treed by the Posleen a couple of times," Mosovich said, glancing down the bluff. It was climbable, with difficulty. "I don't care for it."

As he stepped back Elgars gasped and shook her head. "Now that was a bad one," she said with an uneasy chuckle.

"What was a bad one?" Mueller asked, ducking through to crowd the ledge.

"You ever get flashbacks, Sergeant?" she asked.

"Occasionally," Mueller admitted. "Not all that often."

"Well, I get flashbacks of stuff I've never done," Elgars said with a grim chuckle. "And you know, I've never been to Barwhon, but I've come to hate that cold-assed rainy planet."

"It is that," Mosovich said. "I've only been once and I have *no* desire to return."

"I understand that it has a high species diversity," Papa O'Neal said with a chuckle, reaching up to climb up the bluff. "Every really nasty place I've ever been—

Vietnam, Laos, Cambodia, Congo, Biafra—had the same damned description."

"It does that," Mueller agreed. "It has about a billion different species of biting beetles, all the size of your finger joint. And forty million species of vines that get in your way. And sixty million species of really tall trees that screen out the light."

"And lots and lots of Posleen," Mosovich said with a laugh. "Well, it used to."

"I had this sudden really clear image of a Posleen village, a few pyramids and some other stuff. I was looking through a scope, right eye in the scope, left scanning outside. I know that in just a second a Posleen's gonna come through a door and I have to engage it. Then there were some explosions and, sure enough, a Postie comes right in view. Ah take it out, and some others, then there's a God King and it's all okay, Ah'm in the zone, servicing the targets. Ah've got an IR blanket on and the signature's covered so Ah'm safe, counterfire is not an issue. The gun's big, probably a Barrett, and I have to reposition a couple of times cause Ah'm on this really big branch or something. Then the tree I'm shooting in starts shuddering and Ah look down and there's this line of shot-marks walking up the tree and then it goes white."

"Are you jerking my chain?" Mosovich asked quietly.

"No," Elgars answered. "Why?"

He looked at Mueller, who was standing there, white faced, and thought about simply answering. Finally he shook his head.

"Not here, not now," he said. "Later. Maybe. I have to think about this."

"It's not the only memory where I die," Elgars said with a shrug. "There's another one where I'm running and I've got a burned hand, it hurts anyway, and I'm carrying something and then the ground's coming up at me and I die. And another where I'm up to my waist in water, firing a gun, a light machine gun, offhand. And I die. And another where I blow up and die."

"You die a lot," Mueller commented looking at her oddly.

"Yep," Elgars answered. "Game over, man. Happens to me all the time. Practically every night. It really sucks. Hard to get much confidence going when you die all the time."

"The shrinks didn't tell me about that," Mosovich said.

"That's because by the time the flashbacks started, I'd figured out to stop talking to the shrinks," the captain said with a shrug.

"I have dreams where I die," Papa O'Neal said, spitting over the side. "But it's usually an explosion, usually a nuke. I have that one recurrently. By the way, this is a weird fucking conversation and I need a beer for one of those." He reached up and grasped the tree trunk, hauling himself back up the bluff. "Time to wander down and see if Cally has burned the pig." He turned to give Mosovich a hand then turned back as there was a crackling in the brush.

The Posleen normal had apparently been screened by a holly thicket. Now it charged down the hillside, spear held at shoulder height.

Mosovich had just started to haul himself up and was in no position to respond, but that didn't really matter.

Papa O'Neal didn't bother going for the assault rifle on his back. Instead, his hand dropped to the holstered pistol, coming back up in a smooth motion as the Posleen closed to within feet of him.

The Desert Eagle tracked to just above the protuberance of the double shoulder. Bone over the shoulder, and the shoulder itself, tended to armor the front of a Posleen. But just above and below were open areas; the higher open area, corresponding to the clavical region in a human, also contained a nerve and blood-flow complex.

Papa O'Neal triggered one round and then pirouetted aside, blocking the now limply held spear with the barrel of the gun. The Posleen continued on for a few steps then slid down the hill and off the bluff.

"Heads up," O'Neal called calmly. Then he dropped out the magazine and replaced it with a spare, carefully reloading the original magazine as the Posleen bounced down the hill and off a cliff.

Mueller shook his head and wiped at his face, where a splash of yellow marked the demise of the normal. "God, it's nice dealing with professionals," he chuckled.

Elgars shook her head in wonder. "I don't care if it is difficult to use. That Posleen had a hole I could fit my hand in going all the way through it. I need to get one of those pistols."

"They are nice," Mueller agreed, grabbing the trunk. "On the other hand, they *are* loud."


"We heard you up on the hill," Cally said as the foursome hove into view of the barbeque pits. "I'm surprised you didn't skin it out and bring back a haunch."

"Slid down the hill," Papa O'Neal said with a grin. "Damned bad luck if you ask me. Where'd everybody go?"

"Most of the kids are taking a nap," the thirteen-year-old said, poking at the hickory fire. She had pulled her hair back and put on a full-length apron to work on the fire. Between that and the smudge of ash on her hands and face she looked like some medieval serving wench. "Wendy and Shari are technically inside getting side dishes ready. But I told them there was plenty of time and I suspect they're racked out, too. Any other trouble?"

"These guys are pretty good in the hills," O'Neal said. "Almost as good as you."

"No trouble," Mueller said. "But I've got a question: I've *heard* of people eating Posleen, but . . ."

Papa O'Neal looked sort of sheepish as Cally laughed hysterically.

"Yeah, he ate one," she said. "Parts of a few, actually."

"They really taste like shit," he said with a shrug. "They're tough, they're stringy, they don't soften up when you cook 'em and they really, really taste bad; worse than sloth and that's saying a lot."

"You've eaten sloth?" Mueller asked. "Shit, I've *never* met anybody who's eaten one of those."

"Yes you have," Mosovich said with a grimace. "I did one time. If Posleen's worse than that, they're pretty bad. It's hard to describe how bad sloth is; it tastes sort of like what you'd think a road-killed possum would taste like after a few days on the road."

"That's a pretty good description," Papa O'Neal said. "And Posleen tastes worse. I loaded it up with nam pla even, my *own* recipe for nam pla with added habanero, and the taste *still* came through."

"Oh, Jesus," Mosovich laughed. "That's bad!"

"I finally figured out that I could eat it if I coated it in berbere," O'Neal said with a shrug. "That shit's so hot you can't taste anything at all; it puts Thais on their ass."

"Man, you must have been everywhere," Mueller said with another laugh. "I've heard of berbere but . . ."

"I had it once," Mosovich said. "Somebody bet me I couldn't eat a whole plate of something called 'wat har bo.'" He shook his head. "I took one bite and paid off the bet; I'd rather eat my pride and give up a C note than die."

"Berbere isn't for the faint of heart," Papa O'Neal admitted. "Even I can't stomach much of it and I've eaten more really hot shit than I want to think about. So I don't eat 'em anymore. And I don't let Cally eat it at all; you can get a disease from it, like when cannibals eat brains. It's caused by a little protein they've got that we can't break down."

"Kreinsfelter or something like that?" Mueller asked. "Same thing as Mad Cow Disease basically. I've heard you can get it from eating Posleen. So why did you?"

"That's it," Papa O'Neal said. "But, hell, the onset is a couple of decades normally." He grinned and waved at his body. "One way or another, I don't really think I've *got* another couple of decades."

"I'm hungry," Mueller said with a grin. "But I don't want to die from what I eat. Is there anything else?"

"Well, you sort of missed lunch," Cally said somewhat sourly. "This will be ready in about an hour. But there's other stuff to get ready too."

"We'll get on it," Mosovich said with a chuckle. "Just point us in the direction, O Viking princess!"

She shook her head and brandished a burning brand at him then gestured to the house. "Since the sweet corn is still up, I think we should have that again. Cornbread is in the oven. I had the kids pick some broccoli and that probably should be cut up and put in a big dish and microwaved. We could have a side of fresh beets if somebody went out and picked them. Ditto on tomatoes, they're always good with a little seasoning. What am I missing?"

"Beer," Papa O'Neal said, picking up a large set of skewers and jabbing them in the butterflied pig. "And turning this. How long has it been on this side?"

"About an hour," Cally said. "I got Wendy and Shari to help me the last time."

"I'll take over here," O'Neal said. "As long as somebody brings me a beer. You go rule the kitchen. Give these heathens no mercy! Teach them . . . canning!"

"Ah! Not that!" Cally said with a grin. "We don't have anything to can. And besides, they're guests."

"You take all the fun out of it," Papa O'Neal said with a grin. "Go on, I'll handle the meat." As she left he rummaged in a box by the barbeque and pulled out a large stoneware jug. "Here," he said, offering it to Mueller. "Try some of this. It'll put hair on your chest."

"I've always been proud of my relatively hairless chest," Mueller said, tilting the jug back for a drink. He took a sip and spit half of it out, coughing. As the clear liquid hit the fire, it roared up. "Aaaaah."

"Hey, that stuff's prized around here!"

"As what?" Mueller rasped. "Paint stripper?"

Papa O'Neal took the jug and sniffed at it innocently. "Ah, sorry," he said with a chuckle. He reached into the same box and came up with a mason jar. "You're right, that was paint stripper. Try this instead."

Tommy stood up and raised his mug. "Gentlemen . . . and ladies. Absent companions."

"Absent companions," the rest of the room murmured.

Having released the troops to descend upon the unprotected towns of Newbry and Hollidaysburg, Major O'Neal had decreed that the officers would have a dining in. His stated reason for this was to start integrating the two new officers they had received, but Tommy suspected it was because he was afraid the officers would do more damage than the enlisted.

Major O'Neal stood up and raised his beer. "Gentlemen and ladies: Who Laughs Last."

"Who Laughs Last," the group murmured.

"Sir," Captain Stewart said somewhat thickly. "I think it's important that the new officers become acquainted with the reason for the battalion motto, don't you?"

Mike snorted and looked around. "Duncan, you are our official battalion storyteller. Tell them the story."

Duncan stood up from where he was talking with Captain Slight and took a sip of beer then cleared his throat. "President of the Mess!"

"Yes, Captain?" Tommy said.

"Arrrrgh!" Captain Slight shouted.

"Sacrilege!" Stewart yelled.

"No rank in the mess, Tommy," O'Neal said, waving everyone down.

"President of the Mess!" Duncan continued. "Call the pipers!"

"We don't have any," Tommy complained. "We checked the whole battalion and nobody knows how to play them. And we don't *have* any pipes anyway."

Stewart leaned over and pointed at a device in the corner, whispering in the lieutenant's ear. Tommy went over and, after whispering to his new AID, keyed the controls.

"But it does appear that we have a pirated version of 'Flowers of the Forest,'" Tommy said. "Lucky us."

Duncan cleared his throat and took another sip of beer as the melancholy notes of a uilleann pipe echoed through the mess.

"'Twas the darkest days of the fourth wave, January 17th, 2008, when the sky was still filled with the meteoric tracks of Second Fleet, its smashed remains leaving trails of fire across the sky, when, if you cranked up your visor, you could catch a glimpse of the last task force battling its way through the Posleen wave, towing away the pulverized wreck of the Supermonitor *Honshu*.

"First Battalion, Five Hundred Fifty-Fifth Infantry had been tasked with holding a vital ridgeline outside of Harrisburg, Pennsylvania. From the ridge it was just possible to see the smoke from the final assault on Philadelphia and the millions of fresh Posleen, newly landed from their ships, were even more evident. The Planetary Defense Center to the north was heavily engaged with airmobile landers, and repeated kinetic energy strikes were hammering into it as the battalion sustained wave after wave of suicidal Posleen assaults. Conventional units were heavily engaged to the south, so heavily engaged that they had full priority on all artillery, leaving the battalion to fend for itself. The air was filled with the shriek and silver of grav-gun rounds as the sky was pierced with nuclear fire.

"That was, until the Alpha company began to run low on ammunition. To their front was a gully, and the Posleen waves were, in part by accident, sheltered by said gully. The Reapers had used their grenades to good effect, but the resupply line had been partially flanked and was sustaining heavy interdicting fire. So, slowly, the company got lower and lower on ammunition until they were down to firing individual rounds.

"The Posleen, meanwhile, had through trial and error rediscovered the concept of 'cover' and the survivors were hunkering in the gully, popping up to fire a few rounds, and then hunkering back down.

"The situation was at an impasse; the company did not have the grenade rounds to destroy the Posleen and the Posleen had gotten tired of getting killed in the open.

"It was at that moment that our redoubtable leader made his appearance by running full tilt through the hail of fire that had already garnered three of the resupply personnel. Arriving at the Alpha Company lines he wandered down the slit trench, observing the goings on, until he reached the Alpha Company commander. That would be . . ."

"Craddock," Mike said, taking a gulp of beer.

"Captain James Craddock," Duncan continued, raising his glass. "Absent companions."

"Absent companions," everyone murmured.

"Captain Craddock related their predicament and noted that if they didn't do something, and soon, the Posleen would build up to where they had enough force to engage in hand-to-hand. And that would be . . . unpleasant. He requested that the supply personnel, the medics and techs basically, do whatever was necessary to support his operation, at whatever cost.

"Our esteemed leader, doing his notorious impression of the sphinx, then looks around, picks up a small boulder and rolls it down the hill."

"You could hear the crunch when it hit the horses," Stewart chimed in. "It was nearly as big as he is. . . . He looked like an ant lifting a big chunk of dirt. . . ."

"Then he turns to the company commander and says . . ."

"He who laughs last is generally the one that thought fastest on his feet," Mike said, taking a sip of beer.

"We edited for content and punch," Duncan said. "Using boulders from the surrounding terrain, Alpha Company then proceeded to play 'Bowling for Posleen' for the next few hours."

"Then we got our artillery support back and everything was hunky dory," Mike noted. "Artillery is what has saved this war. But I've noted that surviving these little predicaments is generally a matter of who comes up with the winning tactic at the last possible moment. You go in with a plan, knowing it's going to . . . go awry. And then you adjust. Whoever is the best, the fastest, at adjusting usually is the winner."

"We're very fast at adjusting," Slight said thickly. "And when I say 'we,' I mean the veterans in this room. That's why we're here."

Stewart raised his glass. "To those who think fastest; may they always be humans!"

# CHAPTER 20

*Rabun Gap, GA, United States, Sol III*
*2047 EDT Friday September 25, 2009* AD

"Cally, don't take this as an insult," Mueller said, leaning back from the table with a grin. "But you're going to make someone a great wife some day."

"It's not like I enjoy cooking," Cally said, with a shrug. "Well, not much. But if you want to eat up here, you have to do it all yourself."

Dinner had been a rousing success. Papa O'Neal had cut about ten pounds of moist, succulent pork off the pig, thinking that would be enough and intending to cut the rest up and freeze it for later meals. As it turned out, he had had to go back to the porker twice for more meat. In addition to the corn on the cob and cornbread, Cally had cooked wheat bread, a creamed green-bean casserole and new potatoes, all of which had been eaten. Dessert was pecan pie.

The children, stuffed to the gills, had finally been sent off to bed leaving only the "grownups"—Cally seemed to be included in that group—sitting at the table, picking over the remains of the meal while the CD player cycled in the background.

"I know what you mean," Shari laughed. "There are cafeterias in the Urb, but the food is really lousy; there are days I could kill to just call Domino's."

"I sort of remember them," Cally said with a shrug. "But the last time I ate fast food was the month that Fredericksburg was hit." She shook her head and shrugged. "We went on vacation down to the Keys and there was still a McDonald's open in Miami. We fix pizza sometimes, but it's made from scratch."

"None of the kids even remember fast food joints," Wendy said, pulling a piece of pork off the haunch Papa O'Neal had brought in. "Well, Billy and Shannon do, a little bit. But not really. They sort of remember the playgrounds and the meal toys. But that's about it."

"It all just went away so fast," Shari said quietly.

"It did that," Mosovich replied. "Wars tend to cause that sort of thing. Ask Germans of a certain age about how things change in a real war, or read diaries of Southerners in the Civil War. *Gone With the Wind* is a good example; one day you wake up and your whole life is gone. Some people adjust to it, thrive even. Some people just curl up and die, either in reality or inside."

"Lots of that in the Urbs," Wendy said. "Lot of people that just gave up. They sit around all day, either doing nothing or talking about when the good times will come back."

"Ain't gonna come back like of old," Mosovich said. "I'll tell you that. Too much damage. Hell, even the 'fortress cities' that they made out in the boonies are basically toast. A city is more than a bunch of buildings filled with soldiers. Richmond, Newport, New York, San Francisco, they're just hollow shells at this point. Making them cities again . . . I don't know if it's gonna happen."

"The interior cities ain't any great shakes either," Mueller pointed out. "We were up in Louisville a few months ago at Eastern Theater Command. Most of the people there were trying to get into the Urbs. At least the Urbs were set up for foot traffic; with the shortage of gasoline, getting around in cities is *really* difficult. Just getting to the store is usually a long hike."

"Especially with the weather being as bad as it's been," Shari said.

"What weather?" Papa O'Neal asked.

"Well, we get the reports down in the Urbs; there were record lows all winter. They're already talking about a new ice age from all the nuclear weapons."

"Huh," O'Neal laughed. "Can't tell it by me. If there was an ice age coming on, farmers would be the first to know. Now, the *Canadian* harvests were screwed up, and it probably was in part due to the China nukes, but even that has stabilized out."

"I can't really blame the Chinese, either," Mueller said. "Except for thinking they could beat the Posleen on the plains. Once they lost most of their army, slagging the Yangtze was the only way to keep the Posleen off the stragglers."

"Oh, hell," Papa O'Neal grunted. "They were slagging the stragglers there at the end. That way the Posleen would slow down to eat. And it's not like even that slowed 'em down, it only took 'em a month to reach Tibet. Hell, with all the antimatter and nukes we've built up, better hope *we* never get to that point; we'll end up glazing the whole eastern U.S. And probably to about as much use.

"But as to the weather, we're in a long-term aggressive weather cycle, but that's affected by a pod of warm water in the Atlantic and it was predicted before the invasion. Other than that, the weather's been fine. Great, this year. Rains just on time. Could have been a bit more, but then I'd be wishing they were a bit less."

"We're always hearing these terrible weather reports from the surface," Wendy said. "Record cold, snow in April, stuff like that."

"Well, I've been living here for . . . well, for a long time," he said, looking sidelong at Shari. "And this has been as good a year as we've had. Yeah, it snowed in April. Happens. It was seventy-two two days after the nukes."

"Did that person just say what I think they said?" Elgars asked.

"Who?" Papa O'Neal replied, looking around.

"On the CD player," she said, pointing into the living room. "I think he just sang something about smearing the roast on his chest."

"Ah," said Papa O'Neal with a smile. "Yeah. That. Warren Zevon."

"Warren who?" Wendy asked. Elgars had been picking up socialization fast and she had to wonder if the captain had just done a very deliberate topic change. If so, go with it.

"Zevon," Mosovich said. "The Balladeer of the Mercenary. Great guy. Met him once. Briefly."

"Where?" Shari asked. "I recognize the name, but I can't come up with a song and . . ." She listened to a few lyrics and blanched. "Did he just say what I think he did?"

"Yep," Papa O'Neal said with a grimace. "That's 'Excitable Boy.' It's . . . one of his rougher pieces."

"I dunno," Cally said with a malicious chuckle. "Why don't you sing her a few bars of 'Roland the Headless Thompson Gunner'?"

"I don't think that will be necessary," Shari said with

a smile. "And, believe it or not, I can take a little black humor."

"Oh, yeah?" Cally said with a sly grin. "Why'd the Posleen cross the road?"

"I'll bite," Mueller said. "Why did the Posleen cross the road?"

"To get to the fodder side," Cally said.

"Okay," Mosovich said. "That was pretty bad. Try this one: How do two Posleen resolve an argument?" He waited, but nobody jumped in. "Thresh it out between them, of course."

"Ow!" Papa O'Neal said. "What's the difference between a lawyer and a Posleen?"

"I dunno," Shari said. "One gets paid to eat you alive?"

"No, but that's pretty good," Papa O'Neal said. "No, one is a vicious, inhuman, cannibalistic monster; and the other is an alien."

"You hear the new slogan for the Posleen that fight Marines?" Wendy asked.

"Hah!" Mosovich said with a grin. "I can imagine a few. Oh, that would be *sailors*."

"The few, the proud: DESSERT!"

Cally looked around for a second then grinned. "How do you know that Posleen are bisexual? They eat both men and women!"

"I can't believe you said that!" Papa O'Neal grumped as the others laughed.

"Christ, you have me listening to Black Sabbath and Ozzy Osbourne, Granpa!" Cally said. "And *that* little joke bothers you?"

"What's wrong with Black Sabbath?" he protested. "It's a good group. Great lyrics."

"Oh, I dunno," Cally said. "The *name*?"

"Christian!"

"Catholic, thank you very much."

"Okay, okay, breaking the mood here before bullets fly," Mueller said. "How many Posleen does it take to screw in a lightbulb?"

"I dunno," said Papa O'Neal grumpily. "How many?"

"Just one," Mueller said. "But it takes a really big lightbulb."

"I don't get that one," Elgars said.

"They're hermaphroditic," Wendy said. "They can't really self impregnate, not without help. But any two can reproduce with any other two so since 'go screw yourself' is an insult, people joke about them screwing themselves."

Elgars nodded her head. "I still don't get it."

"Think about it," Cally said. "In the meantime: Why did the Himmit cross the road?"

"I don't know," Elgars said.

"It didn't; it's on the wall behind you," Cally said with a grin.

Elgars regarded her calmly. "This is a joke?"

"Never mind," Wendy sighed. "Then there's the one about the Himmit who sat in his car for three days, in a no-parking zone, blending into the upholstery of the driver seat." She paused for a moment. "He got toad." She looked around. "Get it? Toad. T-O-A-D."

"Aaaagh!" Papa O'Neal shouted. "That's *awful*!"

"I don't get it again?" Elgars said. "What is a Himmit?"

"One of the Galactic races," Cally answered, shaking her head and throwing a biscuit at Wendy. "They sort of look like big frogs. They can blend into the background so well it's like they're invisible."

"Thank you," Wendy said, bowing at the table. "Thank you . . . Or the Himmit in the piano bar? One of the customers says to the piano player, 'Do you know there's a giant invisible frog having a beer on the wall behind you?' And the piano player said: 'Hum a bar or two and I'll pick it up.' Or the one about the extrovert Indowy? He looks at *your* shoes while he's talking to you."

"Those are awful!" Cally said.

"Worse than the bisexual joke?" Mueller asked. "Okay. Two soldiers in a foxhole. One says, 'I heard about two orphans passin' through town today. Those godamn aliens hit their town a week ago, killed their dad—he was a marathon runner, of all things—and ate their Ma. Didn't eat him—just her. Crazy damn aliens, why'd they do that?' The other says, 'You idiot. Their Pa's lean'."

"That's terrible," Shari said. "Nearly as bad as this one. What's a good mascot for the ACS? A lobster: so good to eat, so hard to peel."

"Hey!" Cally said. "My dad resembles that remark! What do you call a Crab on a sugar high? Flubber. It just bounces and bounces . . . You know what they call a Crab studying Marine Biology? Speaker to shellfish."

"How do two hungry Posleen greet each other?" Papa O'Neal asked, not to be outdone. "With salt and pepper of course."

"Why did the Posleen leave an honor stick at the McDonald's?" Cally asked. "They saw the sign '6 billion served.' "

"You barely remember McDonald's," Papa O'Neal said suspiciously. "Who told you that?"

"Just . . . a guy," Cally said with a twinkle in her eye.

"Oh, shit," Mueller muttered. "Hey! How did the bus full of lawyers escape from behind the Posleen lines? Professional courtesy."

"What guy?" Papa O'Neal asked.

"What did the Posleen say when they took Auschwitz?" she asked, ignoring the question. " 'I prefer Sushi.' "

"What *guy*, Cally?" Papa O'Neal asked again.

"Just a soldier," she answered. "At the Piggly Wiggly. He told a joke and so did I and I left. It was no big deal. . . ."

"What do you call Posleen in the open and a Fuel Air Explosion?" Mueller asked desperately. "A Whopper and fries."

"What do you mean, no big deal?" Papa O'Neal said dangerously. "I don't want them changing the song to 'Cally went down to town.'"

"Okay," Shari sighed. "Look at me, Michael O'Neal."

"Yes?" he said grumpily.

"What do the Posleen call Carl Lewis?"

"I dunno," Papa O'Neal said, shaking his head. "You're not going to let me pursue this, are you?"

"No. Fast Food."

He snorted. "Okay."

"What did the Posleen say when confronted by an Ethiopian?"

"I dunno," he said smiling at her. "What?"

"'Nouvelle Cuisine AGAIN?' I gotta million of 'em. What do the Posleen call a doctor?"

"What?"

"Lunch. What do the Posleen call a construction worker?"

"I dunno."

"Lunch. What do the Posleen call a politician? Competition. What do the Posleen call a lawyer? Trouble. Do you know why they substituted lawyers for Posleen in their chemical warfare experiments? Lawyers bred faster. There are things a Posleen won't do. And the researchers were taking pity on the Posleen.

"And last, but not least: Why did the Posleen take less than a month to go through China? Well, you know how it is, you eat Chinese and an hour later . . ."

"Jeeze, you're something," O'Neal said with a laugh.

"You got any Van Morrison in this dump?" she asked.

"I think I've got his 'Best of,' why?"

"Because I want to dance," she answered, taking his hand and standing up. "Come on."

"I've got two left feet," he protested.

"You put your arms around me and shuffle around," she said with a twinkle in her eye. "How hard's it gonna be?"

"You might want to rephrase that," Mueller muttered.

"Oh, shut up."

As the music changed in the background, Elgars poured a small sip of the *better* moonshine. She swirled it in her cup and looked at Mosovich. "I think now is a good time."

"Now's a good time for what?" Cally asked.

"I told Mosovich about a flashback while we were walking," Elgars answered. "There was something about it he really didn't like."

"Yeah," Mosovich said. "You're right." He poured himself some of the moonshine and leaned back. "What I didn't like about it is that the person who had that experience is real, and she's really dead. I saw her die."

"Where?" Cally asked.

"Barwhon," Mueller interjected. "We were both on a recon team that was sent out before the expeditionary force even got there. We were guinea pigs to see how dangerous the Posleen really were."

"You can't remember that time," Mosovich said. "But . . . there was a lot of disbelief. 'Alien invasion? Right, pull the other one.' That got dispelled pretty quick when a high-level delegation on Barwhon got eaten, and the tape got back to the World. Anyway, we were on a recon of Barwhon doing an order of battle and analysis of the terrain and fighting conditions . . ."

"Bad and bad," Mueller said.

"I guess we did our job too well," the sergeant major

continued. "We got a call to capture a Posleen and return it. I figured that we could capture one of the nestlings easier than an adult so we attacked a camp that was also holding some Crabs as a walking larder. When we did, the Posleen turned out to be a bit better at fighting than we had given them credit for. All the stuff we know now; the sniper detection system and the way they just swarm to the sound of fighting. Anyway, we lost a bunch of real legends in the special operations community, including our sniper, Staff Sergeant Sandra Ellsworthy. The description of your flashback correlates exactly to her death."

"Yep," Mueller said. "I thought the same thing. It's like listening to Sandra tell it, complete with the southern accent."

"You know," Wendy said. "That's hardly coming out at all anymore. The accent I mean."

"Anyway, that's why we freaked," Mosovich said.

"What do you think?" Elgars asked quietly. "Do you think that the Crabs put your friend's head in mine? Am I Anne Elgars or this Ellsworthy person? Similar name, both snipers? You think that's it?"

"Not really," Mosovich said. "Ellsworthy was . . . stranger than you are. Spooky weird. You seem a lot . . ."

"Stabler," Mueller said. "Don't get me wrong, on a mission Ellsworthy was great. And she was a good sniper trainer. But she was a wild-child when she wasn't in uniform; you've got ten times her stability in many ways, even with your head not completely screwed on."

"Why thank you, Master Sergeant," she said tartly.

"No offense, ma'am," he said hastily.

"So, how does this affect your report to Colonel Cutprice?" she asked Mosovich.

"I think I'll just send him a message with the whole crazy story," the sergeant major replied. "You move good in the woods and we know you can shoot. If you were a private or a staff sergeant it wouldn't be any question. But for a captain he'll have to make up his own mind. For what it's worth, I think you could learn to do the job."

"Thanks," Elgars said. "I have to wonder. And I have to agree I don't know what *else* might be buried in the depths of my mind. Or, really, who I am."

"Oh, I think you'll get over that," Mosovich said. "Although it brings a whole new meaning to 'getting to know yourself.' Long term, I think you'll be fine. Well, as fine as any of us are these days."

He looked into the living room where Papa O'Neal and Shari were now dancing to "Magic Carpet Ride." "Some of us, of course, are doing better than others."

O'Neal walked over holding Shari by the hand and gave them a sort of wave. "Night, folks. We're kind of tired so we're calling it a night." With that they both walked towards the stairs, hand in hand.

"Well, will you look at that," Cally said bitterly. "Tell *me* not to go downtown!"

"They're both old enough to make a rational decision about it," Wendy pointed out. "Old enough to be your grandfather in one case and your mother in the other."

"And he's old enough to be *her* father," Cally pointed out.

"The Koran says that the perfect age for a wife is half the man's plus seven years," Mueller intoned. "That makes you still too young for me. In fact," he looked at the ceiling and fiddled on his fingers. "I think that means the perfect age for a guy for you would be . . . yours."

"On the other hand . . ." he said, turning to Wendy.

"Hang on a bit," she said, reaching into her back pocket.

"Ah, hah!" Mosovich exclaimed. "It's the notorious boyfriend picture."

Mueller took it and looked at it with a grin on his face. Then he looked puzzled for a moment followed by shock. "Jesus Christ." He passed it over to Mosovich.

Wendy was in the picture, grinning at the camera in a happy-goofy way. She was flanked by a male in Mar-Cam, wearing much the same expression. What was difficult to grasp about the picture was that Wendy, who was no tiny young lady, looked like a baby-doll next to the . . . mountain next to her.

"That's your boyfriend?" Mosovich asked.

"Yeah," Wendy said. "He's an NCO in the Ten Thousand. Six foot eight, two hundred and eighty pounds. Most of it muscle.

"We met during the Battle of Fredericksburg. Well, not really. We went to school together for years. Let's just say I never really *noticed* him until the Battle."

"Well, do I have to wait to be rescued in the middle of a battle?" Cally asked. "Besides, I'm more likely to do the rescuing."

"No, but you should wait a *few* more years before you go making any life commitment decisions," Wendy said with a laugh.

"I get the point," Cally said with a shake of her head. "Noted and logged. Okay?"

"Okay," Wendy said.

Elgars stood up and walked over to Mueller, tilting her head to the side. After a moment she leaned down and yanked one of his arms over her shoulder then got her shoulder into his midsection and heaved him up over her shoulder. She bent her knees a couple of times experimentally then nodded her head.

"I can do this," she said. There was no note of strain in her voice.

"What, exactly, are you doing?" Mueller asked,

hanging more or less vertical. He noted that his head was just about at the level of her derriere.

"As far as I know, I've never been to bed with anyone," she answered, walking carefully towards the stairs. "You'll do."

Mosovich opened his mouth and raised his finger as if to protest, but then lowered it. Since he and Mueller were Fleet and Elgars was Ground Force it didn't, technically, fall under the fraternization regulations. As long as they survived the stairs, everything should be fine. He downed his moonshine and looked at the table with trepidation.

"I think that leaves it up to us to clean up," he said. "Since I choose to avoid the wrath of both the boyfriend and the local farmer."

Cally sighed and started stacking plates. "One of these days," she said, looking towards the stairs.

"One of these days there will be some good news," Monsignor O'Reilly said, looking at his newest visitor.

The Indowy Aelool made a grimace that was the Indowy equivalent of disagreement. "Why should there be good news? It is not the trend by any stretch of the imagination."

The four foot tall, green, "fur"-covered, bat-faced biped was swinging its feet back and forth in the chair like a little child for all it was probably over two hundred years old. Unlike virtually every Indowy in O'Reilly's experience, the Clan Chief of the Triv Clan, all fourteen of them, never seemed worried or flustered by the presence of humans. Either it realized bone deep that humans, omnivores though they might be, were not going to suddenly kill it for some mistake, or it was almost preternaturally courageous. O'Reilly had never figured out which it was.

"Oh, just some *minor* good news would do," O'Reilly

said, waving the message. "Our old friend is on his way back to Earth. He should already be here, as a matter of fact."

"Dol Ron," the Indowy said calmly. "So I had heard. I wonder what mischief he is up to this time?"

"Well, the first visit we lost Hume, shutting down the only official group that was closing in on the secret of the Darhel," the monsignor said. "The second the Tenth Corps was hacked and the hacking was pinned on the Cybers, who were the only group who was working at breaking the GalTech codes. Oh, and an attempt on the life of Cally O'Neal, which would have destroyed her father. The third was the death of General Taylor, and the elimination of two Société branches. Now this trip. I wonder who is going to die *this* time?"

"Not a soldier," Aelool said. "The Cybers would never stop the killing until the last was done. And they are *very* good assassins."

"Perhaps we should send a few groups of our own," O'Reilly said bitterly. "It's not as if we don't know the Devil when we see him with our own eyes."

"Dol Ron is a known quantity," Aelool said with another grimace. "If he were removed, we would have to develop an information network on a completely different Darhel. Not the easiest thing to do. And then, of course, we could lose it at any time if we run into a 'Cyber' moment. It might be well to, sometime in the near future, create *another* 'Agreement.' The only problem being that they are often so entangling."

"Well, I'm going to pull in my horns and teams," O'Reilly said. He knew that Aelool had been against the Cyber agreement. The Indowy was clan chief only by dint of being the senior survivor of over fourteen million other clan members; he no longer tended to worry about the odd loss here and there. "As well as sending a warning to some 'exterior' groups."

"The O'Neals?" Aelool asked.

"Yes, among others," the monsignor answered. "We don't have a team there anymore; we lost Team Conyers trying to prevent the Ontario sanction. So I think they'll be on their own. But I'll warn them that there might be hostile visitors."

"Keeping the O'Neals, and Michael O'Neal specifically, functional has positive long-term implications," Aelool said with a nod, "It is a thread that is being monitored at the very height of the Bane Sidhe. I have methods to contact them discreetly; would you prefer that I do so?"

"Go ahead," O'Reilly said. "And then get ready for a storm."

Shari ran her finger up a long scar on Papa O'Neal's stomach and fingered a twist of gray chest hair. "That was very nice; you're good."

"Thanks," O'Neal said, rolling over without breaking contact and snagging the bottle of muscadine wine he'd left by the side of the bed. "So are you; you wear an old guy out."

"Fat chance," Shari said with a chuckle. "I'm pretty old and tired myself."

"You're not old at all," O'Neal said, pulling her closer against him. "You're no teenager, but I wouldn't want a teenager in my bed; a person who doesn't have any scars isn't worth my time."

"I don't have any scars," she said, deliberately misunderstanding. "See?" She waved down her body. "Well, an appendix scar, but that's about it."

"You know what I mean," O'Neal replied, looking into her eyes. "I think for all the knife slashes and zippers I've got on my body, I've probably got fewer scars than you. Not many fewer, but fewer."

"Liar."

"When you say that, smile," Mike Senior said, but he smiled as he said it. "Seriously, I made a mistake a long time ago thinking that young and pretty was enough. It's not; a person who hasn't been through the fire doesn't know what the world is about. They think that it's all sweetness and light. It's not; the world is at best chiaroscuro. I swear, my ex-wife still believes you can talk to the Posleen and show them the error of their ways. 'Bring them to the Goddess.' It makes me want to puke. Especially when I think about all the time and effort the 'peace at any price' assholes cost us in the early days of the war. And there are people that are, frankly, five times as bad as the Posleen. The horses don't have any sense or a way out of their cycle; humans can *choose*. The fact is that too damned many of them choose evil."

"I don't think that violence settles *everything*," she said. "And calling humans evil is pretty questionable, even my ex-husband who is about as close as it gets. But it is certainly the only language the Posleen understand. I . . . didn't always believe that. But I haven't been the same person since Fredericksburg."

"I know," he said, wrapping his arms around her. "You're better."

She leaned into him and nipped at his shoulder. "You're just saying that to make me feel better."

"No, I'm saying that to get laid," O'Neal said with a laugh. "If you feel better, that's what they call a fringe benefit."

"What? Again? Did you get a Viagra prescription?"

"For you, baby, I don't need no Viagra!" O'Neal intoned with a waggle of his hips.

"What?" Shari yelped. "Now *that* is corny! Not to mention insulting!"

"Sorry," the farmer repented with a laugh. "I must have been channeling Bruce Campbell there for a second."

"Well, as long as you don't come out with something like 'baby, you got real ugly' I'll let you live," she said with a kiss.

Later she ran her fingers up his spine and whispered in his ear:

"'Bad Ash, Good Ash, you're the one with the gun.'"

# CHAPTER 21

"So, Goloswin, how does it go?" Tulo'stenaloor asked.

The Posleen technician looked up from his monitor and flapped his crest. "It is going well. We have received a new piece of . . . intelligence."

"Ah?" Tulo'stenaloor asked. "From the Net?"

"Yes," Goloswin answered, gesturing at the monitor. "From a Kessentai who was on Aradan. It seems he has gained access to control codes for the metal threshkreen communications. We are now 'in their net' as the humans would say. This includes communications between the chief of all threshkreen in this land and the metal threshkreen. Also, there are other threshkreen who use this communications medium; among others your *lurp* friends. I also have their numbers and disposition in the entire U.S.; the only available unit is in its quarters in the area the humans call 'Pennsylvania.' It also permits entry to Indowy

389

communications on the planet, few as they are. The few Darhel are still locked out, but it gives me a starting point to work on them as well."

"Excellent," Tulo'stenaloor said, flapping his crest in reply. "The assault starts tomorrow at midday. With this information we can know when the damned 'ACS' is coming."

"We can change some of their information," Goloswin said. "Make them think that things have been said which have not or tell them false items. But that will quickly be detected. Or we can simply listen in. As long as they do not realize that we are acting on the basis of the information they should never know."

"That is good," Tulo'stenaloor said. "I think we'll just listen for now. Ensure that Esstu has this information."

"I shall," Goloswin bubbled happily. "It is so very timely!"

"Yes," Tulo'stenaloor said, fingering his crest ornament in thought. "Very timely indeed."

"Balanosol, your forces are a mess," Orostan snapped. He cast a baleful eye over the Kessentai's oolt and raised his crest in anger. The oolt'os were half starved, many of them showing prominent shoulders and backbones, and their equipment was falling apart.

The Kessentai, on the other hand, was a resplendent figure in gold and silver harness—he had enough heavy metal on his harness alone to feed his oolt for a month—and his tenar sported the heaviest model of plasma gun.

"I think," the oolt'ondar continued, "that all things considered, you shall have the honor of leading my portion of the assault on the morrow."

The conversation was taking place under the light of a half moon, just north of Clarkesville where the millions of Posleen were opening up and getting in position to begin the assault. It would be a three hour movement for the front rank from this rear assembly area to the forward assembly area in the ruins of Clayton. By the time they reached Clayton, they could be expected to be under artillery fire; not that that should last long for once.

"Well, I don't think so," Balanosol said, raising his own crest in defiance. "I have seniority over half these young nestlings, including your sorlan here. Let *them* take the honor of the front rank; I intend to survive this assault."

"Do you?" Orostan hissed. "Then look you at the woodline."

The Kessentai turned his head to the side and, in the dim light, saw the flicker of metal in the woods.

"You agreed to obey our orders," Orostan hissed quietly. "That was your word. Not to whimper at the first one you were given. You have eaten our rations and drunk our water and breathed our air for the last month; you owe us *edas*. And the reason that you have, that we have permitted your fuscirto oolt to eat up our stores, is that we needed you, and other scum like you, to take the front rank. And if you think you're going to limp along in the rear, scavenging the leavings of your betters, think again. You can either move to your 'jump-off' position, or I will have my oolt'ondai kill and eat you and your pitiful oolt. You see, the humans *may* kill you. But if you don't move out I *will* kill you. If for no other reason than to remove your blot from the race."

As the rag-tag oolt moved up the highway to their designated position, Cholosta'an flapped his crest. "So this is what you meant by 'political units.'"

"Indeed," Orostan said with a snap of his muzzle. "Better to weed out those like him, better for the force, better for the race. If he survives he will just grab the first useless piece of territory he comes to."

"Instead of getting a cut of everything," Cholosta'an said. "But even your 'political units,' even *my* unit will eventually have to brave the Gap. And we will not do so unscathed."

"Oh, if we were far enough back we would," Orostan disagreed. "But I, for one, have no interest in walking up the pass.

"I'm too old to ride tenar everywhere like you young nestlings," he continued, as the first oolt'poslenar drifted over and dropped to the ground, light as a feather. "Nope, no Gap and no tenar for us; we're riding in style."

Shari yawned as she looked out the window of the Humvee. Franklin was coming up and when they got to the Urb it would be back to the daily grind. But, she recalled with a smile, not for long.

"So you're really going to move up there?" Wendy asked. "What the hell am *I* going to do?"

She pulled at the leather pants she'd picked up at the O'Neals', trying to get a better fit. Papa O'Neal had been more than kind and insisted on outfitting the kids. So when she found the pants while digging in the back of a closet, and clearly liked them, he had also insisted on her wearing them. And when Papa O'Neal insisted, people listened. Only later did she find out they were the late Sharon O'Neal's. She had to admit that the lady must have been in shape; she'd had to roll the cuffs up and was still having trouble getting the . . . ahem, stretched out. Sharon O'Neal must have had legs like a giraffe and a butt the size of an ant.

"I thought you were moving out to live with Tommy," Shari answered. "And, yeah, I think I'll take him up on it. He's a very nice man, a very gentle one for being so . . . dangerous. And God knows growing up on that farm will be better for the kids than in the Urb."

"Well, I'm happy for you, even if I'm sad for me," Wendy said. "And we'll just have to see with Tommy. He just made staff sergeant so I *should* be eligible to move to enlisted housing. It's on Fort Knox and the joke is it's guarded tighter than the gold. I can live with that; I'm tired of being in a target."

"That is the base of the Ten Thousand, right?" Elgars said. She was perched on Mueller's lap on the front seat and she gently rotated his snoring face—he had passed out almost immediately on boarding the truck—away from hers. "So that is where I would go if Colonel Cutprice accepts me 'back'?"

"Yeah," Mosovich said. "And I'm going to recommend that."

"Thank you, Sergeant Major," she said quietly. "I'd like to get back to a unit. I feel a real need to get back to grips. Maybe because it's the only thing I know." She looked out the window to the east and shook her head. "What in the *hell* is that? And where did it come from?"

Mosovich looked where she was pointing and nodded. "I guess Eastern Command decided that we needed some backup."

The SheVa gun was just setting into place, to the east of Dillard. To the north, paralleling the highway and occasionally touching on it, was a smashed track of its movement.

"That's a SheVa gun," Mosovich said. "An anti-lander gun. There's another one down by corps headquarters, but you didn't notice it since it was camouflaged."

As he said that, green and brown foaming liquid began to pour out of inconspicuous ports along the side of the base. The foam quickly hardened creating a mound that built up along the base of the gun system.

A large tractor trailer, with what looked like two brass missiles on the back, backed up to the rear of the SheVa gun and tilted one of the "missiles" upwards, sliding it into a port on the rear of the gun.

"That looks like the biggest . . . bullet in creation," Shari said.

"That's more or less what it is," Mueller answered. "They fire full rounds, not projectiles, bullets, with propellant bags or something. They're the biggest cartridges ever made and the most complicated; among other things the system uses a plasma enhancer that requires resistors to be threaded through the propellant. They're not just stuffed with cordite or something."

"In an hour it will look like a big, green and brown mound," Mosovich said. "Then when landers come over the horizon, it just drives out and engages; the foam flakes off relatively easily. And it's a hell of a lot easier to set up than that much camouflage netting."

"What does it fire?" Elgars asked, still staring at the slowly disappearing monstrosity.

"A sixteen-inch discarding sabot with a nuclear round at the center," Wendy said with a smile in her voice. "When you care enough to send the very best . . ."

"Antimatter, actually," Mosovich said. "Much cleaner than even the cleanest nuke. It's a bit of overkill for the Lampreys; the penetrators generally tear them up pretty good. But it's necessary for the C-Decs, the command ships. They're bigger and have more internal armoring. I hear when they hit a lander's containment system it's pretty spectacular."

"Why's it here?" Shari asked nervously. "This corps already had one, right? I thought they were pretty rare."

"They are," Mosovich said thoughtfully. "Like I said, I guess Eastern Command decided we needed some backup."

"So, is something about to go wrong?" Shari asked.

"I *hate* these things," Sergeant Buckley said. "There's a billion things to go wrong."

Sergeant Joseph Buckley had been fighting the Posleen almost since the beginning of the war. He had been in the first, experimental, ACS unit in the fighting in Diess. After Diess, he had been medically evacuated as a psychological casualty; after being caught in a fuel-air explosion, being stuck under a half a kilometer of rubble, having your hand blown off trying to cut your way out, getting swept away in a nuclear blast front and having half a space cruiser land on you, driving you back under a half kilometer of rubble, anyone could tend to go around the bend.

But desperate times called for desperate measures and in time even Joe Buckley was found fit for duty. As long as it wasn't too stressful and had nothing to do with combat suits. It was his only insistence, and he was firm about it to the point of court-martial, that he would *not* have to put on a suit. The series of events on Diess had given him a permanent psychosis about combat suits and all peripheral equipment. In fact, he had come to the conclusion that the whole problem with the war was an emphasis on high technology over the tried and true.

"I tell you," he said, ripping the plastic cover off of the recalcitrant M134 7.62 Gatling gun. "What we need up here is . . ."

" . . . water-cooled Browning machine guns," said Corporal Wright. "I know, I know."

"You think I'm joking," he said, pulling out the jammed round and snarling at it. "This would never happen with a Browning. That's the problem, everybody wants *more* firepower."

The fighting position was on the second tier of the Wall, overlooking Highway 441. Clayton was out of sight around the edge of the mountain, but they had gotten warnings from the Black Mountain observation post that there was a Posleen swarm on the way up the road. So getting Gun Position B-146 back in operation was a priority.

The Wall was a mass of firing and observation ports. Beside the Gatling ports, there were regular heavy weapons, designed for engaging tenar, and rifle ports for the soldiers, whose main job was feeding the guns, to get in the occasional shot if they so desired. But, really, it was the Gatling guns, and the artillery hammering down from above, that did most of the damage.

The gun was mounted on an M27-G2 semi-fixed mount. On command, it would automatically move back and forth across a fixed azimuth, putting out a hail of bullets. The firing circuit was keyed in parallel with all the other guns in the B-14 zone, and at the press of a button, a button located in an armored command center, all twelve weapons would open up, each spitting out either 2000 or 4000 rounds per minute, depending on the setting, and filling the air with 7.62 rounds.

At least, that was the theory. The M134 was a fairly reliable system and the basic M27 mount design was older and more tried than Buckley. But tiny changes in design, necessary to convert both systems to a ground, universal availability, fixed, remotely controlled firing system instead of an aerial, regular availability, firing system, had led to tiny quirks, some of them related to the design, but most of them related to trying to integrate it. To manage those quirks, six soldiers, under Sergeant Buckley, were supposed to keep the guns mechanically functional and "fed" both between battles and during them.

In the case of Buckley's squad, instead of one soldier per two guns it seemed that they needed two soldiers per gun. Buckley, personally and publicly, blamed this on the units that they replaced; duties in the defense line rotated between the three divisions of the Corps and Buckley was *convinced* that the units that had the guns in the other divisions never pulled maintenance and/or actively sabotaged the guns.

The Wall unit, one of the three divisions in the corps, was on duty twenty-four hours per day for four weeks, living in rather squalid quarters within the Wall itself; then it was rotated to the rear. There it went through a maintenance and support cycle, living out of barracks and, in the event of a heavy attack, moving to tertiary defenses that were actually *behind* the corps headquarters. After four weeks in that status, the unit would rotate "forward" to the secondary defense positions, which meant it had to be "on call" for combat. Until recently that had meant sitting in the barracks reading girly magazines and getting into fights. However, since that engineer prick from headquarters had shown up it meant working on the trenches and bunkers twelve hours per day. After twelve hours of shovelling and filling sandbags you could barely make it to the club.

Buckley was morally positive that those bastards in the 103rd had sabotaged his guns. And now they were probably sucking down a cold one in the NCO club and laughing at him behind his back.

Everyone else in the squad, and in the company for that matter, privately blamed the situation on Buckley. Anyone who has a ship fall on them tends to get a bad luck reputation and that condition seemed to have spread to everything he touched. Whether it was an issued Humvee or the guns on the line or even his personal rifle, something odd and unusual always seemed to happen to it.

In this case it was Gun B-146, which absolutely refused to fire in any sort of reliable and continuous manner.

"I think it's a short," Specialist Alejandro said, ramming a cleaning rod with a Breakfree-soaked swab down the number four barrel.

"We checked for a short," Buckley snarled. "The gun's drawing what it should and no more."

"I think it's the ammo," Wright said.

"We replaced the box," Buckley said, pointing to the huge case of belted 7.62 mounted under the gun. "And ran the ammo on 148; it ran fine."

"I think it's a ground fault coming off of the M27," Alejandro insisted, pulling out the cleaning rod. "The M27 is acting funky too."

"I think it's you, Sergeant," Wright said, rotating the gun manually.

"It's those fuckers from the 103rd," Buckley said. "They're fucking with all the guns. I tell you, they just want us to look bad."

"Well, that's not hard," Wright said quietly.

"What's that, Specialist?" Buckley said.

"Nothing, Sergeant," Wright answered. "It's functioning now, let's test it."

"Okay," Buckley said, stepping back. "Reset the breaker, Alejandro."

The specialist ensured the barrels were free of obstructions, took the tags off the breakers for the gun and the mount and threw them over. "We're hot."

"Safe off," Buckley said, plugging in a local controller.

"Weapon is hot," he continued, rotating a round into the first chamber.

"Earplugs aren't in," Wright said hastily, reaching in his breast pocket.

"It's just a short burst," Buckley answered. "Here goes."

He set the gun to four thousand rpm, max speed, and pressed the fire button.

The rounds flew out with a ripping snarl like a chainsaw and the fire looked like nothing so much as an orange laser; every fifth round was a tracer and they were so close together they looked like one continuous stream.

Buckley nodded as the gun continued to fire and then frowned as it clanked to a halt with a shrill scream of disengaged torsion controller. "Shit." The brass cartridge that had caused the latest jam was clearly evident, "stovepiped" in the ejector. "Shit, shit, shit," he continued, reaching for the cartridge.

"Sarge, the gun's hot," Wright objected.

"Screw that," Buckley said, waving Alejandro away from the breakers. "I want to get this over with before . . ."

The two specialists never found out what it was he wanted to get it over with before because the problem *was* a short, but not in the gun or even in the M27 mount. The problem was in the resistor that controlled power flow to the M27.

The resistor coil stepped down the power that was supplied to all the guns so that the voltage going to the mounts was at the proper level. But in the case of Mount B-146, the resistor was slightly flawed, and it was permitting a higher charge through.

This charge had been "bleeding over" to the gun, and since the gun was driven by an electrical motor it was causing the motor to run at a slightly higher rpm than it was strictly designed for. But since the gun was on a controlled ground, the full power of the flawed resistor had never been released.

When Sergeant Buckley grabbed the brass, though, the power, having found a conduit, went to work. And he was suddenly hit by 220 volts of AC power.

Buckley stood in place, shaking for a moment, until all the breakers for the sector blew out.

"Damn," said Wright. "That's gotta *hurt*. You didn't have to blow him to hell to prove your point, Alejandro."

"I didn't," the specialist replied, pulling an injector of Hiberzine out of the first aid case. "Call the medics while I start the CPR. Tell 'em Buckley's having a bad day again."

"Come!"

Lieutenant Sunday walked into the company commander's office and came to the position of attention. "You asked to see me, ma'am?"

"You don't have to pop to attention every time you come in, Sunday," Slight said with a smile. "Bowing will suffice."

"Yes, ma'am," he said, starting to bow.

"Oh, cut it out." She laughed. "Look, Lieutenant, I know it's Saturday, but we're in a bind. First Sergeant?"

It was only then that Tommy noticed First Sergeant Bogdanovich in the corner, lounging like a leopard on the company commander's couch.

Boggle's brow furrowed and she leaned forward urgently. "Lieutenant, several suits in the company have a critical shortage of biotic undergel. Since it's a Galtech controlled substance, it can only be released to a qualified Fleet officer."

"I'm hereby appointing you Armory officer for the

company," Slight continued. "I want you to go over to S-4 and find all the undergel you can lay your hands on. Clear?"

"Clear, ma'am," Sunday said, snapping to attention. "Permission to leave?"

"Go," Slight said seriously. "And don't come back until you have it; we really need to get the suits up to speed."

After the mountainous lieutenant was well clear of the room the two women exchanged glances and then First Sergeant Bogdanovich, veteran of countless battlefields, gave a very uncharacteristic giggle. "Two hours."

"Less," Slight said shaking her head. "He's no dummy."

Lieutenant Sunday marched into the office of the S-4 NCOIC, who started to get to his feet.

"At ease," the lieutenant said waving his hand. "Rest even."

"Good morning, L-T," the staff sergeant said. "What can I do for you this fine . . . er . . . Sunday morning." The combination of the name of the day and the officer's name clearly had him baffled.

"Don't worry about it," Sunday said. "I've dealt with it all my life; I'm used to it. The CO sent me over here to draw some undergel. I've been designated the 'Armory Officer' so I'm cleared."

"Ah, undergel, huh?" McConnell said with a frown. "I think we're about out, sir. The Indowy used it up fitting suits last month. We've got a shipment on order, but . . . well, you know how the Galtech supply line is."

"Damn," said Sunday, nodding his head seriously. "All out, huh? There's not like, you know, one can, someplace? Or maybe a short case hiding under somebody's desk?"

McConnell looked at him sidelong for a second then nodded. "Well, I think there *might* be a can in the battalion headquarters," he answered on a rising note.

"Gee," said Sunday, putting his hands on his hips. "Maybe I should run over to battalion and see the . . . ?"

"Battalion commander," McConnell answered.

"You sure?" Sunday asked, honestly surprised. "It's not like, oh, I dunno, the S-3 NCOIC or, maybe, the sergeant major?"

"Nope, L-T," McConnell answered, definitely. "Major O'Neal. He has the can of undergel. Or so I have been given to believe."

"Right," Sunday said, getting to his feet. "Here I go to see the Battalion Commander to Get Some Undergel. See? And, oh, by the way, Sergeant."

"Yesss?" asked McConnell.

"I think maybe you should call the BC and tell him I'm coming over," Sunday said with a feral grin. "But, maybe, you should leave the . . . overtones of our conversation out." He leaned over the sergeant's desk and smiled in a friendly manner. "Okay?"

"Okay," McConnell said with a grin. "Whatever you say, L-T."

"Apropos of nothing whatsoever, Sergeant," Sunday continued, straightening up. "I feel constrained to mention that I'm something of a student of the Armored Combat Suit. And, if memory serves correctly, the suits generate their *own* underlayer nannites. What do you have to say that?"

"I wouldn't know what to say, L-T," the NCO said with a smile.

"I'm also constrained to mention, *sarge*, that when someone in the military refers to the other by their bare rank, or a negative derivation thereof, such as the name of a bottom-feeding fish, it is generally a sign that that person does not truly respect the individual, whatever their rank. What do you have to say that?"

The NCO laughed. "I wouldn't say a *damned* thing to that, *sir*."

"Call me Tank, Sergeant McConnell," Sunday said on the way out the door. "All my friends do."

# CHAPTER 22

"Major," said Gunny Pappas with a straight face, "Lieutenant Sunday is out here and would like a minute of your time."

"Come on in, Sunday," O'Neal called.

Sunday marched in, came to the position of attention, and saluted. "Sir. Captain Slight has requested that I obtain some undergel replacement! I am given to understand that you have the last available can in the battalion!"

Mike leaned back, returned the salute languidly and tapped the ash off the end of his cigar. "Running low, huh? And, as a matter of fact, I sent the can over to Charlie Company. But I hear they used it up. You can go over to Charlie and ask them if there's any left or you can try to scrounge some up on your own. Your call."

"Yes, sir," Sunday said, saluting again. "Permission to continue my search, sir!"

"Carry on, Sunday," O'Neal said, with another languid wave. "And tell Slight that undergel doesn't grow on trees."

"Yes, sir!" the lieutenant said, spinning about and marching out the door.

O'Neal shook his head as Gunny Pappas came in the door with his hand over his mouth.

"You're sniggering, Gunny."

"I am not," the former marine answered. "I'm snickering. There's a difference."

"I don't think this was a good idea," O'Neal said, taking a puff of the cigar to keep it lit. "Sunday's both smart and former service. I think Slight's in over her head, frankly."

"Maybe she is," the sergeant major said with a shrug. "But this is an old and honorable tradition. What sort of unit would we be if we *didn't* send the new L-T out on a quest for something that doesn't exist?"

"I dunno," Mike said with a smile. "One that doesn't have a piper?"

Sunday stood outside the battalion headquarters, one hand on his hip and the other slowly rubbing his chin, a thoughtful expression on his face. He looked around the small cantonment area, searching for a gleam of inspiration until his eye was caught by a poster advertising the new Ground Forces Exchange. He looked at it thoughtfully for a moment and then grinned.

Whistling, he strode down the road towards main post, saluting the occasional passing troop. Any of them that looked at his face, looked away almost immediately; that was not the sort of expression you wanted to see on a person approximately the size of a bulldozer.

❖    ❖    ❖

Maggie Findley was a short, petite brunette, seventeen years old and in another year, if she was still alive, would graduate from Central High School ("Home of the Dragons!"). She had applied for the job at the Ground Forces Exchange for two reasons; it was a job and jobs were scarce these days and, all things being equal it might be a good way to meet a nice guy.

This was her first shift all alone on the register and, so far, it had been a quiet Saturday morning. A rather large soldier had entered not too long before and headed to the back but, really, they were generally nice guys.

When she saw him headed back to the front she was momentarily a little nervous; he was not just large he was *enormous*. But after a moment she noticed the silver bars of a first lieutenant and stopped worrying; officers were gentlemen after all. So it was in this pleasant state of mind that she blushed bright red when the lieutenant set down the small box he had been carrying.

Tommy smiled at the young lady behind the counter, whose nametag read "Findley." "Would you happen to have any more of this in the back? There were only a few boxes stocked on the shelf."

"Uh," she looked from the box to the officer and blushed again. "You . . . need more?" she squeaked.

"Actually, if you have an unopened case that would be perfect," he said with an unintentionally feral grin. "My company commander and I are . . ." he made some vague hand gestures, " . . . having some difficulty."

"I'll-go-right-now," Maggie said quickly and darted around the counter towards the back.

Tommy stood at the counter, aimlessly whistling through his teeth for a moment, then picked up a copy of *Guns and Ammo*, one of the few magazines to survive the collapse in publishing. He flipped through a couple of pages looking at the new Desert Eagle .65 design. He, personally, thought that anyone smaller than him would be as likely to knock themselves out as be able to fire the damned thing. But some people just had to have the biggest gun on the block.

The clerk came back carrying, as surreptitiously as possible, a small blue-and-white box. "We . . . only have it in the brand name. . . ."

"That's fine," Tommy said, putting the magazine away and pulling out his wallet. "Perfect, actually."

"Will that be paper or plastic?" Maggie asked breathlessly, trying not to meet his eye.

"Oh, paper, by all means," Tommy said with a feral grin. "Please."

"Sergeant Bogdanovich?" Lieutenant Sunday said hesitantly, stepping through the first sergeant's door. "Could you join me for a moment?"

"Certainly, sir," Boggle said, getting up. She nodded at the package. "Is that the undergel?"

"I had to go to battalion looking for it," Tommy said obliquely, opening the door to the company commander's office. "Permission to enter, ma'am?"

"Oh, come in, Sunday," Captain Slight said. "Did you find the undergel?"

"Alas, no, ma'am," Sunday said, coming to attention with a long face. "It appears it has all been expended by Charlie Company, ma'am. However, I remembered in my reading that alternate materials can sometimes be substituted," he continued, pulling the case of K-Y jelly out of the paper bag and setting it on the company commander's desk, "and I thought that, given the specifications, this might satisfy your needs."

Captain Slight blushed bright red as Bogdanovich broke into howls of laughter. "Why, yes, sar . . . Lieutenant. I suppose that . . . could be a useful substitute in some cases."

Captain Slight shook her head in chagrin. "Major O'Neal *warned* me not to do this."

"I think we should listen to him next time, ma'am," Boggle said, wiping the tears out of her eyes. "Tricky, L-T."

"I almost considered it over the top," Sunday admitted. "I considered simple Vaseline, but I was afraid it wouldn't get the point across quite as effectively."

"Don't push it," Slight said with a smile. "We got the pun. Okay, to business. I've decided that the best choice is to put you with the Reapers."

"Yes, ma'am," Sunday said with a puzzled expression.

"The Reapers are almost entirely long service," she said. "However, in Roanoke their former platoon sergeant got hit and is going to be in the Regen tanks for a while. We're short on NCOs so you're basically going to be your own platoon sergeant as well as platoon leader. Normally that's the sort of thing that I'd throw on an experienced NCO . . ."

"But you don't have any," Sunday said with a smile. "And I *am* an experienced NCO. What am I getting?"

"Well, they all know their job," First Sergeant Bogdanovich answered. "And they do it, in combat."

"And in garrison they're impossible," Sunday said.

"Well, we haven't been 'in garrison' in a long time," the company commander said. "But . . . the Bravo Reapers tend to be . . . a bit of a handful. This little charade we went through was, as much as anything, a test to . . ."

"See if I knew how to handle a practical joke?" Sunday said with a huge grin. "They like to play games, huh? I love to play games." He grinned ferally. "I am a *master* of playing games."

"Well, then you should have fun," Captain Slight said with a smile. "You got anything else?"

"No ma'am," the lieutenant said, reaching for the case of KY jelly. "I guess I'll return this."

"No, no," she said, putting her hand on the case. "I think I'll keep it. As an object lesson. You go get ready for the return of your troops; they'll be back tomorrow morning, most of them, hung over and unhappy."

"That I will, ma'am," Sunday said, saluting and stepping out the door.

He paused in the outer office and pursed his lips in thought. "AID, let's start looking at records of the Bravo Reapers. I want both combat reports, live audio-video whenever possible, and personal records." *Know thine enemy*, he thought with a chuckle.

Major Ryan was of the opinion that there was no substitute for checking up on the progress of the defense works in person. Especially on Sundays when it was just as likely that everyone was laying out.

Today they'd probably be busy, though. He could already hear Colonel Jorgensen's precious artillery tubes firing on the approaching horde; he imagined that somebody would be up and ready to receive them. Indeed, the Wall appeared to be a veritable beehive of activity; it even looked a bit like one.

The Wall was over seven stories high at the point that it passed through Black Mountain gap, with each level sporting a different mix of weaponry. These ranged from Shrike light anti-lander systems to giant sheets of directional mines called Longswords. In the last five years only one attack had made it to the Wall, and that one had been repulsed by the Longswords.

He climbed up one of the back stairs and looked out over the secondary defenses. 23rd Division had just replaced the 103rd, and that division was well to the rear, but the 49th was currently at work on the trench lines that backstopped the Wall.

The trenches were supposed to be almost continuous from one side of the defense zone to the other with integrated bunkers. Most important of all, there was to be no direct route to the rear from the primary line of defense. However, because of the difficulties of supporting a division in the Wall, and because nobody thought the Posleen would ever be able to breach it after the first year or so, a road had been put back in, on the base metal for 441, most of which had never been removed, and there was now a four-lane highway that led from the wall to the corps supply depot. In addition, many of the corps units that directly supported the wall had been "forward deployed," that is they were often plunked directly on the secondary and tertiary trench lines. In many cases commanders of these support forces, for a variety of reasons including the ever popular "safety," had filled in the trenches and even disassembled the bunkers. What was left was the most unholy mess imaginable.

In addition to that mess, directly to the rear of the Wall was a large parking area for the hundreds of vehicles the commanders and staff in the wall division felt absolutely necessary for their daily use.

Well, there had been. The parking area was gone; the Standard Operating Procedure for the entire U.S. was that commanders of forward deployed units moved forward with their units and stayed there, with only a few personnel being shuttled back and forth, and transportation for them was provided by "higher." Thus if the Corps commander wanted to talk to, say, the 23rd division commander he sent a Humvee to pick him up. And he didn't keep him away from his unit for long.

One of the first things that Ryan had mentioned on inspecting the defenses was the habit of the forward deployed commanders, and just as often staff officers and even senior NCOs, running back to their quarters to spend the night, rather than in the Wall where they were supposed to be. Taking away the vehicles was one way to prevent it.

In addition the trench lines once again ran across the direct route with a winding road threading through them to the front. The Posleen, if they took the wall, would have to choose to maneuver into and out of trenches, something the equi-form aliens had remarkable trouble with, or take the winding road, adding time to their movement and opening up their formations to flanking shots.

Unfortunately the trenches and bunkers that had once been there had not been replaced and there was hardly any work done yet on the tertiary lines. What that meant was that if there *was* a breach, a serious one, the Posleen, conceivably, had a nearly clear shot at the heart of the corps. And because this part of the front had been stripped of support, there wouldn't be anything to stop them short of the mountains. Certainly there wasn't anything short of Franklin. Which meant making sure the defenses were as ready as possible was high on the list of priorities.

He shook his head as the ambulance pulled away from the base of the wall. Admittedly the pace of work meant that there would be a slight increase in injuries. But that was the price of war; better a few accidents than a breach.

He ducked in through the armored door and threaded his way through the internal maze. The Wall really should have been called the Fortress; it was wider than it was high and filled with barracks, mess-halls, storerooms and magazines. Only the forward portion and a few points along the back were devoted to fighting; the rest was the facilities necessary to support an embattled division including shops and parts to keep the guns running.

Ryan continued on into the bowels of the facility until he came to a guarded door. He showed the MP his key-card and entered the command center for the Wall.

One glance at the status board told him most of what he had to know; the Posleen were pressing forward a solid block up Highway 441 and all side roads. The assembly area was Clayton and some smart Posleen had apparently moved two Lampreys into the area. They were marked on the schematic along with a note that artillery fire was being interdicted over the whole town. There was spot interdiction along the roads as well, indicating the presence of landers, but these were out of sight of the observation post on Black Mountain.

The command post was technically in charge of the division G-3, a bird colonel, but Ryan had long since found that the Division Plans officer, a major like himself, had a firmer grasp on moment-to-moment realities than the G-3. Not that Colonel White was the sort of loser that General Bernard tended to surround himself with. But Major Brandt tended to be more on the up and up.

He stepped over to the major's command console and raised an eyebrow. "Anything I should know?"

"Full court press," Brandt said, glancing up. "If they keep on this way, though, it should be something like Waterloo."

" 'A near run thing'?"

" 'They came at us in the same old way . . .' "

"Ah," Ryan said with an uncertain nod. "Better. I was afraid from the intel we'd gotten about that globe that they *weren't* going to act 'the same old way.'"

"Well, two? no, three years ago, we had a C-Dec get close enough that it could fire directly at us. I understand that was hairy; it had a space-capable plasma cannon and it really gouged up the Wall. But we *still* stopped them. And *it* got taken out by a company of Screaming Meemies. We've got a SheVa now, two from what I hear."

"Yeah," Ryan said unhappily. "I'm still jumpy about some of the stuff that the Lurps reported. There were indications of a massive ingathering, but this looks like it's about the size of a single globe force, maybe four or five million. They've hit us with that before and bounced. I just . . . I dunno."

"Same old same old," Brandt said with a shrug. "Fine by me."

"Just . . . keep your eyes open," Ryan said. "I'm heading back to HQ; that's where I'm supposed to be anyway."

"Okay, have fun," Brandt said with a grin. "I'm gonna be busy killing Posleen anyway."

"Been there, done that," Ryan muttered as he walked out of the command center. "Got the scars."

Ryan wandered out the way he had come in, noting in passing that the level of activity in the hallways was increasing and that the automatic cannons on the top level had opened fire.

He tromped down the stairs to his Humvee and shook his head as the first of the Gatling guns opened up. Next month they had planned on rebuilding the wire and stake obstacles to the front of the wall, but it looked like that would have to wait.

He quickly drove through the serpentine road, slowing whenever groups of soldiers, who should have already been in place, crossed the road to their defense positions. There was a steady stream of vehicles heading to the Wall and the secondary defenses and half the time he felt like he was fighting against a salmon run. Twice MPs waved him off the road to let groups through in the opposite direction, but after a half an hour he finally reached the motorpool on the west side of the corps headquarters.

As he mounted the steps towards the former school he noted that the green-and-blue "hill" to the east was starting to shake and he looked to the south. Sure enough, landers were coming in view. Oh, this should be good.

# CHAPTER 23

*Mountain City, GA, United States, Sol III*
*1113 EDT Saturday September 26, 2009* AD

"I feel . . . uncomfortable watching the assault from a place of safety, Oolt'ondai," Cholosta'an said.

They were both observing through vision screens the progress of the assault. The lead companies, including Balanosol, had been for all practical purposes wiped out. There might be a few members of the surviving oolt that had been lead oolt'os, but none of the Kessentai had survived.

The humans were devilishly effective at finding and engaging the Kessentai, but the mass assault had masked a greater danger; among the "political units" were Kessentai and cosslain who had "taken a leaf" as the humans would say and were sniping the anti-Kessentai defenses.

The first to be removed were the automated cannons on the top. Once the type had been identified their detectors were easy to spot and Kessentai had engaged them, using manual sights since the automatics were overloaded by fire, from beyond the effective range of the human weapons.

Once those were reduced the slaughter of Kessentai lessened, making the attack more coherent, but there were still other guns engaging the Kessentai. These were engaged in order; the front rank Kessentai were now close enough to bring their oolt to bear and that added to the effect. By the time the fourth rank of the assault was in range of the miniguns all of the upper rank heavy weapons had been engaged and destroyed. Most of the guns were recessed, but if enough plasma is pumped into the hole it doesn't matter.

"Ah, well, that relative safety will be reduced soon, eson'sora," Orostan said with a snap of his mouth. The losses had been heavier than anticipated, including among the "political" Kessentai; the human heavy "sniper" weapons had been engaging them as the automatics were engaging the mass assault. "But I think we have their attention well and truly fixed on the front door, do we not?"

"Indeed, Oolt'ondai," the younger Kessentai said. "And now?"

"And now, we slam the door," Orostan answered, waving to a subcommander.

"Well, I guess we don't have to worry about 146," Wright said philosophically.

Alejandro ducked as another wash of plasma gouted through a firing port. "Or 144 for that matter!"

There was a clang from the armored door to the west as it bent inward, the paint on the surface beginning to smoke.

"Jesus!" Wright said, looking to the other two exits. The one to the east was still intact, apparently, but the smoking ruin of gun 146 was in the way to it.

Their last exit was the door to the interior zones of the wall. It was in a "gap" in the firing points and as long as some random round didn't punch out the four feet of rebar concrete they'd still be able to get out that way.

"143 jammed!" Private Gattike called, running to where the two NCOs were huddled in a cool spot. "What do I do?"

"Unjam it?" Wright asked, getting to his feet. "Any idea why?"

"I dunno," the private snarled. "Maybe it was setting up that second battle-box? It's run through fifty thousand rounds so far!"

"Ah." Wright hit the floor as another set of HVMs hit the wall, filling the interior with splinters. The walls had rubber on the interior to reduce the ricochets, but one slammed into the private at his side with the sound of an axe hitting a watermelon. He looked over at Gattike and shook his head.

"DRT?" Alejandro yelled.

"Yep," Wright answered, crawling forward. "I think 143's gone too."

"Okay," Alejandro yelled back. "Where in the hell are Lewis and Schockley?" he continued. "There's nobody on the left side!"

"I dunno," Wright yelled. He got to 145 and noted that it was out of ammo. "Hey, Alejandro! Gemme a battle-box!"

The specialist shook his head and opened up the ammo port, rolling the box out with difficulty—it was a two-man job—and then hitting the ground as the entire massive structure shuddered. The aftershocks continued for a few moments as he tried to keep the four-hundred-pound box from rolling back on him. "Okay," he muttered. "This day officially sucks."

❖    ❖    ❖

Major Jason Porter, commander of SheVa Fourteen, swore bitterly. With some difficulty his driver had hoisted this behemoth to the top of the hill just south of the waste treatment plant and now he could see the Wall, or a portion of it. And the top of the Wall was smoking.

The Posleen were clearly hammering the defenses, but so far there was no sign, from this side, of Lampreys or C-Decs. He considered backing back down the hill; that way they would be out of sight when, if, Posleen ships did come into view. However, as he was getting ready to give the word, the radar pinged with a detection.

One or more ships were moving up the valley towards the Wall. They were staying low, which was unusual enough, but every now and again they popped up for a second. The gun was having a hard time locking on.

"Edwards," he called to the gunner. "Put the gun on a fixed azimuth and elevation that approximates their estimated position and let's see if it can get a lock."

"Roger, sir," the gunner called.

"Come on," Porter whispered. "Get up where we can see you, you sons of mares."


"All ships," Orostan called. "Engage the human defenses."

Despite desperate winnowing on Tulo'stenaloor's part, there were only forty Kessentai who were capable of "fighting" their ships without automatics. Since this required a real "crew," including intelligent and trained persons to man weapons consoles, instead of just hitting the odd flashing button, it was not too surprising. All told, the forty ships were crewed by over four hundred Kessentai. Normally there would have been a bare sixty at most.

But these Kessentai arguably had the second most

important job in the entire "mission"; removing the Wall. And that meant *real* weapons.

The viewscreen went dark as the first anti-ship missile impacted on the Wall.

"Oh, shit," Porter whispered. A section of the Wall the size of a house had just been blasted into the air.

"Solution!" Edwards called.

Porter dropped his eye to the firing sight and hit the confirm key. "Fire!"

"On the Way!"

"Fuscirto uut!" Orostan snarled. "All ships! Stay *low*! Tulo'stenaloor, where are those tenaral!"

"Coming up any time," Tulo'stenaloor said over the circuit. "You *do* want it to be a surprise, don't you?"

"Yes," the oolt'ondai said. "But I have vital missions for every single ship; I need that gun removed. Now."

"Almost there," Tulo'stenaloor said, shifting the data to Orostan's screens. "Almost there."

Pacalostal screamed in pride as the human valley came into view. The sixty tenaral had taken a winding path up and down the valleys of the area the humans called "Warwoman" and now their surprise was complete. The human valley was open to them and they could see both of their primary targets clearly. The hated "SheVa" gun was on a knoll just to the south of them and the majority of the human artillery was to the west, grouped around "John Beck Road" and "Fork Road."

He sent a command to the second division, which swept down to near ground level and increased speed as it entered the corps rear area. Then he took the first division and dropped onto the SheVa gun to the south.

✧　　✧　　✧

The first warning Major Porter had was a garbled call over the corps command frequency. The second warning was when the first plasma blast hammered into his back deck.

SheVas were not, strictly speaking, armored vehicles. They had a lot of really heavy metal pieces on them, some of them quite hard, but they were necessary to support the energies released with each firing of the massive gun. They were *not* designed to withstand close range heavy plasma fire and that became clear on the second hit, when the right rear track separated.

"Son of a bitch!" he shouted as one of the craft flew past a camera. "What in the hell is that?"

The craft looked like something straight out of a 1950s science fiction novel. It was more or less saucer shaped with a small turret on the top. Most of the turrets seemed to have . . . Posleen plasma guns mounted in them. As he panned the camera to follow the craft's flight it fired another bolt into the front quadrant.

"We've lost the right track and drivers fourteen and fifteen," Warrant Officer Tapes called. "I've hit the track release, but we'll have to drive off of it. And that drops our max speed way down."

"Get us out of here," Porter said. "Back us up."

"Solution!"

"Belay that order," he called, dropping his eye to the sight. Without really looking he hit the confirm button. "Fire!"

"On the Way!"

"DOWN, DOWN, stay *DOWN*!" Orostan called. He flapped his crest happily, though, at the sight of the crumbling wall. The massive concrete structure was completely shattered across the center from repeated antimatter and plasma strikes and the way would soon be open. Rocky—the front ranks would have some clearing to do—but open. "And the artillery is dropping off," he added.

"Yes, it is," Cholosta'an said. "Soon we will be through. A real breakthrough. This is amazing."

"It has been years in planning," Orostan pointed out. "We will sweep up the mountains, opening pass after pass . . ."

"And at each point, establishing 'toll booths,'" Cholosta'an said with a flap of humor. "That was brilliant. Anyone who passes through must agree to submit ten percent of their earnings."

"Brilliant indeed," Orostan said. "Tulo'stenaloor feels that these humans owe him much. If he cannot take it from them directly, then indirectly will do as well."

"We should not be too happy yet," Cholosta'an said. "These humans . . . tend to be tricky. And they don't give up easily."

"When we are finished here, we and the tenaral will fly up the valley and take all of the key terrain positions on the initial route. The humans may try to block us, but we shall be there first. As soon as the Wall is down."

"And the SheVa gun taken care of," Cholosta'an said.

"Of course."

Another ripple of plasma fire slammed into the gun and one of the rounds penetrated through multiple layers of machinery into the command center.

The damage control panel came apart like a bomb as the last burst of plasma buried itself in the console. Control runs fused together sending power arcing through the panel and into the primary gun controls.

Sergeant Edwards flew back from his controls with a yell, hitting the chair release and backing away as sparks flew out of the targeting system. The fire control computer sparked on for a moment and then died with a rasp.

Major Porter coughed on the smoke and shook his head. "Is it just me or is this like a bad TV sci-fi show?" He hit his own chair release and pulled the warrant officer's back. In the red emergency lights he could see that the warrant had massive burns across his face and chest, but the engineer was still breathing. "Will the gun fire at all?"

"Negative!" Edwards shouted nervously. "I can't even clear the round in the breech!"

"Oh, this is so very good," Porter muttered, laying the warrant's chair flat and gently unstrapping him.

"Uh, sir," Edwards said, supporting half the weight of the warrant as they lifted him out of his chair. "I think we're mostly getting hit on our back deck . . ."

"I noticed," Porter said, looking around. "Tamby! Abandon ship!"

There was no reply from the driver's position so he slid across the smoking deck and looked down.

The driver's position was surrounded by multiple monitors so that the drivers had an almost 360-degree view at all times. Unfortunately, that meant that when a power surge hit there were thousands of volts all of a sudden going nowhere.

Porter slid down into the position, trying not to put his feet into the carbonized figure strapped into the driver's chair, and checked the drive controls. They, remarkably, seemed to be working so he set them on auto, driving forward, and climbed back out. Then he slid back across the floor and hit the escape hatch. The red painted panel opened with a susurrant hiss and lights came on below.

"Where's Tamby?" Edwards asked, dragging the limp warrant officer towards the hatch.

"Tamby won't be joining us today," Porter said,

taking the warrant's feet. "You drive. And drive like a bat out of hell."

"Who's going to gun?" Edwards asked.

"Who the hell cares?" Porter said. "If we're not at least five miles away before they pound through the magazine *nobody's* going to be driving!"

Atrenalasal flapped his crest and keyed his communicator. "Pacalostal! The gun has stopped firing! We should join the attack on the artillery."

"No," the tenaral commander replied. "The orders are to continue firing until it is stopped and burning. Follow the orders."

"Very well," the Kessentai replied. For some reason, pounding plasma round after plasma round into the burning hulk seemed . . . wrong. But orders were orders.

Major Porter hit the lowering circuit before Edwards was even in his seat, but the gunner had the escape vehicle starting before they had dropped more than a meter. Porter sighed as the scream of the jet turbine engine caused the vehicle to purr like a tiger. Functional power was a good thing.

"Thank God for General Motors," he said. He glanced at the height reading then hit the release as another wash of plasma hit the massive SheVa above them. Fuck it. The torsion bars would handle the drop.

At forty miles per hour and accelerating the still bouncing M-1 Abrams burst from under its larger brethren and headed for the shadow of the nearest ridge.

Behind it, plasma rounds continued to dig into the more recalcitrant armor on the back deck of the SheVa gun, right over its nearly full magazines.

# CHAPTER 24

Far-called, our navies melt away;
        On dune and headland sinks the fire:
Lo, all our pomp of yesterday
        Is one with Nineveh and Tyre!
Judge of the Nations, spare us yet,
Lest we forget—lest we forget!

                —Rudyard Kipling
                "Recessional" (1897)

*Rabun Gap, GA, United States, Sol III*
*1249 EDT Saturday September 26, 2009 AD*

When Major Ryan saw the Abrams burst from under the SheVa he very calmly lowered his binoculars, turned around, spotted the nearest bunker and ran for it.

He was surprised when he dropped through the back door that there were not any other inhabitants. The main headquarters didn't have any structural stability; the main "war room" wasn't even on a ground floor. He considered for a moment going back to the headquarters and trying to convince the commander that maybe, just maybe, being on the second floor of a building in the way of a nuclear blast might not be the best spot to be.

He'd seen SheVas go up before; he was at Roanoke when SheVa Twenty-Five lost containment. But at Roanoke the SheVa had been on top of a mountain and fairly separated from the main force. Not parked practically on top of the tertiary defenses and right opposite the corps headquarters.

He glanced at his watch and wondered how long it would take. It was possible, *possible*, that the Posleen would break off their attack before the containment failed. Actually, if they were *smart* they would break off their attack before the containment failed.

Posleen. Smart.

Not.

As he was looking at his watch and calculating his odds of surviving a run to the motorpool he was joined by a female specialist. She tripped on the entry and tumbled into the far corner.

"Well," she muttered, sitting up, but not getting to her feet. "That was a hell of an entry." She looked over at the officer and shook her head. "You might want to get down, sir. I think a nuke is about to go off."

"Yes," Ryan said, looking at his watch again. He had just noticed that he could faintly hear the "swish-crack!" of the plasma rounds hitting the distant SheVa gun. At least he could between the sounds of secondary explosions from the artillery and the heavy ship's weapons tearing the Wall apart. "But we should have about three seconds to bend over and kiss our ass goodbye after the 'big flashbulb' goes off." He smiled at her grimly. "Don't look towards the light; the light is not your friend."

❖         ❖         ❖

"We're gonna make it," Edwards said, gunning the tank down the streambed of the Little Tennessee River, the water flying up on either side. "I guess that armor is tougher than they thought."

"Maybe," said Major Porter, "if . . ."

What the conditions were Edwards wasn't going to find out because as the major spoke the world went white.

The magazine for the SheVa guns was the heaviest armored container ever designed. The inner layer was simple steel, four layers of hardened case steel coated with "supersteel," a recent development that increased the surface hardness of steel almost fourfold. Outside that were two layers of "honeycomb" armor made of tungsten and synthetic sapphire. The outermost section was multiple layers of ablative explosive plates. These had been found to disrupt Posleen plasma guns, to an extent.

In addition there were four sections that were *designed* to "control" the explosion and "blow out" if a round went off. And there were internal baffles designed to direct the majority of the explosion away from surrounding rounds. In that way it was felt that the explosion could be reduced to at most one or two rounds. Better a minor cataclysm than a major one.

The Posleen had determined that most tanks placed their engines at the front and rear. And since their orders were to keep pounding until the gun stopped and was burning, they had pounded over four hundred plasma blasts into the rear compartment. There was only so much that even the strongest armor could take.

The round that actually penetrated had one last defense to make it through. But at the end it cut through the thin shell of depleted uranium surrounding the antimatter core with relative ease. The antimatter then did what antimatter does when it comes into contact with regular matter. Explode. Spectacularly.

The accidentally targeted round was only equivalent to 10 kilotons and the engineers were relatively sure that a single round exploding would be controlled by the container. At the most, if it was on the outer rack it would blow out and only be a nuisance to any unit within, say, a mile of the gun. A major nuisance to them, but if you weren't *too* close or, say, directly behind the gun, you might survive.

In this case, however, the round was on the inner rack, where there were no available blow-out panels. In addition the plasma rounds worming their way into the gun's vitals had shattered most of the internal compartmentalization, for whatever good it might have done. So when the round went off it set off all the remaining rounds racked in the magazine.

The gun had fired twice and had one round loaded. So there were only five rounds to blow. But they went in a ripple sequence that was effectively instantaneous. And both the nature of the containment vessel and the damage that it had sustained combined to cause a near optimum explosion.

The fireball was noticeable from as far away as Asheville and the overpressure wave from it reached out to swallow the corps, huddled as it was in a valley.

Damage from nuclear weapons comes from three primary sources: overpressure, heat and radiation. Overpressure is generally referred to as the "shock-wave" and is analogous to the effects of a tornado; when the high pressure of the "event" hits a structure, it collapses from the difference in pressure inside and outside its walls. Windows shatter inward, doors collapse and so do walls and ceilings. Combine this with hurricane force winds and close to the center of the blast, everything in its path is destroyed.

The second major cause of damage is from thermal effects. The intense heat of a nuclear, or in this case antimatter, explosion releases an enormous amount of infrared radiation. Any human, or Posleen, in direct view of the fireball, and within a limited distance, could be expected to sustain first-, second- or even third-degree burns. Due to the nature of the fireball, and the momentary containment by the walls of the magazine, thermal damage was minimized.

The third major category of injury was radiation. With antimatter explosions, there was a hard wave of gamma rays, but they were effective only at a limited distance. Like a neutron bomb, hydrogen-antihydrogen conversions gave lots of heat and "power," but very little lingering radiation. This gamma pulse, however, was quite extraordinary.

It was the gamma pulse, as much as anything, which doomed Major Porter and his driver. They were dead before they even knew it, their bodies ravaged by high energy particles that caused massive systems failure as their nerve cells suddenly discovered nothing worked and the proteins in their musculature changed into a non-functional form. But it wouldn't have mattered all that much because they were well within the ten psi overpressure zone. The blast wave picked up the seventy-two-ton tank like a sheet of paper and tumbled it into the air.

However, Major Porter was not the only being in the immediate area of effect. Even closer to the explosion were the tenaral of Pacalostal. The explosion tore apart the lightly armored tenar, sending all forty of them into instantaneous oblivion as it washed out over them and the embattled corps.

The shockwave swept over the tertiary defenses and the barracks of the human corps in less than a second, shattering buildings, collapsing bunkers and filling in the few redug trenches. The overpressure wave was still well above five psi when it hit the former school and collapsed the charming brick buildings in less than a second, scattering the bricks and wood of its structure down the hill and into the valley beyond.

The motorpool at the base was still within the worst effects of the overpressure wave, but the major damage was to the buildings as walls and windows shattered inward. Many of the Humvees and trucks in the motorpool had had their windows blasted out; but, by and large, the overpressure wave left them intact and they were shielded from the worst of the blast by the intervening hills.

The heat from the blast did not cause any flash fires outside the immediate vicinity of the SheVa, but the trees on the surrounding hills were tossed aside like matchsticks and those further out were stripped of their leaves.

Further to the west the explosion washed over the remnants of the corps and division artillery, detonating the remaining ordnance and killing most of the surviving artillerymen. The explosion also caught most of the remaining tenaral, however, tumbling them into ruin on the ground.

The human defense of Rabun Gap had been effectively gutted. The majority of its fighting forces were either under assault at the Wall or already dead from the SheVa detonation. The way north was open.

Well, almost.

Papa O'Neal whistled as he walked back to the house. He'd been whistling or humming Van Morrison's "Moondance" just about all morning and Cally was just about sick of it.

"You're awful smug today, Gramps," she said. She

was feeling edgy from the artillery; it had started up midmorning and had been hammering solidly ever since. From the amount and duration they were hammering a major attack although only recently had the Wall guns started to sound.

"I'm just in a fine mood, young lady," he answered.

"Yeah, I suppose you would be," she said with a malicious chuckle.

"And what's *that* supposed to mean?" he said carefully.

Cally set down the knife she had been slicing with and wiped her hands. Reaching under the table she pulled out a Betamax tape and waved it in the air.

"You *do* recall that the entire house is wired for video," she said, darting for the door.

"GIVE ME THAT!" he bellowed, chasing after her.

"You've got a lot of stamina for an old guy!" she yelled, darting around the woodshed.

"COME BACK HERE WITH THAT, YOU LITTLE VIXEN! IF YOU WATCHED . . ."

"Where in the hell did you learn that thing with the legs in the air?" she yelled back.

"AAAAH."

They both stopped at the sound of a large *crack* from the direction of the Wall. The afternoon was bright, but there was still a visible amount of light thrown off by whatever had caused the sound.

"What in the hell was *that*?" Cally asked.

"I don't know," Papa O'Neal answered. "But it was from the Wall. I think maybe we'd better get ready to lock the farm down."

A second series of sharp cracks, like a string of very high explosives, came from the direction of the artillery park and a very loud *boom* indicated a secondary explosion. Papa O'Neal caught a flicker at the valley entrance of something smooth, silver and very fast moving. "What in the hell was that?"

"I dunno, Granpa," Cally said nervously. "But I agree; time to lock and cock." She tossed him the tape. "For your collection. May there be many more."

It took only a few minutes to get all the livestock under cover and the minefields armed, but they barely had finished closing the last gate when the sky lit with a white flash brighter than the sun.

"Granpa?!" Cally called, running towards the house.

"DOWN, DOWN, DOWN!" O'Neal screamed, hitting the ground himself.

The shockwave, when it hit, was hardly noticeable, but there was a distinct change in air pressure and the trees on the heights swayed as if in a high wind. Then the ground wave hit like a minor earthquake.

"What in the hell is *happening*?" Cally called. She was about fifteen feet from the front door on her stomach.

"*All clear!*" Papa O'Neal called, standing up and sprinting for the house. "Inside!"

"Was that what I think it was?" Cally asked when they got inside the door.

"It was a nuke," Papa O'Neal answered. "I think it was probably the Corps SheVa going; the direction and size was about right if I remember correctly."

Cally beat him through the house connection to the bunker by a hair and started throwing on her Kevlar. "We're not set up for nukes, Grandpa."

"I know," he said, turning on the minefields and electronics before donning his own gear. "What bugs me is not knowing what is going on." He flipped from one camera to the next, but most of them were dead. "Damned EMP."

"So what do we do?" Cally asked.

O'Neal thought about that. If it was just one nuke, specifically the SheVa going off, it might not be that bad. It depended, of course, on where the gun was when it went off. But the Wall shouldn't be affected. There was some fighting from there still; or at least those heavy weapons. Those could be Posleen, but think positive.

There were basically two choices. Plan A was hunker in the bunker, fight anything that came up the notch and wait for the Posleen to get wiped out by the Army. Plan B was run like hell. Since the farm had been in the family for generations, Plan B was not their favorite choice.

Without knowing the condition of the corps he had no idea which plan to go with. He picked up the phone installed in the bunker, but there wasn't even a dial tone. He could hike up the ridge to where he could see the corps, but that would mean either both of them going or leaving Cally alone. And with a potentially nuclear environment, getting out of the bunker didn't make a whole hell of a lot of sense. Finally he decided to just try to ride it out.

"We'll stay here," he said, pulling an MRE out of a cabinet. "We'll have grilled ham and cheese tomorrow."

"Yup," Cally said with a grin. "For tomorrow is another day." She looked at her MRE and grimaced: "Trade ya."

"Pruitt, get the gun up, NOW!" Major Robert Mitchell slid into the command seat and started buckling in, flipping all his switches to "On" as fast as he could.

"But, sir!" the gunner called, looking up from his Visor. "It's the one where Bun-Bun has lost his memory and he's being held by these kids who think . . ."

There was a reason that SheVa Nine, now unofficially

referred to as "Bun-Bun," had a two-story picture of a giant, brown-and-white, floppy-eared rabbit holding a switchblade painted on the front carapace. It, and the "Let's Rock, Posleen-boy!" caption, had taken a few hours to explain to the new commander. After reading the comic, and getting hooked, the commander had reluctantly acceded to the painting; some corps permitted them and some didn't and they would just have to see what the local corps commander was like. As it turned out, they hadn't had time to even *check in* with the corps before the fecal matter hit the rotary impeller.

"NOW, Pruitt!" the major yelled. "Load! Fourteen is under attack! I don't know what they are . . ."

"Major!" Warrant Officer Indy called, popping up out of the repair hatch. "*Don't* move the track!"

"Why not?" the commander called. "Schmoo, are we hot?"

"Coming online now, sir," Private Reeves called back. The private was large, pale, doughy looking and somewhat slow, thus the nickname. But he was a good SheVa driver. From deep in the belly of the tank the sound of massive breakers engaging thundered through the structure.

"I don't have signal!" Pruitt called. "Sensors are *offline*. I'd guess camo. Whoa! Big EMP spike! It was worse out there than Bun-Bun denied his *Baywatch*!"

"Crack the camo!" Major Mitchell called. "Manual rotate the lidar."

"Sir!" the warrant said desperately. "That's what I'm trying to tell you; the camo-foam isn't set yet. Until it cures it's . . . malleable. Heat it up and it sets *hard*; if it seals the sensors we'll *never* have an acquisition system. They'll be frozen solid until we can get a CONTAC team out here. With *a lot* of solvent. I shut them down manually as a safety measure."

"Oh, shit," Mitchell said. His schematic was being

picked up from a corps intelligence section still well to the rear. They, in turn, were still getting information from forward deployed sensors and surviving personnel and he could see the first wave of the Posleen pouring into the Gap, with the Lampreys and C-Decs backstopping them. "We have a serious problem here. Suggestions would be helpful, Miss Indy."

"We can probably move the tracks," the warrant officer answered with a desperate grimace. "If they freeze up they're strong enough to break the plastic. Same on rotating the turret. But until the stuff sets, we can't use the automatics to engage. And it could lock up barrel elevation. So we can't elevate or depress."

"So what do we do, Miss Indy?" Mitchell asked patiently.

"We need to avoid moving the sensors or the gun for about another twenty minutes, sir," the engineer said. "We've got a control run problem with the gun anyway; I'm working on it."

"Do we have *any* solvent?" Mitchell asked.

"I have a couple of five-gallon buckets," Indy admitted. "But it would mean climbing up on top and pouring it on the antennas. And I don't think I could clear *all* the goop; we're either going to have to let it set or find a POL point that can dump gasoline all over us!"

"Pruitt, help the warrant," Mitchell said. "*After* you put a round up the tube. Schmoo, get us the hell out of here."

"Yes, sir!" the private said, engaging the treads. "One foam-covered, screwed up, disarmed SheVa, getting the hell out of Dodge."

"You want me to climb up on top of Bun-Bun while we're *moving*?" the gunner asked.

"Hopefully not," the major said, keying the mike to

call the support units. "But if you do, think of it as Torg and Riff on another adventure." After a moment's thought he started looking for the frequencies for Fourteen's ammo trucks; if they survived this they were going to need more than eight reloads.

"But she looks more like Zoe, sir," the gunner said with a shrug, hitting the key to load the first round. "And is it just me, or does anyone else find it odd calling her 'Miss Indy'?"

"Pruitt, shut up and go help the warrant." He shook his head and checked his schematics again. The landers, now unopposed, were moving in a leisurely fashion to silence all resistance in the valley. "Just how much more screwed up is this day going to get?"

"Just how much more screwed up is this going to get?" Orostan asked, looking at the mushroom cloud rising over the Gap. "Pacalolstal, report!"

"I don't think Pacalostal is going to be reporting ever again, Oolt'ondai," Cholosta'an said. "I suspect that most of the tenaral are gone."

"Thrah nah toll!" Orostan cursed. "Demons of Sky and Fire, I *hate* humans!"

"Oh, this isn't too bad," Cholosta'an said philosophically. "We've only lost two ships, the Wall is down and most of the human soldiers are out of our way. This might actually speed things up."

"The tenaral were to be used against the metal threshkreen as well," Orostan snarled.

"We'll deal with them when we have to," Cholosta'an said with a flap of resignation.

"We shall indeed," Orostan said. "Very well; all ships proceed to the Gap. Time for phase two."

# CHAPTER 25

*Rabun Gap, GA, United States, Sol III*
*1309 EDT Saturday September 26, 2009 AD*

Major Ryan pulled his fingers away from his ears and shook his head trying to clear the ringing. "I swear to God, one of these days I'll remember earplugs," he groaned.

"You okay, Major?" the specialist who shared the bunker with him asked.

"What?" Ryan yelled, standing up. The soldier sounded as if she was speaking from the bottom of a well.

"I asked if you were okay!" the specialist shouted, pulling earplugs out of her ears. "I'm, personally, a little shook up."

"Fine," Ryan shouted back. "Time to see if anything's left."

One corner of the bunker had crumpled, but the rest was intact and the doorway was only partially blocked. Crawling through, Ryan looked out on a scene of devastation.

The picturesque school on the top of the hill had been flattened down to stumps. The bricks of the school were scattered down the western slope of the hill along with various less identifiable bits. Ryan saw a few survivors crawling out of bunkers or, in one incredible case, simply sitting up in the wreckage. But for all practical purposes the corps headquarters was gone. He wasn't sure what might have happened to the three division headquarters, but from his perspective it didn't really matter. The corps was for all practical purposes *bound* to rout, the only question was what he, personally, should do about that.

He looked down at the specialist who, having crawled out of the bunker was now perched on it, looking around at the devastation with an expression of interest on her face.

"What's your specialty . . ." He glanced at the nametag which read "Kitteket" and raised his eyebrows. "Kitkay? Kitta . . . ?"

"You have a problem with my name, Major?" the specialist yelled back with a grin. "It's Native American. It's pronounced Kit-a-kutt. Not, and I want to be clear about this, *not* Kittycat."

"Okay," Ryan answered bemusedly. "What the hell, my sergeant at Occoquan was named Leon . . ."

"I'm a clerk typist, sir," the soldier replied loudly. "You know, all the antimatter in that thing must not have gone up. Otherwise this bunker would have collapsed like a tinfoil hut."

"That's not usually the sort of thing that a clerk typist knows," Ryan pointed out. The motorpool fence had been shredded by the expanding shockwave so he walked around the gate and through a gap.

"I read a lot of manuals."

"Uh, huh. I guess that's why you made for the bunker when they started pounding the SheVa?"

"You betcha," she answered with a grin. "I helped build these things, the hell if I was gonna let 'em go to waste!"

"Well, if we're not all going to go to waste we need to beat feet," Ryan commented, striding down the hill.

"Where are you . . . we going?" she asked. "And shouldn't we be . . . I dunno, organizing the defenders or something?"

"Nope," Ryan said. "In just about five minutes it's going to sink in with most of the support units that the Posleen are coming and nothing's gonna stop 'em. When that happens they're going to rout. And *that* means that all the roads will be jammed."

He pulled open the door of the first reasonably intact Humvee and tried to start it. After he reset a breaker it cranked up.

"What we're going to do is head for the nearest ammo depot," he continued. "Along the way we're going to pick up about four more bodies. And then we're going to head for the hills."

"Like I thought," she said, getting in the other side. "Running away."

"Nope," he grinned. "Hills where roads get steep. Because what we're going to pick up at the ammo depot is all the explosives that will fit in this thing. . . ."

Mueller walked out of his quarters and looked down the valley as the first concussion of the space-based weaponry echoed up the mountains. He couldn't see the SheVa gun from his angle, but he did see the signature of its firing and the track of the "silver bullet" heading down range. Nonetheless it was fairly obvious a major attack was underway and he stroked his chin for a moment thinking about what their mission should be. The recon groups were pretty useless in a heavy assault. But these Posleen were acting out of character already by using the landers to assault the Wall.

He stood there for a moment as other NCOs started to filter out of the barracks until he saw the flight of Posleen flying tanks.

"AID," he said, holding his wrist up where the device could observe them. "Do you see those?"

Most of the group had moved out of sight to the right, presumably attacking the artillery park. But one group could be seen sweeping up and down in singles, apparently assaulting something on the east side of the valley.

"I do, Sergeant Mueller. Be advised, the target of those weapons is SheVa Fourteen. Given their weaponry and the number of passes, it is likely that they are going to penetrate its containment system."

"Map the corps forward areas," he said, glancing at the hologram. "Map probable destruction zone of SheVa catastrophic kill."

The results were not good; if . . . when SheVa Fourteen went, it would gut the corps.

"Oh, shit," he muttered. "Get me Sergeant Major Mosovich . . . and you'd better make sure General Horner is aware of this."

Horner looked at his own hologram and shook his head. He had, indeed, been apprised of the situation in the Gap by a call from Eastern Headquarters, and he had to admit that it looked rather bad. He recalled one of his favorite maxims for a moment like this, coined by one of the few really effective British generals of World War II, to the effect that things are never quite as good or bad as first reports indicate. In that case what had just happened in the Gap was simply a disaster rather than the end of the war.

He also noted that even with an AID, the map was

not the reality. And it never hurt to ask an on-scene observer.

"AID, where is Sergeant Major Mosovich in that mess?"

"Sergeant Major Mosovich is about four miles west of the Corps Bachelors Noncommissioned Officers Quarters."

"Get him for me, please."

Mosovich adjusted the strap of his pack as the team reached the top of the ridge. From there it was easy to see the stream of vehicles that indicated a corps in full "bug-out boogie" mode. Not that he could blame them; the detonation of the SheVa was bad enough, but he could see the rear group of landers swarming over the main valley of the Gap; without a functional SheVa gun there was no way to resist those.

"Sergeant Major," his AID chimed. "General Horner calling."

"Put him through." Mosovich sighed. "Afternoon, sir."

"I notice you don't say 'Good afternoon,' Sergeant." The AID threw up a hologram of the officer in the distant headquarters and he had his habitual tight, grim smile locked down. "Tell me what's going on."

"Full tilt bug-out boogie, sir," Mosovich said. "We're heading up into the hills to try to swing down and take a look at them as they pour past or, if it goes the way I'm figuring, try to E&E out to the west. The AID says they're pouring through one hundred thousand an hour and that matches my rough guess of the ones I can see. And we saw flying tanks; the AIDs have visuals on them now. I don't see the corps rallying either, sir. And there's a Sub-Urb just to the north; I'm afraid that's going to be on its own, sir. I'll tell you the truth, sir, I don't like it at all."

"Neither do I, Sergeant Major," Horner replied. "Normally this corps would be backstopped at some point, but this area . . ." He shrugged. "There's also the fact that, apparently in support of this move, the Posleen all up and down the eastern seaboard are pushing at all the passes, gaps and roads, everywhere. There's even a small incursion that has made it into the Shenandoah between Roanoke and Front Royal. I expect other small incursions as things go by. For that matter, I wouldn't be surprised if we lost *more* than one Sub-Urb in this campaign; we've never been under a full court press before."

"That's . . . not good," Mosovich said. "Among other things, we've got a lot of industry in the Shenandoah, don't we?"

"No, it's not good," Horner agreed. "The area that they are in actually has three SheVas; unfortunately all of them are under construction and none of them are armed; we're looking at losing them half built, which is four months production down the tubes. Move as you see fit, Sergeant Major. If we need you at a particular point, I'll call."

"Can I ask what you intend, sir?" the sergeant major asked diffidently. "In this area, I mean."

"I'll probably try to plug the hole," Horner said. "Eastern Command is moving units to close the roads out of the area; there's a recovering division east of Knoxville that is being spread out and pushed forward. But, realistically, the Gap is like the bottom of a funnel; once you get *out* of the gap, there are roads in every direction. Closing *all* of them against that much Posleen pressure is going to be hard; better to close the Gap again and deal with the landers if and when."

"Plugging the hole will be . . . difficult, sir," Mosovich said, shaking his head. "Whatever unit is in there is going to be hit from four directions at once; there's probably still over five million Posleen down in Georgia trying to force their way up, there's going to be nearly a million at their back, there's landers in the air . . . Just about anybody would evaporate like spit on a hot griddle. With all due respect."

"You're right, Sergeant Major," Horner said with a very tight smile. "Just *about* anyone would."

# CHAPTER 26

Shall we only threaten and be angry for an hour?
When the storm is ended shall we find
How softly but swiftly they have sidled back to power
By the favor and contrivance of their kind?
—Rudyard Kipling
"Mesopotamia" (1917)

*Newry Cantonment, PA, United States, Sol III*
*1405 EDT Saturday September 26, 2009 AD*

Mike touched the next e-mail in the queue, which was from Michelle, his youngest daughter, and the message flashed up on his hologram. Michelle had been evacuated off-planet, along with over four million other Fleet dependents from a variety of countries. The ostensible reason for this was to free up the Fleet personnel from worrying about the security of their children. However, since only one child was taken per Fleet "family," the recognized reality was to create a pool of humans in case Earth was lost. When Mike was feeling really cynical he wondered if they were also hostages to ensure the good behavior of the Fleet. Practically everyone in the service had at least one child being raised by Indowy; it would be easy enough for the Darhel to arrange "accidents" if necessary.

Michelle sent him a letter once per week, whether he needed it or not. In the last year they had gotten . . . colder and colder. Not upset or angry with him, just . . . leeched of emotion. It was starting to bother him enough to want to mention it, but he'd come to the conclusion there was no way to do a darn thing about it from 84 light-years away.

Michelle was as brunette as her sister was blonde and, to make things worse, she seemed to have inherited her father's nose. Other than the nose, however, she was starting to be the spitting image of Sharon O'Neal, down to the voice. It was hard, sometimes, for Mike to remember he was dealing with his daughter; Sharon had occasionally taken that same cold, remote tone when things were bad.

"Good day, Father," she began, giving him a small nod. "There are four items of interest this week. . . ."

She wore mostly Indowy fashions now and the covering that was standard Indowy dress looked something like a Mao jacket. Between that and the expressionless monotone of her delivery it was like listening to a poorly designed robot; she could have written the thing and built in more emotion. The Indowy were an almost aggressively selfless race, making the individual submission to the whole something of a religion. It was probably that influence that was making her so remote, so . . . alien.

He realized he had blanked on what she was saying and re-ran the video. Comments on old earth news, report on the final battle for Irmansul—he had an after-action report, a better one than she did, on his AID—

discussion of a promotion, of a type he couldn't decipher, for an Indowy he couldn't place at the moment. It occasionally occurred to him that as an honorary Indowy lord, more like a duke or archduke, he really *should* take more interest in Indowy society. On the other hand, most of his brain cells these days seemed sort of wrapped up in better ways to kill Posleen.

He realized he'd drifted again and there was something important he'd missed; she'd seemed almost animated for a moment. Ah . . .

*"The fourth and final item this individual has to report is acceptance to level two sohon training. Sohon is, as you should be aware, the Indowy field of technical metaphysics. You are, of course, trained for suit fitting which is a specialized form of level two sohon. However, as far as can be determined, this individual is the first human to be accepted for unlimited level two sohon. It is believed that a level of four or even five sohon may eventually be attained. It is to be hoped that positive acclaim may be accrued to the Clan of O'Neal by this and future accomplishments.*

*"Those are the four items of interest for this week. Looking forward to your reply,*

*Michelle O'Neal."*

Mike reran that part of the tape twice shaking his head. He knew, generally, what she was talking about, but the specifics were sort of eluding him. One of the problems with GalTech was that everything had to be produced by Indowy technicians on an individual, custom, basis. Humans, even humans like O'Neal who had had some training in the technique, generally referred to it as "praying," but that wasn't really what was happening. Because the Indowy had been work-ing with atomic level micro-manufacturing for, literally, thousands of years, their method of manufacture involved using swarms of nannites to build products atom by atom in vats. This gave them the capacity to build materials that violated many "known facts" of materials science; the nannites could make atoms do things that occurred only as low probabilities in any other method.

However, the process defied control by even the most advanced computers. The nannites were best controlled through a sort of direct neural interface. An individual Indowy, or, more commonly, groups, would take seats by the tank and . . . manipulate the nannites. It was not a direct thought process; it involved giving the nannites general directions and then . . . letting them use the individual's brain as a remote processor. For a suit fitting, it mostly involved staying very still and sort of meditating while concentrating on the suit "adjusting" to the person it was being shaped on; the nannites and the suit personality handled the rest.

However, as he understood it, the problem with most forms of class two and higher was that the per-son or team had to hold a perfect image of the item to be produced, down to an understanding of the molecular alignments for all of the individual compo-nents. A suit, for example, was a six-month process of construction involving one level six, a grand master of *sohon*, and dozens of lower level Indowy, all meditat-ing in meta-concert on a perfect image, down to the last atom; that was why a suit cost almost as much as a frigate.

He had to admit that the concept of a human advancing to class two *sohon*, especially an eleven-year-old, even a prodigy like his daughter, was rather amazing.

He thought about how to compose a suitable reply. If he was too positive, too emotional, she might see that as a rebuke of her own distance. On the other hand, if he was too wooden, she might see it the same way. Finally he gave up and gushed.

> **Dear Michelle,**
> It's really great to hear about your advancement. I have to say that your success is a *very* good reflection upon the family and that you should be very proud of it, as I am. I hope to someday be able to congratulate you in person and I look forward to the day that we can all be together again as a family.
> **Your loving father,**
> **Dad**

He always sent his replies as text, typing them into an old word processor program and letting the AID convert them to a suitable format and send them on the military network. A laser transmitter would add them to the queue and squirt them at a deep space satellite. From there they would be transferred to Titan Base, then sit in a Jovian communications buoy until a ship was headed out-system. Every ship carried the mail in and out of the system, dropping it at other buoys until eventually, in about six to ten weeks, faster than any but the fastest military courier, it reached Michelle's planet, Daswan. Given that a transport ship would take over a year to make the journey, that wasn't too shabby.

Mike looked at the message and frowned. There should be more, he should be talking about the battalion and things that they had done. But he knew that Michelle had grown *very* uninterested in the blindsided slaughter that was Earth; she didn't even seem to want to return. He was losing this daughter, probably had already lost her, and he didn't know what to do about it or even *how* to do anything about it. She had been dropped into the Indowy, raised by the Indowy and she was becoming Indowy. And he didn't know what to do about *that* either.

Finally he gave up and hit SEND.

The next message was from Cally and it, too, was everything he had come to expect. Cally's messages were not nearly as frequent as Michelle's and the two sisters were clearly developing in . . . somewhat different directions. Cally also did not have access to GalTech and, therefore, sent a standard text message.

> Hey Daddyo
>
> We had visitors this week; some ladies from the nearby Sub-Urb and a couple of snake-eater buddies of Baldy. They had some kids with them who were, like, totally weird. They'd never been outside or shot anything and the weirdest shit freaked 'em out. I mean, don't even mention Posties around these guys or they got, like, spastic.
>
> No big news other than that. Baldy shot a feral up the hill, but that's no big news. I mean, I got a deer, Baldy shot a feral, Wow!
>
> Oh, Baldy's made some mention of one of the ladies that was visiting shacking up with him. Maybe. I'll believe it when I see it. She's a nice old biddy and I think it would be good for him to get laid once in a while; maybe he'd lighten up. But I'll believe it when I see it.

> Oh, yeah, DUDE! Way to stack some
> horse up in Rochester! Can we O'Neals
> kick ass or what?
> :-)
> Take care and remember: HVMs Smart!
> Cally

Mike sighed, hit REPLY and blanked. All things considered, he preferred the Rampage to the Robot, but replying to Cally had its own problems. Should he point out that referring to her grandfather as "Baldy" was probably not the best of all possible actions? Or that at thirteen, worrying whether her grandfather was getting laid often enough was probably not her business? For that matter, it probably wasn't her business at forty.

For that matter, was *she* sexually active? I mean, Dad would probably pass that on to him, but there wasn't much Mike could do about it if she was. What was he going to do? Sitting the guy down and having a man to man talk with him was out; he was five hundred miles away.

And then there was the whole bloodthirsty edge she had developed. He had noted it in Tommy Sunday as well. The generation that was being raised in the war was a generation soaked in blood; they were desensitized to a degree that he found unhealthy.

Maybe it was a valid reaction to the conditions, but a generation so . . . disinterested in the value of life— it seemed to extend to humans as well as Posleen— was not going to be reconstructing a positive, growing, functional society after the war.

There was some fundamental spark, some flare of optimism, that really seemed to be missing from them. Maybe Horner was right, maybe he just wasn't cold and hard enough for this world. God knew at times like this he just wanted to lay the burden down, to just say "get somebody else." But there really wasn't anybody else. To lead the battalion or even carry the spark; his was one of the last generations that was raised in the "golden age." If they didn't keep their eye on the prize, which was to recover the world not just to a survival level, but to recapture the beauty and art and science, then nobody would. Humanity was going to sink to the level the Darhel chose for them. And the only ones who could stop that were these feral wild-children of the war. Who had as much connection to the basic concept of positive human growth and human rights as they did to . . .

Well, frankly, there was nothing they were *more* disconnected from.

This really sucked.

> Dear Cally:
> Rochester was . . . difficult. We were successful, but the battalion took more casualties than I would have liked. I'm personally and professionally happy that we were able to push the lines back to Cayuga, but all things considered I would have preferred that the necessity not drive it.
> I'm glad to hear that you had some visitors, especially female visitors. I know that it must be hard growing up with only your grandfather for company. I hope that you will be able to learn . . .

He backed up and erased the last sentence unfinished. Using the phrase "ladylike" assumed both that the ladies were and that Cally wanted to be. And assumed that "ladylike" was a useful condition, which was a major assumption. Given the choice between a retiring maid and a little war-child, and given the conditions, he'd take war-child any day. Let the world and the future go hang as long as his daughter survived.

> . . . only your grandfather for company.
> By the way, I hope you're not calling him "Baldy" to his face. If you are, I'm going to have to come down and prove that I can still tan your bottom. And before you say "You and what army?" let me point out that I guarantee I can still pin you in about three seconds *without* armor and if you decide to treat me like the Division Sergeant Major there's always the armor to fall back on.
> :->=
> I've come to the conclusion that I want to resume civilian life after the War. That will give me the opportunity to spend the few years that remain before you flee the nest being "around." I look forward to that and to having Michelle home as well. I think of you often and love you very much.
> > Your Dad.
> > Who is *not* going Bald.

The last one was from his father.

> Mike:
> Rochester looked like a fucking nitemare. I'm glad you survived. And glad it was you and not me. We had some visetors last week. Jake Mosovich, I

knew him in Nma, stopped by with some women from the Franklen Urb. There was some kids and his NCO Mueller. Their both snake-eaters with this corps, but their Fleet. We had a good time and I'm gonna asc one of the women her name is Shari to move in here. I think they were good for Cally she hasn't blown up in to days and I like her. Shes got kids they'll move in to. And Cally will have kids around. Shes doing good to and I think she likes the idea.

I got your last mail. You sound like your burnt out. I hope you get a rest. You need a R&R in Hong Kong and get laid. But I think the Posleen have eat all the whores. Maybe you should try one of the corpswhores in your area. If you show 'em youre metals you might even get it for free.

We got your last cair package and I put it away safe. I appresiate the helop in these trying times. And if you ever need anthing, you no where it is.

Take care and don't forget to duck.

　　　　　　　　　　　　　　　Dad.

It took him the usual two reads to interpret his father's missive. His dad was not illiterate or unintelligent, but when Michael O'Neal, Sr. had grown up in Rabun County, going to the eighth grade was for over-educated nerd-boys. Mike's father had been pulled out in the sixth grade to work the fields and had done so until he was seventeen and could escape to the Army.

And, unlike some of his peers, Papa O'Neal had never improved his writing. He was well-read, indeed he read military history voraciously, but the reading never seemed to translate to his written vocabulary or grammar.

That was okay by Major O'Neal, though. In a way, his father was just about the only person he could open up to, even if his advice was sometimes rough and ready.

He was just beginning to mentally compose a reply to the effect that they *were* getting a Rest and Recovery and that despite the fact that he was the *second* person to recommend that he get laid, he had so far failed to do so, when the AID cleared the screen and threw up a hologram.

"Incoming priority message from General Horner."

So much for R&R.

Mike looked at Horner's image and sighed. "Where?"

Horner opened his mouth as if to start a spiel and then seemed to deflate. "Rabun Gap. It's . . . gone, Mike."

Major O'Neal set his jaw and tapped the AID. "Schematic, Shelly."

When he saw the map of the Gap it had red covering all the zones around the Gap including the O'Neal farm. Mike looked at it a moment in disbelief then dropped his face into his hands. "Did the corps last a whole five minutes?"

"I don't know how well they would have done under normal circumstances," Horner answered, "but these Posleen aren't acting like Posleen at all. They have some sort of armored flying tank that took out the SheVa gun that was forward deployed. It apparently was parked too close to the main force of the Corps and it took out the second and third line of defense. To make things worse, they are using their landers for a straightforward airmobile operation; they used C-Decs to take out the Wall, to literally smash it flat, and look like they're getting ready for a bound forward. Then they have come in and, apparently, rebuilt the road. I'm impressed. And frightened. I don't like the idea of Posleen combat engineers. What next? Artillery?"

"Shelly, how solid is this information?" Mike asked hoarsely.

"Resetting image," Shelly said. "Red is eyewitness reports or video or Posleen transmissions, shading to blue for maximum estimate of expanse."

Modified that way, the O'Neal farm was only a light violet; it was possible that Cally and Papa O'Neal were still alive.

"Shelly, try to raise somebody at the farm and keep an ear out for intelligence as to their condition," Mike said. "So, what do you want me to do?"

"The Gap has to be plugged . . ." Horner said.

"Oh, blow that!" Mike exclaimed angrily. After all the years of fighting it took him barely a second to imagine the broad outline of the proposed mission. And it was *not* survivable. "You're *joking*, right!"

"No, I'm not joking," Horner said coldly. "We still have Banshees, not enough to loft a full battalion but . . ."

"But we're *not* a full battalion," Mike snarled. "God *dammit*, Jack, my middle name may be Leonidas, but it doesn't mean I want to *die* like him! *And* the damned Spartans died because they got surrounded; we'd already *be* surrounded. And just how the *hell* are we supposed to fight our way into the Gap? How? There are, what, fourteen or fifteen million Posleen waiting to move through? Where in the fuck are we supposed to *land*?"

"I need the Gap plugged," Horner said inexorably. "I need it plugged for seventy-two hours."

"Un-fucking-believable," Mike said. "Are you

*listening* to yourself? I've got three hundred and twenty effectives! We couldn't carry in enough *ammo* for three days! And there's no *way* you're going to be able to get anyone to us in three days! Not in the teeth of the Posleen!"

"I'm moving the Ten Thousand, they'll be back-stopped by the best artillery I can find," Horner said. "They'll take positions and wait for the Posleen to come to them then hammer them with artillery. With you in the Gap, the Posleen won't be able to push through any more; they'll only have to take care of the ones that are already through."

"And the ones in the landers," Mike said. "Remember? They're using airmobile, your words."

"SheVa guns," Horner said. "There's one surviving in the valley; it's got some technical problems, but it will get up. I just need the Gap plugged. And you're going to plug it for me."

"Like hell we are," Mike said. "Nobody will be able to. I'd need a damned *brigade* of ACS, which we don't have, and continuous shuttles of ammo *and* power."

"Look, Major, every minute that we spend arguing, sixteen or seventeen hundred Posleen go through the Gap. I'm sending the Banshees to your location. Get your battalion moving."

"Look, *General*, get the wax out of your ears!" Mike shouted. "We're Not Going. The fucking shuttles wouldn't make it to the *ground*! We'd need a *cold* LZ! And we'll need spare shuttles for supplies! *And* we would last about four hours! *We are not going!* Period!"

"God damn you, Mike!" Horner shouted back. "I am *not* going to lose the entire eastern seaboard because you don't want to lose your fucking battalion! You *will* take and hold the Gap to the last man or so help me *God* I will have you court-martialled and shot if it is the last thing I do!"

"Fuck you, Jack! You should have thought of that before you let them put Bernard in charge of the GAP! You got me into this fucking mess! *You* put me in that plasteel fucking coffin, that I've been trapped in for the last nine years, you took away my family, you took away my *wife*! And the only thing I have LEFT is this fucking battalion and you are *not* going to piss that away too, you murdering BASTARD!"

The door practically left its hinges as Gunny Pappas stepped through. "Sir, what in the hell is going on? They can hear you down in the damned *barracks*."

"GET THE FUCK OUT OF HERE, GUNNY!" O'Neal screamed. He grasped the heavy wooden desk, raised it over his head and slammed it into the window behind him. When it didn't fit he let out a shriek of fury and slammed it into the wall repeatedly until the hole was large enough. Then the desk flew through with a bellow.

It was a full-bore rage, as controllable as a hurricane and nearly as destructive. There was nothing between the world and O'Neal's blind anger at reality; if he could have twisted a button and turned off the universe he would have. Instead, he took it out on his office and the battalion headquarters building. In seconds the few scraps of mementoes on the walls had followed the desk. He threw everything in the room through the hole then started widening it by punching the walls.

The headquarters was a simple wood frame structure; the interior walls were gyp-rock and the outer was a layer of pressboard covered by vinyl siding. Despite being only five foot four, Michael O'Neal, Jr. could bench press four hundred pounds and each punch slammed through all three layers as if they were tissue; two by fours shattered with no more than two blows. His knuckles were bleeding within a few punches, but he no more noticed than he noticed the fact that portions of the ceiling were buckling; the pain felt good in his universe of rage. The worst part of the rage, beyond losing his father and his daughters and his life, was that he knew in the end that the battalion would go. And the only thing in his mind besides the rage was that evil plotting bastard at the back of his brain, that little thinking bastard that was already figuring out the mission even as every other fiber of his being was denying that they would *ever* commit suicide in such a clear and stupid fashion.

Finally the rage spent itself fully; there was no emotion left to feel. His office now had a new door, one big enough to fit a car through, and a circle of interested and worried onlookers. He ignored them and strode through the debris path to where the AID still showed a picture of Horner floating in the air.

"Nukes," O'Neal rasped. "We'll go. But only if that entire area is slagged to the ground. I'll have my staff work up a fire plan. You will fire it. If the President balks, tell her it is an *order* of a Fleet officer and she is under treaty to follow military orders of Fleet officers. You will follow our fire plan, and stand by for on-going nuclear support. We will prepare for the mission. We will board the Banshees. We will fly south. If we don't get the nukes, you can kiss my fat, hairy ass before we will go near the Gap. And if at any point I feel that we are receiving insufficient support, I will withdraw on my cognizance alone. Call me when you have nuke release and *only* when you have nuke release, and it had better be *open* release. Shelly, end transmission."

"Yes, sir," she said, cutting off Horner.

"Shelly, I don't ever want to talk to that bastard directly ever again," Mike rasped. "When he sends nuke release, just tell me."

He looked around at the group that had gathered. Most of them were enlisted from Bravo Company—Pappas must have been telling the truth about hearing him at the Barracks—the rest were officers and NCOs from battalion.

"Okay, boys," he rasped, looking around at the group. "Let's all go get kil't."

It had been nearly thirty minutes since the last sound of activity around the Wall. There was sound down in the valley, but it was the sound of thousands of feet and the occasional crack of a railgun or plasma cannon, drifting up the hills on the light wind.

"Damn," Cally whispered as the first Posleen came into sight at the notch. "I don't think there *is* a corps anymore, Granpa."

"Yeah," O'Neal said. "But that's not the worst," he continued, pointing at the tenaral floating up into sight over the eastern edge of the holler. "That's worse."

Cally looked out the firing slit to the west and tapped his arm. "No, *that's* worse."

Papa O'Neal flinched at the shadow that was looming over the farm; the Lamprey was heading west from the Gap at about four thousand feet above ground level. As he watched, a beam of silver stabbed downward into the valley and there was a secondary explosion from the direction of the artillery park.

"Are we gonna get shot by *that* if we fire at them?" Cally asked nervously as the first mine went off. "I don't like that idea at all."

"Neither do I," Papa O'Neal said. "Okay, Plan B is activated."

"Run like hell?" Cally asked.

"Yeah," he said. "Or at least as far as the mine; it *is* reinforced for a nuke; we'll hole up there for a while until the first wave should be past, then we'll head up into the woods."

"Let's go," Cally said, turning around and pressing in the plywood on the back of the bunker. It pushed inward slightly then popped out on hinges revealing a heavy steel door set well into the hill. She undogged the hatch and stepped through. "You *are* coming right?"

"Yeah," Papa O'Neal said, "keep the door open, I've got to set all these command mines on a timer. And rig the final destruct sequence; the hell if these bastards are gonna have *my* house."

"Well, move it," Cally said nervously. "I don't want to go crawling around these hills on my own."

"Be there in a minute," Papa O'Neal said. "Get moving."

# CHAPTER 27

If drunk with sight of power, we loose
>    Wild tongues that have not Thee in awe,
Such boastings as the Gentiles use,
>    Or lesser breeds without the Law—
Lord God of Hosts, be with us yet,
Lest we forget—lest we forget!

>                            —Rudyard Kipling
>                            "Recessional" (1897)

*Near Dillard, GA, United States, Sol III*
*1427 EDT Saturday September 26, 2009 AD*

Major Mitchell looked at the warrant officer as she popped up through the hatch. "Can we start firing yet?" he asked.

The major was a rejuv and, long ago as a newbie officer, had trained to fight the Soviets in Fulda Gap. After his initial shock at this attack he came to the conclusion that this situation wasn't all that different. The "tanks" were larger and one side was flying, but, really, the numerical disparity was about right; there were forty or so landers and only one of them. Perfect.

The technique for fighting forces like this was trained into his bone: shoot and scoot. In boxing it was called "stick and move"; fire off a good, well-aimed blow then move away so that the counter-punch missed. Of course, having friends around in war was good, so the Army also called it "shoot, move and communicate." And Major Mitchell had trained for it most of his adult life. He could jab, he could uppercut and he had the footwork. It was gonna be easy.

Riiight.

The only good news was that they had trained as hard as he could manage over the last few months. The team had been put together even before the SheVa was completed and began working in the simulators and fixed systems at Fort Knox, trying to get a feel for their actions and reactions in a fight. The initial assault had caught him, had caught all of them, off-balance. But he remembered somebody once telling him that surprise was a condition in the mind of a commander. All you had to do was push it aside and play the cards you were dealt.

Now that he was in the groove it was time to do what he had trained for almost his whole life. It was an odd moment, he wasn't sure whether to laugh or cry.

"Yes, sir," Indy said, sliding into her seat and buckling in. "I've taken off the lockout; the lidar should be able to rotate and the guns move."

"I hate this mechanical monstrosity," Pruitt bitched, coming up through the hatch and dogging it down. "We need a bigger engineering crew. Or Riff."

"Engineering?"

"Go," Indy said. "Everything's green."

"Driver?"

"Up," Reeves said. "We are ready to roll."

"Gunner?"

"Up," Pruitt said, sliding into his own chair and slapping on the straps. "Bun-Bun is in the green and ready to kick Posleen."

Mitchell rotated his shoulders and flipped his commander's screens live. "Blow the camo, and let's see what we're in for."

"Tulo'stenaloor, this defensive area is reduced and the humans are in flight," Orostan said. "The support companies have moved up and are gathering what thresh and weapons are salvageable from the pass."

This latter was another innovation. Usually individual Kessentai would have their forces scavenge as they moved. Tulo'stenaloor had put a stop to that; no matter how efficiently a unit did it, it tended to slow them down. Units moving through the Gap had to move steadily, not stop to loot. So special units under cosslain and Kenstain had been detailed to clean up the battle-field.

"The movement through the Pass is going well. We're going to move out to our secondary objectives."

"Agreed," Tulo'stenaloor said over the circuit. "It has gone *very* well."

"Losing most of the tenaral and two ships surely is not 'very well,'" Orostan protested.

Tulo'stenaloor flapped his crest in humor. "I always forget; you've never fought humans before. This was *easy*; fear what is up the valley. The metal threshkreen will be here soon, of that I'm sure. And other humans will do things to torment you as you proceed. Ignore it; stick to the mission and don't get bogged down by resistance."

"I will keep that in mind," Orostan said, gesturing

to his communications monitor to give the orders to move up valley. "Nonetheless, we shall prevail."

"Oh, yes," Tulo'stenaloor said. "We shall. Nothing can stop us now."

"I get six landers up, sir," Pruitt called. "Five Lampreys, one C-Dec. I don't know where the rest are." This would be his first "warshot." He had fired the fixed simulator at Roanoke, where the impact area was all of eastern Virginia. But he'd been told it was different with actual penetrators and in the SheVas; the mobile guns, for all their immense size, were much more susceptible to the shock of firing.

"Probably on the ground," Major Mitchell said, tapping his screen and highlighting the appropriate unit. "Hit this one and this one," he said, flipping them so they highlighted. "Then we get the hell out of Dodge."

"Yes, sir," Pruitt said, laying the gun on a C-Dec almost directly over the former Mountain City. He was nervous on several levels. They were about to make themselves a gigantic target and the death of SheVa Fourteen had been far too noticeable to think that they were invulnerable. And keeping them alive was going to be about hitting these damned maneuvering ships, not the easiest thing in the world. And then there was firing his first warshot. So, as he waited about a half a second until the C-Dec outlined in green his mouth was dry and his palms were sweating. But he was doing his drill and going to by God let them know that Bun-Bun had arrived. "TARGET!"

"Confirm!"

"ON THE WAAAAAAAAAY!" the gunner called and squeezed the trigger. The result felt like being inside a massive bell that had just been hit by a giant. The command center was heavily sound-proofed, but the result of firing wasn't so much "sound" as a vast presence that rang through their bodies, shook the massive structure of the tank like a house made of straw and vibrated every surface. It was the most overwhelming, frightening and invigorating feeling he had ever experienced; like he truly was controlling Shiva, the God of Destruction.

"Target!" Major Mitchell called as the lander stopped in midair and dropped like a stone; that was going to make a nice monument once it cooled in a few years. He laid his aiming reticle on the Lamprey over the western valley. "Second target!"

"TARGET!"

"Confirm!"

"ON THE WAAAY!"

Cally ducked into the tunnel and headed back. The tunnel was cut out of the heart of the mountain behind the O'Neal household. When the first Michael O'Neal had settled these hills, he had been just another fortune seeker in the gold rush. He quickly determined two things; that he could make more money selling moonshine to the other miners than by mining himself, and that having a bolt hole to escape from the revenue agents was a good thing.

Subsequent generations had taken the lessons of the first Michael O'Neal to heart and the bolt hole had, from time to time, been expanded, improved and restocked. The tunnel ran back to a mineshaft that was the center of the complex. Another tunnel ran back to the house, connected through the basement, and three other tunnels ran off to various exits; when Papa O'Neal had complained about no bolt hole he had been speaking from experience.

The mineshaft was reconstructed during the Cold War as a true nuclear bomb shelter, with heavy steel replacing the original wooden supports. It was capable of withstanding a near strike by a nuclear weapon and had been stocked, and restocked as necessary over the years, for three years of almost completely autonomous survival.

Cally opened the inner door to the mineshaft and looked back. "Hurry *up*, Gramps!" she shouted.

"Done," he called. "Coming . . ." and the world went white.

"SON OF A BITCH!" Pruitt shouted as all the viewscreens went black then flickered back on. "What in the hell?!"

The western valley of the Gap had a towering mushroom cloud over it and fires had started in every direction. The devastation area was wider than that from the SheVa explosion and there were no landers visible at all.

"Catastrophic kill!" Major Mitchell said. "Yeeeha! Get us the hell out of here, Schmoo!"

"What in the hell caused it, sir?" Pruitt asked as the shockwave hit. "Whoa big fella!"

"Posleen ships use antimatter as an energy source," Indy said. "You probably managed to penetrate their fuel magazine. I've seen the schematics for them; they're hard to hit and even harder to penetrate. Congratulations. But we've lost some systems from the EMP. Nothing major; most of our stuff is hardened and the EMP really wasn't all that high."

"A couple more of those and we won't have to worry about *any* landers," Pruitt said, patting his control panel. "Good Bun-Bun, good rabbit. EAT ANTIMATTER, POSLEEN-BOY!"

Orostan raised his crest to full height and screamed as the shockwave rocked his C-Dec. "WHERE DID *THAT* COME FROM?!"

"There must have been two of them," Cholosta'an said with a resigned flap of his own crest. "I'm glad we were landed."

"ESSTUUUUUU!" the enraged oolt'ondai yelled.

"There was no report, Oolt'ondai," the Kessentai snarled. "Nothing. It must have just moved into position! I don't know why it waited until then to fire. It is fortunate that we were not all in flight."

"Well, we're all getting up *now*," Orostan snarled. "All ships in the air! Find this damned gun and destroy it! Stay low except when you must cross the ridges, then look for it quickly and drop back down. Tenaral, forward! Find it, destroy it if you can, locate it and cripple it at the minimum. Go!"

"Any station this net, this is SheVa Nine," Major Mitchell called. The frequency was designated for anti-lander units. There was damned little chance that anyone was monitoring it, but just in case there was another SheVa in range to fire he could use some help. "Any unit. This is SheVa Nine."

Of course, with the loss of Fourteen, there were only forty other SheVas in existence and he was pretty sure he knew that the nearest was in Asheville, but it beat chewing on his fingernails.

"SheVa Nine, this is Whisky Three-Five," a female voice replied. "Go ahead."

"We are retreating up the Little Tennessee Valley," Mitchell said as the gun rounded Hickory Knoll. Firing Point Two was on the shoulder of the Knoll, but they needed to get it between them and the Lampreys and C-Decs that were undoubtedly chasing them. It wasn't the landers that he was worried about, though. "We are in engagement with an estimated forty landers of both types. SheVa Fourteen was engaged and destroyed by some sort of flying tank. I don't have a thing onboard to engage them; we could use some cover fire if anyone has anything useful. What sort of unit am I talking to?"

"Uh, SheVa Nine, stand by over," the voice replied.

He flipped through the codes that he had, but he didn't have an AA unit listed for Whiskey Three Five. Since the landers could only be engaged, for all practical purposes, by SheVa guns, there weren't many AA units of any stripe left; most AA personnel had been swallowed by the regular forces.

"SheVa Nine, this is Whiskey Three-Five actual," a different, more assured female voice answered. "We're a Screaming Meemie unit attached to Eastern Command, over. Our orders are to move forward and engage the Posleen forces in direct fire mode. What is your situation and location, over."

"We're at UTM 17 379318E 3956630N. Our situation is we are engaging an estimated forty landers of all shapes and descriptions. We're okay with that, but there are some new flying tanks that are a pain in the butt. I think a Screaming Meemie unit is just what the doctor ordered, over."

"Roger, SheVa Nine," said the other voice. "I'm sending the situation up to Eastern; pending their override we're changing our mission to SheVa support. Just do me one favor."

"What's that?"

"Don't blow the fuck up, okay?"

"Mrs. President, it is not a question of 'will you' release the nuclear weapons," Horner said calmly. His calm wasn't fooling anyone, though; he was smiling like a tiger. "It is simply a question of when you will release them. As Major O'Neal pointed out, you have a valid request from a Fleet officer; you are required by treaty to abide by that request."

"That is arguable, General," the National Security Advisor said. She was colocated with the President, but there were four others in the video conference, and each would be expected to find something to say. Valid or not. "We are required to fulfill any military request for which we have the materials to supply; however, nuclear weapons release are traditionally a *political* request, not a military one. Ergo, it is not necessarily a requirement for us to fulfill it."

"And I have to question the validity," the High Commander said. The former Fifth Army commander had been promoted to replace General Taylor and was still feeling the limits of his authority. Unquestionably, the Continental Army commander was his subordinate; on the other hand, the reason that most people felt that Horner hadn't been promoted to High Commander was that no one dared remove him as CONARC. Fifth Army, on the other hand, for all practical purposes had ceased to exist so the former commander was flapping around at loose ends.

"Major O'Neal is requiring a cold LZ. Very well, let them land outside the Posleen area and assault down from Black Rock mountain. I mean, that's how an air assault is *supposed* to go; you don't land right on the objective for God's sake!"

"And we have to consider the overall effects, Mrs. President," the communications director cut in. "We have a redistricting battle going on nationwide; it's probably not a good idea to give the appearance of panic. If it appears that you're losing in the southeast, and it will if you authorize nuclear release, people will shift towards the other party. . . . And, besides, they're caught in the mountains; surely conventional forces can handle them there."

"Right," Horner snarled. "That's it. First of all, it wasn't a request, it was an order. And a valid one. You can try to parse that, but I guarantee you it falls under the letter of the treaty and the Darhel will well and truly cut your legs out from under you if you try to parse it any other way. That assumes that any of us are around to discuss it with them because if we don't stop this incursion we are all going to be HORSE CHOW.

"Furthermore, Major O'Neal is perfectly correct. There is no way to take the Gap without the Posleen being cleared out. And the only system that conceivably could do it would be using ICBM fire from the upper Midwest.

"I'm so glad that your communications director, with her degree in law from Stanford, is such a military expert! Perhaps she can tell me how I'm supposed to stop the Posleen, who are using airmobile tactics and pouring a hundred thousand troops an hour through the Gap? I have one, repeat, ONE division available to contain them and it will have to cover multiple exits from the zone. Furthermore, they appear to be planning on running up and down the Line, opening up passes. I have *no* units, except for the occasional Four-F militiaman, to stop them from doing that! It's not just Georgia that is having problems; we have over fifty thousand Posleen in the Shenandoah sitting on three half finished SheVas. Perhaps she could tell me what I'm supposed to do about that? If she cannot then I suggest that she SHUT THE HELL UP. This is not a political crisis, this is a NIGHTMARE! And the sooner that you all come to understand that this is not maybe losing a city or maybe losing a division, but MAYBE LOSING THE WAR the quicker we can get done.

"There are times when the proper weapon to use is a nuke. You need to come to grips with that, Madame President. We need to use nukes, not *want*

to use them, *need* to use them. We *should* have used
them at Rochester and at second Roanoke; it would
have considerably reduced the casualties that were
inflicted on us. By *not* using them you probably caused
me to lose a division of additional casualties. But now
we *have* to use them; the choice is that or die. Welcome to the wall.

"This . . . political *squeamishness* has to stop and it
has to stop right now! We have *one* battalion of ACS
left available and they are the *only* unit that can perform the mission and they will evaporate in a *second*
if they don't have a *big* hole to drop into. And that
means using nukes. I am *not* going to piss those ACS
away. We will use nukes in the initial assault and we
will be *on call* with nuclear suppport until the Posleen
are pushed back through the Gap. And if you have a
problem with that, you can have my god damned stars
*right NOW*."

As the High Commander opened his mouth to
respond hotly the President raised her hand.

"Is it really that bad?" she asked.

"Madame President," the High Commander said,
"there is no need . . ."

"Stop," she said, holding up her hand again. "I asked
the question of General Horner."

"Yes, ma'am," the general replied. "It's really that
bad. After the Gap there are multiple routes open.
Some of them, most of them, are pretty nasty, but there
isn't much to block them with. It's . . . complicated, but
I can't get enough forces to all the paths they will
probably take to stop the . . . flow of them. There are
too many exits from the Gap. They are able to turn
towards the west and open up the 129 route and that
will cascade forces onto Chattanooga. *And* they have
enough . . . force-flow to *also* head for Knoxville and
Asheville. I *can't* bottle up all of those forces with

what's in the area; it's gotten drawn down to help all the other emergencies that have occurred. And now they're also starting a full court press up and down the Appalachians: There's just not enough forces to handle all of that *and* the forces in the Gap. I have to . . . bottle them up until I can get forces into the area to push them back.

"I *have* to stop the flow before enough get through to take Asheville or Chattanooga from behind; Madame President, there are three Sub-Urbs between the Gap and Asheville comprising fourteen million people total. And if Asheville falls we might as well all learn to speak Canadian."

"You can't *stop* them with nukes," the High Commander argued. "There are too many Posleen. It's not physically possible to 'glaze the eastern seaboard' even if we could survive it politically or environmentally."

"I don't intend to," Horner answered coldly. "As you would have noted if you had listened. I intend to open up a hole and drop Mike O'Neal in it to plug it. I'd also like to open up their use at other key points."

"Hold on a moment, General Horner," the President said. "I'd like everyone to drop out of this circuit and Mrs. Norris and Ms. Shramm need to leave the room."

She waited as the others reluctantly left the circuit then turned back to the image of the distant general. "General Horner, the Chinese fired over two thousand nuclear weapons and poisoned the valley of the Yangtze for the next ten thousand years. You propose to do much the same to the Tennessee Valley, you understand that? And they still *lost*. That is the greatest part of the problem, the very real *political* and more importantly *morale* problem. Nukes, now, are considered to be the last desperate weapon of someone who is *losing*. Who, in effect, has already lost. That is the *real* reason that I have prevented their use; the image of them being the desperation weapon. Is it worth the . . . social damage that will occur? Is it worth the *physical* damage; the Tennessee drains into the Mississippi. For that matter, it is the water source for the entire lower defense line and it will be poisoned by dropping nukes into that valley."

Horner opened his mouth and closed it then opened it again and sighed.

"First, Madame President, let me say that I appreciate you . . . explaining that. If you had done so before, however, I could have suggested some ways that we could have . . . adjusted that public perception. We could have used them in the 'fortress cities' in the plains, after telling the public that we were simply opening up, effectively and pardon my language, 'the whole can of whup-ass.' I think that would have permitted a reevaluation on the part of the public.

"Second," he paused, unsure of how to phrase it, "let me say that your knowledge of nuclear warfare and weaponry does you as much disservice as your knowledge of geography does you credit. We're not using traditional 'dirty' nukes for this; we don't have them. The warheads in the missiles we'll be using, the last few Peacekeepers we have in silos, are relatively 'clean.' The radioactive exposure for persons downwind of the blast, in the 'fallout zone' will be less in one year than the acceptable exposure for an x-ray technician."

"General, if you're trying to tell me that there won't be any radiation from these weapons, please save it for the talking heads," the President snapped. "Even 'clean' nukes are dirty."

"Madame President, you can *believe* anything you want," the general said coldly. "And I'm sure that the 'Greens' will scream bloody murder. But the radiation left from dropping a couple of billion megatons on that valley, and we don't have that much, more's the pity, will raise the background radiation of the Tennessee to that of, oh, living downwind of a coal-fired power plant. And we have *lots* of those.

"Be that as it may, this *is* a desperation use. If we don't plug the Gap, it's all over but the screaming. You, personally, and your staff and whatever dependents you have there with you, will undoubtedly survive. Something resembling civilization may even continue north of the 'cold line'; the Posleen can't organize a logistics line to save their lives so they're never going to take, say, Athabasca. I understand that Montreal is a very pretty city, but all the survivors in the United States can't *fit* in Canada, not in any sort of sheltered fashion, much less survive for any length of time. We have to plug the Gap. We have to keep it plugged. I need nukes to open it up so I can insert the plug. I'll probably need them again to open up other points and reduce the Posleen in the Valley. We won't have a lot of other choices this time." He paused for a moment. "I don't have any more ACS to throw away."

The President looked at the papers on her desk for a moment and shook her head. "Will it work? Not just putting the ACS in place; I thought the Posleen shot down anything that was above the horizon. Will the missiles even be able to get to Georgia?"

"I don't know," Horner answered. "The remaining silos are all well north of the Posleen lines and there's a strong storm across the Midwest. The combination should permit most of the missiles to fly. They're most vulnerable in boost-phase, of course, but they're going to loft very fast. The Posleen lose some of their efficiency when the targets get into orbital phase. We'll just have to see if they make it."

"And if they don't?" the President asked.

"There's . . . at least one other option," Horner said with a smile that for him indicated extreme unhappiness. "The University of Tennessee has both a SheVa gun enhancement testbed program and a nuclear, antimatter rather, rounds program."

"So . . . they can fire?" the President asked. "Antimatter is *better* than nukes, right? I mean, their fire can *reach* the Gap? And it's a better, a cleaner, system?"

"Possibly," Horner answered. "I'd . . . Both of the systems are experimental, ma'am. And their . . . area denial round has never been field-tested. It's also . . . rather large, a very heavy warhead; you really would prefer *not* to know the megatonnage. The first time I fire something, I don't want the price of failure being the loss of the entire Cumberland Valley."

"Oh."

Horner shrugged at her expression. "I suppose this is what I get for letting rednecks play with antimatter; they just don't know when to say 'Okay, that's 'nough!' Instead, it's always 'Hey, y'all! Watch this!' I only became . . . apprised of the size of the round when we went looking for something to open up the Gap. I've since ordered a 'reevaluation' of the program.

"As for the ACS, the Triple Nickle will be caught in a vise. There will be well over a million Posleen passed through before they land. And there are the airmobile forces. And there are now an estimated twelve million gathered to the south. The battalion, what is left of it, will *have* to hold on to the Gap until we reduce the forces that have passed through and fight our way forward. Whether they survive . . . ? I don't know. I *do* know that there is no other choice."

The President continued to look down at the papers on her desk and then nodded.

"General Horner, you are permitted to fire into Rabun Gap. But Rabun Gap only, understood? All other uses will require my okay."

"Understood," Horner said with a nod. "Rabun Gap only. There may be a need at other times, however. That terrain favors defense; unfortunately we can't stay on the defense anymore."

"I understand that, General," she said tartly. "But *I* approve each use. Understood? I want these *things* used precisely, not at the behest of some . . . officer . . . at the front."

Horner took a calming breath before he replied. "Ma'am, I get the feeling you almost said something along the lines of 'myrmidon' there. The . . . officers at the front are trying to keep us from losing more ground, losing *more* passes. The targets that need to be struck will often *change*; they come and go as fast as the Posleen can manage it. At some point we'll need to reduce the level of authority, Madame President."

"We'll cross that bridge when we come to it," she said, staring the general in the eye. "In the meantime . . . I'm the authority. Only I hold nuclear release." She looked down again and shook her head. "And may the Lord have mercy."

Horner took pity on her.

"Ma'am," he said quietly. "I will say this. The only person I could imagine holding that pass, surviving it for long enough, is Michael O'Neal. It will be worth the clearing."

"I'm glad you feel that way, General," the President said, looking up angrily. "I was just thinking that I didn't care much for the major. I don't care much for someone who is willing to callously slaughter American civilians."

"Excuse me?" Horner asked.

"There are *always* survivors," the president snapped. "There are probably thousands of people in and around the Gap, hiding out. If we drop untold numbers of nuclear weapons on that area, there will be *no* survivors. I guess the vaunted Michael O'Neal doesn't *care* about those poor civilians. The only thing he cares about is his precious battalion!"

Horner's face was as frozen as a glacier and he waited a full fifteen seconds before answering.

"Madame President," he said in a voice as cold as liquid helium, "Michael O'Neal's *daughter* lives in Rabun Gap."

# CHAPTER 28

Cally rolled over and coughed at the dust in her throat. After a few moments choking she sat up and looked around muzzily.

"Shit."

The main shelter was still intact and the lights were on, but that was the only good news. The tunnels to the bunker and the house were both collapsed. The main tunnel was clear, though, and it looked like both exit tunnels were clear. That left the question of how long she had been in here. She felt her head and there was a pretty good goose egg already started on her forehead. Her watch had stopped from either EMP or impact and she hadn't been too sure what time it was when they went in the bunker anyway.

She thought about Papa O'Neal's briefing on nuclear weapons and what to do. They didn't get used much, but Gramps had been thorough. Unfortunately the lecture had been a few years previous and she wasn't sure where to begin looking for a geiger counter or how to use one.

She did recall that people could survive better than structures—something about pressure waves—and that meant that Gramps might still be alive. If the bunker falling in didn't kill him.

So the next job was to get out of the main tunnel and try to find Gramps—dig him out if she had to— then head for the hills.

She stood up then sat down as the ground rumbled to another nuclear detonation.

"Maybe in a while."

"Ooooh, that's gotta hurt!" Pruitt shouted.

Reeves already had the SheVa in reverse so the return fire from the landers, with the exception of one plasma round, tore up the ridgeline. That one plasma bolt, though, ripped into the SheVa's power room.

"Reactors two and three just went offline," Indy called. She unstrapped and headed for the hatch. "I doubt this is going to be a one-woman job."

"We're way down on speed, sir!" Reeves called. He had the throttle all the way open, but the SheVa was barely moving. "Under ten miles an hour!"

"Indy," the commander called over the intercom. "Tell me we can do better than this! Those landers are going to overrun us in about fifteen minutes at this rate."

"Not until I find out what went, sir," the warrant officer called. She slid down the third ladder and grabbed a geiger counter as she sprinted, occasionally being knocked from side to side, towards the reactor room. "We just lost half our power; this is as fast as this thing will go."

"Damn, damn, damn," he muttered. "Pruitt, you have the con."

"What?" the gunner called.

"I'm headed to the reactor room," the commander said. "I think you can ID these things just fine."

"Roger, sir," the gunner replied with a gulp. "Come on, Schmoo, find us another firing position."

"There's one by Fulchertown," the driver said, checking his map. "But it will mean running over a bunch of houses."

"You afraid of getting 'em stuck in our treads?" the gunner asked sarcastically.

"No . . . it's just that . . ." Schmoo looked up and over his shoulder to where the gunner was grinning. "Never mind. I've been trying to stay in the woods so we wouldn't run people over."

"Anybody that's still here *deserves* to be run over."

Mitchell waved a hand in front of his face as he went through the door to the reactor room; smoke and steam were pouring out and the air reeked of ozone. "Indy!"

"Over here, sir," the warrant called from the left side of the room. The room was dominated by the four turbine generators; the smaller reactors were barely noticeable cradled along the sides. Mitchell's background was in Abrams power packs, big jet turbine engines that drove the tanks at speeds upwards of sixty miles per hour. But the power contained in this room would provide electricity to a city of a hundred thousand people. It was sobering to think that all this power could barely get the SheVa up to twenty miles per hour on a flat surface.

"What'cha got?" he asked. "And are we hot?"

"No, sir," the warrant called back, handing him one end of a heavy duty cable. "The shot missed the reactors and the turbines, thank goodness, or we might as well have gotten in the Abrams and run. It took out a transformer, through, and cut one of the main power circuits so even though there was a backup transformer there wasn't any power for it. The reactor went into shutdown immediately."

"So what are we doing?" the commander asked.

"Well, you're holding a replacement power cable," she said impishly. "I'm getting out a really big wrench. Then we're going to replace the circuit and reboot the reactors."

"How long?"

"Ten minutes, fifteen tops," she answered, heading over to where the turbine's power bars joined in the middle. She applied the wrench to a large nut where the cable came out and then, when it wouldn't break free, pulled the wrench off and hammered on it repeatedly until the melted plastic sealing it flaked off. "Just be glad it didn't hit the reactors."

"Yeah," the commander said with a laugh. "Or the track. I'd hate to have to break track on this thing."

"Oh, it's no trouble at all; you just call up a CONTAC team," the warrant said, breaking the nut free. "There's a reason that there's a battalion in a SheVa repair team. A battalion of engineers and three *really* big cranes."

Mitchell dropped the end of the cable on the floor and grabbed a stanchion as the SheVa rocked from a blow. "Uh, oh."

"I can get this," Indy said, grunting as she leaned into the wrench. "Get up top, sir."

"You sure?" he asked.

"Go, I can do this in my sleep," she said taking the nut out and pulling out the burnt cable.

As he darted out of the room she sighed and picked up the cable. "For this I went to MIT. . . ."

✧　　✧　　✧

"Flying tanks, sir!" Pruitt said as the commander flew out of the hatch. "Four of them. And they're spotting for the landers; tracking says they're all coming this way."

"Shit," Mitchell said, looking in his own screen as the flight of tenaral swooped by for another strafing run. The flying tanks each fired several rounds of plasma fire, but only one or two connected. "Concentrate on the landers. Reeves, see what you can do."

"Doing it, sir," the driver said. "The best I can do is get up along the hills, though; we're kind of a big target."

"Is it just me, or do they seem to be staying at a distance?" Pruitt said as the SheVa rumbled down onto the flat. "Oops. TARGET! Lamprey! Fifteen klicks!"

To get to the third firing point required turning the corner of the mountain. By and large the SheVa's position was still covered by the intervening hills, however, the last movement, slow and glacial as it seemed, had rumbled the SheVa fully out into the open.

Pruitt had been more or less ready for it, or something similar, keeping his gun pointed southward towards the approaching landers. Fortunately the Posleen ships moved at a snaillike pace near the ground and had not gotten significantly closer than in the previous two engagements. Unfortunately, there were more of them in sight.

"CONFIRMED!" Major Mitchell called, slipping into his seat.

"ON THE WAY!" the gunner called swinging the turret towards the next target.

"Yes!" Mitchell called. "Cat-kill, Pruitt." The detonation of the Lamprey's fuel source had not been as large as the first catastrophic kill, but it was still quite spectacular.

"TARGET!" Pruitt answered. "C-Dec! Fifteen klicks!"

"CONFIRMED!" Mitchell called.

Pruitt fired just as the dodecahedron dropped below the ridgeline. "Miss! The bastards are maneuvering! Is that legal?"

"Fuck me!" Reeves called as the tenaral swept by for another strafe. "They seem to be firing at the rear of the gun, sir!"

"I noticed," the major said with a curse. "The good news is it's the only part that's heavily armored. The bad news is it's the armor on the magazine."

"No wonder they're keeping a safe distance," Pruitt said, sweeping the gun from side to side, looking for targets. "The *really* good news is that we're nearly out of rounds so if they *do* penetrate the magazine there won't be as large of a boom." He thought about what he'd just said and shook his head. "Mommy!"

Mitchell keyed for the outside line and called the Screaming Meemie unit. "Whiskey Three-Five this is SheVa Nine; we could use some help, over."

"What in the fuck is that, ma'am?"

Captain Vickie Chan shielded her eyes against the westering sun and shook her head. "I dunno, Glenn, I just don't know."

Captain Chan had joined the U.S. Army in 1989 in payment to University of Nebraska Army ROTC. The ROTC had provided the daughter of Fusian immigrants with a scholarship and monthly spending money. So when the Army in its infinite wisdom assigned her to Air Defense Artillery she had put on her soldier suit and wandered into the wilderness.

One fairly successful tour—very few women in ADA made captain in one hitch—had proven to her that a career in the Army was the *last* thing she wanted.

Towards the end of the tour she had looked around at the senior females and determined that there were two types: sluts and battleaxes. She had no desire to be either so she calmly turned in her papers and went back to civvie street.

However, with the coming of the Posleen, she, along with virtually every other human who had ever worn military uniform, received a letter in the mail ordering her to service. Initially she was assigned to an armor unit, but with the need for anti-lander systems and the creation of the initial systems to combat them, a computer had spit out her name near the head of the list. She had ADA background and, at the time she was transferred, was a commander of an armor company. Perfect.

Then her burgeoning career—she had settled on battleaxe—had been nipped in the bud. She was assigned to one of the first Screaming Meemie units, a system officially referred to as the M-179 "Rosser" Medium Anti-Lander System, and, when it became apparent that the system was suicidal and useless against landers, there she had been left. There was no definable utility for the Meemies, but it was too much trouble to reconvert the Abrams tanks that they had been designed around back to direct fire systems and although the Meemies were very effective there were other systems that were just about as good. So for the last five years she had been shuttled around from one corps to another, shoring up a defense here and there, but generally shuttled back out of the way; nobody knew quite what to do with Meemies and few cared to learn.

At the moment she would have happily traded her current position for any of those other corps or any of those boring useless, days. It was apparent that this corps was in full flight, and driving forward to slow the Posleen down sounded like a permanent solution to a temporary problem; there was no way that one Meemie unit could stop a Posleen assault of this magnitude.

However, here she was. And maybe, just maybe, the company would survive. All they had to do was shoot down these . . . whatever they were.

"The computer's balking," Specialist Glenn said. The gunner was a female, like her commander, and had fine, light brown hair that constantly escaped from under her crewman's helmet. She brushed it out of the way and looked up. "It refuses to lock them up. The radar sees them, but the computer won't aim the gun."

Chan sighed and slipped down into the turret. She was fairly sure she knew what was happening. The computer software had been pulled from the long defunct Sergeant York program. That system had been a nightmare from the word go, but it was the closest analogue to the Screaming Meemies, so the software had been assumed to be similar.

"Assumed" had so many connotations. In this case some bug in the software probably was telling the computer that these were not valid targets. She hated the software. If she ever found the idiots who had written it, she was going to line them up against a wall and shoot them.

With the commander's machine gun; the ro-ro would probably miss.

She rolled her shoulders and shrugged. "Okay, Glenn, switch control up here."

"Yes, ma'am," the gunner said. "What are you gonna do?"

"Use up a shitload of ammo," she answered, switching the gun to manual.

She watched the . . . whatever they were for a moment. They would come sweeping in, high, really high, behind the SheVa, fire a few rounds into the back deck then bank off and come around for another shot. She considered it for a moment and hit another control.

"All tanks, flip your guns to remote control," she said over the company net then switched to the SheVa's frequency. "SheVa Nine, I need you to turn to the east and take a constant bearing for a few minutes, please."

Mitchell felt like he was driving a wounded elephant. The SheVa was barely lumbering along and smoke was streaming from multiple strikes. So the call from the Meemie commander fell on welcome ears.

"I'd wondered where you'd gone," he said. "Roger that, will do."

He flipped to intercom and checked his screen. "Schmoo, turn east and head up the slope; don't worry about going at max speed, just keep a constant course."

"Yes, sir," the private said, turning the lumbering gun to the east.

"Major Mitchell," the warrant called. "This is Indy. We're getting hammered, sir. We're taking damage belowdecks."

"I know," Mitchell called back. "How bad is it?"

"We've taken some damage to the gun mounts which is really bad," the warrant called back. "But they've got some redundancy in them. I think we can still fire. But if we take many more hits we're going to be useless."

"What's the status on power?" Mitchell asked. "If we can speed up we can throw them off some. They aren't coming down to engage; I guess SheVa Fourteen's demise has put a scare in them."

"I've restarted the reactors, sir," the engineering officer replied. "But the turbines have a required warmup period; you *really* don't want me to override it. Another five to seven minutes."

"Okay," the commander sighed. "It will have to do." Mitchell considered his readouts and looked over at the gunner. "You gonna be up to this, Pruitt?"

"Yes, sir," the gunner said. "We've only got two rounds left."

"I can read," the commander said, gesturing at his controls. "I'll call for a reload, but we're going to have to put some distance between us and them first." He shook his head at the next series of plasma strikes. "And get rid of our companions; I *don't* want them shooting at our reloads."

"Oh, good God no," Pruitt chuckled.

"If I recall correctly, the fuel bunker for a Command Dodec is just below center," Mitchell mused. "I think the next shot you get, they'll be closer than they have been; under ten klicks. . . ."

"You want me to try to get the fuel bunker," Pruitt said.

"Simply aim with great care," Mitchell said. "Let's see how it goes."

"Okay, here goes nothing," Chan said. She watched the six circles rotating around the sky—she had hooked all six "tanks" together and now had them all under manual control—and picked a point above and behind the SheVa gun. "We *really* don't want to shoot that thing in the ass."

"Oh, no," Glenn said, clamping her hands on either side of her helmet. "This is gonna *SUCK*."

The Screaming Meemie was so named due to its passing resemblance to the WWII German mortar system of the same name. The "gun" was mounted on top of the tank on a very heavy-duty rotating pintle that replaced the turret; the tank commander and a gunner were shoehorned into what had been the bottom of the turret with the driver at the traditional position at the front. The gun itself was more or less circular in appearance with six distinct bulges or lobes on the side. The difference between the systems being that the German weapon, properly called the Neubelwerfer, was a multi-barreled mortar system. The modern Screaming Meemie was a MetalStorm 105 twelve-pack.

MetalStorm's name said it all; each pack could throw up to twelve hundred 105mm discarding sabot rounds into the air in less than a minute. The rounds were packed "nose to tail" into twelve tubes that were both barrel and breach. The system was electrical and could fire either one round or a series at very high rates of fire. Once clear of the "barrel" the rounds, accelerated at slightly different velocities due to the nature of the system, dropped their plastic "shoes" and a sixty-millimeter dart of tungsten headed down-range at tank-killing speeds. With a hundred rounds packed into each tube, and the rounds going off at an electronically controlled sequence, the air quickly became saturated with tungsten and steel.

The amount of energy involved in firing the system led to an enormous number of compromises. One of these was that the system could only shoot "forward" unless it deployed its firing spades or "jacks" as they were called. Otherwise the sheer energy involved in twelve hundred rounds of discarding penetrator heading down-range would flip the massive tank over on its side.

While this had been found to be insignificant against landers, six of the tanks firing into the space the tenaral were passing through was another story.

Tensalarial flapped his crest within the armored enclosure and keyed his microphone. "We need to get lower to destroy this thing; we can't hit it flying by from this height."

"Fuscirto uut," Allansiar replied. "I'm not getting any closer than this! Even this is too close! You saw what happened to Pacalostal!"

Tensalarial flapped his crest again and snarled. It was like something in Posleen was hard coded; when you got one with the sense to do something besides lead an oolt and charge the guns, they also started getting . . . cautious. The smartest Posleen of all seemed to be Kenstain, which he preferred not to consider too closely.

"Our . . . mission is to stop this so the landers can destroy it," Tensalarial said in response, with a tooth snap that was audible over the communicator. "We *will* perform that mission."

"Then shoot the *tracks*," Allansiar snarled in reply. "Not the body: that is where the fuel and weapons are that blow up. There is nothing to blow up in the wheels!"

"Very well," the Kessentai replied after a moment. "We shall shoot the tracks on the next pass."

"Lining up," Allansiar said. "I'll even get lower for that."

"Let us go in one behind the other," Tensalarial commented. "That way the ones behind can gauge their firing on the basis of the leader. I shall lead."

"Why not?" Allansiar said with a grunt. "You're not going to hit anything anyway."

Tensalarial ignored the jibe and turned the tenaral towards the ground, lining up the manual aiming reticle on the slowly moving treads. The groups had had little opportunity to practice firing before the assault and they were learning by trial and error that the rounds did *not* go where the aiming reticle was pointed. The reticle was computer generated, but the system was not an actual auto-aiming device; it was simply a heads-up-display of where Goloswin thought the target was going to be.

Since all Posleen aiming was done with advanced targeting systems—which Goloswin had never bothered to reverse engineer—the tenaral were beginning to realize that there were some basic concepts missing in the aiming system. Two of the missing concepts were "parallax" and "bore-sighting"; configured as they were, the guns were the functional equivalent of plasma blunderbusses and just about as accurate.

Stooping like a falcon, the Kessentai began dropping plasma rounds all over the landscape.

The target recognition system for the Meemies was sometimes a bit messed up and the radar integration system often malfunctioned. But the manual firing system was mostly taken from a standard M-1 Abrams design and worked rather well.

In this case a laser swept the sky until it got a return, estimated the range, found it to be functionally close to the one that Captain Chan had keyed in manually and began a series of calculations. It checked wind-speed, air temperature, humidity and whether the StormPack had been previously fired. Then it ran a rapid series of calculations and adjusted the aiming point appropriately. And the unknown programmer who had originally designed the system *had* heard of parallax.

For Captain Chan it was simplicity in itself. She pointed the red circles at the descending tenaral and waited until they flashed green. This took approximately half a second. Then she flipped the thumb selector from "safe" to "full," closed her eyes, clamped down on the firing lever and held on for dear life.

"Holy shit!" Pruitt called. He had flipped to a screen where he could watch the funny looking tanks arrayed along the top of the ridgeline and now they had disappeared in a wall of smoke and fire. "Did they just get hit?"

"Nah," Major Mitchell said, flipping momentarily to the same screen. "That's what they always look like."

The tanks appeared to have exploded. The air above and to the side was nothing, but smoke, fire and smoking plastic shredding itself on the dense air. Somewhere in there, presumably, were people and functional vehicles, but it seemed impossible that they could have survived. After only a few seconds the firing stopped and the air started to clear, revealing the Meemies, apparently undamaged.

"Holy shit," Pruitt repeated. Then: "We *gots* to get one of them, sir!"

Glenn sat up, groaning. "Ooooh. I hate my job." She pried her fingers off of her helmet and held her shaking hand out in front of her. "I gotta get a transfer."

The Abrams was never designed to mount the MetalStorm 105. The original Abrams tank was designed to fire a single 105mm cannon that was similar in energy. Until the coming of the Posleen and such monstrosities as the SheVa gun, the concept of a mobile MetalStorm 105 would have been ludicrous. The energy imparted by the gun was sufficient to loft a 747, briefly. Lighter systems were considered possible for mounting on medium armor, but a 105mm, high-velocity penetrator was a different matter. It made the 72-ton tank shake like a mouse in the grip of a terrier and rattled the commander and crew like peas.

"Oh, gee, and miss all this fun?" Captain Chan said, rubbing her shoulder where it had banged into a stanchion.

"Clear sky, captain," the gunner said, sweeping her sight around.

Chan popped the commander's cupola and looked

around. The air was still hazy with propellant gasses and the smoke from the thousands of bits of plastic littering the ground and the upper deck of the track. But there clearly were no tenaral in the sky. That didn't mean it was clear.

"All Meemies," she called, dropping back into the tank. "Back off the ridgeline!" She switched frequencies and called the SheVa. "Hey! Big Boy! You've got company south of Dillard."

"I hate humans," Orostan growled as the link from the tenaral went dead.

"So you have said," Cholo'stan pointed out.

"What were those things?" the oolt'ondai asked. "Esstu?"

"I'm still working on that," the Kessentai admitted. "There is reference to them in combat, but not against flying tenar; they are usually used for ground defense."

"Well, we will deal with them after the big gun," Orostan said with a flap of his crest. The oolt'ondai looked at his battlefield schematic and snarled. "Enough of this playing with them, bring us up so we can engage."

"Pruitt, two rounds," the commander reminded his gunner.

"That's all Bun-Bun needs," the gunner replied.

"Major," Indy called over the intercom. "I've got the turbines up to speed; I cut a few corners, but it looks like we're going to be okay. Anyway, we're up to full power."

"Great," Mitchell said. "Reeves, when Pruitt fires, back down the ridge. We've always moved next. This time, back down then wait for my word. We'll pull right back into position then head north of Franklin for resupply."

"Yes, sir," the driver said, checking as his telltales went back into the green. "We're up to full power."

"Okay, engage."

Reeves engaged the drive and threw the multiton tank up the 30-degree slope, leveling it out at the top.

"Oh . . . shit," Pruitt whispered; all the landers were up. In the distance he heard the whine of turbines as Reeves cranked the power until the SheVa vibrated with it.

"Target," Major Mitchell called. Reacting to a training deeper than instinct he had swiveled the gun and laid it on the lower portion of one of the two C-Decs in sight.

"TARGET," Pruitt confirmed. "C-Dec, nine klicks!"

"Confirmed," Mitchell said.

"ON THE WAY!" he called, slamming against his straps as Reeves threw the tank into reverse.

"Miss!" Mitchell called as the round tracked under the maneuvering C-Dec. "TARGET, ON THE WAY!"

The second round, fired from the commander's console, entered the ship on the lower quadrant just as the return fire from the ships erupted around the retreating SheVa. The giant tank still managed to slip away as the top of the hill erupted upward under the flailing of the guns. Despite the heavy fire, the detonation was evident and the fire cut down almost immediately as the hills to either side were lit in nuclear fire.

"NICE SHOT, SIR!" Pruitt caroled. One of the Lampreys was just visible over the ridge they were descending; it was out of control and just as they dropped out of sight it slammed into the side of High Knob. The explosion had easily been the largest so far. "EAT ANTIMATTER, YOU ALIEN *FREAKS*!"

"Reeves, put your foot in it and don't let up until we are north of Franklin," the commander called, manually rotating the turret in that direction. "We've got a reload date to keep." He thought for a moment and frowned. "Swing east of the town; the Sub-Urb is west of it and I'd hate to find out that one of those things acts as a pit trap for a SheVa."

"Oh, damn," Pruitt said suddenly. "The Urb! What about the Urb, sir?"

Mitchell sighed and shrugged. "I think they're on their own, Sergeant. Let's just hope we don't run over any stragglers."

"I *hate* humans," Orostan snarled as six icons dropped off the screen and his own vessels pitched up and down in the shockwave; Chylasarn must have been remanufacturing antimatter already. "Their behavior is bizarre, their reproductive methods are frankly disgusting and they use their weakness as a weapon. There should be a law."

"Yes, so I am given to understand," Cholosta'an said, looking down at the obvious trail leading to the north. The SheVa was out of sight and presumably out of ammunition, but they could easily track it down. "Do we follow?"

"We do not," Orostan said. "We'll deal with it later. For now we are well behind the timetable for us to have taken our positions. Have the ships that are left spread out to take their objectives. Keep maneuvering, but raise up to where they can increase speed; the SheVa appears to have retreated."

"Our reports indicate that one of the human underground cities is just ahead," the intelligence officer said. "It was an objective for Aresseen's oolt'pos."

"Detail another to take and hold the entrances," Orostan said looking at the size of his reduced force again in anger. "The ground forces can detail one unit in three into it. There is much booty and, of course, thresh in one of those; we'll need the materials to continue the drive. The other two forces should turn up Highway 28 and Highway 441 as planned."

"Understood," the S-2 said. "The city will be rich pickings."

"I don't know," Cholosta'an said. "At this rate, I have to wonder if it will be worth it."

# CHAPTER 29

"Sir, I'm looking at this directive and obviously missing something," Captain Slight said. "There's no timetable for the relieving force."

The battalion staff and company commanders had gathered in the briefing room to see if there was some way to make the mission less of a nightmare. Instead, they were finding more and more things not to like about it.

"That's because there's not one yet," Mike said with a grim smile. He leaned forward, steepling his fingers and grinned. "You've taken a look at the terrain, right?"

"Yep," Duncan said. "A troop of Boy Scouts with a .22 should be able to bottle them up in there."

"Normally I'd agree," O'Neal replied. "But in this case, the Posleen are fighting *smart*. The point is that they will be at a really severe handicap; there's not much room for them to maneuver in there and lots

501

of places for dug-in forces and engineers to make their life miserable. But, by the same token, it's the kind of terrain that will eat up assaulting forces."

"So . . . what?" Captain Holder. "They're just going to let us die on the vine?"

"They'll push forces forward until they come into contact," Mike said. "Then they'll hunker down and start killing Posleen. If they kill all or most of them that are in the pocket, they'll push forward. Until they do that . . ."

"We're just going to be left to die on the vine," Captain Slight said. "That sucks, sir."

"Why do you think I lost my temper?" O'Neal said with another grim smile. "The British Airborne in Arnhem kept fighting for nine days when told they only had to hold out for three until relieved; and the relieving forces never *did* reach Arnhem."

"The Germans did not, by and large, eat their captives, sir," Captain Holder pointed out.

"I don't know of a single instance," Mike agreed. "On the other hand, this *is* the mission. Hold until relieved. I, personally, plan on stacking the deck as much in our favor as possible." He pushed his AID forward and nodded at it.

"We are going to need all the shuttles we can get our hands on and all the ammunition, power packs and generators available. But the real problem is going to be that we won't have any anti-lander support. Shelly, how many AM Lances are there that can be transported here within the next, say, six hours?"

"Four," the AID reported. "They are scattered around Minneapolis for the support of Northern Plains Front. One of the shuttles that is lifting from Chicago could pick them up and bring them down. To get here in six hours would require ignoring some safety regulations, but it could be done."

"So ordered," Mike said. "What do we have in the way of shuttles, power packs and generators?"

"There are twenty-two Banshee Two shuttles," Shelly said. "Sixteen will be here within three hours. If we wait for the AM Lances, there will be ample time for all twenty-two to arrive."

"Duncan, start working on a load list," Mike said. "You know what to do: Ensure that stuff is scattered across all the shuttles. Start preparing the load for each. That way when they get here we can just load them. Assume that we will lose shuttles on the way in and that we'll be unloading them under fire."

"I thought that we were going to get area denial support," Captain Holder said.

"We are," Mike answered. "Or we're not going. That doesn't mean we won't be under fire both on the way in and after landing. It just means we won't be wiped out immediately."

"Anyway, Duncan, the AIDs can do most of it, but I want you to ensure that scrap of 'intuition,'" he added with a grin.

"Gotcha," the captain said with an abstracted expression. "We've only got a total of five generators and power packs, though. And if the power packs get hit . . ."

"Biiiig boom," Stewart interjected.

"'There was supposed to be an earth-shattering kaboom, where was the earth-shattering kaboom?'" Gunny Pappas said with a chuckle.

"Don't put anybody on those shuttles," Mike said with a shrug. "I hate to have them be 'noticeable,' but we'll have them fly separately. They can park in the mountains and after we've secured an LZ they can come in and unload. Then we dig the bastards in and hope for the best."

"Like, 'die quick so we don't notice'?" Stewart quipped.

"Something like that," Mike answered. "Duncan, what's operations think we should do?"

"Our best bet for a defensible point is probably the current location of the Wall," Duncan said, flipping up a hologram. "We can dig into its structure and be *very* hard to dig out. But getting to it is going to be slightly tricky."

"We're going to have three or four SheVas that can fire in support," the operations officer answered. "That means a total of six to eight rounds of antimatter area suppression. And *that* means that the actual area we can totally suppress will be low; no more than four thousand meters on a side. We need to prevent direct lines of observation of the landing zone, therefore we're going to have to land *forward* of our objective, up by Black's Creek in what used to be Mountain City. That area is fairly open and flat and what is more important it's a small 'bowl' in the mountains; you can't observe it from the Valley or down on the plains. The only possible observers at that point should be Crispy Critters.

"There's a large enough area that all the shuttles can land together. We take and secure that LZ, then call in the two shuttles with the AM power-packs. Once they are secured, we move up to the Wall and dig in. I'd suggest Charlie Company on the west and Bravo on the east, but that was based on flipping a coin, so feel free to change it around."

He changed the hologram and zeroed in on the Wall structure. "The information we have is that the Posties are doing a number on the wall itself. So until we get there, I don't think we'll know what the actual situation is. But I think we should assume it will be mostly flattened."

"That's a big structure to flatten," Holder said.

"The report said they were using heavy kinetic

bombardment and anti-ship cannons," Mike pointed
out. "They can pick apart a monitor with those; wiping
out the Wall won't be a problem."

"That means C-Decs," Duncan pointed out. "Lampreys can't get their space weapon to bear on a ground
target."

"There was report of both C-Decs and Lampreys,"
Stewart said. "'A large number.' There was also mention of a surviving SheVa engaging them. There's a
Fleet Lurp team on the ground to the west. They're
snooping forward, but we'll probably be to the LZ
before they arrive. . . ."

Elgars looked up from her cards and frowned. "What
was that?"

Billy looked up from where he was kicking her ass
at War and shrugged. He looked at the door, but
obviously couldn't hear anything over the sound from
the other children.

It was just past dinner time and the kids were still
complaining vociferously about the quality of the food.
It only took one trip to the O'Neal farm to spoil them.
But just at the moment she wished they would quiet
down. However, the next rumble from outside the room
was loud enough to cut through to Shari.

"Children! Silence!" she called. She had to repeat
it three times before Shakeela finally stopped talking,
but when she did she looked over at Elgars and
frowned. "Is that screaming?"

"Some," the captain said, getting to her feet and
moving to the door. As she reached it Wendy opened
it from the other side.

"We've got a situation on our hands," she said
breathlessly. "It's another Posleen rumor."

"Rumor or fact?" Shari said nervously.

"Right now it's a riot, so I'm not sure," the younger

woman answered with a shrug. "I was on my way up when I hit the crowd. But there's no alarm so I'd say a rumor."

"How do we know which?" Elgars asked.

Wendy shrugged and went to the communications terminal. "Call Harmon; he's up towards the entrance. He'll have heard."

She tapped in the code for the range and started to talk as Dave's face came on the screen, but he immediately started into his message. "Hi, this is Dave Harmon with Harmony Ranges. I'm not in right now . . ."

"Well, *that* didn't work," Wendy said with a frown. "On the other hand . . ."

"What?" Elgars asked.

"Well, that's only the second time I've ever gotten his answering machine," Wendy admitted. "Okay, Captain, I'd suggest you and I head up towards A Sector. We'll see if we can *find* security for a change; of course they're never available when you want them."

"And what do we do if it really *is* the Posleen?" Shari asked. "If they're already in the Urb?"

"Then we go to the designated defense points," Wendy said. "I hope they're *not* in the Urb, though, because if they came in the main entrances, without a warning, they've got the Armory . . ."

"Considering the condition of your rifle that might not matter," Elgars said, heading for the door. "And neither of us is packed."

"We'll head for the range," Wendy said. "Shari, lock it down; at the least we have a riot on our hands."

"Okay," she said, standing by the door. "Be careful."

"How about 'be back'?" Wendy said. "Here goes nothing."

✧ ✧ ✧

Wendy started to take the main route to Sector A, but the primary passages were choked with underground dwellers. The situation wasn't actually a riot, yet. But the groups were all milling around like cattle that smell smoke but are unsure of which way the fire would come. It wouldn't take much of a spark to start them stampeding.

Wendy shook her head and started off down a tertiary corridor then through a series of turns that quickly left Elgars totally confused.

"I thought I was getting used to this place," the captain admitted. "But if it wasn't for the signs I'd have no idea where you were going or how."

"It takes a native," Wendy admitted, opening a door that was marked "No Admittance." "Preferably a native that has emergency access privileges."

The corridor that they had entered was apparently a maintenance access for the innumerable pumps and pipes that moved the Urb's water and sewage. There was a large pump on the left-hand side throbbing and gurgling and a half a dozen gray pipes over a meter in diameter running into and out of it.

Wendy led the way to a ladder that ran from a lower level upward to the next. "Time to climb."

The ladder stretched upwards at least five levels and Wendy quickly ascended with Elgars following. It was clear that whatever other problems she might have had, the girl could climb.

"Where are we?" Elgars asked.

"Just between the juncture of A and D sectors," Wendy answered moving to the end of a corridor identical to the first. "If memory serves, this should open out into a secondary corridor and *that* should connect to the main route to the range." She stopped as she was about to open the hatch and first put her hand on the door and then laid her ear against it. "Do you hear something?"

"Feel it, more like," Elgars said. The floor seemed to be shuddering at irregular intervals."

"That's . . . new," Wendy said, popping the portal.

The corridor they stepped into was empty, but for the first time there were screams in the distance and then, close, the sound of a gun, probably a shotgun, discharging.

"Okay, that's bad," Wendy said. She looked up and down the corridor unsure which way to go. "Left is to the range," she muttered. That was also the direction of the greatest noise.

As they stood there, the decision was reached for them. A mob appeared at the right end of the corridor and a group of them sprinted down the other direction. On the left, at almost the same time, a large figure in a wheelchair appeared, wheeling in the opposite direction for all his might.

"Oh, shit," Wendy breathed. "Oh . . . *merde*." She felt faint for just a moment and a taste of iron was in her mouth; she really didn't like the way things were going.

"Hi, Wendy," Harmon said, sliding to a stop as the panicked refugees poured by. "Fancy meeting you here."

"Did you *know* I'd come up the tunnel?" she asked and shook her head.

"Well, I didn't figure you'd used the escalators," he admitted. "It was this one or ladder seventeen-B and if you used that one you'd be dead by now, so I fig-ured I'd come over here."

"Oh, shit, Dave," she said, looking into the maintenance room. The idea of lowering Harmon down that ladder was not appealing.

"Let's step inside, shall we?" he asked, rolling past her. "And close the door."

❖   ❖   ❖

"What happened?" she asked, sealing the memory plastic portal. She wished it was a blast door.

"Dunno," Harmon said. "I ran across a security goon; they said that the computer was refusing to recognize the Posleen or declare a system-wide emergency. So other than calling people and telling them to get out, there was nothing to do. And they didn't get the word from the corps *at all*; the Posleen were just on the Urb before anyone knew anything was wrong. I was at my quarters; I couldn't even make it to the range." He reached into his carry bag and pulled out a short barrel pump shotgun. "Of course, nothing says I didn't have a backup."

"But it's like Rochester," Wendy whispered. "If they're on the entrances there's nothing we can do."

"I was wondering about that," Harmon said. "There's more than just personnel entrances; the grain elevators have a completely separate area. If you go down to H level through Hydroponics and into the elevators you'll come out about five miles from Pendergrass Mountain in an industrial park. Posleen can't be everywhere; once you make it up in the mountains . . ."

"That . . . might work," Wendy said, some of the shock coming off of her. "How in the hell are we going to get you down to H Sector, though?"

Harmon laughed and shook his head. "You're not. I *am* going to take the ladder down to D and then head for the cafeteria. But that's as far as I'm going."

"Dave . . ."

"Shut up, will you?" he asked. "We need to move and I need your help. I can climb down the ladder myself, but I need somebody to get the chair down."

"Can do," Wendy said. "But what about . . . ?"

"Wendy, if you can make it out of here, especially with the kids, it will be a miracle," he said. "You will *not* make it out dragging a . . . guy in a wheelchair. Too many ladders, too many small passages that are not exactly 'handicap friendly.' Understood?"

"Understood," Wendy answered.

Getting him down the ladder was easier than it appeared. Wendy found a length of tie-down strap and lowered the wheelchair almost the entire way, then Elgars climbed down and held onto it while Wendy climbed down and repeated the operation. Harmon, as he had said, was able to descend the ladder using only his arms. Maneuvering him into the chair at the bottom was tricky, but even that was accomplished with little trouble.

The corridors had actually thinned out as people gravitated to anywhere they considered safe. They wheeled the former police officer to the cafeteria, which was already filling up with people. As anticipated, many of them had managed to find a weapon "somewhere." Wendy wheeled him into the echoing hall and settled him behind a hasty barricade.

"I still don't like it," she said. She looked around and noted that most of the people in the room were older or infirm. On the other hand, most of them also looked like they were ready to handle anything hostile that came through the door.

"If it's a small incursion and anybody else turns up with a weapon we might make it," he said with a shrug. "And as long as you guys keep out of the way, we'll see each other later."

Elgars walked over and kissed him on the forehead then rubbed his stubble. "Aim low," she muttered. "They might be riding shetland ponies."

Harmon laughed and nodded. "I will. Get out of here."

One of the other defenders came over, a big old man with silver hair and hands that still had the calluses of a guy who had worked for a living. He was carrying a shortened pump shotgun similar to Harmon's and two mugs of steaming liquid. "Coffee, Dave?"

"Damn, where'd you get that, Pops?" Harmon asked with a laugh. "And I see that you are carrying a weapon, in clear violation of Sub-Urb regulation," he added in a stern tone.

"Oh, this?" the old man said, holding up the well-tended shotgun. "I just noticed it lying there in the corridor on my way over here. Undoubtedly it was dropped in panic by some miscreant. Probably at the thought of how angry Security would be if they caught him with it; I'm sure that he was shaking in his—or her, come to think of it—boots." He reached into his cavernous smock and pulled out a handful of twelve-gauge cartridges. "You fixed for ammo?"

Dave just laughed and shook his head. "Take off, ladies. I'll be fine."

Wendy gave him a last pat on the shoulder and walked out into the corridor.

"What we need," Wendy said, "is a plan."

Elgars looked thoughtful for a moment. "'Kill them all; God will surely know his own.'"

"Where did you hear that?" Wendy asked.

"I have no idea, but when you said 'plan' it just popped in my head," Elgars sighed. "We need weapons. Those are in my room."

"Yeah, and we need to get the kids to Hydroponics," Wendy added. "You go for the guns, I'll go for the kids. We'll meet at the entrance to Hydro. Bring all the ammo you can carry."

"Oh, yes," Elgars said. "That part I can guarantee."

# CHAPTER 30

*Near Franklin, GA, United States, Sol III*
*2047 EDT Saturday September 26, 2009* AD

"I don't suppose you're going to let *my* oolt land there?" Cholosta'an said mournfully. Below, the stream of Posleen disappearing into the underground city was clear. As was the huge amount of booty seized from the military forces in the area.

"I don't think so," Orostan said. He was happier now that the plan seemed to be functioning and that the hated, impossible to catch, SheVa gun seemed to have fled. "There are too many objectives to be taken as it is and we are far behind schedule. Your oolt has a mission to perform and that is that."

"As long as I get my cut," Cholosta'an sighed. "But I could wish for some items in hand. I've never been in a *successful* assault before; it seems a waste to just let others take all the loot."

"There will be plenty later," Orostan snorted. "Think of this way; you get a cut of *all* of that. You'll be rolling in funds by the time this mission is done. And everyone who comes through a pass we take owes us a cut; so opening the way through to the plains is more important than sacking one stinking city. I could wish there was a way to stop them entirely. I *need* those oolt'os taking passes and running the human forces down, not looting."

"What is the next objective?" the younger Kessentai asked.

"There is a bridge over a river called the Little Tennessee," Orostan said. "Horrible name. After that, we have to take the road up into the mountains. There are four or five objectives that are very important there. We'll bring the entire oolt'ondar down on the Tennessee then, after we have secured the crossing, we'll break up for the mountain objectives. We have the mission to open the way up the four-four-one route. Sanada will take the route up the twenty-eight road."

"A bridge, huh," Cholosta'an said mournfully. "And mountain roads."

"Don't worry, young Kessentai," the oolt'ondai said. "This time *we* shall have a surprise for the humans."

Major Ryan stood on the slope of Rocky Knob and watched the bridge below. He could see Posleen passing east of Franklin in the dying light, but they weren't to the bridge yet. And there were still refugees on it.

"When do you blow it?" the specialist asked, picking at her hands. Rigging a bridge for demolition had turned out to be hard work

"There's MPs still on it controlling traffic flow," Ryan answered, lowering his binoculars. "I don't know if they're like us, just doing what seems right, or under orders. But if they're still on it when the Posleen get to it, they're going sky high."

"That will be a bit tough on the MPs," she pointed out.

"It will be tougher on everyone else if the Posleen capture an intact bridge," he said. "But I have to wonder what they'll pull."

"What do you mean?"

He sat down on the verge of the road and dangled his feet over the side. They were stopped on a curve on a side road near Cook Creek and the other troopers were taking a break, eating their MREs, soaking their hands in the cold mountain water and wondering what the eccentric engineer in charge of them would have them doing next.

They had slowly picked up the group he was looking for, soldiers who had kept their equipment and were ready to follow a person who stated up front that he was part of a rearguard. He'd gathered eight instead of the four intended, and the bridge over the Tennessee was his first objective. Once it was down they would move on to the next and the next until they either ran out of explosives or luck. He was more worried about the latter than the former.

"These guys are acting smart so they have to know that we'll try to delay them, right?"

"Right," Kitteket said.

"So they've got to have a way over the river," he continued. "I can't imagine these guys just stopping and giving up. Can you?"

"No, sir," the specialist replied. "I can't."

"Well, looks like we're about to find out," he commented as the stream of Posleen, with four Lampreys and a C-Dec hovering overhead, turned in the direction of the bridge. Off in the distance he could see other landers turning towards the west. "I think they're dividing their forces," he mused.

"Well, that's not very smart," the specialist said. "At least if it's not a feint."

"Possibly," Ryan said, turning to look at the specialist again. "Another manual?"

"Sort of," Kitteket answered. "How many troops do you think they can push through the pass in an hour?"

"I dunno," Ryan said, then did some mental calculation. "Probably sixty to a hundred and twenty thousand. Say ninety to a hundred."

"So they're going to push those in two different directions," Kitteket said. "That reduces the forces necessary to stop them on both paths."

"Hmm," Ryan said. "On the other hand, each of the routes will have its own problems; I don't know, for example, if they could push as many on the whole route to Asheville as they can through the gap. Also, by breaking up they're making the task of cutting them off more complex; each individual defense point may last longer and be more effective with the lower numbers, but you'll need more routes covered. All in all I think it's a net positive for them, a negative for us."

"Possibly, sir," Kitteket said. "It depends, I suppose, on whether there are defenders on the other routes."

"I think you just made my point for me," Ryan said with a smile. "And we are now going to find out how effective *we* are going to be," he continued as the MP platoon on the bridge hurriedly boarded their Humvees and retreated, drawing fire from the lead oolt as they did so. Fortunately for Ryan's stomach, there were no stragglers between the MPs and the Posleen; he'd blown up bridges with stragglers on them before and it wasn't his favorite pastime by any stretch of the imagination.

"Are you going to wait until they're on the bridge?" Kitteket asked.

"No," Ryan answered. "And if I did, Sergeant Campbell would blow it up instead. The SOP is . . ."

"Five hundred meters," Kitteket interjected. "Just checking."

"Clerk typist?" he muttered.

"Four years, sir. Right here. Well, down there," she said, gesturing towards the Gap. "I type nearly eighty words a minute."

"If I need any forms filled out, I'll let you know," Ryan said, throwing a hand switch as the first Posleen passed by a street sign he had measured off as just under five hundred meters.

The explosion was the antithesis of spectacular. There were a few puffs of smoke and the concrete and steel bridges dropped into the stream.

"That's it?" Kitteket asked.

"That's it," Ryan answered, packing up the detonation circuit.

"I just expected lots of smoke and fire and the bridge going sky high," she said with a sigh. "We did a hell of a lot of work for a few puffs of smoke."

"I am a master," he said haughtily. "The essence of mastery in blowing things up is minimal force and I have blown up *a lot* of bridges in the last few years. Since we also have minimal explosives, I consider it to be a good idea all around."

"Sure, sir." The specialist laughed. "What next, O Great Master?"

"Next we are going to blow up a road," he answered. "Right after we see what these Posleen are going to do about the bridge."

The first wave of Posleen milled around aimlessly as the lead God Kings lifted up on their saucers and flew over the river. They quickly came back, though, and as new forces joined them the units were spread along the riverbank and the individual oolt'os spaced out.

"Jesus Christ," Ryan said, shaking his head.

"What?"

"They're spreading them out to reduce the damage from artillery. It would be better to start digging in, but I guess they haven't quite gotten that far."

"That's bad," Kitteket said. "Right?"

"Oh, yeah," the major mused as the first Lamprey crossed the river and disgorged its troops. It quickly lifted off and took on a new contingent, beginning a continuous shuttle back and forth. Once on the far side most of the units took up the chase after the fleeing humans, but a few spread out as on the near side, in this case fanning out widely and ensuring that there were no humans in the immediate vicinity.

"And now they're establishing a perimeter," Ryan said. "Why are they establishing a perimeter around the bridge? The *former* bridge."

"They're going to hold a cookout on the remains?" the specialist asked. "Uh, Major, it's getting dark and those Posleen that *aren't* establishing a bridgehead are headed up the road. Towards *us*."

"But the landers aren't moving," Ryan said as if he hadn't heard. One of the other Lampreys had joined the first in shuttling troops, but the other two Lampreys and the C-Dec were on the ground, spread out, as if waiting for something. "What are they *doing*?"

"Sir, maybe we should wonder someplace else?"

"Ah," the major answered with a grunt. "There's some movement."

The Posleen forces had been backing up into the valley, spreading out in a disciplined manner that Ryan still found disturbing, and now the centauroids were moving off the road to let another group through to the front. He focused the binoculars on the formation in the last light and shook his head.

"Tell me those aren't what they look like," he muttered.

"I dunno," Kitteket grumped. "You're the one with the binoculars."

He handed them over and shook his head. "Where in the hell did they get them?"

"Sir," Kitteket said with a gasp. "Are those . . . ?"

"Indowy."

Orostan folded his arms and lowered his crest, the better to keep from frightening the little green one. Tulo'stenaloor had already had one Kessentai killed who had permitted the death of one of the "engineers"; the little creatures had been purchased and transported at great expense and they were a very finite resource. But dealing with them was very difficult.

He pointed to where the bridge had been. "There was a bridge," he said in a hash of Posleen and Galactic. "There must be a new one. If there is a new one, everything will be well. If there is not, your clan will be reduced."

The Indowy sidled around him and went over to the demolished bridge. The supports of both spans had been blown down and the metal girders had been blown in several places. What was left was a tangled mass of pulverized concrete and steel. He examined it for a moment then looked around at the materials in view. Last, he sidled back over to the Posleen commander.

"I will need hands, more hands than we have," the Indowy said diffidently. "Fortunately, there is a source of materials right here. We will not try to reconstruct the bridge, but will make new ones nearer the water level. This will be quicker. It still will take until morning. We cannot work miracles."

"You will have all the oolt'os you need," Orostan said.

He gestured to forestall the question. "They will be controlled by their Kessentai, I will pick the ones to work with you. You may order them in these tasks as you will; there will be no damage to you."

"It will take time," the Indowy pointed out.

"It must go as swiftly as possible," Orostan warned. "No delay."

"We shall start immediately."

"Son of a bitch," Ryan said, getting out his notebook computer.

"What, sir?" Kitteket asked. "They're . . . doing something."

"They're replacing the bridge," Ryan said. "This is going to get interesting."

"So what are we doing?" she asked. "And there are Posleen moving around down in Brendleston."

"Brendle*town*," he corrected pedantically. "We're getting the hell out of here; I've seen everything I need to see."

"Where to?" she asked.

"I was going to blast the face by Rocky Top," he said, examining the map. "But that would be easy for them to clear. So I think we'll find something a little tougher. Unfortunately, we're a bit cut off."

"What!?" Kitteket yelled.

"Oh, nothing we can't handle," the major replied. "But the drive out of here is going to be . . . interesting. On the other hand, it will give us time to think of new ways to amuse our visitors."

"Is it bad?" Shari asked as Wendy came through the door.

"Yep," Wendy answered. "Load the kids up. You have the emergency packs?"

Shari just shook her head and went to the back,

calling for the children to get in line. She pulled out backpacks that were new to the children and passed them out. Each child got one and she put a warm jacket in it along with small packs of food. She admonished them not to go diving in, that the food might have to last a long time. She checked their shoes and in one case changed them out for some better footwear, then had them all line up to go to the bathroom.

Wendy, in the meantime, filled larger daypacks with food and water. She left room for some ammunition, but she hoped that Elgars would be able to bring combat harnesses; they had integral ammunition bags. She considered changing clothes, but the pair of leather pants she had picked up had sort of stretched out to fit and would probably wear as well as anything she had.

By the time she was finished Shari had lined up the kids and thrown Amber into a papoose on her back. Without another word they headed for the door. Looking both ways, Wendy led them out with the kids following in line and Shari at the rear.

Elgars palmed open her door and then strode across to her wall locker, peeling off her clothes as she went. The door popped open as if it had been waiting for her and she started putting on the gear. First was the uniform and boots, then body armor, helmet and combat harness. She considered all the weapons in the locker and frowned. She wanted the Barrett like a junkie wants a fix, but she finally decided that it was the *wrong* weapon for the situation. Finally she pulled out two pistols, the Steyr that Wendy had picked up, the MP-5 and the AIW. She grabbed three combat harnesses and loaded them down with magazines then pulled the sheet off her bed and filled it with ammunition for all five weapons. Fortunately the Steyr and the AIW both used the same type of bullets and the MP-5 used the same as one of the pistols.

Finally she felt that she was set. She was as loaded down as a camel, but once she joined up with the other women the stuff would get distributed.

Without looking back or closing up she strode back out of the room, headed for G sector.

Cally pried up another section of bunker and stopped, dropping down on her heels; in the broken moonlight she could see a still pale hand. She reached out to it and wiped at the thick hairs on the back. One of the fingers was bent back and the skin was gray and cold.

She squatted in the moonlight, quietly rocking back and forth on her heels for what seemed to be half the night. Then she piled rocks back over the hand, picked up her rifle and headed back up the hills without looking back.

After she had left, the Himmit wormed its way out of the wreckage of the bunker, put away the Hiberzine injector and followed her, without looking back.

# CHAPTER 31

When the Himalayan peasant meets the he-bear in
    his pride,
He shouts to scare the monster, who will often
    turn aside.
But the she-bear thus accosted rends the peasant
    tooth and nail.
For the female of the species is more deadly than
    the male.

—Rudyard Kipling
"The Female of the Species" (1911)

*Near Franklin, GA, United States, Sol III*
*2214 EDT Saturday September 26, 2009 AD*

Wendy stopped at the top of the escalator and frowned;
it wasn't working, but what was worse were the yells
and sounds of firing from below.

"I don't think so," she muttered.

The problem was that as far as she could tell the
Posleen had gotten around and below them. To avoid

the Posleen, the group needed to drop several floors, very fast. But most of the elevators were shut down and so were the escalators. That left very few options.

"Come on," she said, heading back down the main corridor.

About halfway down she came to an attack pack and palmed it open. She looked at the array of gear and shook her head; there was no way to carry everything she wanted so she had to decide what she really needed.

Med-pack, among other things, that had Hiberzine in it and she'd used that too many times not to recognize the utility. Doors had already been a problem so she pulled out the door-pack including a tank of liquid nitrogen and a punch-gun. And they were probably going to be climbing some, so a coil of rope with a descent pack attached to it was piled on the top of her pack.

Finally recognizing that she couldn't carry the Halligan tool, or the rescue saw, which had a real appeal, she closed the door and went on.

Entering another maintenance hallway she tied the children together with part of the climbing rope and got them climbing down the ladder. It descended only six levels, but as they approached the base there was a strong wind coming up the ladder shaft.

"What's that?" Shari panted. Wendy could tell that the trip, especially carrying Amber, was already tiring her out.

"Air shaft," Wendy said. "That's how we're going to get to G Sector."

"You're joking," Shari said as they reached the bottom of the ladder. The corridor felt like a wind tunnel, the air hammering against their bodies.

The corridor was lined with ropes and the children grabbed them as they stepped off the ladder.

Shari grabbed one as well and walked to the end of the corridor. The opening there was the width of the corridor with droppable rail well marked with warning signs. On the right-hand side was a massive winch with a spool of cable that looked long enough to reach to China. Well before she reached the end of the corridor Wendy could see the massive airshaft beyond.

Air for a complex as large as a Sub-Urb was always a problem, especially when almost all of it was recycled in one way or another. To facilitate the transfer of fresh air, and to permit mixing of gasses, the Urb had four massive airshafts, each nearly a thousand feet deep and two hundred feet across.

The opening they were at was halfway down B sector, but it still was nearly eight hundred feet to the bottom.

"All I can suggest is don't look," Wendy said, walking to the winch and unlocking the clutch.

"You've *got* to be joking," Shari shouted back. The wind near the opening felt like a hurricane.

"This is long enough to reach the bottom and then some," Wendy shouted back, pulling out the first six feet or so of cable and dropping her climbing gear to the floor. "But we don't really want to do that; the entrance to Hydroponics is on G Four."

"*Tell* me you're joking," Shari said. She felt lightheaded and the dim light from the shaft seemed to be coming from beyond a veil. She'd had this feeling before, when she was walking away from the Posleen assault in Fredericksburg. It was the feeling of utter, bone-drenching terror.

"I'll lower you to G," Wendy continued as if she hadn't heard the older woman. "The cable is rated for three tons at a thousand feet, so you don't have to worry about it taking your weight. The winch I marked for the different openings. When you get down there you'll have to work your way into the opening. Hook the cable up to the take-up spool and then swing it back and forth. I'll watch from up here; when I see you swinging the cable I'll send down the kids. You'll have to work to stabilize yourself on the way down; there's enough cable, though, that we can hook the kids up halfway and you can stabilize from the bottom. Be careful and don't let it pull you out the door."

"This is *INSANE*," Shari said, backing away from the shaft.

"Look," Wendy hissed in her ear, taking her arm and shaking her. "The Posleen have the elevators and most of the escalators. There is no way out going up; there is a *chance* we can find our way out through Hydroponics. But there is *no* other way down. No. Other. Way. Now put the harness on and get ready."

"The children aren't going to like this at all," Shari said, taking the harness with wide eyes. "And I can't take Amber down."

"I'll send Amber on Billy," Wendy said. "And I'll just grab them and tie them to the damn thing. No, they're not going to like it, but there's not much they'll be able to do about it, either: The door is locked."

Shari shook her head at the opening, slowly buckling on the climbing harness. "How are you going to get down?"

"That's . . . gonna be tricky," Wendy admitted.

Shari walked down the wall, resolutely refusing to look down. She had, once, and that had been enough. The bottom of the shaft was shrouded in darkness, but just the sight of lights shining from other openings, deep into the well, was enough to nearly freeze her up.

And that wouldn't have been a good thing because it was taking all her concentration to keep from oscillating. As the cable lengthened it tended to swing back and forth. The one time that she'd slipped and started to swing she had slammed painfully into the wall several times. And that was when she was only a hundred feet down or so; she really didn't want to think about how far and hard she would swing if she lost it now.

The other problem with keeping the descent in control was footing; the walls of the air shaft were covered in slime. It was no great surprise once she thought about it; the air in the shaft had come from millions of human throats. Humans put out a tremendous amount of moisture from their lungs and combined with the dust from dead skin cells the water deposited on the walls was a perfect breeding ground for slimes of all type. Thus not having her feet slip out from "under" her was nearly impossible. She understood that part of her purpose was to prevent the children from oscillating the way she was tending to, but they were still going to get covered in slime.

Somehow she didn't anticipate running across a laundromat any time soon.

She carefully stepped over an opening and read the number. She was at the top of G and, technically, she could stop any time. But there were four openings in the sector and the optimum one was the second from the bottom. Better to drop a little farther, further away from the entrances and further away from the spreading Posleen.

Finally she reached her opening and bounded outward, swinging in and landing on her butt despite all her struggles to avoid that. She quickly stood up and backed into the opening, pulling the cable with her.

There was a take-up winch on the left hand side of this corridor so she first clamped the cable in place then hooked it up to the winch.

There were climbing harnesses and safety lines aplenty in the maintenance packs so she hooked herself off then leaned out and shook the cable.

Wendy had had quite a time getting the children onto the cable. First she had to find clamps for it, then she had to find harnesses that would fit, then she had to convince Billy to take Amber, then she had to run down all the kids who had tried to escape. She had always thought of the expression "dragged them kicking and screaming" as a metaphor, but no longer; Shakeela had actually climbed back up the ladder and was hammering at the door they had come in when Wendy tackled her.

She returned to find that Nathan and Shannon had unbuckled themselves and were trying to pry open the door at the end of the corridor, but she got all three connected to the cable before too long. Finally she took Billy's face in her hands and pointed out the opening.

"Billy, you have to stay with your back to the shaft, facing the wall," she shouted. "You'll have to work to stabilize yourself; otherwise Amber will be crushed against the wall. Do you understand? Face the wall."

The boy nodded looking at her with dark eyes and then pointed at her with a questioning expression.

"I'll follow you down; I have to work the winch."

He nodded and closed his eyes, pointing over the side.

She patted him on the shoulder and then clipped off her own safety line and leaned out into the shaft, swinging the cable back and forth and waving to Shari far below.

Billy caught at the ropes to keep from being pulled out by the weight of the cable, but Wendy had it clamped down and he wasn't going anywhere. Until she released the clamps.

The biggest problem in lowering the children over the lip of the opening was the weight of the cable. Each child was in a harness, either one from the maintenance closet or, in the case of Shakeela and Nathan, a "Swiss seat" made of rope. Each of these was, in turn, attached to a short length of climbing rope and this was attached to clamps on the cable itself. There were two children per clamp and they were currently occupying their remaining free time holding onto each other and, almost to a child, crying their eyes out.

But the cable would pull the children over the lip in an instant if Wendy simply let it slip. And the winch was too far forward to use to attach the children. So she had pulled a section of cable back into the corridor, attached it to a safety ring, set up the tandem rigs and attached the children. Now she faced the problem of slowly lowering them over the side.

She finally took the remains of the climbing rope, looped it through the same ring to which the cable was attached and tied it securely to the last of the children's clamps. Then she set up a complicated but safe method of lowering the cable over the side using the friction of the rope against itself. Furthermore, she could clamp it off to stop the whole process and she could do it all from the edge.

She nodded at Billy, who was strapped in next to Kelly. The younger girl was now more or less catatonic, but when her brother pushed forward and over the edge she let out a strangled scream and grabbed onto him.

Billy managed to keep Amber from being crushed against the side and he did it all while stroking his sister to try to get her to calm down and having his eyes tightly shut.

With the weight pulling them over the side, the rest

of the children were more or less forced to go. Wendy lowered them slowly, ensuring with each that nothing was stuck or pinched as they went over the side. Shakeela managed to get unbuckled again, but Wendy put her back on the line and pointed out that if she did that when she was being lowered it was a long way down.

Once the children were over the side and the rope detached, the lowering went like clockwork. She held the remote control for the winch and leaned outward, lowering them slowly. It was nearly eight hundred feet down and at first she was worried about oscillation. But Shari was on the bottom controlling the take-up and the descent was smooth. Billy lost his footing a couple of times, but each time she stopped the cable until he was set again.

When the cable reached Shari she let out just enough line that Shari could pull the pairs of children into the lower opening. It only took a few minutes and by the end of it, Wendy was shaking. She had to go down next.

How to get down was a huge question. The climbing ropes were only two hundred feet long so rappelling was out. And if there was an eight-hundred-foot rope in the Urb it would be in the security office which the Posleen had already overrun. She had come up with a way to do it, theoretically, but she really didn't like it. It had about a thousand things that could go wrong and all of them ended up with Wendy Cummings as a red blotch on the scum-covered floor of the airshaft.

But it was the only thing she could think of doing and if she stayed there "taking counsel of her fears," as Tommy would put it, she was going to get *et*.

Finally she cut several lengths off of the climbing rope and started tying knots.

The basic method for lowering was called a "Prussik

knot." She took a section of rope and the ends together. Then she wrapped it around the cable and back through itself. When she put weight on one end, the rope would clamp down on the cable and hold itself in place. Theoretically. On another rope it would work fine. On a cable things were different.

The problem, of course, was that the cable was metal. It was both lower in friction than a rope and greased. All things considered, it was not a good candidate for lowering herself using Prussik knots. The answer to that, from Wendy's perspective, was to make several. Thus if one cut loose, the others would start to clamp down.

The last line was tied off to her safety harness and wasn't from the climbing rope, it was one of the safety lines. If she went into freefall, the rope would snag on the cable at the bottom. There were several bad things that would happen then, starting with slamming into the side of the airshaft, but most of them were better than being a red blotch on the floor.

She tested the security of the knots at the edge and they seemed to hold, so she put her foot in one, grabbed two others and stepped over the edge.

And immediately slammed into the side. The good news was the knots were holding, the bad news was that lowering herself was *not* going to be an easy evolution.

Finally she got a rhythm going. She would let go with one hand and loosen and lower the two foot knots. Then she would lower the two hand knots. Using this slow method she had travelled about two hundred feet, or a quarter of the distance, when she heard a Posleen railgun down one of the side corridors. Then one appeared towards the top of the shaft, on the far side. If it looked down, she was dead meat on a string.

She had noted that by grabbing the knots where they

were wrapped around the cable, she could slide them without removing her weight. Sliding the two hand knots down she managed to get all four of the knots side by side and started working them all down without taking pressure off.

What she was unaware of was that the ropes, by sliding over the two hundred feet of cable, had picked up quite a bit of grease. Combined with this, by maintaining pressure, she was significantly increasing the friction generated by the method. Increased friction meant increased heat. Increased heat reduced the coefficient of friction of the climbing rope and under the conditions gravity began to assert its natural hold.

Wendy had gotten another forty feet down when first one foot rope then the other started to slide on their own. She immediately threw her weight onto the two hand lines, but the sudden jerk as she did so changed their coefficient from standing, high, to moving, low, and they, too, began to slide.

She was now on a one-way trip to the bottom of the cable and there didn't seem to be much she could do about it.

She clamped her hands around the upper ropes for dear life. If she clamped down *very* hard she could slow her progress, but already she could smell the ropes beginning to melt and fray. She worked one of the foot ropes up by bending herself into a U, but that rope was smoking as well and the bottom of the cable was coming up fast.

She managed to slow herself to what felt like a hurtling speed just as first one of the foot ropes and then the other gave way. Her glove-covered hands were now for all practical purposes the only things on the cable and she slammed onto the end of the cable at nearly twenty miles per hour.

What saved her from a broken back were several

variables. The first was that she was near the end of the cable, and the weight of the metal above her had put some "stretch" into the line. Thus it gave a bit when she hit the end. The second was that the security line was designed with a give of one third of its length so a bit more of the energy was absorbed by that design. Last, her harness was well designed and transferred most of the energy up along her spine rather than across it.

That didn't mean it was a good experience, simply survivable. She slammed into the wall, hard, and the only thing that kept her from cracking her head was that her shoulder caught the blow. Of course, her left arm now seemed to be out of commission. It didn't seem like anything was broken, it just wouldn't flex worth a damn.

She dangled on the end of the cable for moment and just moaned.

"Are you okay?" Shari asked from ten feet above her.

"No, I'm not okay," Wendy croaked. "I'm alive and . . ." she moved her arms and legs, "everything seems to be working. But 'okay' is not how I'd phrase it."

"I saw a Posleen up there," Shari whispered.

"That damned Postie is about a thousand feet above us, Shari," Wendy said. "And two hundred feet across. If my scream on the way down didn't attract his attention, talking in normal tones isn't going to do it."

"You didn't scream," Shari said.

"I didn't?" Wendy asked. "I could have sworn I screamed."

"Nope, just fell past mostly in silence," Shari said. "I was really impressed. You might have been cursing, I couldn't tell."

"Shari?" Wendy asked, pulling herself up with her functional arm and wincing at the strap bruises.

"Yes?"

"Start winching me up or I'll climb up there and so help me God I'll eat your heart."

Elgars checked both ways on the main corridor and stepped out carefully. The flickering blue sprite leading her bobbed up and down in the air, maintaining a strict ten-foot separation as it led the way to Hydroponics.

The corridor was wide and high with a tram-track running down the center and oversized doors on both sides stretching off into the distance. It also was deserted. She had always noted that there were fewer people in the lower areas of the Urb, but with the Posleen intrusion this sector seemed to have emptied out completely.

She shifted her burden and took a deep breath. The trip to this point had been relatively uneventful, but nerve-wracking nonetheless. And the weight of all the weapons and ammunition was beginning to wear her down; it was at least her body weight of gear if not more.

She trotted clumsily across the corridor, carefully using the crossing points on the tram-track, and over to the twenty foot high door marked "Hydroponics." To the right was a personnel-sized door with a palm pad identifier. She shifted her massive load to get a free hand and slapped the pad.

"Name?" the security system intoned.

"Sandra Ells . . ." She stopped and shook her head for a moment, her eyes widening and a shiver going down her back. "Anne Elgars. Captain, Ground Forces," she said, panting slightly from startlement as much as the exertion.

The door opened smoothly and she bent down and shoved a combat knife into the juncture; it was a blast door—the entire wall was heavy duty blasplas—but with six inches of Gerber steel in the crack it wasn't going anywhere.

She heaved herself to her feet and stumbled into the interior.

This was clearly an entrance for hydroponics personnel. The room was large, sixty feet or so deep and forty across, with lockers down both walls and a deserted security stand against the far wall. The room was filled with benches and tables and there were open wall-lockers and a scattering of personal items on the tables as if the place had been hurriedly evacuated.

She dumped her gear on the nearest table and straightened out her combat harness. She knew that she had to hold the fort until Wendy and Shari got there, but other than that she was at loose ends. Since wasting time in this situation didn't make any sense to her, she started laying out the guns and ammunition, readying the combat harnesses and making small packs for the older kids to wear.

That only took five minutes or so and when she was done Wendy and Shari still hadn't turned up. She wasn't worried, the situation was a simple binary solution set. If Shari and Wendy turned up before she got overrun holding the door, they would all leave together. If not she'd die here. She didn't like the children very much and she could take or leave Shari. But Wendy was the only friend she had; if she left her she would be all alone, without memories and without a purpose. There wouldn't be much point in leaving. Besides, she knew Wendy would do the same for her.

She watched the door calmly for a few minutes, considering her options, then decided that it was not a good use of her time. Keeping one eye on the door she started going through the open lockers, looking for anything useful.

She found a few candy bars and snacks, a few small tools that might or might not come in handy and, most importantly, a physical map of the hydroponics section. She wasn't sure that sprites would work in the area; they tended to stay to the main routes rather than the back ways the group was going to prefer.

At the end of the lockers along the right-hand wall was a box of hazardous material suits and three cases of general respirators. She took one of the suits and filled it with the smallest respirators she could find and a selection of the hazardous waste suits; if they were available to personnel, there was probably a reason. Then she plucked out three of the masks for the adults. The respirators were an emergency type that could filter just about any toxin for fifteen minutes; she suspected that they would come in handy.

Elgars walked back to the front, dropped her acquisitions, peeked back out the door and frowned. There still wasn't anyone around. She wasn't impatient, exactly, just well aware of the need for speed. As she started to duck back into the room she heard a racket of railgun fire down the cross-corridor; the Posleen had arrived first.

She knelt in the doorway and trained the AIW towards the opening of the cross-corridor. As the first Posleen came into sight, she heard a splintering sound to her right. Sparing a brief glance in that direction she saw a portion of the wall shatter and Wendy step into the main corridor.

Wendy spotted Elgars just as the grenade launcher of the AIW chugged. She cursed and pulled Billy through the hole in the wall.

"Go!" she said, pointing at the entrance where Elgars knelt.

The boy nodded his head and sprinted across the

corridor, carefully keeping to the crossing points of the tram-track, but not slowing or stopping at all.

"What's going on?" Shari asked, pushing children through the opening.

"What do you think?" the younger woman snapped. "Elgars took care of the first scouts, but we have to move."

"Get over there," Shari said. "I'll push them through. You go get a gun or something."

Elgars nodded to the boy as he skidded through the doorway. "Left wall," she said, with a gesture of her chin. "Grab the smallest pistol and the three boxes of ammunition by it then line up against the wall. Make sure the other kids line up with you."

Billy picked himself up off the floor and darted to the table, grabbing the Glock and the boxes of .45 ammunition.

Elgars directed the next three children to the side of the room then ducked out of the way as Wendy ran through the door. "About time."

"Sorry," Wendy said. "I was hanging around."

She had been carefully planning the quip so she was mildly annoyed when Elgars just grimaced in anger at the inconsequential.

"Grab the MP-5," the captain said as another child came through the door. "They're going to be back here in a second."

"Nobody has a sense of humor around here," Wendy said with a shrug, picking up the submachine gun and racking in a round. "It's worse than dealing with Danes."

"What are you *talking* about?" Elgars snarled.

"Never mind," Wendy answered, kneeling on the opposite side of the door as the first Posleen came around the corner. "It's a human thing," she added, hitting the shotgun-toting normal in the chest with a three-round burst.

Behind that one, however, there were four more. The first stumbled over one of the bodies in the corridor and was easy meat for Elgars, but two of the others simply jumped the blockage, landing in the middle of the intersection.

Wendy fired at one of them in the air, spreading the fire like shooting at skeet, and hit it on the flank. The damage from the relatively small rounds was not fatal, however, and the normal spun in place and fired its railgun down the main corridor.

The last child, Kelly, was crossing as the normal fired. Most of the rounds flew wide, but one slashed through the back of the child's calf in a bloody mess.

The girl slid to a stop on the hydroponics side of the tram-track, lying on her stomach and screaming.

Wendy emptied the rest of her magazine into the centauroid with a shriek of primordial anger as Elgars neatly dispatched the last survivor.

"Motherfuckers!" Wendy shouted, her nostrils flaring. "I *hate* the fucking Posties!"

"Give me a hand," Shari gasped, dragging her daughter through the opening.

Elgars ripped the knife out of the juncture of the door and sealed it, coding the lock to indicate a biochem emergency on the inside; it wasn't going to open without heavy explosives or a supervisor's codes.

Wendy pulled out her first aid kit and first numbed the wound then wrapped it tight, cutting the flow of blood down to a trickle.

"It missed the artery," she said, tightening the bandage. "It hit the veins, but they'll keep. It's going to be hard to walk on, though."

Shari rocked her daughter, who was still wailing like a lost soul. "It's okay, Kelly. Shhh."

Elgars suddenly leaned forward and struck the child across the face with an open hand slap. "Quiet."

"God damn you!" Shari shouted leaning towards the captain. She suddenly found a pistol socketed in between her nose and her cheekbone.

"We don't have time," Elgars said coldly. "We have zero time. She has to get up and move. And she has to do it without shrieking. Or we all die." She pulled the pistol back and holstered it. "Now go pick up your rifle and harness; we need to go. Now."

Shari nodded after a moment and stood the now quietly weeping Kelly on her feet. "Can you walk on it?"

"It doesn't hurt," Kelly said quietly. "I think so."

"Then let's get out of here," Wendy said, putting the MP-5 on safe with a distinctive "click."

Elgars suddenly realized the younger woman had been standing directly behind her. She turned around and looked at her, but Wendy just returned her appraisal coldly.

Wendy walked over to the table and looked at the remaining weapons and ammo. "Shari, come over here."

Shari took the combat harness from the younger woman and threw it over her shoulders and accepted the Steyr bullpup assault rifle.

"You arm it by pulling back on the charging handle," Wendy said, pointing to the device. "And here's the safety."

"Got it," Shari said nervously. "I've fired before, but not much."

"That's why I want you to take the nitrogen," Wendy added, pulling off the pack. "You've seen how I do it. You open the doors, we'll cover and do the entry on them. I'm also going to pile you with anything that the kids can't carry; that means I can move faster."

"Okay," Shari said.

"Billy," Elgars said. "You're going to have to carry more ammo."

"He's just a boy," Shari protested quietly. "He's carrying enough."

"He can carry more," Elgars pointed out. "Can't you?"

The boy nodded and took the additional boxes of ammunition and a harness.

"You know the different kind of magazines?" Elgars asked. "If you do, when we're running out, come up and give us more ammo. And reload them when you have time. Clear?"

Billy nodded and smiled then pulled out a magazine for the AIW and gestured at the rifle.

Elgars smiled back and dropped her partially expended magazine, replacing it with the one he had offered.

"Okay," Wendy said. "Let's roll."

Wendy looked at the PDA and at the doors; according to the schematic she had picked up there should only be one door at this point, but there were two.

They had passed through a processing area for the fruit and vegetables produced by the section; much of it piled high and already beginning to wilt. Billy had sniffed out a bin full of boxes of strawberries and the children stuffed their mouths full of the tart-sweet fruits. Wendy realized at that point how long it had been since the attack. It must have been at least three hours with the humans staying just ahead of the front ranks of the Posleen.

Now, though, they were in an actual "green" room; the sixty foot high, several hundred meter long room was packed, floor to ceiling, with trays upon trays of legumes growing in nutrient solution. The ones closest to their position were just sprouts, but in the distance she could see full-sized plants and harvester bots passing back and forth across them.

None of which helped her determine which of these two doors was right. The area that they were headed for was the seed and grain loading zone. There were eight supply elevators, most of which the Posleen would have already taken. But there was also a grain elevator that went two ways. It was possible that they could activate it and ride to the surface. Barring that, she was willing to gather some more climbing gear and climb them out. It would take some time, but if they sabotaged the elevator they would have all the time in the world; as long as they were in the tube, the Posleen weren't going to be catching them.

The problem was getting there *without* using any of the main corridors; the two times they had intersected corridors there had been Posleen in the area. To do that they needed to go into the nutrient pumping section next, then into the seed storage which connected. From there it was a hop, skip and jump to the main receiving area. There might be, probably would be, Posleen there. But they'd deal with that when they came to it.

"What's wrong?" Shari asked, nodding at the door. "Left or right?"

"I dunno," Wendy said. "There's only supposed to be one door." She palmed the controls for the right-hand door, but it wouldn't open even after she punched in the override code. Neither would the left-hand door. But they'd dealt with that before.

"Blast the right door," she said.

Shari stepped forward and carefully pointed the nitrogen wand at the center of the door; she had been splashed lightly once, painfully, and had, thereafter, donned one of the hazardous materials suits. The light ramex suits were no proof against Posleen railgun rounds, but they were dandy for keeping off the occasional splashes of hyper-cold liquid.

Normally the door would harden and turn brittle; the memory plastic was not proof against the cold of the liquid nitrogen. In this case it simply cascaded to the floor and ran off to the side, rapidly boiling off.

"Step back," Wendy warned. "That stuff could make you anoxic in a heartbeat. Interesting, the door *looks* like memory plastic, but it's blasplas."

"What's that mean?" Shari asked, exhaustedly. The trek had drained her to the floor.

"It means somebody wants it looking absolutely normal, but impenetrable," Wendy said. "Try the left door; we don't have time for mysteries."

The second door immediately turned to gray and then white, the memory plastic hardening from the cryogenic bath. When the fog began to clear she stepped forward and placed the punch gun against the door, firing it and shattering the brittle plastic.

The Posleen normal on the other side looked down at the suddenly disappeared door then up at the human blocking the doorway and started to raise his boma blade.

Shari let out a yell and pointed the wand at the Posleen, firing a stream of the liquid into his face.

The normal let out a shrill garbled cry that only served to open his mouth to the stream. Shrilling in pain it tumbled backwards into the room as Wendy leaned over Shari and fired two bursts into his chest. The first burst bounced off of and shattered the flattened breast bone that armored the Posleen's chest, but the second burst pierced through to the heart and the normal slumped to the ground as if genuflecting.

Wendy swept the rest of the room but, as far as she could tell, it was all clear.

The vast chamber was obviously a mixing room of

some sort, nutrients from the smell of it. There was a rich stench of ammonia and phosphate in the air and the floor was lined with massive tanks, ten or twelve feet high and thirty or forty feet across. The room was gigantic; the ceiling was high with large fans at the top and it was at least a hundred or a hundred and fifty yards across.

The doorway had opened onto a small metal-grate platform. A catwalk led from it, between rows of tanks, to a door on the wall in the distance. In the middle it was bisected by another catwalk that crossed the room side to side and there was a large control station at the intersection.

Wendy waved the others in and trotted towards the center. It had been decided that since the greatest threat was the Posleen coming up behind them, Elgars would cover the rear. She was backed up by Billy, who had his pistol and reloads for her. Shari had the nitrogen tank and the bag full of uniforms and respirators while Shannon carried Amber. Wendy led the way, both as the second best fighter and the one who knew the route.

The children followed wearily behind her. The trek had been long and extremely tiring, but they understood that they had to keep up. One of the adults, usually Wendy, would carry the youngest ones from time to time. And they slowed down for them when they felt they could. But the children had grown up with the war and the Posleen were the ultimate bogey-men; they would keep running until they dropped of exhaustion or were told to stop by an adult.

Wendy had reached the intersection before the captain entered the room. When she got there she consulted her map, but the last "secure" area would, according to the map, be through the right-hand door. She considered it then walked over, palming the pad.

From the inside, the door opened easily. Sticking her head through, she checked the far room. It was, as the map said, a storage room for the nutrient materials. She waved the rest to follow and waited for them to catch up.

Elgars swept her rifle from side to side, turning to cover back and sides as she closed up the group. As she passed through the intersection something seemed to scream at her from the back of her mind. She had learned to listen to these little internal comments and she did now, looking around the room for whatever threat the voice was trying to tell her of.

After a moment she leaned her rifle up against the console and considered it thoughtfully while rubbing the bridge of her nose.

Wendy checked the far room again, but it was still clear. When she saw Elgars put her rifle down she swore.

"Shari, get the kids through to the other side; I have to go find out what the captain is up to."

"Got it," the older woman said wearily.

"Take a break, but we won't be long." She paused and contemplated the captain again. "I hope."

By the time Wendy had reached the center consoles there was a massive gurgling sound echoing through the room and Elgars had headed to the nearest tank.

She walked over to the ladder on the side of the tank and started to climb up it, drawing her combat knife.

"Hey, Captain America," Wendy said. "We're on our way *out* of here in case you'd forgotten."

"I know, 'twon't take a minute," Elgars said in a strangely deep voice. "Could you possibly rummage me up a spot of wire, baling wire will do well, and a few scraps of duct tape and . . . oh . . . a can of spray paint? There's a good lass."

"Hey!" Wendy said, catching Elgars' eye. "Hello! Anne! We have to make like a tree and *leaf*!"

Elgars shook her head and looked down at her hands, which had started to strip out the wiring harness for the tank motor. She shook her head again and nodded. "I know," she said in a normal, if distant, voice. "But I think the Posties should have a something to remember us by, don't you?"

"So you're mixing up a really nice batch of nutrients?" Wendy asked sarcastically.

"Not exactly," Elgars said with a death's-head grin. "What's *in* nutrients, Wendy?"

Wendy thought about it then said: "Oh."

"*Roight*," Elgars said, her head going back down to her task. "Now go get me a spot of wire and some duct tape, there's a good lass."


"Wire and duct tape," Wendy muttered, shifting the MP-5 to a better grip. "Where in the hell am I going to find wire and duct tape?"

There would be some in a maintenance section, but the nearest one on the map was further away than the elevators and in an area the Posleen were bound to have overrun. She walked to the far end of the room and thought about it. Something one of the long-time "pro" firefighters had told her floated up to the surface of memory and she smiled. She looked at her map and figured out which door an administrative puke would come in. All things considered, either the one they came in or the one they were going out. So, where was the *furthest* away from that you could get?

She climbed down from the catwalk and began hunting along the walls of the room until she found what she was looking for. On the south wall, the furthest from the door they had come in, behind the last tank, carefully hidden from all but a determined search, was a chair.

And a toolbox.

And a pile of oily rags and roll of baling wire. And a can of gray spray paint, half full.

And a pin-up calendar.

"Well, at least he had *some* taste," she said sourly. "Although that chick has *no* idea how to carry a rifle. And I guaran*tee* that's a dye job! If she's a natural blonde, I'm Pamela Anderson."

She opened up the toolbox and, after extracting a hard candy from the bag in the top, found the roll of duct tape in the lower compartment.

"Okay, all the comforts of home," she muttered, rolling the candy around in her mouth. She put the baling wire in the toolbox, closed it up and picked up the can of spray paint. "Now if I can just get it all up the ladder."

"What took you so long?" Elgars asked.

"Gee, sorry, Captain," Wendy snapped back. "I just found a toolbox I thought you could use and all the other shit you asked for. I guess I should have hurried carrying the heavy fucker up the ladder! And trying to breathe in here isn't helping!"

The atmosphere, slightly ammoniacal and earthy before, now reeked of ammonia: it stung the eyes and clawed at the nostrils.

Elgars tossed her a mask and donned one herself. "Sorry, but all I really needed was the baling wire, tape and spray paint," she said, her voice muffled by the respirator. "Thanks for the rest of it, though. What happened to your shirt?"

Wendy's shirt had taken a beating with three of the buttons torn away.

"I caught it on the damned ladder," she snapped,

looking down at herself. "I thought about duct taping it together, but that was just too redneck."

"Don't let Papa O'Neal hear you say that," Elgars said, chuckling.

"You're sounding normal again," Wendy noted, opening up the toolbox and tossing her a hard candy. "You had me creeped out for a second there." She adjusted the mask and refit it carefully. Without careful fitting, masks tended to leak and she could smell a trace of ammonia still.

"What did I sound like?" the captain asked. She had stripped out the primary power leads for one of the mixing tanks and brought it under the catwalk so that it reached the tank on the opposite side. Taking the spray paint can from Wendy she proceeded to tape the three-phase leads onto the can.

"Sort of . . . British I think. All this 'there's a good lass' stuff."

"I sort of remember it," Elgars admitted. "All this stuff is just sort of 'coming' to me as I go along. I think the shrinks were right; I think the Crabs implanted . . . more than just skills, but sort of 'memories' in me. When I dredge one up, the . . . personality associated with it comes up to the front too. Then when I use it for a while, when I get used to it, the personality fades. Sometimes I get real memories along with it. Sometimes I even seem to be the person for a while. I think they might have given me most of my day-to-day skills through a single entity and she's who comes to the fore most of the time."

"So who is the real you?" Wendy asked.

"I dunno," Elgars said softly. "But for the time being I'll take what I can get; better than getting eaten by the Posleen."

Wendy nodded for a moment then grinned. "So, you're channeling the spirit of a British mad bomber?

Does he know any good drinking songs? The Brits usually know all the good drinking songs. . . ."

Elgars laughed and went back to the main control board. "Trust you to see the humor of it."

"Nah, it's just a matter of looking on the bright side of any really fucked up situation," Wendy said with a muffled chuckle. "I didn't know how to do that at first; I really had a hard time understanding how Tommy could be so . . . comfortable in Fredericksburg. I mean, we were all getting ready to be either blown up or killed and eaten. It's because the rest of us had had our heads in the ground for years about the Posleen. But he had been thinking about what fighting them would be like, getting *beaten* by them would be like, for years. So when the time came, he just *did* it while I was running around like a chicken with my head cut off, crying and worrying and half useless."

"That I have a hard time believing," Elgars said. She cut the power to the tank that the leads had been run to and walked back. She carefully leapt to the mixer arm and waved at the wires. "Hand those to me, would you?"

"Sure," Wendy answered, pushing the bundle across the gap. "But really, the difference now is that most of us have been thinking about what might happen down here for years. Oh, there were some that thought the Posleen would never come; just like there are some that planned on getting drunk enough not to notice. But most of us realized that they might, and thought about what we would do about it. Generally, that was 'head for a defense point and hold out until we're relieved,' but even that is wishful thinking; the Posleen will overrun those in an hour or two. There's no way that the Army is going to be back before we're all snacks."

"Was this your plan from the beginning?" Elgars asked. She carefully leaned over the edge and lowered the wires into the ammoniated muck in the bottom, pressing the wires and spray can deep into it.

"No," Wendy said with a sigh that could barely be heard over the grinding of the other motors; the material in the bottom was mostly anhydrous ammonia and the mixture was harder than cookie dough. The motors were designed to drive against liquid and although they were about thirty percent overrated for that, they were quickly reaching the point where failsafes were going to pop out. "My plan had been to be in the emergency crews; they would have been at the front lines, trying to hold the Posleen back for as long as possible. But *that* presumed that we got some warning; I don't know why we didn't."

"So the longest that the defense points could hold out is . . . what?" Elgars asked, wiping her gloves off on a rag and jumping back to the catwalk. She walked back over to the central console and started shutting down the pumps.

"Three to six hours," Wendy said. "That's the estimated time for a Posleen force to eliminate ninety percent of resistance and presence. Of course, nobody *says* that, but I've seen the estimates. That presumes this wasn't just a Lamprey, but if it was there wouldn't be Posleen down here already."

She keyed the information terminal and dove into the database. She had to enter her password twice, but she finally found the appropriate file.

"Two hours after reduction of primary defense—that's the security forces in A section—ninety percent of the population will have been removed," Wendy said, referring to the document. "Within six hours after reduction, ninety-eight percent will have been removed."

"I guess we're in the two percent then," Elgars said.

"I think it's a bit pessimistic," Wendy answered. "But there's one way to find out." She keyed up a schematic of the Sub-Urb then opened up the emergency services database. "I was wondering, earlier, how we could figure out where the Posleen are. I finally realized you could track them by emergency calls." She pulled up the call records and patched them into the schematic. "We've been on the run for four and a half hours. Penetration was about five hours ago, I'd guess." She scrolled the schematic back five hours. "See the red dots? Those are calls, both initiating calls and support calls. There's a bunch of them around the entrances and then they spread out." She scrolled the schematic forward in time and Elgars could see what she meant; the red dots spread out with a solid "outline" for a while then started to dissipate.

"You can see that there's starting to be fewer people to put in calls," Wendy said emotionlessly. "This is by two hours after the entry; we were on our way down at that point. Cafeteria 3-B is already well inside the Posleen perimeter; Dave was gone by then or shortly afterwards." She scrolled it outward further and now there was a light scattering of red dots. "At this point, almost all the population areas have been overrun and the Posleen are scattering into the industrial sectors. And trying to track them is pointless because nobody is calling for help anymore."

"So in four more hours?" Elgars asked, tapping at her console.

"There will probably be three or four thousand people alive, trapped and hiding in various compartments," Wendy said coldly. "Out of two million to start."

"And they're not getting out, right?" the officer said, looking at her sharply. "They're for all practical purposes dead."

"As a doornail." Wendy nodded. "Ground Forces have *not* entered and have *not* responded and the Posleen are going to totally occupy this facility. There might be a Newt or two left, but for all practical purposes they're all dead men walking."

Elgars nodded and hit enter. "Time to leave."

"Six hours?" Wendy asked.

"Yep," the captain said, looking around. "Assuming it works. But we shouldn't dawdle."

"Are you guys done?" Shari asked, coming down the exit walkway. She had donned a mask as well and the voice was muffled and irritated.

"We could do a backup," Wendy said. "I'm not sure that will get it going. What did you use for a fuel-oil substitute?"

"Corn oil," Elgars answered distantly. "What I need is some bloody plastique," she added, rubbing her chin. "That would fix the bahstahds."

"We need to *leave*," Shari asked. "What are you doing?"

"Blowing up the Urb," Wendy answered.

# CHAPTER 32

"The drive out of *here* is going to be interesting," Major Mitchell said.

"No shit, sir," Pruitt said, scanning the independent sight around. "How *do* we get out of here?"

The SheVa had headed down the Little Tennessee River to where it was joined by Cader Creek then headed up that valley to rendezvous with its reload group on Cader Fork. The reload teams were well into the process and the spare drivers that accompanied them were working with Warrant Indy to repair some of the damage done to the gun.

"You mean other than going back to the Tennessee?" Mitchell asked.

"Yes, sir," the gunner said patiently as the gun shuddered to another round being loaded. The word had already reached them that the Posleen had bounded forward to Oak Grove; indeed, the landers would have

553

been cold meat as they passed the valley opening. But what it meant was that there were now Posleen on both sides of the valley entrance. For that matter, there could be Posleen pushing up the valley by now. However, Major Mitchell had detailed the Meemies to screen in that direction so they shouldn't be caught reloading. "I think by the time we get back there we'll be *way* too popular if you know what I mean."

"Major!" Indy called. "We've got company."

"Shit!" Pruitt said, sweeping the sight around. "Not when we're *loading*! Where? Bearing!"

"No, I mean we have *company*," Indy said with a nervous laugh, climbing up out of the hatch. "Get your finger off the trigger before you give our position away."

Following her was a short, muscular female captain. Mitchell smiled when he saw the ADA insignia on her uniform.

"Whisky Three-Five I presume," he said, offering his hand.

"Captain Vickie Chan, sir," the captain said, taking it.

"Thanks for your assistance, Captain," the SheVa commander said. "I thought we were goners."

"Captain, I *want* one of y'all's guns," Pruitt said, spinning his seat around to face her. "They are *bad*. Not as bad as Bun-Bun, mind you. But pretty damned tough."

"You can have it," the captain laughed. "You have *no* idea what it's like to fire."

"Bad?" Mitchell asked.

"That's an understatement, sir," the captain replied with a smile. "Let's just say we tend to wait until we *have* to fire. So what is the plan?"

"Unfortunately, I think it's to go up there," Mitchell said, panning an external monitor up into the mountains.

"I've been looking at a map. And it's even worse than it looks on the screen."

"That's nearly vertical, sir," the Meemie commander said hesitantly. "I think that Meemies can handle the *slope*, but it's also covered in trees, which we *can't* handle. And isn't a SheVa a little top-heavy for those slopes? Not to mention . . . wide?"

"I think we're about to find out," Mitchell answered. "I think I've plotted out a course that we can take; up through Chestnut and Betty Gap and down Betty Creek. It's not going to be fun or easy—the slope in particular around the back side of Panther Knob is going to be a special nightmare—but it's all wide enough for us to fit, according to the map, and with nothing worse than a thirty-degree slope. With all our rounds loaded, we actually have a fairly low center of gravity, despite the look. I think we can make it."

"And if you can't?" Captain Chan asked.

"Well, if we go back, we're going to run into the Posleen," Mitchell answered. "At least, that's a very good chance. And if we go . . . up, there are a series of possible bad outcomes. For one thing, we don't know that the Posleen aren't on Betty Creek in force. But it's also the only path that doesn't involve getting immediately overrun. If the Posleen *are* there, but not in force, well . . ." He grinned ferally.

"What about your resupply units?" she asked, thumbing over her shoulder. "And us, for that matter."

"I've updated a map," he said, handing her a flash card. "Do you have a . . ."

"I've got a map module," she said with a smile, pulling out her map reader and popping the chip in. "We've got all the modern refinements."

"You'll go up by Mica City and over Brushy Fork Gap; there are some roads. On the map the path is usable by my trucks, your tanks . . ."

"Are pretty damned heavy."

"Yes," he said. "There are some hairpins I'm not sure about you being able to make. I'll be honest about that. If you get permanently stuck, I suggest you get out and board our trucks. But I hope you're able to meet us on the far side. God knows we can use the help."

"We might take a different route," Chan said scrolling around the map. "I really don't think this road will take us."

"I agree," Mitchell said with a sigh. "But I don't see another way out of the valley."

"I do," Chan said with another smile. "We'll follow you."

"Uh," the major paused. "We . . ."

"Make a hell of a mess," Chan said. "I know, we followed you here, remember? But you smash stuff more or less flat; heck, sir, you smash tree stumps into sawdust. It's bumpy, nearly impossible, for most vehicles. But an Abrams doesn't have a problem with it at all. So we'll just tag along behind you."

"Okay," Mitchell said. "Sounds like a plan."

"Well, sir, this was a hell of a plan," Kitteket said sourly. The Humvee was perched on the edge of a precipice that did *not* appear on the map.

The path up to this point had been no picnic. It was a forestry road and hadn't been maintained in years, certainly since the war had started. The road had not been particularly good to start with and washouts and fallen limbs had slowed them considerably. But this was certainly the icing on the cake.

"Good stop there, Specialist," he said, considering his map again. "This certainly is not what is supposed to be there. Or, rather, what is supposed to be there is not there."

"Whichever it is, we need to find someplace that *is* there," Kitteket said grumpily.

"Ah," he reached into his briefcase and pulled out a bottle of pills. "Take one," he said, handing it to her.

"What is this?" the specialist asked.

"Provigil," he answered, taking one himself. "It's getting late and it's been a long day and we're all tired, right?"

"Right," she said, taking the pill.

"Not anymore," he said. "What, you never read a manual on Provigil?"

"No," she said. "I've heard the name, but I don't know what it is."

"It makes you 'untired,'" he said. "It's not an upper; it's sort of the reverse of a sleeping pill. You don't get sleepy. You do tend to get stupid and you don't notice, but tomorrow some time, assuming that we don't get to sleep, which is likely, I'll pass around some uppers and those will increase our thought speed as well. We'll be *almost* good-to-go. Right up until the spiders start crawling all over us."

He considered the map again and frowned. "If we back up and head downhill there's another road that heads over towards Betty Gap along the ridge. It should be passable."

"If it's even there," she grumped, putting the Humvee in reverse.

"Oh ye of little faith," he said, leaning back. "Things could be worse, things could be much worse."

"Oh really?" she asked sarcastically.

"Trust me," Ryan said, fingering the 600 insignia on his chest. "Been there, done that, got the scar."

"You're doing *what*?" Shari asked. "Are you *nuts*?"

"Well, I'm not sure I'll *tell* anybody we did it,"

Wendy answered. "Assuming we live to get out of here. But, no, we're not nuts."

"You must be," Shari said angrily, looking around the room. "You can't blow this place up! There are survivors all through the Urb!"

"It took them four years to retake the Rochester Urb," Wendy pointed out. "The estimate is that after two weeks there will be less than two hundred survivors and I think that is being generous; I'd say less than two. Compare that to the Posleen losses if the whole Urb comes down on them; there are probably fifty or sixty thousand Posleen in this place right now."

"You can't blow the whole thing up anyway," Shari countered. "It's designed to survive a close explosion of a nuclear weapon."

"It's designed to be hit from the *outside*, lass," Elgars answered. "The supports aren't designed to take side damage. Plus the bleeding bombs will start fires; lots of them. If the Posleen aren't all burned out they will still weaken the supports and the whole thing will come down."

Shari looked at Elgars with a sidelong expression. "What bombs? And why do you have an English accent?"

"She's channeling a Brit," Wendy said. "Probably one of their demo experts. And the bombs are all the tanks; each of them is filled with ammonium nitrate fuel oil bombs."

"They look like . . . gray gunk," Shari said.

"Don't worry, it's a bomb," Wendy said. "A big enough one that it's going to gut the whole Urb and any Posleen that are in it."

"And all the human survivors," Shari said.

"And all the human survivors," Wendy agreed.

"That's sick," the older woman spat.

"No, it's war," Wendy answered coldly. "You remember where we came from?"

"I *survived* Fredericksburg," Shari snapped. "And there will be people who would *survive* this! But not if you detonate that bomb!"

"What was important about Fredericksburg was that it gave the Posleen a seriously bloody nose!" Wendy snapped back. "After that, they knew we could and would fuck them at every opportunity. With this we're going to cut the head off of their advance and take out a sizable chunk of their force. And that is *worth* the casualties. *Worth* the dead. In war, people *die*. Good people *and* bad people. If I thought most of them would survive, no, we wouldn't detonate the bomb. But almost all of them are going to die in these tunnels and be turned into *rations*. Not. On. My. Watch."

"So are you going to stick around to be blown up?" Shari asked bitterly.

"Hell no!" Wendy said. "I'm going to get the fuck out, if I can. And bring you and the kids with me! And we're setting the bomb for six hours from . . ."

"About four minutes ago, actually," Elgars said, looking at the controls. "So I suggest you ladies get this discussion done."

"Shit," Shari said quietly. "Okay, okay. Let's go." She looked upwards to the rest of the Urb and shook her head. "I'm sorry."

"I'm sorry I didn't die in Section A," Wendy said, putting her hand on Shari's shoulder. "That would have been . . . clean. But we're going to fuck up the Posleen, and that's the bottom-line."

"Well, you two can talk about it all you'd like," Elgars said, heading for the far door. "But I'm getting the hell out of Dodge."

"Agreed," Wendy said, following her. "Agreed."

Shari took one more look at the controls and turned to follow the other two as the north door opened up.

The Posleen normal took one look at the three

women and started trotting down the swaying catwalk, burbling a cry as it pulled its railgun around.

Wendy turned and let out a shout as she pulled her MP-5 to the front.

"NO!" Elgars yelled, ripping the submachine gun from her hands. "This whole place would go up!"

"Eat nitrogen, asshole!" Shari shouted, firing a stream of the cryogenic liquid at the catwalk and the Posleen.

The normal paused to look at the liquid flying in a foaming arch. It seemed confused as to why the thresh would spray white liquid all over the walkway. But as the catwalk began to shatter from tension and brittleness the Posleen let loose a stream of railgun rounds then fell screaming into the ammonia tank.

"Oh crap," Wendy said, getting up from having thrown herself on the floor. "Ah, hell, Shari."

Shari was lying on her back, hands clamped over her stomach, with blood pouring through the catwalk and onto the floor below.

Wendy walked over and rolled her onto her stomach, exposing the massive exit wound of the railgun round.

"Aaaahhh," the older woman yelled in pain. "Oh, God! Wendy, I can't feel anything from my waist down."

"That's because it went right through your spine," Wendy said sadly. She put a pressure bandage in place and waved for Elgars to come over. "Put your hand on that."

"We need to leave," Elgars said, putting pressure on the bandage.

"Yep," Wendy answered. "And we will, in just a moment." She ripped open a Hiberzine injector and applied it to Shari's neck.

"What's that?"

"Hiberzine," Wendy said. "I can't move you awake like this."

"I don't want to be out," Shari panted. "The kids need me."

"Not with a great damned hole through you they don't," Elgars replied. "You're not going to be doing them any favors screaming every time we move you."

"We're nearly to the elevator," Wendy said desperately. "We can get you out; getting you up to the surface won't be that hard."

"Oh, God," Shari said, her lips turning blue and going cold. "I can't die now."

"You won't," Wendy promised. She jammed the Hiberzine injector against her neck and watched as the woman went limp. Her color improved almost immediately as the nannites directed blood to the brain. In moments her face was flushed and her tongue protruded horribly.

"Okay, let's go," Elgars said.

"Fuck that," Wendy answered. "We need to find a medical facility and a stretcher." She pulled out the medical pack and withdrew some clamps. "If I can put her together even a bit the Hiberzine will keep her from bleeding out while we move her."

"We can't *operate* on her!" Elgars snapped. "We have *six hours* to get out of this place or we'll all be jelly. We have to *leave*."

"WE ARE NOT LEAVING HER!" Wendy screamed coming to her feet and putting herself nose to nose with the soldier. "*NOT!* DO YOU UNDERSTAND ME?"

Elgars met her stare for stare, but after a moment she backed off. "Most of the Class One facilities are where there are *people*. And there's not much we can do, unless you've been taking night courses as a trauma internist."

"We can stabilize her," Wendy said, waving at the console. "Go find a medical facility, one that won't have the Posleen all over it."

"This is impossible," Elgars said, shaking her head. But she keyed in the information request anyway, asking for the nearest full-scale medical facility. Strangely, the database asked her for her username and password. Keying both in, it noted that there was a Class One Plus facility only three quadrants away. The map showed it as being carved out of the wall of the main sector.

"There's a facility practically next door," Elgars said. "That door that didn't appear on the map you down-loaded? It's the way into the facility."

"Well, then we're fucked," Wendy cursed. "We can't open it."

"Let's go back," Elgars said. "Maybe I can come up with something."

"What?" Wendy asked.

"I don't *know*," the captain said. "I'll say 'open sesame' or something."

"Fine, you go get the kids," Wendy said. "I'll start dragging her."

"Great," Elgars said. "Send me after the kids."

"They'd argue with *me*," Wendy pointed out heaving Shari up into a fireman's carry. "Oof. You'll be there before me, I think."

Elgars placed her palm on the doorpad as Wendy carried Shari through the door to the tank room. As soon as she placed her hand on the pad, the door opened.

"What did you do?" Wendy asked. She was sweating and panting already carrying the older woman; it had been a long day.

"I just put my palm on the pad," Elgars said with

a shrug. "I'm military; maybe it was designed to open for any military personnel."

The far room had lockers against both walls and the far door appeared to be an airlock.

"You *did* ask for a medical facility, right?" Wendy asked, shifting the body on her shoulders. She looked around, but it looked more like the entry to a computer chip clean room.

"Yes," Elgars said leading the line of children to the far door. It, too, opened at a touch. "It's supposed to be this way. The map showed a winding path; we'll have to see what that means."

The group crowded into the airlock and Elgars keyed the next door, which opened into violet darkness.

The light from the airlock illuminated the far wall and Elgars felt an almost unholy dread shiver down her spine. The wall was clearly a made thing, but it looked organic and the tunnel drifted off to the right in a fashion that made her think, uncomfortably, of the inside of an intestine.

A purple intestine at that; the light that seemed to emanate from the walls was a deep violet. In the distance was a gurgling sound, not quite like a brook or a fountain, but more like an upset stomach and closer to hand there were high, shrill whistles. The smell was odd and alien, and acrid sweetness that told hindbrain that it was no longer in a human environment.

"Well, this is odd," Wendy said.

Elgars hefted her rifle and looked around the violet tunnel. "I don't like this. I don't like it at all." She was panting quietly.

Wendy shifted the inert lump of Shari on her shoulder and shrugged as well as she could. "I don't care if you like it or not; there's supposed to be a trauma facility in here and we're going to find it."

"Where's an info terminal?" Elgars asked rhetorically.

"Do you need information, Captain Elgars?" a mellifluous voice asked out of the walls.

Elgars pried one of the children's hands off of her uniform and looked around. "Who asked?"

"This is the facility AID, Captain," the voice answered. "Do you require assistance?"

"We have a patient," Wendy answered. "We need a medical facility."

There was no answer.

Elgars looked at Wendy and shrugged. "We have a patient, we need a medical facility," she repeated.

"Follow the sprite," the AID answered. One of the blue glowing micrites appeared and bounced in the air. "It will lead you to the facility."

The group followed the sprite as it went through a series of turns. The shrill piping and gurgling in the distance never seemed to go away or even change, but the light would brighten in the areas through which they walked, getting dimmer as they passed.

There were occasional low, mostly empty rooms to either side of the passageway. In a few there were low stools or cushions that looked amazingly like toadstools and one had a low bench and table set that could have been for children. There were many puckered spots that could have been openings to additional chambers or simply odd architecture.

Finally they came to a room that was somewhat higher than most. In the center was a small dais with what looked like a glass-covered altar on it.

"Please place the patient in the chamber," the AID chimed in as the sprite flickered out and flew away. The top to the chamber seemed to disappear rather than receding or even folding away as memory plastic would have.

"What is this going to do to her?" Wendy asked.

"AID, could you answer that question, please?" Elgars said impatiently. "And future questions from that person that are permitted."

"The nanochamber will repair the subject," the AID answered. "The choices are repair, repair and rejuv or full upgrade."

Wendy slowly lowered Shari onto the altar and shivered uncomfortably. "Computer, what is the nature of 'full upgrade'?" she asked.

"The patient will be given nano-enhanced musculature, fast-heal and bone-structure," the AID answered emotionlessly. "Along with implanted combat skills."

"Oh, shit," Elgars said. "Computer, what is the nature of my access to this facility? Is it because I'm a military officer?"

"No, Captain," the AID answered. "You are an ongoing patient."

"Oh, Jesus Christ," Wendy said bitterly. "How long does repair take, computer?"

"Repair will take approximately ten minutes for the damage that is detected. Full upgrade will take approximately fifteen."

"Son-of-a-bitch, son-of-a-bitch, son-of-a-bitch," Wendy muttered. "SON OF A BITCH!"

"It's been here the whole time," Elgars said bitterly.

"They could have repaired David any time they wanted to."

"Or rejuved any of the old people."

"'It would take months in the regen tanks to fix,'" Wendy quoted bitterly. "The question is whether Shari wants somebody else's memories."

"Improvements have been emplaced in the system since the experiments on Captain Elgars," the computer burbled happily. "Secondary memory and personality effects have been severely decreased. In addition, it was necessary to implant a full personality core in

Captain Elgars due to complete loss of original function."

"Say that again in English," Elgars snapped.

"Anne Elgars no longer existed; she was dead," the computer said. "Due to extensive brain damage it was necessary to dump all but hindbrain functions and reload a complete personality core. This patient has not suffered significant neurological damage."

"Oh, shit," Elgars said quietly, sitting down on the floor. "Who was it?"

"That information is not available to this facility," the computer answered. "Some personality cores were brought to Earth by !Tchpth!, others were collected on Earth."

"Computer," Wendy said. "Full upgrade."

"That command needs to come from Captain Elgars," the computer said.

"Concur," Elgars whispered. "Do it." At her words the top closed and went opaque, obscuring the view of the badly damaged woman.

"Annie," Wendy said, sitting down and putting her arm around her. "Don't take it so hard. They saved you. That's all that matters."

"Whoever 'me' is," Elgars said. "The fuckers. They wouldn't even tell my doctors. No wonder they thought I was nuts; I am."

"Of course they didn't explain it to your doctors," Wendy said archly. "They would have had to explain this facility. And you're not nuts, we've all got multiple 'people' running around inside of us. We just show different ones at different times."

"Sure, but that's just a way of *saying* it," Elgars said. "I'm *really* multiple people. Like . . . Frankenstein, but in the head. A patchwork girl."

"That's not the way it appears to me," Wendy argued. "You seem to . . . manifest a few of the personalities then they go away. You hardly ever have an accent any-more. And that probably explains your speech impedi-ment; you couldn't decide which accent was 'you.' Lately you seem more . . . whole. I think you're going to end up okay. Just . . . Anne Elgars. But . . ." she snorted. "But 'upgraded.'"

"I thought I was naturally strong," the officer said, flexing a muscle. "And all this time it's nannites."

"And working out," Wendy corrected. "I imagine it gives you a . . . a sort of a stronger *baseline*. You have to improve it from there."

Wendy looked over at the group of children and shook her head. "We're gonna get out of here, kids. *All* of us."

"Is Mommy going to be okay?" Kelly asked tearfully. The children had been following in near silence since having a rather severe talking-to at the hands of Elgars.

"According to the computer she should be as good as new," Wendy said, taking her up on her lap and hugging her. "Better, she's probably going to start looking younger."

"Can it do that?" Shannon asked, shifting Amber's carrier. The ten-year-old had been keeping up like a trooper, but she was obviously flagging.

"According to the computer," Elgars said, pulling the backpack off of the girl and setting the baby on the floor. "We'll just have to see. Speaking of which—computer, are you smart enough to know that we're invaded by Posleen?"

"Yes," the AID said.

"Are there any in this facility?"

"Negative; the closest are in the Hydroponics section."

"Lemme know if that changes, okay?"

"Hey, computer," Wendy said. "Where'd all the techs go?"

"Clarify, please," the computer said.

"Well," Wendy said looking around. "I didn't see any Crabs or Indowy running around. And most of the gear in here is theirs. So where did they go?"

"The primary entrance to this facility is separate from the Sub-Urb," the AID answered, flashing a hologram up in the room. "The exit is on the southeastern face of Pendergrass Mountain."

"*And* there's a back way out," Wendy snarled. "If I ever find out who set this up and kept it secret I will rip their heart out and eat it while they watch."

"Well, that's a bit excessive," Elgars said. "Wouldn't it make more sense to just kill them?"

"No, I don't want anybody to fuck us over like this again," Wendy said. "God, I'm mad."

"At what?" Shari said sitting up.

The top had disappeared again so soundlessly that no one had noticed. Except Billy who was sitting up with an amazed expression on his face.

"Mo . . . Mommy?" he croaked.

"Billy," Shari said. "You talked!"

"Y . . . " The boy swallowed and cleared his throat. "Yo . . . you're young."

Shari looked as she must have when she was in high school. Her hair had actually lengthened slightly, as if time had been dilated inside the shell, and was a brilliant white-blonde. Her breasts were large, high and firm and any sign of an age blemish or wrinkle was gone as if it had never existed. She looked down at the bandages still on her clothes and shook her head.

"Even the bloodstains are gone," she whispered.

"It didn't fix the hole in your shirt," Wendy replied, looking at the tear and fingering the skin underneath. "There's not even a scar, though. How do you feel?"

"Fine," Shari said looking at her hands in wonder.

"Good. Better than I've felt in years. Strong. What in the hell happened?"

"This is apparently the facility that repaired me," Elgars answered. "We thought you might prefer the full upgrade. Among other things it included a rejuv."

"Wow," Shari said, looking at the fineness of her skin. "Mike is going to . . ." She suddenly stopped and grimaced. "I guess not." For just a moment her eyes teared up.

"Hey, he's tough," Wendy said. "We'll head out to the northwest; we should be able to get around the Posleen that way. When we get someplace safe we'll check on them in the refugee database."

"If we can get out of here," Shari said pensively.

"It turns out there's a back door," Elgars said dryly. "Just another little item whoever built this facility failed to mention to the rest of the Urb."

"We can go directly to Pendergrass Mountain," Wendy said with a nod. "No waiting."

"Then let's go," Shari said, standing up and pulling off the bandages.

Wendy suddenly looked at the altar with a speculative air. "AID, how long until the first Posleen gets close to here?"

"There are Posleen in the Hydroponics area. Due to the chaotic nature of Posleen movement, precise timelines for their movement to this area are impossible to generate."

"Hmm," she said. "Do you think there is enough time for a full upgrade?"

"Do you think that's a good idea?" Shari asked.

"You hearing voices in your head?" Wendy asked. She took Shari's Steyr and tossed it to her. "Catch."

Shari caught it and jacked the chamber to see if there was a round in place. Then she flipped it on safe and held it barrel to the floor in a tac-team carry position. "What does that prove?"

"Look at how you're holding it," Wendy said with a grin. "Say 'fire.'"

"Why?" Shari asked warily, looking at how she was holding the weapon. It looked odd but . . . it *felt* right.

"Just say it," Wendy said.

"Fire."

"See," Wendy said with a grin. "Not a trace of an accent. They fixed the bugs testing it on Elgars."

"Color me guinea-pig," the captain said sourly.

"So, computer," Wendy said. "Do I have time?"

"Unknown. And when Posleen breach the outer door, my orders are to shut this facility down with prejudice," the AID said. "I will then require that you leave."

"What happens if I'm in the chamber when that time comes?" Wendy asked.

"You *don't* want to be," the AID replied.

She looked at the other two women. "It's probably the only chance I'll ever get for a rejuv. If it's not eternal life, it's a close equivalent."

Shari sighed. "Go for it."

"Computer," Elgars said. "Please do a full upgrade on this patient."

"Very well," it said, opening the cover. "Get on the slab."

There was another wait as Elgars got the computer to download a schematic of the exit and Shari ensured all the children were ready to run. She settled the children and convinced them that, yes, she was really Miss Shari. After checking out the route and determining that there shouldn't be any Posleen between their current position and the surface she took over carrying Amber and started giving her a bottle.

About then the cover came off and Wendy sat up.

"Dang," she said. "It's like going into and coming out of Hiberzine. No time passed at all."

"Feel any different?" Elgars asked.

"Stronger," Wendy said. "It feels like . . . I dunno, my 'wind' is better. I feel charged up is the best way to put it."

"Well, let's go," Shari said, cradling the child in one arm and the bullpup in the other. "I don't want this place to 'shut down with extreme prejudice' on our heads."

"Do we know where we're going?" Wendy asked.

"We do now," Elgars said, holding up the pad. "But . . . computer, could we get a sprite?"

"Certainly," the AID responded as one of the micrites appeared and flashed on.

"Ready to go," Elgars said.

"Okay," Wendy replied. "Let's roll."

They exited the chamber to the left and went through a series of turns and twists, twice passing through large sphinctered openings that reminded Wendy of nothing so much as heart valves, until they came to an even larger chamber than where the rejuv device had been. In the center of the chamber, which was nearly fifty meters across and nearly as high, was something that looked just exactly like a purple loaf of round bread.

"What is that?" Elgars asked, as the sprite vanished into the distance.

"That is the transport pod," the AID answered as an oblong door opened in the side. The oblong was horizontal so the entrance was well below normal human height. In fact, Elgars had to duck so she wouldn't hit her head.

The interior was just as unpleasant and unprepossessing as the exterior, consisting mostly of purple-blue foam with occasional washes of green that looked brownish in the odd light.

"Please take a seat," the AID intoned. "This transport is leaving the station."

The group sat on the floor and looked around waiting for the device to start to move. There were no external windows so there was no way to see what was going on outside; it was for all practical purposes its own little universe.

"AID?" Elgars said after a moment. "When will we start moving?"

"You are halfway to Pendergrass Mountain, Captain Elgars."

"Oh." She looked around again and shrugged.

"Inertial dampers," Wendy said. "The sort of thing they have on spacecraft; it 'damps' the motion."

"Okay," Shari said with a shrug. "So when do we get there?"

"Now," Wendy said as the door opened into blackness.

"That's not so good," Elgars said, stepping out onto the barely visible floor. Looking around she saw a chamber that was a large and apparently natural cavern. But there was no visible entrance deeper into the mountain; it was as if the transport had gone through solid rock. "Okay, now I'm freaked."

"It's just before dawn," Shari said. "We need to let the children sleep. I could use some rest myself for that matter."

"It's cold out here," Wendy said, pulling at her torn shirt. "Maybe we could sleep in the transport."

"And have it suddenly go back to the Urb?" Elgars asked. "I don't think so."

"We've got some blankets," Shari said. "We can bed down in here. If we all huddle up together it won't be too bad."

"Okay," Wendy said looking around. "Up near the walls. Can we light a fire?"

"Probably a bad idea," Elgars said. "The light and heat could attract attention. We just need to make it through this night; we'll find some better materials tomorrow."

"Okay," Wendy said. "Let's get some sleep. And hope it gets better tomorrow."

# CHAPTER 33

They sends us along where the roads are,
      but mostly we goes where they ain't:
We'd climb up the side of a sign-board
      an' trust to the stick o' the paint:
We've chivied the Naga an' Looshai,
      we've give the Afreedeeman fits,
For we fancies ourselves at two thousand,
      we guns that are built in two bits—'Tss! 'Tss!
                              —Rudyard Kipling
                                    "Screwguns"

*Betty Gap, NC, United States, Sol III*
*0714 EDT Sunday September 27, 2009* AD

Pruitt stared into the rising sun, pretty sure he'd never been this exhausted in his life. Whatever the drugs were telling him.

"I feel like I haven't slept in a week," he muttered. "Or at least like I could sleep for a week." He wasn't exactly tired; the Provigil was making sure that he wouldn't feel that way and a tiny bit of methamphet-amine was ensuring that he was alert. But it had been a *long* day with a lot of stress and it didn't look to be ending any time soon.

The route over the mountain had been a long drawn out nightmare and one where he couldn't do anything except hold on and hope for the best.

The SheVa gun had not been designed to climb mountains and a couple of times he was pretty sure they were just going to go tumbling back down a slope; once just west of Chestnut Gap when they had to ascend a ten-foot bluff while already on a very steep slope and another time when the mountainside was just a *bit* steeper than it looked on the map. The SheVa often felt like it was going straight up and knowing that there was a multiton gun and two stories of steel above you, pulling the gun over and backwards, was pretty nerve-wracking. It was almost worse the few times that they had had to straddle a ravine with one giant tread half supported on either side; the undercarriage would creak and groan, sounding like it was going to shatter at any moment.

It had been worse for Reeves; the large and airy compartment occasionally got thick with the fear sweat from the driver. But every time that Major Mitchell told him to take a slope, he'd just nod his head and put his foot to the floor. It took a special kind of courage to simply place your faith in a hunk of machinery, that it would take the hill and not turn into a gigantic iron boulder.

The trek had to have been nearly as bad for the Meemies. The Abrams tank was certified to negotiate a sixty degree slope—amazing what placing most of sixty tons of metal near the ground could do for center of gravity—but that didn't mean that anyone but an idiot *liked* to go up them. And in places the laboring

SheVa had torn the slope to such an extent that its tread holes, which were the only clear route for an Abrams, easily approached sixty degrees. But the commander of the MetalStorm tracks had taken them into and out of those ersatz fighting positions without any apparent qualm.

It would almost have been better if he'd just turned off his screens and gone to sleep, but they didn't know when the Posleen might do a flyover. And now that he was reloaded, he was ready to kick some Posleen butt.

Where the Posleen were was a big question. Between Major Mitchell and the Storm commander they had managed to scrape up a few other surviving units on the radio. It turned out that the horses had taken the Rocky Face slope and Oak Grove, cutting off a good part of the surviving Corps. But engineers had blown the bridges at Oak Grove and Tennessee before the horses got there and at both points the Posleen were rebuilding the structures while laboriously ferrying troops across.

That last was bad news; nobody liked to think about Posleen having combat engineers; among other things that meant that the entire lower Tennessee was potentially crossable. But it was taking them a few hours to do the structure and the advance was slowed down in the meantime. Currently Major Mitchell intended to head down into Betty Creek and then over Brushy Fork mountain to Greens Creek. After that they would practically have to debouche into the Savannah Creek valley; they had to get ahead of the Posleen and filtering through mountain passes wasn't going to let them do that.

They had reports that a company of mixed MPs and infantry were holding the bridges over the Tuckasegee River. It wasn't a big deal to the SheVa—there wasn't a bridge in the world that would support Bun-Bun—but the Storms needed one to cross the river. If they could make it to the crossing ahead of the horses all would be relatively well. If they didn't, on the other hand, things would get sticky.

There was also the issue of destroying the bridge. The MPs indicated that they didn't have any engineers; they had piled explosives around, but the bridge was pretty sturdy and they weren't sure it would go down. If worse came to worse, of course, Bun-Bun could take care of that little detail as well.

It was near the Tuckasegee crossing, at Dillsboro, that the roads forked. There, Highway 23 separated off and went to Asheville. That was a critical juncture; just up the road at Waynesville was another Urb and if the Posleen got that far it was a mostly open plain all the way into the city. For that matter, at Balsam Gap the road crossed the Blue Ridge Parkway. Since that was a support road for the majority of the Appalachian Line, getting up onto it would permit the Posleen to spread nearly at will. And just east of Waynesville they would hit Interstate 40; that would permit them just about unrestricted movement.

There was part of a division out of Asheville headed towards the Balsam mountains. But Asheville was under heavy attack on two fronts and couldn't spare much in that direction. Major Mitchell had, therefore, decided to head up the road to Balsam, using the SheVa and the MetalStorms to slow the Posleen advance. This program was not without its detractors; the main road to Balsam Gap was not going to be usable by the SheVa, which meant going off-road. And the terrain around Balsam Pass was worse than what they were crossing at the moment.

But that obstacle was far off. For now it was simply a matter of surviving the descent.

"Good Lord," Indy said, looking at her own screen. "It's even worse in daylight!"

The route down from Betty Gap was a normal Appalachian mountainside, carpeted in a mixture of moutain laurel and deciduous trees with a thin covering of loam over schist and gneiss rocks; the morning light had brought with it a thin layer of the wispy fog that gave the Smoky Mountains their name and the pearlous light made the scene almost unreal. Especially since it also was an almost six-hundred-foot drop to the valley in less than a mile, a good bit of it relatively unbroken slope. They had discovered to their occasional despair that the thin coating of loam tended to strip off and act as a lubricant when a seven-thousand-ton tank tried to cross it.

"Sir?" Reeves said in an exhausted tone.

"Go slow," the major replied. "If we start to slip just . . . put it in reverse."

"Yes, sir," the private said, gently revving the tank in idle. "Of course, I could just put it in forward and try to go down *really* fast."

"Please don't joke," Indy said. "I'm surprised we haven't blown a track or a bar yet; I don't want to think about what hitting the valley floor at ninety miles an hour would be like."

"Just . . . take it slow, Reeves," the major repeated, gripping the arms of his chair and leaning back.

"Bun-Bun would have something quippy to say right about now," Pruitt said, leaning back like the major. "But at the moment I'm too terrified to come up with anything."

"Just think of it as skiing?" Reeves muttered.

"I don't think this will slalom very well."

"Captain Chan," Mitchell said, switching to the Storms' frequency. "We're going to have to attempt this slope. There is a road along the ridge that should handle your tanks; I suggest you try that first, rather than trying to toboggan after us."

"Agreed," Chan replied. "And . . . good luck."

Wendy slid from between two of the children and walked to the entrance of the cave. She should have been out like a light, but for some reason she had started awake about ten minutes before and been unable to get back to sleep. Elgars was standing watch, staring off to the east where the first faint glimmer of light could be discerned. The lights of Franklin had been extinguished, but fires had been set throughout the valley, the Posleen being nearly as incendiary as Old World mercenaries. She could barely see the forms moving down below, but she knew that thousands, tens of thousands, millions of Posleen were pouring past to the north, headed for Knoxville, headed for Asheville. Many of them perhaps pouring into their former home.

She looked at her watch and nodded. That was probably what had awakened her.

"Has it gone off yet?" she asked.

Elgars shook her head. "I thought it should have gone off about five minutes ago."

"'There should have been an earth-shattering kaboom,'" Wendy intoned. "'Where was the earth-shattering kaboom?'"

"The Martian, right?" Elgars asked.

"You remember?"

"Nah, I saw it while I was watching the kids the other day," the captain said. As she did, there was a faint shudder in the floor of the cave, and then a second stronger one. It felt like a very small earthquake. To the east, there was a gout of light and a section of land settled slightly then formed a giant, smoking crater.

"I feel, really ambiguous about this," Wendy said

after a moment. "I just lost quite a few friends. People that I care about. On the other hand . . ."

"On the other hand they were already dead," Elgars said, standing up and brushing off her butt. "Or as good as. Most of them would have become rations for the Posleen, a use that we have prevented. And we got who knows how many Posleen in there. Yes, it wasn't pretty. War isn't."

"Easy enough for you to say," Wendy snapped. "Those were my *friends*."

"Wendy, with the exception of you, and Shari, and the kids, and . . ." She stopped and counted on her fingers then nodded. "And Papa O'Neal and Cally and Mosovich and Mueller, the people we just buried are all the people I know in the *world*. We, I, just buried all my nurses, all my doctors, all my therapists under a billion tons of rubble. They'll probably never be pulled out; they'll just put up a monument with a list of names. I did that. With my hands. And if you think I don't have some problems with that, you're not the friend I thought you were. But if I had it to do over again, I'd do it over again. Because it was the right decision. Morally and tactically."

"You're so sure," Wendy said quietly.

"That's why they pay me the big bucks," Elgars said with a snort. "It's your turn for guard anyway. Go ahead and think it over for the next few hours. Then get some rest; it's a long way to Georgia."

Orostan had found that patience was like a tool with the Indowy. It was clear that the engineers were going as fast as they could, so simply being there and watching patiently was his best bet. But with the coming of dawn, the bridge, a hastily constructed span of I beams torn from buildings and wooden planks, was nearly complete.

"You have done well, thresh," the oolt'ondai said. "There will be other bridges to build; there is one to the north that will be more difficult. I want you to look at the human maps and make plans to create one more swiftly there. Understood?"

"Yes, lord," the Indowy replied.

"Your clan yet exists," the Posleen commander said. "Continue to serve me well and it will be permitted to continue. Fail me, and the last of your clan will be eliminated. It shall be as if you were never born. Understand?"

"Understood, lord," the clan chief replied. "We will need maps and any pictures of the next bridge that are available."

"I will ensure you have them," Orostan replied.

Cholosta'an's head came up as there was a rumble to the southwest. "What was that, lord?"

"I'm not sure," Orostan said. "Perhaps this area is prone to earth movements," he added, forgetting that Cholosta'an was a native-born.

"Not that I'm aware of, lord," the Kessentai said. "And . . . I hate to say it, but that is from the direction of the underground city."

"Arrrrrh!" the oolt'ondai shouted, pulling up his tactical net. "Telenaal fusc! Aralenadaral, taranal! I will *eat* these humans, body, blood, bone and SOUL!"

"The city is gone," Cholosta'an said, looking at his own display in disbelief.

"I CAN READ THE NET! Gamasal!"

"Yes, Oolt'ondai?"

The younger Kessentai had been waiting impatiently the entire night; at one point Orostan had wondered if he would have to order him removed when he threatened an Indowy. Now, with the sun coming up and the host about to move again, it was time to release him.

"We can handle bridges, but when these humans

get dug into passes they are impossible. Take an oolt'poslenal and oolt'ondar. Move carefully forward, staying away from both the heavy defense points and this damned gun, to take and hold this position." He brought up a human map. "This is Balsam Gap...."

# CHAPTER 34

"Oh, shit," Reeves said calmly and threw the giant tank into reverse as a shudder rumbled through the ground. Then he slammed the accelerator to the stops as it started to slide.

The first part of the descent had been uneventful; the SheVa had started down the steepest part of the slope, towards the upper end, and handled it quite well. But just at the top of Betty Branch, where it first issued forth from a shallow spring, Reeves had had to traverse the tank slightly to negotiate the bluff above the spring and the slope had given way.

Now the SheVa had started to ski down the mountain and there didn't seem to be a thing to stop it.

"Oh, I don't like this," Pruitt whined. "I don't like this *at* all."

"Reeves . . ." Major Mitchell said, but he knew there was nothing the driver could do to stop the slide that wasn't already being done; the treads were tearing up the bare rock of the hill and not getting any traction at all.

"SheVa Nine!" Captain Chang called. "Warning! Posleen landers, three o'clock!"

"Shit, shit, shiiit . . ." Pruitt said slamming sideways as the SheVa hit a solid chunk of rock and bounced. "Our center of gravity is going to shift if I rotate the turret!"

"If we haven't fallen over by now, we're not going to!" Indy said.

"Go for it," Major Mitchell called, starting the rotation.

The crew compartment was in the base of the turret, so the ride just got stranger as the tank went one way, jouncing up and down on the rough slope, and they turned another.

"Oh, shit," Reeves said in a muffled tone. "I'm gonna ralf!"

"What happens when I fire this thing?!" Pruitt yelled, locking in a round.

"I don't *know*," Indy said tightly. "We're on a forty degree slope, sliding downward in max reverse, firing *sideways* at about forty miles per hour. We're not designed to do *any* of those *at all*!"

"Shit," Mitchell muttered.

"I'm losing it here, sir!" Reeves called. "We're headed for a bluff!"

"TARGET! Lamprey, two thousand meters!" Pruitt sang out.

"Danger close!" Mitchell called, indicating that the explosion of the gun's own penetrator could potentially damage it; the minimum recommended distance for a SheVa to engage was over three thousand meters. "FIRE!"

❖     ❖     ❖

"Take the pass, he says," Gamasal complained. "Where is the honor in that? Where is the loot?"

"We get a higher cut," Lesenal replied. The two were nest mates, an unusual occurrence in Posleen society, and instead of taking individual oolts had chosen to colead a single company. It was perhaps this oddity that had led them to attach themselves to Tulo'stenaloor; compared to a Posleen trying to make himself a general, coleaders of an oolt was nothing. "A cut specifically of everyone who uses the pass."

"But once they swing around and open up the other passes, everyone will use those," Gamasal grumped and adjusted the oolt'pos to clear the ridge as low as possible. "I still say we could take that other gap, the one the humans call 'Newfound.' "

"Ah, but the way there is too easy to close," the coleader pointed out. "In those hills the humans and their snipers can pick off the Kessentai like so many abat. The way to Balsam is clearer. And with us in place, the humans will be scrambling to find a way to escape. Follow the plan. And watch out for that gun. We were lucky yesterday, I don't want our luck to run out."

"Oh, fuscirto uut," Gamasal replied. "You mean *that* gun?"

The round from the SheVa gun hit the Lamprey high and silver fire jutted from every opening. The skyscraper-sized ship dropped out of sight immediately, but there was another right behind it.

The second Lamprey was, however, the least of SheVa Nine's problems.

"Aaaaah!" Pruitt screamed as the overstressed vehicle slid sideways on the slope, bounding off a bluff and hitting at an angle with a sound like a thousand junkyards being dropped from the sky.

Major Mitchell opened his eyes to red emergency lights and swore. "Indy!"

"I'm here, sir," the warrant officer said. "We just blew every breaker in this thing; if this was a *Star Trek* episode, Pruitt would be flying across the compartment. But we didn't lose the tracks!"

"I got *nothin'*, sir!" Pruitt called. "And we had another Lamprey up!"

"I saw," Mitchell said. "Are we functional? What's our *status*, Indy?"

"I'm working on it, sir," she said. After punching a few buttons lights started coming back on. "So far, everything is working. But if you want me to certify the gun as functional, I can't, sir. We just took a hell of a beating; we're almost sure to have stress damage on the supports."

"I'm up!" Pruitt said. "Where's the Lamprey?"

"I'm not!" Reeves said, gunning the SheVa as his treads spun in place. "I think we're *stuck*!"

Gamasal slammed the Lamprey down through the trees and opened the assault door. "Let's go!"

"Why are we doing this?" Lesenal asked. "Our mission is to take the pass!"

"The gun is in the way!" his coleader said. "We'll cross this ridge and destroy the gun. Then continue on our mission. Oh, and since we're here and have taken out the defenders . . ."

" . . . The net will designate it as our fief," Lesenal said. "Clever. You realize, of course, that we could just drop below the level of the ridge and fly around. And so will Orostan."

"We are but simple oolt-Kessentai," Gamasal replied with a flap of his crest. "How could we have thought of that?"

❖          ❖          ❖

"No, no, NO!" Orostan swore. "Go *around*!"

"And miss a chance to kill it on the ground?" Cholosta'an said. "Not to mention getting that as a fief for taking out the defenders? No chance."

"Besonora!"

"Yes, Oolt'ondai?" The Kessentai had been with him from before he joined Tulo'stenaloor and Orostan preferred to have him available. But he was running out of trustworthy Kessentai that could handle ships. "Take an oolt'poslenal. Gather the best of the local forces. Take Balsam Gap. Hold it until I get there. Do not fail, do not get distracted and do not get *high*; there is a heavy defense center nearby."

"Yes, Oolt'ondai," the Kessentai replied. "I go."

"All other ships," the oolt'ondai called over his communicator. "Get that GUN!"

"Major Mitchell?" Chan called. "What's your status?"

"Oh, we're stuck," the SheVa commander said calmly. "We're jammed between two bluffs, stuck in a ravine. There's a company of Posleen on the ridge above us. We expect they'll be attacking any time now. And there are, presumably, other landers around. They should be showing up just as soon as it goes from bad to worse."

"Any chance of you getting out?"

"Oh, sure," the major said sarcastically. "If we had an engineering team to blow up the cliffs."

"Jesus! What was that?" Kitteket said. The concussion of something had echoed across the mountains.

"SheVa gun," Major Ryan answered. "I'm pretty sure anyway; nothing else sounds quite the same. I think it's down by Betty Creek. How in the *hell* did a SheVa gun get down by Betty Creek?"

The night had been a long series of tiny roads on knife-edge ridges. It would actually have been easier in a smaller vehicle than the Humvee; one of the old Army jeeps would have been perfect. But the Humvee was what they had. Often the team had had to unload and either rapidly widen the road, under the major's expert direction, or even in some cases make temporary bridges across otherwise uncrossable gaps. At each obstacle the major had been right there, blowing up the rocks, cutting down the trees and filling in the holes; nobody could complain that he was a hands-off officer.

Now the engineers were past the worst of the ridges and on the downhill. And apparently driving back into the battle.

"I thought the SheVa blew up," Kitteket said.

"I heard they were bringing in another one," Ryan said in thought. "Let's head towards Betty Creek," he continued, scrolling up his map-board. "There's a forest road that turns off to the left up ahead. Take it."

"We're headed for a SheVa," the specialist said wonderingly. "In the middle of a battle."

"Oh, by the time we get near it the battle will be over," Ryan said. "One way or another."

"Major!" Chan called. "You have two more landers coming over the hill: a Lamprey and a C-Dec. From where you are pointed they'll be at two o'clock and eleven!"

"Got it," Mitchell said calmly as the first railgun rounds punched into the stranded SheVa. "I don't think we're going to have to worry, though; we're about to be nibbled to death by Lilliputians."

"Don't worry about the dismounts, sir," Chan answered with a grin that could be heard over the radio. "We're coming in on their flank."

"Look, it's stuck!" Gamasal chuckled. "Easy meat!"

"Yes," his coleader said. "But how do we kill it

without having it blow up? This is a nice valley; I would like it more or less intact."

"Hmm," Gamasal said, waving to the oolt'os to cease fire. "That is a good question. Perhaps we should board it?"

"That is probably a good idea," Lesenal said, pulling out his boma blade. "I prefer the blade anyway."

"Mommy," Reeves muttered. "They're pulling out their swords."

"This is a good thing," Mitchell pointed out in a too calm voice. "That gives us a few moments more to maybe survive the landers."

"There's only two of them," Pruitt said tightly. "I can do this." He set the radar to max gain and pointed the gun at the two o'clock position. "Come to Poppa."

"All Storms," Captain Chan called as the company crested the ridge and began negotiating the narrow path downward. "Engage Posleen as they bear. When you're shot out, try to get off the trail to let following units engage."

She could see the SheVa out her left vision blocks and the first of the landers no more than a thousand meters away through her right vision blocks. It suddenly occurred to her that if the lander exploded, or if Pruitt missed a little low, say from the gun being knocked askew by their wreck, things were really going to suck.

And in just a few seconds she was going to have to fire the Storm. She knew intellectually which would be worse, but she'd never been killed before and she'd had to fire the Storm way too many times. Being caught in a nuclear explosion, as an alternative, had its positive aspects.

"Glenn."

"Yes, ma'am," said the gunner, peering through her sight for the first look at the Posleen dismounted company.

"I have to agree with you. I need a transfer; this job sucks."

A moment later the tank rounded a corner and the Posleen company, spread out across the ridge and trotting downhill, came into view.

"Fire," she said, slewing the gun onto the group of Posleen.

"Aaah," said Glenn, grabbing the trigger and setting the MetalStorm to "Full." "AAAH!"

The slope was lightly wooded, but that didn't really matter; the penetrators tore the trees apart without being appreciably slowed. They also tore into the Posleen without being appreciably slowed.

And the true test of how bad the system was to use was that the Storms never even noticed the SheVa firing right over their heads.


"Target C-Dec! TWELVE HUNDRED METERS! TOO CLOSE!"

"FIRE!"

"TOO *CLOSE*!"

"IT'S KNIFE-FIGHTING RANGE! WE'RE BUN-BUN! *FIRE THE DAMNED GUN!*"

The round tracked straight and true into the top of the ship, actually punching out the back side before exploding.

The detonation was the equivalent of ten thousand tons of TNT, but both it and the flash of gaseous uranium and spalling would have been survivable by the C-Dec; the explosion wasn't actually in contact and wasn't at a particularly vital or vulnerable point. However, the compression wave was above the lander. And that drove it downward into the hard and unyielding ground. C-Decs were designed to survive much, but slamming into North Carolina mountains at over a hundred miles per hour was not one of them. Internal compartmentalization gave way throughout the ship. Not from the *acceleration*, but from the *deceleration*.

A ten pounds per square inch compression wave, strong enough to damage or destroy heavily constructed buildings, also washed across the MetalStorm tracks. But compared to the damage they took from firing their own weapons . . .

"What was that?" Glenn groaned.

"What was what?" Chan answered, pulling herself out of her fetal crouch.

"That last 'bang,'" the gunner answered. "Did we break something?"

"I don't know," Chan said. "It wasn't that bad, though. Brandon, get us out of here, we need to open up the way for the rest!"

"Ma'am, I would, but I can't," the driver answered. "Look at the road."

Glenn straightened up and looked through her vision blocks then whistled. "Wow, did we do that?" The entire slope was covered in fallen trees. "Nah, we couldn't have."

"You sound disappointed," Chang said scanning for Posleen. "I think the lander must have blown up."

"And we survived?" Brandon called over the intercom.

"Either that or this is hell," Chang said. "And I'm beginning to wonder."

"TARGET LAMPREY SIXTEEN HUNDRED METERS!"

"This is hell, right?" Reeves shouted with his fingers in his ears; at this distance if the lander exploded there was no way they would survive. "Please tell me this is hell!"

"FIRE!"

"'Cause it's gotta get BETTER!"

The round entered through the lower quadrant, but was travelling upwards at a sharp angle and missed the fuel bunker. However, it, too, exited through the rear of the ship and exploded above it. This time, though, the smaller Lamprey was effectively killed by the kinetic energy of the depleted uranium warhead passing through its engine-room. With the loss of lift and drive it dropped like a rock onto the ridge, toppling sideways and began to roll. Straight towards the stuck SheVa.

"NO!" Pruitt screamed, aiming the gun down as the SheVa rocked in blast-wave.

"DON'T!" Major Mitchell screamed, but it was too late; the gunner had already fired.

The DU penetrator had barely had time to shed its boot when it entered the soil of the mountain. Pruitt had been aiming at the Lamprey, but he had fired low and the ten kiloton round penetrated almost two hundred meters into the gneiss and schist of the mountain before detonating.

Major Ryan was still blinking spots out of his eyes when he saw the top of the mountain erupt skyward; with a Lamprey mixed into it. "GET OUT AND UNDER THE HUMVEE!" he yelled, putting words into action as he grabbed the detonator kit, kicked open the door and piled out.

The explosion was almost graceful. The round had penetrated to near the center of the hilltop and it scooped out a section of soil and rock that was a near perfect circle; eventually it would be a very nice lake. However, it was tons of overburden that tended to tamp and reduce the energy of the relatively small nuclear explosion at its core. The material closest to the antimatter detonation was simply vaporized, becoming plasma that added to the energy transfer and would eventually dissipate as gaseous silica and the other constituent elements of the rocks.

Outward from the plasma zone the rock was finely pulverized and then the condition graded outwards until in the outer layer there were rather large boulders . . .

. . . That the explosion in their center tossed thousands of feet into the air.

"For what we are about to receive," Major Mitchell said as the side of the mountain started to slip their way. "May we truly be thankful."

"Oh damn," Pruitt said. "Bad things are supposed to happen to *other* people when Bun-Bun is around."

"I've got traction!" Reeves shouted.

"Go!" the major replied, watching the landslide building up.

"I'm going!" the driver shouted, as the SheVa lumbered up out of the suddenly widened hole. "I think the shots loosened us up!" Then he swore as the ground gave way again and the SheVa stopped abruptly. "NOOO!"

But the mountains they were traversing were old; the hillsides worn by millions of years. The slope-ripping slides of the Rockies were virtually unknown in the Appalachians; even when started by a nuclear explosion. The crumbling mountainside continued about halfway down the hill and then came to an abrupt, tree-crunching halt in a cloud of dust.

At which point, everyone started to notice the bonging sound on the top of the turret.

"I think you're about to get your wish, Pruitt," Indy said sourly.

"What?" the gunner said, looking up as if in disbelief that they were alive.

"Bad things are about to happen to other people."

"I don't like this!" Kitteket shouted as the boulders continued to rain on the bouncing, jolting Humvee over their heads.

"Neither do I," Ryan replied equanimably. "It could be worse, though!"

"How?!"

"You want a list?" he asked. "We could be stuck in a basement, surrounded by a Posleen force that has already overrun everything in its path and with them pounding on the last door!"

"We're about to get crushed by a rain of boulders!" she shouted. "That counts as really bad in my book!" But even as she said it the worst of the shower had passed.

"Everybody okay?" Ryan asked, rolling out from under the vehicle despite the continuing rain of small debris. "And ready to walk?"

"Oh, man, it's trashed," Kitteket said, getting to her feet and looking around. "What a mess!"

Rocks ranging from pebbles to boulders large enough to have crushed the Humvee were scattered in every direction and most of the trees had been swept off the mountainside. From their perch at the edge of Betty Gap they could clearly see the SheVa gun down in the holler, apparently wedged into a ravine. A unit of MetalStorms was picking its way down the slope towards the gun. And a Lamprey, crumpled like so much foil, was well down the holler.

"It's a mess, all right," Ryan replied, keying his code module. "Dig around in the gear and find anything salvageable. A radio for choice."

"Well, this is another fine mess you've gotten us into, Ollie," Pruitt said.

He was standing on one of the boulders, looking down at the SheVa stuck like a cork in the gully.

Gully was something of a misnomer; the small valley could have easily have contained a few single-family homes if the area was a subdivision. But the SheVa was still stuck.

"Look," Reeves said defensively. "I did my best." The edges of the gully were barely above the treads and didn't, quite, intersect the turret. But some of the boulders that had tumbled down the slope were piled on the sides of the machine. "At least I didn't blow a mountain down on us."

"I prefer to think of it as blowing a Lamprey *off* of us," Pruitt said. "And here's our Greek chorus . . ."

"Damn, sir," said Captain Chan, walking over to the group peering at the SheVa. "I've seen some tanks get stuck in my time but . . . Damn, sir."

"Yeah," Mitchell said, walking back and forth and looking at the gun. "I think that the big problem is the lip in front of it; it can't get any traction to pull itself out."

"We could hook some of your tracks up to it, ma'am, and try to pull it out," Reeves said.

She looked at him in amazement. "Did you actually think before you said that, Private?"

"Uh . . ."

"A Meemie weighs just over sixty tons; how much does one of these things weigh?"

"Errr, just over seven thousand," the driver admitted. "I hadn't realized there was that much difference."

She looked over at her track then up and up at the SheVa towering nearly two hundred feet in the air. Tanks made her feel small; SheVas made her feel like an ant.

"I don't think that will help, son," she said. "It would be like trying to move one of my tracks with a tricycle."

"You know, they're talking about making one of these as a close combat support vehicle," Mitchell said. "Think about how much one of *those* will weigh; especially covered in armor."

"Ouch."

"And, golly gee," Pruitt said with a grin. "We've proven that they can be used in mountain warfare."

# CHAPTER 35

*Betty Gap, NC, United States, Sol III*
*0829 EDT Sunday September 27, 2009 AD*

"I think they're stuck, Major," Kitteket said.

"I do believe you're right, Specialist," the major replied with a chuckle.

It had taken the group nearly a half hour to travel down the hillside, during which the group around the giant weapon had performed a thorough study of the area. Along the way Ryan's small group had obviously been spotted.

As he walked around the back of the monstrous piece of machinery, a female soldier appeared out of a hatch over the treads and walked down them. After a brief moment's inspection she saluted.

"Warrant Officer Sheila Indy," she said. "Engineer for SheVa Nine."

"Major William Ryan," the engineer replied. "I'm a combat engineering specialist attached to Ninety-Third Corps. Right now I'm in charge of this motley crew.

Until recently we were trying to make things hard for the Posleen."

"And what are you doing now?" Indy asked.

"We're looking for a ride; a rain of boulders seems to have destroyed our Humvee."

The warrant officer laughed and looked at him with interest. "Did you say combat engineers, Major?"

"Yep," he answered. "And it looks like you need some earth moved."

"That we do," the warrant said. "Could you come with me, sir?"

He popped the straps on his ruck and gestured at the mixed group of soldiers. "Rest; I think we'll be working in the near future."

He and Kitteket, who seemed to be acting as his shadow, followed the warrant officer around the SheVa to the front where a group of officers were wrangling over the situation. The SheVa was in a crack with both of the treads only partially on the ground—they were mostly supported by rock on both sides of the gully— and with a high mound of earth directly in front of the treads. It was this friable mixture of rock and loam, well mixed with the water from the stream, that was preventing the tank from getting a good grip. With a car the answer would be to pile branches under the treads. With a SheVa gun, that wouldn't work.

Ryan didn't approach the group of officers, but walked over in front of the gun, stooping to pick up the occasional bit of debris then stopping and pulling out his entrenching tool. He dug into the stream bank until he hit rock, then chopped at it until he had a sample; at that the sample was small. Last, he walked to the far side of the gun and got a good look at that side.

By the time he did approach the group they had stopped talking and were watching him.

He approached and, not knowing if he had date of rank on the major in the group, saluted. "Ryan, Army Corps of Engineers."

"Mitchell, SheVa Corps."

"If I may ask, who is the genius who jammed the shit out of this thing?" Ryan asked with a laugh. "Because it is, pardon the pun, caught in a crack."

"My driver," Mitchell said with a shrug. "Not his fault," he added, gesturing at the lander in the valley. "We were a little busy at the time."

"I noticed," Ryan said with another grin. "And I'd guess it was your gunner that decided that Chestnut Mountain needed a swimming pool."

"That would be him," Mitchell said with a nod. "And while I was wishing for an engineer, I was really wishing for one that had a heavy engineering battalion behind him. As it is . . ."

"Oh, we can get you out," Ryan said. "I've thought of three or four ways. I don't think that the Meemies would like the best one though."

"What would that be, Major?" Captain Chan asked. "Vickie Chan, I'm commander of the MetalStorms."

"Well, I think we could more or less jam one of your guns under each tread and drive the SheVa out over them . . ."

"You were correct," she said, "I don't like it. . . ."

" . . . The SheVa has an integral crane for doing some of its maintenance. I've used them before for engineering purposes and we can use it to decouple your guns first. *Probably* it wouldn't cripple your system; the Abrams chassis is a remarkable piece of engineering."

"I really don't like that idea," Chan said unhappily.

"Okay," Ryan said. "At least one of you fired earlier, are any of you loaded? I assume your reload teams aren't right behind you."

"Both our reload teams are over by Dillsboro by now," Major Mitchell said.

"Well then, the alternative is that we use one of the loaded systems to punch holes in the rockwall," Ryan said. "Carefully. Then we load them with explosives and blow up the rock. That will open up a cavity for you to move out. We'll do the same in front, blasting off this overburden; there's solid rock under it almost at the level of your tracks. Getting out then is easy. We can blow out the walls further down, using the same techniques, to ensure you don't get stuck again."

"Hold on," Indy said. "You want to set off explosives in rock that is *in contact* with our tracks?"

"There will be some impact waves," Ryan said. "But nothing that will affect the tracks or the gun."

"You want a *MetalStorm* to fire into rock that's in contact with the *SheVa*?" Mitchell asked.

"They can fire on single shot," Kitteket interjected. "We're not suggesting that they open fire full out."

"It will make a forty millimeter hole," Ryan pointed out. "Admittedly one that's quite hot and filled with uranium dust, but beggars can't be choosers. We'll then pack it and seal it and blow the rock down."

"You *do* intend to blow up rock that is in contact with my tracks!" Indy said.

"Warrant, I've been blowing up everything in sight for the last five years," Ryan said wearily. "I've blown up bridges and buildings and I don't know how many sidings. I blew up the Lincoln Memorial. Don't tell me I can't blow in a little embankment without hurting your precious tracks."

"But we're not talking driving away in the next fifteen minutes," Major Mitchell said. "Either way."

"Fifteen, no," Ryan replied. "For the assisted maneuvering method . . . forty minutes to an hour. For the other it will depend on whether we can find some secondary explosives. My men and I have a few hundred pounds of C-4, and that would do the job, but we will need it for other missions; I can't in good conscience use it all to extract one stuck tank."

"Not to blow my own horn," Mitchell said. "But this is a very big and very expensive tank."

"I know," Ryan answered. "But there are a lot of bridges between here and Asheville."

"I know," Mitchell smiled thinly. "But I *guarantee* I can take them down faster than you can."

Chan had been talking with Glenn and finally she shook her head.

"Okay," she said. "I have an alternative. Worse or better I'm not sure. We can easily fit two or even three of our guns under the treads, especially if we use a little of your explosives to blow out some of the overburden in front."

"That's true," Ryan said. "I didn't think that you wanted to sacrifice *all* of your units."

"The thing weighs seven thousand tons, admittedly," Chang said. "But *all* of that won't be on the tracks at first. And if it is, only for a little while. If we roll it up *slow* and roll it down *slow*, you're right, they might just survive. And if they don't . . ."

"We never have to fire one again," Glenn said with a sigh. "Could you drive it fast? And maybe bounce it a little?"

Pruitt engaged the crane and started lifting the first MetalStorm away from its chassis as the first explosion sounded from the front of the SheVa. The crane was mounted on the upper deck of the gun, nearly two hundred feet over the tank at its feet, and the MetalStorm turret swayed back and forth wildly as it came out of its mounts. As Pruitt waited for the oscillation to subside, he keyed his throat mike.

"Hey, Warrant, you still got that welding set handy?" he asked thoughtfully.

"Don't even think about it, Pruitt," the warrant officer called. "Besides, a weld would never hold."

"It just seems a shame. I mean, it's the whole turret, isn't it? Weld it on, hook up the controls, hell, not even controls, just power . . ."

"Don't make me come up there and hurt you," Indy said with a laugh.

"I'm serious!" he protested. "It could work! Maybe seat it or something . . ."

"Put it in the suggestion program," Indy said. "And leave me alone!"

Pruitt looked down at the now stable gun mount and realized he had no idea where to put it. The Meemies were on a slope; if he just set it down to the side, the area would both get "filled up" rather quickly and the guns might fall over and roll downhill. There had been *enough* disasters for one day.

He looked around and noticed that there was a "lip" and fence, a safety measure as much as anything, running around the top of the SheVa.

His face lit with an evil grin as he engaged the crane. "It's always easier to ask for forgiveness," he muttered.


"There's probably some sort of regulation against this," Chan muttered. "I know that my bosses aren't going to be happy with me."

"Well, they'll be happier than if your driver hadn't thought to *back* it in," Mitchell pointed out. "Seriously, I don't want to lose your tracks; we need the firepower."

"We're going to lose some, that's for sure," Chan said grimly. Then she brightened. "On the other hand, we're going to lose some."

"And this is a *good* thing?" Mitchell asked.

"Firing them is pure hell; there's just nothing good about it," the captain answered. "Any rush involved in all that tungsten going downrange is totally absorbed by the pain inflicted while it's going on and the utter terror that the whole thing is just going to blow the hell up."

"Well," Major Mitchell said after a moment. "I'll make sure I don't get a transfer to Meemies."

"When you guys shot one of the landers, we came up from firing to find every tree around us down," she said calmly. "And we didn't notice when it happened."

"That's pretty bad," he said.

"The second time I was in one that fired, I wet myself," she continued.

"Not the first time?" he asked.

"No, the first time I was knocked unconscious," she admitted.

"That's pretty bad," he said again.

"The flechette missions aren't too bad," she said. "Those just make you think you're a steel pinata. It's the anti-lander packs that really take some getting used to."

"Have you gotten used to them yet?" he asked, feeling very masochistic.

"Not yet," she admitted.

"And *how* long have you been doing this?"

"I've been commander of this unit for three years," she answered simply.

"Hmm . . ."

"Two months, seventeen days and . . ." she glanced at her watch, " . . . twenty hours."

"You *really* don't like these things, do you?"

"Come to think of it, I don't know why I protested in the first place," she admitted. "Could you run over them a few *more* times?"

❖　　❖　　❖

"Major, we're ready to try this out," Pruitt said over the radio. "All the Meemies have had their packs pulled and the chassis are positioned."

"Okay," Mitchell called back. He was at the back hatch, conferring with Indy. He looked to the front where Chan was waving at him. "Pruitt, where *are* the MetalStorm packs?"

"On the top deck," the gunner said. "There wasn't anywhere else reasonably flat to put them down. I chained 'em down; they're not going anywhere."

"Uh, huh," Mitchell said, giving Indy a nod. She rolled her eyes and made a very rude gesture. "Miss Indy says that we're *not* going to hook them up."

"I understand that, sir," the gunner replied with a butter-wouldn't-melt-in-his-mouth tone. "It was simply the safest place to put them. Each of those weapons systems is a significant investment."

"So is a gunner for a SheVa," the major said, walking to the front of the gun. "On the other hand, so is the chassis for an Abrams and I'm about to use six of them like so many wood-chips. Keep that firmly in mind."

"Yes, sir."

"So how's it going, Major?" Mitchell asked.

"Great," Ryan said, climbing out through the treads of the SheVa. "This might actually work. And if it doesn't, we can always blow it out."

"So I understand," Mitchell said sourly. "Okay, is everyone clear?"

"My team is up the hill," Ryan said, pointing to where the engineers were clustered.

"My guys are breaking out the champagne," Chan said, pointing to her formation.

"Okay," Mitchell said. "Let's get out of the way and see how it goes."

They walked up the slope until they were at the level

of the upper deck of the SheVa and Mitchell stopped to catch his breath. "Christ, did we actually drive *over* these slopes?"

"Yep," Chan said. "I sort of figured that the only thing keeping you going was it was dark and it was hard to realize how stupid we were being, even with third generation night vision systems."

"Well, think of it this way," Ryan said, gesturing at the torn slope to the west. "You made some dandy ski slopes!"

Mitchell let out a belly laugh and keyed his throat mike. "Okay, Schmoo, try it nice and slow."

Reeves carefully ran the motors up to ten percent and then engaged the transmission. The SheVa had originally been designed without the latter system, but it was added late in the game in recognition that sometimes "throwing it into gear" was the best way to handle a situation.

In this case the SheVa rocked up on its ersatz traction enhancers then rolled backwards. There was a massive metallic sound from the six Abrams chassis and the loud, sharp *sprong* of a fracturing torsion bar.

Captain Chan gave out a whimper and grabbed her helmet with both hands. "I just started thinking about what this loss report is going to look like." Behind them the officers could hear the crews of the MetalStorm guns cheering. "My career is toast."

Mitchell tried not to laugh as he turned to the side and keyed his mike. "Okay, Schmoo . . ." He paused for a moment and snorted before keying the mike again. "Gun it!"

"Are you sure, sir?" the driver asked.

"Oh, yeah," the major replied. Behind him the driver

could faintly hear cheering. "The nature of the mission dictates that whatever means necessary are used to get the SheVa out; that looks like it means gunning it. Whatever the cost in materials."

"Yes, sir!" Reeves answered, turning the power to thirty percent. "Here we go!"

The treads of the SheVa began thrashing against the rear decks of the Abrams chassis, tossing them up and down to the screams of torn and abused metal. The gun rocked forward, partially up on the smaller tanks, then back down as treads and road-wheels began to spring off of the smaller vehicles.

"It looks like your tanks' treads are humping mine," Chan said unhappily. "I wish the crews would stop cheering; that's not a very good testimony to my leadership."

"I think it's a great testimony," Mitchell said as the SheVa rolled back down then accelerated forward and up. "They kept getting in them."

With a final surge the SheVa pulled up out of its entrapment and, to the sound of tortured and stressed metal from the abused tanks, it pulled out of the gully and up onto reasonably solid ground.

"Now as long as we don't have to dig ourselves out again," Mitchell said grumpily, "or run into any more of those flying tanks, everything should be fine."

"Well, I don't think I have to worry about getting back in *that* tank again," Chan said; the rear deck had crumpled on hers and the power pack was in pieces on the ground. "I guess we're walking from here on out."

"Only if you want to," Mitchell said. "Your turrets are on our top deck; you can ride in those."

"That's an . . . interesting idea," Chang said.

"You might have a little vertigo and motion sickness

problem," he admitted. "It's *high*. And you can tag along as well, Major," Mitchell continued, turning to Ryan. "Although I guarantee I can take a bridge down faster than you."

"Sure," Ryan said. "But can you do it from out of sight of the Posleen?"

# CHAPTER 36

*Dillsboro, NC, United States, Sol III*
*1514 EDT Sunday September 27, 2009* AD

Major Ryan stepped off the SheVa as it began the complicated process of crossing the Tuckasegee River without killing anyone.

They had run into the rear ranks of stragglers near Dills Gap and many of them had latched on to the SheVa. The gun had four "loading points" and each of them was now covered with soldiers.

The good news was that they seemed to have gotten there ahead of the Posleen and, for a wonder, there was a gap between the rear of the stragglers and their pursuers. The word was that some snipers were slowing the Posleen advance, but they were working from the ridges and wouldn't be crossing at Dillsboro. That meant he probably wouldn't have to blow the bridge with people on it.

About a platoon of soldiers with a captain leading them was headed for the cautiously maneuvering SheVa and Ryan touched the dismount communicator Major Mitchell had loaned him.

"I think we've got a welcoming committee, Mitchell."

"I see them on the external," the SheVa commander replied. "We'll hold up until we find out what they want."

"Captain," Ryan said. "Major William Ryan, Corps of Engineers. And you are?"

"Captain Paul Anderson," the officer replied. "I'm in charge of the crossing, sir, and I'm afraid the personnel riding on the SheVa will have to dismount and be processed."

He had the crossed flags of a Signal Officer which, strangely enough, made him a line officer. In a situation such as this he could give orders to even a colonel of, say, the medical corps. However, engineers were line officers as well.

"I'll give you the guys hanging on the outside," the major said with a faint, cold smile. "But I'm taking my guys over to make sure the bridge is properly prepared to blow."

"Ah, that would be good, sir," the captain said with a relieved smile. "I . . . didn't mean to come on so strong, but I've been holding down this crossing for the last eighteen hours and trying to keep the groups crossing organized; it hasn't been fun."

"Been there, done that," the major smiled back. "How, exactly, were you going to classify the SheVa?"

"I'm going to treat it like the proverbial eight-hundred-pound gorilla, sir," the captain said. "Sergeant Rice," he continued, gesturing at the staff sergeant who was with him. "Get the rest of them across the bridge and sorted out."

"Yes, sir," the sergeant said, waving the platoon after him.

"We've got ammo trucks parked north of town," the captain said. "*Widely* dispersed. We also had two groups of SheVa reload trucks, accompanied by some MetalStorm reloads, come in. I sent them up the road to Sylva; there just wasn't anywhere around here to put them."

"Those would be Major Mitchell and Captain Chan's," Ryan said, touching his communicator. "Mitch, good news. The reload group is just up the road, over."

"Good," the SheVa commander replied. "With only eight shots, you get nervous when you're down to four. Now, how do we get there without killing anyone? There's only about three routes and it looks like there are people on all of them."

"How does the SheVa get there?" Ryan asked.

"That's going to be tough, sir," Anderson admitted. "We're reconstituting units on both flanks of the town. That probably means running it straight through. We've mostly cleared it because it's too hard keeping units in control in there."

"There won't *be* a town if we do that," Ryan pointed out. "Or any roads."

"We're running most of the traffic through on the bypass 23," the captain said, pulling out a map-board. "If he crosses the Tuckasegee east of 23, then turn . . . well *on* the town, he can head up 107. We're running tanks down that anyway, to keep from tearing up the main road; it's already trashed. His reload group is just to the south of Sylva, off of 107."

"Gotcha," Ryan said, conveying the message to Mitchell. "And could you have my boys unload at the same time?"

"Roger," Mitchell replied. "Could I keep Kittekut, though?"

"I suppose," Ryan replied, nonplussed.

"I've installed her in the commander's chair. Which means I've finally got a commo person."

"Feel free," the major said. "I'm going to go check out the bridge."

"Are you going to be reboarding, Major?" Mitchell asked.

"I doubt it," the engineer replied. "I've got other things to do. I might call you back to knock down a bridge depending on how much demo I have."

"Well, we'll be seeing you," Mitchell said as the SheVa whined back to life. "Keep the dismount commo; I somehow think we'll be seeing you again."

"Good luck."

"Thanks, you too."

Ryan turned back to the captain and shook his head as the SheVa *slowly* trundled off to the east. "We met up in the mountains; they took that thing over one of the smaller gaps."

"*That?*" the captain asked waving them towards the bridge. "How?"

"Not very well on the way down," Ryan replied with a smile. "They got it stuck as shit. Of course, that was while they were taking out two landers at point blank range. It's a long story."

"I can believe it. How did they get out?"

"You see those things all the way up top?" Ryan grinned.

"Yeah, they looked like MetalStorm turrets, but I never heard of those on a SheVa."

"They're not attached; they're just chained down," Ryan said with another, wider, grin. "We got it unstuck by driving it over the chassis."

"Holy shit," Anderson said in turn. "That was one expensive goddamn fix! I assume the chassis didn't survive."

"Nope, busted 'em bigger than shit," Ryan replied, stopping and looking off the bridge at the water below. He was suddenly struck by an intense sense of déjà vu, but he couldn't place where it was from.

"So how did you get stuck with this shit detail?" Ryan said with a smile, gesturing at the bridge as they reached the far side. "Not to be nasty. But playing rearguard on a bridge is right up there with antimatter injector cleaner."

"Oh, it's a shit detail, I agree," the captain said, shaking his head. "The answer is General Keeton."

"Eastern Commander?" the major asked. "How in the hell did that happen?"

"I was laying in cable when the word came that the Posleen had taken the Gap," the captain replied. "I took a look at the map and figured out where the chokepoint would be for most of the corps. I headed over here to try to . . . I dunno, help out or something since the headquarters I was laying the wire to was gone. But there wasn't anybody in charge and there were already problems getting the groups straightened out. So I grabbed the more stable looking units and started to get organized. Then, about the time I had to order around a major, I realized I didn't have authority for any of it. The cable was laid back to Eastern. I called up there and got ahold of a friend of mine in Operations. He apparently busted in on the meeting when they were trying to figure out what to do and who to send. The next thing I know I'm talking to General Keeton and he's telling me to do whatever I have to do; I've got full authority."

"Go to your head?" Ryan asked.

"More like hit me with a douse of cold water," the captain said. He gestured to one side where a group of privates and sergeants were clustered around a mass of tactical radios. "I suddenly realized I was Horatius.

And I had to coordinate about a division's worth of personnel, materials and vehicles."

"Hah!" Ryan laughed. "That was me in Occoquan, except the coordination part. Don't let *that* go to your head, either. It won't be the last time, hopefully."

He stopped and looked around. The town was run-down—it was apparent that the economic downturn of the war had hit it hard—but it still was fairly antique looking and, the term that came to mind was "quaint." Most of the houses seemed to date to the early twentieth century or the late nineteenth. Many of them needed a coat of paint, but obviously before the war the place had been a rather prosperous tourist center. That was when it hit him.

"Damn," Ryan said, shaking his head. "It looks just like Occoquan."

And it did. The town was very similar to the site of his first battle. It was clustered around the river on a major highway and had the exact same look. He would bet a month's pay that before the war the town had been packed with antique shops and little cafes.

Now though, it looked as if it had been mostly abandoned *before* the arrival of the retreating corps. Hopefully it would get fully cleared out before the SheVa drove over it.

"About Bun-Bun," Ryan commented to the captain.

"I've got a platoon making sure the town is cleared," Anderson replied. "And they'll pass on to Sylva and do the same."

"You know who Bun-Bun is?" the major said with a quizzical smile.

"Well, Bun-Bun is a homicidal rabbit with a switchblade and a bad attitude," the captain replied with a grin. "But I assumed you meant the SheVa with the great big Bun-Bun painted on it."

"You're a fan," Ryan said. It was not a question.

"Oh, a huge one," the signal officer replied with a grin. "But the first guy to call in the sighting was confused as shit."

"Sighting?" the engineer asked. He looked up at the precipitous hills around the valley. "Of course you've got scouts out."

"There's a local militia," the captain replied. "They were actually at the bridge before I was. I sent them out to spot for us; by now they're all over the hills on four-wheelers."

"So you'd already figured on clearing the town," Ryan said, shaking his head. "You're on the ball."

"Why thank you," the captain said with a grin. "I may look like Torg, but I'm Zoe inside."

"So, what about the bridge, Zoe?"

"I'd appreciate you handling it, sir," the captain said. "I turned it over to a sergeant who had experience working with demo, but he admitted he'd never rigged something like this to blow. And Eastern is pretty adamant that they want it down. In the meantime, I've really got to get back to what I was doing."

"I've got it, Captain, good luck."

Ryan made sure that what he had mentally termed his "eight pack"—he hadn't even figured out what most of their names were—had dismounted from the SheVa. The group had moved over by the bridge guards and he was pretty sure would soon be racked out; sleeping on the metal floor of a pitching SheVa was not particularly easy. Fairly certain that they were okay and he knew where they would be if he needed them, he started really inspecting the explosives laced on the bridge.

The bridge was a heavily constructed concrete and steel structure, rising on four pilings about a hundred feet off the river. The river was both deep and swift so it would be impassable to the Posleen once the bridge was down. And bridging it would be difficult for the Indowy; this obstacle would severely hamper the movement of the force. That presumed that the bridge would actually come down.

He wandered down a side road and under the bridge, looking up at the explosives laid on the pilings. After a moment he shook his head. He could see what the captain had attempted, the explosives were laid— as you often saw in movies—at the juncture of the bridge and the pilings. However, they were insufficient in quantity to separate the bridge at that point. The junctures were actually fairly strong and flexible; breaking a bridge at them was tough.

The pilings themselves, however, were round concrete "x"s, about four feet in cross section. If they had taken the explosives they had emplaced up above and simply wrapped the pilings in them, the bridge would come down for a treat. *Relaying* the explosives was going to take a while. Time they might not have.

But, if worse came to worse, they could always have Bun-Bun knock it down.

"Okay, Schmoo," Major Mitchell called. "The nice people who are running the bridge have cleared out the town. I want you to cross the river to the east of the bridge then turn into the town and turn again up 107. Our reload team is out there someplace."

"Got it, sir," the private replied. "Say goodbye to Dillsboro."

The driver gunned the SheVa, carefully lowering the front into the river. The stream, which at that point was about six feet deep with a ten-knot current, would have been impassable to most tanks. But the SheVa didn't even notice; its rearmost treads had barely had time to enter the water before the front treads were climbing out on the far side.

There was a steep ridge on the far side. Before the

attack it would have looked like a real obstacle, but after crossing Betty Gap it wasn't even worth commenting on; Bun-Bun just went straight up, crushing a few houses, and down the other side. It was fortunate in one way that the famous "Home Defense Scorched Earth" policy had only held for the coastal plains; otherwise each of the houses would have been a potential anti-tank mine.

"Sir," said Kitteket. "I've got a group that says they are our escorts. They have Dillsboro completely clear, but they're having some trouble getting everyone out of Sylva."

# CHAPTER 37

*Dillsboro, NC, United States, Sol III*
*1623 EDT Sunday September 27, 2009 AD*

Ryan set the demolition team, augmented by his own
people, to work rearranging the demolitions, then
walked back over to Captain Anderson's command post.
When he arrived there he could tell something had
gone wrong; the captain had a set look on his face and
the collection of RTOs was almost silent instead of
communicating and chattering as they had been when
he came by the first time.

"What?" Ryan asked.

"The Posleen airmobiled again," Anderson answered,
looking off into the distance in thought. "A C-Dec force
just took Balsam Gap. They landed on the Blue Ridge
Parkway and assaulted the force that was holding it.
They're, the force, it's gone."

"Oh hell," Ryan said, thinking about the map of the
area. There were only three routes over the line of
ridges between them and Asheville or Knoxville. U.S.

23 went over Balsam Gap and straight to Asheville. U.S. 19, which crossed 441 in Cherokee, more or less paralleled it, crossing the ridges at Soco Gap. And 441 crossed the ridges at Newfound Gap, then descended into the Cumberland Valley. The forces could head for 19, but that route, and 441, were narrower and thus slower. And pushing all the gathered groups through that single road would be, in his professional opinion, impossible. And there was no way for vehicles to "filter" out as they had from the Gap; the ridges in this region were so steep and high that there were *no* other roads crossing the mountains.

"What's responding?" he asked.

"There's a division moving up from Asheville," Anderson said. "But they're having a bit of trouble getting their act together; they're pretty green and they had to pull out of the line around Asheville to head this way. They might be able to force them out of the Gap. But the reports are that these Posleen were last seen *digging in*. And the C-Dec was giving them covering fire during their assault. I . . . don't think they're going to be able to force the pass in any short time."

"Damn, damn, damn," Ryan said. "Do you know what you're going to do?"

"More or less," Anderson said. "I've had a few minutes to think about it. I'm going to take all the really nonessential personnel and equipment and push them up 441; that's the worst route and it won't help us when they're in friggin' Pigeon Forge, but they'll be out of the way."

"And the ones we really need you're going to push up U.S. 19, right?" Ryan said.

"Yes," the captain confirmed. "All the supply vehicles. Gas trucks, ammo, food. All of that. Nothing slow, nothing not strictly necessary. I'm even going to send all the commo and intel up 441."

"Concur, what about the combat forces?" There were a few of those who had made it out of the Gap, a small group of M-1E1 tanks, some artillery and Bradleys as well as a small group of infantry that had walked or ridden trucks.

"I'm going to push them up to Balsam," the captain said coldly.

"That's . . . suicide," Ryan replied after a moment. "They're not even a formed unit."

"The unit on the far side isn't into position yet and attacking from that side won't be any easier than this," Anderson said with a grimace. "We have a little artillery and a fair amount of infantry. It . . . won't be easy, but I'm sure we can do it. The local militia snipers are still slowing the Posleen up in the Savannah Valley. But if we get caught in between the forces . . . we'll get wiped out. So taking out the force in the pass, and retaking it, has to be a high priority."

"Oh, my yes," Ryan nodded after a moment. "We *really* don't want them linking up."

"We might be able to hold them off," Anderson said dubiously. "We'll try anyway."

Ryan looked up at the sky and rubbed his chin in thought. "I . . . have a thought."

"Yes, sir?" the captain said.

"We have a SheVa, and it has been reloaded."

"Oh, ow," Anderson replied. "Does it have area denial rounds?"

"Yep. You still have commo with Eastern command?"

"Yep," Anderson said. "Heck, we've even got video."

"Good," Ryan said with a grin. "I want to see General Keeton's face."

General Keeton nodded in the jerky manner that denoted a slow internet connection. To Ryan it always reminded him of a cartoon his dad loved called "Max Headroom."

"Major Anderson, still got your finger in the dike I see."

"Yes, sir," the captain replied. "And it's captain, sir."

"Not anymore," the general said. "Who are these other gentlemen?"

"Sir, I'm Major William Ryan, Corps of Engineers. I was the corps Assistant Corps Engineer."

"And I'm Major Robert Mitchell, Commander of SheVa Nine."

"That the one with the great big rabbit painted on it?"

"Yes, sir," the major replied with a slight sigh.

"Indications are that you've been blasting the shit out of the whole valley for the last couple of days, Major," the general said severely. "Care to comment on that?"

"Yes, sir," the major replied. He suspected he was just about to get an ass-chewing which, all things considered, didn't seem fair. On the other hand, the military was like that sometimes. "It was, in my position as responsible for air defense of the corps, necessary operations of war."

"Get any?" Keeton asked.

"Sir, our records will indicate over the last two days we have eight confirmed kills of Lampreys and C-Decs and we estimate an additional nine to ten that were too damaged to continue. Those are all on camera. Frankly, I think that we might have stepped on twice that, but that will require an evaluation after we have retaken the valley."

The general considered that for a moment and then nodded his head. "So, what you're telling me is that, as usual, Bun-Bun's been kicking ass and not even *bothering* to take names?"

Mitchell paused and blinked. "Yes, sir."

"I'm going to do something here, and if you fuck with Anderson because of it I'll have your ass, understand?"

"Yes, sir?" Mitchell replied.

"You're a light colonel. Everybody in your crew is bumped one grade. We'll talk about the medals later."

"Yes, sir," the colonel said with a slightly choked tone. "Thank you."

"Don't get all teary on me, you realize you're probably fucked. There's no way to get that big bastard out of that valley. And according to all the intel I have you have about a billion Posleen about to butt-fuck you."

"That's what we're here to discuss, sir," Major Ryan interjected.

"Ryan, you're that hotshot who blew up the Lincoln Memorial, right?"

"Yes, sir," Ryan replied.

"You in charge of the bridge now?"

"Yes, sir, about that . . ."

"Don't blow it up until we're done talking, I'm not sure I want it down."

"Yes, sir," Ryan paused. "I . . . I think we're in agreement here, sir. Sir, we have a plan of action we need to discuss with you."

"Go ahead."

"Sir, you're aware that Balsam Gap has been taken?"

"I've got a shitload of forces on the way," Keeton replied. "Unfortunately, getting them down to you will require Balsam Gap. And they're mostly trained in positional defense. Which means they're gonna be lousy in the assault. It may be a while before you have any friends in the area."

"Sir," Major Anderson replied. "I've started an evacuation of the forces in the pocket, using secondary routes. But we think we can clear the Gap."

"Go ahead."

"Sir," Colonel Mitchell chimed in. "We've mated up with the reload teams for two SheVas . . ."

"I've got multiple reloads and the best SheVa repair battalion in the U.S. on the way," Keeton interjected. "Don't get Bun-Bun blown up and ruin all that work."

"I appreciate that, sir," Colonel Mitchell replied. "But it's going to take a while for them to mate up with us. The nearest SheVa repair batt was in Indiana last time I checked."

"Not if you can retake Balsam; they're both in Waynesville. I got them moving the minute that I heard about the Posleen taking Rabun Gap."

"Oh."

"Sir," Major Ryan said again. "Bun-Bun has four area denial rounds available in his reload team, two from his reloads and two from SheVa Fourteen."

"Yeah," the general said slowly. "Tell me the rest."

"I have a short company of Abrams and about the same of Bradleys," Anderson interjected. "I've also got a couple of batteries of artillery; the Brads and arty were from a recon unit that tacked down the Long Wall. The Bradleys are short on bodies, but I have plenty of infantry personnel."

"Sir, our plan is for Bun-Bun to approach Balsam Gap using cover to prevent taking fire," Ryan continued. "Simultaneously, our mechanized forces will take a hide position near, but not too near, Balsam Gap. Bun-Bun will fire one air-burst into the Gap whereupon the artillery will follow it with airburst and penetrator shells while the mechanized force performs a ground assault. Bun-Bun will then move forward to provide cover fire from the C-Dec if it has survived the assault."

"Classic prepared assault," the general said. "With one little fillip."

"Yes, sir," the three of them chorused.

Keeton laughed and shook his head. "You haven't had *time* to practice that much. Okay, I can't give you a friggin' release. So I'm going to call Jack Horner and the two of us are going to . . . counsel National Command Authority."

"Yes, sir," Colonel Mitchell said.

"This may take a little while; the President really hates nuclear weapons. In the meantime you get your assault forces together," the general continued. "And get everything you can out of that pocket. I'll get you the release. If I have to send a company of MPs down to sit on the President. Clear?"

"Clear, sir," the colonel said, wondering how serious the general was.

"Sir," Major Ryan said, "it is my intention to move up other roads and render them unusable."

"You're talking about 19 and 441?" the general asked. "After the support groups have passed through?"

"Yes, sir," Ryan said. "But there's no way to do that effectively and still be able to use them on the way back."

"Don't worry about coming back," Keeton said, tapping at his computer for a moment. "23 will be enough for that. Rip them to shit. That's an order. While you're out there, keep an eye out for a company of MetalStorm tanks. We lost contact with them right after we ordered them in. They should be a help if they survived."

"Er . . ." Mitchell said.

"Yes?" Keeton asked. "Did they survive?"

"Sort of, sir," the colonel replied. "Their turrets are lashed on top of Bun-Bun."

"On . . . top?" the general asked. "I suspect there's a story there. Have you put them into operation?"

"No, sir. Not for want of my gunner asking for it. And, yes, sir there's a story."

"I have to ask; where are the chassis?"

"Betty Gap, sir," Ryan replied. "We have them precisely located. They're not going anywhere."

"Let me guess," Keeton said. "You blew them up?"

"Not blew them *up*, sir," the engineer said.

"Later. I can tell it's bad. Gentlemen, you have your orders. Carry them out. As soon as we've retaken the Gap and Bun-Bun is repaired, I expect you to begin an advance down the valley."

"Yes, sir," Mitchell said.

"General Keeton, out."

"Madame President," General Horner said. "We now have the situation I discussed."

The President shook her head at the image on her monitor; unless the hookup was badly distorting the image the officer was gray. "General, are you okay?"

"Yes, ma'am, I am," Horner replied. "However, the remainder of the Rabun Gap forces are not. The Posleen have taken Balsam Gap by a coup de main and have them cut off. Our sole remaining SheVa is in the pocket among others. Most of them could get out by secondary routes, assuming the Posleen don't take those positions as well, but we need Balsam Gap to push forces back down into the valley."

"You want to nuke that Gap as well," she said.

"Yes, ma'am, I do," Horner replied. "Furthermore, I would like full tactical release for the remainder of this campaign."

"So you can call the fire?" she asked bitterly.

"No ma'am," he said with a smile like a tiger. "I intend to give it to a colonel."

"Now I wish we were hooked up," Captain Chan said. "This is going to be bloody."

The SheVa was swaying from side to side as it

maneuvered up the Scotts Creek valley, more or less paralleling Highway 23. The valley was a twisted complex of small hills and hollers that was the equivalent of a SheVa obstacle course; Reeves had had to back up and refigure his route twice in the last few hours of slow, careful movement. But the same broken terrain that was slowing the SheVa should help the human forces caught in the vise to defend their positions.

"And close," Pruitt said over the intercom. "Although some of it had better not be *too* close; my AD rounds are 100kts. The explosions in the mountains were love taps compared to that."

"Oh, hell, those *were* love taps," Chan snorted. "We didn't even notice them until afterwards."

"Well, you were firing at the time, ma'am," Kitteket broke in. "Trust me, in anything but a Meemie they didn't seem like love taps. Okay, I've got all the units plugged into the database along with their commo codes. The mech team is in movement to its ORP. And I've got an update on the repair batt; they're not only carrying repair gear, they're carrying slap-on armor."

"Cool," Pruitt said. "It sounds like they're intending for us to fight in-close."

"We could use it now," Mitchell said uncomfortably.

"Well, I've also updated the Posleen position," she added. The map they all had been looking at suddenly blossomed with data. The area around Dillsboro was red with Posleen indicators.

"We need to get some support here or we're going to be a melting puddle of slag," Reeves said.

"All it will take is one plasma round the wrong way through the treads and we're in trouble," Indy pointed out.

"Then we'll need to stay hull down," Pruitt pointed out. "Not that hard around here."

"Where's the data coming from, Kitteket?" Colonel Mitchell asked.

"There are still scouts on the hills," she said, highlighting scout positions. "Their positions are guesses; they're not obviously telling us where they are exactly. But they've been calling in PosReps. All the intel guys didn't leave with the main group; there's a small intel team collecting and analyzing with the assault force. I'm feeding off of them."

"I wish we could be in the assault," Pruitt said. "That'd be cool."

"We can't *fit*," Reeves said. "And we don't have any direct assault weapons; it would be like taking an artillery piece along."

"I think I've figured out a way to hook up the MetalStorms," Indy said.

"Really?" Chan said over the intercom. "Direct or remote?"

"You'd have to stay in them," Indy said. "But I've been looking at your manual CD. We pulled the whole turret assembly, including your control motors. All we have to do is provide a mount—and really that can just be a circular piece of steel—and power. I think if the repair group has lance cutters, which it should, we might be able to drop you into the turret. It would also require some bracing, we'll see what the repair batt people say."

"Well, at the least, they should be able to recover our parts," Chan said with a sigh. "I don't know what we'll do after that."

"Like I said, ma'am, we'll see," the warrant replied.

"Sir, I think this is about as close as I can get," Reeves said. "At least and have an angle to fire." He carefully backed the gun up and shoved it into a gully. The ravine on the edge of Willits Hill—there had been a very small unincorporated town until the SheVa came through—was pointed in more or less the direction of the pass.

"Pruitt?" Colonel Mitchell asked.

"I think I've got an angle from here, sir," the gunner said. "It's not detonating at ground level after all."

"I neglected to ask," the colonel continued. "Do you know the protocols for firing one of these things?"

"Yes, sir," Pruitt answered. "I read about them when I took over the position and I just reread the section. It's pretty automatic. I need your codes for release, though."

"Uh, oh," Kitteket said, looking at the skip receiver. "Codes coming in."

"What's it say?" Pruitt asked.

"It comes in slow," the clerk said. "But the first group is in. It's the release type. Three, one, five."

"Three one five," Mitchell repeated, tapping the command into his database. "It says that's an ROE change . . ."

"ROE?" Pruitt said. "Rules of Engagement? But that's . . ."

*"Oh my God."*

"Did we just get a full engagement change to nuclear active?" Pruitt asked carefully. The colonel had gone all ashen faced.

"Yeah," Mitchell croaked then cleared his throat. "We're clear for nuclear release, unlimited fire levels, unlimited targeting, at my discretion only."

"Oh my God," Kitteket whispered in unthinking repetition.

"Well, sir," Pruitt said quietly. "The first thing to do is clear out Balsam Gap, don't you think?"

"Okay," the colonel said taking a deep breath. Removing a key from his dogtags he opened up the safe over his head, removed a manual and turned to the back page. "I need verbal confirmation. I have release codes. Does everyone agree? Schmoo?"

"Yes."

"Pruitt?"

"Yes."

"Indy?"

"Yes."

"What about me?" Kitteket asked.

"You're not an official crew-member," the major said. "But I do need that second set of codes you received."

He pulled a purple hard plastic package out of the back of the book and broke the back of it along a perforation. Inside was a red piece of plastic that looked somewhat like a credit card. Turning to the appropriate section of the manual he took the codes from Kitteket and, using the numbers and letters on the card, determined the correct codes to enter.

The program was referred to as "Positive Action Locks." To get the area effect rounds to work required codes from the President. But the presidential codes were then put through a "filter" at the actual system. The method was cumbersome, but when talking about nuclear weapons it only made sense.

He keyed the final sequence into a box by his head then waited until it gave a "Go" code. Normally the "Go" was a green number. Instead, in this case, there was a small infinity symbol that made the bottom drop out of his stomach. Trying to ignore it he entered "One" as the number of rounds released. "That's my code. Warrant Indy?"

Indy followed the same procedure, pulling out her own manual and keying in her translated codes.

Pruitt for once looked properly chastened. "I'm green on one area effect round."

"Very well," Colonel Mitchell said. "I want one round, at optimum airburst, right over Balsam Gap."

"We're keyed to transmit nuke warnings," Kitteket said.

Pruitt turned and opened up a new control panel, using the same key to unlock and then lift a red, semi-transparent cover. He ran his fingers over it for a moment then brought up a map of the local area, tapping Balsam Gap as the target. He cross-checked that it was the correct UTM coordinates then keyed for airburst and let it compute optimum height. Finally the system flashed confirmed.

"We're prepared, sir," Pruitt said. "Coordinates set. Permission to load?"

Mitchell checked the cross-linked information and then nodded. "Load."

There was a series of thunks as the SheVa switched out the anti-lander round that was "up the spout" and loaded the explosive round.

"UP."

"Kitteket, send the nuke warning."

And, unfortunately, the next Lamprey that was hit blew up rather spectacularly.

He had come to lying in the Little Tennessee River. How he had gotten there was a mystery until he saw the Humvee lying sideways on a shattered tree. He was, however, cleaner. The rest of the retreat was a bit of blur. The Posleen actually got ahead of him at one point, but he managed to get a ride on a five-ton that snuck around them to the east. Then, in Dillsboro, they'd all been unloaded and segregated out.

Technically he was probably still a patient, but he didn't make any fuss about being handed a rifle. They'd even given him a "squad." All eight of the soldiers were clerks with an infantry military operational skill rating. The way that worked was that after going through training to be infantry, some desk jockey would grab them to push papers instead of carry a rifle. So the guys had been trained to be infantry, but only one of them had ever spent any time in the line.

He, and the one specialist with some line experience, made sure that all the clerks knew how to load and fire their weapons. Then he found some rations and they sat around waiting for somebody to get their thumb out of their butts. Hurry up and wait was all well and good, but the Posleen weren't all that far back; if whoever was in charge of this cluster-fuck—it looked like a captain which was just crazy, there must have been a brigade's worth of gear and personnel in the area he was looking at—didn't get a move on, the Posleen were going to overrun the lot of them.

Then the rumor got around that the main exit had been cut off. He managed to get his guys to help quell the near riot that erupted, but it turned out it wasn't just a rumor this time; the Posleen really *had* cut off their escape route.

Then they got the word that *most* of the personnel,

and gear, was going to go out by the two alternate routes. Great. He was all for fighting, he'd been doing it for damn near ten years, but it helped to have a way *out* in case things went south. However, it turned out that "most" did not include the "combat arms" forces.

The next thing he knew he and his squad were in the back of a Bradley headed up the road to the pass the Posleen had taken.

Now, he wasn't a coward by any stretch of the imagination. But he'd gotten a look at the map and taking that pass with the pitiful little force they had was just suicide.

They finally had a real meeting, where the lieutenant who was in charge of the Brads called all the squad leaders together and told them the plan, such as it was. The SheVa gun, probably the same one that had killed the Lamprey that blasted him into the drink, was going to fire a nuke into the pass. Then they would charge into the pass and clean up the survivors.

"It'll be easy," the lieutenant concluded. "All the Posties will be toasties from the nuke. We just have to secure it until the brigade on the other side makes it up the road."

Sarge Buckley had been beating around the Army since before the Posleen had been heard of and he knew when somebody was lying. "The check is in the mail" is nothing compared to "the trucks are on the drop zone." But the worst military cliché of them all had to be "the artillery is going to pound them flat then we'll just go in and paint the lines."

Buckley looked up as the radio in the track began to honk.

"NUKE WARNING. NUKE WARNING. TARGET COORDINATES: UTM 17 311384E 392292N. 100 K-T. THIRTY SECONDS!"

Life just got worse.
"FIFTEEN SECONDS. TEN . . ."
They were all gonna die.

Pruitt inhaled, then: "Initiate."
The area effect weapons had similarities to the anti-lander penetrators and differences. Since the gun remained a smooth-bore and the round therefore had to be fin-stabilized, they were discarding sabot. But they were thicker in cross section than the penetrators and flew at a lower velocity. Last, but not least, since they were not penetrators, they were made out of simple carbon steel. Since the metal they were made out of was going to be distributed as a fine dust, better to have it composed of materials the human body could metabolize.

The round flew out of the tube in a river of fire, dropped its sabots and headed for Balsam Gap.

The weapon detonated seventy-three hundred and twenty feet above sea level, two thousand feet above and just about one thousand feet to the northeast of the pass. They say that close only counts in hand grenades and hydrogen bombs, but in this case close didn't quite count. The fireball swooped down over the Posleen defenses, devouring the trees to either side and gouging out the sharp walls of the pass, especially on the eastern side. However, on the northern side of the pass, the expanding fireball was partially blocked and deflected by the shoulder of Balsam Mountain.

The Blue Ridge Parkway crossed over U.S. 23 at Balsam Gap. The overpass was heavily constructed and many of the Posleen defenses had been built underneath it for additional overhead cover from the expected artillery fire. While the antimatter warhead was very strong, it had been placed as a "personnel killer" rather than a structures killer; therefore between the deflection of the corner of the mountain and the construction, the compression front that hit the structure tore down the southern span, but the northern span remained intact.

Furthermore, Posleen under the bridge were shielded from the thermal pulse and at least some of the radiation release. The result was that although the majority of the oolt'ondai had been swept away in the atomic fireball, a small, but very angry remnant suvived.

Sergeant Buckley hefted his rifle as the Bradley gunned towards the pass. His "squad" was virtually unknown to him, and he knew darned well that humans mostly fought for the people in their "tribe." When they hit the objective it was just as likely that most of these guys were going to either hit the dirt and stay there or run.

Which meant that actually getting them to fight was up to him. He never asked for this, but the stripes on his shoulder meant he had the responsibility. And he was going to, by God, discharge it.

He looked out the small porthole by him and considered the map. They were probably less than three hundred meters from the objective; he had a hard time telling from the terrain because everything had been so churned up by the nuke strike. But he was pretty sure they were just about on the straightaway for the gap.

He pulled out a magazine and waved it to get everyone's attention then inserted it in the magazine well. Riding with magazines in meant that some idiot was bound to lock and load. If somebody locked and loaded, they were bound to have an accidental discharge. To prevent that, before loading he had had them take out their magazines and clear their weapons. That way while they were waiting around and bored somebody wouldn't accidentally fire on full auto; he'd cleaned up a Brad where that happened and it wasn't pretty. Now they reversed the procedure, slipping in the magazines and pulling back their charging levers. In the dim light he had each of them show him that the weapons were on safe, then looked outside just as the Brad next to them ate a plasma bolt.

Major Anderson wasn't sure what he was doing leading the charge; he was pretty sure that if General Keeton had heard he would have prevented it. But when he joined the Army it hadn't been to lay T-1 cables; it was just a fluke of the placement board that put him in Signals.

Now he had that chance that most officers only get to think about, that Patton had phrased as "the opportunity to lead a lot of men into a desperate battle." It would probably be the only chance he got and, furthermore, he was just about the only officer that most of the group knew. So this time, *Signals* got to lead the way.

The problem being that the last time he had looked at how to do something like this was in ROTC. He had ordered the tank unit to drive through the objective and then swing back through while the Bradleys, who were supposed to follow right behind, stopped on the objective and unloaded.

Now, however, it was apparent that part of the Blue Ridge overpass had stayed up. And some of the Posleen on the objective were still alive. As the first M-1 that went up could attest. For that matter, those Posleen who were alive were being shielded from the variable time fire by the overpass. Basically, the artillery was useless.

If he had thought there might be significant resistance he would have had the artillery fire smoke; the Posleen generally couldn't deal with obscurement rounds very well. But it had been assumed that a nuke would do the job. Bad assumption. And by the time they shifted types of fire, the assault would have succeeded or failed; when they passed the last curve and came under fire they had less than four hundred yards to go.

He made an instant decision; the tanks didn't have any real utility to the mission, it was only the Bradleys that mattered. Getting the infantry onto the objective was the mission.

"Armor team, stream smoke and drive through the objective. Infantry, unload and move forward by fire and maneuver."

He stooped down and stepped towards the troop door just as the hypervelocity missile impacted on the front slope of his Bradley.

Buckley rocked forward and back as the Bradley screamed to a stop then rolled to the rear as the troop door dropped open filling the interior with streaming red light from the setting sun.

"Come on, you apes! You wanna live forever?!"

He jumped out of the troop door and stumbled to his knees as he tripped on the end. When he stood up and turned around he could see the rest of the squad frozen on the inside.

"Okay!" he yelled. "You're in the biggest fucking target around!"

He dove into the median and rolled into the ditch down its center. The good news was that now all the plasma bolts and railgun rounds were going overhead. The bad news was that it looked like he was pinned down.

A moment later one of the privates from his squad followed him into the ditch, landing on him and knocking the breath out of the sergeant.

"You wanna get off my back, Private?" he snarled.

The private rolled off to the side with an apology as a second member of the squad rolled into the ditch. However, right after that their Brad, which had just started to move again, ate an HVM.

Buckley shook his head to clear his ears and looked around. The tanks had apparently blown smoke and headed into the pass, but none of them had made it. There had been four. One was on fire, with its ammo cooking off, behind him in the median. The other three were scattered across the front, the closest to the objective less than a hundred meters from it. That one had suffered a catastrophic kill and the turret was fifty feet to the side, buried halfway into the moutainside.

There were two privates with him and that was it. He could hear somebody ahead and to the right firing at the Posleen in the Gap, but he couldn't see who it was. For that matter, the only thing he could see was an overpass that was apparently shielding the Posleen from overhead fire. Oh, and a C-Dec. Which was just lifting off from the left of the intersection.

Joy.

"But I'm *not* in a suit!" he growled.

Besonora tapped the younger Kessentai on the shoulder as the oolt'poslenar staggered into the air. "Try to stay low; we must find and destroy that gun or all is lost."

"I shall try, Oolt'ondai," the Kessentai answered. "But I have flown very little."

"Do the best you can."

The oolt'ondai left the command deck and laboriously

headed for the outer levels. He was not one of those who cursed the Alldn't designed spiral gravity ramps that were the primary method of movement between areas; someday the Posleen would be able to modify and not just copy Alldn't equipment. Until then, they had to make do with the way it was.

One of the items that would change, if he had his way, would be the fact that things were scattered through the ship apparently at random. Thus, the personnel quads were found almost anywhere throughout the vessel. In the case of the section holding the last "reaction" oolt, it was in the upper "west" quadrant, a silly place since they then had to go to the lower "north" to unload.

He greeted the Kessentai of the oolt and gave him his instructions. As soon as they landed he was to unload, pass around the oolt'poslenar and attack the gun to destroy its ability to fire, in other words, aim at the barrel.

Having done all that he could to prepare, he ordered the Kessentai to begin the laborious movement to the exit and started back to the command deck. As he did, alarms went off throughout the ship.

"Sir!" Pruitt said. "I've got anti-grav emanations."

"Sir," Kitteket interjected. "I just got word from one of the scouts; a C-Dec lifted off and is headed this way!"

"Where?" both Mitchell and Pruitt asked.

"He doesn't know right now sir," the specialist answered. "He says it's staying low and he lost it in the hills. He's up on Rocky Face and he said he just saw it for a second by Joe Mountain."

"I don't have a direction, sir," Pruitt said. "I'm up on penetrators. And I'm more or less on vector," he added, glancing at his map.

"Elevate the gun a bit," Mitchell said. "Captain Chan, are you listening?"

"I'm here," the MetalStorm commander replied.

"This may turn into a knife-fight," Mitchell said. "How well are you chained down?"

"Not well enough to fire," Captain Chan answered. "Even if we *had* power. Which we don't. As for secondary effects . . . we'll have to see."

"Do you want to exit your turrets?" Mitchell asked.

"No," the captain replied after a moment. "Better the devil you know."

"Sir, emanations are strong," Pruitt said. "I get the feeling they're close."

"The fire came from near here somewhere, Oolt'ondai," the pilot said. He gently tapped the controls so the ship wouldn't slam into the side of the mountain. "Should we unload the oolt?"

Besonora looked at the view from the outside; the side of the mountain was steep and covered in trees. To let them down would require backing up. However, the map showed an open area ahead; they could put them down there just as well.

"No, follow the road around this ridge and drop them here," he said, showing the Kessentai the map. "In the bend of this creek which is marked 'Scott.'"

# CHAPTER 39

For heathen heart that puts her trust
      In recking tube and iron shard,
All valiant dust that builds on dust,
      And guarding, calls not Thee to guard,
For frantic boast and foolish word—
Thy Mercy on thy People, Lord!

              —Rudyard Kipling
              "Recessional" (1897)

*Near Balsam Gap, NC, United States, Sol III*
*1952 EDT Sunday September 27, 2009 AD*

Despite the danger, Captain Chan had ordered all her tank commanders to stick their heads out of their hatches; when it came down to it mark-one eyeball was probably going to be faster than anything else. And each of them had been given an assigned sector to watch.

As luck would have it, the first person to spot the slow-moving C-Dec was Captain Chan. And when she saw where it was she cursed fluently.

"TARGET, C-DEC, TWO THIRTY, LEVEL, THREE HUNDRED METERS. All TCs! Close hatches!"

"Oh shit, oh shit, oh shit," Pruitt cursed, frantically slewing the gun down and around.

"Fire when you bear," Major Mitchell said calmly.

"We're under three hundred meters, sir," Kitteket said.

"Understood," the major replied. "That's the breaks."

"I understand, sir," the specialist replied. "But you know that these rounds have a minimum arming distance, right?"

"Put it down! Put it down!" Besonora shouted.

"I am!" the pilot said. "But there's no place flat."

"Fuscirto uut to flat!" the oolt'ondai cursed. "Just get the oolt on the ground!"

"All guns, fire as you bear!"

Eleven "facets" of the twelve sided C-Decs had weaponry on them. Unlike the Lampreys, which only had one face with an anti-ship weapon, the command dodecahedrons sported a mix of heavy and "light" weapons.

In this case, the facet that was pointed right at Bun-Bun mounted quad plasma guns.

"This is gonna suuuck!" Reeves shouted, bending down and putting his fingers in his ears as the gun finally leveled on the C-Dec.

The first plasma round entered the gun system low, punching through a road-wheel and the compartment wall of the engine room. Plasma rounds transferred enormous amounts of energy, but like bullets that shatter when they hit a wall, they didn't have a lot of "penetration." In this case, the plasma vented into the engine room, raising the temperature notably, but otherwise doing no damage. The second round did much the same, hitting slightly to the side and taking out a section of track. The SheVa was now effectively immobilized, but maneuvering hadn't been an issue anyway.

The third plasma bolt hit the upper deck of the engine system and boiled twenty feet of steel into the air. The fourth missed entirely.

Then it was Bun-Bun's turn.

"TARGET!"
"FIRE!"
"ON THE WAY!"

By the time Pruitt was finished with the "on" the round had already struck the C-Dec, centerline vertically and just off center to the right.

The round penetrated the outer layer of armor and the portions of it that had not already been converted to plasma and gaseous uranium proceeded to crash through the interior and break apart.

This was the point where most rounds would have detonated their antimatter charge. However, as Kitteket had pointed out, the rounds had a minimum arming distance of six hundred meters. What happened instead is that about halfway through the ship, the containment vessel shattered. The result, from the outside, was very like an antimatter explosion, but in reality it was a very fast flash-fire.

"Hooowah!" Pruitt yelled in relief. No huge explosions, just lots of plasma gouting out of all the ports. Some of it washed over the SheVa, but it was not much more than a wall of flame by the time it got there; Bun-Bun could shrug it off. "The Rabbit strikes again!"

"Captain Chan, you with us?" Mitchell called.

"Oh, yeah," the MetalStorm commander answered. "Did you guys fire yet?"

"Sir," Kittekut said, "the force in the pass is getting cut up. I've lost contact with Major Anderson, but all but one of the transmitters from the tracks has cut out and the last word I got was that there were still Posleen in the pass. Some of the militia scouts say they see columns of smoke and what look like secondary explosions in the area."

"Oh," Colonel Mitchell said. "Keep trying to raise them. And try to get ahold of the force on the Asheville side; maybe they can clear it."

"Yes, sir. A few of the militia scouts are headed over to see what they can do."

"Good," Mitchell said, not adding *for what it's worth*. "Anybody seen Indy? Or know what the damage report is?"

"We're dead in the water is the answer, sir," the warrant officer replied, coming up through the engineering hatch. Her face was covered in soot, but she appeared uninjured. "We've got full track severance on the right side and probably some major damage to the drive train; there's a huge hole in the side of the gun where a drive wheel used to be. I think we might have taken a hit on one of the firing support struts as well. But it looks like we kept all the motors this time."

"Oh," Major Mitchell said again. "This is such a good time."

"So, what you're saying," Pruitt said with a manic grin, "is that we're dead in the water, we're surrounded and the only combat forces around, the guys who would normally be holding off the million or so Posleen coming up the valley at us, are getting wiped out trying to clear the Posleen in the pass?"

"Pretty much sums it up," Major Mitchell said with a nod.

"By Jove, I think he's got it," Kitteket agreed.

"Nice recap there, Torg," Reeves said.

"Just trying to be clear, here," Pruitt answered. "Why do the words 'we're fucked' resonate through my head?"

Sergeant Buckley considered his situation carefully as he looked to the front. Now that things were a bit less chaotic it was obvious that there wasn't *a lot* of fire coming from the overpass. He counted maybe three missile launchers, a pair of heavy plasma guns and some, not many, railguns. There didn't seem to be any shotguns at all.

Which meant that the pass was held by one of the Posleen "heavy" companies. That meant experienced God Kings and veteran troops.

Better and better.

He looked around, but all there was in view were the two privates with him and burning tracks. There was a blackened body hanging out of the one they had unloaded from and another was in sight in the middle of the road. That one was near torn in half and Buckley recognized the sure sign of a close encounter of the worst kind with a plasma round. He'd finally figured out what had kept him and the other two alive; the tank the Brad had been following had started to blow smoke right after the first plasma fire came in. That had given them just enough concealment that the Posleen hadn't fired up the Brad for a few seconds. Which meant that if those dumb-fucks in the Brad had followed him out right away, rather than stopping to debate it, they might still be alive.

The price of cowardice was just getting unacceptably high.

"You guys see anybody else?" he asked.

"No," one of the privates replied. "But I heard firing off to the right earlier."

"Hey!" he yelled. "Somebody out there!"

"Over here!" a voice replied. "Who's that?"

"Sergeant Buckley!" the sergeant replied, knowing it wouldn't mean a thing.

"You seen Major Anderson?"

"No! Anybody with you?"

"No!"

"You got a radio?"

"Yes!"

"Hot diggity," Buckley said quietly. "Stay the fuck down! You may be the only thing that keeps us alive! Anybody else out there?!"

He listened for a moment, but all he heard were moans behind him somewhere, the crackle of ammunition cooking off in the vehicles and the whistle of wind in the pass.

"That's it?" one of the privates asked. "Just *us*?"

"Looks like it," Buckley replied. "Could be worse."

"How?!"

"We could be in the ACS. Hey! RTO! You got anybody on that radio?"

"No!"

"You got the frequency Major Anderson was using?"

"Yes!"

"Switch to it!" He looked around at the two privates with him and at the drainage ditch. It led to within twenty yards of the overpass, but then it rapidly shallowed out. The three of them could probably low-crawl to within a few yards of the Posleen positions. He hadn't gotten a good look at them yet, but it looked like the Posleen had blown a *trench* across the road, under the overpass. Which was way more smarts than he wanted to see out of the horses.

The Posleen basically had stopped firing, there was only the occasional round going overhead. He wasn't sure if it was intended to keep their heads down, but it had the effect. Really, though, now that he got a look at the situation, they might be able to pull it out. All it would take was a little luck.

He thought about that for a moment then whispered: "*Good* luck. All it will take is a little *good* luck."

"Sir, I've got contact with a survivor up in the pass," Kitteket said. "There's not many of them left, this guy says he only knows of four including himself."

"Well, that's just ducky," the colonel said.

"He says the sergeant up there wants some artillery support. He wants an . . . 'individual tube adjustment.' That's one I haven't heard before."

"Put him through." Mitchell waited until he could hear the carrier frequency then replied. "Infantry, this is SheVa Nine. How do you want that artillery?"

"This is Lima Seven Nine," the RTO replied. "Sergeant Buckley says he wants an individual tube adjustment, right in front of the Posleen positions. Get this, the horses are *dug in* under the bridge and half the bridge is still up. The overhead's not getting near 'em. You got that, over?"

"Roger," Mitchell called. "We'll give you the frequency for the artillery and monitor; the only thing we've got to throw would kill you quicker than the Posleen."

"That's a big ten four, good buddy," the RTO replied. "We *don't* want any nukes, clear?"

"Got that. Do you have a count on the Posleen?"

"Negative, we're taking some heavy fire and having to keep our head down. But it doesn't look like many.

A few railguns and some plasma cannons sure did for the tracks, though. They're all *gone*."

"Understood. I'm sending you back to the commo officer, she'll put you in touch with the artillery. Write when you get work."

"Roger, out here."

He waited until Kitteket turned over the frequency to the distant RTO and then gestured for everyone to turn to the center.

"Okay, Kitteket, we've got contact with one or two infantry in the Gap, the artillery and a few of the militia. Anyone else?"

"Not so far, sir," she answered. "I don't have frequencies for the units on the far side of the Gap and everyone else is out of range. I . . ." She stopped and shook her head. "I've got an idea, but I'm not sure it will work."

"What is it?"

"The nuclear control system," she said. "It's a two way system that . . ."

"Bounces off of the ionization tracks of meteors," Mitchell said. "But it's only for sending code groups."

"Yes, sir," the specialist replied. "And you can only send three text characters at a time. But it can send *any* set of text characters; you could type out the dictionary, slowly."

"Do it," Mitchell said. "Get us the frequencies for the unit on the far side; we need them to clear the pass. Either that or we'll have to leave it up to the militia."

"Somehow, I don't think assaulting passes is their forte," Kitteket said.

# CHAPTER 40

Thomas Redman was one pissed Injun.

It wasn't bad enough that the war had forced the shut-down of the casino that had been his place of employment for over fourteen years. It wasn't bad enough that his younger brother had been killed on fucking Barwhon by these Posleen sons-of-bitches. Now they'd went and overrun Dillsboro where his "certified Indian Made Posleen Scalpers" store *had* been.

Well, admittedly, that damn SheVa gun had run it over first, but it wasn't like they had much of a choice.

*Whoever* had wiped out his store, it was the fault of them Posleen and they was, by God, gonna pay. His family had been in continuous residence in these mountains since they'd run the Creeks out about the time when Columbus was conniving Isabella out of her jewels. And he wasn't going to be the last Redman to screw the white man out of money in them.

653

Up to this moment his resistance to the Posleen had consisted of telling the babe in the SheVa gun where they were. When they'd first gotten word the Posleen were coming up the pass he'd sent the wife—he only called her "squaw" when he wanted to get her *really* mad—up the road towards Knoxville. Then he'd gotten out his militia radio, his four wheeler and his rifle and headed up onto the ridges.

Now, though, it was looking touch and go. He hadn't been able to see much of what was happening in the Gap, but the columns of smoke made most of it pretty obvious. He knew a spot where he could get a bead on the Posleen. But that was going to involve a technical violation of the laws of man.

In the rush to enact legislation at the beginning of the crisis, one of the big debates was over formation of militias. Finally the Congress had passed laws that effectively repealed most of the anti-weapons regulations that had grown up, substituting a series of laws to "regulate the several militias." One of the laws had to do with militia boundaries, in that no member of a militia "formed in one territorial area should pass for militia purposes into another territorial area without the clear wishes of the government of the second territorial area." What they meant was that if a group of, say, Virginia militiamen were practicing, they shouldn't go into Maryland.

Unfortunately, the bureaucrats of the Bureau of Indian Affairs correctly interpreted that to mean that there would have to be a "Reservation" militia and the militia of the rest of North Carolina. And, technically, the only area that one Thomas Redman, sergeant in good standing of the North Carolina Cherokee Tribal Milita, could make war on the Posleen in was reservation territory. And he was just about to clear the reservation line.

A series of not particularly funny John Wayne movie jokes went through his head as the four wheeler crested the last bit of rock and rumbled onto the Blue Ridge Parkway headed to cut the Posleen off at the pass.

"Y'all better WATCH out!" he yelled to the night. "This Redman is *off* the reservation!"

"Sir, I'm in contact with Eastern Command," Kitteket said, tapping rapidly for a moment then stopping.

"And what's the word?" the colonel asked.

"I'm still giving them our situation, sir," she continued, tapping again. "I have to set up the words three letters at a time, then wait for them to transmit then set up the next set of three letters. It's a real pain."

"We'll get that fixed in the next upgrade," Pruitt said, scrolling his tactical map around. "Assuming we're *here* for the next upgrade." Things were not looking so hot.

"Okay, what about the Posleen around Dillsboro?" Mitchell asked.

"That's looking pretty bad. They're having some trouble with the torn up road and about half of them headed up 441, but the rest are headed this way. There's also a huge buildup across the river. The scouts can't get a good estimate on the numbers in there, or they don't want to believe their math. Either way, it's a lot."

"ETA?" Pruitt asked.

"About an hour, the way Posleen travel," Kitteket said. "I'm telling Eastern that, too."

"Oh, the hell with this," Mitchell cursed. "No more Mister Nice-Bunny. There is *no* reason we should have to worry about getting overrun with Posleen. Pruitt, we've got three more rounds of area denial, right?"

"Yes, sir," the gunner said. He tapped a control and the turret began to track smoothly to the rear. "And there ain't no humans to worry about back there. Up on three one-hundred kiloton nukes, at your command . . . Sir!"

"Kitteket, find out where the main concentrations are and an estimate of where the leading forces will be in . . . oh, ten minutes," Mitchell said. "And find out why it seems we're the only ones fighting for this pass!"

The Blue Ridge Parkway is one of those American icons, like Route 66 or the Appalachian Trail. It runs along the crest of the Blue Ridge, which is really a series of smaller mountain ranges, from the Great Smoky Mountains in North Carolina to the Shenandoah Valley in Virginia. Along the way it passes through some of the prettiest, and most rugged, country in Eastern North America. Running, as it does, along the spine of various ridges, it is not easily accessed. Nor is it usually the quickest way to get from Point A to Point B.

But it was as good as it got for Thomas.

He'd gotten up on the parkway near Woodfin Creek, using a little known track that connected to the *old* parkway, and then up the hill onto the new one, and now was closing in on the Gap. But his target wasn't actually in the Gap. From what the babe in the SheVa was saying, half the overpass was up. While it sounded sort of fun to climb out on it and fire down on the horses, it made more sense for him to get where he could fire under the overpass. There was a ridge running out from the parkway, the one that made the last bend in 23 necessary, that could be accessed from the road. From the end of it, if he could find a good hide, he thought he would be able to fire right under the bridge and take some of the pressure off the troops caught in the Gap.

He noticed the tops of trees gone as he rounded a curve then slowed down when he saw some of them in the road. Towards the end of the curve the parkway was littered with them and many of them were already beginning to wither and yellow from intense heat.

All things considered, it was good that those harbingers were present because as he rounded the curve, still doing nearly twenty miles per hour, he slammed into the first of thousands of fallen poplars blocking the road.

"Oh, shit!"

"Sir, I've got a message from Eastern Command," Kittekut said. "More good news."

"Go ahead," Colonel Mitchell said, pointing to a spot on the map for Pruitt.

"There's a reason we're the only ones fighting for the pass, sir: Our nuke caused a rockslide on the road up to the pass on the Asheville side. The brigade that was supposed to be up there by now is blocked off. They're clearing the road, but it will take at least another hour. There's some light infantry trying to climb past it, but they're going to be a while too."

"Fine," Mitchell replied, tapping in his secondary release codes. "Tell them we're just about to clear the Scott Creek Valley of Posleen."

Pruitt finished setting the firing commands and turned to look at the SheVa commander. "All three rounds, sir?"

"You were perhaps saving them for a more festive occasion, Pruitt?" the colonel asked. "All three rounds. One on the crossroads, one on the head of the Posleen and one on the mass backed up on the other side of the river. If *that* doesn't slow them down, nothing will."

"Yes, sir," the gunner said, keying in the last command and hitting the firing sequence.

❖     ❖     ❖

Between them, the BIA and the United States Congress may have come up with some really silly regulations, one of which Thomas was now limpingly in violation of, but they did spring for the militia's equipment. Especially once it was pointed out that with the casino closed "for the duration," the Nation didn't have much in the way of income. And, being a government agency, they didn't stint. Which was why he *used* to have a nice, camoflage painted Honda ATV.

But he'd survived the wreck and so had his rifle in its case, and his binoculars and his ammunition. So he was ahead of the game. Sort of. Getting to the ridge where he could fire down on the Posleen was going to be tougher than he'd expected; that nuke had really torn the place up.

The whole area around the intersection was a tangled mass of fallen timber. It looked like some of the pictures from Mount St. Helens. He'd done a paper on that disaster back when he was in the eighth grade and he still remembered the pictures of the elk picking their way through the fallen trees. Well, now he knew how they felt: pissed.

He pulled his right leg over another log and swore. He'd wrenched his knee in the wreck and clambering over this pile of twisted sticks wasn't helping one bit. Especially in this nearly pitch black dark; the sun was fully down and the moon was running in and out among the clouds. But he was pretty sure he knew where he was: the gully down below should be one of the headwaters of Scotts Creek and that meant the ridge he was on should overlook the intersection.

Just down from the ridge, along what one of the sniper instructors had termed the "military crest," there was a line where some of the trees had stayed up, sheltered from the blast. It wasn't exactly a "path," but it was better than what he'd been crossing and it gave him a chance to angle up the ridge out of sight of the Posleen.

Finally, *finally* he limped up to the top of the ridge and got down on his stomach. The blast had dropped many of the trees more or less parallel to each other and for a change it was the direction he was going. So he was able to belly up through the gaps in between until he could see first the overpass, then the Posleen positions under it.

He also could see the burning tracks on the road; the infantry guys had really gotten the shit kicked out of them from the looks of it. But he could see two of them low-crawling towards the Posleen position.

Time to give them some covering fire.

The last time Joe Buckley could remember low-crawling was the last time he took an EIB test. That would have been in the dawn of man when the only thing he had to worry about was breaking his leg on a jump or wrecking his bike or getting into a fight over some fat chick on Bragg Boulevard.

Man, those were the days. No Posleen. No skyscrapers falling on you. No ships exploding. Just the occasional pissed-off sergeant and watching *Pinky and the Brain* while waiting for afternoon formation. It just didn't get any better.

He tucked his butt lower as a round skittered off the pavement and whistled by overhead. Frankly, it was lots better then than now.

One of the two privates had gotten a little too high and was toasted by a plasma gun for his mistake. The other one had frozen halfway and was now belly down and shivering in the median. Buckley wasn't sure why he was still going. It might have been sheer stubbornness; these Posleen had started to really piss him off. Or it might have been that he knew if they didn't clear the pass, they were going to get royally corn-cobbed anyway.

He snuggled even closer to the ground as the first artillery shell plunged out of the sky. If all went well, his approach would be covered by the fire.

On the other hand, if the gunners or FDC screwed up, it was just as likely to land on him.

It didn't, though; it hit on top of the overpass. He waited impatiently as the RTO walked it down off the overpass and onto the ground. Falling as it was now, the majority of the fragmentation from the round should be thrown under the overpass and onto the Posleen. It didn't mean it stopped them, but it should keep their heads down a bit, making it a tad easier for him to move. As he moved out, a round from the next gun came screaming in.

The ditch he was crawling in, which had *really* shallowed out for a while, had started to deepen. Enough that he felt he could raise up just a tad and move a little faster.

He got partially up on his elbows and knees. Not a high crawl, not enough cover for that. But not a low crawl either. Call it a really fucked up medium crawl. He started to shimmy forward, spread out like a crab, when there was a racket from the Posleen lines and all of a sudden his butt felt like it was on fire.

Dropping onto his stomach again he felt behind him and swore as his hand came away wet. Either he had the worst case of hemorrhoids in the world or some Posleen son of a bitch had just shot him in the ass.

Thomas shook his head at the poor brave son of a bitch down in that ditch. It was pretty clear in the thermal imaging scope that he'd just got shot in the ass—there was a noticeable blood splatter giving off residual heat—but he was still crawling forward.

Another one was down on his stomach, not dead by the temperature, probably just too scared to move. And there was another bright white, headless body in the ditch. That one was so hot, and obviously dead, that it must have eaten a plasma round. Other than that, it looked like most of them had been killed in the first few moments.

He swung his scope around to the Posleen position and shook his head. All the fire from their plasma guns had left noticeable trails on the road and heated up the air under the bridge. And every time an artillery shell hit, the flare of light from it shut down the scope for just an instant. But he could still pick the horses out; they were slightly cooler than humans, but much warmer than the increasing chill of the evening and the cold ground under the overpass. And there weren't many of them, fourteen it looked like, maybe fifteen; there was one who was down on the bottom of the trench not moving.

Now to figure out which ones were the God Kings.

He noticed a haze around the head of one for a moment and switched off the thermal scan for visible light. In the green haze he could just barely see that that one had a crest; it must have lifted it for just a moment and created that thermal halo around its head.

He nodded to himself and switched back to thermal. Taking a breath he flipped the Barrett off of "safe," placed his finger on the trigger and began to gently squeeze.

Sergeant Buckley ducked as Posleen fire began to rave out of the trench, but it didn't seem to be directed at his position. Risking a quick look, it was clear they were firing everything they had at the ridge behind him and to his left.

Taking another risk, he got up on his hands and

knees and shimmied towards a chunk of concrete that would make for good cover. It was probably a piece of the south span that had been blasted free by the nuke, but it looked like heaven and a womb to Buckley; he might even be able to sit up behind it.

He rolled into the shelter of the chunk as the fire died down and considered his position. He was within twenty yards of the Posleen trench, but the fire that had come out of it was from more guns than he had thought were there. And the artillery wasn't taking them out, only keeping their heads down. A bit.

It seemed like there was somebody else out there, maybe a sniper up on the ridge. If he had survived the counter-fire. That would be nice, it would be good to feel that he wasn't completely alone.

He rolled over to the south side of the chunk and thought about his options. There was another chunk, this one most definitely a piece of the bridge with a big hunk of steel sticking out, about five meters closer to the bridge. And it was lying against the center pylons. If he could make it to the cover of that chunk, he could work his way to where he would be on the flank of the Posleen, in a position to rake their trench from end to end. And with the way the south portion had fallen, he would be in "good rubble."

Good rubble was a special term for infantry. Rubble was the infantry's friend; armor couldn't negotiate it, it shed most artillery and Posleen hated it. Good rubble was rubble like the bridge, fallen and twisted with holes a person could worm into for protection and concealment. The south span looked like *great* rubble.

There were two problems with making it to that rubble, though.

The first was the artillery. The rounds were falling dead on target—they actually seemed to be digging holes in the concrete of the road—but they were also falling just a few meters from the route he would have to take to reach shelter. If he had a radio, he would have them switch to smoke. But he didn't and the RTO was way too far behind him to yell to. Even if yelling *wouldn't* give away his position, which it would.

He had heard that it was possible to move within a yard or two of artillery like this, if it was falling "away" from you, which this was. There was a solid "thump" of concussion from each shell, but what killed you with artillery was the shrapnel. Most of that was being thrown towards the Posleen positions. Technically, very little of it should be coming back towards where he was going to be crossing.

Technically. Very little.

The second problem, assuming that the artillery didn't get him, was that there was *no* cover or concealment between his current position and the next block. None. It was flat, level ground, stripped of any vegetation that might once have been there, directly in sight of the Posleen position and less than twenty meters away.

He could *try* to run it. Just get up and dart across. The problem with that was that Posleen tended to react much better to something like that than humans; it would be the equivalent of trying to dodge past a professional skeet shooter. They were sticking their heads up, bobbing up and down, even *with* the artillery. He'd have the chance of a snowball in hell of making it across.

The only other alternative was to try to sneak past.

The lighting was . . . confused. There was the sudden flair of the artillery, the moon scudding in and out among the clouds, but other than that not much. A few fires that had probably been started by the artillery gave a bit of flickering light, but none of them were nearby.

Posleen had good night vision, but not perfect. And

# CHAPTER 41

Cheer! An' we'll never march to victory.
Cheer! An' we'll never hear the cannon roar!
        The Large Birds 'o Prey
        They will carry us away,
An' you'll never see your soldiers anymore!
                                —Rudyard Kipling
                                "Birds of Prey" March

*Near Balsam Gap, NC, United States, Sol III*
*2025 EDT Sunday September 27, 2009* AD

Thomas rolled over a log and started to crawl back up
to the top of the ridge. He'd *heard* about the Posleen
reaction to snipers, but that was the first time he'd
experienced it. He'd also heard that they didn't react
if other people were firing or if artillery was falling.
Well, artillery was falling so he was pretty whipped how
they had spotted him.

It didn't really matter. He had been pushed back by
the recoil of the Barrett so most of the fire had gone

over his head. He'd been hit in the face by a splinter, but that was just going to add another scar. No big deal.

He carefully nudged the rifle back over the edge and lifted himself to where he could look down into the target-zone again.

The one soldier had gotten up to the beginnings of the rubble pile from the bridge and was sitting up with his back to the Posleen doing . . . something. Thomas zoomed in and switched to light intensifier, but he still couldn't figure out what was going on. The guy seemed to be mixing something in his hand.

Figuring it wasn't worth worrying about, the Cherokee lined up another shot. One down, fourteen to go. Forget about the God Kings, just take 'em out one by one.

He lined up the first target just as the sky behind him lit up like God's Own Flashbulb.


Buckley used his knife to shave some of the rock-hard camouflage paint into his cupped palm. The stick of issue paint that he had been carrying since who knows when had dried to the consistency of coal. That was annoying, especially since he figured his only chance of making it was if he coated every inch of skin so nothing showed. If nothing was reflecting, he might be able to inch his way across the gap. Especially if he timed the start for the next shot from the sniper. While they were concentrating on the ridge, he could crawl out and, hopefully, if he moved slow enough, not set off their internal alarms.

If he just could get this camouflage paint mixed with a drop of bug-juice, that would permit him to camo up and maybe make it across alive. It was worth a shot. Of course, a distraction would help, but nothing else came to mind.

For just a moment, the light was so bright he could

see *through* his hands, except where the camouflage paint was resting in the palm of the left one. He shut his eyes, but it didn't matter, the after-image was burned into his retina. He knew he was going to be effectively blind for at least five or ten minutes, but that didn't matter either. All that mattered was that so were the Posleen.

He dropped the tube of paint and the dust in his hands and snatched up his rifle. Grabbing the corner of the concrete block he heaved himself to his feet and darted across the opening between the two bits of rubble.

He expected at any moment to hear the crackle of a railgun or the brief belch of a plasma gun before turning into a carbon statue. But they never came. Instead, a moment after his foot told him he had reached the concrete block, his nose told him that it had reached the piece of steel sticking out of it.

Stifling a scream, Buckley fell behind the concealing concrete, clutching his bleeding nose and waiting for his vision to return.

"I'm beginning to agree with you, Pruitt," Colonel Mitchell snarled. "It's times like these that I wish we had some decent armor and direct fire weapons."

"Well, we *have* a direct fire weapon, sir . . ." the gunner said.

"One that wasn't a national disaster every time we fired it, son," the colonel replied. It had taken the militia scouts a few minutes to reset their radios, but it looked like the back of the Posleen advance was well and truly broken. It had been at a terrible cost, though.

Both Dillsboro and Sylva, even the bits that hadn't been destroyed by the passing SheVa, were gone. God only knew what damage had been done to the bridge, the bridge that Eastern had specifically wanted to stay up. They'd targeted the closest nuke so that the full "ground zero" effect would not encompass the bridge, but that didn't mean it was still tank-worthy. It would take someone like Major Ryan to certify it before they could push much over it.

On the other hand.

"Whenever the guys from the other side *do* get through, it will just be mopping up," Pruitt said.

"Mopping up Posleen is manpower intensive, Pruitt," Warrant Indy said. "Major Anderson was just going to 'mop up' a few Posleen after a nuke strike."

"Time to find a better way," Captain Chan chimed in. "I've got a great view up here, but I'm about ready to get back to fighting. We need to figure out how to get these turrets in action."

"Maybe after the repair batt gets here," Indy said. "*If* they ever get here."

"Let's just hope they get here before the remaining Posleen do," Reeves pointed out.

"What Posleen?" Mitchell chuckled. "I doubt there are four hundred alive between here and Savannah. I, personally, am going to go take a nap. Wake me up if anything happens."

Thomas held his hand up in front of him and squinted. Yep, he could sort of see it, time to get back to work.

The nuke had trashed his sight. He didn't know if it was the EMP or the light overload, but the sight was flickering like a bad TV. Which meant he had to do the rest with iron sights. Okay, he'd grown up with iron sights. He could do it. If he could see at all.

The moon was coming up, but it wasn't going to shine under the bridge. And the Posleen weren't making any light. What he needed was a flare down there or something. If he could just see to shoot.

Finally he decided to just try putting one in the area to see what happened. The worst that could happen is they'd tag him on the return fire.

This time Buckley heard the crack from the ridge before the Posleen opened fire. Their fire was also much less directed; they seemed to be firing in every direction. He hunkered down for a moment then used the disturbance to move again.

His vision wasn't really back; he still had much of his field of view blocked out by a negative image of his hands. He'd heard about "knowing something like the back of your hands," but he seemed to have the *inside* of his hands superimposed over everything.

But he could sort of see and he sort of knew where he was going so it was sort of time to move. He squatted down and duck-walked to the end of the chunk of granite and then paused. When he stuck his head out he would probably be looking at Posleen from less than ten *feet* away.

The question as usual was fast or slow. Finally he decided on fast. Pulling a grenade out of its pouch he pulled the pin and took a breath.

"Once the pin is pulled, Mr. Grenade is no longer your friend," he whispered and leaned out.

Thomas pushed himself back up the hill and wiped at his mouth. That time a plasma round had impacted just to the side and a big chunk of oak had hit him square in the lips. He would be spitting teeth for weeks.

As he leaned into the rifle, though, a grenade went off under the bridge. In the brief light from the explosion he could see three forms right in his target line. He squeezed off a round then ducked back awaiting the return fire, but the Posleen seemed to have a different aim. Pushing forward again and getting a good brace he started to hunt for more targets.

Joe waited for the expected flurry of fire to subside then leaned around the concrete pylon and hammered off all five grenades in his AIW as fast as he could pull the trigger. The Posleen were firing before he even pulled back, but over the racket of the railguns—all the plasma gunners seemed to be gone—he could hear a Barrett punching out round after round. Pulling another grenade from his harness he tossed it in the general direction of the trench as he reloaded. One more burst should do it.

He jacked the first grenade into place and leaned around the concrete obstacle just as the HVM round hit it.

Thomas closed his eyes at the explosion, but it was too late; his vision was gone again. Blinking through the tears, though, he could see that the Posleen were gone too. He wasn't too sure what had just gone off under the bridge, but the north span had collapsed as well and was now lying canted to the west side so he didn't have a shot at all. It looked like the whatever it was had blown down the west, center pylon. Just smashed it in half. There might be Posleen under there, but it didn't really matter; the road was so blocked it would need a heavy engineering unit to clear it.

There was no sign of that last soldier and no fire from the Posleen. So he decided it was time to limp his ass down there. He got to his feet, but his knee buckled immediately. "That's what comes of being old and fat and wore out," he muttered.

He sat down on a tree and shook his head. Let somebody else take the pass. He'd just sit here till his leg felt like moving.

# EPILOGUE

Cally fit the last package in the rucksack and prepared to exit the cave. Cache Four was designed to provide all the materials necessary for just such an escape and, after crying her eyes out and then sleeping, she had carefully prepared for a long journey. The route seemed to be up through the Coweeta area then cut across to Highway 64, assuming it was clear, then west to the defenses around Chattanooga.

Now it was time to leave but she hesitated. Despite finding Papa O'Neal's body, she was still having a hard time believing he was gone. Or that that life was over. She just wanted one more argument, one more morning. And once she left the cave it would be an acceptance that there was no more farm, no more Papa O'Neal.

Finally, she set the pack down and pulled out a book. There was enough food and water for her to sit here for a year and the cave was both secluded and secure.

She'd think about leaving tomorrow.

The Himmit watching her from the top of the cave gave an internal shrug of puzzlement. She had been well on the way to leaving and now had paused. This made no sense to the Himmit. But that was why humans were so endlessly fascinating; they did things for no apparent reason.

He settled in for a long wait. But Himmits were good at that. And this was going to make a fine story someday.

Mosovich paused as Mueller raised a closed fist and settled on his heels. Then the master sergeant cocked his head quizzically and Jake could hear the sound as well. There was a large stream just ahead, part of the Coweeta Hydrological lab area, and the rush of the waters overwhelmed most other noises. But, faintly, he could hear what sounded like female laughter.

Wendy sat up sputtering and lowered the MP5 she had managed to keep out of the stream.

"Very funny, Shari," she snapped, shivering. "This water is frigging freezing."

"I can tell," the older woman said with another laugh. "*Anybody* would be able to tell."

Wendy looked down and had to chuckle. Her clothes had taken a beating in the exit from the Urb and from the vegetation of the mountains. So between the tearing and the water and the thinness of her shirt it was . . . more than evident that the water was cold.

"I look like a friggin' Packed and Stacked girl," she said, shaking her head.

"You sure do," Mueller said, sliding down out of the underbrush. "I wish I had a camera!"

"Jesus!" Shari said, spinning in place. "Don't *do* that to me!"

Mueller raised his hands at the three leveled weapons. "Hey, friends."

"Lord, Mueller, I never thought I'd say this," Wendy said, standing up and lowering the barrel of the submachine gun. "But you are a sight for sore eyes."

"Likewise, I think," the master sergeant replied. He glanced over at Shari and shook his head. "Who's your . . . Shari?"

"It's a long story," Elgars said, raising her hand. "We're headed to the O'Neal caches. You?"

"We're supposed to scout forward to the Gap," Mosovich said, coming out upstream. "But we're moving fairly fast and light."

"Were," Elgars said. "We're moving fairly fast, but we could use some help. And you're hired."

"Captain," the sergeant major said severely. "We've been given our mission by the Continental Army commander."

"Okay," she said, gesturing at his AID. "Call him up. Tell him that you've been shanghaied by a bunch of guurrls with their kids and you don't like it."

"I'm supposed to be *scouting*," Mosovich said. "I can't do that dragging a bunch of refugees."

"Oh, yeah?" Wendy said. "Just watch you."

Sergeant Patrick Delf swept his AIW from side to side, using the night scope on it to look for targets. The area around the Blue Ridge overpass was a mass of heat signatures, but none of them were moving. Most of them were unrecognizable. He stepped forward carefully, his feet shuffling for good footing on the rubble-strewn road, and searching for threats or targets. But there wasn't anything. Both spans, contrary to their intelligence, were down and down hard; clearing the road was going to be a bitch.

He moved closer, waving for the rest of his squad to spread to either side. The recon team opened out, each of them looking for Posleen and finding nothing.

Under the shadows of the bridge they found a trench filled with dead Posleen. Most of them were too fire-blackened to determine what had killed them, but several had had their lights punched out by a large caliber gun, probably a sniper.

The cental pylon was gone at the base. It looked like it had taken heavy fire, probably plasma or HVM, from the Posleen trench. Which didn't make any sense unless one of them had gone completely ape-shit. There was a cooling smear at the base, but he wasn't sure what that meant until he went to one knee, wiped at it and and sniffed his fingers. The odor of human blood, as opposed to Posleen, was distinct.

"Sir, this is Sergeant Delf," the team leader called, touching his communicator. "The pass is clear. Some poor bastard got all the way up here and then got waxed by an HVM. But the HVM collapsed the bridge and blew plasma back on the Posleen; they're gone."

"Any other survivors?" the brigade commander asked.

"Not so far, sir," the sergeant replied. "It doesn't look good. We're not on the other side of the bridge yet, but we can see some tracks; they got wasted, sir. I see three Abrams and two Brads from here and they're all toast. The pass is blocked by the fallen bridges, it's down all the way across. And the tracks are in the way. But no Posleen. The survivors kicked the shit out of them."

"Roger," the colonel said softly. "Is the area clear for aircraft?"

"I can't guarantee that, sir. I don't know what's down the valley."

"According to Eastern Command just a very pissed off SheVa. I'm sending a dustoff up for anyone you find, complete your sweep and get back to me. Be careful, though, it's a long way to Rabun Gap."

❖    ❖    ❖

Cholosta'an shook his head as his pupils started to widen back out. Despite the secondary lids and the tightening pupils he was sure there was some eye damage. Better than what would have happened if the oolt'ondai had chosen to move forward.

"I will eat their get," Orostan growled angrily. But even to the younger Kessentai it had a defeated sound to it.

"We're out of elite oolt," Cholosta'an pointed out. "And trained pilots. We have no remaining tenaral. Besonora's oolt'ondar has been wiped out and the humans will soon retake Balsam Gap. The damned *engineers* have destroyed the other roads out of *this* valley. And Torason says that he is held from advancing up the Tennessee Valley. We must retreat while we have any oolt left at all."

"No, we must drive forward," Orostan snarled. "We *will* take that pass. And the lands beyond. We have the forces still. Take your oolt forward, gather all the scattered oolt'os that you find. Drive forward for the pass! I will gather all that are left in this area and follow."

"Your wish, Oolt'ondai," the Kessentai said. "I go."

He waved for his oolt'os to attend him and moved forward. As soon as he had crossed the rickety bridge and into shattered Dillsboro he turned right, paralleling the Tuckasegee.

"Let Orostan die in his quest to 'save the race,'" the Kessentai whispered. If there was one thing this world had taught him it was that to survive was enough. Let the brave die "for the good of the race." Cholosta'an would just survive.

Tulo'stenaloor shook his head at the report from Dillsboro. He considered, briefly, telling Orostan to withhold his attack. It would take him hours to gather his forces again, what forces he had left. Finally he decided against it. First of all, the old idiot would probably ignore him and attack anyway. Second, slowing the advance of the forces headed for the Gap was a worthwhile goal. When the metal threshkreen finally arrived, he was going to lose the pass to the humans, temporarily. But just give him some time and he could get it back. They would be low on ammunition and power and he could push them out with time.

"All I ask is time."

Mike walked out the hole where the back wall of his office used to be and didn't look back; he was pretty sure he'd never see it again.

The battalion was drawn up in "chalks" before their shuttles. All twenty-two shuttles had landed on the parade field and had been loaded with weapons and equipment, including the critical power packs and antimatter Lances. All that was left to do was load the troops and maybe give a little speech.

The problem with that was that even the "newbies" knew they were going on a suicide mission. It was an important suicide mission, one that couldn't be more vital. But if any of them survived it would be fairly remarkable.

There was also the fact that even the newbies had been on darned near continuous combat operations for between two and five years. These were troops that had walked into the fire, eyes open, over and over and over again. And most of them had heard his speeches before.

But it was a little tradition.

Mike removed his helmet, but set the AID to amplify his voice and faced the assembled battalion.

"On October 25, 1415, near Calais, France, a small band of Englishmen under the English king Henry the Fifth faced the entire French army. This battle was called 'Agincourt' and it occurred upon St. Crispin's Day.

"Although outnumbered by five to one odds, they inflicted terrific casualties upon the better armed and armored French, thereby winning the day.

"An offhand remark of King Henry was later modified by William Shakespeare into the famous 'St. Crispin's Day Speech.'

"This day is called the feast of Crispian:
He that outlives this day, and comes
    safe home,
Will stand a tip-toe when the day is named,
And rouse him at the name of Crispian.
He that shall live this day, and see old age,
Will yearly on the vigil feast his neighbours,
And say 'To-morrow is Saint Crispian':
Then will he strip his sleeve and
    show his scars.
And say 'These wounds I had on Crispin's day.'
Old men forget: yet all shall be forgot,
But he'll remember with advantages
What feats he did that day: then shall
    our names.
Familiar in his mouth as household words
Harry the king, Bedford and Exeter,
Warwick and Talbot, Salisbury and Gloucester,
Be in their flowing cups freshly remember'd.
This story shall the good man teach his son;
And Crispin shall ne'er go by,
From this day to the ending of the world,
But we in it shall be remember'd;
We few, we happy few, we band of brothers;
For he to-day that sheds his blood with me
Shall be my brother; be he ne'er so vile,
This day shall gentle his condition:

And gentlemen in England now a-bed
Shall think themselves accursed they were
    not here,
And hold their manhoods cheap whiles
    any speaks
That fought with us upon Saint Crispin's day.

"Throughout the history of man, small forces facing overwhelming odds have been remembered in storied song. The small Greek force at Marathon that defeated a Persian force that outnumbered it a hundred to one. The Rhodesian SAS team that accidentally ran onto a regimental review of guerrillas and wiped them out. The Heroes of Thermopylae. The Alamo. The Seventh Cavalry."

He paused and looked around at the silent, blank-faced suits. He knew from experience that better than half of them were composing an e-mail or listening to music or looking for some new and better porn. But what the hell.

"Given our situation, I think the last three are most significant," he continued, pulling out a dip and putting it in. Spitting to clear his mouth, he looked at the sky. "Today we fly to take and hold a pass. We will do so until we are out of bodies or power or ammo. I'm not sure which we'll run out of first. All things considered, probably bodies.

"We few, we happy few, we band of brothers. In years to come, men at home now in their beds will think of this day and do you know what they will say? 'Jesus, I'm glad I wasn't with those poor doomed ACS assholes or right now I'd be dead.'

"But what the hell; that's why they pay us the big bucks. Board ships."

# AUTHOR'S AFTERWORD

There was supposed to be, there originally was, a long, mildly humorous acknowledgments section here. Of course, I was working on this novel on 9/11. And then, as "they" say, the world changed.

Well, "they" are wrong. "The world" did not change on 9/11, our country did. In the author's afterword to *Gust Front* I commented that "we are living in a Golden Age, with all its strengths and ills." That Golden Age met a distinct reality check on 9/11. The event, more than anything, woke many of us up.

It didn't wake *me* up, I was already awake. I'd been awake since I was eleven or twelve and an ammunition ship blew up in Beirut harbor. Of course, I was about ten blocks away at the time, so it was . . . rather noticeable. "Loud" doesn't cover it. The world has always been a very hostile place, more so for Americans in the latter half of the twentieth century than for any other group (with the possible exception of Jews). People in the developing nations come in two distinct brands: they love America or they hate it. I never, in all my travels, met one person who was just flat ambivalent. Being awake was one of the reasons I gave my body to Uncle Sammy. I knew there were barbarians at the gates, even if nobody else heard the thumping.

What has always seemed distant to many Americans has always been real and close to me. I have had to wonder how many of my schoolmates were in the crowd that stormed the embassy in Teheran. I've had to wonder if my best friend from fifth grade died in the Bosnian conflict. And I've always wondered what "it" was going to be. What "it" was that was going to sufficiently shock my fellow countrymen out of their complacency. Was "it" going to be a nuke in Washington? Or smallpox? Or anthrax?

As things turned out, "it" was destroying the Twin Towers.

In WWII, for the British, "it" was the invasion of Poland, and even more so the invasion of France. For the U.S. "it" was Pearl Harbor. Democracies require an "it," a defining moment when the call to arms is so clear that the most complacent hear the trumpets.

Where we are going in the future is uncertain. We may yet descend into cataclysmic warfare to dwarf my books. Or we may "change the paradigm" and hammer through on the backs of our elite. I don't know what we shall find in the tunnel ahead. I do know this, though. That is all that it is. A dark tunnel. There *is* a light at the end; it is not another train, it is the future. We will create that future as Americans always have: a better, brighter future.

All we need do, as a nation, is drive through to the end.

They shall not grow old, as we that are left grow old,
Age shall not weary them . . . nor the years condemn.
At the going down of the sun, and in the morning,
We will remember them!

—Lawrence Binyon

John Ringo
Commerce, GA
October 5, 2001

# GLOSSARY

| | |
|---|---|
| abat | Small, generally inoffensive Posleen pest. |
| Attenrenalslar | Five percenter Kessentai in Rochester. |
| Blastplas | Material that blastdoors are made from. |
| Castleman Avenue | One side (the east) of the "box" in Rochester. |
| Chengdu | City near western limit of Posleen advance in China. |
| Cholosta'an | Junior Kessentai. |
| chorho | Birthplace. |
| cosslain | Superior normal. |
| defib | Defibrillator. |
| devourers | Digging machines. |
| Drasanar | "Patrolmaster," operations officer in charge of patrols. |
| edas | Set-up debt. Also any general debt. |
| eson'sora | Junior officer/protégé. |
| Essthree | S-3, Operations. |
| Esstu | S-2, Intelligence. |
| estanaar | Greater Warleader/Khan. |
| Forty-Three | Uncompleted SheVa. |

| | |
|---|---|
| Forty-Two | SheVa in Rochester. |
| Galplas | Standard Galactic structural material. |
| grat | Malicious Posleen pest. Only eats abat. Similar in appearance to a large wasp. Very territorial and aggressive. |
| Halligan | Type of entry tool. |
| Irmansul | Darhel planet currently under attack by the Posleen. |
| Kenstain | God Kings who act as castellaine. |
| Kerlan | Posleen name for Barwhon. |
| Luoxia Shan | Mountainous region in China. |
| micrite | Small UAV, larger than a nannite. |
| oolt | Posleen company. |
| oolt Po'osol | Lamprey. Holds Posleen company and Kessentai. |
| oolt'ondai | "Colonel," brigade/battalion commander. |
| oolt'ondar | Brigade (B-Dec unit)/battalion (C-Dec unit). |
| oolt'os | Posleen normal. |
| oolt'po'slen'ar | C-Dec. Holds four Posleen companies (oolt'ondar). Commanded by an oolt'ondai. |
| orna'adar | Posleen Ragnarok. |
| Orostan | Senior Posleen. Oolt'ondai. |
| Pendergrass Mountain | Mountain near Franklin, N.C. |
| plasteel | Galactic armor. |
| polylon | Galactic weaving material. |
| Po'oslena'ar | Posleen. |
| PreserFilm | Weapon sealing material. |
| Ramsardal | Kessentai. Casualty in Clayton. |
| Staraquon | Posleen S-2. |
| Teneral | Flying tanks. |
| thresh'c'oolt | Posleen iron rations. |
| Westbury | Area on the Ontario Plain. |
| Xian | City in Eastern China. Last major defensive action on the part of the Chinese. |

# SHEVA I SPECIFICATIONS

*Height*: 170 ft. ground to top of turret
*Treads*: four
*Tread height*: 27 ft.
*Tread width, individual tread*: 150 ft.
*Weight of individual tread*: 37 tons
*Total vehicle width*: 385 ft.
*Total vehicle length*: 468 ft.
*Gun length*: 200 ft. including barrel and breech
*Gun bore*: 16"
*Round weight*: 16 tons, projectile, cartridge and propellant
*Cartridge length*: 14.7 ft.
*Cartridge diameter*: 27 inches
*Reactors*: 4 Johannes/Cummings pebble-bed uranium/helium
*Drive motors*: 48
*Total power*: 12,000 horsepower
*Unloaded weight*: 7,000 tons approximate

# CALCULATION OF PSI OVERPRESSURE WAVE FOR NUCLEAR EXPLOSIONS

r_blast = Y^0.33 * constant_bl are:
constant_bl_1_psi = 2.2
constant_bl_3_psi = 1.0
constant_bl_5_psi = 0.71
constant_bl_10_psi = 0.45
constant_bl_20_psi = 0.28

# RECOMMENDED MUSIC LIST
## FOR *WHEN THE DEVIL DANCES*

| | |
|---|---|
| Bat Out of Hell | Meat Loaf (Mike O'Neal, Jr.) |
| Born to Run | Bruce Springsteen (Mike O'Neal, Jr.) |
| Born to Be Wild | Steppenwolf (Mike O'Neal, Sr.) |
| Brothers in Arms | Dire Straits (Mike O'Neal, Jr.) |
| Brown Eyed Girl | Van Morrison (Shari O'Reilly) |
| Conquistador | Procol Harum (Mike O'Neal, Sr.) |
| Copperhead Road | Steve Earle (Mike O'Neal, Jr.) |
| Don't Pay the Ferryman | Chris DeBurgh (Mike O'Neal, Jr.) |
| Don't Fear the Reaper | Blue Öyster Cult (Mike O'Neal, Jr./Sr.) |
| Fire on High | ELO (Mike O'Neal, Jr.) |
| Fire and Rain | James Taylor (Mike O'Neal, Jr.) |
| Flowers of the Forest | Traditional (Tommy Sunday) |
| Heavy Metal | Don Felder (Mike O'Neal, Jr.) |
| Immigrant Song | Led Zeppelin (Mike O'Neal, Jr./Sr.) |
| Invincible | Pat Benatar (Mike O'Neal, Jr.) |
| Jungle Love | Steve Miller Band (Mike O'Neal, Jr./Sr.) |
| Lawyers, Guns and Money | Warren Zevon (Papa O'Neal) |
| Magic Carpet Ride | Steppenwolf (Mike O'Neal, Sr.) |

| | |
|---|---|
| More Human than Human | White Zombie (Cally/Stewart) |
| Never Been Any Reason | Head East (Mike O'Neal, Sr.) |
| No Surrender | Bruce Springsteen (Mike O'Neal, Jr.) |
| On the Dark Side | John Cafferty and the Beaver Brown Band (Mike O'Neal, Jr.) |
| Over the Mountain | Ozzy Osbourne (Mike O'Neal, Jr./Duncan) |
| Paint It Black | Rolling Stones (Mike O'Neal, Jr./Sr.) |
| Promises in the Dark | Pat Benatar (Mike O'Neal, Jr.) |
| Rebel Yell | Billy Idol (Mike O'Neal, Jr.) |
| Renegade | Styx (Mike O'Neal, Jr.) |
| Riding the Storm Out | REO Speedwagon (Duncan) |
| Right Here, Right Now | Jesus Jones (Mike O'Neal, Jr.) |
| Roland the Headless | Warren Zevon (Papa O'Neal) |
| Separate Ways | Journey (Duncan) |
| Shadows of the Night | Pat Benatar (Mike O'Neal, Jr.) |
| Slow Ride | Foghat (Mike O'Neal, Sr./Duncan) |
| Smells Like Teen Spirit | Nirvana (Cally/Stewart) |
| The Mob Rules | Black Sabbath (Mike O'Neal, Sr.) |
| The Unforgiven | Metallica (Mike O'Neal, Jr./Cally/Duncan) |
| Thunder Island | Jay Ferguson (Mike O'Neal, Jr.) |
| Thunder Road | Bruce Springsteen (Mike O'Neal, Jr.) |
| Veteran of the Psychic Wars | Blue Öyster Cult (Mike O'Neal, Sr.) |
| Waiting for Darkness | Ozzy Osbourne (Mike O'Neal, Jr./Sr.) |
| With Arms Wide Open | Creed (Cally) |

Got questions?  We've got answers at

# BAEN'S BAR!

**Here's what some of our members have to say:**

"Ever wanted to get involved in a newsgroup but were frightened off by rude know-it-alls?  Stop by Baen's Bar.  Our know-it-alls are the friendly, helpful type—and some write the hottest SF around."
— Melody L  melodyl@ccnmail.com

"Baen's Bar . . . where you just might find people who understand what you are talking about!"
— Tom Perry  perry@airswitch.net

"Lots of gentle teasing and numerous puns, mixed with various recipes for food and fun."
— Ginger Tansey  makautz@prodigy.net

"Join the fun at Baen's Bar, where you can discuss the latest in books, Treecat Sign Language, ramifications of cloning, how military uniforms have changed, help an author do research, fuss about differences between American and European measurements—and top it off with being able to talk to the people who write and publish what you love."
— Sun Shadow  sun2shadow@hotmail.com

"Thanks for a lovely first year at the Bar, where the only thing that's been intoxicating is conversation."
— Al Jorgensen  awjorgen@wolf.co.net

**Join BAEN'S BAR at**
# WWW.BAEN.COM
**"Bring your brain!"**

# DAVID WEBER

**The Honor Harrington series:** *(cont.)*

## *Ashes of Victory*

Honor has escaped from the prison planet called Hell and returned to the Manticoran Alliance, to the heart of a furnace of new weapons, new strategies, new tactics, spies, diplomacy, and assassination.

## *War of Honor*

No one wanted another war. Neither the Republic of Haven, nor Manticore—and certainly not Honor Harrington. Unfortunately, what they wanted didn't matter.

## *AND DON'T MISS—*

The new <u>Honorverse novel</u> (*Shadow of Saganami*) and the Honor Harrington <u>anthologies</u>, with stories from David Weber, John Ringo, Eric Flint, Jane Lindskold, and more!

---

## HONOR HARRINGTON BOOKS by DAVID WEBER

| | | |
|---|---|---|
| ***On Basilisk Station*** | (HC) 671-57793-X /\$18.00 | ☐ |
| | (PB) 7434-3571-0 / \$7.99 | ☐ |
| ***The Honor of the Queen*** | 7434-3572-9 / \$7.99 | ☐ |
| ***The Short Victorious War*** | 7434-3573-7 / \$6.99 | ☐ |
| | 7434-3551-6 /\$14.00 | ☐ |
| ***Field of Dishonor*** | 7434-3574-5 / \$6.99 | ☐ |

continued ☞

# DAVID WEBER

continued